PRAISE FOR JUDITH MICHAEL'S
A TANGLED WEB

A Literary Guild Main Selection
A Doubleday Book Club Main Selection

W9-BUV-632

Books by Judith Michael

Deceptions
Possessions
Private Affairs
Inheritance
A Ruling Passion
Sleeping Beauty
Pot of Gold
A Tangled Web

Published by POCKET BOOKS

JUDITH MICHAEL

A TANGLED WEB

POCKET BOOKS

New York   London   Toronto   Sydney   Tokyo   Singapore

This book is a work of fiction. Names, characters, places and incidents are products of the author's imagination or are used fictitiously. Any resemblance to actual events or locales or persons, living or dead, is entirely coincidental.

POCKET BOOKS, a division of Simon & Schuster Inc.
1230 Avenue of the Americas, New York, NY 10020

Copyright © 1994 by JM Productions, Ltd.

ISBN: 0-671-53288-X

First Pocket Books printing October 1995

10 9 8 7 6 5 4 3 2 1

POCKET and colophon are registered trademarks of Simon & Schuster Inc.

Cover art by Brian Bailey

Printed in the U.S.A.

Once more, for Cynthia, Andrew and Eric

"I think it's the most special blessing of all: to like our children as companions."

—Garth Andersen

"Oh, what a tangled web we weave,
When first we practice to deceive!"

—Sir Walter Scott

Part I

Part I

_S_abrina took a deep breath and blew out the birthday candles—thirty-three and one for good luck—closed her eyes and made a wish. *Please let everything stay the same. My children, my dearest love, my friends, my home: close and safe. And truly mine.* She opened her eyes, smiling at everyone around the table, and picked up the antique silver cake cutter she had brought back from her last trip to London.

"What'd you wish, Mom?" Cliff asked.

"She can't tell us," Penny said. "Wishes don't come true if you tell them."

"They don't come true anyway," Cliff declared. "Everybody knows that. It's all a myth."

"Oh, too cynical," Linda Talvia said, putting her hand on Marty's arm. "Lots of my wishes came true."

"And all of mine," Garth said, his eyes meeting Sabrina's down the length of the table. "Even one or two I hadn't thought of."

"They can't come true if you don't wish them," Cliff scoffed.

3

"Sure they can," said Nat Goldner. "Dolores and I didn't even know we wanted to get married, all those years ago, and then all of a sudden we were and it was exactly right."

"And I wished for wonderful children," Sabrina said, "smart and fun and full of love. Was that a myth?"

"Oh. Well, sometimes they come true." Cliff grinned as the others laughed. "I mean, if you make the right wish . . ."

The right wish.

I made a wish once. So did Stephanie.

Oh, Stephanie, look where it took us.

Sabrina folded into herself as the others talked, remembering Stephanie, longing to hear her voice, to look into her eyes and see her own eyes gazing back at her, her own face, her mirror image, her identical twin. *It's your birthday, too, Stephanie, not just mine; you should be celebrating today; you should be—*

Here. She should be here. If Stephanie were alive, she would be sitting at this table, surrounded by the family and friends that were hers long before she and Sabrina dreamed up their plan to switch places. It had been a mad and careless idea, though at the time it had seemed like a lark, a daring adventure. One year ago, only a year, they both had had troubles in their separate lives and lightheartedly wished for a chance to live a different life, just for a little while.

And then it became serious. And so, at the end of a trip to China, Sabrina went home as Stephanie Andersen, to a husband and two children and a shabby Victorian house in Evanston, just outside of Chicago. And Stephanie became Sabrina Longworth, divorced and living alone in the elegance of a Cadogan Square town house in London. Just for a week, they said, one week of escaping into another life, and then they would switch back, with no one the wiser.

But they had not switched back. Sabrina broke her wrist in a bicycle accident, and Stephanie, her marriage to Garth

4

already shaky, pleaded with Sabrina to stay in Evanston until her wrist was healed, the final X-ray taken. Then, when once again they were identical in all ways, they could safely return to their own lives.

But the weeks of healing turned their lives upside down. Sabrina fell in love with Garth with a passion she had never known, and found a deep love for Penny and Cliff, while Garth discovered a wife quite different from the one who had been drifting away from him, whom he had barely looked at for many months. He found her enchanting and exciting, and told himself she was consciously changing herself since her trip to China, to save their marriage.

Stephanie, in London, made new friends, and began an affair with Max Stuyvesant, a man of wealth and mystery and social connections who was involved with the world of art and antiquities. And she managed Ambassadors, Sabrina's exclusive antique shop, growing more self-confident with each day that she pretended to be her glamorous sister. Still, they would have changed back, but first Stephanie begged for just a few more days for a cruise with Max on his yacht. One last fling, she told Sabrina. One last fling.

And then she was dead. The yacht exploded off the coast of France, and the news came that everyone on board, including Lady Sabrina Longworth, had been killed. Sabrina and Garth went to London, where everyone mourned the loss of her sister, and in the funeral home Sabrina said goodbye to Stephanie, almost blinded by tears of loss and guilt. At the funeral, trying to tell the truth, she fell to her knees beside the grave, crying, "It wasn't Sabrina who died . . . It wasn't Sabrina . . . !" But no one would listen; they said she was unbalanced by grief. And Sabrina, in a turmoil of despair and confusion, could not fight them.

And so she returned to Stephanie's family. She knew it could not last—she could not build a life on a deception—but for the next three months, weaving through her grief was a happiness greater than any she had ever dreamed of:

passionate love with a strong man; warmth and cherishing and humor with two bright, loving children.

But by Christmas, almost four months after the sisters switched places, before Sabrina had gathered the strength to tell Garth she was leaving, he unraveled the deception himself. Enraged, he ordered her out of his life, out of his children's life. She fled to London, her world in ruins from that mad act she and Stephanie had so carelessly committed.

But, alone in his home, Garth slowly came to understand the depth of Sabrina's love for him and his children. He understood that she, too, had been trapped by the deception. And he knew that he loved her more deeply than he had ever loved before.

"Stephanie? You still with us?"

Sabrina started slightly and saw Nat Goldner looking at her with concern. Nat, the close friend, the doctor who had set her wrist when she broke it one year ago, looking at her with affection. "I'm sorry," she said with a small smile, "I guess I drifted away."

Garth came to sit on the arm of her chair. "It's usually professors who get accused of that, not professors' wives." He put his arm around her. "This isn't an easy time."

"You're thinking about Aunt Sabrina, aren't you?" Penny asked. "It's her birthday, too."

"I miss her," Cliff said. "She was lots of fun."

Tears filled Sabrina's eyes, and Dolores Goldner leaned forward. "How awful for you, Stephanie; such a happy day, but filled with sadness, too."

"I guess I need to be alone for a few minutes," Sabrina said, standing up. "Cliff, you're in charge of cutting more cake." She leaned down and kissed Garth lightly. "I won't be long."

She heard Cliff taking orders for seconds as she climbed the stairs to the bedroom. The bedside lamps were on; the sheet was turned back on either side of the four-poster bed; their clothes had been put away. Wonderful Mrs. Thirkell,

Sabrina thought. I brought her from Cadogan Square in London, where her only concern was Lady Sabrina Longworth, and plunged her into a family of four in an old three-story house that always needs repairs, and in the eight months she has been here she has never once seemed flustered.

Lady Sabrina Longworth. Sabrina sat on the curved window seat and looked into the front yard, palely lit by streetlights and the windows of neighboring houses. There is no such person as Lady Sabrina Longworth anymore, she thought. Mrs. Thirkell calls me, from habit, "My lady," to the children's endless amusement, but Sabrina is dead; to the world, she died on a cruise with Max Stuyvesant last October. To me, she died when I realized I could never go back to my own identity, because that would give away the deception to Penny and Cliff. They would know that their mother had thought it would be a lark to pretend to be Sabrina Longworth, free and on her own in London while her sister took her place at home. They would know that their mother had been traveling with a man not their father when she was killed. I could not let them know that. And so there is no more Sabrina Longworth. And often I miss her, miss being her, miss living her life.

But she had been Stephanie Andersen for a year of love and discoveries, and most of the time she missed her other life simply as a child misses a bedtime fairy tale: something dreamlike and perfect, not real. Not real, Sabrina told herself. Not real. Below, on the dark grass, she spotted Cliff's T-shirt, tossed to the side that afternoon in the heat of an impromptu soccer match. That's what is real: all the little things and the big ones that make a family. That was my wish, a year ago, when I wanted to live Stephanie's life. And it came true.

But it came true with a terrible dark side.

Because Stephanie died. And because she was murdered.

"You're not responsible," Garth said from the doorway. "You couldn't know what would happen, and there

7

was nothing in your life that led her inevitably to her death.''

"I tell myself that," Sabrina said, her voice low. "But I keep wondering . . . How did the police know that the bomb was put on the ship just to kill Max? What if it was to kill Stephanie, too? Because to them she was Sabrina and she might have gotten involved in something. Once, when I was at Ambassadors after the funeral, I was sure that was what happened, that she had said something that made them feel threatened. I don't know, I just don't know. But if I hadn't been so happy here, I might have pushed her to tell me what she was doing, what Max was doing, and whether she knew anything about it. Maybe I could have warned her. I *knew* those people and she'd just met them. But all those months I was living her life, happier than I'd ever been and turning my back on everything over there. *I never asked.*"

Garth sat behind her on the window seat, his arms around her, and Sabrina rested against him. "Maybe I couldn't have done anything. I don't know. But I do know that all I really cared about was you and the children—"

"Listen to me, my love." His voice was patient; they had gone over this so many times, but still he went through it each time as if it were the first. "You told me you'd talked to her about the forged artworks and she handled the whole thing brilliantly. She kept Ambassadors out of that scandal; she protected its reputation as if it were her own shop. You did warn her to stay away from Max, not because he was the head of a smuggling operation—none of us knew that until it was too late—but because you'd never liked him or trusted him. She had plenty of information from you, and she probably had learned a lot more that you didn't know. She was a smart, grown-up woman who chose her own path. You can't hold yourself responsible for the choices she made.''

"I know, I know. But"—she looked around the room— "I have all this, I have everything, and she—"

"Yes, I think of that." Garth turned her in his arms and

kissed her. "My dear love, I think of that more than you know. But I cannot feel guilty for what we have found."

"Mommy, don't you want to open your presents?" Penny stood in the doorway, her eyes wide and worried. "Are you sick or something? Everybody's worried about you."

Sabrina smiled. "Everybody?"

"Well, Cliff and me. 'Cause if you forgot about your presents . . ."

"I must be sick." She laughed and hugged Penny, her somberness lifting.

Garth gazed at her beauty and thought of all she had been to him since last Christmas, when he had brought her back from London. She had played the shabbiest trick that could be played on someone close and vulnerable, but it had not been done from malice, and in the end, she had been trapped by her love for them and theirs for her. And who could have foreseen that? he mused. We'd never even liked each other very much.

But she had changed in the years since he had first met her, and she changed again, living with them, so that, after a while, she truly was not always sure which sister she was, and that was another way she was trapped. Once Garth realized that, he let himself love her with a passion greater than any he had ever known with Stephanie or anyone else.

"So can we go?" Penny asked. "We've been waiting and waiting . . ."

"You're right, it's time," Sabrina said. "But where are the presents?"

"We hid them in the best place! Guess where!"

"Oh, Penny, can we play guessing games later? Why don't you just put them in the living room? Then Mrs. Thirkell can clear the table."

"Okay. On the coffee table or the couch or . . . ?"

"You decide," Garth said firmly. "We'll be down in a minute."

Penny gave them both a swift look, seeking reassurance, then gave a little nod and dashed out. Sabrina turned again to Garth and kissed him. "I love you. I'm sorry I get so . . . lost, sometimes."

"It's not something you choose. But it is getting better, isn't it?"

"Yes. Oh, yes, of course. Time, and so much love, and wonderful kids who demand a lot of attention . . . Do you know, I find myself thinking about Stephanie and then I tell myself, 'I'll think about her later, after I have my conference with Cliff's teacher or take Penny shopping or help Linda with an estate sale . . .' and I do, in snatched minutes, but then you come home and everything seems wonderful because you're here . . ."

Garth's arms tightened around her. "Everything *is* wonderful. And I won't allow us to deny what we've found, and that it gets more astonishingly wonderful all the time."

"Do you know what I wished when I blew out the candles?"

"Penny says you're not supposed to tell anyone."

"You're not 'anyone,' you're my love, and I can tell you anything. I wished that everything would stay the same. You, the children, this house, our friends. I want it all to stay just as it is." She gave a small laugh. "Dolores would say that's because no woman wants to have any more birthdays past thirty."

"But the truth is, you wished it because it took us so long to find what we have. I wish it, too, you know, every night when I'm falling asleep with you in my arms. I'd hold back the clock for you, my love, but that's not my branch of science. Come on, now, we'd better get to those presents. Mine isn't there, by the way. I'll give it to you later, when we're alone."

"Is it so private? The children will be disappointed. Remember when I tried that with your birthday present."

"Oh, Lord, I suppose you're right. Where do children get these ironclad ideas about appropriate family behavior? Well, okay, but it is private and special; you'll understand when you see it."

"How mysterious." Sabrina took Garth's hand and they walked down the stairs and into the living room, where the others waited.

"Thirteen years married and still holding hands," said Marty Talvia. "We should drink a toast to that. And it so happens that I brought a special port for the occasion." He reached over the back of the couch and retrieved the bottle he had hidden there. "And the admirable Mrs. Thirkell has provided glasses, so I shall pour while Stephanie opens presents. You'd better start, Stephanie, or your kids will explode with waiting."

Penny had placed three packages on the coffee table, and Sabrina removed the wrapping paper from the two top ones, opening them at the same time. "Oh, how lovely!" she exclaimed. "I've been wanting a new necklace, Penny, how did you know? And is this candleholder made of walnut, Cliff? It's perfect with our new tablecloth; we'll use it tomorrow night."

"We made them in school," Cliff said. "Dad said it was better to make things than buy them."

"Of course it is. I love whatever you give me, but it's special when you make something yourself. And I love you. More than anybody in the whole—"

"Except for Dad," said Cliff.

"Always except for Dad." Over their heads, Sabrina met Garth's eyes. "Always."

"Port," said Marty Talvia, handing small glasses to the six of them. "Penny and Cliff, you'll have to wait a few years."

"Mom lets us take a sip," Cliff said. "She never used to, but all of a sudden, you know, lately she started—"

"It's because you're twelve," Garth said.

"But I'm only eleven and I get a sip, too," said Penny.

"Those are the magic ages: eleven and twelve," Sabrina said lightly, sliding past another observation—one of so many in the past year—that she did things differently from the way Stephanie had done them. "Now, what's going to happen to that large, elegantly wrapped gift still sitting on the coffee table?"

"Open it!" cried Cliff.

"Please open it," Linda Talvia said. "I'm going crazy, waiting."

"So am I," Dolores said. "We bought it together. Of course you can buy any of these things for yourself now, but we thought—"

"Not necessary," said Nat, his hand on her arm.

Sabrina pretended to be absorbed in working open the gilt wrapping paper. There had been difficult moments among the six of them when the others became aware of how much money and property the Andersens now had, since Sabrina's will had left everything to her sister. *I've left everything to myself,* Sabrina had thought, frantic with despair and bitter humor the previous October, in those awful weeks after Stephanie's funeral. But she and Garth were careful to keep their life much as it had been except for a few changes. They had had the house painted, and she had gradually brought in some fine antiques from London and from Collectibles, the shop in Evanston where she had become a partner. She had linked Collectibles to Ambassadors, and occasionally she went to London to buy at auction and to watch over her shop. She and Garth took more short trips together, and of course Mrs. Thirkell was there, the perfect housekeeper, the envy of everyone.

Those had been the only changes, and as the months went by, everyone seemed to forget that Garth and Stephanie Andersen had become wealthy, at least compared with other academics in Evanston.

But now Linda said, "We think about it, though, buying you things. It used to be so different. Remember when we bought you that bathrobe? Dolores thought it was too loud, but I said you'd been wearing brighter colors since you got back from China, so we bought it and you loved—"

"Oh, wonderful," Sabrina breathed, lifting from its

cushioned box a Penrose Waterford decanter. From the early nineteenth century, it was etched with eight-pointed stars, its stopper shaped like a small umbrella above three doughnut-like rings. "It's absolutely perfect. Where did you find it?"

"The Charteris estate sale. I knew you liked Waterford."

"Oh, I do. And I've never had a Penrose."

"You've never had Waterford, period. Until lately, that is."

"That's true." Sabrina barely noticed her small slip; no one else did, either. By now she did not guard her tongue as she had in the beginning; if she spoke occasionally from Sabrina's background and experience, or did not know what they were talking about when they reminisced together, the others found ways to explain it away. They explained everything away; they always had, from her first night home when they were in the kitchen and she'd asked Garth and the children where they kept the pot holders. After that there had been dozens of mistakes and slips of the tongue, but no one was suspicious or even curious because, Sabrina realized, people see what they expect to see and they find reasons for oddities to protect the comfortable order and predictability of their lives.

Now, in her living room, she set the decanter on the coffee table and stretched her arms wide. "What a wonderful birthday. The best I've ever had. It's so perfect, being here with all of you, knowing this is where I belong . . ."

"Dad, you didn't give Mom a present," Cliff said accusingly.

"Where is it?" Penny demanded. "You told us you got it."

Garth grinned at Sabrina. "Right again." He pulled a small velvet box from his shirt pocket and put it in her hand. "With all my love. For now, for always."

Sabrina kissed him, then opened the box. A long sigh broke from her.

"What is it? What is it?" Penny cried.

"Hold it up, Mom!" said Cliff.

"It's a ring," Nat said, looking into the box over Sabrina's shoulder. "Stunning. A star sapphire, yes?" he asked Garth.

"Yes," Garth murmured, his eyes holding Sabrina's. She put her hand along his face. "My engagement ring."

"But you're already married," Penny protested.

"I never had an engagement ring," Sabrina said.

"Neither did I," said Dolores. "Probably for the same reason: Nat couldn't afford it."

"Neither could Marty," Linda said. "Garth, what a nice idea."

Garth pulled off Sabrina's gold wedding band and slipped the engagement ring and wedding band together onto her finger. Sabrina closed her eyes. This ring was for a wedding the others knew nothing about. This was for a rainy December day when Garth had come to London to say he loved her and wanted her and it no longer mattered what she and her sister had done; and for another rainy day two days later, when they took the train to Canterbury, where no one knew them, and bought two gold wedding bands and found a magistrate to marry them. The narrow streets and stones of that ancient town were dark gray, streaked and dripping in the steady downpour, but Sabrina wore a red raincoat and rain hat and she bought Garth a red carnation for his lapel, and when their eyes met as each slipped a ring onto the other's finger and the magistrate said "husband and wife," they saw in each other the sun, and spring, and hope.

"Thank you," Sabrina said, her lips close to Garth's. "It's the most wonderful gift I could have imagined. And the most private; you were right about that. So when we're alone . . ."

The telephone rang, and abruptly she began to tremble. She knew Penny and Cliff were watching, but she could not stop. She could not hear a late night ring without recalling in terrible detail the night last October when Brooks had called from London, crying, to say that Max Stuyvesant's yacht had gone down and everyone on board . . . everyone on board . . . everyone on board—

"It's all right." Garth drew her tightly to him. "It's all right, my love, we're all here, it's all right."

"My lady," Mrs. Thirkell said from the doorway. "There's a call for you, from London—"

"No," Sabrina cried involuntarily.

"—Miss de Martel. Though of course she's Mrs. Westermarck now; I must try harder to remember that."

"Gaby," Sabrina said. She forced her body to stillness. "At three in the morning London time. What in heaven's name is she up to? Excuse me," she said to the others, and left the room behind Mrs. Thirkell's ample back, her muscles tight, her heart pounding.

"Gaby," she said, picking up the telephone in the kitchen. "It must have been quite a party, if you're just getting home."

"I haven't been to a party in two weeks." Gaby's high voice was clear and close. "We've been in Provence, bicycling. I've had an inordinate amount of fresh air; I can't believe it's healthy for anyone to have that much all at one time. You didn't tell me you'd be there; we could have spent some time together."

"That I'd be where?"

"In Provence. Avignon, to be exact. About a week ago."

"I wasn't there, Gaby, I was here. What are you talking about?"

"Oh, God, am I being indiscreet? Stephanie, were you there to see somebody? I can't believe it; I thought you were head over heels for your professor. Have you got something going on the side? You can trust me, you know; I'd do anything for you because you're Sabrina's sister and I adored her and she saved Brooks and me when—"

"I'm not having an affair; I haven't got anybody but Garth. Gaby, what is this all about?"

There was a silence. "You weren't in Avignon last week?"

"I just told you. No."

"But I saw you. Or your double. It was some festival or other, hordes of people—"

Or your double. Sabrina was trembling again. Once she had had a double. Once she had had a sister.

"—and I couldn't get to you—you were across the square, walking in the other direction, with a guy, very handsome, very attentive—and you took off your hat, one of those wide-brimmed straw ones with a long scarf tied around the crown, red and orange, and you were brushing back your hair—you know, combing it with your fingers?—and then you put on your hat again and you were gone."

Brushing back your hair. She and Stephanie had done that all their lives: taken off a hat, combed their hair with their fingers, feeling the air lift and cool it, then replaced the hat. Their mother had not approved; a lady kept her hat on, she said. But Sabrina and Stephanie went on doing it long after they were grown up and far away from their mother's strictures. *Brushing back your hair*.

"My lady?" Mrs. Thirkell pulled a chair up and put her hands on Sabrina's shoulders, settling her into it. "I'll get you some tea."

"So either you've been identical triplets all this time, without telling anybody," Gaby said, "or something very weird is going on."

"Of course we weren't triplets, don't be absurd." She was trembling again; she could not hold herself still. It was as if the earth were shifting beneath her feet. "This whole thing is absurd," she said, biting off her words. "You saw someone who reminded you of me, that's all; I can't imagine why you'd make something of it—"

"Stephanie, listen, I'm not joking, this is very weird and a little scary. I've known you and Sabrina since she and I were roommates at Juliette; I lived in her house on Cadogan Square when Brooks and I broke up, and she and

I talked every night; she even took me on her lap once, and I cried like a baby, and I loved having her hold me, and I loved her, and I know what the two of you look like and I'm telling you, I saw you, or her—oh, God, how could it be her, she's dead—*but I know what I saw, and it was you or her. Or a ghost.*"

CHAPTER *2*

---

*N*oontime crowds filled the streets of London, and Sabrina merged with them, a Londoner again, Sabrina Longworth again, free and independent, on her way to Ambassadors, the exclusive antique shop she had created after her divorce from Denton. She never thought of Denton except when she was in London, and she thought of him briefly now: his round, rosy face, his fascination with himself and his pleasures, his love of women and gambling. He had been gambling in Monaco when Max Stuyvesant's ship went down; he was the one who identified the body of Sabrina Longworth. Max's body had never been found.

Sabrina's hands were clenched. Beneath a cool, early-October sun, she walked along Pont Street, wearing a black and taupe plaid skirt and matching cape that furled about her with each step. She wore a black narrow-brimmed hat angled low over her eyes, and fine black kid gloves. She looked sophisticated, purposeful and calm, but beneath the cape she was tense and withdrawn, her thoughts swinging from the past to the present, from one life to another, from Stephanie to herself, from the memory of a funeral to Gaby's telephone call, and always, always, to Garth.

She had told him about the call, but made light of it. "She saw someone who looked like me and wondered why I hadn't told her I'd be in Europe. I'll call her next time I'm there." And then, casually, she had added, "I think I'll go next week. I want to check on Ambassadors and . . . just be there. Would you mind?"

"And our October trip?" Garth asked.

"Oh, of course we'll do that." She had planned her trip to Ambassadors for the end of October, while Garth gave a paper at the International Biogenetics Conference in The Hague; then they would meet in Paris for a week to themselves. "Of course we'll go; I wouldn't give up a week in Paris with you. But I'd like to be there now, too. I was thinking of next Monday; would you mind?"

Of course he said he would not mind. Garth had always given her plenty of space in which to merge her two lives. "We miss you more each time you go," he said, "but you've given us the formidable Mrs. Thirkell, and if anyone can ease the pain, she can."

Mrs. Thirkell had taken firm control of their house, keeping it so well lubricated that none of them could imagine how they had functioned without her. And so when Sabrina moved up her trip to London, there was only a brief conversation with Mrs. Thirkell to go over shopping lists, schedules, the window washer, who was due on Tuesday, and the landscaper, who was coming in a week to cut back the gardens for winter. And then she asked, as she always did, if there was anything she could bring back from the London house.

"Why not bring the dessert forks, my lady? You don't entertain there anymore, and we seem to be doing more all the time here, and what a shame to keep such handsome silver locked away."

"A good idea." Sabrina thought of the steady westerly movement of possessions from Cadogan Square to Evanston, matching the steady fading of Lady Longworth into Stephanie Andersen.

"And then there's the fish poacher, my lady; I certainly could use that."

Sabrina laughed. "I am not about to carry a fish poacher across the ocean. Buy a new one, Mrs. Thirkell; I'm surprised you haven't already."

"You do get a fondness for certain familiar things. But of course I'm sure I'll get attached to a new fish poacher, too."

It doesn't take long to get attached to new things, Sabrina thought, approaching Ambassadors, already missing Garth and the children even though her plane had landed only that morning. But she was still attached to Europe, too, where she and Stephanie had grown up. Their life had been nomadic as they moved from city to city whenever their father was assigned to a new embassy. They had learned half a dozen languages, speaking all of them, including English, with a faint, unidentifiable accent, and they had become experts in antiques and decorative arts during leisurely afternoons browsing with their mother in castles, stately homes, and out-of-the-way shops where they would come away with dusty hands and some wonderful piece that their mother would clean up to reveal its hidden beauty and value.

Then their father was named U.S. ambassador to Algeria. Their parents decided the country was a dangerous place for American girls, and sent them to Juliette high school in Switzerland, where Sabrina roomed with Gabrielle de Martel and Stephanie with Dena Halpern. They earned blue ribbons in fencing and sailing, and then, in their last year, they quarreled, bitterly and painfully, over Stephanie's feeling that she was always in Sabrina's shadow, outshone by her more dramatic, more adventurous sister.

And so they separated, Stephanie to Bryn Mawr College in America, Sabrina to the Sorbonne in Paris. And then they found each other again, after Stephanie married

Garth and Sabrina married and divorced Denton. The ties that bound them, so that each felt her sister was the other half of her, could not be torn apart for long, and in the years that followed, they visited in America and London and talked for hours on the telephone. And then they joined a group of antique dealers on a trip to China, and while they were there, away from everything familiar, Stephanie—it was Stephanie, the less adventurous one, who thought of it—suggested changing places.

Such a simple idea; such a lark. They spent a week memorizing details of each other's life, and on the last day of the tour, in a Hong Kong hotel, they exchanged clothes and luggage, Stephanie took off her wedding ring and gave it to Sabrina, and they handed each other the keys to their houses. And then they went home.

Home, Sabrina thought, turning the doorknob of Ambassadors. It wasn't my home then; it was Stephanie's. But it became the most wonderful home I've ever had. The only home I ever want. She opened the door into the softly lit warmth of the shop, waiting for her eyes to adjust after the brightness outside. "Mrs. Andersen!" said Brian, coming forward. As he came closer, he sucked in a sharp breath of surprise. "Forgive me, Mrs. Andersen; it's still such a shock, seeing you. You could tell me you're Lady Longworth, back from the dead, and I'd believe you."

"Yes, Brian." She began to walk around the shop as if she were a customer. The room was patterned after an eighteenth-century salon, long and narrow, fronted with a square-paned window. The walls had dark oak wainscoting; the ceiling was molded in plaster octagons. Sabrina made a circuit of the room, then stood in the center, turning in place, eyeing the placement of furniture, the arrangement of small objects on shelves, the lighting.

"Very good, Brian," she said at last and heard his quick sigh of relief. Every time she walked in the door, Brian held his breath, even now, almost a year after Ambassadors had been taken over, as far as he knew, by Lady Longworth's sister from Evanston.

At first he and Nicholas Blackford had been condescending to the housewife from America, but Sabrina had stopped them cold. She had behaved like Sabrina, which confused them, and she had recklessly demonstrated her vast knowledge of antiques and even of London and the people in it. And they had accepted it. Everyone accepted it.

Because London was just like Evanston. Here, too, everyone found ways to explain away her mistakes. Well, they thought, Sabrina must have told her sister everything; she must have talked about us all the time. How else would Stephanie Andersen know so much? And while they were amazed by that astonishing conclusion, they were also satisfied by it.

So Brian sighed with relief and Sabrina went into her office and sat at the cherrywood table she used as a desk. *I could call Gaby now. That's what I'm here for, the only reason I came to London now instead of waiting until the end of the month. I'll call her now; she might be home.*

"There is a fair bit of mail I haven't had a chance to forward to America," Brian said, and brought in a basket piled high with letters, announcements of sales, and even invitations, on the off chance that Stephanie Andersen would be in London for various balls and dinners and country weekends.

It can wait; after all, it's not really urgent, it's just something I'm curious about.

She spent the afternoon at her desk. When the front bell rang and Brian left to take care of the casual customers who wandered in, mostly tourists at this time of year, Sabrina stayed behind the partition, refilling her teacup, nibbling on crackers, deep in the affairs of the shop. It was a place she loved, a place she had created when Denton's circle was snubbing her, calling her an American adventuress who had taken Denton for huge sums of money. In fact, she had refused money from him and when society ignored Ambassadors she had been in despair. But Princess Alexandra Martova rescued her. She hired Sabrina to renovate and furnish her new town house, and Sabrina's brilliant design won such wide attention and lavish praise that society could no longer ignore her. And Alexandra gave a series of parties that made her house and her character—once thought irrevocably tarnished because of the men in her past—respectable and intriguing. From that beginning they had grown to be the closest of friends, Alexandra became the center of London society, and Ambassadors was a stunning success.

Almost done. I can call in a few minutes. But . . . not from here. I'll call from home.

Of course it wasn't urgent, so she methodically worked through the pile of papers on her desk, then stood and fastened her cape with its single ebony button. "I'll be in tomorrow, Brian, but I don't know what time. I may stop in at Blackford's on the way."

Outside, beneath the streetlights that had come on in the early dark, she merged again with the crowds, this time office workers rushing to their tube stations to go home. She would stroll home, she thought, and call Gabrielle. Not the minute she got there; there was no reason to do it immediately, since it wasn't urgent. She would hang up her cape, put her hat in its box in the cloakroom, pour a glass of wine, climb the stairs to her fourth-floor sitting room, perhaps make a fire in the fireplace, settle herself on the chaise, then reach for the telephone.

But as she walked, her steps grew faster until she was out of breath when she reached her front door, and as soon as she was inside, she sat down at the telephone, still wearing her hat and cape, and called Gaby.

"I'm sorry, Mrs. Andersen," the secretary said, "Mr. and Mrs. Westermarck are driving through Italy; I can't even tell you how to reach them. They should be calling in, but I don't know when."

"Ask Mrs. Westermarck to call me," Sabrina said. "I'll be here for a few days; at least until Thursday or Friday."

She hung up, frustrated and more disappointed than she

would have expected. *What do I think she'll tell me?* She removed her gloves and hat and took them to the cloak-room, nestling them in their tissue-lined boxes, then hung up her cape. It doesn't matter, she told herself, it's just a day or two; I'm sure she'll call in a day or two.

She was sharply aware, as she was each time she came to London, of the emptiness of the house without Mrs. Thirkell bustling about to make her comfortable. Four floors of large, perfectly proportioned rooms filled with the finest antiques from England and the Continent: the walls covered with silk, the floors with Oriental rugs, the furniture with shantung and velvet and loose cashmere throws. A warm, sensual house, but empty, with a chill in the air. Mrs. Thirkell would have banished the chill. Mrs. Thirkell would have stored Sabrina's gloves and hat and hung up her cape; she would have said, "You look tired, my lady, why don't you go upstairs and I'll bring you a good tea in a little while. I'll wager you had no lunch; you don't take proper care of yourself."

But Mrs. Thirkell was now taking proper care of Sabrina's family, so Sabrina gathered up the mail she'd found scattered on the floor inside the front door, poured a glass of wine, and climbed the stairs to her sitting room. The velvet drapes were closed and the room had a hushed stillness that made her feel alone. She settled herself on the chaise and looked at her watch. Five-thirty. Eleven-thirty in the morning in Evanston. Maybe, she thought, and dialed Garth's office number.

In a minute she heard his voice. "Andersen," he said absently, absorbed in whatever he was doing, barely aware of the telephone, faintly annoyed at being interrupted.

"Are you too busy?" Sabrina asked, smiling, knowing the answer. "Shall I call back?"

"Never too busy, you know that. How are you? God, it's wonderful to hear your voice. I was thinking about you."

"You were thinking about science. At least I hope you were; I'd hate to hear about other scientists forging ahead while Professor Andersen daydreams about dalliances with his wife."

"Ah, but I wasn't daydreaming; I was thinking scientifically. I calculated the percentage of space that you occupy in our house, the space that's empty right now. It turns out to be one hundred percent. The house is empty, no matter how much we dash from room to room to create the impression of purposeful activity and therefore of occupancy. I miss you. We all miss you."

"There's a lot of empty space here, too." Sabrina could feel his arms around her, his body fitting itself to hers in bed. "What have you been doing?"

"We went to Nick's Fishmarket for dinner; I thought it was the only restaurant in Chicago that would be a match for Cliff's appetite. But I was wrong; he cut a swath through his plate like a tornado and asked for more. Penny ate like a lady, and made conversation like one. She's a good companion. Almost as good as her mother. And almost as beautiful. Did you find everything all right at Ambassadors?"

"So far. They sold a desk and a commode for good prices, even though the economy here is slow, and they've bought a few new pieces that are very fine. And the shop looks lovely, warm and attractive and inviting. I felt very good about it."

There was a pause. "Like coming home."

"Oh." She was still taken by surprise at how well he knew her: better than anyone ever had, except Stephanie. "No, not home, it can't be that, ever again, for me; not the shop or my house. But they're more than just a shop and a house; I've got a lot invested in them in time and energy and emotions; it's not as if I'm a tourist."

"They were home to you, for a long time. So they have familiarity. And freedom."

Sabrina winced slightly. *If I hadn't thought it this morning, he wouldn't have picked up on it.* "If you mean freedom from you, I don't want it. I want to be with you, I want to live with you and be part of you and make love to you. I miss your arms around me and your eyes smiling at me and the way we laugh together—"

"Wait a minute." Sabrina heard him put down the telephone; she heard a door close, and then he was back. "I don't want anyone to see the distinguished professor looking lovelorn, woebegone and awash in tears."

"Oh, my love." She caught her breath at the note in his voice and blinked back her own tears.

"Well." She could hear his voice change; he was settling back in his chair. "Tell me more about London. Have you seen any of your friends?"

"No. I may not even try; I'd just like to be quiet. I did call Gaby, but she and Brooks are driving through Italy. Did Penny get her art project in this morning? She didn't like it; she said the assignment was too restrictive . . . my fierce little free spirit—" Her breath caught again.

"She showed it to me; it was fine. Not her best, but she's learning that she can paint what someone tells her to paint and still be herself, with her own style, and that's not a bad lesson. And Cliff actually wrote a longer book report than he was assigned; he got energized when I suggested he compare one character's crisis to a game of soccer."

"Oh, wonderful; what a good idea. If it's soccer, it has to be interesting and important. Oh, Garth, I miss them. I miss you. You sound so close, as if you're around the corner."

"I wish I were." There was a pause. "When are you coming home?"

He was always reluctant to ask, but he always did. "As soon as I can." *As soon as I talk to Gaby. I know it's crazy, but I can't leave until I talk to her.* "There are a few things I have to do; I'll let you know. I hope in a couple of days. Garth, don't you have a class about now?"

"My God, what a memory. Yes, but I can be late."

"You hate to be late. You think professors have an obligation to give their students the full hour of class and all their attention."

"This woman forgets nothing. That's why I can never

26

lie to you; I'd forget which lie I told when, and with what degree of fervor, but you never would. Goodbye, my love; shall I call you next?''

''I'd like to talk to Penny and Cliff; I'll call tomorrow around breakfast time if that's all right.''

''Hectic, as you know, but very much all right. Until then. I love you.''

''I love you, Garth.''

She sat very still after they hung up, as if, by not moving, she could freeze the moment and prolong the spell of their talking: the warmth of Garth's voice, the palpable feeling of his arms around her. *I could go home tomorrow,* she thought. *There's nothing to keep me here.*

Nothing but Gaby. And if I don't talk to her, I'll never get that phone call out of my mind; it will jump around inside me and keep me from thinking of more serious things. Just the way it is now.

But Tuesday and Wednesday came and went and Gaby did not call. ''I haven't heard from them, Mrs. Andersen,'' the secretary said when Sabrina called on Thursday morning. ''I'm sure Mrs. Westermarck will call as soon as she knows you're waiting to hear from her.''

By Thursday noon she was so impatient she could barely sit still in her office. She thought of Garth and the children, and the three breakfast conversations they had had. *I want to go home. I want to be with my family.*

Well, then, forget it, she told herself. It was exactly what I told Garth: Gaby saw someone who looked like me. That's all it was. It was crazy for me to come to London, to try to talk to her . . . there's nothing she has to tell me.

She gazed at the yellow leaves swirling around the entrance to Ambassadors and, beyond them, gardens of russet and gold chrysanthemums across the street. A year ago she had watched the leaves turn in Evanston; it had been a glorious week of crisp fall days and she had moved smoothly through them, thinking it would be her only time there before returning to London. That was before she broke her wrist, before she knew Stephanie was having an affair with Max, before Stephanie wanted one last fling with him on his yacht. Before Stephanie was killed.

I know what I saw, and it was you or her. Or a ghost.

But it wasn't any of those. Not Sabrina, of course not Stephanie, and they all knew there were no ghosts.

You could tell me you're Lady Longworth, back from the dead, and I'd believe you.

"Stop it!" she said aloud. Ridiculous, crazy imaginings; what was wrong with her?

Something was driving her, something that would not leave her alone. *Jumping around inside me, keeping me from thinking of more serious things.*

I could go look, she thought.

Look for what?

I don't know. Someone who looks like me. A ghost.

And then she knew that all week she had been moving to this point; that it might be ridiculous and crazy—of course it was ridiculous and crazy—but she was going to try to find out for herself whom Gaby had seen.

She was going to Avignon.

CHAPTER *3*

---

*T*here was a plane to Marseilles early the next morning, and then the TGV to Avignon. Sitting on the upholstered seat of the high-speed train, Sabrina barely saw the landscape; she was telling herself how foolish she was. But even as she repeated it, she knew there was nothing else she could do. And when she stood in front of the small brick train station fronting on a circular drive jammed with cars and taxis, she knew exactly what her schedule would be. The hotel first, she thought. And then a tour.

The old walls of Avignon encircle the city, the huge stones worn by centuries of rain and wind to an indeterminate brown. Broad gates that had seen processions of Roman legionnaires, popes and their retinues, favor seekers, bandits, marauders, farmers, merchants, refugees and settlers now look down on traffic jams and strolling tourists, their heads tilted back to see the watchtowers spaced along the walls and, in the distance, the great towers of the Palace of the Popes. The narrow, twisting streets open onto small, intimate squares or large public ones; the stone

29

buildings hide their secrets behind shutters of wrought iron or wood mottled with flaking paint.

Sabrina left her small bag in her room at L'Europe, barely glancing at the antiques with which it was furnished, or at the view, beyond paned windows, of the square that could be glimpsed through huge trees in the hotel courtyard. She walked out onto the Place Crillon, then stood in place, getting her bearings. She had never been to Avignon, but she had studied maps and books on the plane, and now, in search of a hat, she turned toward the Place de l'Horloge. *You took off your hat, one of those wide-brimmed straw ones with a long scarf tied around the crown, red and orange, and you were brushing back your hair . . .*

She had searched for such a hat in London, but no shops had summer hats in October and so, beneath the blazing Avignon sun, she walked to the shopping enclave, free of autos, just off the Place de l'Horloge and found Mouret, where every wall, floor to ceiling, was filled with every kind of hat ever dreamed of, from fur hats and hunting hats to opera hats and walking hats, summer hats, winter hats, and hats for every holiday.

Sabrina took three wide-brimmed ones and tried them on, angling them differently while the shopkeeper made admiring comments and adjusted the mirror for her. "Fine," she said, choosing one, "but I need a scarf as well."

"Alas, Mouret has no scarves," the shopkeeper said, "but DJ Boutique on Rue Joseph-Vernet . . ."

So she doubled back, almost to her hotel, and found the shop, where a riot of sun-drenched colors greeted her. She bought a long narrow scarf and wound it around the crown of the hat, letting the ends float free, just as she and Stephanie had done all the years they were growing up in Europe, just as their mother had taught them to do on a limited budget: to change a hat with scarves, feathers, flowers, so it always looked new.

She went out into the slanting rays of the late afternoon

sun, softer than before. People walked more slowly here than in Paris or London; they stopped to chat and gave way when others approached. Children in school uniforms with book-filled backpacks walked hand in hand or ran across the squares, chased by yapping dogs. *You were across the square, walking in the other direction.* Which square? There were several, linked by narrow streets or gracious esplanades, and Sabrina walked slowly, looking into people's faces, beginning at the highest part of the city, where, almost six hundred years earlier, a succession of seven popes had made Avignon their Rome, building a huge palace of domes and spires and great windows fronting on an enormous square that dwarfed everyone in it. So many people, Sabrina thought as she walked across the square; so many families, so many generations standing on these granite slabs, all with their own stories, their own problems, hoping for answers. And so am I.

She went into the small hotel at the edge of the square; she walked in and out of shops in the streets leading from it. What did she expect to find? Someone who would look at her with recognition; someone who would greet her. But no one did; she was anonymous. And so she went on, leaving the palace behind, walking purposefully, as if she knew exactly where she was going, and found herself once again at the Place de l'Horloge with the great clock for which it was named.

This time she paused and let herself enjoy the scene. It was the largest square in Avignon, like a small town lined with trees and shrubs, outdoor cafés and shops, with the magnificent white stone theater at one end and, nearby, a carousel of brightly painted horses and elephants and great throne-like seats, turning to the accompaniment of hurdy-gurdy music. Sabrina stood beside it, wishing Penny and Cliff were there, wishing she and Garth could sit on a matched pair of elephants and circle in stately grace for hours with no past, no telephones, nothing to break their private rhythm, while people came and went, filling the square with shifting colors and the soft French pronunciation of the south.

A stillness came as evening fell: the carousel still revolved, but the children went home to their supper, taking the dogs with them; shopkeepers swept up and straightened their shelves with slow, dreamlike movements; in the cafés people sat at small metal tables in a kind of reverie, reading newspapers and talking softly while waiters glided among them with trays held high.

Sabrina found a table and sat down. She felt she was waiting for something. No one questioned her being alone, as did the maître d's in London; cafés were a place for those who had no one with whom to share a meal. But I have a family to share my meals, Sabrina thought. A whole family, waiting for me.

Not yet, not yet. She was the one who was waiting now.

The next morning she had a brioche and coffee in the courtyard of her hotel, then went out again and walked again, up and down the streets, looking into shop windows, looking into people's faces, asking directions. She was waiting for someone to recognize her. But no one did; she wore her hat, grateful for it in the hot sun, and walked through Avignon, a stranger.

Just before noon, she walked on the cobbled street along the Sorgue River, cooler than the open squares, admiring the mossy waterwheels on the river's edge and the antique shops on the other side of the Rue des Teinturiers. Almost as mossy as the waterwheels, she thought with a smile, and went into a secondhand bookshop, a shop that offered embroidered waistcoats and decorative fabrics, and then into one crammed with antique maps. She had never dealt with maps and knew nothing about them, but she went in.

No one was in the small room, though she heard rustling and footsteps beyond a doorway in the corner. She moved slowly around a large table, idly lifting heavy folios, each map encased between protective sheets of plastic. The air was cool and musty, the only sounds the rustle of papers in the other room and Sabrina's steps on the dark wood floor as she moved to a wall of shallow drawers and began to pull them out, glancing at the maps inside. She had no reason to be there; she had no idea of the value or rarity of the maps she saw in drawer after drawer, but she did not want to leave. Twice she thought about it—*there are other places to go; it's a big town and I have only today*—but both times she stayed where she was.

"Good morning, madame, may I be of service?" A small man came through the doorway, stooped over a cane. His white hair was in disarray; his white beard was trimmed to a neat point. "I'm sorry I kept you waiting; I was wrapping some maps for a customer— Ah, madame, have you come for the Tavernier? Perhaps your friend could not wait to have it shipped; it is not surprising: he was so excited about it. I have it wrapped for you; I will get it."

Sabrina's heart began to pound; she felt herself sway.

"Madame! Here, a chair, oh, I'm so sorry, only a stool, but still . . . please, please, madame, it is perhaps the heat outside?"

He was holding her arm, but Sabrina gently moved away. "Thank you, I don't need to sit down; I'm fine." A map had fallen from her hand and she saw its delicate traceries and pale colors waver as she stared at it.

"There is a doctor, madame, not far from here; I can take you to him."

"No, really, I don't need a doctor." She smiled at him. "You're probably right; it was the heat." She paused, then made a decision. "However, I must tell you that I am confused. I was not here recently; I have never been in your shop. Whoever was here must have been someone who looked like me."

He was frowning at her. "Madame makes some kind of joke? Everything is the same, the hat, the scarf, the hair . . . and the face! Someone so beautiful, madame, so in love, so eager to learn, is not quickly forgotten. And your friend, who knows so well the world of maps; I do not forget him either." He bent to retrieve the map from the floor. "It was a pleasure to talk to him; not many these days have such knowledge. And he is a painter, not a cartographer! It astonishes me still."

Sabrina shook her head. "There is some mistake. Did they tell you their names?"

"You are asking me if you told me your name, madame? You did not. I asked your friend if he had a card, but he said no and made a little joke, that painters have canvases but not cards. No, madame, your friend did not tell me his name and neither did you." He looked at her pointedly, waiting for her to tell him, and end whatever game she was playing.

Whoever they were, Sabrina thought, they had some reason for not telling you. A long conversation about a shopkeeper's wares, a possible purchase, almost always led to an exchange of names.

"My name is Stephanie Andersen," she said, "but that is not the name of the woman who was in your shop."

"Madame!" he exploded. He turned away to replace the map in its proper drawer, then turned again to face her. "If you have changed your mind about buying the Tavernier, that is one thing. I understand that you are not especially interested in maps—that you deal with antique furniture instead—but . . ."

"What?"

"I beg your pardon, madame?"

"You said antique furniture."

"*Mon dieu!* Madame, I am baffled that you insist on playing this very strange game; it is nothing to me what your name is—"

"Did they say where they live? What neighborhood in Avignon, or nearby town?"

He flung up his hands. "No, madame, you did not tell me that."

"What kind of painter is he?"

"As you know, he did not tell me."

"Did you watch them after they left your shop? Where did they go?"

"I do not know where you went, madame. Nor am I interested in finding out. Now, if you will excuse me, I have work to do." Furious with her, he returned to the other room.

Sabrina stood indecisively, then slowly left the shop and retraced her steps along the river and returned to the center of town. The shops would be closing soon for the afternoon break, and by the time they reopened, she would be on her way to Marseilles to catch her flight to London; otherwise she would miss the morning flight to Chicago. But what difference did it make whether the shops were open or closed? If this woman, this *impostor*—for what else could she be?—was determined not to tell her name to shopkeepers, and her friend was determined, too, what good would it do to go from shop to shop to try to find out who they were and what they were doing and why?

But he's a painter. If he was telling the truth about that, he would have wanted to go to galleries. Or maybe he needed more supplies.

Suddenly filled with energy, she went to the tourist office on Cours Jean-Jaurès and got a list of art galleries and artists' supply shops. There were only two supply shops, and the first, Monet Fournitures Artistiques, was a few blocks away. She walked quickly, ignoring the heat, her face shaded by her hat.

"Ah, madame, I am so glad you return," said the tall woman behind the counter. She had broad shoulders, her cheeks were round and full, and she wore oversize glasses that made her look like an amiable owl. "I left out one brush in wrapping your package; I have it here." She brought a narrow box from behind the counter and held it out to Sabrina with a wide smile. "Otherwise I would have had to go looking for you, which would have been a long process, since I did not know where to look."

Sabrina avoided the truth; it was too difficult. "I didn't tell you where I live?"

"No, madame, the subject did not come up." The woman tilted her head and contemplated Sabrina's pale face calmly and with sympathy; she was prepared to accept any kind of infirmity or eccentricity. "Did you think you did?"

Sabrina laughed. "No, I know I didn't. Did I tell you my name?"

"No, madame, and neither did your companion."

Sabrina frowned slightly. "How do you know he was not my husband?"

"In fact, madame, at first I thought he was, from your closeness, your joy at being together, so very evident, especially to someone recently widowed, but I overheard a conversation when I left the room for a moment and it was clear that someone else was the husband."

Their eyes met. They liked each other. "I'm sorry about your husband," Sabrina said gently, and the woman bowed her head in acknowledgment. Her hands gripped each other; tears were in her eyes. A loving woman, Sabrina thought. So loving that she was willing to indulge a stranger in a bizarre conversation rather than issue a challenge and perhaps cause distress. A wonderful woman, a caring woman.

And Sabrina knew she could not intrude with her own concerns on memories of a dead husband.

Slowly, reluctantly, she turned to go. But the woman's voice stopped her. "Madame asked me if you told me your name."

She turned back. "Yes."

"As I said, you did not." In gratitude for Sabrina's sympathy, the shopkeeper no longer spoke as if it had been Sabrina in her shop. "The woman did not tell me her name. But when I was in the other room—I was searching for a kind of gesso that I thought I had, and indeed I did—she and her friend were talking together and he called her by her name. And she spoke her husband's name."

Sabrina looked at her, waiting.

"Her name was Sabrina," the woman said. "And the husband's name was Max."

Part II

CHAPTER 4

The explosion ripped open the *Lafitte*'s staterooms, flinging debris in a wide arc above the Mediterranean. The roar echoed off the white and pink buildings on the shore, causing cries of alarm in the streets and cafés of Monte Carlo. Those who had binoculars grabbed them, but saw little in the turbulence of waves and wreckage. On the ship, within seconds, water flooded the elegant quarters where Max Stuyvesant had entertained and made love, and the crew's quarters below, and within minutes the ship began to sink. It was five-thirty in the afternoon of an overcast October day.

Stephanie and Max were flung across the lounge by the force of the explosion. Stephanie's head struck a corner of a steel-and-glass cocktail table, and she lay beside it like a rag doll. Max was thrown against the end of the mahogany bar, and he huddled there, trying to catch his breath, the words *the bomb, too early, the bomb, too early* . . . pounding through his head.

He heard no screams or cries for help, only an eerie silence broken by the angry slapping of waves against the ship as it rocked and shuddered beneath him. *Christ, blew the whole thing* . . . He forced himself up on all fours and shook his head like a dog shaking off water. Pain shot through his left shoulder, and he shifted his weight to his right arm as he tried to stand. He fell back and, muttering a steady stream of curses, crawled across the room to the high, wide window, not thinking of anything now but getting away. He pulled himself up to the windowsill, grunting, swearing, soaked with sweat. The glass was shattered; he had a clear way out.

With his right arm he pulled himself up to the sill, then he swiveled and swung one leg out. And as he turned, he saw Stephanie on the floor, her eyes closed, blood running down her face.

"Sabrina—" It came out as a gasp. *My God, they've killed her.* He wiped away the sweat running into his eyes and thought he saw her move. Or it might have been the rocking of the ship. "Christ!" he burst out. He swung his leg back into the lounge to go to her, then stopped. He couldn't wait; he had to get away. She was dead and he was alive; his men would be waiting for him, and he had to get the hell out of here before the ship went down. He pushed his other leg through the window and tensed to leap into the water.

But he could not stop himself from taking one quick look back, and when he did he saw Stephanie's head roll to the side into a thin stream of water trickling in beneath the door. As he watched, the water flowed faster and then the force of it burst the door open and a torrent gushed in. Max knew he could not leave her like that. He had to know if she was alive, and if she was, he had to keep her with him.

He swung his legs around and dropped back into the room, gasping with the pain. Broke something, he thought. No, probably not that bad. He knelt in the water beside Stephanie. "Sabrina! God damn it, Sabrina, wake up, help me . . .

"*Merde.*" He was cursing now in whatever language

broke through the panic building inside him. He held his fingers against Stephanie's neck and found the thread of a pulse. Alive. God damn, she's alive. A wellspring of joy sprang up within him, so powerful it stunned him. Wait. Think about it later. Got to get us out of here.

He gripped Stephanie's hands and, crawling backwards through the water, dragged her to the window, fighting dizziness and the pain in his leg and left shoulder. She was deadweight, and he slipped on the wet floor as he struggled to push her up until she lay over the windowsill like a burlap sack. Gasping, coughing, he pulled himself up to sit beside her and catch his breath. No time, he thought; no time to breathe. He pulled off his shoes, and Stephanie's, then lifted her and shoved her through the window and into the sea. And as she dropped, he dove in, just behind her.

It had been two minutes since the explosion.

He hit the water clumsily and fought his way to the surface. Debris churned around him in the waves rolling outward as the ship went down; he felt a piece of metal cut his hand, another struck his thigh. Treading water, he looked around. He was on the side of the ship away from shore, and except for some small boats speeding in his direction, he seemed to be alone. "Sabrina! Sabrina, for Christ's sake . . ." Sputtering, coughing, he took a few lurching sidestrokes, favoring his bad shoulder, and found himself at the stern of the ship. He saw the hole in its side—*the bomb, the fucking bomb, wasn't supposed to go off until*—and then he saw Stephanie, floating face down in water red with her blood, shards of wood and metal swirling around her.

He reached her in an instant and twined his fingers in her thick hair to yank her head back and out of the water. He rolled her over, then hooked his left arm beneath her chin and swam with his other arm away from the ship. His clothes dragged him down, the water was colder than he had imagined, his head and shoulder throbbed, and he had to force his legs to keep moving. "*Bastardos*, fucking *bastardos,''* he said aloud, meaning all of them, the ones who had set the bomb to kill him, and his own men who should have been there by now to pick him up.

Stephanie floated, her face colorless, pale veins tracing across her dead white eyelids. Max could see the gash in her forehead now; he thought it was not as bad as all the blood had made it seem. She'll be all right, he thought. She'll be fine. She's tough; I always liked her toughness.

But he was so tired he could barely stay afloat. It would be easier without her. Easier alone. He'd known that all his life: it was easiest to go alone. But he held on to her. He remembered that spurt of joy when he knew she was alive, though he could not recapture it now. *Verfluchen,* he swore wearily. Sons of bitches. Said they'd be close by . . .

The motorboat was beside him before he saw it; the men had cut the engine and maneuvered through the debris to come close without setting up high waves. "Sorry, boss," one of them said. "Didn't think it'd go off this early. You want her, too?"

"Fuck it!" Max exploded.

"Okay, right." The two men reached down and dragged Stephanie into the boat. "Grab my arm," the first one said to Max, and pulled him in as the other man started the engine. The small boat leaped away, its prow high out of the water. Max lay beside Stephanie in the bottom of the boat, out of sight, while the men kept fishing poles and nets raised high and looked straight ahead as they tore through the water.

Max slid a life preserver beneath Stephanie's head, then ripped off his shirt and pressed it to the bleeding gash in her forehead. Holding it there, he lay back again, breathing deeply. Now, he thought; now I can breathe. But then he heard one of the men say, "She's gone," and he raised himself and looked behind them. He stared at the widening circle of debris and the motorboats bobbing a little distance away. Rescue boats were approaching from shore. That was all he saw. The *Lafitte* was gone.

"A beaut, that bomb," one of his men said cheerfully.

Max looked at him until the man's cheer faded. "Why the fuck did you wait so long to tell me about it?"

"I didn't wait! I told you as soon as I knew! I didn't hear word one about a bomb, about any *plans* for a bomb, until today. I don't know; maybe they were starting to wonder about me—"

"I pay you so they don't wonder about you. I pay you to make them trust you. I pay you to get information to me in time for me to use it."

"Well, you did; you got out in—"

"None of us should have been on board in the first place."

"I didn't hear a thing until this afternoon, boss, honest to God. I called you on your plane, but you'd landed and the pilot said you'd just left for the dock. I got down there as soon as I could, but you were gone, so I called you on the ship's radio; what else could I do?" There was a silence. "So you went forward, right? I mean, when you knew the bomb was under your stateroom . . ."

"We went forward."

The others had been unpacking in their rooms, but Max had insisted on going to the lounge. "You can unpack later, Sabrina," he had said. "I want a drink; I want you to see Monte Carlo in this light." And they had gone forward.

In fact, he'd thought he had plenty of time. His man, who had worked his way into Denton's organization, had told him the bomb was set to go off at seven, when everyone was dressing for dinner. But Max was not one to sit calmly on top of a bomb without doing something about it. He had planned to leave the lounge after a few minutes and get the engineer to go with him to find the bomb. But then it had occurred to him that the engineer could be part of the plot. Whoever brought the bomb on board and found a place to hide it and then left the ship without anyone being suspicious . . . whoever did that couldn't have managed it without help from someone on the crew.

He had been thinking about that while pouring drinks in the lounge. "It looks like a little girl's birthday cake," Stephanie had said, looking at the pastel colors and rococo designs on the buildings of Monte Carlo, stepping up the hill from the shore.

Max brought her a drink and saw the sudden cloud that shadowed her face. "What is it?"

"I was thinking about little girls' birthdays," she said, and he grasped her hand, angry at her for letting her thoughts take her away from him. He put her glass in her hand and curved her fingers around it. And then the bomb went off.

In the small motorboat, Max cradled Stephanie's head against him to protect her from the pounding vibration of the engine. They were racing west, toward Nice, the beaches and harbors of the Côte d'Azur on their right. The sun was still bright, but the beach was emptying as bronzed men and women gathered possessions, packed them into brightly striped raffia bags, and strolled to the hotels lining the shore.

"Almost there, boss," said the man at the wheel. "Burt's waiting at the dock; he took care of the helicopter. Trouble is, we didn't know you'd need a stretcher or an ambulance or, you know, so there won't be anybody waiting when we get to Marseilles."

"Burt can call from the helicopter. An ambulance and a hospital."

"Right; he'll know where to go; he's lived there all his life."

Nice was a jumble of buildings behind the forest of ships' masts in the harbor; the cafés on the Promenade des Anglais were crowded with people settling in for late afternoon drinks. Max looked at them, thinking that that familiar life was closed to him for a long time. Then he turned away as his small boat chugged slowly to a deserted part of the harbor near a cluster of squat warehouses, and eased into place at the far end of the dock.

A black Renault was parked close to the dock; beside it

stood a short, slender priest with a brown beard. He squatted as Max's men tied the boat to the dock. "I heard you were coming in today; I came to greet— *Mon Dieu*, Max, you're hurt!" He leaned into the boat, his hand extended. "But who is this? She's bleeding . . . Max, what happened?"

"An explosion; the ship went down." Max grasped the priest's hand and clambered out of the boat, gritting his teeth against the pain that shot through his arm. "I'm glad to see you, Robert. We'll need a hospital in Marseilles."

"You need one now. We'll forget Marseilles for today; it can wait—"

"It can't wait. Another half hour, Robert, that's all. Do you know a doctor in Marseilles?"

"Of course. But, Max, this is not wise; we don't know how badly she—" He saw Max's face darken. "Well, then, to Marseilles. Gently, my friends!" he said as the men in the boat lifted Stephanie's inert form and laid her on the dock. The gash on her head was bleeding again, her sodden hair dripped water mixed with blood, and bruises and small cuts covered her swollen face and arms. "Into the car. Max, you first, the back seat, and hold her when we put her in . . . Now, my friends, lift her gently but speedily; the helicopter is waiting."

Stephanie lay against Max, her head rolling from side to side as Robert careened around corners until Max held her tightly to his chest. He watched the buildings that seemed to race past on both sides, the palm trees and flower gardens and policemen directing traffic, but his eyes were dulled by exhaustion and a low, throbbing anger that held him in its grip. *Fool, fool, to let them get ahead of me.*

They had never been able to do it before; they'd never been able to touch him. I got lazy, he thought, stupid, let down my guard; didn't give a damn about anything but—he looked at the woman in his arms—about anything but Sabrina.

It wasn't quite true: he had conducted his business and made careful plans to wind up his activities in England and disappear when the time was right, but for the past few weeks he had let himself be distracted from business and the survival and prosperity of Max Stuyvesant; he had been absorbed by thoughts of this woman, so different from the Sabrina he had known years before, when she was married to Denton.

As if she mesmerized me, he thought: Max Stuyvesant so mesmerized by Sabrina Longworth that I forgot to keep looking over my shoulder, forgot to watch and wait and listen . . . and so the bastards almost killed me. Almost killed both of us.

He tightened his hold. She was alive. He let himself recapture the joy he had felt on the ship when her pulse had fluttered beneath his fingers. She was alive and she was his. And he knew he was more than mesmerized. He was fiercely, possessively in love with her.

"All right, Max," said Robert, and they pulled up beside the helicopter. Two men were waiting; they helped Max and Robert bring Stephanie inside, and in a moment the blades were spinning in the muggy air, singing a high, sustained pitch and lifting the helicopter from the ground.

They flew low, over the hotels and villas of the Côte d'Azur, one of the great playgrounds of the world, to the dense, industrialized sprawl of Marseilles and, directed by Robert, to the roof of a hospital built in the shape of a cross. The helicopter door was opened and a team of men and women in white coats took Stephanie from Max, lifting her onto a stretcher. He did not see her again until the next day.

She lay in a narrow bed in a narrow whitewashed room, with the morning sun streaming in. She wore a white gown beneath a white coverlet; a wide white bandage was wound around her forehead; a clear, shiny ointment and small white patches were on the cuts and bruises all over her face and arms. Her eyes were closed, the eyelids quivering as she slept. Her magnificent hair had been cut short; it was a curly halo, chestnut gleaming red and gold in the sun, the only color in the room.

Max sat in a hard metal chair beside the bed. He took her hand from beneath the coverlet and held it between his. Tubes ran from her other hand to three clear plastic bags hanging from a metal stand at the foot of the bed. Max could see the slow drip of fluid from the bags into the tubes, and he thought of the other time he had seen that, when he was nine years old, sitting beside his mother's hospital bed in London. He had not thought of his mother for years; he had not thought of himself as a boy since his father had disappeared when he was twelve. Max had been a man all his life.

But the clutch of fear he felt as he watched the fluid drip into the plastic tubes brought back the child he had been, and he had to wrench his thoughts away from that terrified boy and away from his mother. She had died; this woman would live. He sat in the metal chair as the hours passed and the nurses replaced the empty bags with full ones, and the drops moved slowly down their channels, agonizingly slowly, into the veins of the pale hand lying motionless on the bed, and he held the other hand, moving away only when the doctor made his twice daily examination. Each time, as soon as he was gone, Max moved back to the hard chair and again took that unresponsive hand in his.

He was willing her to live and recover, even as he spent the hours trying to figure out what to tell her if she did. They had to go into hiding and change their names; he had already used her new name when he filled out the forms admitting her to the hospital. They had to go into hiding and stay there until he found a way to eliminate those who had set the bomb. Until he knew they were safe.

He had made plans for hiding. He had known for some time that he would have to leave England and change his operations. When newspaper stories began appearing on the smuggling of antiquities, he had known it would have to be soon. At the same time, he was being pressured by Denton to expand their operations just when he knew he had to cut back or stop altogether, at least for a while. And then, because the damn fools who worked for him had started a little sideline of selling forged art to galleries, and the reporters were after that story, too, he knew another spotlight could be turned on him. Every week he moved up the date for disappearing. He had made plans and everything was in place . . . but the plans were for one person, not for a couple.

Now he had to rethink all of it. He could handle their living arrangements: Robert would help him find a larger place for them to live than the small apartment he had rented for himself in Aix-en-Provence. But to keep her with him, to persuade her to give up her life in London, her antique shop, her friends, her very identity, required either that she loved him so passionately that nothing else mattered—loved him as he knew now he loved her—or that she was afraid.

She did not love him. He knew that. But he was sure she would, if they had time. And so he would have to convince her that she was in danger, and that safety lay only in staying with him.

His thoughts raced, then settled on this solution while he sat beside her and watched her as the hours passed. He ate, dully and automatically, the food the nurses' aides brought him, and answered their questions in his fluent but oddly accented French that made them look at him curiously, wondering where he came from; and he dozed through the nights on a cot they put beside the bed. And then, on the third day, Stephanie opened her eyes.

Max felt again that leap of joy and he leaned over her, his hands clasping hers, and started to say her name. But then he stopped. She was staring straight up, at the ceiling, not moving, and something about that blank stare and the stillness of her body made him fearful and kept him silent. He tightened his grip on her hand, and waited.

The minutes stretched out. Finally, very slowly, she turned her head. Their eyes met in a long look, and Max knew that she had no idea who he was.

In an instant, everything changed. It might be only temporary—a few days, perhaps only a few hours—but if it was not, if she really had lost her memory and it held, it would be as if he had been given a gift. Max had lived a lifetime on his wits, on the ability to incorporate new information instantly and adapt it to that moment's situation. Now, meeting Stephanie's blank stare, he knew that this was far better than his other solution. He would not know for sure for a while yet, but he had an alternative now, and if it worked out, he could not have planned events more perfectly. "Sabrina," he said, and watched her face.

She frowned and echoed it, her voice thin and tentative. "Sabrina . . ."

"You don't remember?" He spoke in French, silently willing her to reply in French. Her command of the language was as good as his and her accent was better, and he assumed that if, indeed, she had no memory, she would follow what she heard and saw. He would make sure that she followed him in everything, and clung to him, and belonged to him. "Well, if you don't remember, we won't worry about it now; we'll deal with it later. You've had a shock, you've been hurt." He bent down and kissed her cheek, then kissed her lightly on the lips. "You'll be all right, Sabrina; you'll be fine."

"Sabrina." She tested it on her tongue, then shook her head. "*Je ne comprends pas . . .*" Max let out his breath. Perfect. Stephanie's eyes widened as the enormity of it struck her—*I don't understand*—and she began to cry. "I don't understand. I don't know anything. Why don't I know?"

"If you please, monsieur." The doctor was behind Max. "If you will wait outside . . ."

Max did not look at him. "I'm staying with my wife."

Stephanie's eyes widened. She stared at him.

"This is my patient, monsieur; I intend to examine her."

After a moment, Max relinquished Stephanie's hand and backed away from the bed. He leaned against the wall, making it clear, by his folded arms and unwavering stare, that that was as far as he would go.

The doctor fastened a blood pressure cuff around Stephanie's arm. "You do not know your name, madame?"

"Go away." Still crying, Stephanie rolled her head back and forth, as if trapped, then looked away, through the narrow window at the blue-white sky. "Go away, go away, I don't want you here. I don't want anybody here."

"Madame has had an accident," the doctor said calmly. "It is necessary that we discover the extent of the damage, physically and mentally." He bent over Stephanie, holding her eyes open to shine a tiny flashlight into them. He took her pulse, pulled out his stethoscope to listen to her heart, thumped her chest. He pulled back the coverlet and struck her knees and Achilles tendon with a tiny hammer. He raised and lowered her arms and legs, examining her bruises, then covered her again, neatly, laying her hand gently at her side on top of the coverlet.

Stephanie lay still, unresponsive, almost unaware, staring at the ceiling past the doctor's fringe of gray hair. She winced when he began to unwrap the bandage around her head. "Ah, *très bien,* this will heal," he murmured, and rewrapped the wound with fresh gauze.

He gazed at Stephanie's profile. He could not place her nationality. She spoke perfect French, but with a faint, unidentifiable accent that made him sure she was not French. The man most assuredly was not French; he spoke fluently but with an accent that was vaguely German. Two people who probably have spent their lives in many places, the doctor mused; intelligent people who are quick with languages. The world has more of them every day: sophisticated chameleons. The woman, even bruised and injured, was extraordinarily beautiful, and her beauty and fearfulness drew him, but he knew he could help her only as much as the husband permitted.

"So, madame." He spoke to Stephanie's profile, aware of Max's unwavering stare on his back. "Physically, you improve. You are a fortunate woman; your wound will heal, your hair will grow and cover the scar, your bruises will disappear. We have superb plastic surgeons who can repair the damage to your face. But now we must talk about the other injury, to your memory. There are many things you do not remember?''

Stephanie did not reply.

"Your name, madame. Tell me your first name. And your maiden name."

She stared at the ceiling.

"Or any name that comes to you, madame, a friend's name, perhaps, an acquaintance, someone who works for you; it might lead you closer to your own. Madame, I cannot help you unless I know the extent of the problem. Can you tell me your name? Or anything else about yourself, your friends, your life in . . . where is it you come from, madame?''

"I don't know, I don't know, I don't know!" Stephanie held up her hands, one of them trailing the plastic tubes, and turned the palms toward her, then away, then toward her again. "Hands," she said. "My hands." Her gaze raced around the room. "Wall. Window. Sky. Bed. Hands. Is that right? Doctor," she said, and pointed at him. She pointed. "Left. Right. Up. Down. Is that right? Was everything right?"

"Yes, madame, yes, yes," the doctor said. "What else do you know?"

"Ceiling," Stephanie said. "Door. Sheets. Pillow."

"And your name is Madame . . ." The doctor let the word dangle. "Quickly, madame. Your name is Madame . . ."

Stephanie shook her head. "I don't know. I know *things*. Why is that? Why don't I know anything else? What am I going to do?''

"You'll get well," Max said. "You'll be with me and you'll get well." He came to the bedside and spoke to the doctor. "How soon can you arrange for the plastic surgeon? Everything else I can take care of.''

The doctor ignored him. "Something has made you forget many things, madame. Perhaps not for long, and perhaps not everything; I would like to help you find out. It may have been the blow to your head or the trauma of the accident—"

"What accident? Nobody said anything about an accident."

The doctor looked at her closely. "A few minutes ago I said madame had had an accident. You do not remember that?"

"No. You said an accident? I don't remember. What accident?"

"Your husband said your motorboat rammed the end of a dock and there was a fire . . ." He turned to Max. "You're sure that was what happened, monsieur? A ship exploded off Monaco last week; you were not involved in that?"

"I told you what happened. I didn't hear about a ship exploding; when was it?"

"Oh, Monday or Tuesday, I don't remember. It must have been about the time of your accident. But of course you could not have been in that other one; I understand there were no survivors. A terrible thing." He turned back to Stephanie. "You remember nothing about a motorboat?"

"No." Stephanie turned her head to look at Max. "My husband." She held up her hands again, spreading the fingers wide, looking at the bare third finger on her left hand.

Max moved in, bringing Stephanie's hands down to the bed, holding her free one between his. He had had time, standing there, to think everything through, and now it was all in place; everything that he had planned for the past year reformulated to a new life not just for Max Stuyvesant but for Sabrina Longworth as well. He spoke to Stephanie, but his words were for the doctor, too. "We met five days ago, at a party in Cap-Ferrat; we were married the next day, and we went for the boat ride that afternoon. You've been unconscious for three days. We didn't take the time to buy a ring; we planned to wait until we found the perfect one. We planned a honeymoon, too, and we'll have it, and you'll have your ring, but first we'll get you well and take you home."

Stephanie was watching him through the tears still welling in her eyes. "I don't know who you are."

"Max Lacoste."

"And I—?"

"Sabrina Lacoste."

"What was madame's name before she was married?" the doctor asked.

"Robion," Max said promptly.

The doctor sighed. "There must be half a million Robions in France. But you, monsieur, you can tell madame who she is, where she comes from, who is her family . . ."

Max was shaking his head, still looking at Stephanie. "We didn't talk about our past; we thought there was plenty of time for that. We talked about the future. We had so many ideas about what we would do together, so many hopes and dreams . . . and all of them can still come true."

"Sa-bri-na." She said it as she had before, testing it. "Sabrina. Sabrina. Sabrina." She shook her head. "It doesn't seem right."

"Where do you live?" the doctor asked Max.

"Not far. I asked you about a plastic surgeon for madame; I'm anxious to get her home."

"I want to give her a week to get her strength back; then we'll have the plastic surgeon come in. But I also urge you to let me bring in a psychologist for counseling. She should be evaluated—"

"If we're married," Stephanie said, "what was my name before?"

"I told you," Max said. "Robion."

"You did? Robion? That was my name?" Her eyes widened. "When did you tell me?"

"A few minutes ago; it isn't important."

"It is, it is." Her voice rose. "I can't remember *anything?*"

"You must not be alarmed," the doctor said quickly. "This is not unusual, this form of amnesia; it often occurs after a trauma. It is called anterograde amnesia and it almost always disappears within a few days. But, madame, you also have a kind of amnesia known as retrograde amnesia, which can be more persistent. I think you should be fully evaluated by skilled professionals who can diagnose the particular form your amnesia has taken and help you with the trauma you have undergone, perhaps help you find ways to jar loose your memories."

"My wife and I will deal with her trauma," Max said.

"But there are those, monsieur, who are so familiar with cases like this . . ."

Leave me alone! The thought was in English, not French, and as she realized it Stephanie was engulfed in a wave of terror. She jerked her hand from Max's grip and slid it beneath the coverlet; she closed her eyes and shut both men out. Their voices rumbled above her, deep and antagonistic, but it was like trains going by—trains, Stephanie thought; was I on a train? Where did I go?—a rush, a roar, with no meaning, and she lay stiffly beneath the sound, her hands clenched, afraid to move. She was alone in emptiness—a fog, a cloud, the sky, all of space, infinity—with nothing to gaze upon or touch or grasp. She tried to think of a place where she belonged—a house, a room, a chair, a bed—but there was nothing. She tried to picture a town, a neighborhood, a street, but there was only emptiness: no scenery, no roadway, no guideposts. Only a muffling, terrifying emptiness.

Sabrina. Sabrina . . . what? What did he say my last name was? He told me, didn't he? Oh, God, I can't . . . She began to shiver. The name Sabrina meant nothing to her, and she could not remember her last name.

"What is my last name?" she asked without opening her eyes.

54

"Lacoste," said Max.

Sabrina Lacoste. And he is . . . he is . . . Max. He said Max. Max Lacoste. Her shivering would not stop. That name meant nothing to her, either. She felt she was falling soundlessly through that terrible fog of nothingness, absolutely alone, unconnected to anything or anyone. She saw herself reaching out her hand, searching for someone to clasp it, but there was no one. *Oh, help me,* she cried silently, tears stinging behind her eyelids. *Help me find a place to belong.*

"Sabrina." Max's voice was the only sound in the room, and she opened her eyes. He towered above her, tall and broad-shouldered, with shaggy red eyebrows and frizzled red hair. He had slightly bulging gray eyes, a heavy, sensual mouth, and large, well-shaped hands. He carried himself with purpose and moved with a restless energy that seemed to create eddies in the air around him, unsettling the room. *My husband.* The thought sank into the muffling fog, and Stephanie repeated it, trying to make it seem right.

"We'll go home soon." His voice was relaxed; he seemed to control everything around him, and Stephanie stared at him, conscious of his strength. "I'm going to buy a house in Cavaillon." The idea had come to him just a few minutes before; he knew the area, a perfect one for privacy, and Robert ran a Catholic school there; he would find them a house. "You'll love it; it's very beautiful and quiet."

"Cavaillon?"

"Where we're going to live."

"Did you tell me that, too?"

"No, why should I, in front of the doctor? No one needs to know where we're going. You'll like the town and our house; you'll be very happy."

"I don't want to go there."

"Indeed. Where would you like to go?"

There was a long silence. The tears came again, running soundlessly along her cheeks, wetting the pillow and disappearing into the emptiness where she was suspended, alone. "I don't know."

"Of course not. And in fact, where else would you go but home, with your husband, where you belong? Listen to me, Sabrina. I love you. And you love me. You belong with me, and you'll stay with me, and do as I say; that's the only way I can guarantee your safety and your happiness. Do you understand that?"

His voice pierced the thick fog that swirled around her. *Safety. Max will keep me safe.*

From what? she wondered. But then it was gone, and all she knew was that she was not alone after all. Someone would be there when she reached out her hand. Max would be there. Max loved her. And Max would keep her safe.

C H A P T E R 5

*F*or two months the hospital was Stephanie's whole world. The people she talked to were doctors and nurses and other patients in the solarium, but much of the time she was in her own room on the top floor, where Max had had her moved after the first week. At one end of the room stood a brightly patterned armchair and chaise and a low table with books and magazines, and after each of the three operations on her face, Stephanie spent the days curled up in the armchair, reading, or lying on the chaise. She would gaze for hours at the blue of the Mediterranean blurring into the blue of the sky, and at the boats moving in and out of the harbor while great gulls swooped around them in widening circles and then, with a flapping that could be heard above the creaking of the ships' masts and the boisterous calls of fishermen, flew out to sea and disappeared in the mist.

Twice a week a psychologist came to her room after Max finally allowed it. Max did not join her for any of their talks, though Stephanie often asked him to; his excuse was that he had a great deal of work to do. And it seemed that he had: he had begun leaving the hospital as soon as she moved to her new room, at first for an hour or two, then for a whole day and, once, for almost a week.

He had put off going because he thought she would die without him there to watch over her. He had come to believe that it was only his presence that kept her alive: he had saved her when the ship exploded, and now he was saving her again, hour by hour, day by day, by willing her to live. The first time he left to go to the warehouse on the dock with the sign Lacoste et fils over the door, he had fought with himself the whole time not to rush back. But he told himself it was a weak, childish fantasy, and because he abhorred anything that was weak or recalled childish fears, he pushed the thought from him and stayed away all that day, and next morning left again and did not look back after saying goodbye.

In fact, he had to go; he had no choice. He had to know what had happened to the people on the yacht, and what the police had found. He had told the doctors that the accident had occurred in a motorboat when it struck a dock, but he maintained that fiction only within the hospital; he needed Robert, and so Robert had to know the truth.

The day after Stephanie awakened, when for the first time he had let himself think of something else, he had asked Robert to go to Monaco for him; now Robert had returned, and they were to meet in a café in a corner of town where no one would know them. The newspapers had reported almost nothing beyond the bare story of an explosion on the French-registered *Lafitte* with apparently no survivors. The doctor in the hospital had said the same thing. *No survivors.* How could they know that? No one in Monte Carlo knew how many were on the ship, or who they were. The *Lafitte* was registered under the name of Max's French company, Lacoste et fils, and his crew chief signed either Max's name or his own when registering with the dockmaster. If he had signed Max's name and the police had found bodies in the water but not Max's, why wasn't that in the newspaper stories? None of it made sense, and Max chewed on the ambiguities while Robert made arrangements to go to Monte Carlo and then was there for three days.

"Max." Robert took his hand and held it, searching his face. "You look much better than the last time I saw you. How is the lady we took to the hospital?"

"Still there; she'll be there for a while." They sat in a booth and the waiter brought them two beers. "I want to talk to you about her, Robert, but first tell me what you've found."

"Yes. Well, you've read the newspapers; you know that the police reported that everyone on the ship was killed." His gaze was fixed on Max's face. "They're not absolutely sure about you; they say you are missing and presumed dead."

Max spread his hands. "You think I should call the police in Monte Carlo and tell them I'm alive."

"Of course I do. Why would you not? You must have family who will worry about you—"

Max shook his head. "No one."

"Well, then, friends. And the authorities must keep open the investigation into the explosion until they know for sure that you are alive or dead. Why would you not tell them?"

"Because it suits me right now to have people think I am dead."

Robert contemplated him. "What caused the explosion?"

"I don't know. I suspect a malfunctioning boiler; we'd had trouble with it before."

"A malfunctioning boiler is no reason to keep secret the fact that you are alive." He waited. "Max, listen to me. You know very well that I cannot continue to be your friend if you are hiding a crime."

"I am not hiding a crime. I was in a business in London that others were trying to take over. I've shut that business down, but I don't want them to know where I am."

Once more Robert waited. "You could provide more details."

"I'd rather not. Robert, we've been friends ever since I started my company here, over a year ago. Do you have reason to think I'm not worthy of your friendship?"

"Ah, what a cleverly phrased question. No, my friend, I have had no reason to doubt it, in our relationship. But now what you are doing goes far beyond our relationship. Pretending to be dead . . . that means you are in hiding, yes? And the lady in the hospital? She hides with you?"

"Of course."

There was another silence. "I've overlooked much secretiveness in you, Max," Robert said at last. "Your wariness, your caution, what I thought was your occasional prevarication . . . But the world is full of secretiveness and lying, and it does not have many men who are as good and kind and generous as you. And I like you. I suppose nothing has really changed, except that I have one more piece of information about you. You understand, however, if someone should ask me, I could not lie to keep your secret."

"I understand that. I don't think anyone will ask you."

"And one more thing. I will not be used by you."

"I wouldn't do that. I think the reverse may be true, however."

"You think I am using you?" Robert grinned. "I am using your money, which you give willingly. Men who do good works always turn to those who have money; where else would they turn?"

"Perhaps to prayer."

"Well, yes, of course, and I do. And one of my prayers is that you remain wealthy and generous."

Max chuckled. "You're a practical man, Robert. It's one of the traits I find most admirable in you." He nodded to the waiter who brought two more beers. "Now tell me what else you learned."

"Well, the bodies of the crew were found and identified, and seven others, presumably the guests, were found and also identified. I don't understand—"

"Seven? There were nine of us."

"The police said the ship had four staterooms."

"One couple brought a friend; they made up a bed for her in the sitting room off their stateroom."

"Well, they are assuming there were four couples in four staterooms, and they have accounted for three of the couples and one single woman, a Lady Longworth, who—"

"What? What are you talking about?"

"—who would have been your companion, is that right? But then, Max, I don't understand. Who is the lady we took to the hospital?"

Max was staring past Robert, his mind racing. "Who identified her?"

"Denton Longworth. Her former husband. He happened to be in Monte—"

"Jesus Christ."

"Max."

"Sorry." He sat stiffly in his chair, locked in a fury of frustration. What the hell was Denton up to? He knew damn well the woman he identified was not Sabrina; why would he . . . ? Or *did* he know? One of the women on the ship had looked vaguely like Sabrina—in fact, they all had teased her for mimicking Sabrina, wearing her hair the same way, copying her makeup, buying her clothes and jewelry at Sabrina's favorite shops—but a former husband would not have been misled.

Unless . . . He recalled the scene in the water, and Sabrina's face when he held her in the motorboat: colorless, swollen, blood running from her forehead and oozing from dozens of small cuts. A man might be misled if a woman who looked vaguely like his former wife was so badly bruised or burned or cut by debris that he could not be absolutely sure. And he most definitely would assume—

"Max?"

—definitely would assume it was his ex-wife if he wanted to believe she was dead. And Denton wanted very much to believe Sabrina Longworth was dead, she and Max both, because they knew too much.

"Max? The woman who was with you . . . ?"

Max Stuyvesant missing and presumed dead. The body of Sabrina Longworth identified by her former husband. *No one would be looking for them. Max and Sabrina Lacoste, living quietly in a small town in Provence, were home free.*

He turned back to the priest. "She's my wife, Robert. We were married in Cap-Ferrat the morning of the explosion. Her name is also Sabrina; it was Sabrina Robion. The other people on the ship were from London and Paris, not close friends, simply companions for a few days."

"Your wife." Robert smiled and covered Max's hand with his. "You once told me you would never . . . Ah, but we should not remind ourselves or our friends of rash statements in our past. I am very happy for you, my friend. But she was gravely injured, Max; will she recover?"

"She will, I think, physically. But she has no memory."

"You mean, of the accident?"

"Of anything except the names of objects. But she's a remarkable woman, very strong; she'll make a new life here, I'm sure of it. In fact, I'm looking forward to it."

"But you can tell her her past, and the more you tell her, the more likely that she will remember all of it."

"I don't know it. We were acquainted only a few days before we were married. But she doesn't miss her past, Robert. She has a new life to create, a completely new life; most of us would give everything we have for that chance."

Robert's eyebrows rose. "Would we? I think, my friend, you'll find that she misses it very much."

Max shrugged. "She'll do what she has to do. That's true of all of us. Robert, I have another favor to ask. The last one, I hope."

Robert smiled. "Another rash statement. What can I do?"

"You know I rented an apartment in Aix. It won't do for both of us. I need a house. I want to buy one, and I was thinking of the plateau above Cavaillon."

"A beautiful spot. You want me to look for one."

"A private one; you know I don't like being crowded."

"You mean I must remember that you're in hiding. Well, I'll see what I can do. The father of one of our students sells houses in the Lubéron; I'll ask him. Now I must go; tomorrow morning is our weekly faculty meeting." He looked closely at Max. "If you need to talk sometime . . ."

"I would not burden our friendship. It's all right, Robert, I've never needed to talk about my problems, or my successes, either. You understand"—he hesitated, a man who had difficulty expressing emotion of any kind—"my friendship with you is the closest I've ever had. I appreciate it." He stood up, as if he had said too much. "When Sabrina and I are in our own home, you'll dine with us. I want her to meet you."

"And I want to meet her. May I visit her in the hospital? I would be pleased to."

"No, I'd rather wait. They've got doctors and psychologists running in and out of her room; she's barely alone and she's exhausted from all of it. You'll come to our home."

"Fine. But if you change your mind . . . priests are good at hospital visits, you know."

Max nodded, barely hearing; he was suddenly frantic to get back. He sped through the streets, repeating his words to Robert. *She will, I think, physically. She will, I think, physically.* But he had been away from her for two hours, and in that time . . .

He raced to her room and found her sitting in her chair, talking comfortably to a doctor he did not know. There were always new doctors in her room, sometimes chatting about the weather or sailing in the Mediterranean or dining at fine restaurants, but most often asking questions, giving Stephanie tests, noting with approval the steady healing of the gash on her head. Much of those conversations she did not remember from day to day, or even hour to hour, but the doctors were patient: they always began again.

"Your amnesia, madame," said one doctor, "is of two kinds. The anterograde, which causes you to forget what I said this morning, will pass, I can positively assure you. But the other, the retrograde, that is more serious. I cannot make any predictions about how long it will last."

"No one told me that," Stephanie said.

"Your first doctor did. You forgot. It happens."

"We find it puzzling," said another doctor to Stephanie on a day when Max was there, "that your type of memory loss does not fit the usual pattern of posttraumatic amnesia. We think it possible that you are primarily suffering from psychogenic amnesia—that is, an amnesia that results when a patient attempts to hide from an overwhelming psychic trauma by totally dissociating the self from the environment. In which case your amnesia would have little to do with the accident on the boat."

Stephanie stared at him. "Are you saying I *want* to forget everything? I'm keeping myself from remembering?"

"You are not consciously preventing yourself from remembering, madame, but it is possible that your unconscious is doing just that. You may have been involved in circumstances that caused you much conflict, that you had not resolved, that, in fact, caused so much pain when you tried to resolve them that it took only a blow on the head to make you cut yourself off from them entirely."

She shook her head, then stopped because it made her headache worse. "What kind of circumstances?"

"I have no way of knowing, madame."

"Something . . . criminal?"

"It is possible."

"It is not possible," Max cut in. "She's not a criminal; she's not capable of criminal acts. I think we've had enough of this; we won't have any more of these sessions."

"Why do you think that?" Stephanie asked the doctor. "That I'm repressing the personal parts of my whole life."

He looked at her with interest, noting the level of intelligence that allowed her to reformulate his theory in that way. "Your memory, madame. It is intact regarding language—in fact, we now know that you speak Italian, English and French with equal fluency—and it is intact regarding the names of objects and how to perform many functions. You buttoned your blouse this morning."

Stephanie looked down at the white buttons on the blue and white striped silk blouse Max had brought her the day before in a large box that also contained a dark blue skirt, underclothes, silk stockings, high-heeled blue shoes. "I didn't realize I was doing it."

"Precisely; it was automatic. Something you knew from before. But what of the rest of your life, madame? Can you think back to buttoning your blouse at other times, perhaps when you were a child and your mother was helping you? Think about your mother, madame, holding you on her lap—yes?—and showing you how to button your blouse. Or taking you to the store to choose a blouse, or perhaps not a blouse, perhaps a doll or a coloring book. Or anything else. You and your mother shopping together, think about that, madame, you and your mother in a shop, choosing something to buy and take home, can you think about that, can you concentrate on that? Think about your mother, madame, and doing things together, shopping together, going in and out of shops, or it does not have to be shopping, it could be—"

"Laura," Stephanie said.

"Madame!" Excitedly, he took her hand. "Is that your mother's name? Don't stop, madame, please go on, concentrate: your mother is Laura and your father is . . . Come, madame, tell me the name of your mother and father."

"I don't know."

"Come, I will help you. Your name is Sabrina. Your mother's name is Laura. Your father's name is . . ."

"I don't know! I don't know if Laura is my mother's name; I don't even know if Sabrina is really my name. Max says it is, but it doesn't feel like my name—"

"What does feel like your name, madame?"

She shook her head then stopped, as she always did, because the pain became worse when she moved her head in any direction, and then she said no more.

In January, Max took her home. The doctors and nurses said goodbye with affection and regret: they had wanted to help her, no matter how long it took, but she was still locked in her empty space, with no past, and her husband said she would not return to them.

Stephanie looked back at the hospital as they drove away. "Home," she murmured. It was the only one she knew, the doctors and nurses and other patients her only friends. She clasped her hands in her lap and sat quietly in the velvet interior of a dark blue Renault driven through streets completely strange to her, by a man who said he was her husband, toward a future he had arranged. She wore a country tweed suit he had given her, part of a complete and lavish wardrobe he had brought to the hospital over the past two months, and as she watched him maneuver easily through the traffic of Marseilles and into the rolling countryside, she felt like a child in a small boat carried by the current to a place so distant it could not be guessed at or even imagined.

They did not stop when they reached Cavaillon, but drove through the town and beyond it on a road that climbed to a plateau overlooking the valley. On the plateau, a large plaque, mounted beside stone gates, commemorated the history of the village and the plain. Max turned into the gates and drove past homes spaced widely apart, set back from winding roads amid tall trees and shrubs, each one shielded from its neighbors. Within that small discreet community Robert had found for them the most discreet spot of all, a stone house set within wooded acres at the end of a road, well hidden behind a high stone wall with a wrought-iron gate.

"Home," Max said, echoing Stephanie's word of two hours earlier, and opened her door to help her out.

And then, almost without effort, she was living there. Madame Besset, the housekeeper, unpacked and put away her clothes; the gardeners touched their caps and one of them gave her a bronze chrysanthemum from the greenhouse. The maintenance man pulled a chaise to a protected corner of the terrace where she could look down upon the town with its orange tile roofs crammed together between narrow, angled streets and bustling squares, its slender church steeples silhouetted against the fields beyond. The terrace was made of white stones, pale beneath the winter sun and the deep blue sky; behind Stephanie the stones of the house were smooth and warm; below, a cliff fell away in huge rock outcroppings surrounded by dense shrubs and pines that clung tenaciously to the steep slope.

I could jump, Stephanie thought the first time Max settled her in the chaise and she gazed over the low wall bordering the terrace. I could just float off the wall and disappear. No one would miss me because they wouldn't know I'd died.

She shivered in the pale rays of the January sun. *No one who ever knew me knows where I am.*

Each day she lay on the terrace and listened to Madame Besset's purposeful clattering in the kitchen, the low rumble of Max's voice on the telephone in his office, the gardener pushing a wheelbarrow to and from the greenhouse, the maintenance man whistling as he repaired some broken tiles on the roof. Those were the only people she had heard since she arrived in Cavaillon. No one came to see them; they did not go out. "We will when you're strong," Max said. "There's no hurry, and in the meantime this is hardly an unpleasant place to be."

It was a beautiful place, the stone house bleached white by the sun, with bright blue shutters, red and pink geraniums on the windowsills, and strings of garlic and dried herbs hanging in the kitchen. Stephanie's bedroom was on the ground floor, a small room with a high four-poster bed, a painted dresser, and fresh flowers brought every day by Madame Besset to her bedside table. Max had taken her to the room when they arrived. "While you recover," he said.

And so she divided her time between her bedroom and the terrace with its sheltered corner and its view of the roofs of Cavaillon, listening to the sounds from the house and the garden. She lay on the chaise, and the sun settled deep within her, easing the last, lingering pain from surgery. She wore a hat to keep the sun from making her headache worse and to protect the sensitive skin grafts on her face, and the days merged into each other as she lay motionless for hours at a time, listening to the silver trills of the birds and the snapping of clippers as the gardener trimmed the holly hedge, and smelling saffron and garlic in the bouillabaisse Madame Besset was preparing, and the fragrance of the red rose Max had brought her that afternoon.

She took the rose from its vase and held it to her nose, breathing deeply of the heady fragrance. *Roses. I've cut roses . . . with a scissors, a silver scissors, and put them in a vase, a tall vase with a design . . . some kind of design . . .* But Max's voice from the study grew louder, repeating something to make a point, and she lost the thought.

His voice wove through her days. Every morning and afternoon he was in his study, on the telephone. But he joined her at lunch and dinner and after dinner, when they sat on the couch in the living room, finishing their wine while Max talked. He told her about his travels, his acquaintances on four continents, his art collection, his childhood in Holland, Belgium and Germany. "I was always a loner; I never stayed anywhere long enough to make friends."

"I moved around, too," Stephanie said.

"Where?" he asked quickly.

"I don't know." She looked at him with puzzled eyes. "I don't know."

They were sitting at either end of the long couch, and all the living room lights but one had been turned off. The room was large and high-ceilinged, with a floor of square white stone tiles and scattered Bessarabian rugs patterned in bold flowers in oranges and greens and browns. Hand-hewn beams ran the length of the ceiling, the slipcovered furniture was deep and soft, and paintings of the lavender fields and vineyards of Provence hung on the walls. One large painting, a wild scene of the Alpilles range signed with the bold signature of Léon Dumas, stood in the most prominent place, on an easel near the fireplace. It was almost midnight and the house was quiet, the housekeeper and gardener gone, the birds still.

"What did I wear?" Stephanie asked abruptly. "When you met me, what was I wearing?"

"A long skirt and a blouse, off the shoulders, I think."

"What color were they?"

"I don't remember. I don't notice that much about clothes."

"That's not true. You've bought everything I have and it's all the right size and the styles are right for me and so are the colors. Max, please, what colors was I wearing? What was the skirt made of? And the blouse?"

"Cotton. The blouse was white and the skirt was striped red and black."

"Where did I buy them?"

"I have no idea. Probably in France."

"You didn't see a label on them?"

"No." He contemplated her. "You didn't ask any of these questions in the hospital."

"I didn't think of them then. Did you see labels on any of my clothes?"

"You unpacked a Valentino evening dress on the ship, and two Christian Dior blouses."

"That's all?"

"We didn't finish unpacking. I wanted you to see the

skyline of Monte Carlo from the lounge and we went forward.''

''That was all you saw? No private label?''

''What made you think of that?''

''If I had a dressmaker, she would know me.''

''There were none.''

Stephanie was frowning, studying his face. She did not believe him. Something was wrong; she knew it, even though she had no idea what it could be or why he would lie to her. She felt ungrateful, doubting him after all he had done for her, but she could not shake this certainty. ''Did I have a purse?''

''Of course, but I wasn't in the habit of rifling it.''

''Did I wear makeup?''

''A little. Not very much. You didn't need it.''

''What was my hair like?''

''Long. Magnificent. You can let it grow again, if you like.''

''I think I will.'' She looked at her hands. ''You said I hadn't been married. When did I tell you that?''

''Soon after we met. Why?''

''I don't know. I think . . . maybe . . . it might not be true.''

''Indeed. Why do you think that?''

She fell silent, suddenly reluctant to confide in him the new thoughts that came to her each day. ''What did you do after your mother died?''

He paused, wondering if he should pursue his question. Not necessary, he thought; the less we talk about it, the better. ''My father and I kept moving: Spain for a while, then London. I told you about my mother yesterday. You remembered.''

''Oh.'' She sat forward. ''Max, I remembered!'' For the first time since she awoke in the hospital, she smiled, a slow smile that caused Max to draw in his breath on a wave of desire that made him dizzy. He had wanted her every minute of the past week, since coming to Cavaillon, but he had held back and given her her own bedroom, put off by the distant look in her eyes when she turned to him: the look of a stranger, the look of someone who had no desire to be close to him. He knew that was not true of her; their affair in October, in the weeks before the yacht exploded, had been the most passionate he had known in a lifetime of sexual encounters.

They had met again, in London, years after Max had first met her, when she and Denton, newly married, were guests on his yacht. She was unused to their ways then, resisting the drugs and casual sex that the rest of them took for granted. When he saw her again, at the end of September, sitting with Brooks and Gabrielle at Annabel's, there had been a hunger in her eyes for adventure, and a kind of recklessness, as if she were trying to squeeze everything into a short time. He had liked that; it was the way he had always lived.

He had asked her to decorate and furnish his new town house, and she had done it brilliantly, and then she had made it hers as well by staying there for a weekend that had struck him with that same kind of intense recklessness: as if it were to be their only time together.

He had fallen in love with her then; her presence haunted him after she left. But at the same time he had been preoccupied with his company, Westbridge Imports, with Denton's trying to take it over, with rumors of reporters working on stories about smuggled antiquities and forged works of art. He had been busy winding up his London operations, setting up Lacoste et fils in Marseilles, and getting out of England while he could, to make a new life with a new identity in France, and so he did not recognize the fact that he had fallen in love with her and, in fact, probably would have asked her to marry him if the explosion on the yacht had not happened.

Now, in Cavaillon, seeing her smile, seeing her eyes come to life, he could not wait any longer. He took her in his arms. "My beautiful, adorable Sabrina," he said, and covered her mouth with his.

She let him hold her, but her mouth was slack beneath

his and her hands stayed in her lap, and after a moment he let her go. "What we had was so memorable," he murmured, but then he realized the irony of it. Nothing was memorable to this woman, and that was the way it had to be: they could go on together only if she remained locked in her amnesia, believing she was his wife and knowing nothing of the bomb on the yacht, or that it had been put there to kill not only Max Stuyvesant but Sabrina Longworth as well.

"Memorable," Stephanie said wryly. "It would have had to be a lot better than that."

"It was better, and we'll have it again. Listen to yourself, Sabrina: this is the first time you've been able to look at yourself with humor. You're getting better." He took her unresisting hand. "If you still want to wait, if you insist on sleeping downstairs . . ."

"Yes."

"Well, for a time." He kissed her fingers and her palm. "I adore you, Sabrina; you're everything I want. You'll come to me, and I promise you we'll be everything to each other. We don't need anyone else; all we want, all we need, is here."

Stephanie gazed at the top of his head as he kissed her hand. She felt his lips brush her skin, but that was all. *I ought to feel something if he's my husband. I ought to want him.* And she knew then that she knew what sexual desire was and that she had felt it once, but felt nothing now.

Two weeks after they arrived, the weather changed: the sky lowered into a solid gray and the wind rose, bending the trees and making the shutters creak. Rain spattered on the white stones of the terrace, and chill air crept into the house. For the first time, Max and Stephanie ate lunch indoors, in a small room off the kitchen with a round olivewood table and four cushioned wicker chairs. Madame Besset had been making bread, and the room was fragrant and snug while the wind flattened the grass beyond the windows.

Something let go within Stephanie. The tense fearfulness of the past two weeks began to ease, her body relaxed against the flowered cushions of her chair, and she picked up her glass and saw how beautiful was the pale gold of the wine in the golden light from the chandelier. I'm alive and I'm getting better, she thought. And if·I keep getting better, pretty soon I'll remember everything. I'm already remembering things that happened yesterday and the day before, and I do know some things about myself. She ticked them off in her mind. I knew someone named Laura and she may have been my mother, and I cut roses with a silver scissors and I moved around a lot. She felt a sudden sinking. It isn't much. It really isn't anything.

"Sabrina?" Max was looking at her.

"I'm sorry. I didn't hear you."

"Dreaming again." He looked up as Madame Besset came in.

"There is a man waiting to see you in your study. Very serious, very intense. He calls himself Father Chalon, though you would not know he is a priest to look at him, and he says he will wait until you have finished your lunch."

"No, bring him here; he'll join us for lunch. A good friend," Max said to Stephanie. "I've been wanting you to meet him."

Stephanie looked up as he came in: he was short and slender, with a neatly trimmed brown beard shot with gray and dark brown eyes set close together above a thin nose. He bent over her hand. "I'm so pleased to meet you. Max speaks of you often."

"Join us," Max said. "Madame Besset is bringing a plate."

"Thank you." Robert sat down, his eyes still on Stephanie. Quite young, he thought. Thirty? Perhaps thirty-one or -two. Slender, holds herself well; perhaps she has been an athlete. He recognized the clothes she wore: the white turtleneck sweater and blue jeans that Max had bought on a shopping trip in Marseilles. Robert had been with him, watching with amusement Max's sureness with sizes and styles: he knew how to dress a woman.

But more than anything, Robert was struck by her beauty, a vibrant beauty enlivened by the curiosity and intelligence in her eyes. That had not been visible when he helped bring her to Marseilles; he had known only that she probably had once been beautiful. Now, looking at her as if he were viewing a Botticelli in the Uffizi, or one of Titian's glorious women in the Louvre, he felt the tug that beauty exerts: the desire to draw close to it, to absorb some of its perfection, to believe that, because it exists, the world can become a place without pain or sorrow or grief. He became aware that the silence was stretching out and he said, "I am delighted to see you so much improved."

Sabrina looked at Max questioningly.

"Robert accompanied us to Marseilles and to the hospital," he said.

"And would not have predicted such a rapid recovery. I can see that your bruises have faded, as has the swelling; how is the wound on your head? That frightened us very much."

Instinctively, Stephanie's hand went to the scar, hidden by her hair. "It's much better. I'm getting better."

"And remembering, too?"

"No." She looked swiftly at Max. "You promised you wouldn't—"

"I told only Robert because he's very close to us. We'll tell no one else; I promise you that."

"Close to us?" Stephanie waited as Madame Besset arranged a plate and cutlery for Robert and placed a casserole nearby so he could serve himself. Max poured his wine as Robert broke off a chunk of bread from the large round loaf in the center of the table.

"Robert and I do some work together," Max said. "It's something that would not interest you. But—"

"Why not?"

"Well, it might, someday, but not today. Anyway,

Robert has had a most unusual life; he might tell you about it.''

"If madame would be interested," said Robert.

"Oh, not 'madame,' " Stephanie said. "It doesn't sound like me."

"Ah, thank you. Sabrina, then. A very lovely name. If indeed you are interested . . .''

"Yes." And to her surprise, she was. It was the first time since she had been in the house that she had felt a spark of curiosity. She had not opened any of the books that filled the library; she did not look at *Figaro* when it arrived each day on their doorstep, nor had she read *Madame Figaro*, the glossy magazine that came with the Friday edition. She had thought idly of going into Cavaillon, especially on market days, but Max said they could not go yet, and she did not care enough to press it.

But today the wind howled, the breakfast room was cozy, and it was exciting to talk to someone who was not a doctor or a nurse or Max. Today, over the deep sadness that lay like a weight inside her, and over the terrors of emptiness that haunted her nights, she felt a ripple of being alive and of being glad that she was. She smiled at Robert. She liked him. He wore corduroy pants and a dark blue sweater over an open-necked shirt, and his raggedly cut hair reached his collar. He looked like a schoolboy. "How old are you?" Stephanie asked.

"Forty-one," he said promptly. "Forty-two next month."

"You look younger."

"I feel younger. Probably from bicycling up Mont Ventoux once a week. Perhaps you'll do it with me one day."

"I don't know if I know how to ride a bicycle."

"The easiest way to find out is to start pedaling. If you find you can't do it, I'll gladly teach you."

Stephanie looked at Max. "I'd like to try. Is it all right? May I buy a bicycle?"

"Of course, if that's what you want. We'll wait," he said to Robert, "until she's stronger."

"She's strong enough now for many rides around here. The postal roads that circle the vineyards and cherry orchards—empty except once a day when the postman comes in his car—even you could do them."

Max smiled. "I thought you'd given up trying to turn me into an athlete. But if Sabrina wants it, of course she'll have it."

Stephanie felt like a child between two grown-ups. They knew everything, and she knew nothing. She imagined curling up between them, letting them take care of her. Then, perversely, she felt stirrings of anger. *Don't treat me like a child.*

But in a powerful way, she really was like a child. She had no history, no framework of experience in which to maneuver and hold her own and make decisions about the future.

Then I'll pretend, she thought, and said to Robert, "You were going to tell me your story."

"And so I will." He wiped his plate with his bread, finished his wine, and sat back. "My father was a pirate." He smiled at Stephanie's expression. "It amuses me to say that, and in fact, when I was growing up, that was what he told me and my brothers: he was a pirate on the high seas. But he was something less dramatic: a clever and rather lucky thief who worked as a steward on a very posh cruise line. He was quite short, but extraordinarily handsome and well-muscled, and he charmed everyone; I never knew a man before or since who was so loved—adored, really—by everyone. Including, of course, his wife and six sons."

"That I hadn't known," Max said. "Six boys. No girls?"

"My mother often said her character was forged by having to hold her own against seven men. And she was indeed a woman of admirable fortitude. She was a maid in the Hôtel Fouchard, an elegant place with a restaurant that Michelin gave three stars every year. That was my favorite place in the world, that kitchen."

"What did your father steal?" Stephanie was leaning forward, her chin on her folded hands, for the first time happily absorbed in someone else.

"Whatever he could. Small amounts of money that were not likely to be missed; jewelry, always from women who had brought such an enormous cache of gold and jewels on board that a bracelet or brooch or jeweled hair clip might not be missed until they were back on shore. It was highly risky and stupid, because his tips were extremely generous, and of course it was immoral, but he was convinced he could not support his family in fine style in any other way. And then, you see, he had so many successful years that it all began to seem quite normal. After a while he saw himself as an entrepreneur; his business, with regular routines and accounting systems and steady hours, was piracy."

Stephanie laughed. Max and Robert looked at her as if she had been transformed. And in a way she had: her face was alight as it had not been before. For Max, it was as if the woman he had known in London had come back to him, exuberant, vivid, living life as if everything she found was new and wonderful. For Robert, the moment when Stephanie laughed was the moment when he began to love her with the protective love of an adult for a child caught in a world filled with dangers.

Of course her world is filled with dangers, he thought. Why else would Max pretend to be dead? From whom was he fleeing? What if these people, whoever they are, found out that he was still alive? Where could this child-woman go? To whom could she run for help? She would come to me, Robert thought. And I would take care of her.

It was a promise.

"Where is your father now?" Stephanie asked.

"Dead, for many years. It becomes a sad story. You see, for all his legendary charm, my father was a man of vicious temper. My mother kept him under control at home, but away from his family he was a coiled spring, waiting to explode at any provocation. It did not happen often, but it happened a few times that I knew about before the last time, when I was sixteen. Some man tried to blackmail my father into sharing his loot. They had a fight. The man had a knife, and my father was killed.''

Stephanie was staring at him, wide-eyed. ''He was very young. And your mother was left with six boys to bring up.''

''Spoken like a mother,'' Robert said, smiling.

Stephanie gave a small gasp, and Max said, ''Sabrina has no children.''

''How do you know?'' Stephanie demanded.

''You told me you'd never been married. I assume you had no children. You never mentioned any. I got the impression you didn't want any.''

There was a pause. ''You never told me that. What else did I say that you haven't told me?''

''A few things, nothing that would help us fill in your background. I was waiting until you were better to tell you all of them; I thought if they triggered some memories, you would handle them more easily if you were stronger.''

''Max, I'm strong now.''

''You're still recovering. We'll go over everything, Sabrina, at the right time. You said you would trust me; I expect you to do that.'' He refilled their wineglasses. ''Robert, finish your story.''

Robert looked from Max to Stephanie. He saw Stephanie clasp her hands—in despair? he wondered, or resignation?—and he pulled his chair closer to the table to drink the coffee Madame Besset had served. ''Well, then, my mother was left with six boys. I was the oldest and by then I was earning a little money, so I could help her.''

''But you were in school,'' Stephanie said.

''No, I left school when I was twelve. I made a fuss and my mother did not argue. I was not a good student; what I really wanted was to be in the kitchen of the Hôtel Fouchard. So I would go to work with my mother, and while she cleaned the rooms, I hung around the kitchen. I washed dishes, I folded napkins and polished cutlery, I ran errands, and then one day the sous chef said I could help cut up vegetables. I did that for all of my fourteenth year. When I was fifteen I was allowed to help make salads. By the time I was sixteen, when my father was killed, I was assistant to the pastry chef and they were paying me, not much, but something.''

"And then?" Stephanie asked.

"Well, eventually I became a chef with my own three-star restaurant. I had a reputation equal to that of the Troigrois brothers, Paul Bocuse, Michel Guérard . . . all the masters of French cuisine. We were all good friends, compatriots, dedicated to our art. And after a while I had a wife and a child.''

"Oh. But then . . .''

"But then, one day, just ten years ago, I was working late and someone came to rob the restaurant. And my life changed.''

He paused, and Stephanie murmured, ''Another thief.''

Robert gazed at her with pleasure. ''You understand how curious it is that my life was shaped by two thieves. Well, yes, another thief. He broke in a side door while I was at my desk off the kitchen. I heard a sound—he was breaking open the safe in the maître d's office—and when I confronted him we fought. And I killed him.''

Stephanie gasped. ''You had a knife. From the kitchen.''

"Ah, my dear, you are quick. Yes, this time I was the one with the knife. But he had a gun, and though he had no chance to use it, everyone agreed that I had been defending myself and therefore should not be convicted. So I was free and my restaurant had a soupçon more publicity, and all should have been well. But it was not. Because, you see, when I fought with that man I discovered in myself a fury I did not know I had, and a great joy in the attack. I became my father, exploding into murderous rage, and nothing, *nothing* could have stopped me from killing. When it was over, I understood my father and I understood that I was indeed his son.''

There was a silence. Robert was looking at his hands,

clasped on the edge of the table. "I understood, too, that all of us harbor some seed within us that is fundamental to our being even though we have no suspicion it is there, something so deeply a part of us that even when we claim, in our arrogance, that we can predict how we will behave in this circumstance or that, and can control our actions, in truth we do not have the proper eyes to see that seed, nor do we have the self-knowledge that would allow us to plumb deep enough to reach it. And so we know only a part of ourselves and often cannot control even that part. I did not know the man who killed that thief. His name was Robert Chalon and he inhabited my body, but he was unknown to me. That terrified me. And I thought then that it was essential to learn who I was, and to use my knowledge to help others know truly who they are, to help them understand their fundamental nature and use it for good."

"You've upset her," Max said, and Robert looked up to see tears glistening on Stephanie's face.

"Ah, Sabrina, forgive me." Robert held her hand between his. "I did not realize . . . Of course, that is your loss, too: you do not know the person who inhabits your body. Well, then, let me help you, let us try together to bring back your past and return to you your true self."

"I don't know how," Stephanie said.

"Nor do I, but perhaps we can learn together. And do you know what else? I will teach you to cook. Shall I? I would make a bet that you knew how in the past, and it may come back and help us find the rest of you. What do you say to that?"

"Madame Besset will not be happy," Max said, and Stephanie knew that though he said it lightly he was not pleased with the discussion.

"I'd like that," she said firmly to Robert, not looking at Max. "I'd like that very much."

"Then we'll do it. Perhaps two mornings a week? Would that be all right?"

She smiled ruefully. "I'm not busy; that would be wonderful. But I don't want Madame Besset to find out that I have no memory."

"Can you give her the day off?"

"Oh, yes, that would be perfect; I'll tell her she can have two mornings— Oh." She turned to Max. "I'm sorry. Is it all right? We could give Madame Besset two mornings a week off, couldn't we?"

"If it would make you happy."

"Thank you," Stephanie said, and no one commented on the fact that twice, during lunch, she had asked Max's permission as if, indeed, she were a child.

Robert stood up. "I must leave. I thank you for lunch; it was excellent. We should decide on which mornings—"

"Why didn't you say anything about God?" Stephanie asked abruptly. "If you wanted to help people find themselves, you could have become a psychologist or a psychiatrist; you didn't have to become a priest."

He sat down again. "You know about psychologists and psychiatrists."

"From the hospital."

"And you know much more than that, I'm sure. Well, you want to know about God. Long ago, in ancient times, when men tried to map the world, they would draw as much as they knew from sailing along the coastlines of countries, but without airplanes, they could not know all there was. And so the rest of the map was left blank. In that blank space they drew dragons and other fire-breathing creatures, and wrote, 'Where you know nothing, place terrors.' After I killed that man, when I knew that I knew nothing, my world was filled with terrors. And the only way I could live with my ignorance and those terrors was to acknowledge that there are mysteries that pervade our lives and we will probably never understand them. People like to think they can understand everything, given enough time and money, but of course that is not true. So I accepted the great mystery in what makes us human and unique, and, like others throughout history, I gave it the name of God. And within that name lie all the unknowns and powers and potentials that make us what we are; the fears and dreams and terrors that visit us; the love we give and the love we are so grateful to receive; the spirit that lets us soar—unless we fail to nurture it, and so we sink. I could not look inside myself or help others to do the same without acknowledging the dominance of that mystery in my life. Psychiatrists and psychologists seem able to do it; I know many of them are sensitive and superb in their helping professions. But I cannot. Does that answer your question?''

''What happened to your wife and child?''

''My wife died two years ago. My child lives with a family in Roussillon. Sometimes we count our gains in losses. We will talk about that sometime. Now I will say goodbye, my dear Sabrina. And I will see you . . . day after tomorrow? At nine in the morning?''

Stephanie looked at Max. ''Fine,'' he said. ''I'll see you out, Robert.''

She watched them go. She heard the shutters creak and the house groan beneath the onslaught of the wind and she saw the trees whip wildly, like dancers gone mad. *Sometimes we count our gains in losses.* She had lost her past, but the house sheltered her, and within it Max and Madame Besset cared for her. She was alive; her body grew stronger each day; she remembered someone named Laura and the smell of roses, and a silver scissors, and moving around a lot, and she knew about psychiatrists and psychologists.

And now she had a friend who would help her remember the rest.

CHAPTER *6*

Sabrina and Garth stood in the round, dimly lit main room of the Shedd Aquarium, greeting their guests. It was February, almost four months after Stephanie's funeral, and by now Sabrina found it so natural to be with Garth, to stand beside him hosting a university function, that she no longer wondered at her life, or her sureness in making it her own. Her grief over Stephanie's death was a permanent part of her, clutching her at unexpected moments, but her love for Garth and the children was more powerful, always new and wondrous, a kind of magic she had never known.

In the aquarium, she and Garth stood close together, smiling and greeting everyone by name. On the circular wall around them large windows looked into the bright underwater worlds of exotic fish, crustaceans, corals, and undulating plants that made the aquarium on Chicago's lakefront famous. Garth had chosen it as a unique place for a reception to honor major donors to the Institute for Genetic Engineering, and to welcome potential ones, and now he watched the guests move from window to window, murmuring through their sophisticated veneer at the wondrous iridescent colors of rare fish and the fantastic shapes of crustaceans from all the oceans of the world. He and Sabrina shared a smile. "I'm glad you're here," he said. "Even with the fish, it would have been as dull as every other reception, without you."

"It wouldn't be dull for me," Sabrina said. "I love to watch you work a crowd and make speeches, and I love you, and there's nowhere else I'd rather be right now."

Their guests commented on what a striking couple they were, Garth in his tuxedo and Sabrina in a gold sweater and long white satin skirt she had brought from her closet in London, and when Claudia Beyer, the president of the university, arrived, she eyed them with approval. "Stephanie, Garth, you do us proud. Do we have a goal for tonight?"

Garth shook his head. "We're just making everyone feel wanted and loved. We'll go after them in the next six weeks, the end of the campaign, I hope. February and March are good times to ask for money; by then most people have forgotten how much they spent on Christmas."

Claudia smiled. She was tall and very thin, curved like an archer's bow, with slicked-back gray hair and oversize tortoiseshell glasses. She wore a black pants suit with a ruffled white blouse and was almost a twin to her tall, thin husband, a professor of French history. "And the goal for the end of the campaign?" she asked.

"Three million four," Garth said patiently, knowing that she knew exactly how much everyone in the university was seeking at every moment of the year. "That will bring us up to fifteen million and we won't have to ask for any more until we decide to expand."

"It's taken a lot of entertaining," Claudia mused.

"All of it in the budget. We haven't gone over."

"I know. It's a very big budget. But tonight looks like a good evening; I like your idea of the aquarium."

"I can't take credit for that," Garth said, glancing at Sabrina.

"Ah." Claudia nodded. "I always did like Stephanie's ideas. I'll call you about another lunch, Stephanie; there's something I'd like to talk to you about. Shall I call you at your shop?"

"Yes. If I'm not there, Madeline will be. I'd like lunch; I enjoyed our last one."

"Good." She left as abruptly as she had arrived, moving purposefully to a group of guests watching a school of anglerfish glide through the darkened water, their bands of color as luminous as neon.

"What did she mean about a very big budget?" Sabrina asked.

"That we're spending a lot to raise a lot and she'd rather spend a little to raise the same amount. I'd do it if I could, but I haven't found a good way to get someone to write a six- or seven-figure check without some socializing to smooth the way."

"Claudia ought to do it. You should be thinking about science and running an institute, not going around with your hat in your hand."

"She does do it, and she's one of the best, but people who write checks with lots of zeroes usually want to see the person who's going to spend them. I can understand that. You look extraordinarily beautiful tonight. You look wonderful in gold, and I like your hair; you've cut it, haven't you? It looks shorter."

She was laughing. "I have cut it and it is shorter, and I'm glad you like it." But beneath her laughter a sudden stab of grief cut through her and she shrank into herself, almost breathless with pain. Stephanie had had long hair; the two of them had always worn it tumbling loose to their shoulders and when one of them felt like braiding it or pinning it up, the other had done the same. Why did I cut my hair? she wondered suddenly. I started thinking about it in January and I knew it was the right thing to do. Why was that? Why am I so sure it was right?

"My love," Garth said gently.

"I'm sorry." She put her hand on his arm. "I don't mean to go off like that and leave you."

"I know you don't; it's not something you can control. I think we should leave as soon as possible; how do you feel about that?"

"Wonderful."

But Garth and Claudia Beyer were hosts for the evening and so they stayed, through dinner and brief speeches, and then dancing. "We're stuck," Garth said as he and Sabrina moved in a smooth rhythm at the edge of the dance floor. "I can't leave until Claudia does."

Sabrina slid her hand farther around his shoulders. "I love to dance with you. I'm very happy where I am."

"I'm very happy with where you are, too."

They danced in silence. "Sometimes I miss Ambassadors, though," Sabrina said slowly, almost tentatively, knowing Garth did not like to talk about the past. "That whole crazy business of antiques in Europe, the competition, so much more fierce than here."

Garth's eyebrows rose. "You want more tension in your life?"

She laughed. "I can't imagine why I would. But I've been thinking about Ambassadors, Garth; I think I ought to go there, just for a few days. It's been two months since I was there, and that was Christmas and they were so busy . . . Anyway, I don't think I should stay away more than two months at a time."

"You don't trust Nicholas and Brian?"

"I trust Brian; he's worked for me for a long time. But I've never worked with Nicholas and there's so much going on, merging his shop with Ambassadors and both of them with Collectibles in Evanston, it almost feels as if I'm starting over again, and I don't feel I have any real control unless I can be there, at least once in a while. I want to make this work; it means a lot to me."

"I know it does. Of course you should go. And you've got your house to stay in; that makes it easier."

"And Mrs. Thirkell. I've decided to bring her here, Garth. She has nothing to do there and—"

"Bring her here?"

"It's that or let her go, and I don't want to do that; she's been with me even longer than Brian has. And why shouldn't we have someone full time to take care of the house, and all of us? You know how wonderful she is; she'd make everything a lot easier."

The music stopped and they stood still, holding each other lightly. Garth looked beyond Sabrina, at the other dancers. "There's a lot of hostility on a campus when professors seem to be living higher than they should."

Sabrina stiffened. "Who decides how high they should live?"

"No one; you know that. It's a kind of unwritten community standard that everyone recognizes. And it's not always a bad—"

"So everyone who lives in that community has to fit that standard, is that right? What if I hired Juanita for two days instead of one, or served better wines, or bought a fancier car—would the tongues start wagging? Would somebody paint a hex sign over our front door?"

"Look, I didn't make this up. It's part of the world we live in. And it's not always a bad thing. When you're part of a community you don't lord it over everyone else or give them reasons to think you are. I have more important things to do with my time than deal with whispers and wounded egos. I'm not saying they're inevitable, but—"

"You said, 'There's a lot of hostility.' "

"Well, it's happened. It isn't a sure bet that it would this time, but it's a possibility. And why chance it? Hostility makes a lousy atmosphere for research and building a new institute, especially if the people who are hostile know they're not likely ever to have the kind of resources we have."

"Garth, this is ridiculous; I can't believe you're saying this. If they can't afford a full-time housekeeper, they can't afford one. That's all. It isn't a commentary on their character or scientific brilliance; all it says is that different people have different bank accounts. And we don't judge people by their bank accounts. At least I don't.''

They had walked a little distance away from the dance floor to a quiet corner, their heads close together, their voices low. Their bodies were tense, and no one interrupted them.

''You haven't lived on a campus,'' Garth said impatiently. ''You might try to understand how people feel when they make just enough to support a family without a wagonload of frills.''

''I might try to understand? There was a time when I didn't earn enough to support anyone but myself, and sometimes I wasn't sure I could do that. It took me a long time to make Ambassadors a success; there were a lot of years when I didn't have one frill, much less a wagonload. And I never stopped being careful. You know that; I've told you about it. Are you accusing me of being extravagant or profligate, Garth? Do you think I've been throwing our money around?''

''No, but you don't know—''

''I know enough to run your house, and I have no intention of lying down and letting a bunch of hidebound professors tell me how to do it with their unwritten rules and regulations. I haven't—''

'' 'No intention'? What does that mean? That you'll do what you want, come hell or high water? That you don't give a damn what's important to me?''

''You know how much I care what's important to you. I think I pay a lot of attention to that. I haven't failed, you know; I've done a pretty good job with your family.''

''It's your family, too.'' He took a deep breath. ''What the hell are we talking about?''

''The elegant, high-toned, exclusive Mrs. Thirkell.''

Their eyes met and they burst out laughing. ''Well, she's more homey than high-toned,'' Garth conceded. ''Christ, I'm sorry, my love; I went overboard, didn't I?''

88

"I'm sorry, too. I shouldn't have gotten angry. I'm never angry at you; how did I do this?"

"Maybe you've got the tension you were looking for. I don't know what got into me, though."

"I think you're under a lot of pressure about the institute and you worry too much about fitting into your community. But you're good enough to be whatever you want to be, Garth. Everyone likes you and admires you; why are you afraid to be different? What would happen if some people think that we're living too high for our station in life?"

"They could make life unpleasant. It's a very small community, you know, and we all need each other, for support, for getting funding, for bouncing ideas off each other, even for convincing the administration we need another secretary. It isn't as simple as it seems to outsiders."

"Am I an outsider?"

"No, my God, no. Look, go ahead; bring her back from London if you want. It won't cause an earthquake, just a small shift in the earth's crust. Everyone will get used to it."

"Fine." They were silent. "Have we really been talking about Mrs. Thirkell?" she asked.

"Well, not entirely. I suppose I'm jealous of London. You tend to wrap a place around you, my love, and make it part of you, and it was your home for a long time. I think of you there with your friends, and nothing to remind you of us, and it's occurred to me—it occurs to me often—that they might seduce you into coming back."

She put her hand along his face. "Not one chance in a million. The only seduction I'm interested in is my husband's. If we were home now, I could prove that with a few very interesting moves."

He chuckled. "I'll hold you to that." The music began again and they moved into each other's arms and onto the dance floor. "So, let the marvelous Mrs. Thirkell come to

Evanston; you're right, it would be wonderful for you, and I think the kids would love her.''

"I think so, too.''

"When do you want to go?''

"In a week or two. I may do some buying while I'm there, if Madeline agrees. I don't want her to think I'm taking over, but we have clients who are looking for particular pieces that I might be able to find.''

"Let her go next time.''

"She doesn't know Europe. I'll have to do it a few times a year. You really don't mind?''

"I'll miss you. But of course you should go.''

Her hand curved around the back of his neck. "Would there be a lot of hostility if I kissed you here? Would people say it wasn't appropriate for your station in life?''

"If they do, the hell with them.'' They kissed lightly, smiling. "It is amazing and wonderful to me how much I love you,'' Garth murmured, and then Claudia Beyer came up to them and Sabrina and Garth had no more time alone until almost midnight when, finally, everyone left, buttoning fur and heavy wool coats against the bitter end-of-February wind that whipped in off the lake and buffeted them as they walked down the broad steps to their waiting limousines.

"Nice of Claudia to do this,'' Garth said as he and Sabrina saw the limousine waiting for them. "I like her style.''

"I like her,'' Sabrina said. "We had a good talk at lunch last week. She's smart and she cares about people and she cares intensely about the university.''

The driver held the door and Garth slid into the back seat after Sabrina. "More than she cares about people?''

"You mean, would she sacrifice people for the good of the university? I don't know. I'm not sure she does. I hope she doesn't have to make the choice.''

"I hope not.'' Garth put his arm around her and held her as the limo merged with the traffic on Lake Shore

Drive. "If you had married a rich man you could travel like this all the time."

Sabrina did not say that she had married a rich man once, and it had not been enough. There was no reason to talk about Denton; he no longer had any part in her life, and she had had no reason to think of him for years. "I like the man I married," she said, "with or without limousines. Do you think tonight was a success?"

"I know it was. They all loved you, you know; they think if you're connected with the institute it's well worth their hard-earned or hard-inherited money. But right now I want to stop thinking about money and just think about us."

He pulled her closer and they kissed, a long kiss of familiarity and contentment, and of a love and passion that grew with each day they were together. Five months, almost six, Sabrina thought, settling back against Garth in the warmth of the car as snowflakes began to streak past the windows. *Almost six months since I came here, deceiving everyone, and stayed and stayed and fell in love and then Stephanie . . .*

Stephanie.

It was a low cry within her. Stephanie was gone, and it felt to Sabrina as if the place where she had been was a vast emptiness, a fog, a cloud, all of space, infinity. All that was left was a memory, a longing, a love.

But there were many other loves—Garth, the children, her work, a way of life. She felt she was living on two planes, pulled in two directions: *My sister is dead, but for the first time I have more than I ever dreamed could be mine.*

"Do you know," Garth mused, his voice a soft murmur at her ear, "once in a very rare while there comes a time when our lives settle into perfect balance, when everything is in its perfect place. I never really believed that could happen. Now I know that it can. Because right now, my love, now is our perfect time."

"Yes." The word was a long breath, like a prayer of

thanksgiving. The flare-up with Garth, all the little flare-ups and tensions of learning to live together while pretending to the world that they had been married for twelve years, all faded away. They were not important. What was important was that even though she had lost the person closest to her in all the world, she had found Garth, and a family, and a love between a man and woman beyond imagining. *I don't know how that can be. Unless somehow I've become both of us in a way that's beyond logic. If that's true, then, look, Stephanie, we both have short hair now.*

She sighed, a little ashamed of her fantasy, and settled deeper into Garth's arms as the car headed north to Evanston, and the snowflakes streamed past the window, blotting out the lights of the city and the rest of the world.

"Sounds like a fishy evening to me," Cliff said and guffawed as he poured a small pond of syrup over his waffle.

"It sounds like fun," Penny said wistfully. "Like, if nobody talked to you, you could look at the fish and they'd keep you company."

Sabrina gave her a swift glance. "Has that happened lately? People not talking to you?"

"Oh, sometimes. You know."

"No, I don't know," Garth said. "You and Barbara were best friends, I thought. What's going on, Penny?"

"Nothing." Penny looked at her plate. "It was just, you know, I was just thinking about the fish."

Cliff stuffed waffle into his mouth. "A lot of your friends look sort of like fish; you know, mouths going all the time, and staring at you like they're looking for dinner."

"They're not like that!" Penny cried. Tears appeared in her eyes. "They're my friends."

"I thought you just said they don't talk to you."

"They do! It's just . . ."

"Okay," Sabrina said, "I think we've talked enough

about Penny's friends. Maybe Penny and I can talk about them later, by ourselves.''

Trouble here, she thought as Penny threw her a quick, grateful glance, but we'll take care of it. Whatever it is, it hasn't been around long enough to become deep-rooted or I would have heard of it.

She watched Cliff spear a piece of waffle on his fork and swirl it around his plate, making figure eights through the pool of syrup. He looked absorbed, but something about the tilt of his head told her he was listening. He's waiting for us to say something, she thought. About what? About last night?

"It *was* fun," she said. "Everybody said it was the best place to have a party because it was so different, even a little mysterious. You know how they keep the rooms dark so the fish tanks show up better; it's probably the only university party where people were in the dark."

Garth smiled. "Some people say academics are always in the dark."

"Not the academic in this family," Sabrina said.

"Was what's-his-name there?" Cliff asked. His voice was casual, but Sabrina saw his grip on his fork.

"What's-his-name?" Garth echoed.

"You know, Lun or Lon or Loony or whatever."

"*Lu*," Penny said. "Lu Zhen. He's only been here for dinner a hundred times."

"Six or seven," Sabrina said. "And you do know his name."

"*Was* he there?" Cliff asked Garth.

"No. There weren't any students. Would it make a difference if he had been?"

Cliff shrugged.

"You're jealous," Penny said.

"I'm not! I just was *wondering;* you don't have to make a big deal out of it."

"More waffles?" Sabrina asked. "Cliff? Do you want another piece to sop up all that syrup?"

"Sure."

"Cliff doesn't like him," Penny said.

"I never said that!"

But you don't, Sabrina thought. You don't like your father's star graduate student and maybe that shouldn't surprise us. Another piece of trouble to watch out for; I guess we'll have to talk about it before we invite Lu to dinner again. "What I want to know is, what is everybody doing this afternoon?"

"We could go to the aquarium," Cliff said brightly. "That's a good thing to do on Sunday afternoon."

"Good idea," Sabrina said quickly, to forestall the impatient exclamation she saw Garth about to make. "I didn't get to see much last night; we were too busy talking to people. You'd better bundle up, though; it's unbelievably cold walking there from the car."

"We're really going?" Cliff asked in disbelief.

"It's okay with me if it's okay with everybody else."

"Can I take my paints?" Penny asked.

"They're too messy to carry around, Penny. Take crayons or chalk. You can paint at home. Garth? Is the aquarium all right?"

"Only if Cliff can find me a coelacanth."

"A what?" yelped Cliff.

"I'll show you." Garth took out a pencil and pad of paper and began to draw. Penny and Cliff hunched near him, and Sabrina watched the three of them. *There comes a time when our lives settle into perfect balance, when everything is in its perfect place.* Wonderfully true, she thought. Because Penny's and Cliff's problems are part of growing up and children grow up bumpily, not smoothly—that's something I've learned in the last five months—and one of the perfect parts of our life is sharing our children's growing up: shaping, nudging, helping, guiding. Something I never had and always wanted. And, Stephanie, these are such lovely children, so full of love and life, so bright and curious and eager to learn. You did that. You and Garth. Before I ever got here.

"Well, I think it's ugly," Penny said. "You can look

for one if you want, but I'm only going to look for beautiful things that I can draw. I only want to draw beautiful things."

"There's lots of unbeautiful things in the world, though," Cliff said.

"But I don't have to paint them. Do I, Mommy?"

"Not now," Sabrina said. "Maybe, if you decide to be an artist when you grow up, you might paint more of the whole world, the good and the bad, the beautiful and the ugly, and the happy and the sad, too."

"You don't do that," Penny objected. "You and Madeline don't buy ugly antiques; you only buy beautiful ones."

Sabrina met Garth's amused glance. "That's true. But do you think I'd have a lot of customers if I bought ugly things?"

"No, but nobody would buy my paintings if they were ugly, either."

"I think it's different with art. Artists give us their visions of the world and we look at them to find whatever we can in their paintings or sculptures and books. Every work of art probably has as many meanings as it has people looking at it, because each of us sees it in our own way. Sometimes what we see helps us understand the world a little better, or maybe understand ourselves better, know who we are and what we want . . ."

Penny was watching her intently, trying to grasp it all. "It's more complicated than antiques," Sabrina finished. "One of these days we'll talk about it again." She spooned a few strawberries from a glass bowl to her plate. "But I did want to talk about antiques, and maybe this is a good time."

"Gonna watch television," Cliff said and pushed back his chair.

"No, I want you here," Sabrina said. "And you don't watch television in the morning, ever, you know that."

"Yeh, but, Mom, *antiques.*"

"I know they're not your thing, but I want you to stay

because what I really want to talk about is my shops.''

"Collectibles," Penny said.

"She said *shops*," said Cliff.

Sabrina nodded. "Collectibles and Ambassadors and Blackford's.''

"Yeh, but those other ones are in London," Cliff said. "You don't work in them; you work in Collectibles."

"But I own half of each of them. So I have to keep track of what we buy and sell, and how much money we make, all that sort of thing. And it isn't enough to do it on the telephone; owners have to check out what they own in person, at least once in a while.''

The breakfast room was silent. Then Penny cried out, "You can't! You can't go there!''

"You're going to London?" Cliff demanded. "You can't; you have to stay here!"

Penny burst into tears. "Mommy, don't go! Please don't go! Please stay here!''

Garth and Sabrina exchanged a look. We should have expected this, they told each other silently. "Hey, you two," Garth said firmly, "listen for a minute. Your mother is going to London for a few days, three or four, that's all, and then she'll be back."

"Last time you went to London you didn't come back," Cliff said loudly. "You sent presents, but you didn't come back. You didn't even write to us."

"I did come back," Sabrina said quietly.

"Well, yeh, finally, but it took forever and Dad had to go over there to get you."

"He won't this time," Sabrina said.

"Dad, are you going to let her go?" Cliff demanded.

"I won't try to stop her, if that's what you're asking."

"I'd stop her if she was my wife!"

"You couldn't!" Penny wailed. "Husbands can't stop wives from doing things anymore."

"Then ask her!" Cliff cried to Garth. He glared at Sabrina. "If you really loved us, you wouldn't go. Nobody else has a mother who goes to London; they all stay home.''

"You sent me those paints and things," Penny said through her tears, "and I loved them but I didn't want them, I mean, I didn't want them if that was all I could have, I mean, *I wanted you and you were gone and you didn't even call us!*"

Because your father thought you should forget me, Sabrina told her silently. Because I was the interloper, taking the place of the mother you did not even know was dead, and I had no right to be here . . . until he came to understand how I loved you, how I loved him, and that the three of you had become my whole life. And then he came to bring me home.

"—few days," Garth was saying. "I told you: three or four, that's all. It's a business trip; it's the same as when I go to conferences. I always come back, right? And your mother will come back."

"There's no scientific proof of that," Cliff said flatly.

"*Listen to me.*" Sabrina held her hands toward them. In a minute Penny and Cliff each put a hand in hers. "You and your dad are the most important people in the world to me. My work is important and that's why I'm going on this very short trip and that's why I'll go again, a few times a year, probably, but I promise you this—are you listening?" She waited until they nodded. Their eyes were fixed on hers, Penny's filled with tears, Cliff's intent and somber. "I promise you I will always come back to you. I will never leave you for good. You are my whole life and nothing could ever make me give you up. I love you, I love you, and nothing will ever change that."

Penny jumped up and threw her arms around Sabrina. "I love you, Mommy."

Over Penny's head, Sabrina met Garth's eyes again. "I love you," she said quietly.

"Hey, Mom, listen, are you in trouble or something?" Cliff asked. "I mean, are your shops losing money? 'Cause we could help, like maybe work after school at

Collectibles and you wouldn't have to pay us as much as somebody who isn't in your family, and if you save money, maybe you wouldn't have to go over there.''

"Oh, Cliff, you're wonderful.'' My sweet, mercurial son, she thought: one moment a child, the next so close to being a man. "No, I'm not in trouble, but I appreciate your offer, and if things get bad, we'll talk about it. All right?''

"Right.'' Cliff jumped up. "I've got an idea. We'll go with you!''

Sabrina laughed, marveling at his stubbornness. "It's a wonderful idea and one of these days you will, and we'll see a lot of London and maybe other places, too. That's another promise.''

"When are you going?'' Penny asked, still anxious.

"In a few days. But something wonderful is going to happen before that. I was going to keep it a secret, but I've changed my mind; I'd rather you knew about it now. We're getting a present for our house named Mrs. Thirkell.''

"She doesn't belong here,'' Cliff declared, automatically opposed to anything that had to do with London. "She lives over there and she takes care of Aunt Sabrina's house. We don't need her here.''

"Will she make our beds?'' Penny asked.

Cliff wheeled in place. "*Will* she? And set the table and do the dishes?''

Sabrina smiled. "She'll help us as much as we want her to, but I think she'd be very unhappy if she thought she was taking away all your jobs.''

"No, she wouldn't; she doesn't have to know we do those things.''

"Let's talk about it when she gets here,'' Garth said. "Right now, since she's not here, you have to clean up your rooms by yourselves and if you get going we can go to the aquarium.''

"Yeh, but—''

"Now, Cliff. No more talk.''

Cliff gave an exaggerated shrug and he and Penny turned to go. Sabrina and Garth watched them run up the stairs. "I should clean up the kitchen."

"They'll do it before we leave. You were wonderful with them. It's astonishing how much reassurance children need. Did I need that much? I can't remember. Did you, do you think?"

"Probably, because we moved around so much we never felt we belonged anywhere. Until Juliette; four years of high school in one place. But we made most of our own reassurance: we always had each—" The words caught in her throat.

Garth drew her out of her chair and onto his lap, and held her like a child. His love for her was so deep and encompassing that he could not imagine life without her, but he did not know how that had happened. Two women, he thought, two halves of one woman, and now somehow both of them are here, part of me in a way Stephanie never was when we were married. There is a mystery to this: to what they were individually, and to what Sabrina is now that Stephanie is dead, and to what Sabrina and I have forged. And though it is hard for me, a scientist, to say this, perhaps this is a mystery that we will never understand. This is a mystery we will live with, and in our more fanciful moments we will call it magic.

"I'm all right," Sabrina said, her face against his shoulder. "Thank you, my darling. Thank you for everything." She sat up. "We really should plan a trip to Europe for all of us: London and Paris, maybe Provence. Do you know, I've never been to Avignon or Arles or Cavaillon . . . Oh, Garth, let's plan a trip."

Garth smiled. "All those places in one trip?"

"No, we can't; you're right. But let's think about it. Maybe spring vacation? Or this summer?"

"One of the above. Or October; I have a conference in The Hague. We could keep the kids out of school . . . except that I want some time for the two of us."

"Oh, so do I. But we can't just go off after I've promised . . ."

"We'll do both. We'll figure it out." They smiled at each other. *So many plans; so much time for so many wonderful plans.*

She was still thinking about that two weeks later as she drove to Chicago: that once she had thought she was only borrowing this family, but now she knew she would have them always. And stay with them, she thought, amused, because she had put off her trip to London again and again and finally had abandoned it for the foreseeable future. She had too much to do here, and London no longer seemed urgent or attractive, especially since Mrs. Thirkell had arrived and had plunged into organizing their house and their family.

The great organizer, she thought, smiling, as she walked into the Koner Building and saw a man leaning against a pillar, waiting for her. "Koner," he said, and held out his hand. He was short and square, with a flat, pugilist's nose, black eyes constantly darting back and forth, heavy whiskers, and a custom suit and shirt that he wore with dark blue suede shoes. A gold watch chain stretched across his generous paunch.

Sabrina shook hands with him. They had talked on the telephone, but she had never met him, and now they looked at each other for a long moment, to see if they liked what they saw enough to take the next step to working together.

William Koner had bought the abandoned ten-story warehouse in Chicago's Printer's Row neighborhood a few months earlier. It had been renovated once in its long history by Ethan Chatham but then had fallen into disrepair, and Koner had hired Vernon Stern, an architect, to design the renovation, with shops on the ground floor and loft apartments above, and he had asked Sabrina, in a telephone call, to do the interiors. This was the first time Sabrina would meet both of them and walk through the building.

Koner paced, waiting for Stern, anxious to start. Sabrina, wearing faded jeans, a black turtleneck sweater and a tan corduroy blazer, perched on a windowsill littered with paint and plaster chips. "Why do you want me for this job, Mr. Koner? I've never done a building of this size; I haven't worked with loft apartments at all."

"Right, I know all that." He pulled out a pipe and stuck it between his teeth. "Madeline Kane took me to the house you're doing in Lake Forest. Good job. Old on the outside, old and new all mixed up on the inside. I liked it. My wife liked it. And Madeline says you're the best."

"And you'd give me this job because of one home I've designed and Madeline's recommendation?"

"Why not? My first two wives bought a lot from her; they said she knew her stuff. My wife, my current wife, says you've made that shop world class and you've got some kind of deal with a couple of shops in London, so you know Europe, too. I'd say you're ambitious and smart and you've got class; I don't need a wife to tell me that. So why shouldn't you do this job?"

Sabrina laughed. "I think I should."

They smiled at each other. "And cut out this 'Mr. Koner' business," he said. "My friends call me Billy. And I call you Stephanie, unless you have a problem with that."

"I have no problem with that."

The door swung open and Vernon Stern arrived. He was tall, blond, tanned, as perfectly handsome as if he had stepped from the pages of a magazine. His hair was carefully tousled, he wore jeans and cowboy boots and a tweed jacket over a purple silk shirt open at the neck; he was impeccably casual. Sabrina found herself smiling. He had designed some of Chicago's most striking buildings, but it seemed that his most loving creation was himself.

His eyes widened when they were introduced, as men's eyes always did when they met her; she barely noticed it anymore. But he also made their handshake last longer than necessary and studied her as if he were evaluating a painting. "Beautiful," he said. "It's rare these days to find beauty that hasn't been carved out by a plastic surgeon or layered on with cosmetics. A pleasure to meet you, Stephanie."

"I admire your buildings," Sabrina said and slipped her hand from his.

He nodded, still gazing at her, then unhurriedly unrolled the set of plans he carried. Sabrina took out her clipboard and pencil and a steel tape measure and they began to walk through the building. Koner's secretary had arrived and trailed invisibly behind them, taking notes. When they reached the ninth floor, Sabrina stopped at a window. "What an amazing view of the city. We ought to do something spectacular up here. May I see the plans for this floor?"

Stern spread them on the floor and the three of them knelt in the dust and littered plaster to bend over them. "But it's the same as the other floors," Sabrina said.

"Your job is to make it spectacular," Koner said.

"What did you have in mind?" Stern asked Sabrina.

She looked again at the vast space. "I was thinking of two apartments instead of four. It's hard to find five- or six-thousand-square-foot apartments in the city." She looked at the high ceiling. "Or you could get the same size apartments by making them two stories, with a two-story living room, the windows extended all the way, and—maybe a winding staircase? Then you'd get the full impact of the view, and incredible light."

"Good idea," Stern said dryly.

Sabrina drew back. "I'm sorry. This is your field, not mine."

"You'd be good in it. I presented both of those ideas to Billy and he vetoed them."

"I want the most apartments I can get," Koner said. "Two thousand square feet is plenty big enough for a city apartment, and there's more money in four on a floor than two."

"Not necessarily," Stern said. "We talked, if you recall, about how much of a premium you could get for larger apartments on the top two floors. In fact, I brought those plans, just in case." He flipped through the plans to the last few pages.

Sabrina leaned over them. "Oh, I like this; you found a way to combine them. But how would they share a central foyer and elevator?"

"This way." Stern took out his pencil, and he and Sabrina bent closer to the drawing. "We'd enlarge the foyer here and add an elevator behind the existing one . . ."

She nodded as he talked and sketched in bold, swift lines. After a moment she made a tentative sketch of her own in a corner of the sheet. Stern frowned, changed it, changed it again, then smiled. Their voices were murmurs, their pencils busy. Sabrina forgot everything except the joy of creating a space, envisioning it, and manipulating it with her pencil and her imagination. She followed Stern's lead, but whenever she offered a suggestion, he treated it seriously and once flashed her a smile that made her flush with pride. But then Koner, standing above them, broke in. "I told you: four apartments to a floor."

"Which is exactly what you'll get if you insist," Stern said, clipping his words. He stood and slapped dust off the knees of his jeans. "But Stephanie has some fine ideas and I think you should consider them very seriously."

"You think they're fine because they agree with you."

Stern grinned. "I inevitably admire people who agree with me."

Sabrina stood with them, holding the plans. "The Koner Building could get a lot of attention with this design. And Billy Koner would be called a visionary."

"That doesn't buy groceries," Koner said.

Sabrina met Stern's eyes and saw an impatience and frustration that matched her own. All designers and architects probably wish they could do without clients, she thought; at least some of the time. "Well, maybe you're right," she said at last. "Maybe ordinary apartments sell more easily than dramatic ones."

"Ordinary is exactly what people want," Koner said. "They don't want surprises; they want things they're comfortable with." He watched Sabrina roll up the plans. "I can get three hundred thousand for a twenty-five-hundred-square-foot loft apartment in this neighborhood; it's hot now; young couples like lofts and they like the city."

"I imagine they're adventurous, too," Sabrina said casually. "Maybe they like surprises instead of always being comfortable. Maybe they'd choose your building over another one if it was exciting: something that's fun to furnish and to show off to their friends."

Koner contemplated the empty space. He stood for a long time, his head bent in thought. Sabrina met Stern's eyes, and they waited, willing Koner to change his mind. "Well, maybe," he said at last. "The right people, if you can find them, pay for prestige. They don't enjoy paying for ordinary. I'll give it some thought; massage some numbers in my office. I'm not promising anything, but maybe."

Sabrina and Stern exchanged a smile. "Well done," Stern murmured. Then he said to Koner, "We'll put together ideas for the lower floors while you play with your numbers, but let us know as soon as you can."

Koner nodded. "Right. Absolutely. No time to lose."

"I have to finish the house in Lake Forest," Sabrina said quietly.

He frowned. "How long?"

"Two to three weeks."

"But that's finishing up a job; it's not full time, right? You could be meeting with Vern at the same time."

"Finishing a job is often the busiest time. I'll do what I can, but I won't have much time until April."

"This is a big job, Stephanie. People make time for big jobs."

She took a breath. "I have a family. I run Collectibles with Madeline; I have a project in Lake Forest that I intend to finish in the best way I can. I'll do my best, Billy; that's all I can promise.''

He peered at her. ''Maybe you're not hungry enough. Maybe I need somebody who's willing to toss everything else over to do my job.''

''Maybe you do,'' she said, her voice turning cold. ''I've never let anyone down, I've never had a project run over in cost or time unless my clients made too many changes, but I can't guarantee any of that unless I have control over when I start a new job. If that isn't good enough for you, I suggest you find someone else.''

Scowling, he tried to stare her down, then nodded, as if to himself, and stuck out his hand. ''I don't want anybody else. Vern? You okay working with Stephanie?''

''Very much so.''

''Well, so okay.'' They shook hands. ''So that's done.''

''I'll send you my contract,'' Sabrina said. ''You'll want your lawyer to look at it.''

''Shouldn't be too complicated, should it? You're not the architect, after all; you're doing the simple part: paint and carpets. That shouldn't take more than a simple contract. Fixed price, too; we talked about that.''

''And I said I didn't work that way.'' Sabrina walked to the center of the vast open space. The painted brick walls were flaking, long cracks ran like lightning through the plaster, electrical conduit hung from steel beams in the exposed ceiling, the window frames were splintered and most of the windows were broken, the lavatories had been vandalized, the painted steel columns that marched from one end of the building to the other were pitted and peeling, the floor was a wild mosaic of linoleum, carpet strips, paint, and the original wood planks.

''The simple part,'' she repeated thoughtfully. ''I'll tell you what, Billy. I'll send you my contract, which is probably pretty standard, and when I've gone over Vern's plans I'll give you an estimate of the number of hours I'll spend on it—an estimate, not a fixed-price bid—and when we're finished, if you think I've made the job overcomplicated or billed you for too many hours, I'll refund ten percent of my total charge.''

"You mean you're making a bet?''

"Something like that.''

"Who decides how complicated it was or how many hours it should have taken?''

"You do.''

"How about that. Well, it's a deal. You're okay, Stephanie. You believe in yourself. I like that.''

"So do I,'' Stern said. He shook Sabrina's hand. "I'm looking forward to working with you.''

She drove home in a haze of euphoria. *Oh, Garth, I can't wait to tell you . . .* That was the core of her life now: that at the end of a wonderful day, or any kind of day, what she wanted most of all was to share it with her husband. *I'll always need this: to tell you all of it so we can make it ours, not just mine.*

She treasured her excitement as she drove home and pulled into the driveway, but as she came to a stop she saw Penny flying toward her, sobbing. *Oh, not now. Later, but not now; I really want this time just to be happy with Garth . . .* But she saw that his car was not in the garage, and then, the minute she opened the car door, Penny was in her arms, so she pushed her exhilaration aside and knelt on the driveway, holding Penny close. "Hush, hush, sweet Penny. We'll take care of it, whatever it is.''

After a moment, Penny's shudders eased and her breathing slowed. "Let's go inside,'' Sabrina said. "Otherwise, we'll freeze to the driveway and Daddy will have to chisel us loose. I'd like a cup of tea; how about hot chocolate for you?''

Penny nodded. "She wanted me to have tea.''

"You mean Mrs. Thirkell? Well, she's only been here for a few days and I guess nobody told her that the best thing in a crisis is hot chocolate. Come on, love, then we'll talk.''

Sabrina made hot chocolate while Mrs. Thirkell made fresh tea and then Penny and Sabrina carried their mugs to the living room and curled up in one of the deep couches near the bay window. The wind had risen and tree branches whipped against the house as low clouds gathered. "Doesn't Chicago have springtime in March?" Sabrina murmured. "Well, I ought to be used to it; London doesn't, either."

"What?" Penny asked.

"Nothing important, sweetheart. Now tell me what happened."

But Penny, clutching her mug, was suddenly unable to talk. Her face grew flushed, she huddled in the corner of the couch, and then she was crying again.

"Penny," Sabrina said sharply. "I can't help you if you don't tell me what it is. Is it about school? Or . . ." She looked at Penny's drooping figure and remembered their dinner conversation two weeks earlier. *Like, if nobody talked to you, you could look at the fish and they'd keep you company.* "Is it your friends?"

"They're not my friends! They don't want me!"

"Well, why don't you tell me about that?"

"I can't. They just, well, you know, they get together and talk and look at you, you know, like they're talking about you and they laugh but you don't know why, or what they're saying . . ."

"Where, Penny?"

"Oh, all over, but mainly the playground, at recess. They stand real close together, you know, sort of bunched up, all the girls, and the boys, too, and they smoke, you know, they roll these cigarettes, grass, and they say these things . . . like they're going to some kid's house after school and do I want to come, and I can't—I mean, I want to but I'm scared, so I say I have to go shopping with you or something and the girls call me a baby and say I'm not their friend and then . . ."

Through her anger, Sabrina said quietly, "Then what? What happened today, Penny?"

Penny struggled with it and then the words poured out. "Greg, he's one of the boys, gave me his cigarette, there was just a little piece left, and I took it because . . . you know . . . I didn't want them to laugh at me, but I couldn't put it in my mouth, it smelled and it was soggy and *I couldn't do it*, so he grabbed it back and said in this disgusted voice, 'oh, shit'—I'm sorry, Mommy, but that's what he said, and then he pushed me backwards until I was against the fence and he rubbed against me, you know, down here, and he said I need a lot of teaching and he called me Henny Penny and then everybody called me that and they were laughing and pointing and I started to run away but Greg grabbed me and he put his hand here and said how flat I am and then he . . . he sort of threw me to Wally and Wally pushed me to Cal and they all did that, like I was a . . . a *football* or something, and I got dizzy and I was crying and then the girls said they should leave me alone and then I ran away.''

Sabrina was cradling her, so enraged she could not speak. She kissed Penny's forehead and her wet, closed eyes and rocked with her.

"So I went to the bathroom and washed my face, I didn't know what else to do, I was so hot, Mommy, but I was cold, too, and my teeth kept chattering, and then in math Mrs. Thorne asked me if I was sick and I said no and in history Miss Daley said I looked sick but I said I was okay and then when I came home you weren't here and Mrs. Thirkell said I should have cookies and some tea, but I just wanted you.''

Sabrina held her, rocking gently, sick with anger and fear. What can we do, she thought: how can we protect her? Every day she leaves this house and the people who love her and try to make her feel good about herself, and she goes into the world and it's so big and harsh, and there are only the two of us, Garth and me, trying to protect her. How can we do it?

Penny's tears had stopped; now and then she hiccuped. Sabrina brushed her heavy black hair back from her forehead and saw, as if for the first time, how beautiful she was, her face a perfect oval, her deep blue eyes wide spaced over high cheekbones, her hair a mass of black curls. Her body was wiry and tough; she was a strong swimmer and was becoming a fine tennis player, but all Sabrina saw was a fragile child who needed protection.

"Penny, do you want to be friends with those girls?"

"Well, sure. I mean, everybody does."

"Why?"

"Because they're the best." Penny looked up at her earnestly. "They know more than anybody else about everything, and they're so grown up and they decide who gets first in line at lunch and who goes inside first when it's raining . . . you know, all those things. If you're their friend you always get the best and you have the most fun, 'cause they have the most fun of anybody."

"Do they get the best grades?"

"No, but that isn't . . . I mean, I get good grades, but I'm not popular the way they are."

"But they don't sound very nice."

There was a pause. "They're nice if they like you."

"Well, anybody can do that. It's harder to be nice to people you *don't* like a lot. The people who can do that are the people I admire and want to be friends with."

Penny sighed and was silent.

"How many boys and girls are we talking about?" Sabrina asked.

Penny closed her eyes and counted. "Six boys and five girls."

"That's not very many. What about all the others in your class? Don't you want to be friends with them?"

"They're okay. They're just not . . . exciting."

"What about Barbara Goodman? She was your best friend a couple of months ago."

"We still are, sort of. She kind of hangs around them sometimes, and then she says she just wants to be with me . . . it's sort of confusing. I don't think she knows what she wants."

"Have you talked to her about it?"

Penny shook her head. "I mean, how can I tell her I

want her to like me better than them when I . . sort of
. . . want to like them better than her?''

''It sounds as if neither one of you is sure of what you
want.''

Penny nibbled on a fingernail.

''Well, let's talk about the rest of it.'' Sabrina moved
back a little so she could watch Penny's face. ''They use
drugs at school and also, I'm sure, after school, and that's
what they're asking you to do when they ask you to come
with them to somebody's house. Is that right?''

''I guess. I've never gone, but they talk about it.''

''And they drink, too?''

''Mostly beer. At least that's what they say. And Scotch
sometimes.''

''And what else do they do after school?''

There was a long pause. Penny reached for her mug of
hot chocolate and drained it. ''They have sex,'' she said.

Sabrina drew in her breath. *These are eleven-year-old
children. What has happened to speed up their lives so
that they've become children who have no childhood?*

She and Penny had talked about this in October, on
another day when Penny had come home from school
embarrassed and afraid that her classmates would think
she was a baby ''because,'' she had said, ''in the gym
locker room they whisper and giggle and talk about . . .
you know . . . fucking and screwing . . . and I don't want
to do it! Ever!''

Sabrina had let pass for the moment the words Penny
used. There were more important things to talk about.
''You will, Penny,'' she had said. ''But wait for it. Don't
turn lovemaking into fucking; don't make it as ordinary as
a handshake. Wait until someone is so important in your
life that you want to share the things you feel in this one
way that is like no other.''

And Penny had seemed to accept it, to understand that
she could have her own ideas and feelings about lovemaking and not be ashamed if they were different from those
of her classmates.

But when they had had that talk, in October, Penny had been worried about what the others in her class were talking about, not what they were doing. Now, it seemed, they were doing it.

Sabrina looked through the window at the sedate street where they lived. Tall, serene elms and maples formed a long tunnel of bare branches with the first spring buds just beginning to push their way to the sun; solid houses were lined up on both sides, all of them exactly the same distance from the street, all of them neatly painted, roofs tight against rain and snow, windows hung with shades or drapes, lawns free of weeds, sidewalks free of cracks. Everything looked snug, settled, secure, protected. But the children of those houses, and of other houses on streets that looked just like this one, were making their own way in a world that was not settled or protected, and who could predict what way that would be? *What was I doing when I was eleven?*

Oh, we were so insulated, she thought. There must have been drugs at Juliette, but no one that we knew used them, at least not openly; Stephanie and I didn't know anyone who drank more than a daring glass of champagne at school dances; we didn't know anyone who had any serious plans for sex, at least before we graduated. Somehow we thought we wouldn't be grown up until we graduated from high school. Penny's classmates think they're grown up at eleven.

"Mommy?" Penny was looking at Sabrina, her eyes wide with worry. "Are you mad at me?"

"No, sweetheart, of course not. I'm thinking about those boys and girls in your class. If you don't want to do those things—"

"I don't! I told you a long time ago—remember?—only now they're always talking about it and if you don't do what they do, they make fun of you and it *hurts,* and they don't talk to you and they walk right into you, you know, like you're not even *there,* you're just nobody . . ."

"Or they throw you around," Sabrina said when Penny

fell silent. "Why didn't you come home when they did that to you?"

"I couldn't. They would have laughed at me and called me a baby and told everybody."

"Yes," Sabrina murmured. Power plays and mocking peer pressure had been a fact of life even at exclusive Juliette. "But, Penny, you said you wanted to go with them after school, but you were scared. Does that mean you're thinking about doing the things they do?"

There was a long silence. Penny twisted a strand of hair around her finger, frowning fiercely in concentration.

"Penny?"

"No," she said at last.

Sabrina sighed. "Have you ever lied to me, Penny?"

Tears filled Penny's eyes. She shook her head.

"How about now?"

Penny twisted her hair and looked at her lap and was silent.

Sabrina finished her tea but held on to the mug, as if for support. *I've never had a daughter; I've never helped anyone grow up. What if I say the wrong things?* She saw herself earlier that day, with Vernon Stern, excited by her own competence, proud of her ability. Now she was filled with anxiety. It's easier to design a building than to help a young person grow up, she thought ruefully. She looked at Penny's lowered head and nervous fingers, the tense line of her neck, the slim body curled tightly in the corner of the couch. *What does Penny want me to say?*

The back door slammed and Cliff came in, pulling off his backpack. One sleeve of his soccer shirt hung loose, ripped at the shoulder. "Mom, can you fix this? I need it for tomorrow."

"You could say hi," Sabrina said over her shoulder.

"Oh, yeah, hi. Hi, Penny. Are you guys having a private talk?"

"Yes," Sabrina said.

"Can you fix my shirt?"

"Later. Do you have much homework?"

Cliff shrugged.

"What does that mean?"

"A little bit. It won't take long."

"Even in science?"

"Okay, okay, I'll do it. Shall I leave my shirt?"

"Put it in the washing machine. I can't sew through mud."

"Okay. What's for dinner?"

"I don't know. Why don't you ask Mrs. Thirkell?"

"How come you don't cook anymore?"

"Because I'm having a private talk."

"*Okay.*" He turned to go. "Wash the shirt," he mumbled, "talk to Mrs. Thirkell, do my homework . . . God, they really keep me busy around here."

Sabrina stifled a laugh. She turned back to Penny and took in her doleful face and tense posture. *Still waiting.* But Cliff had provided a respite and Sabrina's anxiety had faded. She was Penny and Cliff's mother and they trusted her and loved her, and the best she could do was tell them what she felt was right and important. And if she made mistakes, she hoped they would someday forgive her.

"Penny, I think you aren't telling me the truth. I think you want this group to like you so much that you're on the way to joining them even if it's scary." Penny sat still, the muscles in her neck and arms taut and quivering. Sabrina took a breath. "Well, you're not going to do that."

Penny's head shot up; her eyes were wide.

"It's illegal for young people to use drugs and alcohol, but besides that, it's incredibly stupid. You've got good bodies and clear minds, but you can mess them up before you've even begun to know who you are and how you can be part of all the worlds that are waiting for you. Everything is waiting for you—friendship and learning and adventures and love—but you have to come to them gradually, making discoveries all along the way and learning how to fit them into your life. But those kids in your school are willing to put all that at risk because they think it's cool to pretend to be grown up. And they don't even know what that means."

Penny was staring at her, and Sabrina realized how intensely she had been speaking. "Sex isn't for eleven-year-olds, Penny," she said quietly. "They can brag about it from here to the next county, but they don't know the first thing about it. They're too young. I told you last time we talked about this that intercourse isn't an after-school sport or a way of scratching an itch; intercourse is a language, it's using your body to say, 'I love you.' You remember that, don't you, Penny? Well, those kids in your school haven't the vaguest idea how to do that; they're like Tinkertoys that somebody put together with a few gears that turn, but they have nothing inside—"

A giggle broke from Penny, but Sabrina was in full flight and barely noticed.

"They're not all put together yet, their hearts and their heads, their emotions and their understanding of themselves and the world; they have no insight into the value of their bodies. They're going through motions and thinking they're pretty great, but they're not finding out how to make intercourse loving and joyful and fun. And I am not going to let you mess up the wonders of sex and everything else that's waiting for you just because a bunch of kids talk big and laugh at you. They may talk big, but they're babies. In fact, I'll bet they're laughing because they're just as scared as you are, but they've gotten in too deep to admit it."

Penny's lips were parted; she had not taken her eyes from Sabrina's face.

"So if I find out that you've gone to anybody's house, even your girlfriends' houses, without my permission; if I find out you've been doing drugs or drinking or having sex—and I'm very good at finding things out, Penny, you know that—I'm grounding you for a year. Not a week or a month; a year. No more art classes or art supplies, no more friends over to spend the night, no more movies on Saturday afternoons or trips to the Art Institute or the planetarium or the aquarium or the Field Museum with Daddy and Cliff and me. Is that clear?"

"That's not fair," Penny said, but it came out weakly: not a cry of defiance but a standard complaint so intrinsic to adolescence that young people could utter it in their sleep. Penny's rigid muscles, Sabrina saw, had relaxed; she was no longer quivering.

"I think it's fair because I think it's right. And I think it's important for your growing up. When you're ready to leave home you'll make your own decisions about what's fair and right and important, and your father and I won't be a part of it, but until then—"

"I don't want to leave home!" Penny flung herself into Sabrina's lap. "I want to stay here forever, with you and Daddy and Cliff and our house and everything just the same!"

Sabrina laid her cheek on Penny's hair. "You'll grow up, my sweet Penny, and you'll create your own life; you'll believe in yourself and trust your decisions, and you'll know who you want to be and how you're going to become that person. But for now we're all here, we're together in our family and our house, and it's going to stay that way for a long time. I promise you that."

She looked up. Garth was standing in the doorway, carrying his raincoat and briefcase, watching her. He raised his eyebrows in a question, and Sabrina shook her head. "No, you're not interrupting; we've had a good talk and we've just about covered everything. Haven't we, Penny?"

Penny sat up. "I guess."

"But?" Sabrina asked.

"I don't know what to say when they . . . you know."

"Say your mother told you you'd be grounded for a year if you go with them. I did that with Cliff last fall and it worked like a charm."

"With Cliff? You did? Why? What did he do?"

"Well, that's between Cliff and me. But it worked for him and I'm sure it will work for you. In fact, now that I think about it, it's amazing how a few basic ideas can be used in dozens of situations, like ingredients in recipes. It makes being a parent a lot easier than one would think.''

Garth chuckled. ''It's only easier when you're smart enough to figure out how to use the ingredients. Penny, I saw two of your puppets in a display in Kroch's window today; you didn't tell us they'd be there.''

Penny leaped up, everything else forgotten. ''In the window? My puppets? Why?''

''There was a precariously balanced tower of books on arts and crafts, and in front of it were two extremely beautiful puppets and a sign saying they were made by Penny Andersen. I told everyone who was walking by that that was my daughter. They were very impressed.''

Penny was jumping from one foot to the other. ''Can we go see them? Mrs. Casey must have loaned them, but she never told me. Can we go? Please? Right now? *Please?*''

Garth and Sabrina exchanged a quick look. Five o'clock was their time, a quiet hour for a glass of wine and talk about their day. ''Okay,'' Garth said, ''a very quick trip to Kroch's, and then your mother and I want some time together.''

''Okay, but can we go *now?*''

Sabrina watched them go, Garth tall and lean, his hair a little too long, his jacket patched at the elbows, his shoes scuffed. We have plenty of money for him to buy a new everything, she thought, but we don't do that because he's still worried about comments from his colleagues. Peer pressure. Not so different from what Penny faces. Maybe we never escape it: wondering what others see when they look at us, what they want to see, what we want to show them. Poor Penny, to have to deal with all of that at her age. But when Penny and Garth returned, Penny was talking only about the display and the manager who had complimented her on her artistic skill. ''I'm famous! They're going to put my picture in the paper! I have to tell Cliff!''

When she had run upstairs, Garth sat with Sabrina on

the couch. Mrs. Thirkell appeared, and set a bottle of wine and two glasses and a gold-rimmed platter of hors d'oeuvres on the table before them. "There were a number of calls today, my lady; the messages are on your desk. I would have told you earlier, but I didn't want to interrupt you and Penny."

"Thank you, Mrs. Thirkell. Seven-thirty for dinner, please; we're running a little late. And would you make sure that Cliff really washes his hands? He seems determined to keep part of the soccer field with him at all times."

Mrs. Thirkell smiled. "I have a photo of England's top cricket player accepting an award with impeccably clean hands. I'll show it to Cliff." She made minute adjustments to the placement of the wine bottle and the platter, made a swift survey of the living room to see that nothing else required her attention, and then was gone.

Garth poured the wine. "Does she lie in wait like a cat, watching for the perfect moment to pounce?"

"She probably timed it to Penny's going upstairs." Sabrina contemplated him. "Are you really annoyed? I know she hasn't been here long, Garth, but she's settled in so completely and it's so wonderful to have her, I can't believe you're upset."

"It doesn't bother you that she stands around and chatters when we ought to be having our own time?"

"She chattered, as you call it, for a little less than one minute."

"And why the hell does she hang on to her royalist 'my lady'? It doesn't belong in this country and the kids don't understand it."

"The kids find it vastly amusing. She's always called me that, Garth, and it seems to give her pleasure to go on doing it."

"She has never called Stephanie Andersen 'my lady.' "

"No, but she looks at me and thinks I look exactly like Lady Sabrina Longworth, and maybe she doesn't want to think of that woman as being dead. Maybe she'll get over it after she's been here awhile, but if she doesn't, I don't think it's anything to worry about. What is it that really bothers you? Is it being waited on?'' She gazed at him. "That is it, isn't it? Deep inside, the Minnesota farm boy feels guilty because he's living like a capitalist and therefore he must be exploiting labor. Good heavens, Garth, Mrs. Thirkell is doing a job she loves and does superbly; her job is no different, really, from yours at the university or mine at the Koner Building. Why not let her enjoy it and let yourself enjoy the fruits of it?''

"The Koner Building. I meant to ask you about that as soon as I got home. Was it a good day?''

"Yes.'' Sabrina felt a spurt of anger. "Damn it, it was a wonderful day, and I couldn't wait to tell you about it—''

"I'm sorry.'' Garth put his arm around her. "You were right about there being too much going on, and I'm more wound up than I think. But I don't mean to take it out on you.''

Sabrina slid her hand to the back of his head and brought his lips to hers, and they kissed with an intensity and passion that was the greater for the tensions that sprang up between them. "I love you,'' Garth said. "I never want to hurt you; what we're building is so good, if I thought I was destroying it—''

"You couldn't do that. All the way home this afternoon I kept thinking that nothing I did was complete until I'd shared it with you; I felt I'd explode with all the things I had to tell you. And I want to hear about your day, everybody you talked to, and I want to know when what's-his-name from the congressman's office is coming—''

"Dinner, my lady,'' said Mrs. Thirkell from the doorway.

Sabrina felt Garth's muscles tense. She stayed still; he would have to handle this himself. "Good timing,'' he said after a moment, with an irony that only Sabrina caught. He put his lips beside her ear. "And you and I, *my lady*, my dearest lady, will sit before the fire later on, just the two of us, while the rest of our world sleeps, and whatever we need we will give to each other with no one's help."

Sabrina gave a low laugh. She turned her head and kissed him lightly. "You are a most wonderful man, and I love you, and I am so very glad that I have a lifetime to share with you."

Turning back to the kitchen, Mrs. Thirkell nodded with approval. It was a wonderful thing how love grew. She had reason to know it: already she loved Mrs. Andersen fully as much as she had loved Lady Longworth. And in fact it was as if Mrs. Andersen *was*, in a strange way, her sister. Mrs. Thirkell was not a mystic; she prided herself in seeing clearly what was what, but the truth was that she saw both sisters in Mrs. Andersen and if that was strange and impossible to understand, then that was the way it was. And thank goodness, Mrs. Thirkell thought, carrying the soup tureen to the sideboard in the dining room. This family is better for it, and heaven knows, so am I. "Penny," she said, "how about helping me serve the soup?"

CHAPTER 7

Stephanie was alone. Max was in Marseilles, Madame
Besset was at the market, and the house was silent, except
for the drumming of a hard early March rain on the tile
roof. "I'll only be a couple of days," Max had said that
morning as he packed a small bag, and after he left,
Stephanie wandered through the rooms, trailing her fingers along the furniture, catching glimpses, through the
rain-streaked windows, of the misty hills in the distance.
"My house," she said aloud. "This is my house."

She liked the silence. It was the first time she had been
alone since she and Max had arrived, a month earlier, the
first time she could listen to her own thoughts for a whole
day, without interruption. "I live here. Even if I don't
know anything about myself, I have these rooms where I
belong, and a name—Sabrina Lacoste, even if it feels
somehow wrong—and a housekeeper, a gardener, a maintenance man, and . . . a husband."

In the kitchen, Madame Besset had left a platter of
baked Provençal tomatoes and sliced roast veal for Stephanie's lunch; the table in the breakfast room was set for

one, with a bottle of wine and an espresso maker ready to be switched on. The kitchen was immaculate, the house was clean, the laundry folded and put away, the plants watered. There was nothing left to be done.

Stephanie walked out of the kitchen and up the stairs to the large bedroom Max had been using, alone, for a month. Madame Besset had been here, too: the bed was made, the clothes put away, the bathroom scrubbed. But Max's presence hung in the room, in the book on his bedside table, his hairbrush and a tray of tie tacks and cuff links on the dresser, a pile of coins on the rolltop desk—he never carried loose change, Stephanie had learned—beside an embossed pen rising from a heavy gold penholder and Stephanie's picture, snapped by Robert in front of the fire in the living room, framed in silver.

Idly, Stephanie pulled up on the handle of the closed rolltop. It was locked. How odd, she thought; I guess he doesn't trust me. Or Madame Besset. She tried the drawers; they were all locked. Maybe he doesn't trust anybody.

When, at breakfast, he had told her he would be taking a trip, on business, she had asked, "What business?" "Exports," he had said briefly, and changed the subject. "No, but I really want to know," Stephanie had insisted. "You said once that you and Robert work together, but when I asked him about it, he said you meant that you give money to some of his causes. You're both so secretive; I hate that."

"Not secretive; I thought you'd find it boring. I export farm and construction equipment to developing countries. Tractors, forklifts, backhoes, whatever they need and can pay for."

"Do you go there, to all those countries?"

"Sometimes. Usually not. I use my office and warehouse in Marseilles, and I work from here."

"But what do you *do*?"

"I just said—"

"No, I mean, if you don't travel to those countries to make sales or negotiate contracts, and you don't type up the contracts or go out and buy the tractors and forklifts yourself—at least I assume you don't—and you don't deliver them in person to your customers, what do you do?''

He chuckled. "Not much, it seems. Well, I do make sales and negotiate contracts, as it happens, usually by phone; I have local agents who take care of the details. But mostly I deal with government agencies. The poorer the country, it seems, the more devious and obstructionist the government is, and even the best governments are a hierarchy of agencies staffed by people committed only to holding on to their jobs. Usually they're someone's brother or cousin or nephew, and that gives them a certain confidence; those are the ones who get things done. The ones without connections are usually the smartest and most interesting ones, but they spend their time protecting themselves by tying knots in every step of every negotiation to a degree of complication so dense that no one but they can unravel it. I spend my time unraveling their knots.''

Stephanie was smiling. "I like that. I like listening to you; you make everything a story.''

His face changed and he reached for her hand. "I don't like leaving you. I'd take you, but I couldn't spend time with you.''

"What about Robert? He said you work together.''

"Robert has assigned himself the task of saving the youth of the world. He has a few cohorts, priests in various countries, and they go about educating and training and finding jobs for young people. I give him money; that's all I do; it's very simple.''

Simple, Stephanie thought, standing in his bedroom with her hand on the rolltop of his desk. Very simple. So why does he lock everything up?

She sat on the edge of the bed and gazed at her picture on the desk. "I love you,'' Max said every night when he kissed her on the forehead and cheek and let her go to the small first-floor room she still made her own. The night before, he had embraced her, holding her tightly before giving her that chaste kiss on her cheek and forehead. And when he had released her, Stephanie had felt, for the first time, a sense of loss, and had almost reached out to return to the warmth of his arms.

But she had not. Because nothing else had changed: she still believed he kept things from her. And she still could not trust him.

Sitting on his bed, she listened to the drumming of the rain. She was beginning to feel uncomfortable with the silence that she had treasured only a little while before. The air in the bedroom seemed heavy, stifling the sound of the rain; Stephanie clapped her hands, and the sound was muffled. She began to tremble. It was as if once again she was lost in the fog that had enveloped her when she was in the hospital.

"I don't want to be alone," she said aloud. "I've never been alone and I don't want to be now." She drew in her breath. *I've never been alone.* Was that really true? If it was, then she must have lived with her parents until she went to college—*if* she went to college—and then gone on living with them or gotten married right away—*if* she had gotten married; Max said she'd told him she hadn't been married—and then lived with her husband . . . and children? But Max said she didn't have children.

And then what? How did she get from there, wherever that was—parents, maybe college, maybe marriage—to being Max's wife, on a yacht off the coast of France?

The fog closed in, the silence wrapped itself around her. *Oh, please come back! My past—my own life—my self— please come back! I want to know who I am!*

She jumped up and ran down the stairs. Her soft shoes made almost no sound on the polished wood, and in the crushing silence she ran faster, back to the kitchen. She turned on the faucet and listened to the splashing of water; she opened the freezer and dropped ice cubes into a glass, the clink loud and comforting. On the counter, her lunch waited for her. She took the platter of tomatoes and veal to the breakfast room and sat at the place set with blue-glazed Provençal dishes and a country wineglass, heavy and solid in her hand. She served herself and poured a glass of wine, then sat still for a long time, holding the glass and looking at the heavy raindrops bouncing as they struck the terrace, splashing in pools of their own making, running like tears down the trunks of trees. "I don't want to be alone," she said again, and looked at the empty chair to her right. She wanted Max.

In the afternoon she lit a fire in the library and curled up in a leather chair, leafing through a book of French paintings and sculpture. But when she heard Madame Besset return, she rushed to the kitchen for companionship. "Oh, how wet you are!" she cried.

"Like a duck, Madame Sabrina," Madame Besset said cheerfully. "One would think the good Lord had turned the ocean upside down, just over Cavaillon. A strange thing for the Lord to do, but then, many things connected with the Lord frequently seem strange, do they not?" She dropped her raincoat on the tile floor and toweled her hair vigorously until it stood up like a black fringe above her round black eyes and high brows. Her face was round with full cheeks, her figure was round and ample, and her arms were muscled from working on her family's farm. "Perhaps, in the spring, I will grow tall, like our crops, from all this good rain." She laughed as she began to put away her purchases.

"Let me help," Stephanie said.

"Ah, no, madame, you sit there. Perhaps you would like a café au lait?"

"No, I want to do something; I want to help you put everything away."

Madame Besset tilted her head to the side in thought. "No, madame. It is not right."

"But I want it and that makes it right."

"Madame, forgive me, but some things are correct and some are not. I was taught very thoroughly what was correct, and you must not ask me to forget all that I was taught."

"What is correct on your farm may not be correct in this

house. While you work here, all you need to remember is that what monsieur and I say is correct. And I'm tired of sitting around and doing nothing, Madame Besset, and you will make me very happy if you move to one side so that I can work with you."

It was the most authoritative speech Stephanie had made, and Madame Besset's eyes were wide with surprise. Until now she had felt she worked for the husband, since he was the only one who gave orders. Now she saw that there would be two people to please: a man of strong opinions and a woman who changed with the rain and wind. But the position was good and paid well and so of course Madame Besset would adapt; she came from a line of French farmers and vintners who had learned, through the bloody centuries of Provence's history, to adapt and adapt again, and survive. She smiled. "You are recovered, Madame Sabrina. I am pleased to see it. And I would find it pleasant to share this task."

Madame Besset hummed a folk tune as they emptied the large woven baskets she carried to the market three times a week. The kitchen was cozy and cheerful, with a white tiled floor and white cabinets. The countertops were tiled in red, and so was the large island with a built-in grill, and Stephanie took pleasure in the colors as she and Madame Besset piled up the food they took from the baskets: shiny purple eggplants, oranges, lemons, leeks, russet potatoes, red cabbage, wrinkled black marinated olives, pale green endive, and dark green spinach and chard. All the lights were on, and the food and the copper-bottomed utensils and the jars of jam and vinegar shone brightly against the leaden windows streaming with rain. Stephanie felt a long, slow sense of comfort fill her as she and Madame Besset worked together. I wonder if I had many women friends, she thought as she put away green-gold olive oil and goat cheese wrapped in chestnut leaves. I'm sure I did. I'm sure I had a very close woman friend. Sometimes that's the best thing of all.

"Madame will have chicken stew for dinner," Madame

Besset pronounced as she closely examined two pale chickens spread-eagled on the counter, searching for feathers the butcher had overlooked. "And endive salad. Is there anything else madame would like?"

Stephanie was piling tiny white potatoes in a basket. "I would like it if you would stop calling me madame."

"But then what would I call you, madame?"

"I have a name."

"Call you by your given name? Oh, madame, that would be very wrong. It is as I said: I was taught what is correct and what is not correct, and that is most definitely not correct. Your name would be a piece of glue on my tongue. No, madame, it is not possible."

Stephanie sighed. "So many rules, so much formality . . ." Two of the potatoes fell to the floor and she bent to retrieve them. "You and Mrs. Thirkell, you're just the same: so strict with formality . . ."

"Who, madame?"

Stephanie stood up. Her eyes were bright. "Mrs. Thirkell," she repeated.

"And who is that, madame?"

"Oh . . . someone I once knew." She spoke casually, but inwardly she was filled with excitement. *Mrs. Thirkell. She must have been a housekeeper, like Madame Besset. Where was that? I don't know, but it doesn't matter for now, because I'm remembering. I'm remembering.*

"It does not sound like a French name," Madame Besset said dismissively. She found a feather and plucked it vehemently. "One cannot trust a butcher these days."

Stephanie watched her. "I want to learn to drive," she said.

Madame Besset looked up. "Yes, madame."

"And I would like you to teach me."

"Oh, madame, Monsieur Lacoste would be angry. He would say that that is his responsibility, not mine."

Stephanie piled more potatoes into the basket. Max did not want her to leave the house. He found reasons for her to stay at home whenever she suggested an excursion to

Cavaillon or the surrounding countryside or even to the Auberge de la Colline, the small café at the far end of their street.

They had been there once for dinner, seated near the huge open fireplace with its grill jutting over the raised brick hearth, but that was all, only once. But Robert had said it was possible that she would remember more if she saw more. I need to see and hear, Stephanie thought; anything to jog my memory. I've got to see more than this house and these gardens; I've got to be part of the world. Then the world will come back to me. I've got to get away from here. So I have to be able to drive.

"Ask him, madame," said Madame Besset gently. "All women drive now. Even the most backward men get used to it."

Stephanie laughed. "I will ask him. But he's not here, and I don't know for sure how long he'll be gone, and I'm anxious to start. I want this very much," she said strongly.

"Well. It is of course very difficult, living here, so far from town. One does need a car. Well, madame." She pondered it. "We could begin, and then monsieur, as soon as he returns, would continue. You never drove, madame? At all?"

I must have driven a car; I must have cooked. Women do those things. But I don't remember . . . Oh, God, if I could only remember . . . "No," she said to Madame Besset. "I never learned. But I want to. Right away. This afternoon."

"But the rain, madame! It is not the best—"

"We'll go slowly. Just up here. Please; it's very important to me. We won't drive into Cavaillon today."

"I should hope not," Madame Besset said under her breath. She shrugged. "Well, then, if you will wait just a moment . . ." She dropped the chickens into an iron pot with chopped vegetables and water, threw in a handful of herbs, propped a lid halfway over the pot, and turned on a low flame beneath it. "Now, madame. The chickens cook and we drive."

Max had taken the large Renault, leaving a small low-slung Alfa Romeo in the garage. Madame Besset shook her head as she and Stephanie walked past it. "Most definitely not that one." She opened the garage door and the two of them, wearing slick raincoats and hoods, ran the few steps to Madame Besset's small Citroën.

Stephanie sat behind the wheel. "Now, madame," said Madame Besset, and visibly began to swell with the importance of what she was doing. She sat straighter, her fingers emphatically jabbing. "The key. The clutch. The brake. The gas pedal. The gearshift. The radio. Ignore the radio, madame; you must not be distracted." She named all the parts of the car, pointed out the five positions for the gearshift, then told Stephanie to turn the key. "Fortunately, I have backed into the driveway, so you have only to drive forward."

For the next hour, in the pounding rain, the small Citroën lurched along the main street that circled the plateau above Cavaillon. Stephanie sat rigidly, her hands gripping the wheel, her face set with concentration, lifting her foot too fast or not fast enough, pressing too lightly or slamming the brake or releasing the clutch with a jerk that caused Madame Besset to cry out, turning too sharply on the curves or not sharply enough, yanking the steering wheel to left or right when a tree loomed ahead. But soon the drive became smoother, Stephanie's movements grew more sure, her body began to relax.

"Very good, madame," said Madame Besset. "One would think you had done this before, you learn so quickly."

"Yes," Stephanie murmured, "it feels very comfortable." In fact, it felt wonderful. The bulk of the car, its steady hum and enclosed warmth in the pouring rain made her feel strong and powerful, and exhilaration filled her as the Citroën obeyed her commands, spurting forward, stopping, turning to left or right or forging straight ahead. She sat tall and looked straight ahead. She was going ten miles an hour; the drenched stone walls and iron gates guarding miles stone houses, the sodden gardens, heavy bushes and tall trees moved past in dignified slow motion, but Stephanie felt she was flying. I can go anywhere, she thought. To Cavaillon and all the other places Max and Madame Besset and Robert talk about: Aix-en-Provence, Roussillon, Arles, Saint-Rémy, Gordes, Avignon. I can go anywhere. I'm free.

She drove one more smooth circuit, then came to a gentle stop at the driveway of the Auberge de la Colline. "Well done, madame," said Madame Besset. "A good, smooth stop. But we are not home yet."

"We're not ready to go home," Stephanie replied firmly. She contemplated the driveway, gauging its width between two stone pillars, then took a deep breath and drove between the pillars into the parking area. There were only a few cars at this time of day, but Stephanie had not considered maneuvering into a parking place, and while she tried to consider it now, the car kept moving forward.

"Madame!" Madame Besset said, alarmed, and Stephanie turned to ask her a question, but there was no time: the car reached a row of bushes at the far end of the lot and came to an abrupt stop with its headlights in the branches.

"Oh, no! Oh, how could I—" Stephanie's shoulders slumped as she looked at the bushes embracing the front end of the car. "I'm so sorry, Madame Besset; look what I've done to your car. I'm so sorry—"

"Please, madame, do not be upset. You did so well—"

"But look what I've done. Why didn't I step on the brake? I just forgot about it." Her voice rose. "Forgot, forgot, can't remember . . . that's what's wrong with me!"

"Madame, please!"

"We'll buy you a new car, I'm so sorry, I should have known I couldn't drive—"

"Madame."

Stephanie turned and Madame Besset put a hand on her arm.

"You drove very well. You did excellently for one who has never driven. I am sure you have not destroyed my car; it perhaps will need some new paint. It does not worry me, and it must not worry you, either. It is a small matter and all will be well."

In a minute, Stephanie gave a small smile. "Thank you. I think I'd better back out of here."

"Ah, no, madame; do not attempt any more right now. We have not practiced driving in reverse. I will get us out of here and then perhaps I should drive home."

Stephanie shook her head. I did do well, she thought, I did excellently, and I'm not going to give up. "I'll get us out of here and I'll drive home. But not right away. First we're going to have a glass of wine. We've earned it. Poor Madame Besset; were you afraid for your life?"

Madame Besset opened her mouth to object, then closed it. They were in her car and it certainly was not proper for her to drink wine with madame in a café—or anywhere!—but she worked for madame and madame had become very stubborn suddenly, and more sure of herself, and it seemed unlikely that madame would change her mind about the wine, or perhaps about anything, just because Madame Besset objected.

The café was almost empty, the tables neatly set with pink patterned tablecloths and napkins, the ladder-back chairs pushed in, the stone floor swept clean, poised for the dinner crowd. Stephanie and Madame Besset sat near the fireplace, the flames rising inside a tepee of logs, plates warming on the brick hearth. "Red wine," Stephanie said and looked at Madame Besset, who, after a moment, nodded. They were silent, gazing at the fire, Madame Besset with her mouth in a thin line of resignation, Stephanie smiling to herself, once again feeling wonderful.

The owner of the café brought the wine and two slices of pear tatin—"to fortify two lovely ladies on a very wet day, with my compliments."

Stephanie watched him walk away. "What a nice thing to do."

"He most likely remembers madame from her dinner here with monsieur and is looking for more visits," said Madame Besset, knowing that there was only one lovely lady at the table.

"Oh, how hard you are. I think he was just feeling generous and wanted to brighten a rainy day." Stephanie tasted the wine. "This is very good. Well, we will come back. I like this room and I like the owner and this wine is excellent." She took a bite of the pear tatin. "Everything is excellent. I think we'll come here often for dinner, certainly on your days off, Madame Besset."

The room was quiet. Two men sat at a table in the back, reading Provençal newspapers; two men nearby were playing chess while a third watched; in a corner a man sat alone with a carafe of wine and a small dish of walnuts. The clatter of dishes and pots and pans could be heard from the kitchen. Stephanie saw herself and Madame Besset sitting at their small table, two women sharing a glass of wine on a winter afternoon, the warmth of the fire curling around them, their rain slickers and hats dripping from a nearby coat tree, and she felt a rush of affection for Madame Besset. This is how women become friends, she thought, and asked, "Madame Besset, are you married?"

"Yes, madame."

"And? Do you have children?"

"Yes, madame."

"Are they young? Do they still live at home?"

"No, madame."

"Oh, I will not have this!" Stephanie exclaimed. "I want a conversation, not questions and answers as if you're a student taking a test. Surely we can talk to each other as two women; what would be wrong with that? I promise to ignore you when we're at home, if that's what you would like. I could even order you around quite haughtily, if that is what you were taught to think of as correct."

A smile flickered on Madame Besset's lips and the muscles in her face began to relax. She was aware of the warmth of the fire and the excellent red wine and pear tatin, and she liked—more today than before—this very beautiful and kind lady who was so strangely childlike one moment, seeming lost and bewildered, and so much a woman the next. And always lonely, Madame Besset thought, and found herself leaning forward. Two women having a conversation; there could be nothing wrong in that. In fact, it could be very pleasant. "Well, madame, I have seven children, three boys and four girls, born between the time I was sixteen and twenty-eight. Of course they are grown now, and four of them have families of their own, but still one thinks always of one's children as children."

"And your husband? He owns the farm where you live?"

"He and my father and uncle. It is large enough to support two families—my uncle's and ours—"

"Your mother is dead?"

"For thirty years. Some tumor . . . no one knew what it was and she did not trust doctors. And then it was too late."

"So she was not with you to help with the children."

"No one helped me with the children. I am fortunate in that I have a large lap, madame, and much good humor. And I know what is correct, so I could teach my little ones and then they knew how to behave and they were no trouble."

Stephanie smiled. "It sounds so simple."

"It is simple, madame, if one is firm and has a loving heart."

"And do you—"

"Pardon, madame, do you wish more wine?" The café owner had materialized beside their table, his balding head shining beneath the ceiling lights, his curved black brows raised in inquiry.

"Not for me," Stephanie said. "But Madame Besset . . . ?"

"No, no, I am content, madame."

"You are, aren't you?" Stephanie asked. "I mean, with your life and your family and your farm."

"Of course, madame; I am greatly blessed. I was born on my farm; I have traveled a little—"

"Where?"

"What, madame?"

"How far have you traveled?"

"Oh, I went once to the sea, to Nice and to Marseilles, but they were far too crowded; I like fields and hills and the sky without interruption. I have been to Orange and Vence, but nowhere was any better than right here; in fact, nowhere was as good. You see, madame, we all have a place that is right for us, with people who are right for us, and when we find it, and recognize it, it is foolish to waste time searching for something else. I know there may be many excitements in other places that I have never even dreamed of, and perhaps riches and perhaps sorrows, but I think I would lose myself if I were not in my own place, and then what would I be?"

Tears stung Stephanie's eyes and she looked away, staring at the fire.

"Madame?" Madame Besset was leaning forward. "I have said something wrong?"

"No, of course not." Stephanie turned back, and met Madame Besset's worried frown. "I was just thinking that I envy you. Your life is so clear, to you and to your family; you all know yourselves: where you come from and where you're going, where you belong and . . . who you are."

Madame Besset gave a slight shrug. "It is of no great difficulty; we are ourselves and we do not try to behave like others. We are comfortable together. As for me, I have a good husband and good children, a good position with you and monsieur, and good health. That is enough to make anyone content."

"But why do you work for us? Didn't you say the farm takes care of your uncle's family and yours?"

"Indeed it does, but our sons and their families will want it soon for themselves; always the younger generation itches to pull free of the old. My uncle has no children, so our three boys will take the farm and we will retire to a house we have bought, with a large garden, in Saint-Saturnin-lès-Apt, perhaps thirty kilometers from here. So I put away the money monsieur pays me, for that future time. And you know, madame, I enjoy my work. It gives me pleasure to make a home—it is what I do best— and you and monsieur need me. So there you are."

"Why do we need you?" Stephanie asked curiously.

"Because I think you have not found your place yet. Monsieur, perhaps, but you are still searching. So it seems that you do not know what to expect of each other, almost as if you are strangers, getting acquainted. And of course you do not— But forgive me; that is not to be spoken of."

"We do not sleep together. Is that what you were about to say?"

"It is not for me to speak of that, madame."

"But surely there have been times in your married life when you did not sleep with your husband."

"Madame!"

"Oh, I didn't mean . . . I didn't mean you were sleeping with someone else. I meant, you might have been ill, or your husband was, and one of you went to a different room, so the other could sleep."

"Well. Perhaps, now and then . . ."

"And that is how it is with monsieur and me. I was injured, and I was sleeping badly, and so we thought it would be better for me to have a separate room."

"Forever, madame?" asked Madame Besset boldly.

Stephanie shrank from the question. "Everything changes. Perhaps not for you and your family, but for most of us. I can't predict next week or next month, as you can." She looked at her watch, the gold watch Max had given her when they arrived in Cavaillon, saying that now she would want to know the time, to make her own schedule instead of following the one the hospital made for her. "We should go home. Monsieur will be calling, and he will worry if I am not home."

"Yes, madame." Her lips pressed tightly together again, Madame Besset withdrew into her earlier stiffness. "If madame wishes me to drive—"

"No, I want to drive home. And I have to learn to back out, don't I? I can't drive forward all my life."

Madame Besset smiled slightly. "That is true, madame."

"Then you'll teach me. Madame Besset, I have many things to thank you for." Stephanie took her hand, clasping it against Madame Besset's instinctive withdrawal. "But mostly for this afternoon. I've had a wonderful time. And I think we're friends. Perhaps sometime you'll take me to your farm. I'd like to see it. And meet your family."

"If madame wishes . . ."

"I just said I did," said Stephanie impatiently, and went to get her rain slicker. The mood of the afternoon had been lost: they were simply two women in a café with a fire that was dying and the sound of dishes in the kitchen, and it was time to go home.

Outside, darkness had fallen and they scurried across the parking area beneath tall light poles that illuminated the rain still splashing in puddles and bouncing off leaves. Stephanie sat behind the wheel, thinking of driving in the dark, of driving in the rain, of driving backwards, and she turned to Madame Besset, to suggest that perhaps, after all . . .

No, she thought. This woman has never been more than fifty kilometers from her home. If she can drive, so can I.

And so, with Madame Besset giving instructions, Stephanie put the car in reverse, pressed cautiously on the accelerator and very slowly released the clutch. Looking over her shoulder, she backed the car in a half circle until she faced the stucco pillars at the entrance. She looked at

Madame Besset, who nodded solemnly and repeated her instructions about first and second and third gear. And Stephanie drove through the gates and turned right onto the main street.

Her headlights pierced the darkness and streaming rain only a few yards ahead, and there were no streetlights, but she drove steadily, guided by the stone walls on her right that led her to her own wall, her own gate, and she drove through it and stopped just short of the garage door. She turned the key in the ignition, and a long sigh broke from her. *I did it. Without crashing into anything. Maybe a few scratches, but I didn't destroy this wonderful, wonderful car.*

They ran the few steps from the car into the garage. Madame Besset went on into the kitchen, but Stephanie stayed in the garage, standing beside Max's sports car. I'll drive this one, too, she thought. And his Renault. Or . . . why shouldn't I have my own? I can't ask his permission every time I want to go to the market. I'll ask him as soon as he gets back.

She laid her hand on the shiny car and stroked it gently, as if it were alive. *I'll go everywhere, I'll meet people, I'll go into shops, I'll buy things for myself. I'll talk to everyone. And after a while I'll find out where my place is, the place that is right for me. And then I won't be lost anymore.*

CHAPTER 8

$\mathcal{M}$adame Besset was away, and Robert and Stephanie had the bright kitchen to themselves. A March wind rattled the windows, but the sun shone, flowers were thrusting up through newly raked gardens, and tiny buds had appeared on the short stumps of plane tree branches, pruned back in the fall and ready now to grow again, and spread out. In Provence, summer was almost here. Robert stood before the stove, Stephanie beside him, and he dipped a spoon into the pot of simmering sauce and blew on it lightly. "Now, Sabrina, let us see what we have wrought." He took a small sip. "Ah, yes. It is a miracle, how a few ingredients can blend to such sublime harmony. What a pity people and their governments cannot learn to do the same."

"If it's a miracle, how can they learn it?" Stephanie asked.

He chuckled. "You have me there. They can only pray. But that seems an inadequate solution for the problems of the world."

"Robert, you must believe in prayer."

"And so I do. But I do not trust prayer on its own strength and fervor to bring about the great changes the world needs. People must take action if there is to be progress and hope. Now, taste this and tell me if there is some way we can improve it."

Stephanie took the spoon and sipped from it. "Oh, wonderful. But . . . perhaps a little flat?"

"Good. Very good. What a pleasure to have such a quick student. We shall add a soupçon of lemon juice"—he was slicing a lemon as he spoke—"and then a touch more salt and pepper . . ."

"Robert, don't you ever measure anything? It's always a handful of sugar or a touch of cayenne or a soupçon of lemon juice or a few capers . . . How can I follow recipes like that?"

"You will not follow recipes; you will create by understanding the relationship of one ingredient to the other. Cooking is like life, you know: you do not strive for rigidity and absolutism; you seek variety, flexibility, freedom. Without them, you cook insipid dishes and live a narrow life. You are already learning this in our lessons. I think, my dear, that you have done a considerable amount of cooking in your life, probably not haute cuisine, but simple everyday meals that were most likely very good, because you are comfortable in a kitchen. Do you not feel this?"

"No. Everything is new." She picked up a lemon zester. "You had to tell me what to do with this, and I thought the poultry shears were just an odd kind of scissors, and I didn't know how to use a boning knife, and"—her voice caught—"*I couldn't even peel a potato until you showed me how to hold*—"

"Hush, now, hush, my dear Sabrina." He took the zester from her and put his arms around her, holding her gently. "I know this is terrible for you, and worrisome, but you are doing well. This is only our second lesson, and look how much you've learned. As for your past, I don't think you can force it or command it to return to you; it will come in its own way, in its own time. You must have patience. Do not try so hard. Relax and enjoy this lovely home and the people who care for you.'' He moved away from her in a way that made it seem they had simultaneously stepped apart. ''So. Max will be here in two hours and we have not finished our dinner. Now that we have the sauce for the coquilles Saint-Jacques, we will make coq au vin, and then marquise au chocolat for dessert. You understand, I do not eat this way every day; if I did I would have a paunch that would be memorable, even in Provence. But for a small party, to welcome Max home and to celebrate your second very successful cooking lesson, it is a good menu. Now, my dear, we first reduce the chicken stock, and while it is cooking we prepare the pearl onions.''

I love Robert, Stephanie thought. And I love Madame Besset and I love this room, all white and red and shining, and I love the sun after a week of rain. She felt light and happy, moving purposefully about the kitchen, using her hands, thinking, planning, creating. She found it incomprehensible and frightening that her moods swung so wildly from fear and depression to happiness and then back again without warning, as just now, when the full weight of what she did not know about a kitchen had struck her, but as soon as Robert comforted her, she swung again to joy. She felt now just as she had the week before, driving Madame Besset's car: she was a real person, a whole person, thinking about now and not about a past that was lost to her.

She watched Robert's hands move surely and swiftly, with perfect economy of movement, and she tried to match him. As he worked, he described each step, and even told her the history of the foods and spices they were using and anecdotes about them. ''It was Lewis Carroll, you know, in *Alice in Wonderland,* who had the walrus say that a loaf of bread and pepper and vinegar would—''

''Alice in wonderland? What is that? A story? About a

talking walrus? How strange; do you have it? I'd like to read it.''

Robert was sliding a covered dish into the oven and he waited until he turned around to answer. He was filled with pity for this woman, so strikingly beautiful, so full of life and curiosity, her mind quick and open . . . but with nothing to cling to but the things of here and now. How much we take the past for granted, he thought; without being aware of it, each day we stand on top of yesterday, reaching back a week, a month, years, perhaps, to pluck out memories that give us assurance of our place in the world and a foundation for tomorrow. How would it be to awaken and have nothing to reach back and grasp, not even my own name? I cannot imagine it; it seems it would be a form of death.

But this lovely woman was not dead: she was young and vibrant and she was making a life. With our help, Robert thought. We must all be very good to her, and very careful; she is dependent on us for all of the todays that will become her yesterdays, for the foundation she is building for the future. We can give her security and time to become a new Sabrina Lacoste. We can give her love. And if we are steadfast in that, she will remake herself with the grace and style that are hers, even if she never recovers her past.

His thoughts had been swift, and he was speaking even as he turned back from the oven. ''I think I have a copy of *Alice in Wonderland;* I'll look for it. It is a fantasy filled with wisdom, written by a British mathematician who knew a great deal about human foibles, including his own. If you have questions when you read it, you must ask me. Or Max, of course. Now, my dear, everything has been prepared, and I am going to clean the kitchen while you change into something festive. We'll have drinks in the library as soon as Max arrives.''

''Madame Besset will clean up tomorrow,'' Stephanie said.

He smiled. ''I'm sure she would. But I have invaded

her kitchen, and the only way to ensure a pleasant encounter the next time is to leave it as I found it. Better, if possible, though with Madame Besset that is very difficult. Go on, now, get ready; Max said six o'clock and he is always punctual.''

"You like him, don't you?" Stephanie asked. She was reluctant to leave.

"Very much. He is a man of his word."

"Do you know . . ." She hesitated. "Do you know what he does on his business trips?"

"He tells me he exports farm and construction equipment."

"Do you believe that?"

"I have no reason not to. Do you?"

"I don't know. He keeps a wall around himself; I never know what he's thinking."

"He loves you. You know that."

Stephanie was silent. After a moment she said, "I think you don't really believe him when he tells you what his business is."

"Sabrina, I do not call my good friend a liar."

"But you said, 'He *tells* me he exports equipment.' "

"Ah. You have a quick mind; you hear subtleties. Well, he does tell me that and I do not doubt it, but I think Max is a man who would not be content with that, and so it seems possible to me, even likely, that he also is involved in other endeavors that challenge his wits more than construction equipment."

"He said he gives money to you and other priests around the world."

"He does. We have some programs that are very important to us and Max helps fund them. In fact, I rely on him greatly for the money he contributes; it is substantial."

"Programs of education and job training."

"Yes, for young people. And finding housing for them, helping them help their parents and younger brothers and sisters, teaching them to be involved in the political system, if there is one.''

''If there is one?''

''Many countries have only a dictatorship.''

''So you don't teach them about politics in those countries?''

''Well, we do, in a different way. My dear Sabrina, if you do not get cleaned up, Max will find you looking like the chef instead of the mistress of this house. He might even confuse you with Madame Besset.''

Stephanie did not return his smile; she was looking at him closely. ''All right, I will, but I'm not through asking you questions. It seems to me you go into the tiniest details when you talk about food and cooking, but as soon as I ask you about yourself, you get very vague.''

''Go on, now,'' Robert said gently. ''This has been a good day, filled with many lessons.''

''Oh.'' Stephanie made a gesture of frustration. ''You and Max, so mysterious sometimes.''

But when she was taking her bath she forgot Robert and thought only of Max. He had been gone for eight days, and the house had seemed to grow larger and more silent with each day. Well, I got used to him, Stephanie thought, stepping out of the tub and reaching for her bath sheet. He's a big man; he takes up a lot of space. And he's interesting to talk to.

She dressed in an ivory silk sweater and wide ivory silk pants that Max had bought one day in a boutique in Aix-en-Provence while she was in the hospital. It was the first time she had worn them, and the cool, clinging smoothness of the sweater and the swirl of the pants felt so good that she spun about in a brief whirl of pleasure. Very sexy clothes, she thought, fastening a gold necklace that Max had given her just before he left for Marseilles. Whatever that means: sexy clothes.

She ran a comb through her hair; it was beginning to grow long. Max had mentioned it a few times after she had asked him about it—how magnificent it had been—and she had known it would please him if she wore it long, but that was not the reason she was letting it grow. She wanted to see the other person she was, the one she could not reach or even imagine.

She lifted her hair to look at her forehead. The scar was long, but tight and neat, and it was fading; the doctor had said it would become silvery in a few months and then almost disappear. Her cheeks and neck and the area around her eyes were still scarred, but each week the lines grew fainter; by now, from a distance, they were barely visible. Pretty soon I'll look as good as new, Stephanie thought, stepping into ivory silk shoes. All patched up. The only thing missing will be my real self.

She looked at her image in the mirror and knew that she was beautiful and that she had dressed to make the most of her slender figure. She picked up a heavy gold link belt and threaded it through the loops on her pants. It fastened intricately in front, with a cluster of pearls. "Smashing," she said aloud, in English, and saw her eyes in the mirror grow wide with surprise. "Smashing," she repeated. "Where was I that people said *'smashing'*?"

The glare of headlights swept across her window; she heard a car stop and a door slam. I'll think about it later, she thought. Max is here. She ran from her room and was in the foyer when the front door opened and he walked in. She was in his arms before the door had swung shut. "Too long," he said, his mouth on hers. "Much too long away from you."

Stephanie's body awoke. Within her, small flames flickered, reached higher, then caught in a burst of heat and light. They danced wildly inside her; her fingers dug into Max's back, and she gave herself to the crush of his arms, feeling herself dissolve into wanting him.

"My God," he muttered and swept her off the floor. "You're back, my magnificent Sabrina . . ."

He turned to the stairs, cradling Stephanie in his arms, her face buried against his neck. But just then, faintly, came the sound of a casserole lid being replaced and an oven door closing. Stephanie's head came up; her body tightened. "Oh, Max, I forgot. Wait. Robert is in the kitchen—"

"The hell with him."

"No, you don't understand; he and I made dinner. He's waiting for us."

"Let him wait."

"*No!*" She was struggling to stand up.

He let her go. "Well, what the hell do you want, then?"

"Robert and I made dinner. It's very special, he cared very much about making a special meal for you, to welcome you home, and I want us to eat it together. And then, when Robert goes . . ."

"Dinner. One fucking dinner is so goddam important you put it ahead of—"

"Don't talk like that!" She was trembling with wanting him, but angry at him for not caring about Robert. "This is important to Robert and he's the best friend we've got, and we are not going to keep him sitting in the kitchen like a servant after he spent a whole day teaching me and cooking for you and telling me how much he likes you. Dinner will take two or three hours, and if you can't wait that long to go to bed with me, then we won't go to bed at all."

Max stood at the bottom of the stairs, looking at her through narrowed eyes. Stephanie gazed back at him steadily. After a minute he smiled and lifted her hand to his lips. "My fiery Sabrina. You've come back to me. What happened this week to wake you up?"

So I was like this before, Stephanie thought. Standing up for things; saying what I think, even if it isn't convenient. I'm glad. I hated feeling helpless all these months.

"I learned to drive," she said, and turned her hand within Max's to twine her fingers in his and lead him to the kitchen.

He watched her all through dinner. At first he let Robert do much of the talking, about events in Cavaillon, but after the soup he opened up, praising the food and the chefs who had prepared it, admiring the choice of wines, talking easily and amusingly about Marseilles. At one time he mentioned a trade representative from Guatemala whom he had met there, named Carlos Figueros. Stephanie thought there was a quick look between him and Robert when he talked about him, but she could not be sure. What she was aware of mostly was Max watching her, his eyes on her face for the two and a half hours they sat at dinner.

Then Robert left, promising to come back in two days for another cooking lesson, and the instant Max locked the front door Stephanie was in his arms and then, for the first time, they went upstairs together, to his room.

He pulled her sweater over her head, caressing her breasts as he did; then he fumbled with the clasp of the gold and pearl belt. "Why the hell you wore this . . ." he muttered, and Stephanie broke into nervous laughter. "Maybe I wanted a chastity belt." Panic was rising inside her. *I don't know what to do; I'm not even sure I want this.* But he bent to take her breast in his mouth, and a gasp broke from her. She opened the belt and stepped out of her pants and then, wide-eyed, stared unseeing across the room while he undressed her completely. She kept her gaze away from him, hearing him take off his own clothes, until he pulled her to him and she gave a start at the shock of his skin on hers. Her breasts were flattened against the thick hair on his chest; his large hands moved over her back, her buttocks, her waist, her thighs, as if shaping clay, and then her long sigh broke the silence. She remembered nothing about making love to him in the past, but his hands were insistent and her body, fervid and open, rose to meet his. It knew what to do.

At dawn they put on two of Max's silk robes, Stephanie rolling the sleeves up to her elbows, and they went downstairs to the breakfast room and ate cold coq au vin and slices of marquise au chocolat, and finished a bottle of burgundy. "An excellent dinner twice excellent," Max said. "I'm in Robert's debt, and even more in yours. I haven't been this hungry or this satisfied since October twenty-fourth.''

"What was October twenty-fourth?'' Stephanie asked idly. She was drifting on the languor of the night, remembering how it had felt to live fully in the moment, as if neither of them had a past and so finally were equals.

"Nothing. It was a slip of the tongue.''

"No, it wasn't. It was a specific date. Tell me what it was.''

"It can wait.''

"Max.''

"Well. That was the day the yacht exploded. Since then I haven't been sure when we would find each other again, and so I haven't felt satisfied. Until tonight. That was all I meant.''

"But you've never told me what happened. Every time I ask, you put me off.''

"There's no rush; it might be a shock to you to hear the details. Anyway, this is not the time to dredge it up; I'm sorry I mentioned it. You talk to me instead. Tell me what you meant about learning to drive; a joke, I assume, but I seem to have missed the point.''

"It wasn't a joke. Madame Besset taught me to drive.''

"Madame—'' He frowned. "I told you I would teach you when the time came.''

"Well, the time came, and you weren't here.'' A spark of annoyance cut through her languor. "Max, I'm not a child, and I'm not a prisoner. Am I? Do you plan to keep me locked up forever?''

"Of course not; don't be absurd. I wanted to make sure you were well and strong.''

"I've been well and strong for at least a month.''

"But you still get headaches, and you're frequently depressed—''

"And driving makes me feel better. It makes me feel wonderful.''

After a moment he shrugged. "Where have you driven?''

"Only up here. Twice. Once in a torrential rain and once with blue sky and puffy clouds and birds flying all around us and I felt as if I was flying with them. It was absolutely wonderful; I loved it. I didn't want to stop. I wanted to go into Cavaillon, but Madame Besset thought it would be best to wait for you."

"The first sensible thing I've heard about her tonight. I should fire her; she had no right—"

"Max, you will not fire her! She taught me because I insisted, and I like her and I want her here. And I don't know what we'd do without her."

He gazed at her for a long moment. "Well, then, this time she stays. But you understand, Sabrina, I will not have servants breaking my rules in my home. I do not give directions frivolously, and I expect everyone to understand that they are to be scrupulously followed at all times."

"Everyone?" Stephanie sat back in her chair, putting space between them. "You're not talking only about servants; you're talking about me, too, isn't that right? I'm to obey all your orders, *scrupulously*, in your home. Isn't this my home, too?"

"Of course it is. We share it as we share our lives, which gives both of us satisfaction and enormous pleasure. But you have no knowledge of the world, Sabrina; you know that you have everything to learn. Until you do, you're in my care and you'll defer to me and let me guide you. Good God, do you know how I worried about you in the hospital—that without me to watch over you, you would die? You've been entrusted to me, Sabrina, and I will decide how to protect you so that nothing can harm you."

She was stunned, almost buffeted, by the force of his words.

"And I need order in my life," he went on. "This house is a refuge for me, and for you, too. I promise I'll take care of you; you will never lack for anything. Whatever I can do to make you happy and content, I will do; I promise you that. But you can't fight me, Sabrina; I've lived by my own rules for a long time, I've never lived with anyone else, and I have no interest in learning to live with chaos.''

''All I did was learn to drive. What does that have to do with chaos?''

''Nothing; you're right, of course. I exaggerate. But I will not have a breakdown of authority.''

''Your authority.''

''My dear, you can't believe that I would bend to anyone else's. As for your driving, would it have been so painful to wait another week or two? If you had asked me, I would have been delighted to teach you. In fact, I was looking forward to it.''

Stephanie was silent. Her week-long exhilaration at learning to drive, her pleasure in standing up to Max regarding dinner with Robert, the night's sensual languors were all gone. She felt as helpless and vulnerable and alone as she had in the hospital and in the weeks after Max brought her to this house.

I will decide how to protect you so that nothing can harm you.

I've lived by my own rules for a long time.

I will not have a breakdown of authority.

She looked at her hands, folded compliantly in her lap. The only thing he hadn't said was that if she didn't like it she could leave.

But where would I go? I don't know anything, I have no money, I have no other place. I have no one but Max to take care of me.

Her throat tightened and she closed her eyes to prevent tears from forming. No one but Max. Robert was there and he cared for her, but he had his own life, restricted in many ways; Madame Besset was there, but she had a husband, a family, a farm, and she knew what was correct and what was not, and her employer coming to live with her, even temporarily, would definitely not be correct.

The silence dragged on; Max would not break it, and

Stephanie could not. The sky was brightening. She could see the kitchen come to life, but what she saw most clearly was that she was alone with a man she barely knew in a small town nestled in the fields and hills of southern France, and she had nothing of her own, not even a name. She had only what Max gave her. Somewhere in the world there were people who knew her and who were wondering what had happened to her, but she had lost them. She had no connections, except to Max. She had no family, except for Max. She was lost to everyone, even to herself, except for Max.

"My dear," he said at last, and took her clasped hands between his. "We will do many things together, go many places. You will learn so much it will be as if you never forgot anything. You will never feel deprived. Now come. We're going to move your things into my room."

She followed him from the breakfast room, the fine silk of his robe brushing her skin, wrapping her, enfolding her. I belong to him, she thought, and shivered.

In the small room that had been hers, Max pulled clothes from the closet and laid them on the bed. He piled cosmetics into one box, shoes into another, lingerie and sweaters into a third. "We can do this in two trips." He draped clothes over Stephanie's outstretched arms and picked up two boxes. "You'll decide where everything goes; I bought an extra armoire and bureau for you."

Surprised, she stopped on the bottom stair and looked back at him. "I didn't see them."

"I put them in the dressing room. If you want them in the bedroom, we'll move them."

On the second trip, Max paused beside the wide arch to the living room. It was daylight now, and he saw the room for the first time. "What have you done here?"

Behind him, Stephanie stopped short. "I changed a few things."

"So I see." He put down the box he was carrying and walked forward. Stephanie watched from the doorway. He strolled around the room, examining the arrangement of the furniture, the lamps and bowls of fruit, the groupings of small sculptures, the paintings and patterned rugs, as if he had never seen them before. He came back to the center of the room. "Why did you do this?"

"It wasn't right before."

"What was wrong with it?"

"It wasn't harmonious."

"What made you think that?"

"I don't know. I just knew it."

"You just knew it? The idea just came to you out of nowhere that this room wasn't harmonious?"

"It wasn't an idea. I felt it. I *knew* it. And I knew I could make it better. I would have liked to change some of the furniture, but I worked with what was here and a couple of pieces I found in the attic."

"What made you think you could make it better?"

"*I don't know!* That's just what I thought!"

"Based on nothing else?"

"Oh." She caught her breath. "You think I did this before. You think I knew what to do because it was my profession. But you said I never talked about a profession. Did I ever say anything about designing rooms?"

"No," he said flatly. "And I have no reason to think that was your profession. You might have done it as a hobby, but we have no way of knowing that. We'll have to see what other inspirations you come up with. Did you have any while you were cooking with Robert?"

"He says he's sure I've spent a lot of time in kitchens."

"An easy guess, true of most women. Where did you get the rug in front of the fireplace?"

"In the attic. Madame Besset took me up there. I think it may be very fine; the weave is tight and the colors . . ." Her voice trailed off.

"Why didn't you wait for me, to ask me if you could do this?"

Anger flared within Stephanie. She had worked hard to make this room beautiful, and she knew she had succeeded. He had not thanked her, or even acknowledged that she had improved it. Instead he had put her through a quiz and treated her like an ignorant servant. *Whatever I can do to make you happy and content, I will do, I promise you that.* Well, he has a hell of a lot to learn, she thought, and snapped, "Change it back."

"No," he said musingly. "I wouldn't do that. It is indeed far better, far more pleasant than it was. In fact, it is superb. You have an excellent eye. Thank you, my dear. I hope you'll look at the other rooms of the house without waiting for me to go away again."

Stephanie's anger simmered, with nowhere to go. Damn him, she thought, and wondered if she had been able to keep ahead of him before she lost her memory. But they had known each other for only a few days. *I didn't know him then, and I don't know him now. I wonder how long it will be before I figure him out.*

He was looking at her, waiting for her to respond. "Of course," she said. "I'd like that," and followed him up the stairs.

It took only half an hour to make her a part of his bedroom. Max hung her clothes in one of the closets in his dressing room and in the new armoire; Stephanie laid sweaters and silk underclothes in the new bureau and arranged her jewelry box and cosmetics on the dressing table. Max replaced the burned-out bulb in the lamp on one of the nightstands. "Max," Stephanie said, piling her books beside the lamp, "do we have a copy of *Alice in Wonderland?*"

"I have no idea; I don't read fantasy. Why?"

"Robert mentioned it. I'd like to read it."

"Then we'll buy a copy if we don't have one."

Stephanie yawned, her eyelids suddenly so heavy she could not keep them open. "I think I need to go to sleep." She looked at him curiously. "Aren't you even tired?"

"No, I've stayed up all night many times. You lie down; I'll be downstairs in my office."

Stephanie wanted to say, *Stayed up for what?* but she was too sleepy; her body was shutting down, legs, arms, neck, eyelids, all drooping, letting go. She lay down on Max's bed—*no, now it's my bed, too*—and felt him cover her with the quilt before she sank into sleep.

Max stood over her, gazing at her beauty, still astonishing to him when he came back to her, even from another room of the house. His face darkened when he focused on the small scars on her face and the large one on her forehead, partially visible through her hair; that anything should diminish her beauty enraged him. He saw her beauty as art, and he was a collector of art; he had studied it all his life and had made acquaintances around the world with whom he could talk in the private vocabulary of those who were familiar with art and could afford the greatest works of the present and the past.

And art had been his business, too, for two decades, until last October. He had been perhaps the world's most successful smuggler, arranging for his people in Central and South America and the Middle East and Far East to rob museums, tombs and ancient temples—sometimes whole sections of the temples themselves, dismantled for shipment—and to smuggle them out of their countries and into Europe and America, where collectors willing to pay huge fees were waiting. He had been preeminently successful because he was far more than a businessman: like his clients, he knew the intrinsic value of what he was obtaining, and often they came to him for advice on filling out a collection or selling something they had tired of.

Now, as he looked down upon the woman in his bed, his rage was the same rage he would feel if one of those irreplaceable works of art had been damaged, not grossly, but enough to cast a pall over its perfection and reduce its value to anyone who might have wanted it.

Still, he felt a certain satisfaction in that: the scars on her face and her loss of memory made her less perfect and therefore more dependent on him. And he needed her dependence. His love for her had grown in the past months to an obsession, desire eating at him wherever he was, whatever he was doing, and he had known, through the night just ended, that he had to possess her completely and permanently, and to receive from her a passion equal to his.

He was sure that would come, had already begun, and so when she came to his office after her nap, and he stood up and confidently took her in his arms, he was stunned and then infuriated by her instinctive withdrawal. His arms tightened. "Well?"

Stephanie saw the flat coldness in his eyes and her body went slack; she stood passively within his arms. "I don't know. I was just . . . surprised."

"By your husband embracing you in the house you share after a night of making love."

She did not answer. He made it sound absurd, but something in the way he had taken her to him, as if he had the right . . .

But didn't he have the right? She had married him. She lived with him. She had made love to him all night.

"Well?" he demanded again.

"I don't know." She moved away from him, and he did not try to hold her. "I don't *know* you," she burst out. "You never let me know who you are, inside."

His eyebrows rose. "What would you like to know?"

"Oh . . . so many things. What you really want, what worries you, what makes you happy, what you're afraid of."

"Are *you* afraid? Is that what's worrying you?"

"No, should I be? Of what? The explosion on the yacht? You won't tell me about it. Or everything you know about me—"

"Why do you think I haven't told you everything I know about you?"

"I don't know. I feel it."

"The way you felt the living room was not harmonious?"

He was smiling, but Stephanie's face was somber. "Yes. Exactly. Something between us isn't harmonious, and there has to be a reason for that. And there are other things I want to know. I think you're hiding something, and I want to know what it is and why you're doing it; I want to know if maybe you're not as absolutely sure of yourself as you pretend to be, if you're worried about not always being in control of things around you, of what happens to you."

"I'm not afraid, I'm not worried, I'm not hiding anything," he said flatly. "You know as much about me as anyone does, probably more. I don't show my feelings the way Robert does; you'll have to accept that. Now, that's enough; I don't fritter my time away speculating about motives. What would you like to do today?"

She thought of trying again to make him understand how important this was to her: that as long as she felt he was hiding things, as long as she felt they were not harmonious, she could not love him. Then, with a small gesture of resignation, she dropped it. Later, she thought, as she seemed to think so often with Max. Later she'd make him understand, and then, perhaps, she would love him.

"Could we go for a drive?" she asked. "I mean, would you come with me while I drive into Cavaillon? We could have lunch and I could see the town; I haven't seen it at all."

"Whatever you'd like. Give me a few minutes to finish up here."

He went to his desk and began to sort through papers spread out on the large blotter. Stephanie watched for a minute, trying to see from his face if he was angry, but he showed nothing but concentration, and after a moment she left and went to the kitchen. Madame Besset was opening and closing cabinets, a deep frown on her face. "Is something wrong?" Stephanie asked.

"No, madame, though I had my fears. Everything is exactly where it belongs and nothing is broken. I am very pleased."

"I'm glad you're pleased," Stephanie said gravely. "We didn't want you to think we'd invaded your kitchen."

"An army invades, madame. Two people simply displace. I felt displaced. Do you anticipate that it will happen often?"

"As often as possible," Stephanie said, more sharply than she intended. Everyone wanted to be in charge of something: Madame Besset wanted to be in charge of the kitchen; Robert wanted to be in charge of the school he headed and of their cooking lessons; Max wanted to be in charge of her and of the house. And I ought to be in charge of something, she thought. But I don't know what that would be. If I were really good at something—if I'd earned my living in some profession—wouldn't it have come back to me by now? Some hints, at least?

Well, maybe I did have a hint. I redesigned the living room and Max said I had a good eye. An excellent eye, he said. *You might have done it as a hobby.* But even if it was only a hobby, I still knew exactly how I wanted everything to look. And it looked just the way I'd hoped and I felt so happy doing it . . .

Maybe I could get a job. I could help people make their homes beautiful. I wouldn't even charge them; I'd do it just because it makes me happy. And because it would give me another name—interior designer —an identity. I'd know exactly who I am.

Maybe then, what I would be in charge of is myself.

She became aware of Madame Besset's scowl. "I'm sorry," she said gently. "I meant, I enjoy learning from Father Chalon—you remember I told you he'd been a three-star chef?—and I hope he'll come often to give me lessons."

"I know who he is, madame; Chalon's was famous everywhere. People mourned its disappearance. I would not have allowed anyone else in my kitchen."

Oh, wouldn't you? Stephanie thought. This is my house and my kitchen and I'll decide who occupies it. I saved your job today.

But she heard Max walking down the gallery and knew it was not worth arguing about. She and Madame Besset would get along most easily by skirting difficult issues, letting things slide into place almost as if arranged by someone else, and finding ways not to dwell on who really made the decisions in that house.

I wonder if that's how other people do it, she thought, and then Max was there and they were on their way to the garage. "If you could, we need flour for tonight," Madame Besset called after them. "I thought I had more than enough, but for a pie, and bread—"

Max closed the door on her voice. "Shall we bring flour for our chef?"

"Oh, absolutely," Stephanie said. "She needs to shine tonight, to outperform Robert. I predict a memorable dinner."

"The battle of the foie gras." Max opened the car door on the driver's side. "Well, let's see what you can do."

Stephanie sat behind the wheel, momentarily frozen. She felt Max's eyes on her face and hands and she could not remember the first thing to do.

"The key," he said.

"I know," she retorted coldly, and then everything came back, and she was all right. She started the car, backed smoothly out of the garage, and drove through their gates to the street. "But I don't know how to get to Cavaillon."

"Turn right just beyond the gateposts and follow the road down the hill." He was amused, and Stephanie realized that her hands were gripping the steering wheel and she was gritting her teeth. I probably look like a warrior about to scale the ramparts, she thought. I'll feel better if I can pretend it's Madame Besset sitting beside me. A laugh broke from her.

"What is it?" Max asked.

"I was trying to pretend you're Madame Besset, but that was more than my imagination could manage."

He chuckled. "I'm relieved to hear it."

The exchange had relaxed her; now her hands lay lightly on the wheel and, for the first time, she let herself look at the landscape. Her eyes darted to left and right, hungrily taking in scenes she had glimpsed only once, when Max brought her here from the hospital.

From their terrace, her view had been of Cavaillon from above: a jumble of orange tile roofs, a few concrete apartment buildings, a highway. Beyond lay a valley where small, neat fields of grapes and melons and potatoes nestled between Cavaillon and the gentle hills of the Lubéron range. Now she saw the town and the fields from the street: new shapes, new colors, a real town.

She slowed down as she drove into town and along its tree-lined streets. "Where shall I go?"

"Wherever you like."

She smiled and drove at random, turning wherever it pleased her. She passed the Grand Marché supermarket, its parking lot filled with cars, and the trailer park behind it, some with added porches and tiny gardens; she passed small shops and bistros, homes and apartments, and then saw the shops change: their windows sparkled; they displayed elegant gowns and shoes, jewelry and kitchenware. Then Cavaillon's main square opened up before them, with its fountain topped with a sculpture of metal spikes like the rays of the sun. Trying to see everything, Stephanie drove more slowly, barely crawling, and soon other drivers were honking angrily, shouting at her, throwing up their hands in Gallic frustration and telling her in various ways where she should go and what she should do with herself.

"Ignore them," Max said, and she nodded, but in fact she barely heard him or the shouts of the other drivers; she was in her own small shell, trembling with the rapture of discovery. Oh, the people, so many people, old and young, skinny and fat, strolling or striding purposefully along the sidewalks, pulling off jackets and coats in the March sun to reveal a kaleidoscope of patterned shirts and plaid pants like flashes of light amid sober business suits and casual dresses. And so many cars crazily swerving around her, the drivers gesticulating when her eyes met theirs; and so many cyclists weaving casually and cheerfully through the treacherous traffic; and the shop windows beckoning with bright displays, and sidewalk cafés with white-aproned waiters holding trays high as they slid sideways between crammed tables where people sat reading the newspaper or talking, their heads close together, striking the table to make an important point . . . how wonderful it all was, how noisy and alive and *busy* after the silence of the stone house on the hill.

Stephanie was buoyant, as if she had broken free and had just been born into this wonderful world. *I love it; I love being part of the world, I love being alive and being me, here, now . . . whoever I am.*

Joyous, growing confident, she drove more easily, speeding up to join the movement of traffic. She turned into the main shopping areas of town, no longer fearful that she would scrape the sides of parked cars or run over curbs when she turned corners. By the time she turned onto the cours Gambetta, she was allowing herself swift glances into the windows of the shops on both sides of the wide street. And then she looked, and looked again, into the windows of a shop in the middle of the block and stepped on the brake. "Max, I have to stop; where can I park?"

"Nowhere," he said dryly, looking up and down the street. "Well, perhaps over there. Have you ever parked anywhere but in our garage?"

"Not really. Would you do it? I'll wait for you in that shop."

He followed her glance. It was the largest shop on the street, its slightly dusty windows flanking a wide door beneath the name Jacqueline en Provence spelled out in tall gold decorative letters. In the windows Max saw furniture and ceramics, floor pillows, dishes, draperies and tall glass hurricane lamps crammed together. "For refurnishing our house?"

"Oh. Yes, if there's anything . . ." She opened the door and stepped from the car. She had not thought of furnishings for their house; she had not thought of anything except seeing what was inside the shop. It fascinated her, and she did not even hear Max's grunt of annoyance as he circled the car and sat in the driver's seat.

"Wait for me there," he said. "Don't wander off."

"Yes." She was already crossing the sidewalk, heading for the door.

Just inside, she stopped and looked around. There was barely room to move: antique sideboards and hutches held displays of old translucent china and vases; antique sofas, chairs and rockers were grouped around tables and desks mellowed by age, set with silver and glass bowls filled with old marbles, napkin rings, candle snuffers, salt cellars. Wherever a few inches of space had been found on the floor there were baskets holding folded tablecloths and sets of place mats and napkins. Everything in the shop contained something which contained something else; the floor was carpeted, the walls were hung with draperies and tapestries, chandeliers hung from the ceiling. The air smelled of silk and wool and freshly ironed cotton, the lemony scent of furniture polish, and the sweet, slightly musty scent of old velvet and tapestries and faded rugs. Like someone's attic, Stephanie thought, and she knew that this was the most wonderful place in the world and that she felt she had come home.

"Yes, madame." A tall, slender woman, austerely beautiful, had come from another room. She wore a gray silk dress, perfect in its simplicity, and her ash blond hair was held loosely back from her face. "What may I show you?"

"Oh, the desk," Stephanie said, choosing a piece at random. "It looks very old."

"Seventeen-thirty, perhaps -forty. The construction of the drawers and the curve of the legs . . ." She pulled open a drawer and Stephanie bent to look. The dusty smell of the wood enveloped her and suddenly she felt dizzy. Without thinking, she knelt on the floor and ran her hand over the smooth wood of the legs and around the carvings of the feet, like a blind person identifying features. "It's in very fine condition," she said at last, standing up.

"Yes." The woman was peering at her closely. "Madame knows something about furniture?"

"No, I don't know anything, but I'd like to. I like old pieces, working with them, arranging them . . ." She moved to a bureau and touched a candelabrum centered on it. Fanciful animals played at its base and its arms stretched upward like tree branches, holding eleven candles. "Can you tell me about this? And what it costs?"

"It was made by Ladatte, about 1770. As you see, it is gilt bronze and the candles seem to rise out of flowers. It is a favorite piece of mine; its twin is in the Palazzo Reale in Turin."

"And the price?"

"Fifty thousand francs, madame."

Stephanie touched the candelabrum again. "Is that a good price?"

The woman smiled. "It is a very rare piece."

Stephanie turned. "And it will be perfect for someone's home, and then cost will not be an issue."

"As madame says." They shared a smile. "Is there anything else I can tell you, madame?"

"Oh, I want to know about everything. I love this place, just being here . . . I never want to leave."

She looked everywhere, her gaze coming to rest on a coat tree hung with boldly designed tablecloths in brilliant yellows and blues, ochers and splashes of vermilion. "Would you let me work here?" she asked abruptly. "I'd do anything, whatever you need, and I know I could learn, I'm *sure* I could learn and be useful, and I want to be here so much; I want it more than—" She saw Max pushing open the door and lowered her voice. "Well, I don't really know if I could . . . I mean, I'd have to ask . . . someone, but if I could work here, would you let me?"

The woman watched Max walk toward them; then she turned her back to him, facing Stephanie as if forming an alliance. "I wish I could, madame. I like you very much, but you see I have two women who help me now and I cannot afford anyone else, especially someone I must train. I am truly sorry. Perhaps you would wish to ask me again in a few months. Who knows? Something may have changed.''

Max heard the last few words. "Ask what in a few months?" he asked Stephanie.

"If I can work here.''

"Why?"

"Because I love it, I love being here . . ." She was holding back tears, feeling as if a door, briefly opened on enchantment, had swung shut. "I don't have anything to do, Max, and I want to do something, and it would be so wonderful if I could work here . . .''

"Just here, or anywhere?''

"Just here.''

"There are other shops.''

"Not like this one.''

"You said you would redesign our house, buy new furniture; that should keep you busy for a long time.''

"I can still do that. But I want to be here, too.''

"I'd rather you were at home. Now that you can drive, you can visit other towns, buy anything you want for the house and for yourself. There's no need for you to work.''

"Oh, you're talking about money. I'm talking about something else. I want to work. I want to work here.''

"Why?"

"I don't know. What difference does it make? Max, I want this so much. Is it that you don't want me to work? Why shouldn't I? I'd like to find something I'm really good at, something I can be proud of. It really isn't the money, you know; I'd work for nothing just to be here.''

There was a silence. Max looked past her, seeing nothing of the shop, seeing instead Ambassadors, Sabrina Long-worth's shop in London. He had considered from the time she was in the hospital the possibility that she would regain her memory, and he had worked out several scenarios for dealing with that if it happened, all of them built around the central fact that there had been a bomb on his yacht and he—and probably she, too—had been the target.

He did not know how much she had known of the forged porcelains that had been a private sideline for Ivan Lazlo and Rory Carr, who had worked in his smuggling operation; for some time he had not known himself. He wondered if Sabrina had unknowingly bought one of the forgeries and then found out about it; if she had, and if she then confronted Lazlo or Carr, they would have been delighted to get rid of both Max and Sabrina with the same bomb. But it did not really matter if she had known something or not: she was with him and therefore Carr and Lazlo probably thought she was a danger to them, too.

He could tell her that much: that she had been a target because of him. But he could not explain why he did not want her to work in a public place, even in a town as small as Cavaillon, the center of the region's melon farming, not a place where tourist buses or hordes of visitors came in the summer.

Because he had realized, soon after they moved there, that they were not home free after all. As long as there was no body of Max Stuyvesant, whoever actually set the bomb would be wondering whether he really was dead. And looking for him.

He could not tell her that because she knew nothing of Max Stuyvesant. She did not know that Max Lacoste had dyed his hair and grown a beard to go with his new name, and lived more quietly than ever before and avoided places popular with English tourists. There was no reason for her to know any of that. But now she was asking him for something that seemed so simple he did not know how to continue to refuse. Something had broken free of the locked rooms of her amnesia and brought her here. Inwardly he shrugged. One more risk. And it will please her.

"Well, madame," he said to the proprietor, who had walked a few steps away to give them privacy, "my wife seems to want to be an apprentice in your shop. For no salary. That eliminates the problem of your payroll. I would expect, however, that you would reopen the discussion of a salary in six months or so, when you both know what she can do.''

Stephanie looked at him with such gratitude that the woman drew in her breath. What made a beautiful young woman so dependent on a man? She stood before him, her face as eager as a child's, her body bent forward slightly as if she could draw from him the answer she longed for. There is no way I can say no, the woman thought; I have to help her get away from her husband, if only for a few hours a day.

''It would give me great pleasure to have you here, madame,'' she said. ''My name is Jacqueline Lapautre; you will call me Jacqueline and I am sure we will work together in perfect harmony.''

''Oh.'' Stephanie's breath came out in a long sigh. She held out her hand. ''Sabrina Lacoste. Thank you, thank you; I'll do anything you want. Could I come every day?''

''Two days a week would be sufficient,'' Max said.

Jacqueline glanced at him. ''For stability and continuity, monsieur, it would be best if Sabrina came in every day for a few hours.''

''Well, we'll try it for a month. I want you at home for lunch, Sabrina.''

Stephanie's eyes met Jacqueline's; then she looked at Max. ''I can't do that if I'm working. But you said you'd be traveling more . . . and we'll still have dinner . . . and breakfast. That's really quite enough, Max.''

''Is it,'' he said. ''Make your arrangements, then; I'll be in the car, just down the street.''

When he was gone, the two women looked at each other. ''He wants to protect me,'' Stephanie said.

Jacqueline smiled. ''To my knowledge, there are no threats here.'' She held out her hands and Stephanie took them. ''Welcome, my dear. I think we are going to have a very good time.''

CHAPTER 9

Sabrina climbed down from the ladder in the window of Collectibles and adjusted the antique lace curtains she had just hung from a rod at the ceiling. They filtered the April sunlight streaming through the glass, patterning the Italian silk armchair and needlepoint footstool she had placed in front of them. She contemplated the arrangement, then brought a heavy bronze Art Deco lamp to a spot beside the chair.

"Oh, Stephanie, I like that," Madeline Kane said, coming from the back room. She was small and slender, with a thin, delicate face dominated by sharp black eyes. "I wouldn't have thought they'd go together at all."

"It still needs something. What did we do with those old eyeglasses someone brought in last month?"

"They're on the Louis Quinze desk, aren't they? I'll get them."

When she brought them back, Sabrina hung them over the arm of the chair, their round, spidery wire frames and glass lenses glinting in the sun. "And a book," she murmured, and went into the shop and found an 1870 leather-bound copy of *Alice in Wonderland* with faded gilt lettering and frayed edges. "Stephanie and I loved this book," she murmured, and leafed through it until she found a page she liked, then laid it on the seat of the chair, opened to an illustration of Alice and the Caterpillar.

"What did you say?" Madeline asked.

"Oh, I was just talking to myself. I loved this book when I was growing up and I was thinking that I haven't read it in years. I'm not even sure Penny and Cliff have read it. I'll ask them." She glanced at her watch. "I've got to change and get out of here; how did it get so late?"

"You were having fun. I like what you've done; it's so cozy I could move right in."

Sabrina laughed. "You're our best customer." She heard the telephone. "I'll get it; I'm going back there anyway."

At the refectory table they used as a desk in the back room she picked up the telephone.

"Stephanie, it's Brian."

"Oh." It took her a minute to switch from Evanston to London, from Collectibles to Ambassadors. "Brian, I'm running late; can I call you back?"

"I just wondered when you'd be coming to see us."

"I've been thinking about it; in fact, I'd planned on coming in February, but I couldn't get away. Is anything wrong?"

"I think it might be a good idea for you to pay us a visit. It is your shop, you know. I mean, I'm sure you're busy with your own life, but you said you'd be able to handle both, and if you expect me to manage here and deal with Nicholas—"

"Just a minute." They're not getting along, she thought, and Brian is working himself up to hysteria, and who knows what Nicholas is working himself up to? "Brian, I'll be there; I'm just not sure when. I'll call you tomorrow; I'm sure we can handle this over the telephone, whatever it is."

"Stephanie, I really would prefer it if you were here."

I can't get away; I have too much to do. This had happened in February, when she had told Garth she was going to London: everything in Evanston had tugged at her and so she had canceled her plans. I'll go in March, she had thought, but that was the month she began the Koner Building, and so March had come and gone. And now it was April and Brian said he needed her and all she felt was impatience with his demands.

It occurred to her, as it had before, that it might be a good idea to sell Ambassadors and cut her ties to London altogether. But immediately she thought, No, not yet. Some time in the future, maybe, but not yet. It's too soon. I want to know they're there for me.

She was ashamed of the thought and pushed it away. It was too soon to decide anything; there was plenty of time. But for now, with Brian's voice rising in anguish, she could not turn her back on her shop and on Blackford's, Nicholas's shop. "I'll do my best to get there, Brian. I have a project here. Can you wait a couple of weeks?"

There was a pause. "If absolutely necessary."

"Good heavens, Brian, all these intimations of disaster . . . I can't imagine that you'll be unable to cope with Nicholas or anything else for two more weeks. I rely on you for your skill and ingenuity, you know."

"Well. Yes, of course. I do know that. I'll do my best. When do you think—"

"I don't know. I'll call you when I've decided."

In the dressing room she and Madeline had carved out of their work space, she washed her face and hands, pulled off her blue jeans and sweatshirt and opened the small overnight bag she had brought to work that morning. In a few minutes she came out wearing a red tweed suit and a pale gray silk blouse. "I'll be back at two," she said as she walked past the refectory table where Madeline sat, a sandwich and a thermos in front of her.

"Have a good lunch."

Sabrina caught the wistful note in her voice and turned

back. "Am I keeping you from something you wanted to do?"

"No, of course not. You told me about this date last week."

"But something's bothering you."

"Is it that obvious? What a lousy poker player I'd make. It's not important, Stephanie."

"It's important if it bothers you. *Is* it my lunch date?"

"Oh, in a way. It's more who it's with. In fact, it's *all* the people you know. They're so interesting and important; they do things, they make things happen. I don't know anyone like that. I don't have one friend who's ever had his picture in the paper."

Sabrina smiled. "Criminals get their pictures in the paper."

"You know what I mean. It's all right. I'm jealous, but I'm glad for you. You have fun at everything you do; you make your own excitement. That's an art, and I guess I never learned it. I keep thinking that if I just knew how to go about it, my life would be a lot more exciting and fun. It isn't that my life is bad, you know; it's just that I know there are adventures out there, but I don't know how to grab them. Well, what the hell, you shouldn't have to listen to me complaining; go on, now, Stephanie; you don't want to keep a college president waiting."

Sabrina bent down and kissed her cheek. "I'll be back soon."

Claudia Beyer lived a few blocks from the campus, and as Sabrina approached her house, she saw her walking toward it from the other direction. They smiled from a distance. "Perfect timing," Claudia said as they shook hands. "I'm glad to see you. I hope you don't mind coming here; it's the only place I can be sure of privacy."

"I like it here." Sabrina followed her through the cool house into the bright solarium. "And it's nice to see it in the daytime; we've only been here at night."

"For faculty functions that are too big, but absolutely

necessary. I'm hoping to get you and Garth here for a small dinner party one of these nights.''

''We'd like that.'' Sabrina breathed deeply of roses and geraniums, basil, thyme, and seedlings ready to be transplanted to the garden. ''This is a wonderful room.''

''My therapy center. It always restores my soul, no matter how frustrated or furious I get at work. But it needs new furniture and I'm hoping you'll help me with it.''

A young girl in a white dress put a bowl of salade niçoise on a table near a tall fig tree. Beside it she put a basket of bread and a small decanter of green olive oil. ''*Merci*, Violette,'' Claudia said. ''*Nous aurons notre dessert immédiatement après, s'il vous plaît, et ensuite notre café.*''

''*Est-ce que madame désire du vin?*''

''*Non, merci*,'' Sabrina said, smiling, and went on, still in French: ''I couldn't work in the afternoon if I drank wine at lunch.''

''Once again you amaze me,'' Claudia said as Violette left and they sat at the table. ''Your French is perfect.''

''I grew up in Europe. It was fun to slip into it; I don't get to speak it often. And how lucky you are to have a little bit of France in your house.''

''And you, I understand, have a little bit of London.'' Sabrina's eyebrows rose. ''News of Mrs. Thirkell has even reached your office?''

''I hope I hear everything, at one time or another.''

''And did you hear it from someone who resented it?''

''Yes, but also from others who didn't. There will always be those who think that it somehow dilutes the purity of research if professors have fun or indulge in luxuries. And there are those, not all of them on campus, who question where the money to pay for a housekeeper comes from.''

''Where it comes from? I don't understand.''

''Well, we'll talk about that later. Help yourself to salad, please.''

Sabrina considered pursuing it, then let it go. She was a guest here. "Tell me about Violette."

"When Philip and I were first married, we lived in Paris while he studied at the Sorbonne and we made many good friends. We see them when we visit France, and all of them seem to have at least one daughter who wants to come to America and learn English and go to college and, of course, live with us. And so we've had several helpers over the years. I like it, you know; they're lovely girls. Violette arrived just last week, which is why we're still speaking French. You'd told me you grew up in Europe, but you didn't tell me much more. You talk about yourself very little."

"I'd rather listen to other people."

"Yes, you're good at that. So am I, but it's part of my job. I get the feeling you've cultivated it because you have a past you don't want to discuss."

Sabrina smiled faintly and poured a small pool of the fragrant olive oil on her plate. "I'm very happily involved in the present; it's quite full enough without bringing in the past. Sometimes I think the present is like walking through the Luxembourg Gardens in Paris: so many choices of where to go and how to get there, so many new sights and things to think about around every corner, with such beauty everywhere that it's almost possible to forget there are such things as ugliness and sadness in the world, and pain and loss."

"I like that image. Life as the Luxembourg Gardens. And yours must be very happy indeed if that's how you see it. But ugliness and sadness and pain do exist beyond the gardens; you can't wish them away. And perhaps you've had your share."

Violette returned with a carafe of mineral water and two stemmed glasses, and Sabrina watched her arrange them. "We all have our share; I think the hard part is finding a way to balance them, or the memory of them, with the wonderful things around us. It seems to me we spend most of our lives searching for something to balance pain and then something else to balance happiness, because we feel just as disoriented by perfection as we do by sorrow. My work is all about balance, you know; every house I design depends upon it. And I'd like very much to help you with this room. In fact, I've got a glass-and-steel Italian table that would be perfect in here.''

"You do balance your life; I've watched you. You're young, but you have a strong sense of who you are and how you want to direct your life. Too many people, too many women, take a long time to discover that; some of them never do.''

"You must have discovered it very early. Not many major universities have a woman as president. Were you always aiming for that?''

"Not anything like it. When we married I had much more traditional goals. Did you expect to be married to a professor and have your own career?''

"I'm not sure what any of us expected; we had so many different dreams. Did Philip go along with your traditional goals or was he the one who expected them?''

Claudia laughed. "That's very perceptive. He and his family expected them, and I was young and didn't fight back. His family descends from the French nobility going back to the Crusades, and they know exactly how the world should be ordered, so they simply assumed I'd be a perfect wife and mother and fit in with their twenty-odd generations of women. I found them completely daunting. Did you and Garth agree on all your goals from the beginning?''

"Not in the way we do now. We've changed, and so has everything around us. Did you get along with Philip's parents?''

"I was very good with them and they approved of me. I was writing poetry in my spare time, and they thought that was a sweet, rather feminine hobby. But I began to publish, you see, and then I went back to school, and then taught poetry and eventually became dean of students at

Massachusetts College for Women and then president of Midwestern, and here I am.''

''And Philip? Did he approve of all that motion on your part?''

''Oh, I like that. *All that motion*. Philip would like it, too, now; in the old days he would have scowled, thinking you were being flippant about his attitudes.''

''He would have been right.'' Their eyes met and they laughed. ''But now he applauds your success?''

''More or less. It isn't easy for a man, French or American or otherwise, to stand in the shadows, so to speak, while his wife gives the speeches and gets the attention and earns considerably more than he does.''

''And has more power.''

''To the extent that anyone connected with a university has power.''

''But within the campus.''

''Yes. It's interesting that you see that; so many people think only of the public position and of the fact that I make more money than he does.''

''But you've worked it out; he doesn't resent the fact that you have your own life. You're happy together.''

Claudia smiled slightly, as if looking into herself. ''It depends on the day of the week. Men seem to need predictability more than women do. They like life to be a sheet of graph paper with clear lines showing directions and trends and everything staying close to center: as it was, as it will be. If they suddenly find those lines not so clear and not in the center—you know what Yeats wrote: 'Things fall apart; the center cannot hold'—then they feel caught in something that defies the laws of nature, or at least the laws that they want to live by, and they have trouble facing it, much less accepting it.''

''And then what happens?''

''I think that must be a subject for another day. As it is, I've spent our time talking about myself, and I planned this lunch so that I could listen to you. I give up, for now;

you're too stubborn for me. Tell me about the Italian table you want to put in this room."

Sabrina described the table she had bought at an estate sale in Lake Forest, and then they talked of other things. Their low voices were the only sounds in the sun-washed room. Beyond the glass walls two puppies played on a flagstone terrace and robins and sparrows flew circles around each other above a broad lawn bounded by honeysuckle and lilac bushes, their branches bent low beneath the weight of their flowers. Sabrina felt a deep sense of well-being. The beauty around her, her family, her home and work, her health, the strength of her body when she played tennis and bicycled and climbed ladders at Collectibles, and her friends, including the intelligent and powerful woman sitting across from her, all buoyed her up. *Our perfect time.* Garth had been right. Because even her grief over Stephanie's death, which ran like a subterranean stream beneath all her thoughts, could not drown out all that was wonderful in her life. She was too young, too resilient, too vibrant not to embrace such an exhilarating world.

That was why she was reluctant to go to London, she thought, even though that life of freedom still called to her on occasion, like the siren's song. She did not need London; this life was enough. *Our perfect time.*

"And we treasure Garth," Claudia said as they finished their espresso and biscotti. "He brings prestige to the university, not to mention a lot of money in research grants. Does he ever talk to you about them?"

Sabrina heard the too-casual note behind the question and her head came up, as if a warning bell had sounded. "Sometimes. He's very proud of them, but I think he's just as proud of the money he's raising for the new institute."

"Yes, he's doing an extraordinary job." There was a silence. "This is a difficult time for universities, Stephanie. I don't know how much you and Garth talk about it, but it's a time to be cautious. And careful."

"Of what?"

"Of what others think of us. A lot of people don't understand what we do, and if some self-styled crusader says we're wasting money on foolish projects—wasting taxpayers' dollars, that is—they tend to believe it."

"And then what?"

"Then the crusader gets more attention from television and the press and after a while Congress backpedals when it comes time to renew funding for research. Congressmen don't know the first thing about research, of course; they can't think further than the next election, so how can they understand projects that can take years and sometimes result in something as dramatic as a polio vaccine, and other times turn out to be a dead end with no payoff at all?"

"You're talking about Congressman Leglind," Sabrina said.

"You've been reading your newspapers, I see. Yes, Oliver Leglind, but he's only one of several. He's the worst, but without others he'd have no influence at all."

Sabrina set her coffee cup in its saucer. "What does this have to do with Garth?"

"I'm not singling out Garth; it has to do with all of us. But the professors on the front line, so to speak—the most visible, the most involved in government-funded projects—should be the most aware of what is at stake and how vulnerable the university can be."

"You think Garth is not aware of these dangerous times?"

"I didn't say dangerous; I said difficult. And I'm sure he's aware of them."

"Then I don't understand this conversation," Sabrina said flatly. It seemed clear that there was a threat somewhere in Claudia's remarks, but she could not identify it; it was as if shadows had closed in: a warning of something to be fought off.

Claudia sighed. "You know, Stephanie, it isn't only Garth we treasure; I'm very glad to count you as a friend.

There aren't many people a university president can talk to openly.''

"But you're not being open.''

"I've told you that I'm concerned about influential congressmen who single out universities to attack when they're looking for a hot issue dealing with money. I don't know how serious this might be; I'm trying to be prepared, in case it is serious, so I need to talk, even though I have nothing specific to say right now.''

"Do you talk to Philip about it?''

"Philip is easily bored by administrative matters.''

Sabrina felt a little jolt. So that was one of the problems between them. Either Philip was genuinely bored by administrative matters and not willing to endure boredom for his wife's sake, or he fabricated boredom to keep his wife from discussing her work at home, because even now, after all this time, he still could not acknowledge her position, more visible than his, more powerful, robbing his world of predictability. And so, in this lovely home made by two people of intelligence and grace and sophistication, Claudia could not talk about her work or her worries, because her husband would not listen. And Claudia had to wonder who would listen sympathetically and not repeat to others what was said in the quiet of her solarium. She was taking a chance today, but she was not ready to take a bigger one and be as honest as she could be. As she might be, Sabrina thought, if our friendship grows.

She stood and held out her hand. "I must get back; Madeline expects me. Thank you for lunch and for our conversation. I hope we can do this often.''

Claudia stood with her, their hands clasped. " 'Often' is a word I like. I'll call you soon.''

"I hope you'll come to my house next time. Mrs. Thirkell knows no French, but she'd be delighted to cook for us.''

"Thank you, I'd like that.''

Sabrina strode down the sun-dappled street through flickering shadows cast by new leaves unfolding on the maples and elms arching overhead. Shadows, she thought. I'll have to tell Garth. The spring air was soft and smelled of freshly turned earth and clipped grass, lilacs and daffodils, and she felt again the sense of well-being that had come to her in Claudia's home. But now a dark thread ran through it. I'll have to tell Garth.

She waved to the owner of the pharmacy across the street and stopped briefly to greet the manager of Sorenson's Fireplaces. In the next block she met a neighbor shopping for a dress for her granddaughter. "Eighty dollars is too much, don't you think?" the neighbor asked when Sabrina stopped in the doorway of the shop. "For a three-year-old, I mean."

"It's a very impressive price."

"My daughter would say I threw my money away, because how long will a three-year-old wear it? But it is pretty, isn't it? The French are so good with fabrics; it's from Provence, you know, and I love it."

"Then you should buy it. Dresses like that aren't really made for children or even for their parents; they're made for grandparents."

"You mean we're soft touches."

"What's wrong with that, if it's for someone you cherish?"

"Not a thing. Well, I'll do it. Thank you, Stephanie; I'm glad you were here."

I'm glad I'm here, too, Sabrina thought, walking on. Claudia said it: I've made a place here.

She was half a block from Collectibles when she saw a young boy standing on the corner, kicking stones, waiting. Her heart lurched. "Cliff, what's wrong? What's happened?"

"Nothing much."

" 'Nothing much'? What does that mean? If nothing much is happening, why are you standing around waiting for me—you are waiting for me, aren't you?" When he nodded, she said, "And why are you doing that when you ought to be in . . . math, isn't it? Next to last period, and then American history. And then soccer practice.''

"Jeez, Mom, you remember everything."

"I don't remember this being a holiday."

He kicked another stone. "I got bored."

"Bored?"

"I knew all the stuff they were doing."

Sabrina studied his closed face. "Let's take a walk," she said, and they turned toward the lake. Cliff was almost as tall as she, and she felt a rush of pride in her handsome son, striding along beside her, still a boy but with a sense of decency and honesty and humor that showed what kind of man he would be. But there was no humor in his face now, though Sabrina thought he looked more confused than angry. "You walked out of class because you were bored?"

"I didn't go. I knew what they'd be doing."

"Because of the homework you did last night?"

"I didn't do— I didn't have any homework last night."

"I thought you always had homework."

He shrugged.

"Well, how did you know what they'd be doing in class today?"

"Somebody told me."

"Who?"

He shrugged again.

"Cliff, a shrug is not a good conversational tool."

"I don't remember who told me. Somebody."

A string of sailboats on the lake stretched out like the tail of a kite, white triangles against the dark blue water: a sailing class. I miss sailing, Sabrina thought. Maybe we'll teach Cliff; he seems ready for something new.

"You think school isn't as good this year as last year?" she asked as they began to walk along the lake.

Cliff shrugged.

"Cut it out, Cliff; I won't tolerate that. If I talk to you with respect for your ideas and feelings, you can do the same for me."

He threw her a sidelong glance, almost of relief, she thought, that she would not allow him to be rude to her. "It's okay. The same as ever, I guess."

"But last year you seemed more enthusiastic."

He started to shrug, caught himself, and mumbled something.

"I didn't hear that."

"Sometimes things change."

"Do you want to tell me what things you're talking about?"

"Not really."

"Why not?"

"You wouldn't understand."

"I could try. Sometimes I'm pretty good at understanding. And weren't you waiting for me so you could talk to me?"

"It's . . ." Cliff struggled. "It's that guy."

Sabrina started to ask which guy, but then she knew. "You mean Lu Zhen." She paused. "I know you don't like him, Cliff, but he's a pretty small part of your life, isn't he? He's your dad's student, but he's here only until he gets his Ph.D. and goes back to China. He really doesn't have much to do with you."

"He's coming to dinner next week."

"Well, is that so terrible? He's in a strange country and your dad thinks it's nice to give him a feeling of family once in a while. He's always very pleasant, even though he's so uptight about his work it's hard to get him to relax. You don't think we should welcome him?"

"I hate him."

"That's hard," Sabrina said after a moment. "Hatred is awfully heavy to carry around, like an overloaded backpack. Or it gets inside you and it's always there, whatever else you're doing; even when you wake up in the morning, there's a lump inside you and you know something's really wrong and after a minute you remember what it is: you hate someone."

Cliff was staring at her. "How do you know all that?"

She put a casual arm around his shoulders. "I've had a few bad times of my own: things I was afraid of, people I didn't like, people I thought I hated . . . mostly people I envied."

"I don't envy him," Cliff said in a rush.

"Well, then, what is it?"

"I just hate him. I don't want him around. He doesn't belong in our family. He's too different."

"Cliff! You mean because he's Chinese?"

"He's too different. We should just be with people like us; that's best for everybody. All the kids in school say that."

"Good heavens." They walked in silence for a moment. "I find that pretty surprising. Do you mean that if somebody from Antarctica or New Zealand—or how about a Martian or somebody from Venus?—if any of them showed up, you wouldn't let them in the front door because they're different from us?"

"That's different."

"How is it different?"

"They could tell us about where they come from."

"Lu Zhen does that. He tells us about growing up in Beijing, and how his government sent him here to—"

"That's right! He talks and talks and everybody listens and you think he's so *fascinating* just because he comes from somewhere else!"

Sabrina's arm was still around Cliff's shoulders and they walked slowly, their steps synchronized. "I guess we do give him a lot of attention. Maybe we feel sorry for him because he's lonely and we have each other."

"He's not lonely!"

"Oh, I think he is. It seems to me that when somebody talks a lot, it's because he doesn't have many people who'll listen to him. So he stores things up until he finds himself at a table with friendly people and then everything just pours out."

Cliff kicked a stone and watched it skitter along the path

and into the grass. "I can't help it if he's lonely. I still hate him."

They came to an intersection and Sabrina turned to circle back toward Collectibles, bringing Cliff with her. "I'm not asking you to love him, Cliff, or even like him. But it's important to your dad that we help him. I gather that he's a brilliant student, and your dad—"

"Right! And I'll never be as brilliant as him, or even close, so it doesn't matter what I want; nobody gives a damn!"

"We do give a damn, though I'm not really thrilled when you use that word. We love you, Cliff, and we want you to be happy. Just because a student is brilliant—"

"And I'm not!"

"What does that have to do with whether we love you or not?"

"It just does. 'Cause the people Dad likes best are big deals, high grades and scholarships and super special research, all that shit."

"Oh, Cliff." She stopped and put her hands on his shoulders. "You know perfectly well your dad loves you more than any student he's ever had or any he will have. Do you really think there's a chance that some student is going to sit down in one of Professor Andersen's classes and Professor Andersen is going to say, 'Well, how about that, I've found somebody to love more than my son'?"

A short laugh broke from Cliff. "Well, but—"

"Because if you think there is, you're dumber than I think you are, and I think you're pretty smart."

"Not as smart as what's-his-name."

"I don't know exactly how smart you can be, and neither do you; you haven't really pushed yourself yet. You're a good student, Cliff; you're curious about the world, and when you put your mind to it, you learn a lot and I think you have a good time doing it. But I don't see how you can be any kind of student—good, bad, or brilliant—if you walk out of school in the middle of the afternoon and if you're not honest about how much homework you have.''

Cliff shot a glance at her. "Like what?"

"Like last night. I think you had homework. I think you didn't do it. And then a little while ago you told me you didn't have any.''

"Well, I might have had a little, but not a—"

"Cliff.''

"I just didn't feel like doing it! Don't you ever feel like not going to work?"

"Well, I love my work, so that's not a good comparison. But sure, there are lots of things I don't feel like doing.''

"So you don't do them.''

"Unless I have to. Homework is something you have to do.''

They walked again, to the next corner, and turned left. Cliff saw where they were headed. "Are you going back to work?"

"I have to stop by and see if Madeline needs anything. She's been alone all afternoon.''

"Can I come?"

"Sure. But I think you'd better stop at school on your way home and get your books, don't you? And you can find out what your homework is for math and American history.''

"I don't know what to tell them.''

"Tell them you had to talk to me. That's pretty much the truth, isn't it?''

"But you're not supposed to leave without permission.''

"That would have been a good thing to remember before you took off. You'll have to deal with that yourself, Cliff.''

"What about soccer practice?"

"What about it?"

"Can I go?"

"It's all right with me if it's all right with your school.''

"But what if they say I can't because I sort of . . . walked out?"

"That's something else you'll have to deal with. As far as I can tell, you were upset and you wanted to talk to me and you didn't want to wait, so you left without thinking it through. But you've never done it before and you won't do it again, so I'm not worried about it. That doesn't mean that's how they'll see it at your school."

They had reached Collectibles. Cliff scuffed his feet. "You could call the principal and tell him it was an emergency."

"I won't do that, Cliff. This is your problem." Sabrina put her arm around him again and kissed his cheek. "You'll do fine. I have great confidence in you. And I love you and I'm very proud of you."

"You are?"

"Of course I am. You're a big deal and very super special in our house."

Cliff grinned weakly. "Yeh, but you're a mom." After a moment, his head down, he turned and walked slowly away. Sabrina watched him; at the next corner, his head came up and his stride lengthened. *Good boy; always go in with your head high.*

And that was how she described Cliff—striding away with his head high—when she told Garth about it later that night. Everyone had gone off, Penny and Cliff and Mrs. Thirkell tucked into their bedrooms, and the two of them were sitting alone in the living room, a thermos of coffee and the rest of the wine from dinner on the low table before them. Sabrina was wearing a dark blue velvet robe Garth had given her when he brought her back from London at Christmas.

"I like the feel of this," Garth said, his arm around her as she rested against his shoulder.

"The velvet?"

"The lady inside the velvet."

She gave a low laugh and looked up, and they kissed, quietly at first, a kiss of companionship, then more deeply:

two people still discovering each other. "I love you," Garth said.

Sabrina sighed. "I spend a whole day running around, being busy, talking to people, and as soon as I slow down, the first thing I think about is you."

"Scientifically speaking, I'd say that's the right reaction." Without taking his arm from her shoulders, he leaned forward and filled their wineglasses. "I thought about you today while I was playing tennis with Nat, and while I was lecturing on autoimmune diseases, and when I met with Lu Zhen to talk about his research, and when I was eating lunch with the dean, and when I was walking home."

"It sounds like the professor is having trouble concentrating. It must be his advanced age."

"If it is, it means I've grown mature enough not to let small matters interfere with my passion for my wife. Do you want to tell me about your day?"

"Oh, not really."

"Problems?"

"There are always problems. Just when I think I have Penny pretty much taken care of, there's Cliff."

"Other than being a short-tempered and sullen twelve-year-old, what's wrong with Cliff?"

"He was never short-tempered and sullen before, Garth. He's not happy about your favorite student."

"He's jealous. He'll get over it. I tried to talk to him but he wouldn't listen."

"He'll listen if you get him in a quiet corner. He's unhappy and he needs you and all he sees is Lu Zhen getting your attention when he's here for dinner."

"He's our guest. Cliff knows I haven't forgotten him just because I don't coddle him for one evening. My God, he's my son; he doesn't need proof every single day that I love him."

"We all need proof every single day that we're loved."
Garth gazed at her. "Do I give you that proof?"

"Yes, always, it's part of what is so wonderful between

us. And you give it to Cliff and Penny, too, but they don't always see it. I think you can't be subtle about love with children that age.''

"Well, I'll talk to him. I'm not sure what I'll say, other than to tell him again that I love him, but I'll try.''

"He wants you to think he's special.''

"I do. He must know that. I look at him sometimes and wonder how I was so blessed to have such wonderful kids. And not just to love them but to like them. In fact, I think it's the most special blessing of all: to like our children as companions.''

"Have you ever told him any of that?''

"Probably not in those words,'' Garth said after a minute. "I assumed it showed in everything we did together.''

"A big assumption.''

"But they don't like to be slobbered over, you know. Twelve isn't a great age for expressing lots of emotion.''

"Do you think you could find a middle ground between praise and slobber?''

He chuckled. "I'll work on it. Anything else about Cliff?''

"He's picked up from his friends at school the idea that we should only be with our own kind.''

"Good God. Don't they teach kids about a shrinking world these days? And about getting fresh ideas and making a leap forward from being a melting pot and all that sort of thing?''

"I'm not sure what they're teaching; I guess I'll have to find out. It is dismaying; you might bring it up sometime. I mentioned Martians at the door and whether he'd let them in and so on; you could build on that.''

He chuckled again and kissed her. "A good place to start. Didn't you have lunch with Claudia today? How was that?''

"Wonderful. I like her so much. She needs someone to talk to; I hope I don't disappoint her in that.''

"Why would you?''

"I might not have good answers when she needs them. Right now she's worried about Congress, among other things."

"University presidents always worry about Congress. Too many congressmen vote on whims and political fears, so they can't be reasoned with or predicted. That confuses anyone who believes in a life spent training minds to think clearly, and it worries the hell out of anyone who relies on them for funding. Is there anything special she's concerned about?"

"Oliver Leglind. And she thinks you ought to be aware of the dangers. Difficulties, she calls them."

"Does she think I'm not?"

"She says she's sure you are. It's just one more thing, though, distracting you. And us."

"It's not earthshaking, my love; it's part of the crazy political and academic climate I work in. You're not worried, are you?"

"A little. Claudia told me to be watchful; she had a reason for that. And she's worried; that was pretty clear."

"Well, we're always watchful where government grants are concerned, and there are a lot of us keeping our eyes open: we'd lose too many projects if we lost that funding. But it's not something that has to invade our home; we have enough people demanding this or that from us without adding Oliver Leglind to the list."

"Oh. That reminds me. People making demands of us. There seems to be a crisis at Ambassadors. Or at least Brian thinks there's one."

"So you want to go to London."

"I don't, really, but I think I'd better. I didn't go in February, you know, and—"

"My love, you don't have to explain it. Just don't stay away too long."

"I can't; I have to work on the first spec sheets for Billy Koner, and Madeline and I are expecting a new shipment in about ten days. Oh, but why don't you come with me? We could make it a holiday."

"Not this time. You'll be worrying about Brian and Nicholas and Billy Koner and I'd be thinking about Lu Zhen's research project and Cliff and maybe even Oliver Leglind. We'll go soon, though; I'd like some time in Europe with you. When we're both ready, just the two of us and no projects dangling like loose ends back home."

He put his arms around Sabrina and brought her to lie back against him. They were quiet for a long time in the quiet house that drowsed in the late night hush when creaking floors were silent, the busy kitchen put to rest, the day's voices and laughter stilled; when the street in front was a clear black ribbon running straight through the sleeping town; when lampposts cast blue-white circles of light on deserted sidewalks and the houses across the way stood like dark sentinels against a cloudy sky faintly pink from the glow of Chicago's skyscrapers, just a few miles away.

"Isn't it amazing," Garth murmured, "how every lover thinks he's invented love? People fall in love in the most unlikely times and places, and they wonder at the magic of it, and sing with the joy of it, and think no one else has ever known what they have discovered." He held Sabrina close, one hand inside her robe holding her warm breast. "And everyone who thinks that is absolutely right. We've invented it, we've created the words for it; it's our love and no one else's. It becomes a mirror of the two of us, and no matter how many poets write about it, it can never be fully shared with anyone but the two people in the mirror." He kissed her, his mouth opening hers. Sabrina turned within his arms and they fitted their bodies to each other like travelers coming home, knowing the door would always be open to them. When they pulled apart they were smiling, letting desire fill them, and they held it close, wondrous and wild and theirs alone.

"Whatever else happens in our life," Garth said, "whatever the intrusions, we've created ourselves as we are to each other, part of each other, and nothing can diminish that. Nothing can ever take that from us."

"Garth," Sabrina said, her hand along his face, "it's time to go to bed."

He stood, bringing her with him, and they walked to the foot of the stairs, their arms around each other. *You have a strong sense of who you are and how you want to direct your life.* Oh, yes, Sabrina thought, remembering what Claudia had said. Yes, with this man, in this place, and with no one else, ever.

They climbed the stairs, their steps in unison, and the lights of their house, the last to be illuminated on the street where they lived, went out one by one.

CHAPTER *10*

---

*S*tephanie was making a life. Each day, each week, became part of a new past, and when she woke each morning with Max beside her and the sun streaming through uncurtained windows over the familiar contours of the bedroom, she no longer had the sinking feeling of being lost and alone in emptiness; now she had yesterday to remember and today to plan and tomorrow to anticipate.

She had a schedule. Five days a week, from nine to one, she worked at Jacqueline en Provence. One afternoon a week she cooked with Robert. The other afternoons were for Max, unless he was away, and then she worked on redesigning the rooms of the house or chatted with Madame Besset or lay on the chaise in the sitting room, reading books from Max's library.

She had found an illustrated copy of *Alice in Wonderland* on a high shelf, an old leather-bound copy in perfect condition, with a gold ribbon for a marker, and she opened it one day after lunch, when Madame Besset was at the market. She began to read and it was a moment before she looked up, her heart pounding. She had read ten pages, in English, without hesitating or stumbling over a word.

But why would she be surprised? In the hospital they had discovered that she was fluent in three languages.

But it's so easy, she thought, and looked again at the page before her.

Alice took up the fan and gloves and, as the hall was very hot, she kept fanning herself all the time she went on talking. "Dear, dear! How queer everything is today! And yesterday things went on just as usual. I wonder if I've been changed in the night? Let me think: *was* I the same when I got up this morning? I almost think I can remember feeling a little different. But if I'm not the same, the next question is, 'Who in the world am I?' Ah, *that's* the great puzzle!"

Stephanie drew in her breath. *I guess I'm not the only one who wonders that.* She read the book through, then turned back to the beginning and read it again, stopping for a long time at a page in the middle.

The Gryphon added, "Come, let's hear some of *your* adventures."

"I could tell you my adventures—beginning from this morning," said Alice a little timidly; "but it's no use going back to yesterday, because I was a different person then."

Maybe there are a lot of ways we can lose ourselves, Stephanie thought, gazing at the picture of the Gryphon. And Alice finds herself at the end; she gets back to where she started. Maybe that's what Robert wanted me to discover when he talked about this book.

She put the book on the table in the library and kept it there, where she could pick it up and read it whenever she felt like it. *I wonder if I read this before. Maybe, if I just concentrate, it will remind me of something.*

She was always trying to be reminded of something, straining to dredge up memories from associations. "House," she would say aloud, and close her eyes, picturing a house, rooms, furniture, gardens . . . but the only rooms and gardens she could picture were her own. When she thought "house" she tried to picture a family, but no faces came to her and she felt a great sadness. But as the weeks went by, she stopped struggling to tear down the curtain that hid her past. The doctors at the hospital had said everything might come back to her someday; Robert had said the same thing. Until then she had a life, and that would have to be enough.

When Max was home, they spent the afternoons driving to nearby towns, exploring twisting streets and browsing in the shops and talking. As Stephanie built a new store of memories and worked and drove and felt her life building around her, she became bolder. "You don't really tell me anything about yourself," she said one afternoon as they took shelter from an April rain in Les Deux Garçons in Aix-en-Provence. "You always put me off, as if I'm a child."

"What do you want to know?" he asked. They were sitting just inside the café, facing the cours Mirabeau, and he watched Stephanie's profile as she gazed at the fanciful ironwork on the balconies of the buildings across the wide, tree-lined street. She was wearing white jeans and a black turtleneck sweater with a silver necklace and long earrings he had bought only an hour before; her scars were barely visible, her beauty almost as pure and striking as before, and Max felt a surge of pride. He had done this. He had saved Sabrina Longworth from death and the destruction of her beauty, and he had re-created her as Sabrina Lacoste, whose beauty and spirit were now truly his. Sitting in the café, he felt relaxed and expansive; everything was going so well he could almost believe it would always be this way. "I've told you about my mother's death and my wanderings with my father . . . you do remember all that?"

"Yes, of course," she said impatiently, as if memory had never been a problem. "And Holland and Belgium and Germany and Spain . . . of course I remember. And then you went to London. But how did you feel when it was just you and your father? Did you love him?"

"I can't remember. We stayed together because we didn't have anyone else. I was afraid of him for a while; he had a bad temper and he hated staying in one place for long; a bad combination because he was always looking for excuses to move on and the excuse was usually a fight with someone. Once I got in the middle, I don't remember how, and was thoroughly beaten up. He took me to London, and when I recovered, I left him."

"Such a cold listing of facts," Stephanie said. "No feelings, nothing but facts. Wasn't there any love or fun in your life?"

"There was necessity. That's what gets most people through their days; how many do you think are fortunate enough to find love?" He took her hand. "When it comes, and comes late, it's all the better."

"And the fun?"

"I've never been sure what that is. I don't ask myself if I'm having fun. I take great pleasure in what I do; is that good enough?"

"What do you do?"

"I live with you and introduce you to Provence; I spend time with Robert and business associates in Marseilles—"

"I meant, what do you do for a living?"

"I told you. I export farm and construction equipment to developing countries."

"Did you tell me that before I lost my memory?"

"I don't remember. It's possible, but as I told you, we talked mostly about the future."

"Well, I think you do more than export equipment."

"Do you indeed. And why do you think that?"

"Because you take great pleasure in what you do. And you're not a dull man; you like challenges. So I think you do something more interesting than exporting machinery, and I'd like to know what it is."

The waiter brought their coffee and Max waited until he left. "Do you know, Sabrina, that is the first compliment you have paid me since you were injured."

She looked startled. "Is it? I'm sorry; you've been very good to me."

"There is a difference between compliments and gratitude."

"You mean you want me to admire the person you are. I do, from what I know. Robert says you're a man of your word. I admire that. But how do I know whether there is more to admire, or less?"

Max was growing bored. He loved her, he was obsessed with her, but not even she would know any more about him than he was willing to share. He had never been open with anyone; he had no intention of starting now. But what would she say, he wondered idly, if he told her what he did? *My dear Sabrina, I own a small printing job shop in Marseilles where we print party invitations and letterhead stationery and thousands of other innocuous jobs, but our main job is to print money. We ship the equivalent of hundreds of millions of francs' worth of counterfeit money to customers all over the world, packed neatly and efficiently inside farm and construction equipment . . .* He had no idea how she would react.

But it was only an idle thought. He would not tell her; he would not tell anyone, because he trusted no one but the few men who worked with him. And it would have no effect on their life together; they would be happy and she would love him, knowing exactly as much as she knew and no more. It was as much as she needed to know.

But for now he was not interested in playing games; he would not waste time dancing around her questions. "I'll try to make sure you find more to admire, the longer we're together. Now tell me about your work; what did you do this morning?"

"Oh, stop it!" Stephanie cried. "I'm not a child; I

won't be treated like one. You build a wall of secrets around yourself; do you expect me to admire that? I hate secrets—my whole past is a secret—and I refuse to live with them now.''

She pulled on her raincoat and rushed out of the café. The rain had stopped, and she made her way between the few soggy tourists sitting doggedly at the rows of tables and chairs lined up as if in a theater. On the broad sidewalk that ran the length of the street she turned toward the main square, walking rapidly, pulling on her rain hat as protection against the drops falling from the trees. When she reached the main square with its enormous fountain, gray-green with wet moss, she sat on the broad stone edge, looking away from the direction Max would come when he followed her.

Her back was rigid, her hands clenched, and it was a moment before she realized that what she felt was not aloneness or anxiety, as so often before, but a cold, hard anger. She sat in the windswept square, the gray plumes of water behind her splashing invisibly into the gray sky, wet stones gleaming faintly beneath dripping trees, and let her anger grow, knowing that it was important to her: that anger at being treated like a child was the beginning of standing alone in this new life she was making. She remembered that she had felt like a child the day she met Robert, as she sat between him and Max at lunch; she remembered feeling like a child when she first began to cook in the kitchen, when she first sat behind the wheel of the car, when she first moved into Max's arms and grew panic-stricken at the thought of making love to him.

But I'm growing up, she thought; I'm learning my way around. And Max and everyone else will have to treat me like an adult, like one of them.

In front of her, three women led a long line of schoolchildren across the square. The children, wearing yellow slickers, were strung together like beads, holding on to a bright red rope that trailed on the wet stones behind the last child. Their high-pitched voices rang excitely through the square above the sound of the splashing fountain. Stephanie watched them, and suddenly she was swept by a wave of longing so powerful she stood up and started toward them, following them partway across the square before she realized what she was doing and came to a stop. *What a crazy thing to do; why am I doing this?* She watched them file into a narrow street and disappear around a bend. *I wonder how old they are. Eight? Nine? Such a lovely age, so open and full of love.*

A child ran past her, one child alone, wearing a yellow slicker, tears streaming down her face. Without thinking, Stephanie reached out and stopped her, and knelt down to hold her close. "It's all right, I'll help you, don't cry. Tell me what happened. Did you lose your friends?"

The child nodded, gulping through her tears. "I saw a puppy and I stopped to pet it . . . I wasn't supposed to . . . they said hold on to the rope . . . and now I don't know where they are!"

"I saw them go past. We'll find them." Stephanie smoothed the child's hair from her wet face and kissed her forehead and her cheeks. Through the bulky slicker she felt the trembling of the small, wiry body and she tightened her arms and felt that the child had become part of her. She could not hold her close enough; she never wanted to let her go.

"But where are they?" the child cried. "They will be so angry . . . and my mama and papa will punish me if they find out . . ."

Reluctantly Stephanie stood up and took her hand. "What is your name?"

"Lisa Vernet."

"Well, Lisa, let's find your class and perhaps no one will tell your mama and papa that this happened."

Lisa looked up, her eyes wide. "Is that possible?"

"I don't know. But we'll try." They set off, walking rapidly toward the street where the class had gone. The buildings here were of old mottled stucco with shutters streaked and faded from rain and sun, the heavy wooden doors deeply grained and scarred with age. The street was barely wide enough for a small car and there was no sidewalk. Stephanie and Lisa walked down the center on wet cobblestones until they came to a tiny square with three streets leading from it. Lisa looked up, waiting for Stephanie to show her which way to go. Stephanie had no idea. "This way," she said firmly, and took the street to the left, in every way identical to the one they had just been on.

"—and we always go somewhere on Thursday," Lisa chattered as they walked. "Madame Frontenac, she's our teacher, you'll like her, she's very pretty, like you, and she has a daughter of her own, so she is very kind to the girls, very understanding, you know, and then she *was* one, too, when she was growing up and she remembers what it was like, but with the boys she is much more firm, but then that is proper, they need it, they are very rough— some of them are bullies—and they need to be told—"

Stephanie was walking as fast as she could with Lisa clutching her hand. There was no sign of the class. How far ahead could they be? It had only been a few minutes . . . Her heart was pounding; she could have guessed wrong, she could have gotten them both lost. Lisa would stop her cheerful chattering and become frightened again, and it would be Stephanie's fault for pretending she was grown up and could take care of a child.

The street bent to the right and they followed it and then, above Lisa's chattering, Stephanie thought she heard the babble of young voices.

"Hush, Penny, just a minute," she said. "I want to listen."

"What?" Lisa asked.

"Wait," Stephanie said, and they stood still and heard the sound of voices and laughter.

"Oh, we found them!" Lisa cried and ran on ahead, around another corner. Stephanie followed and found the class clustered around Lisa, everyone talking at once.

One of the teachers stepped forward. "Are you the good person who found our naughty girl?"

"Oh, but she isn't naughty at all," Stephanie said. She held out her hand. "Sabrina Lacoste."

"Marie Frontenac," the teacher said.

Stephanie smiled. "And you have a daughter, so you are very understanding with the young girls and very firm with the boys, especially the bullies."

"Ah, Lisa is a chatterbox. But how interesting that she thinks that I am gentler with the girls because of my daughter. Do they all, I wonder? Probably, if Lisa talks of it. And perhaps I am. Well, but now we must do something." She looked at Lisa, surrounded by her friends, all of them talking at a high pitch of excitement. "We cannot let our young people wander off; she must be punished."

"She was terrified," Stephanie said. "She felt alone and lost, and the square seemed strange to her, like a world she didn't know. Isn't that punishment enough?"

"Perhaps, but I cannot let the incident vanish. I must say something to the others."

"Ask Lisa to tell them how frightened she was. She'll probably exaggerate—they all do, at that age— and it will become a better lesson than anything you could say."

Their eyes met and they laughed. "Ah, Madame Lacoste, how well you know children," said Marie Frontenac. "Are you a teacher?"

"No."

"But of course you have children of your own."

"No. And I didn't think I knew . . ." Her voice trailed away. "I work in an antique shop in Cavaillon," she said abruptly. "Jacqueline en Provence."

"Ah, I know that shop, it is exquisite. Oh, madame, perhaps you will consent to speak to our class sometime on what that means—antiques. Children cannot comprehend the past, and perhaps you can help them understand how it still lives and comes to us in furniture and buildings and art and other antiquities."

''I'm not an expert,'' Stephanie said. ''I'm just beginning.''

''But you know more than we do. Would you consider it?''

Stephanie thought about it. She wanted to see Lisa again; she wanted to be with children. *Maybe I was a teacher. Or I did have children after all. No, Max said I didn't. How strange this is.* ''Maybe I will,'' she said. ''I'll call you when I decide.''

''My address and telephone . . .'' Marie Frontenac wrote on a pad of paper and tore the top sheet off. ''I look forward to it. Now I must leave. I thank you from my heart, Madame Lacoste—''

''Please. Call me Sabrina.''

''Ah, Sabrina. I thank you from my heart for returning Lisa to us. Lisa, come here; you of course wish to say goodbye to this good lady who rescued you.''

Stephanie bent down and Lisa kissed her on one cheek, then the other, then back to the first. ''Thank you, madame. But could I ask you a question?''

''Of course.'' Stephanie's arms were around her and she was thinking of nothing but the good feeling of that slender body against hers.

''Why did you call me Penny?''

Stephanie pulled back. ''I didn't know I did. I called you Penny?''

''When you told me to hush. You said, 'Hush, Penny.' I think you were trying very hard to hear if my class was nearby. And it was.''

''Yes. I don't know, Lisa. Perhaps you reminded me of someone named Penny. But I do know your name and I'm coming back to see you one day.''

''Oh, how lovely.'' She looked at Stephanie searchingly. ''And no one is going to tell . . .''

''It doesn't seem at all necessary to tell Lisa's parents, does it?'' Stephanie asked Marie Frontenac. ''If Lisa talks to the class as we discussed . . .''

''Well, no, I think this time it will not be necessary. Of

course if Lisa makes a habit of running off whenever she feels like—"

"I didn't run off!" Lisa cried. "I stopped to pet a puppy, but then I got lost and it was terrible!"

"Yes, that is what we are counting on." Marie Frontenac held out her hand. "Thank you again, Sabrina. I hope, when you return, we will have time to get acquainted."

"I'd like that very much." Stephanie bent down and kissed Lisa's forehead. "I'll see you soon." She turned and went back the way she had come, trying to remember the twists they had taken. Here and there, like guideposts, she saw a broken shutter, a strange pink door, a toppled flowerpot, and she followed them, thinking, I remember, I remember; I remember everything now.

But in a few minutes the silence of the narrow streets closed in upon her. No one was about; she turned and turned, but behind her and ahead of her the street was deserted. There were no clues in this part of the walk, nothing that looked familiar; she could have been ten miles from the square or a few feet from it. Fear built inside her. *She felt alone and lost, and the square seemed strange to her, like a world she didn't know. Isn't that punishment enough?*

But I'm not being punished, she thought. I haven't done anything wrong. Or have I? What did I do, in those years I can't remember, that led me here?

She began to run, turning a corner, then turning another and another, looking for anything familiar, but by now all the buildings looked identical, and there were no guideposts, and she wondered if perhaps she only thought she was running but in fact she was standing still. The thought made her dizzy and she leaned against a building. *I don't know where I am or where I'm going.*

The fear grew inside her and she ran again, trailing one hand on the stucco buildings crammed together, leaning into the street. And then abruptly, as she turned another corner, she saw, framed by the buildings on all sides, the square opening before her, with the fountain, and Max standing beside it.

"Well? Did you have a satisfactory excursion?" he asked coldly.

"I'm glad to see you," Stephanie said, her breathing beginning to slow with relief. She kissed him. "I took a lost child back to the group she'd been with. I hope you weren't worried."

"It occurred to me that you might not come back."

She looked at him somberly. "Where would I go?"

"I have no idea. Do you stay with me only because you have nowhere else to go?"

She gave him a long look. "I don't know."

He took her hand and they walked toward the side street where he had parked the car. "I told you, you will love me. You did once; you will again."

"Not if you treat me like a child."

"I treat you like a woman. I do not talk about myself, Sabrina."

"You told me about your mother, about Holland, about Spain—"

"And that should have been enough."

As he unlocked the car, Stephanie asked, "Is it criminal? Is that it? You don't tell me what you do because it's illegal?"

"Would it make a difference?"

"And that explosion on the ship? Was that part of it?"

He sat behind the wheel, rubbing the car key with his thumb as Stephanie sat beside him. "I've told you that the explosion was an accident."

"But you said, in the hospital, that you would keep me safe."

"You remember that," he said musingly. "You forgot so much else in those early days."

"I remember your voice saying it. I thought about it every day I was there. That you said you would keep me safe."

"And so I will." He started the car. "In a world where

people are cold and hungry and without the help of friends, I will make sure you are warm and fed and close to people who care for you.''

"And is it illegal, what you do?"

"Would it make a difference?"

"No. If I loved you, it would."

"Brutal but honest. Well, you will love me, Sabrina, and someday I may tell you what I do, but not today. Tell me about the child you found."

This time, when he brushed aside her questions, there was nowhere to run; nor did she want to. She did not want to be alone, in Aix or anywhere else. Max was her anchor and the center of her life. He took care of her and was a good companion; they had a marriage even if she did not love him. At least for now, she thought. At least for now.

"Max, did I ever mention someone named Penny?"

"No." He drove around the main square and headed out of town. "Do you know someone named Penny?"

"I think I did. And I'm sure she was a child. Someone I taught, perhaps, or . . . perhaps my daughter."

"You told me you had no children. And you never mentioned being a teacher."

Stephanie sighed. "I don't know."

"What was the name of the child you found?"

"Lisa." She told him about the class of children holding on to a red rope, and about Lisa Vernet and Marie Frontenac, and the invitation to speak to their class. "Marie Frontenac said children can't comprehend the past; it seems strange that I would be asked to talk about it, when I don't have one."

"She didn't ask for a personal history; she asked for a discussion of how the past comes to us in antiques."

"She said, 'how it still lives and comes to us.' It does still live, doesn't it? It's there somewhere, like another floor in a house, but closed off. If I could find the way to it . . ."

They were silent. They were driving through a misty landscape, the distant colors muted but the nearby fields bright green beside vineyards of rich black earth, where skeletal grape plants stood like sentinels in perfect rows. Along the road, the plane trees were sending out new shoots, the first irises were blooming along stone walls, and the *genêt* bushes were just beginning to bloom, pale yellow but already hinting at the deep canary they would become, with a pungent fragrance that would fill the air for miles.

"I've collected art and antiques for thirty years," Max said casually. "The pieces in our house are mine."

"Oh." Stephanie nodded, as if to herself. That was the way she would learn about him, in small bits of information that came out almost incidentally. Except, she thought, that Max never does anything incidentally. "You could help me, then. I don't know how to talk about antiques."

They discussed paintings and furniture, silver, porcelain, old lace and cut glass, as Max took back roads, extending their drive. Stephanie was astonished by the extent of his knowledge; it was as if he had spent a lifetime studying these things. "There are a number of books in the library that will help you," he said. "I'll give you a list."

The late afternoon sun broke through the clouds, spilling over the houses of Roussillon, nestled high in the hills, intensifying their color: vivid orange, pink, red, ocher climbing the slope like a construction of children's playing blocks. "Robert's son lives there," she murmured. "I'd like to meet him someday."

"Don't count on it. Robert keeps his lives carefully separated."

Stephanie smiled. "How many does he have?"

"A few that I know of."

More secrets, she thought. What is the matter with these men?

But she could not be angry, not with so much beauty all around her: the sun-burnished houses of Roussillon and the tree-covered hills where it perched, the fields and gardens bursting with new life, the clouds pulling apart like curtains on a stage to reveal blue sky and a pale crescent moon. Her earlier anger was gone as well, wiped out by the adventure with Lisa and Marie Frontenac. As they approached Cavaillon, she was feeling lighthearted, all her fears gone. Everything would be all right; everything she wanted could truly come to pass.

And Max was beside her: she was safe and protected, enclosed in his car as if she were in his arms. As if she were that crescent moon, shining because of the light from the sun, she felt herself absorb and reflect his confidence and power, and make it her own.

But I don't want to be a reflection of Max. I want to be myself.

And what if he is a criminal?

Oh, of course he's not, she thought, without pause. He likes to be dramatic and he was angry at me for walking out on him, and so he hints and pretends and tries to make me nervous. But Robert wouldn't be his friend if he were a criminal.

But still she could not give Max the trust he wanted. She could not brush aside the feeling that even though he was exciting and passionate and seemed truly to love her, there was something dangerous about him. Today was the first time she had thought he might be doing something criminal, but every day something about him made her think that he lived with danger or put others in danger, or perhaps both.

And every day she thought he lied to her about what he knew of her past.

And so she did not trust him or love him. She reserved the small self she had—the few months of experience that were her entire history—for herself.

I don't even know if I can really love anyone until I'm a whole person again, she thought. And who would it be, even if I could? I don't know anyone. I'd like to, though; I want so much to know what love feels like.

She remembered greeting Max after his first trip away

from her. She had been sure she loved him and wanted him and was happy to be his wife. But that was the only time; she hadn't been able to feel that way again.

So if I did love him and trust him once—and I must have if I married him—it's gone.

"You're very quiet," Max said as he drove up the hill to their house.

"There's so much to think about," she said vaguely.

"Well, right now let's think about dinner. Would you like to go to Goult? You liked La Bartavelle last time we were there."

"Oh, I loved it. Yes, that would be wonderful. But we shouldn't go if Madame Besset has already begun dinner."

"She has not; I called her from Aix."

"Oh. This was planned in advance?"

"I wanted to make sure we did something special. I'm leaving tomorrow, for a week."

"Where are you going?"

"Marseilles and Nice."

"Why can't I come with you? I haven't really been to either one."

"I'd like to have you with me; I hate the idea of a week away from you. But we couldn't be together; I have meetings day and night. And I want to show you those cities in my own way, when we have plenty of time. We'll go soon, when I have only you to think about." In the garage, he turned off the engine and took her in his arms. "Sabrina, you know I love you. If I could change my life to be with you all the time I would." He kissed her, his hand on her breast, his arm enclosing her so that she felt submerged within him. Stephanie let herself respond; it was easier than debating with herself whether she really wanted to make love to him, and it was much, much easier than telling him she wanted to think about it. So her body warmed and opened to him even as her thoughts were cool and separate, and as they walked upstairs to his room she told herself that she was his wife and he took care of her and she owed this to him. She knew there was something wrong with that, but she let it go; she could think about it when he was gone.

Max watched the shore recede as Carlos Figueros raced his small motorboat out to sea, past sailboats, past other motorboats, past yachts moving with stately grace through the choppy water. "Now we have absolute privacy," Figueros said, cutting the motor. He leaned forward. "What do you have for me?"

"A list of shipments." Max took from inside his slicker a sheaf of papers clipped together. "And you have for me . . ."

"Payment for the last load of counterfeit we shipped. And a record of what has been donated." He searched in his pocket and brought out a business envelope and a small notebook, no larger than his palm. He gave the envelope to Max. "Eighty-five thousand francs."

"How much was donated?"

"Max." Figueros pouted. "You think I am not honest? We donated eight thousand five hundred. Ten percent. Were not those your orders? Ten percent of your share for the priest's people, the rest to you."

Max held out his hand and Figueros put the notebook in it. He leafed through the small pages, squinting to read the tiny handwriting. "Guatemala, Haiti, Chile. Nothing in Africa this time?"

"No, nor in Russia or Eastern Europe or the Middle East or China. Father Chalon said he didn't want us to spread the money too thin; he says that would be almost the same as giving them nothing at all. Do you want us to do it a different way?"

"No, it's Father Chalon's game; you'll do whatever he says." He pocketed the money without counting it, as well as the page he had been reading, and gave Figueros the sheaf of papers. "The schedule. It begins next month, the first of May, and runs through the end of July. You should be able to handle that."

Figueros turned the pages slowly, reading each line. Max watched a nearby sailboat with four young people practicing raising the spinnaker. He was impatient to get back to shore, but he kept it well hidden; Carlos Figueros was valuable to him.

"There is no figure for the shipment to England," Figueros said at last.

Max took the sheaf. "It should be here. My secretary was supposed to get it before she typed this. I'll talk to her when we get to shore."

"She is not there."

"In her office? You checked?"

"I stopped in to say good morning before I met you. The office was locked."

"That doesn't mean she isn't there now. She's never missed a day. Well, let's go back and find out. If she's ill we can call her or go to her home."

"Good." Figueros started the motor. The boat vibrated beneath them, then shot forward, making a wide arc as he pointed it toward shore. They wove through other boats, and Max recalled the last time he had been in a motorboat, speeding from Monte Carlo to Nice with Sabrina bleeding and unconscious and the sunken remains of his yacht behind them. No more danger from there, he thought; they think we're dead.

On shore, he and Figueros went to the Lacoste et fils warehouse at the end of the dock. The office was in a small building attached to one side. Max turned the knob, but the door was locked. "Peculiar," he muttered and took out his key. Inside, the room was damp and still; the desk empty, the files locked, telephone directories and atlases and maps neatly lined up on the bookshelves. Max looked at the calendar on the desk. "Saturday, four days ago. We talked that day; it was the day I left for Nice. Where the hell is she? I don't remember any talk about a vacation."

He picked up the telephone and dialed her home number and heard her voice on her answering machine. Without leaving a message, he hung up. "She lives not far from here; I think I'll run over there."

Figueros nodded. "I'll come with you."

There was no answer when they knocked on the door of the apartment in a tall concrete building a few blocks from the harbor. But as Max knocked again, the door across the hall opened. "It will do no good, monsieur," said the small man standing there. His eyes looked up at them with sadness. "The police were here; the young lady was in an automobile accident, she and her young man, and they are both dead."

"These are Valdrôme," Jacqueline said, unwrapping a package of quilted place mats. "Excellent quality, as is this . . . ." She tore open another wrapping from the shipment that had arrived that morning. "Martine Nourissat: some of the finest tablecloths I have found."

Stephanie ran her hand over the fabric, cotton as smooth as silk, the patterns ranging from a small floral on the place mats to bold stylized flowers and branches on the tablecloths. She and Jacqueline were sitting on the floor beside stacks of packages, a knife and scissors and café au lait on a low table nearby. The shop was not yet open and the high-ceilinged room was in shadows where lights had not been turned on. Beyond the windows, the cours Gambetta was crowded with office workers leaving the cafés to go to work, shopkeepers unlocking their doors, and trucks and cars and motorcycles jamming the street in an early morning rush punctuated by horns and the squeal of brakes.

Inside Jacqueline en Provence, all was hushed and peaceful, the furniture and fabrics crowded together as if in a warm, familiar living room, Jacqueline and Stephanie talking in low voices and sipping their hot coffee. Jacqueline had asked her to come in early to unwrap the shipment, and so for the first time in the two weeks Stephanie had worked there, they had a quiet time for talking. Two women talking together, Stephanie thought. Two friends.

At first there was only Madame Besset; now there is Jacqueline.

"Of course these are all new," Jacqueline went on as they unwrapped other packages and laid the folded tablecloths and place mats in baskets for display. "The old pieces, mostly lace but a few silk and linen, are in the armoire across the room. We'll talk about them next."

"I looked at them yesterday when you were out," Stephanie said. "And I found a book in the back room on antique fabrics; I read it last night."

Jacqueline smiled. "Soon I'll have nothing to teach you. But, my dear, it wasn't necessary to read the whole book in one night; you don't have to study as if I'm going to give you a test."

"Oh, but I liked doing it. I always read late when my husband is out of town."

"He's an impressive man, your husband; I'd like to know him better." Jacqueline folded a large tablecloth, laid eight matching napkins on top and tied them all together with a wide green crepe ribbon. "I was sorry you couldn't come to my dinner party the other night."

"Dinner party?"

"On Saturday. I mailed the invitation; it was foolish, of course, since I see you every morning, but I like the formality of written invitations, and the element of surprise." She tilted her head and contemplated Stephanie. "And you *are* surprised, but not the way I anticipated."

"Max didn't tell me. We were in Aix on Saturday, but we had plenty of time . . . in fact, we went out to dinner that night. He wanted us to be together because he was leaving the next day. But he should have told me."

"Husbands often think their decisions need no explanation."

Their eyes met and they smiled. "I didn't know you were married," Stephanie said.

"I am not. But I have been, twice. It embarrasses me to say it. Marriage is not like folding tablecloths: it is of such greater proportions that one should take care to learn from one's first mistake and never repeat it. But I did. When I realized it, two years into my second marriage, I could not believe it. I have always been proud of my intelligence. How could it fail me so completely? I did not even have youth as a defense; I was over fifty. I had no excuse at all."

Stephanie gazed at her in surprise. "How old are you?"

"Sixty-two in a few weeks. A very good age in most regards, though I find I am not as patient with fools as I once was, and every year it seems that there are more fools than one would have thought possible."

"You don't look sixty-two."

"And what does sixty-two look like?"

Stephanie laughed. "I don't know. Just . . . older. Someone who doesn't move furniture around the way you do, and climb ladders and talk about skiing off-piste at Chamonix and keep moving for hours without sitting down. And, I suppose, gray hair."

"Ah, well, as for the hair, that needs some help, which I give it regularly; otherwise you would see gray, perhaps not all, but enough to create an impression. The rest, however, is me. I am blessed with health and energy. And sixty-two, you know, is, after all, quite young; there is nothing one stops enjoying at that age. And you, my dear? How old—"

"Do you think you'll marry again?" Stephanie asked.

Jacqueline looked at her curiously; already she knew enough about this woman to know that she would not be deliberately rude. But now she was rude. Why would it bother her to be asked her age, when she was clearly so much younger than Jacqueline? Well, another time, perhaps; meanwhile the question was easily answered. "No, most certainly not. I do not need the financial support of a man and there is always the possibility of another failure. And I like living alone; I like to live to a pattern and rhythm I make for myself. I don't get lonely; I have many friends and resources. And a man, of course. It is essential to have a man when one wants him. Or men, on occasion, though I prefer one at a time, and at the moment there is only one.''

Stephanie had stopped opening packages and was sitting very still, her eyes fixed on the fine sculpted lines of Jacqueline's face. She felt very happy because Jacqueline was being so open, and in that way making her a part of her life. Stephanie felt that she was learning what it really meant to have a woman friend. She thought of Max and realized how alone she had been until now, without a woman to talk to and learn from. And so, thinking still of Max, she asked what would have seemed an impermissibly intimate question but now was not, because Jacqueline had made it permissible. ''And do you love him?''

''No, nor does he love me,'' Jacqueline said easily. ''That part of it definitely is not essential. We like each other and we have a pleasant time together, and that is quite enough.''

''But you trust him.''

''Trust? I think that is a word for marriage, not for an arrangement of convenience. It is a question I have not asked. Do you ask it about your husband?''

''Yes,'' Stephanie said, and felt a wonderful sense of relief as the word came out and she knew that Jacqueline had made it possible for her to say many things. ''Not that he won't take care of me; I know he will. But that he is . . . what he says he is.''

''Oh, well, my dear, how many of us are what we say we are? We all have hidden pasts, hidden lusts or fears or hatreds or loves . . .'' She gazed at Stephanie for a moment. ''But you mean more than that. You mean you think he is not as honorable as he seems.''

Stephanie nodded.

''That should become clear the longer you live with him. One thing I discovered about marriage was that almost always one learns far more about a spouse than one ever wished to know.''

''I want to know everything,'' Stephanie said. ''I don't like blank spaces.''

"Well, we all have our own needs. I think a little mystery keeps us on a fine edge of interest. It is like the sun slipping in and out of great dark clouds; suddenly the world is brilliantly transformed, and if we have been drowsing or inattentive we are brought back instantly to beauty, and to life."

"Do you feel that way about the man you're with now?"

"Ah, no. If I did, we would have a grand passion instead of a pleasant friendship. We are very different, and neither of us feels the need to share too much or to enjoy the mystery of each other. That does not mean we do not have a good time and, in fact, need each other. If we parted tomorrow I would miss him very much for a while, but I would wish him well for the pleasure we have had, and he would do the same for me. That is all I want."

Jacqueline picked up another package and slit the wrapping paper carefully along one end to avoid cutting the fabric inside. "Have you been married long?" she asked.

"No. A few months." Stephanie's hands rested in her lap; a small frown was between her eyes.

"Well, you will find how very much you learn in the first year. Probably you will fill in most of those blank spaces you don't like." She slipped the fabric from the wrapper and began to separate the tablecloths and the napkins. Without looking up, she asked casually, "How old are you, my dear?"

There was a silence. "I don't know," Stephanie said at last.

Jacqueline's head shot up. "Why is that?"

"Because I don't know anything about myself except what I've done since October. Because I have no memory. Because I've lost myself."

"Oh, my poor little one." Jacqueline swept aside the tablecloths and place mats and took Stephanie in her arms. "What a terrible thing. You remember nothing? Nothing comes back to you?"

"A few bits and pieces. I think my mother's name was

Laura. I knew someone named Penny, probably a little girl. I never lived alone. I cut roses with a silver scissors."

"And you know design."

"Maybe. Just because I rearranged—" Stephanie pulled back within Jacqueline's arms. "How did you know I rearranged our living room?"

"I didn't know it. But I'm not surprised. I've been watching you in the two weeks you've been here; you've been moving things around the shop since the day you arrived."

"Oh. I didn't realize . . . I'm sorry."

"Why should you be?"

"Because it's your shop, not my living room."

"But the more you treat it as your living room, the better it looks. Sabrina, I could have stopped you at any time; I did not, because you have a very good eye and an excellent sense of harmony. I like everything you have done. I would guess that you were an interior designer once, or at least you worked with furnishings. Tell me what happened. Did you have an accident? You were injured?"

Stephanie brushed aside her hair to expose the scar on her forehead. "There was an explosion on a boat. Max got me away and held me in the water until another boat picked us up. That's what he says; I don't remember any of it. I was in a hospital in Marseilles for two months; there was a wonderful plastic surgeon there and Max says I look the same now as I did before. But . . ."

"Yes? There is more?"

Stephanie nodded. She had not told this to Robert or to Max, but she wanted to tell Jacqueline. "About a week ago I called the hospital in Marseilles and spoke to one of the doctors who took care of me. I can't remember most of what happened there, either, you see, and I wanted to know what he had said about my memory. And he said he thought it wasn't only that I was struck on the head, but that there's something I don't want to remember, something I want to block out, so I've blocked out everything. He called it psychogenic amnesia."

"He cannot be sure of that."

"He said they had discussed my case and they all agreed."

"Well. And how do you feel about that?"

"I don't know. I think about it all the time; what could I have done that made me so ashamed I forced myself to forget it?"

"Perhaps it was something else, something you saw or heard," Jacqueline said gently. "Why do you blame yourself?"

"Because I feel that something is my fault." The words were almost inaudible. "I can't explain it, but I wake up in the morning and the first thing I think is that I've done something wrong. And I can't remember what it was. Because I can't remember anything."

"My poor little one," Jacqueline said again, and held Stephanie close. Stephanie let herself sink into Jacqueline's strong embrace; she felt safe and protected and wished she could stay there forever, not having to worry about who she was or what she had done, just staying close and soaking up Jacqueline's assurance and control of her life.

A knock on the door made them start. "Oh, my Lord, look at the time, and these packages not finished." Jacqueline put Stephanie gently from her and stood up, smoothing her wool skirt, adjusting her silk blouse, sweeping her palms along her perfectly smooth hair. "I'll unlock the door, Sabrina; would you take the rest of these packages to the back room and open them? We'll put everything away later. And, my dear"—she put her hand on Stephanie's arm—"we'll talk again. This time together has meant a great deal to me."

Stephanie was trembling with the shock of returning to the normal day. "Yes, it was wonderful. Thank you." She scooped up the remaining brown-wrapped packages and made her way through the crowded room to the back. "I'll turn on the lights."

"Good." Jacqueline was at the front door, and as she swung it open, Stephanie flicked the switches and all the lights came on, illuminating the curves and angles of the furniture, the translucent china displayed in old painted armoires, the small stitches of cashmere throws and the worn threads of antique tapestries. *It is like the sun slipping in and out of great dark clouds; suddenly the world is brilliantly transformed, and if we have been drowsing or inattentive we are brought back instantly to beauty, and to life.*

Oh, I'd like that, Stephanie thought, filled suddenly with a longing that took in the whole world beyond Cavaillon and Max's house and Max's bed. I wish I could know what it's like to feel that.

She stood beside a long oak table in the back room amid the clutter of gifts to be wrapped, lamps to be repaired, draperies to be hung, and unopened boxes that had arrived in that morning's shipment. On a small desk was a computer used for recording and ringing up sales, an empty coffee can holding pencils and pens, and a mug half full of coffee left over from the day before. Absently, Stephanie took the mug to the sink in the corner and washed it and set it on the edge to drain. She picked up a spool of iridescent ribbon that had fallen to the floor and dropped it into a box with others like it. She pushed lamps and vases and memo pads aside to make a place on the oak table and used the space to open the packages she had carried in. And all the time she was thinking, I'll never know what that feels like as long as I'm with Max. But I'm tied to him; the only life I know is with him. And it's a good life; I should be grateful; I haven't any right to complain.

Besides, how can I think of not being with Max? I'm too afraid. I don't know how I'd manage without protection. She remembered feeling safe and protected in Max's car, driving back from Aix, as if she were the moon reflecting his sun, making his confidence and power her own. And then she had wanted to stay in Jacqueline's embrace forever, soaking up her assurance and control.

When am I going to be myself, with my own strength? When am I going to be more adventurous?

She heard voices from the shop: two women talking animatedly about an eighteenth-century sofa, a man's voice saying something about a group of paintings, and Jacqueline saying, "Good, very good, we sold all the last ones so quickly, and I have customers waiting. They want especially the landscapes."

The man chuckled. "Too bad. The new ones are abstracts. I've brought slides of them; if they're not right for your shop I can take them to Galerie Le Fèvre."

"You will not! Léon, good heavens, I represent you; you agreed to that."

Someone was standing in the door to the back room. "If you please, madame, this tablecloth, what is the price?"

Stephanie looked at the cloth draped over the woman's arm. "Fifteen hundred francs. That includes the napkins, of course."

"Well, I adore it and I must have it. And I want one for a housewarming gift; which would you suggest? Something a little smaller. And definitely not as expensive."

Stephanie suppressed a smile as she led the customer into the shop. "We have several on this rack; if you wish to look through them . . ."

"Oh, whatever you choose. She won't invite me to dinner so often that I'll have to look at it very much. Here, what about this? Yellow. A color I detest, but she'll probably like it."

"Not just yellow; aureolin," said a man's voice, "deep, luscious, lustrous, filled with sunlight and fresh breezes, youth, love, and the promise of good food and wine."

Stephanie and the customer had turned around. He leaned against the wall, smiling easily, a small man barely taller than Stephanie and about her age, lean, broad-shouldered, blond and deeply tanned, wearing blue jeans and an open-necked white shirt. His face was thin, with faintly hollowed cheeks; his eyes were green and they met Stephanie's with a look of amused conspiracy. His voice was the one she had heard in the shop, talking to Jacqueline about paintings.

They stood looking at each other while the customer said, "Aureolin? Aureolin? I never heard of it. I don't even know how to pronounce it. What is it?"

"Chrome yellow," said Jacqueline, coming up to them. "A pigment painters often use. You wish to buy these two tablecloths, the red and the yellow?"

Stephanie took them from the customer. "I'll wrap them for you."

"Unless there is something else madame wishes," Jacqueline said.

Stephanie flushed. She was not concentrating; she still felt the man's eyes on her and she wanted to look at him. "Yes, please look around; I'll have these for you when you're ready."

"Well, I will; I saw a vase I rather liked . . ." The customer drifted away.

"I'm sorry," Stephanie said to Jacqueline.

"Oh, Léon has a way of derailing conversations. Sabrina Lacoste, Léon Dumas. You may have seen some of Léon's paintings in the shop, Sabrina; I think the last one sold just after you began to work here."

"I did see it and we have one in our living room," Stephanie said as she and Léon shook hands.

"Which one?" he asked.

"The Alpilles. The little house in it reminds me of van Gogh's painting of them."

His eyes brightened. "I put it there in homage to him. Have you been there? Or climbed them?"

"No." Stephanie was confused and she took a step back, and then another. "Excuse me, I have to take care of this; I have to wrap these . . ." She turned and fled to the back room. *I know about van Gogh. I know about his painting of the Alpilles. But in all the months I've lived with Max and looked at that painting, I never thought of van Gogh. Maybe I'm beginning to remember. Maybe it's coming back.*

Léon was in the doorway. "Was it something I said?"

"No." She pulled out a length of wrapping paper and cut it off. "I just wanted to take care of this."

"Not quite true, I think, but we'll let it go for now." He watched her wrap the red tablecloth and napkins. In the silence, they could hear Jacqueline's voice in the shop. "You said, *'We* have one in *our* living room.' Are you married?"

"Yes."

"And who bought the painting? You or your husband?"

"My husband. Before we met."

"I admire his good judgment." He came into the room and held out his hand. "I'm happy we met. I hope to see you again."

"Yes," Stephanie said. Once again they shook hands, and their hands stayed clasped while their eyes met. He was not handsome, Stephanie thought, but she liked his looks; his face was alive with curiosity and intelligence and humor, and he looked at everything with intensity. Right now he was looking at her as if he wanted to know all about her, not just in a casual way with carelessly spoken social phrases—*I hope to see you again*—but in a way that took what he said and did seriously. And Max had said he was one of the finest young painters in the country. He held her hand too tightly, but then, she was not trying to pull away. They looked at each other steadily, as if they were speaking together, getting acquainted.

When am I going to be more adventurous?

Oh, Stephanie thought, perhaps beginning right now.

CHAPTER *11*

Mrs. Thirkell pushed forward the platter of roast chicken and potatoes she was holding at Lu Zhen's right hand. "Of course you'll have seconds," she scolded. "A growing boy is an engine that needs a constant supply of petrol. Especially if he's also a student, and a skinny one at that. Come on, now, two or three slices, young man, you'll be the better for them. And more potatoes, too."

"He doesn't want any more," Cliff growled.

"Yes, he does," Penny said, watching Lu. "He's just being polite. Can I have some more, Mrs. Thirkell? After Lu?"

Sabrina and Garth exchanged a smile. "Our diplomat," Garth said. "Go on, Lu, dig in; you're outnumbered and Penny's made it accepted practice."

Lu smiled his thin, cautious smile and heaped chicken and potatoes on his plate. Mrs. Thirkell sighed with exaggerated gratification and took the platter to Penny. "It's really delicious," Penny said. "Is it different from the chicken in China?"

"Their eyes are different," Cliff said.

"Cliff—" Garth began, but Sabrina forestalled him. "Not a good joke," she said lightly.

"Do you know, I think they look exactly like your chickens," Lu said seriously. "I lived in a village once and I saw them being slaughtered, and they seemed quite ordinary to me."

"I thought you grew up in Beijing," Sabrina said. "When did you live in a village?"

"When I was a child. There was a time when the government ordered people from cities to work in the fields and villages, and I went with my family to the west."

"Masses of people uprooted," Garth said, "whoever they were, whatever their profession. Including Lu's father, who's a physicist, and his mother, who teaches English."

Lu smiled again, the smile that barely stretched his lips. "My father shoveled manure for five years; my mother did laundry."

"Why?" Cliff asked, curiosity cutting through his sullenness.

"The government felt that intellectuals and professionals should return to the people because they'd forgotten who they were."

"What does that mean?"

"The government said intellectuals and professionals thought of themselves as better than the peasants when really everybody should be the same."

"But people aren't the same," Penny said.

"The government said they were."

"But they were wrong. Didn't anybody complain? People here complain about the government all the time."

"That is not the way in China."

"Well, I know you can't complain out loud; we learned about that at school. But don't you, when you're at home? You know, when you talk about things at the dinner table, the way we do."

"Sometimes."

"Does the government still think everybody's the same?" Cliff asked.

"Not so much, it seems."

"So where are your parents now?"

"In Beijing. My father teaches at the university and my mother is in a middle school."

"Did your mother teach you English?" Penny asked.

"Yes, but I also studied it in school. Everyone wants to learn English. Especially if you want to go into science. English is the language of science all over the world."

"I'd like to learn Chinese," Penny said. "It sounds sort of like singing."

"I could teach you some words, if you like."

"Really? Would you? That would be so neat; nobody at school knows any Chinese at all. Tell me a word now."

"*Ma.*"

"What does that mean?"

"Mother."

"But that's the same as English. Who cares about that? Tell me a *Chinese* word."

"That is the Chinese word. But I will give you this one: *hen hao chi.*"

"What's that?"

"Tasty. That's what this dinner is. And here's another one: *youyi.* It means friendship."

Penny repeated them. "Will you teach me lots more?"

"If you like."

"Lots. So I can talk, you know, not just words and stuff, but a few sentences that really sound like I'm talking in Chinese. Then I can do it at school and everybody else will just be *totally out of it.*"

Sabrina looked at Penny thoughtfully, wondering which problems, old or new, were behind her vehemence. She'd bring it up when they were alone; right now she was enjoying the conversation, pleased that Cliff had joined in. There had been a swift moment of pain when Lu first arrived—it happened every time he entered their house—when, looking at him and hearing his accent, she was swept back to China last September, China for two weeks with Stephanie, ending in Hong Kong when the two of them took the first step in the game they had decided to play and handed each other the keys to their front doors. China: the last place she had seen her sister alive.

The pain subsided when they sat at the table; it always did, when the conversation began and she was once again Stephanie Andersen, making a foreign student feel at home. "Does speaking English all the time make you feel different about yourself?" she asked Lu. "Language seems to me to be so deeply a part of our identity: the way we view the world, the way we see ourselves, the subtleties of words that can't ever be perfectly translated . . . Would any of us be the same person if we spoke another language all the time?"

"You did, Mom," Cliff said. "You told us you and Aunt Sabrina talked French when you were in school in Switzerland."

"Yes, but only in classes and whenever we were with the faculty. In our rooms we always went back to English. I think if I were living in Switzerland now, or France, and speaking only French, I might be confused about my identity. Lu, what do you think?"

"I speak Chinese to other Chinese students at school. It is very important to me; it makes me feel I am not drowning in America and the sloppiness of English."

"Sloppy!" Cliff exclaimed.

"So it seems to me. It is very casual, very fluid, like the American people. Chinese is very specific, very rigid, very clear at all times."

"English isn't sloppy," Cliff insisted.

" 'Sloppy' probably isn't the best word," Garth said. "I'd think 'casual' is better. But whatever English is, I'm glad Lu learned it, because if his research comes out as we hope it will, he has a brilliant future as a scientist."

Lu gazed fixedly at Garth. "Thank you."

There was a silence. "Can you tell us about it?" Sabrina asked.

"I think you would not find it interesting."

"Make it interesting," Garth said. "The other day you told me you want to do ~~research~~ when you go home, and run an institute of genetic engineering and teach. The most successful teachers are those who make their subject interesting for everyone, even people who aren't in their field."

Lu gave a barely perceptible shrug. "I am interested in problems in immunology. The lymphocytes—the white blood cells—are some of the best understood cells in the body and this is a field where some very advanced research is being done. For my postdoctoral project I am working on autoimmune disease. This is when the body's B and T cells—"

"The what?" Penny asked.

"I'm sorry. B and T cells are the names of lymphocytes that recognize foreign cells in our bodies and destroy them. It is because of them that we recover from a cold or the flu—that is, when they do what they are supposed to do. But it is a very complex system and it can fail if certain genetic defects exist, and then the system turns against the body."

"Turns against the body?" Sabrina repeated. "What does that mean?"

"The B and T cells can no longer tell the difference between foreign cells that invade our body, and our body itself." Penny was frowning, and Lu said, "I mean, the lymphocytes that are supposed to save us by attacking invading cells turn on us and start attacking *us*. Then we get diseases like rheumatoid arthritis, diabetes mellitus, multiple sclerosis, myasthenia gravis, and Addison's disease. These are all autoimmune diseases. The one I am working on is rheumatoid arthritis; I am trying to find out if we can replace the defective gene that controls the growth of lymphocytes with a healthy one so that the body can produce new lymphocytes that won't attack joint tissue."

"Could you cure AIDS that way?" Cliff asked.

"No, AIDS is caused by HIV. Anyway, I am not working on AIDS."

"Why not? AIDS is killing people."

"And rheumatoid arthritis is crippling millions . . . including my mother. I promised her I would bring back to China a cure for her and so many others."

"It would be a medical revolution," Garth said. "There's tremendous excitement in the department; this is the frontier of research in how genes specify the immune system, and Lu is doing the kind of work that will push it even further ahead. We're very proud of him; his research program is excellent and he has good ideas about the nature of the problem and ways to attack it. If his experiments pan out, it will be a very big feather in the cap of our new institute."

Sabrina saw Lu's face close up. He wants the glory for himself, she thought—not for the department, not for the institute, certainly not for Garth Andersen, just for Lu. He probably thinks he's going to get the Nobel Prize. And from what Garth says, maybe he could. "But others must be working on this, too," she said to Garth.

"At least a dozen, but I don't think they're as close as we are. Farver Labs in San Francisco is probably the closest; I talked to Bill Farver a couple of weeks ago and he sounded about as excited as we are. Of course they don't have Lu, which puts them at a distinct disadvantage."

Cliff made a retching sound. "Oh, Cliff," Sabrina sighed, but at the same time she felt a rush of pity for him. She met Garth's eyes and shook her head slightly. She didn't know why he always seemed to go overboard about Lu, as if he had to make him feel loved and admired over and over again, as if it weren't enough to tell him once that he was on his way to being a fine scientist and leave it there.

Well, if he has to, for whatever reason, he can do it on campus, she thought; he doesn't have to do it at home, especially in front of Cliff. We just talked about this; I guess we'll have to do it again.

"I did want to ask you, Professor," Lu said, "about the polymorphisms within the peptide-binding cleft: how much of the variation in individuals is determined by the ability of the MHC protein to bind different antigens . . ."

They slipped into their own language, their own world. Smiling, Sabrina watched them, feeling a great tenderness for Garth, a man driven by so many passions, and for Lu, never capable, perhaps, of passions as intense as Garth's, but somehow understanding how rare and wonderful they were. His face was absorbed and even adoring, she thought, as he kept his eyes locked on Garth's face.

She looked around the table, set by Mrs. Thirkell with a patterned Provençal cloth, yellow candles, white and yellow daffodils, and bright blue and yellow Provençal pottery that Sabrina had found years before at the marché aux puces outside Paris. It was as if the sun shone within the room, bringing a brightness to the faces around the table, and Sabrina felt a tenderness for all of them—her husband, her children, Mrs. Thirkell, Lu—and for the place where she was: the dining room with its furniture rubbed golden and satiny from centuries of loving hands, the house that enclosed her in well-worn comfort, the town where she greeted friends as she walked down the street.

Oh, everything is so good, she thought. The good things in her life piled up ever higher, never erasing the sadness inside her but dulling it, keeping it out of sight except for the quiet times of very early morning, when she often woke and ached for Stephanie. But at times like this, with her family around her in their bright dining room, she felt herself stretching inside, like a cat in a warm circle of sunlight, and thinking, Oh, everything is so good.

It struck her that she thought that more and more often lately, so often that it had become a refrain beneath everything she did. It was almost as if she were cataloguing and memorizing the glories of autumn, knowing they would be snatched away in the cold sweep of winter. But that was a foolish fantasy, and she brushed it aside. I'm happy, she thought, and I'm grateful for happiness, and I thank goodness for that. The riskiest thing one can do with happiness is to take it for granted.

But Garth and Lu had talked long enough in their private jargon; Cliff's face had tightened and Penny was fidgeting. "We're feeling a little left out, here," Sabrina said lightly. "The conversation has gotten a trifle technical."

"More than a trifle," Garth said ruefully. "I'm sorry. The problem is that I'm so busy with the new institute I don't get much time with Lu. In fact, I haven't been paying much attention to him at all. So it was fun to catch up." Then, as if going back over their dinner and hearing himself praise Lu and withdraw with him into a scientific discussion, he turned to Cliff. "We haven't heard much about your work lately; what are you doing in your lab course these days?"

"Nothing much. It's pretty boring."

"I thought you liked it."

Cliff shrugged, then threw a glance at Sabrina and hunched his shoulders. "Can I be excused?"

"Before dessert?" Garth asked. "That's a first. I think you should hang around, Cliff. We have a guest and it would be nice if we could finish dinner together."

"I *know* we have a guest!"

Mrs. Thirkell came in and began to clear the dishes. "Cliff, how about helping out?"

"Do I have to stay?" Cliff asked Sabrina.

She nodded. "I agree with your father."

"Jeez," he muttered, and began to stack plates.

"Not too high," said Mrs. Thirkell, and the two of them went into the kitchen.

"Cliff does not like me," Lu said. "Have I done something to offend him?"

"A lot of ideas and feelings get stirred up in a twelve-year-old," Sabrina replied. "Cliff will work them out. Didn't you have a lot of mixed-up feelings when you were twelve?"

He shook his head. "We don't have time for things like that. We owe our country all our energy and attention. It is making it possible for us to be educated so we can lead productive lives, and we have no right to fritter away any of our time."

"*What?*" Penny asked.

"Well, we feel honored that you took time out for dinner," Sabrina said, amused, and then was ashamed as she saw confusion on Lu's face.

"I take it very seriously. My government and my family expect me to bring great credit to our country, and then to come home to help all of China."

"Quite a burden for anyone, much less a young man of twenty-two," Garth said. "I hope you don't feel that all of China will condemn you if you do less than brilliantly."

"But why would I do less? You told me I have a brilliant future."

"If everything goes well, I think you do. But I'm sure that your government will support you, and your family will always be behind you whatever—" Garth saw the confusion deepen on Lu's face, and he cut his sentence off. "That's enough shop talk for tonight, I think. Let's have coffee. Lu?"

"Yes, thank you." His voice was muted, and then he was silent as Garth poured coffee and talked about plans for the groundbreaking ceremony for the Institute of Genetic Engineering.

"A little over three weeks away and Claudia and I haven't written our speeches," he said as Mrs. Thirkell and Cliff finished clearing the table and brought in a cake. "The hope is that the longer we wait the shorter they'll be. Do you know, if we could find the gene for brevity we could create universal happiness by shortening ceremonies all over the world."

Sabrina smiled. She cut the cake and handed around the dessert plates, and as they talked of other things, Lu's face relaxed, though he remained quiet. But when he stood up to leave, he stopped beside Cliff's chair. "I guess you don't want to learn Chinese, but I played soccer in China and we could talk about some things I learned from my coach. I mean, if you want to. They're a little different from the stuff you're doing."

Sabrina heard the plea in his voice and held her breath, watching Cliff struggle between jealousy and his love of soccer. "I guess," he said at last; then, as if he was ashamed of his grudging reply, he added, "Sure. Thanks." Sabrina breathed a sigh of relief. She met Garth's eyes. He needs our help, she thought, and then, as they stood and went with Lu to the front door, she wondered which young man, Lu or Cliff, she had meant.

Garth watched Lu walk down the porch steps. A light May rain was falling; there was no breeze and the warm air was soft on their skin. Lu put up an umbrella and turned to wave goodbye, and then Garth closed the door and put his arm around Sabrina as they went back to the dining room. "Thank you. It is a joy to watch you keep a conversation going."

"Everyone helped. He loves you, you know."

"Lu? Why do you think that?"

"I saw it in his face."

"I haven't seen it. Or much of anything else; he hides most of his feelings. I've known him for two years and he's never talked to me before tonight about proving himself worthy of his government's expectations."

"Still, I think he thinks of you as a father."

"Well, I can live with that if Cliff can."

"We'll talk to Cliff. But, Garth, you really do go on about Lu; does he need all that stroking all the time?"

"I don't know. You're right; I realized I did it again tonight, but he's so tense most of the time I find myself trying to make him feel better about himself. There's a kind of desperation to him, almost a recklessness. He can't really relax; he can't really enjoy himself. One time when he was in my office I wanted to hold him on my lap and tell him everything would be all right."

Sabrina smiled. "He would have been very surprised."

"He would have thought the eminent professor had lost his mind. Well, I'll be careful at home from now on, and I'll talk to Cliff." At the door to the dining room, he stopped and took her in his arms. "I love you."

"I'm so glad of that." They glanced into the room and saw an empty table, and heard Penny and Cliff talking to Mrs. Thirkell in the kitchen, and they held each other close and kissed.

"Stolen kisses," Garth murmured as the kitchen door swung open and Penny and Cliff came back.

Sabrina stayed in his arms. "It's when parents stop kissing that children get upset."

"Not a problem, then, since kissing you is the first item on my agenda for the next fifty or sixty years."

"What's the joke?" Cliff asked as Sabrina and Garth smiled together.

"Sixty years of kissing," Sabrina said, and as Cliff came close she put her hand on his hair, chestnut-colored, the same as her own, and pulled him closer. "We plan to kiss you and Penny for at least the next sixty years."

"You'll be ninety-three," Penny said. "That's really old."

"Not too old to kiss."

"We're hot on the trail of a gene that makes kissing as potent at ninety-three as it is at thirty-three," Garth said, and he stood in his dining room with his wife in his arms and his children close by, and felt the abundance of his world and of his own powers: he was just forty years old, healthy, respected in his field, loved in his home. He had everything he wanted; there was nothing he could not do.

A week later he reached back to retrieve that feeling as he sat in his office facing a staff attorney for Congressman Oliver Leglind.

"Roy Stroud," the attorney had said as he walked in. "Glad to meet you, Professor; I've been wanting to for a long time. Ah, this must be the grand new building we've heard so much about." He walked to a square table beneath the window and looked down at a model of the Institute for Genetic Engineering. He was short and stout, with a small brush mustache, wire-rimmed glasses that slid down his small round nose, and a watch chain across his paunch, and he rocked back and forth from toes to heels to toes as he contemplated the Styrofoam model set in Styrofoam-landscaped grounds. "Very handsome. Handsome indeed. That's a handsome monument to you, Professor."

"To science," Garth said.

Stroud was moving a model car along the road circling the institute. "Takes me back, oh, it does take me back. I had a collection once: every model car they made. I don't think I missed one. Not one model car did I miss. Well." He turned back to Garth. "Let's sit down, Professor, I don't want to take too much of your time."

Garth pulled out a chair for Stroud, debated briefly taking the one next to it, then sat in his leather swivel chair instead, putting his desk between them. "It would be helpful if I knew what this is about."

"Well, it's about universities; I guess you could guess that. Congressman Leglind, as I'm sure you know, is chairman of the House Committee on Science, Space and Technology, and he's been bombarded lately with a flood of mail from constituents who are worried about balancing the budget and wondering if maybe Congress is giving too much money to universities. Nobody watches over universities, you know; there's nobody out there signing off on how you spend the funding you get from your government, so nobody really knows where the money goes. So the congressman thought, in response to this avalanche of mail—an outcry from the people if we ever saw one—that he'd hold hearings on the way universities use the money Congress gives them."

"A bombardment, a flood, and an avalanche," Garth said reflectively. "How much mail is that, exactly?"

Stroud guffawed. "I do use a lot of words; I confess it.

I don't have an exact count, Professor, but I assure you it was definitely a torrent."

Garth did not smile. "And what is it you want from me?"

"Information. The hearings start next month and you're on the list of those we'll probably call to testify, but right now we're just gathering information. The congressman likes information up front; he doesn't like a lot of surprises, so we're into fieldwork in a heavy way before the hearings begin. We're curious people, Professor, and we're mainly curious about the way other people spend the government's money. So what I want first is to ask—"

"It is not the government's money. It's our money; it comes from our taxes. The government wasn't transplanted here from Mars: the government is us, all of us who vote and pay taxes. And the government doesn't give our money away; it invests it. In this university, the government invests in genetic research that can change people's lives: how long they live, how comfortably they live, how productive they are, how secure an environment they can provide for their children—the next generation. Most people would call that a wise investment."

"And indeed it might be, it might indeed be, if the money is used wisely. The wise use of money, as of course you know, is numero uno when there isn't enough to go around. So, Professor, I'd ask you first about a party you gave at the Shedd Aquarium in Chicago on February twentieth of this year."

Garth stared at him. "You can't be serious."

"I am always serious, Professor."

"You come in here talking about balancing the federal budget and then you ask me about a fund-raising event that cost five thousand dollars."

"Is that what you call it? A fund-raising event? I understood that it was a party."

"Who called it that?"

"Well, it doesn't really matter. Someone who heard about it. Renting the aquarium, you know, that's a class act, and class acts tend to get around. Good food, music, limos to take some of you home . . . doesn't sound very academic, does it? I mean, I went to college and law school and I never heard of my professors dancing around with fish and catered dinners and riding home in limos."

"Entertainment is in the budget," Garth said, and heard himself saying it to Claudia at the aquarium. "People who give substantial sums of money like to be appreciated. We hold these events in the most pleasant atmosphere we can find to thank those who've helped fund our programs and to describe to them and to prospective donors the programs that still need funding. Our guests always know we'll be coming back to them for more at some time in the future; a convivial evening is part of the whole process."

"But you've got the government giving you—sorry, investing in you. That money is supposed to be used for research, not for renting the aquarium. And not for putting on a dinner at the Ritz-Carlton last December eighth, or for a dinner at Le Français on January the twentieth, or for renting a cruise ship on Lake Michigan for dinner on March tenth. One thing we've noticed, Professor, is how well you all eat."

Garth gazed at him. "The entertainment budget is one half of one percent of the money we spend on research. It pays for itself many times over."

"So far. You don't know that, going in; that's just a hope and hopes sometimes crash; hope is not a way to do business. Especially with the government's money. But I agree: these aren't the biggest items. The biggest—no contest—is this handsome institute you're building for yourself."

"For the university. And for science."

"But there's a kitchen in this building, and a lounge that's sort of like a faculty club, and an auditorium, and some pretty nice offices and reception rooms. So what we're curious about here, Professor, is what does all that have to do with science?"

Garth was so still it seemed he barely breathed. Anyone

who knew him would have known how his anger was building. "Since we're asking questions, I have some for you. Why is Congressman Leglind hostile to science? Is he afraid of it? Does he think that attacking science somehow makes this a better country? Or does he believe that the fortunes of his political career rest on finding something to destroy?"

He was on his feet now, leaning over the desk, his voice rising. "Or is he simply the kind of politician who makes Congress a laughingstock, the kind who creates circuses instead of legislation, the kind who believes in nothing but getting reelected by means of whatever demagoguery it takes?" He paused. "I'm waiting for an answer."

Stroud shook his head. "Shame on you, Professor. You're talking about a congressman who spends his life in the service of his country and doesn't have anything like the cushy life you professors have, and you still can't leave him alone. Congressman Leglind cares about science, he cares deeply about it, but he also cares about the government's money, how it gets spread around college campuses and frittered away on dinner parties and fancy buildings. He's determined to root out anybody who isn't doing science. Real scientists spend the government's money on equipment, not fripperies; they don't need kitchens and lounges and auditoriums and fancy parties. Real scientists care about science. Period. And that's what the congressman cares about."

Garth circled his desk and went to the door of his office. "If your congressman gave a damn about science, you'd be asking what that institute is for, how many students and faculty will use it, what lab facilities it will have and what kind of a library, what guest speakers will use the auditorium and who will be in the audience from local high schools and other universities, what space it will free up in other buildings that can then be used for other branches of science."

Stroud had turned to face him, and Garth opened the door. "That's what an inquiring mind would ask; that's what a truly curious person would want to know. A curious person would not spend his time fabricating plots to whip up the anger of voters. A curious person would want to search out the best ways he and his constituents can make this a more informed, more intelligent nation. And there are people like that around: people who understand the value of science and how desperately this country needs to increase its commitment to it, for our own good and for our place in the world. They know that if some universities are guilty of excesses, that's not a reason to undermine all the work that's being done by serious scientists across the country, and I can't believe those people will let you get away with a slash-and-burn rampage across the campuses.''

He looked at his watch. Be polite, he told himself. At least be polite from now on. ''When we made this appointment I thought I'd have another hour, but as it happens, I have to take a class in a few minutes for a colleague who is ill. If you think we need a follow-up, my secretary will find a date.''

Slowly Stroud stood and retrieved his briefcase, which he had not opened, from beneath his chair. ''I'd be more respectful, Professor, when you testify before the committee. Just a friendly warning. If the congressman wants me to come back, I'll call.''

Garth watched him disappear where the corridor turned a corner, and after waiting another minute he too went out, turning the other direction to a door that led to a small courtyard behind the science building. Patches of May sunlight dappled a stone bench beneath spreading trees; beside it was a dry stone fountain, its basin filled with last fall's papery maple leaves and brittle black locust pods. In a warm corner beside a brick wall, a student slept, his head on his outstretched arm, his book face down in the grass. Garth watched two butterflies chase each other in fluttering circles around his motionless body; then he sat on the stone bench, legs outstretched, and put his face up to the sun, letting his anger seep away.

For all his intelligence and sophistication, his world travels to scientific conferences, his work and friendships with an international array of biologists and chemists, he still had a naive astonishment that he could not lead the simple life he wanted without interruptions from people who had no idea what he did and had not the slightest interest in finding out. He had thought he was insulated on a campus, secure behind walls that enclosed a community dedicated to the life of the mind, but in that, too, he was naive: campus walls were easily breached and universities had become big business, involved with corporations and the government and a host of government agencies like NASA and the National Science Foundation and the National Institutes of Health, contracting with them for research and development with huge sums of money involved.

But still Garth Andersen, professor, came to work each day and returned home each night thinking that his clearly defined life was all he needed to concentrate on: his work and his family, the two passions that drove and exhilarated him and made him whole. He had never cared about the fray of competition. He knew Sabrina missed it and was looking forward to returning to it when she went to London, and he knew that his children were learning to handle it in school, from necessity if not from desire. But he was bored by it and did all he could to avoid it.

He always had done, in his own way, what he wanted to do and what he was best at. And, because he had always excelled, he had never known failure or even second place; he had not had to consider what they would mean in his life. He knew he was lucky, but he was also confident: he knew himself and he knew what he could do excellently and what he could not do at all, like painting, sculpting, singing on key, or building a fine cabinet, though he admired, extravagantly and sometimes with envy, those who did all those things. He was interested in politics and sports; he loved literature, movies, theater, the opera, but none of them were absolutely essential to his idea of a complete life. His family and his work were.

And so when a little round man with a watch chain across his paunch walked into his office looking like a bill collector from the London of Charles Dickens, Garth's immediate reaction was to brush him aside. The hell with it, he thought; it will die away. They'll probably find something on other campuses to spice up their hearings, but there's nothing here and they know it. It was a fishing expedition and it's over.

He checked his watch. Five minutes before his first class. As he stood up, he glanced at the student on the grass. He was awake, stuffing his book into his backpack, preparing to leave. The sun had moved behind the corner of the building, and the courtyard was in shadow. Garth turned toward the door of his building, then glanced back one more time. The student had left, and the butterflies were gone.

It was raining in London, wet streaks on gray buildings, gusty May winds flinging sheets of water against the windows of Ambassadors. Sabrina opened the front door, snapping her umbrella shut as she backed into the shop. She stood on the Bokhara rug just inside the door shaking the water from her hair, feeling exhilarated, as if she had confronted Poseidon and won. Or at least prevailed, she thought; one never defeats the gods—they always have another trick up their sleeve.

"Mrs. Andersen!" Brian said, coming from the back room. His voice was surprised and also relieved. So whatever it is, it's still going on, Sabrina thought, and everything else fell away: she became alert, thinking of possible problems, noticing changes in the shop: a new Empire sofa and Directoire chair, a pair of French clocks . . . with a price tag visible on one of them. She went to it and tucked it out of sight, knowing Brian was watching, knowing he would remember and not let it happen again.

She unbuttoned her raincoat and waited for Brian to

help her slip out of it. He held it, dripping, in front of him, and carried it to the back of the shop, partitioned into her office and a smaller one for him, and hung it on an antique coat tree in the corner. Sabrina eyed it. "Where did that come from?"

"Nicholas found it. Or rather, Amelia did, for Blackford's, but he doesn't acknowledge that. Such a strange marriage, you know: I almost never see them together, and the few times I do, they pay absolutely no attention to each other."

"We will not discuss Nicholas's marriage," Sabrina said calmly, though she was angry. Brian would never have made that statement had he thought she was Lady Longworth; he said it only because he knew her as Stephanie Andersen, American, and therefore eager for gossip and unaware of the fine distinctions of social status. She sat at her cherrywood desk. "I'll look at the ledgers now."

His face flushed, Brian brought them from his office. "Is there anything else you need, Mrs. Andersen?"

"Yes, sit down." She flipped the pages back to December, when she had last been there. She ran a finger down the columns of purchases and sales, then looked at Brian, seated across from her. "I'll go over it more closely later on, but at first glance everything looks fine. All right, Brian, let's talk about your problem."

He shifted in his chair. "Nicholas wants to fire me."

"Oh, I doubt it; he'd have to deal with me on that, and he hasn't said a word. Why would he want to?"

"He thinks I'm spying on him."

Sabrina kept her gaze level. "Are you?"

"Well, yes, as a matter of fact. But only on behalf of Ambassadors."

"And what activity requires you to spy on him?"

"I think he's buying very special pieces and shipping them directly to clients, not bringing them through Ambassadors or Blackford's."

"You'd hear from the clients. They always call to discuss a piece they've bought."

"Not if Nicholas told them we've slipped badly, lost our touch, our expertise, since Lady Longworth's death."

"*Is* Nicholas telling them that?"

"I've heard that he is."

It was possible, Sabrina thought. Once before, in the turmoil after Stephanie's funeral, Nicholas had tried to take Ambassadors from her. She had stopped him then: stunned him by understanding immediately what he was doing and cutting him off exactly as Sabrina would have done. If he was trying again, he must believe Stephanie Andersen was too absorbed with her life in America to pay attention. Or to care. Stubborn Nicholas, she thought. But perhaps formidable.

"Olivia knows it's not true that we've lost our touch," she said. "Her friends know it's not true."

"Some of them are loyal," Brian replied gloomily.

"I'll talk to Olivia; she'll take care of it," Sabrina said at last. "It used to be Alexandra who stopped rumors for me; now it has to be Olivia."

"For Lady Longworth," Brian murmured, almost apologetic at reminding her that Alexandra had stopped rumors for her sister, not for her.

Sabrina ignored it. "Is there anything else I should know about?"

"There's an auction on Thursday, Lord Midgeford—"

"Riscombe Park? You didn't send me the catalogue."

"I was late mailing it; I imagine it's arriving in Evanston about now."

"Well, I'll be here on Thursday, so I'll go. Please get another catalogue and reserve a seat for me. And I'll need a limousine."

"Nicholas will have his, my la— I'm sorry. Mrs. Andersen."

"If what you tell me is true, I don't want to be in Nicholas's limousine; I want him to be in mine. I'd like the names of clients you think will be interested in specific pieces at Riscombe, especially Regency silver; Abner Midgeford collected it. I've lost touch with a lot of the people who will want it." She wondered if Brian would correct her again, asking how Stephanie Andersen could have lost touch with anyone when it was Sabrina Longworth who had lived in London and owned Ambassadors and known the people who collected Regency silver. But he was silent. He probably thinks I've gone crazy, Sabrina thought; what a test of Brian's reserve. "Please call Nicholas; tell him I'd like him to have dinner with me tomorrow night at the Savoy. Eight o'clock; please take care of the reservation."

She spent the afternoon at her desk, going more deliberately through the ledgers, reading the mail. She kept looking at her watch, and when it was dinnertime in Evanston she called Garth and the children, and closed her eyes, seeing them, feeling their arms around her. "Soon," she told them. "I'll be home very soon."

Brian left early for a dentist's appointment, but Sabrina stayed on. She was not in a hurry to return to the empty house on Cadogan Square and she liked the atmosphere of her shop, the faintly cloying scent of furniture polish in the still air, the stuffy smell of old wood and old fabrics. They were odors she remembered from the shopping expeditions of her childhood, with her mother and Stephanie, and they were exactly the same as those at Collectibles in Evanston. The universal air of antique shops, she mused with a smile; one could be anywhere in the world and always be at home.

She heard the front bell ring and the door open. Brian should have locked it, she thought, and stood up quickly to go into the shop. "I'm sorry, we're closed for the— good heavens," she said as she saw who it was. "Denton." She walked toward him. *I'm Stephanie; I'm not Sabrina. He'd expect* . . . She held out her hand and Denton took it and pumped it up and down.

"Delighted to see you again, Stephanie; how well you look. Much better than the last time we met, at Sabrina's funeral. In fact . . ." He leaned forward, scanning her face. "My God, you could be Sabrina. I never realized . . . It's quite amazing, you know; it quite takes one aback. Did you look like this all those years ago when she and I were at that barbecue at your house in . . . where was it? Evansville?''

"Evanston."

"Of course. I didn't think I'd ever forget that day. Years ago, of course, but if you'd looked like this . . . well, I would have noticed . . . said something . . . I didn't say anything, did I? No, of course I didn't; I would have remembered. Well, then, that's the answer. You didn't look like this. You couldn't have."

Sabrina gazed at him in silence.

Denton cleared his throat. His sharp black eyes slid left and right and he wandered vaguely around the shop, trailing delicate fingers across clocks and lamps and furniture. "Wonderful things. Sabrina had superb taste, and so do you, I see. I always admired her taste."

That is a lie. You paid no attention to it at all.

He looked at her from across the room, bouncing slightly on his toes. "Look here, why don't we dine together? It would please me very much. I was passing by and I saw you in here, and it occurred to me that you probably don't know many people in town, and I have a free evening, and why should you be lonely?"

Dinner with Denton? What a depressing thought; it would be like seeing my life go by in reverse. "Thank you, no, Denton; I have too much to do in the short time I'm here. I'll work right through dinner at home."

"Alone? You can't do that. The worst thing for your digestion, you know, and for your state of mind. People have gone mad from eating alone."

Involuntarily she smiled. She wondered how he had managed to stay exactly the same for almost fifteen years. His round face and rosy cheeks, his little mustache, his fascination with himself, his desperate need to be surrounded by people at all times to convince himself that he was happy . . . they were all familiar to her. As if preserved in plaster of paris, Denton seemed the same today as on the day she married him.

"There, that's the ticket; you're magnificent when you smile, you should never frown or even look too serious. Sabrina had the same smile, you know—well, of course you know; you knew her better than anyone—it was one of the reasons I adored her and could never tear myself from her." Sabrina's eyebrows rose. "Truth," Denton said, raising his hand. "I couldn't look at another woman when I had my Sabrina."

That is a lie. You slept with any woman close enough for you to sniff her perfume.

"And we were incredibly happy, you know. Two people—"

That is a lie.

"—who adored each other. We were the talk of London society, the envy of everyone because we were perfect."

That is a lie.

"I miss her, you know. In spite of the fact that we couldn't make it, I loved her and admired her; I still do. I want you to know that."

Why are you telling me these lies?

"And it was unbelievably ghastly, you know, when they asked me to identify her. I could barely look at her; I broke down like a baby, shaking all over; I nearly fainted away."

I'd be willing to bet that's a lie, too.

"It was bad enough that it was my own wife they were telling me to identify. But dead bodies, you know . . . I never could look at them; I can't even think about death, much less look at it . . ."

That part I believe.

"Stephanie, forgive me. I didn't mean to talk about this, but seeing you . . . My God, it's even worse for you than for me and I go on and on . . . I'm a blithering ass. I do beg your forgiveness; I am truly contrite. Tell me I'm forgiven. Tell me it won't stop you from having dinner with me. Tell me we're still friends."

"I forgive you, Denton, but we've never been friends, and I think it highly unlikely that we ever will be. And I won't have dinner with you because I would much rather be at home."

There was a pause. "You sound just like her, do you know that? The same voice, the same odd accent that nobody could ever place, the same way of saying 'I think it highly unlikely . . .' Of course with twins it's hard to fathom . . ."

"I'm closing the shop now. Good night, Denton."

"You'd really rather eat alone?"

"Yes."

"She was like that, too, you know. Sometimes she'd say she just didn't want to go to another dinner; she wanted to be by herself. She said it quite a lot after a while, and then I'd go by myself . . . of course we were having some problems by then."

"Good night, Denton."

"Well, then. Good night, Stephanie." At the door he turned back casually, as if something had just occurred to him. "I don't suppose you've heard from Max Stuyvesant, have you?"

Sabrina froze in shock. "Max? What are you talking about? He's dead."

"Presumed dead. They never found a body. I thought if he turned up somewhere he might have tried to contact someone. You know."

"No, I don't know. If he were alive he would have come home; where else would he go? He would have called you; you were one of his friends. You introduced u . . . them, didn't you? I thought Sabrina told me you took her on a cruise on his yacht and that's when she met him. That must have been the same yacht—" She took a breath. "He would have called you, not me."

Denton nodded. "I suppose so. But you know, Stephanie, if he does surface—good Lord, what an unfortunate choice of words; I'm so sorry. But if he does come back—it probably won't happen, of course, everyone else was killed; they found everyone else—but if he does and if he happens to call you, would you let me know? I would appreciate it. I somehow can't believe he's really dead, you know. He always seemed indestructible to me."

"I'll let you know, Denton." She said it almost soothingly. "Now I'd like to lock up."

"Yes, right, sorry." He opened the front door, then reared back as wind and rain gusted in. He slammed it shut. "Damn, I can't go out in this."

"You did it once, to get here; you can do it again," she said coldly. "Go home, Denton. I don't want you here."

"Yes, well, that is abundantly clear, isn't it? It's too bad, you know, Stephanie; I did think we could be friends. I might stop in again sometime, just to make sure you're all right. I feel a sense of responsibility . . . Sabrina's sister . . ." He waited for her to say something. When she did not, he girded himself, ducked his head as he opened the door, and flung himself into the storm.

Sabrina was shaking. What was going on? What was he looking for? Or afraid of, she thought suddenly, recalling the quivering of his mustache and the nervous thrust of his lower lip as he said, "I might stop in again sometime . . ."

Still shaking, she pulled on her raincoat. My hat, she thought; I had one, a long time ago . . . Oh, it can't be here; Stephanie would have found it, or someone . . . She reached up to a high shelf in the supply closet and her hand closed on a Burberry rain hat, neatly folded. Oh, Stephanie, you left it for me.

She was crying. She grabbed her umbrella, turned out the lights and left the shop, the hat pulled low over her eyes, her open umbrella close to the top of her head. She walked to the taxi stand and stood there for a long time until, through the rain, she saw one of the familiar tall black cars pull along the curb. She got in and put her hat and umbrella on the floor. "Kensington Cemetery."

"They close pretty soon, miss, and it's no place to be in a rainstorm."

"I want to go. I won't stay long; can you wait for me?"

"If you was my daughter, I wouldn't let—"

"Please."

He looked at her closely. "All right, then."

Inside the cemetery, the taxi moved slowly along the curved road until Sabrina told the driver to stop. "You will wait?"

"Not likely I'd leave you, miss."

"Thank you."

She walked along the road. She had thought she would come here the next morning, but she found she could not wait. It was strange, but she found more of Stephanie in London than in Evanston: this was where she had spent the last month of her life and Sabrina felt her presence everywhere. Now she looked for her as the rain stung her face and whipped her coat about her ankles. It had been gray last October during the funeral, the clouds lowering against skeletal trees, the cold wind cutting through the mourners' coats. But why should the sun ever shine on Stephanie's grave?

Sabrina tilted her umbrella against the wind and walked slowly along the road until she found the white marble stone. She had ordered it in February and sent to the stonemason the lines to be carved on it from Yeats's poem, one of Stephanie's favorites. This was the first time she had seen it, and she ran her wet hand over the deeply chiseled letters.

LADY SABRINA LONGWORTH

Through hollow lands and hilly lands,
I will find out where she has gone,
And kiss her lips and take her hands;
And walk among long dappled grass,
And pluck till time and times are done
The silver apples of the moon,
The golden apples of the sun.

Rain streaked the marble like cold tears. Sabrina knelt on the sodden grass, the umbrella resting on her bent head, and wept.

"Miss," the taxi driver said. He put his hand on her shoulder. She had been there for ten minutes and she was shivering so violently she could barely look up at him. "They're closing, miss, and you're going to catch your death."

She let him help her up and stumbled beside him back to the taxi. She was not aware of the streets through which they drove: the sidewalks undulating ribbons of black umbrellas, the lights of shop windows and apartments wavering drunkenly through the rain-lashed windows of the taxi. Sabrina huddled in the back seat, numb and cold, the tears flowing silently down her face.

She let herself into the empty house on Cadogan Square and dropped her umbrella and drenched coat and hat in the foyer. A stream ran from them to the serape rug in the center. She looked at it with unconcern and climbed the stairs to her sitting room. The fireplace was dark. On my own, Sabrina thought ruefully. I told Denton that was what I wanted.

She laid a fire and lit it, then turned on both faucets in her tub, pouring in a stream of bath oil. She boiled water in an electric teakettle in her sitting room and stripped off her clothes while the tea was steeping, then carried the cup and teapot into the bathroom and lowered herself slowly into the fragrant, steaming water. Her tears had stopped and now, gradually, her shivering stopped. Her body soaked up the heat and the slow caress of the bath oil; she put her head back until only her face was exposed, her hair floating on the surface of the water.

Stephanie was here, too: it was as if Sabrina could see her coming in that first night, walking around the room, opening closets and drawers, discovering all that would be hers for the one week they had crazily decided to steal from their lives, standing before the mirror in a dress from the closet that made her look, suddenly and astonishingly, exactly like Sabrina, the same tilt of the head, the same confident pose . . .

I can't do this, Sabrina thought; it's so real it's as if she's alive.

She forced herself to think of London, of Ambassadors and Brian, and of Nicholas. Dinner with Nicholas tomorrow, and she had to be prepared. She thought often of selling Ambassadors and she knew she would one day, but no one, certainly not Nicholas, was going to steal it from her.

And so when she met him at the Savoy the next evening, she was cool and watchful. At first Nicholas was not aware of it. "A small gift, Stephanie," he said, handing her a box wrapped in silver and gold paper. "Sabrina found them amusing." They were sitting at a small table beside a window looking out on the Thames and the long span of Waterloo Bridge. The view was framed by velvet draperies and figured wallpaper, and Nicholas, in suit and vest and starched cuffs, had settled into his upholstered chair with a sigh; it was his favorite room, as Sabrina had known. "I thought you might find it amusing, too. It's a little gift to welcome you to London. It was a surprise to hear from Brian—you never told us the exact date you'd be coming—but how pleasant, Stephanie . . . and of course you have a birthday coming up—in September, isn't it?—and you may not be here then. And I always remembered Sabrina's birthday with some little token."

No, you did not. And this is only May; a very long time to September. Sabrina opened the box. "Well, Nicholas," she said after a moment. "A Fabergé egg is more than a little token." She lifted it from its box, a golden egg decorated with jewels that swung open beneath her fingers to reveal a tiny basket of flowers carved from precious stones. "In perfect condition," she murmured.

"Well, only the best," said Nicholas gaily.

"Thank you. It's very generous of you." And not bad, she thought, as an attempted bribe. She smiled at him, suddenly enjoying herself, reveling in being back in the fray, fencing with people who always had hidden motives. "Such a clever idea, to open a conversation with such a gift."

Nicholas's look sharpened; he never liked it when people understood him.

"Tell me about the winter season," she said. "I've gone over our books and it seems to have been rather quiet."

"Yes, rather. The economy, you know, people are holding back, waiting for a clue to the future. I wouldn't worry, though, dear Stephanie; we're solvent and we can wait out a bad season, or even two, if we have to."

"Even two," Sabrina repeated thoughtfully. "And what are you doing to change a bad season to a successful one?"

"Well, you know, one talks to clients, as always, one meets new people, one gathers information for the future; the main thing is to make sure that one's clients and their friends don't forget one."

"You mean you continue to build goodwill for Blackford's and Ambassadors."

"Exactly. Exactly. One is always at work, always."

"But the question seems to be, Nicholas, for whom?"

"I beg your pardon?" He finished his martini, waved to the waiter for another, and picked up his soup spoon, absently tapping it on the table. "You tend to talk in riddles, dear Stephanie; many of us find it disconcerting—even, on occasion, unpleasant."

My God, Sabrina thought, is that the best he can do to try to make me afraid of him? "If that's true, I regret it," she said evenly. "I've not heard that from anyone, but of course you deal with rumors far more frequently than I do." She watched several expressions flit across his face. "I'm concerned about our reputation, Nicholas. I've been thinking of expanding from our three shops, adding two more, in New York and Paris"—she had not been thinking of any such thing, but as she said it, she thought, Why not?—"and I will not tolerate anything that might tarnish our good name. There are only two things we have to offer our clients: expertise and trust—you know that as well as I do—and it takes a long time to establish both of them. I worked too hard to create that for Ambassadors to allow anyone—''

"Well, but my dear Stephanie, surely you mean your sister did.''

Abruptly, Sabrina struck the table with her hand. "It's the same thing!'' She stopped, astounded at her lack of control. Nicholas was staring at her in amazement. And, in fact, she had never before raised her voice in a business discussion, nor had she done anything as untoward as striking the table in a discreet restaurant. *It's being back here for the first time in months, but not really being back, because I have another life now.*

"Stephanie?''

"I'm sorry,'' she said. "That was uncalled for. Of course my sister built Ambassadors, but I often find myself speaking for both of us, especially when it comes to business. As you know, we were very close. My point remains, Nicholas: I will not tolerate anyone making the slightest attempt to undermine my reputation or that of the shop.''

"Of course, of course.'' His head tilted, Nicholas looked at her through narrowed eyes. "Forgive me for getting a trifle personal, Stephanie, but you seem to be under a strain; I think you're trying to do too much. Why don't you go back to your husband and children—you're obviously a fine housewife and mother—and let me manage Ambassadors? I'll continue to report to you at regular intervals, and I assure you, you will be quite satisfied.''

"What satisfies me,'' Sabrina said softly, "is working with the three shops we have now, and any others we decide to purchase, and being kept informed on all major purchases and sales at Ambassadors and Blackford's. What satisfies me, Nicholas, is trust.''

"Yes, yes, of course, but really, Stephanie, you cannot run a business from across the ocean. There are major decisions that must be made every day involving hundreds of thousands of pounds—millions, on occasion. These are not small dealings such as you handle from your little shop in Chicago—"

"Evanston."

"Evanston, yes, of course." The waiter placed another martini in front of him and refilled Sabrina's wineglass from the bottle on the table. "The point remains—"

"And I intend to keep doing it, Nicholas, with help and cooperation from you and Brian. I do own Ambassadors, as I hope you remember. I think there's nothing more to be said about that."

"*Nothing more to be said?* My dear Stephanie, that is not for you to decide." He took a long swallow of his martini. "The fact is, I am bringing new clients to Ambassadors far more prominent than those Sabrina dealt with before her death. I am commissioned to locate and purchase pieces of furniture, jewelry and paintings that are among the most precious in the world."

"I thought business was down. The economy and so forth."

"Even in a slow season, I am finding the best clients. And you are in no position to deal with them. Sabrina might have been able to, but beyond the physical resemblance you are nothing like her. You are quite out of your depth here; London is really no place for you. You're far better off in Evanston with your family and friends. I promise you, at regular intervals, your share of the profits—"

"Excuse me, Nicholas," Sabrina said as the waiter approached again, "may we order now?"

His face was flushed. "I haven't decided . . . well, what are you having?"

"Scallops and then the duck."

He nodded. "Fine. The same."

The sommelier had joined them. "And perhaps a red wine to accompany the duck?"

"Châteauneuf-du-Pape," said Sabrina. "Do you still have any of the 'fifty-eight?"

"Ah," he said approvingly. "We have a few bottles, madame."

As he left, Nicholas spread his hands. "Did she tell you everything?"

"Yes. Now, if I heard you correctly, you were talking about profits. You alone would send my checks? With no one else looking at the account books?"

"A ship has one captain, Stephanie. I will take care of you, I promise."

Sabrina laughed. "Oh, Nicholas, a Fabergé egg isn't enough."

His face reddened again. "Don't play games with me. You're a very pleasant woman, Stephanie, but—I regret having to repeat this, but it is important—you do not have your sister's class and sophistication. You're a housewife and a mother, both admirable occupations, but they do not prepare you for dealing with wealth and royalty. You can wear Sabrina's clothes and live in her house, you can even order wine that she told you about, but you're still a poor imitation of Sabrina Longworth. You're not as experienced as she was, not as socially adept, and because of that, I am the one who should be concerned about our reputation, and I cannot allow you to continue to interfere in the workings of these shops, putting everything at risk. Too much is at stake."

Sabrina had leaned forward so that their faces were a few inches apart. "A poor imitation?" she echoed seriously. "Everyone else has trouble believing I'm not really Sabrina." She held his gaze for a long moment, then slowly shook her head. "Poor Nicholas, to be so desperate. I won't ask you what is at stake; you'll have to deal with whatever you've done that has made you so anxious to be rid of me. But I will tell you what I've decided. I'm going to write letters to all our clients and to others—those prominent people you mentioned—assuring them that our services are as complete as ever and that we act on their behalf from the moment an item is purchased to the time it is delivered. That means we will not allow any item, however small or large, to be shipped to a customer without a thorough inspection of its condition and a search of its provenance in our shop. Any sale at auction is contingent on the item's condition being as stated in the catalogue—you know that, Nicholas, but many clients do not—and one of our most important duties is to fulfill that part of the sale. Those letters will go out this week over my signature. It would be appropriate, if we are to remain partners, for your signature to be there as well."

His face had darkened; his eyes were bulging. "You can't do that."

"Why not?"

"It undermines my integrity; it makes me look a fool."

"How does it do that if your signature is on the letter?"

"You must not write it; it would be a mistake."

"I don't think so."

"You don't have to explain yourself to clients who already know what you can do for them."

"I think perhaps I do."

"You are absolutely determined to do this?"

"Absolutely."

He sat frozen, then abruptly shoved back his chair. "We have nothing to talk about." And with only the slightest hesitation as he realized he was deserting a woman in the middle of his favorite restaurant, he turned and walked out.

Sabrina sat alone. The sommelier brought the red wine and held the bottle for her to read the label. She nodded and he uncorked it. The minutes passed. The waiter put a dish of scallops before her and set another at Nicholas's place. "You may remove that," she said. "Mr. Blackford has been taken ill and has gone home."

The waiter's brows went up. In a moment, the maître d' sped to her table. "If madame is uncomfortable and wishes to leave, we would understand . . . there would be no charge . . ."

Sabrina smiled at him. "I'm not at all uncomfortable. But I am very hungry."

He stood looking at her, wondering why a beautiful woman forced to eat alone in a fine restaurant was not uncomfortable. But she continued to smile at him, and so, after a moment, he bowed. "If there is anything I can do . . ."

"Not at the moment." She watched him walk away. In fact, she was very uncomfortable, but not for the reason he thought. Nicholas's hostility had shaken her; it wound itself around her and made London seem unpleasant, even treacherous. She sipped the superb red wine and felt depressed. She didn't really love being back in the fray, fencing with people who had hidden motives; it was a terrible waste of energy and she resented having to do it when she could be concentrating on making a marriage, building a home, bringing up children, spending her time loving instead of parrying thrusts from greedy or frightened people.

The waiter brought a plate of duck and wild rice and she contemplated it. She had no appetite but she would eat some of it, to prove to Nicholas and Denton and the waiters at the Savoy that she could eat alone anywhere. But she missed her family. She missed her home. She missed Garth. She wanted to look up and meet his eyes down the length of the dinner table. She wanted to hear her children chatter and even squabble over the things of their day. She wanted her house to creak about her and know that the windows were tight and the doors secure. I don't want two lives, she thought. I only want one.

But she would not let Nicholas win. She would find someone to buy Ambassadors and she would withdraw from her participation in Blackford's. She had known the time would come to do this; now that it had come, she realized how anxious she was to cut these ties. But she would not rush: now that she knew what she wanted, she would do it properly, even if it took a few months. I'll sell the house, too, she thought. Maybe by September I'll have sold them both.

September. My birthday. And I'll be home for good.

*S*tephanie and Léon met on the sidewalk on the cours Gambetta as she was wheeling her bicycle from the shop and he was striding toward her.

"I was watching for you," he said as they shook hands. "Perhaps you will let me join you on your ride."

Her heart had lifted when she saw him and she was smiling. "But you have no bicycle."

"Behind you, in the shop. We use the same repairman; it's a good sign, I think. May I join you?"

"Yes, I'd like that."

"I'll be right back."

In a moment he was wheeling his bicycle from the shop, unhooking his helmet from the handlebars as he stopped beside her. "Have you a destination?"

"No. I thought perhaps some of the hill towns. I've only ridden to three of them."

"Have you been to Fontaine-de-Vaucluse?"

"No. I haven't even heard of it."

"Then that is where we go. No, I'm sorry; that was high-handed. I'd like to show you one of my favorite spots, but since what I want most is to spend the afternoon with you, I'll go wherever you choose."

"Fontaine. Is it really a fountain?"

"An underground one, a spring that is the source of the river Sorgue. A beautiful spot; magical, I think."

"Then that is where we go."

He chuckled and they put on their helmets and began to walk the bicycles to the corner. "I saw you leave your shop; have you had lunch?"

"No, I didn't want to take the time. I brought an apple."

"Have you the time when we get to Fontaine-de-Vaucluse? I'd like to show you Café Philip; another of my special places."

Stephanie thought about it only a moment. "Yes. Not all afternoon, but for a little while."

"Good." They parted to allow a woman with a baby buggy to pass between them. "Where have you ridden around here?"

"Mainly around the vineyards, but last week I rode to Maubec and Robion and up to Oppède-le-Vieux."

"A steep hill; you're very strong. But isn't it a wonderful ride? And beyond, to Ménerbes and Bonnieux as well."

"How do you ride so much, and paint?"

"I almost always ride in the morning, seven, six, even five o'clock. I recommend it; perhaps we'll do it together. The traffic is light; the air is cool. By now, the end of June, it really is too hot to—" He stopped. "I just realized. Have you recently come to Cavaillon?"

"Yes, a few months ago. Doesn't the traffic seem worse than usual today?" They had reached the corner and stood on the curb, waiting for the light to change.

"It is bad, but I try to ignore it when I'm riding. My theory is that since no driver is anxious to hit me, nor I him, we'll manage to take appropriate action to avoid each other. So far that's been the case. When we cross, we'll ride straight ahead and turn at the first cross street; it will be quieter then. I'll go first if you'd like."

Stephanie nodded. She was feeling young and free and very happy. She had not seen Léon since the day they had met six weeks ago. He had not come again to Jacqueline en Provence; his new paintings were delivered by his friend who owned a large van. As she and Jacqueline had unwrapped them, Stephanie had asked casually if Léon would come to see how they were displayed in the shop, or if he would be bringing new ones.

"Oh, one cannot be sure," Jacqueline replied. "He is totally unpredictable. But aren't these fine? So different from the landscapes, but with that same power, as if he could cut with his brush through all pretense . . ."

That was the last time Stephanie mentioned him. And after a while she stopped thinking about him; she was ashamed of feeling she could be adventurous with him. I'm married, she told herself; how did I plan to be adventurous with Léon? Just what did I have in mind?

But I shouldn't use Léon or anyone else to break away from Max; I have to do that by myself. I have to learn to do everything by myself; I can't always let other people clear a path for me.

"Green light," Léon said, smiling at her, knowing her thoughts were far away.

They rode across the highway, then stayed close to the edge of the road as cars and trucks whizzed past. Stephanie gritted her teeth, her eyes on Léon's back, willing herself to ignore the noise and the rumble of the pavement as trucks barreled down upon her from behind. Her muscles were knotted and she cringed as she rode, certain every moment that the next truck would fling her aside like a piece of debris. But nothing happened; she and Léon pedaled furiously and it was only a few moments before he turned, and she followed, onto a narrow road that cut a straight line between high solid walls of cypress trees.

The sounds of the highway stopped as if a door had slammed; the air was still and hushed. Stephanie heard the swish of their tires, the slow drone of bees, the distant call of a rooster, the descending scales of birds silhouetted against the silvery blue sky. She relaxed and caught up to Léon, who had slowed for her.

"Better?" he asked.

"Much. This is lovely."

They rode in silence to the end of the cypresses, then between vineyards whose rows of vines, sprouting new leaves, seemed to radiate in perfectly straight lines from the farmhouse in the center. The sun blazed upon them and Stephanie wiped her forehead with the back of her bicycle glove, then reached down for her water bottle and drank from it as they rode. She liked Léon's silence and his smile when their eyes met; she liked letting her thoughts float, absorbing all that surrounded her: sprinklers spraying high arcs of water that glittered in the sun, wild thyme lining the road with tiny pale purple flowers, and rosemary bushes blossoming with pink flowers amid their pinelike needles, men walking on the road wearing undershirts and black pants that fell in folds over the tops of their boots and calling out an amiable *bonjour* as they passed, cherry trees with lush bunches of fruit peering through the dense foliage, the small postal wagon scooting along back roads like a child's toy. She felt strong and healthy, part of the earth, propelling herself through a landscape so serene and timeless that she could believe nothing existed beyond it, and she and Léon were the only two people in the world.

Oh, how happy I am, she thought, and she knew that whatever else she had felt, with Max and Robert, with Madame Besset and with Jacqueline, she had not said those words to herself in that way before.

The road widened, became busier; soon it was bordered by a low stone wall and there were power lines, light poles, signs of a town. Stephanie and Léon rode around a curve and saw just ahead an enormous stone bridge of tall arches, and they flew beneath it and then past high dark gray cliffs pocked with deep caves that led directly into Fontaine-de-Vaucluse.

"We can leave the bicycles in the square," Léon said, and asked a policeman where they could lock them. "Now we walk." They skirted the crowded square shaded by ancient trees and strolled up a long inclined promenade with the river on one side and booths on the other filled with souvenirs to catch unwary tourists. When they reached a row of cafés, Léon stopped at the one with a sign that said Café Philip. "One moment." He ran down a small stone stairway and quickly returned. "We have a reservation for lunch in half an hour."

As they came to the top of the promenade, Stephanie caught her breath and moved ahead, forgetting Léon. She stood beside a pond as still as a mirror, reflecting a giant curved cliff behind it. But the stillness was only in the pond; at the edge, where the earth fell away, the water plunged straight down in a thunderous fall, flinging spray high in the air, churning foam over huge boulders and spinning in whirlpools and eddies as it roared down the steep grade. Then, as the land leveled, the river widened, moving in rapid currents, and then widened still more, tossing up little waves that caught the sun. Small waterfalls like silver ribbons lined its banks and it grew steadily calmer as it flowed: one of the mighty rivers of Provence, the Sorgue River.

Stephanie sat on the rocks beside the edge of the pond where the still water fell into the deafening waterfall. Around her, children ran and shouted, dancing on the rocks, daring the water, screaming to make themselves heard; their parents clicked cameras and dragged the children back, warning of danger. Stephanie was unaware of them. She stared at small rainbows in the river's dancing droplets, at rocks glistening purple and brown and black from centuries of polishing by that relentless flow, and she felt herself become part of it, merging with it, fighting it, being carried away by it. It was as if she were back in the hospital, imprisoned in a fog, unable to break out or even move; it was as if she were in bed in Cavaillon in those early morning hours when she would wake from a dream and try to recapture it, to find in it a clue to her past, but would find instead an emptiness as loud, in its way, as the roaring water beside her.

Standing a few feet away, Léon watched her. She was very beautiful and he knew he wanted to paint her, but he was more interested in the impression she made of tentativeness: a woman unsure of herself, of who she was, where she was, even how she got here. He knew that was fanciful, but Léon believed in fancy: he believed in the furthest stretches of the imagination, in coincidence and unlikely circumstances, in events that seemed impossible or, more likely, unexplainable.

He knew that art could not be created or enjoyed without the unexplainable, nor could love and friendship grow, and so he trusted his emotions and his senses, his imagination, and his delight in complexity and perverseness to lead him, ultimately, to some kind of truth. Because of that, when he saw Sabrina Lacoste, stunningly beautiful, charming and intelligent, looking in this pensive moment like a woman who did not know who she was or where she belonged, he believed it was possible that indeed she did not know those things, and instead of brushing that idea aside, he found himself wondering about her past, and what part he could play in helping her, if help was what she wanted.

His painter's eye framed the landscape: a woman sitting on gray-white rock in front of a dark cliff where tenacious trees grew outward to catch the sun, the black water of the still pond, and the woman herself, wearing dark blue bicycle shorts and a white bicycle shirt open at the neck, her chestnut hair barely brushing her shoulders—it had been shorter when he met her six weeks ago—her slender body, her long legs, and a regal bearing that must have been drilled into her when she was young, so natural did it seem. Her gaze was fixed on the tumbling water, and he wondered what compelling memory it had brought to life.

And then he saw that her hands were clenched, the muscles of her arms taut, as if she were trying to swim against that fierce current, or to escape whatever thoughts were roiling within her.

He took a small sketch pad and a piece of charcoal from his backpack and drew swiftly and surely, first the landscape—crowds milling about the motionless woman, leaving a small private place for her as she stared at the water— and then the woman herself. Sabrina, he thought. A lovely name. A lovely mystery. Tantalizing and irresistible.

And married.

But I am involved with someone, too, Léon thought. Not a marriage, but still complicated. So we shall not look too far ahead, Sabrina and I. Not yet.

After a time, he went to her and put a hand on her shoulder. "If you're ready, we can go to lunch."

"Yes." She came out of her reverie and took his hand and stood up. "Thank you for bringing me here; you were right: it is magical."

"It reminds you of something." Their heads were close together, in order to hear each other. "Something beautiful . . . or overwhelming?"

"It's overwhelming on its own—don't you think?— without reminding anyone of anything. How deep is the spring beneath the pool?"

"No one has found it yet, though Cousteau and many others have tried."

"No one has found it? But isn't that amazing, that its beginnings are hidden, that only part of it is revealed, but still it has such strength and beauty . . ."

Léon was looking at her with curiosity. "Most of us reveal only parts of ourselves."

"Yes. Of course." As they turned, she looked back at the torrent. "I wish we didn't have to leave."

"But we aren't leaving. You'll see."

They walked back the way they had come, down the stone staircase to a glassed-in restaurant, and beyond it, a broad flagstone terrace shaded by an awning and extending over the water. "Oh, perfect," Stephanie said as they were shown to a table at the railing, with the river just below them. "What a lovely discovery."

"It often seems that most of the world has discovered it," Léon said with a smile as the waitress brought their menus. "When I want to be truly alone here, I come in the winter; it's truly magical then, with steam and snow and not a human voice to be heard, nor any presence but my own. Except, of course, for whatever gnomes and elves inhabit the caves in the cliffs."

"Gnomes and elves. Do you see them? And have conversations with them?"

"Not so far. But one doesn't have to do either to believe."

Stephanie rested her chin on her folded hands. "You believe in things that are invisible."

"I believe that there are things beyond our knowing: mysteries, magic, the shape of the future, the whole meaning of the past."

"And that doesn't frighten you?"

"It makes me very happy. How poor life would be without mysteries and miracles. And they fill my life, so I must believe in them."

"You mean your painting."

He took her hand. "Do you know, you are the first person who has understood immediately what I mean when I say that. Most people think I take a brush and paint what I see in front of me, just as they think writers write about people they know and scientists weigh and measure what they can pick up or trip over. Which is all nonsense. We paint and write and study what we cannot see; we leave the rest to the camera and the journalist. And we don't even know how we do it. Something inside us—or outside of us, who knows?—guides the brush and the pen and the scientist's thoughts, and we never fully understand what that force is, where our vision comes from. Why should we even try? We should only be grateful that it's there. I think our waitress would like us to order. I recommend the omelet with truffles and the Provençal tomatoes, unless you don't like—''

"It sounds perfect.''

Léon ordered, and chose a bottle of Côtes du Rhône, and in the flurry of ordering and the setting of cutlery and napkins at their places and the pouring of wine, their hands came apart, and when they were alone again, Stephanie was holding her wineglass, and her other hand was in her lap.

They gazed at the water in a comfortable silence. "Have you been to the top of Mont Ventoux?" Léon asked.

"No. I'm waiting until I can do it on my bicycle."

"A formidable trip.''

"I have a friend who does it every week. He says in a month or two I'll be strong enough if I work at it.''

"And is it so important that you ride to the top?''

"Yes.''

"It would be a triumph over . . . what?''

"It would be a triumph. Tell me about your painting. Have you always been a painter?''

"Since I was four. In fact, I remember the day and my first box of colored chalk, a birthday present. I took it to my room and stayed up through my naptime covering the walls as high as I could reach—and standing on chairs— with drawings of people, pets, animals in the zoo, and of course goblins and elves. I think they all may have looked alike; that part I can't remember. I do know that I used up every bit of the chalk.''

"Your parents told you about that later.''

"No, it's quite astonishing, but I remember it. No one was with me, but later I described the room exactly as they saw it when they walked in. As far as I know now, that's the only day I remember from my early years, but I do remember it: one ecstatic afternoon with four blank walls and a fresh box of colored chalk. The dream of every painter, and the birth of this one. I'm sure I have never been more perfectly happy.''

Stephanie's eyes were on his, but she was seeing beyond him. "Wonderful," she said softly.

"It is a wonderful memory." He knew, without being able to define it, that they were talking about different things, but he had decided that he would ask her nothing about herself. It seemed clear that she would fend off any personal questions, as she had several times today, and so he let it go. Next time, perhaps, or the time after that. He would wait until she was ready.

"And you went on drawing and painting?" she asked. "No time out for sports or mischief?"

"None. I was an exceedingly dull boy. I was an only child and my parents had many ambitions for me, but I had only one for myself and I never wavered, though, for their sake, I did give some thought to medicine, law, science . . . all the respectable professions. It did no good; I always came back to what my mother called 'making pictures.' "

"Are they pleased now with your success?"

"They're very pleased that I'm successful, but they think I've come to it by a dubious route, through play rather than hard work and purposeful activity."

Stephanie smiled. "Where do they live?"

"In Lyon."

"Is that where you were born?"

"Born and grew up." Léon sat back as the waitress refilled their wineglasses and served their lunch. "I left high school after my second year and hitchhiked and worked on freighters—Europe, England, America, Africa, India—and then settled in Goult, which astonishes my friends and dismays my parents."

"I've been to Goult, to La Bartavelle, for dinner."

"An excellent restaurant. You were a few blocks from my house when you were there."

"It's a strange town. So tiny and . . . ghostly. It makes me think of a medieval town that everyone has fled because marauders are storming the walls."

He chuckled. "A perfect description, and the very reason my parents are dismayed. They think I've holed myself up in a village of stone walls, shuttered windows and hermits, cutting myself off from the world. In fact, I've found a perch from which to view it, and swoop down now and then to capture what takes my fancy.''

"And what is it that takes your fancy?"

"You do," he said quietly.

Stephanie caught her breath and looked away, to the blue-green river with sunlit froth dancing on the surface. Léon's eyes were the color of the river, green and blue; she could see them in her mind and feel them watching her. He had let her lead the conversation and she had been lulled by that, thinking it extraordinary but somehow natural that he knew she did not want questions about herself. A few times he had tried to turn the conversation to her, but when she changed the subject, he had moved smoothly on, and had not asked again.

She felt a small twinge of disappointment. If he had persevered, she might have answered. But that's foolish, she thought. I made it clear I wouldn't answer; I changed the subject and he allowed me my privacy. But that odd disappointment lingered. She felt again the warmth of his hand on her shoulder as she sat beside the waterfall, and his hand holding hers on the table, and she knew she wanted to talk to him.

I want to confide in him and trust him. I want to tell him whatever is inside me. Because I think he'll understand.

I want to make love to him.

She felt a sinking within her. I can't think that. I'm married to Max. I have a home with him, he's given me the only life I know. I owe him—

"And opera," Léon went on easily. "Theater, the circus, market days, bookstores, toy shops, antique shops, bicycle riding, hiking, good movies, good food, and good friends. Not, of course, in that order." He saw Stephanie watching him with a small frown. "You did ask what takes my fancy."

"A long list for someone who was a dull boy."

He smiled. "I picked things up along the way."

"And you didn't finish high school or go to college?"

"No, I couldn't handle it—classrooms, teachers, assignments. I'm sorry now, because there is so much about literature and history and science I'd like to know in an organized way instead of the haphazard way I teach myself, but when I was young I couldn't do it. I hated having other people organize the world for me. I knew that when I painted I created worlds and images that made sense to me and I knew, even when I was very young, that I had to believe in myself and my way of doing things or I would never be a painter. I still believe that, but I went too far, and with all the arrogance of a young person, I decided that the only worthwhile and important thing in the world was my painting. So, in school, I got myself into trouble, doing my damnedest to get expelled, and though my father tried everything he knew, even threatening the principal with the wrath of God—as if my father could direct God's wrath—and giving me regular whippings—"

"He whipped you?"

"He thought that would make me understand that life is harsh, filled with obstacles, pain and disappointment, and that the only way I could make my way in its tangles was with diligence, concentration, constant application, and automatic obedience to authority. I could handle the first three if I could apply them to art, but of course that wasn't the lesson he was trying to teach me. And then, as you may imagine, I was a total flop when it came to automatic obedience."

Stephanie laughed. "I can't imagine that you even tried."

He smiled. "I didn't. It seemed to me that obedience would require great amounts of energy and offer a meager reward. I was working and saving my money to buy paints; that was where my energy went."

"Where were you working?"

"I modeled for other artists from the time I was ten. The pay was not bad and I liked being around them. They gave me things, too—sketch pads, canvases, extra tubes of paint—and introduced me to dealers and gallery owners. After I was expelled—because of course I was—and came back from my travels, I showed the paintings I'd been making to some of the dealers I'd met and they took almost all of them. It was a very lucky time for me.''

''Or the paintings were very good.''

''Luck always plays a part. The fates play tricks on us, and all our talent and experience piled up together often can't deflect them. We forget that at our peril.''

The sunlit river ran swiftly past their table, the restaurant emptied, the waitress served coffee with small wrapped squares of bittersweet chocolate, and Léon and Stephanie rested their arms on the table, leaned toward each other, and talked all through that long summer afternoon.

Max waited in a dim corner of a café in Carpentras, drinking marc and cursing silently as the time dragged on. Everyone who worked for him knew that he was never kept waiting, but Doerner was—he looked at his watch—four minutes late. Only four minutes, he thought; it had seemed like twenty. He told himself to relax, but he could not; he had not relaxed since the death of his secretary, and that was why he was here now, waiting for Hermann Doerner, whom he had sent to find out what the police knew about it.

He had told Sabrina he would be late, but would be home for dinner. She had gone bicycling the day before—to Fontaine-de-Vaucluse, she had told him—but today she was working on their house, and he pictured her walking through the rooms, making sketches, talking to Madame Besset, gesturing as she described to the gardener new plants she wanted along the terrace. His body strained to escape from the grimy booth, the secretive dark, and go to her. But he sat, locked in place, waiting for a fool who was late, because he had to know what had happened to his secretary before he could decide what to do next.

"*Es tut mir leid.*" Doerner slid into the opposite side of the booth. He was as tall as Max, slightly stooped and balding; he wore square glasses and his mouth was wide, with a full lower lip.

Max nodded shortly; apologies sounded the same in any language. He signaled for two drinks. "Well?"

They spoke German, falling silent when the bartender brought their beers.

"They think it was an accident. No sign of foul play."

"They *think?*"

Doerner drew an envelope from inside his jacket and held it out to Max. "They'd been to a party in Toulon. They were driving back to Marseilles, late, and they'd told their friends they'd take A-Fifty, but for some reason they took N-Eight instead. Probably not thinking; they'd had a lot to drink. It looks like they realized their mistake and tried to cut back to the highway at Le Beausset, but they never made it; just outside town they lost control of the car. It turned over a few times and they were both thrown out and killed. Instantly, the postmortem says."

"No witnesses."

"No, but someone who was on the road behind them said a car came toward him and slowed down at the place where they were thrown out and then turned and went back the way it had come. You know, as if making sure . . ."

"The police think someone followed them from the party?"

"They don't know. Everyone denies it, all the guests. They all say it had to be an accident; you know, three a.m., lots to drink, a difficult road. But the police are leaving it open."

"Were all the guests from Toulon?"

"Most. A few from Marseilles, a couple from Aix, three people from Nice. Some of them stayed the night."

"Did you talk to any of them yourself?"

"Eleven of them: the names checked on that list. I couldn't tell if anybody was lying."

Max read the list of names. None of them were known to him. "No one else was at the party?"

"That's the whole bunch."

"Are the police going to watch them?"

"They said they would. But who knows? Most of them think it was an accident."

"But they're not sure."

"They won't say they're sure."

Max tossed down the glass of marc, letting the fumes fill his head. "Is there anything else in the report?"

"Details. Nothing I haven't told you."

He drummed his fingers on the table. "Keep in touch with them; they may find something else. Meanwhile, you're interviewing secretaries?"

"I may have found one. I'll know by the time you come to Marseilles."

"Thursday. I'll see you then."

Max put money on the table for their drinks, and left. Doerner would follow later. *They won't say they're sure. I couldn't tell if anybody was lying.*

He drove through the town. None of the names had been known to him, but that meant nothing; Denton could have sent someone who'd never been in the area, someone who could follow a secretary, get friendly with her, get invited to a party . . . or not be at the party at all, but simply follow the secretary to Toulon and wait until she and her boyfriend came out to drive home.

He knew no more than he had before.

Outside Carpentras he picked up speed. He turned on the air conditioning, found some music on the radio, and settled into the seat, absently watching the needle climb to 175 kilometers an hour. Speed helped him make decisions. And he was not far beyond Carpentras when he knew that he would have to leave Provence.

He did not believe in coincidences, and so he did not

264

believe that his secretary's death was accidental. Somehow Denton had arranged it, probably as a warning.

But perhaps not. It had been eight months since the explosion, and not a sign of anyone interested in him. How could Denton have found him? There was no way he—

There was always a way.

But Denton was a fool and a dilettante; he'd preen himself on successfully blowing up Max and Sabrina, and wander off to another playground.

He was also stubborn and vindictive and afraid. A dangerous combination.

Max had known all this from the beginning, when he began making his plans to disappear, and so he had never expected to stay in France for more than a few months. He had started Lacoste et fils and had run it from London for a year; he had planned to leave it in the hands of Hermann Doerner and Carlos Figueros as soon as he was convinced they could run it without his close presence. Then he would move on, open another company, probably in the United States or Latin America, and settle there.

There had been no room in that plan for buying a house and living with Sabrina Longworth. But once he made that decision, he had been lulled into complacency. His business was thriving, he had a comfortable home, and he knew Sabrina would want to stay there.

But he was not in a position to be lulled into complacency. Not with Denton; not even completely with Sabrina. He had carefully rehearsed what he would tell her if her memory suddenly returned, but she would accept his story of danger only if she loved him. And he knew that, still, she did not.

He believed that the longer her amnesia lasted, the more likely it was that it would be permanent. But he could not rely on that: there was nothing scientific to support it. It seemed he could rely on less and less lately. All his life he had trusted his tough instincts; now, suddenly, instincts, toughness, even brutality, seemed feeble tools for survival.

We'll get out of here, he thought. Robert will sell the house and everything in it; we can't risk a trail of furniture. Carlos will buy a new place for us—Buenos Aires? Los Angeles? Maybe Toronto—and rent a warehouse and create a life for us to step into. We can't change our names; I couldn't explain that to Sabrina. But it doesn't matter. It's not certain that we're running away from anything. Not yet.

I won't tell her tonight, he thought as he turned into their driveway and saw the house waiting for him, the windows brilliantly lit. It can wait for a week or two, until I have a schedule, a place, a plan.

A question came to him, but he brushed it aside. Of course she would go with him. There was nothing else she could do.

She was very quiet at dinner, but it suited him not to talk. And that night he could not sleep, and so spent the hours in his study and, in the morning, had locked the door, as he always did when he was working, before she was awake. Later he caught a glimpse of her car as she drove to work, and then he left the study to greet Robert when he arrived.

"You look tired," Robert said. "Another night of insomnia?"

"It has nothing to do with insomnia; I had work to do. You can analyze and prescribe for your students and your flock, Robert, and for your revolutionaries, but not for me."

"Not revolutionaries, my friend, though the vocabulary is often similar. And so is the need for money; thank you for your last deposit; it was an extraordinarily generous one."

"We had a good quarter. And I added some of my own."

"I thought so. I didn't see how you could reap such profits from your small printing shop and your exports.

But obviously I know nothing about it. Max, as usual when I come to you, I need help.''

"What do you need?''

"A passport, a visa, a driver's license, two or three letters with envelopes canceled at post offices in Haiti.''

"A difficult country, Robert.''

"The easy ones don't need me.''

"What name for the passport and visa?''

"Wallace Lambert. Does that sound sufficiently stuffy for the son of a successful British businessman?''

"Is he?''

"Of course not. But the people in Haiti will think he is. Is the name a good choice?''

"Very good. You want the letters addressed to him, I suppose.''

"Yes.''

"And when do you need all these documents?''

"Is one week too soon?''

"Can the letters be waiting for your person in Haiti?''

"No, they must be here.''

"Then I need two weeks. Everything else is easy, but that takes time.''

"Two weeks, then. Thank you, Max. And something else. There will be someone coming out of Chile soon. I don't know if you have current business there . . .''

"I do, as it happens. We'll be shipping them two front-end loaders in a month or so, about the end of July, and bringing back one that was the wrong model. Will that fit in with your plans?''

"We'll make it fit. It's a young woman, Jana Corley. She's quite small; I think she would manage easily if the equipment is of a size that requires a large crate. And a front-end loader would, I imagine.''

"A woman. I hadn't thought of women; it's always been men, until now.''

"More women are coming to us lately. They're as idealistic as men, you know, probably more so, and certainly they like adventure as much as men. And they're very good: they speak softly, but they work with the local priests—"

"*Your* local priests."

"The ones in our network, yes, of course. They work with them to help the people in these countries feel they have some power."

"Starting a kindergarten," Max said, amused.

"Does that surprise you? In a village where no one provides education, a kindergarten is a victory. If they can add another grade each year—"

"A revolution would be faster."

"And bloodier, and not at all certain of victory."

"But you're moving an inch at a time. You help these peasants protest when the government stockpiles food for the wealthy; you open clinics where their kids can be vaccinated. It's window dressing; it doesn't change a damn thing."

"It changes the way they feel about themselves: they begin to think they can have some power over their lives. Until they think that, what can they do for themselves? They rely on outsiders."

"Your idealistic boys and girls."

"Young men and women. Children of God. If you could work with them you would not be so cynical. They are so beautiful, Max, and they truly become part of the poor people's lives."

"Until the governments come after them, and you have to smuggle them out."

"You and I smuggle them out. You know all this, Max; we've talked about it before. I think you like hearing me repeat it as a child likes a familiar bedtime story told over and over."

Max smiled thinly. "Perhaps."

Robert shook his head. "Max, you should not be so angry when someone understands you. There is no attempt to understand where there is no love." Max was silent. "Look, my friend, I don't pry into the dark corners of your life. Whatever you may regret or fear or try to deny is your affair, unless you ask me for guidance. I would rejoice if I could help you with any troubles you have, should you ever ask me. But I see your pleasure in helping me in my cause, however small and slow you think it, and I think that your pleasure comes from doing good, perhaps because it balances other things that you do or have done. And so you ask to hear about it now and then for comfort or for reassurance that your money and your help are still doing good."

Max said nothing. He was angry, with the visceral defensive withdrawal that came whenever anyone saw beneath his surface, but he was also impressed. And for the first time he felt a warming toward Robert far different from the casual affinity he had felt until now. *There is no attempt to understand where there is no love.* It occurred to him that Robert might—in time, and if he let him—become more than the kind of arm's-length acquaintance Max had had all his life; he might become a friend.

Except, of course, that soon Max would be half a world away.

"Well." Robert sighed. "I'll have the details about Jana in a couple of weeks; I'll tell you as soon as I have them. Last time, when it was Afghanistan, you used a cargo plane; I assume this time you'll use a freighter."

"Since it's Chile, yes."

Robert grinned. "I feel sometimes that we are like two boys smoking behind the barn. Smuggling . . . Not something one learns in the kitchen or the seminary. You handle it well, you and Carlos and Hermann. I could almost guess you had done it before, but I know nothing about these things. I should simply thank you for using what you know to help me. I seem to be thanking you all the time. What can I do for you? I'm going to Marseilles this afternoon; is there anything I can do for you there?"

"Stop by the shop and tell them exactly what you want for whomever you're sending to Haiti. I'll call to tell them you're coming. You know, a post office canceling machine isn't a bad idea. I'll look into it."

Robert laughed. "You'd need one from every dictatorship in the world."

"Not impossible."

They shook hands, smiling, more comfortable with each other than at any time in their year-long acquaintance. "By the way," Robert said. "I saw Sabrina in town this morning, on her way to work. She looks very well; beautiful, as always, and also happy."

"Hasn't she been happy in your cooking lessons?"

"It seems so, but when we're together I sometimes wonder whether she might be pretending so I won't worry about her. This morning, however, she was alone in her car and her face had a lovely brightness I haven't seen before. So things go well with the two of you?"

"Very well."

Robert searched his face. "You know, Max, I love her. She has so many needs, but she doesn't demand that we satisfy them; she doesn't cling or complain. I admire her and I want her to be content, with herself and with the world. I hope indeed that things go well with the two of you. I do know that she is happy in Cavaillon; in such a short time she has truly made it her home."

"I'll see you out," Max said abruptly, and led Robert to the door. "I have some calls to make," he said in a kind of apology. "I'll see you tomorrow, won't I? Isn't that the next cooking lesson?"

"Not this week; I'll still be in Marseilles. Next week."

They shook hands and Max watched Robert walk to his car. It was probably a good thing that he was leaving: Robert often understood too much. Max felt a sinking in his heart. It did not really matter where he was or how comfortable he might begin to feel with another person; there never would be a time when he could completely relax.

Watching the small car follow the curve in the road and disappear, he wondered for the first time if Robert might be in danger. Probably not; there was no trail leading to a small, quiet priest in Cavaillon who organized a network of activist priests all around the world and smuggled other activists, mostly students, into and out of their countries. We're two of a kind, Max thought; that's probably why we get along so well. Two smugglers in a world of police, border guards and identity papers. And if my smuggling has always been to increase my own wealth, and Robert's is to enhance the lives of the poor and the helpless, we still have our bond. And we need each other. He saw that, even if I didn't want him to.

The telephone was ringing in his study and he went to answer it.

"The contract came, from Bimerji in Iran," Carlos said. "Will you be here soon, or shall I send it up?"

"I'll be there Thursday." Iran, he thought with satisfaction. He had been talking to the Iranians for months, and now they'd taken the last steps, bringing in Bimerji to buy the construction equipment, and sending the contract to Lacoste et fils in Marseilles. He'd known they would come through; everyone knew there were factions in Iran trying to undermine the government, and what better way to start than to flood the country with counterfeit currency? But to know the contract was there . . . that was the satisfaction he had waited for.

He pictured Carlos sitting in the office that everyone, including Robert, thought was a small print shop connected to Lacoste et fils. Carlos would be at his small desk behind the counter beside steel shelves stacked with paper, envelopes, inks and rubber stamps. Through a nearby door one could glimpse the large copy camera with its anachronistic-looking bellows, two offset printers, and a small laser scanner; the closed door of the darkroom was just beyond. On the walls of the front room, with its counter for customers, hung samples of party invitations, announcements, business cards, letterhead and printed envelopes: the kind of careful work the shop did so well.

Everything was neat, orderly, modest: an unobtrusive windowless wooden building jutting from one side of his warehouse. But in a room behind the darkroom sat Andrew Frick, an American of genius—so the judge had called him when sentencing him the last time—a man who called himself a true artist. Frick was passionately absorbed in the romance of copying, engraving and printing money in dozens of currencies. He had invented an ink mixed with magnetic metal powder that duplicated the inks used throughout the world, and he had found a way to use nonfluorescent pigments to simulate the whiteness of cotton fiber instead of using the bleach that less artistic counterfeiters used, which fluoresced beneath ultraviolet light, showing them instantly to be counterfeit.

Andrew Frick's counterfeit money was so fine it had been compared by experts to the delicate purity of a Botticelli. And Andrew Frick had never been as happy in his life as he was in Max Lacoste's back room, where he could make his own hours and have the most modern equipment to do what he loved best, and receive in return generous pay, an apartment near the harbor and a charge account, billed to Max, at Fauchon and Galeries Lafayette.

Frick had burned all his bridges in America, moved everything he owned to France, and thrown in his lot for all time with Max Lacoste. He never wanted to be anywhere else.

Seeing all of it in his mind as he stood at his desk in Cavaillon, Max thought ahead to Thursday. "How much do they want in Iran?" he asked Carlos.

"One hundred fifty million rials."

"When?"

"A month. I suggested a shipment of three backhoes about the end of July. If they find they don't need one of them after all, the contract specifies that they can send it back."

A hundred fifty million rials would take no more than two or three cubic feet of space, Max calculated. The Iranians would convert thirty-seven and a half million rials—his fee—to francs and ship them to him in the backhoe that they would find they did not, after all, need.

"You're satisfied?" he asked Carlos.

"I think everything is there. I want you to go over it."

"Good. I'll be there early on Thursday, eight or eight-thirty. By the way, Father Chalon will be there tomorrow. He needs identity papers; he'll tell you about them. I'd like them rushed through."

"They always are, for him. Anything else?"

"No, I'll see you Thursday."

He stood beside his desk after he hung up. Of course Robert is in danger, just as I am. There is always the chance that someone will talk, someone will recognize a face, someone will follow a trail that seems so faint as to be invisible but that, to just one person, is as clear and straight as an arrow.

Which is why I have to move.

And which is why a priest in Cavaillon, who believes prayer is good but prayer with action is better, might also have to move one day.

Maybe three of us will go, Max thought. Or Robert will join us later. That would make leaving Cavaillon easier for Sabrina to accept. I'll mention that to her as a possibility. He locked his door and went back to his desk, to return to work.

"I thought perhaps a hike and picnic," Léon said on the telephone. "It's been five days since Fontaine-de-Vaucluse and I am badly in need of exercise."

"No five a.m. bicycle rides?" Stephanie asked. She was in the back room of Jacqueline en Provence an hour before the shop would open. She had begun coming in early every morning, to work alone and to feel, for that brief, wonderful time, that it was her shop, her own place, to mold any way she wished. It was like a secret she carried with her. And now Léon was another secret. It was the first time he had called since their afternoon at Fontaine-de-Vaucluse.

"I haven't even thought about bicycling; I've been working on a new series of paintings, very different and exciting. Perhaps you'll come to the studio to see them.''

"I'd like that.''

"After our picnic, then. Are you free this afternoon?''

"No. I'm sorry. But on Thursday . . .''

"Three more days.''

Stephanie was silent.

"Well, then, Thursday. You choose the place; I'll bring the food. I'll call you the day before, about this time, if that's all right. I've missed you, Sabrina; I've replayed last Tuesday in my head a dozen times. It was a very special day.''

"Yes. For me, too.'' Stephanie's hand shook as she hung up. Max was going to Marseilles on Thursday. She had made a date with Léon for a day when Max would be away.

"You're very quiet,'' Jacqueline said later that morning as they unpacked and arranged a display of china. "Is something troubling you?''

Stephanie nodded. "But it's something I have to work out; it's complicated.''

"Then it involves love. And it is probably less complicated than you think. Love always seems to create so many tangles, but in fact there is usually a single thread that can be pulled to make everything clear. Though I admit that finding the thread is sometimes difficult and painful.''

"And have you found it, with your friend?''

"Certainly, but he and I have no tangle. The thread is friendship. Are you worried about finding it with Max?''

"I don't know what it would be. I couldn't give it a name.''

Jacqueline looked at her thoughtfully. "Perhaps because you don't know what you have: marriage, friendship, companionship, a living arrangement, a business relationship—''

"Business!''

"Well, because he offers you his home and his name and his protection and you offer him eight months of memory, and affection but not love. I don't know how many men would consider that satisfactory for a marriage, though for a business transaction it would do."

"I think he likes it that I have no memory."

"Indeed? Why?"

"I don't know. But he doesn't urge me to make connections, to try to reach back, the way Robert does."

"And you do not . . . when you are making love, at that time when we are most open and most receptive to stimuli, you do not recall anything?"

Stephanie concentrated on aligning pearl-handled knives and forks with the china. "I'm . . . not open then."

"Ah. And what keeps you guarded?"

"What I told you before. I can't believe what he says. I can't trust him."

"Yes, but just for the pleasure of it . . . Well I see that that is not enough for you. You need more. I hope you find it with someone, my dear. Or . . . perhaps you have found it and that is the tangle that bothers you now?" She waited, but Stephanie did not answer. "You know you can always talk to me, Sabrina."

"I know. I love talking to you. And I will, but I have too much to sort out."

The doorbell rang as a customer came into the shop, and Stephanie went to greet her with relief. She did not know why she was uncomfortable; she could always talk to Jacqueline. But today the words stayed inside her.

"And what have you planned while I'm gone?" Max asked that night at dinner.

"To work on this room," Stephanie said. "If you don't mind, I want to get rid of most of the furniture; it's too heavy for a dining room, especially this one. We've got a table in the shop that I'd like to try, and Jacqueline told me about some places that may have chairs and a sideboard."

He did not want to hear about her plans for the house. "And what else?"

"A chandelier—"

"No, I mean what else will you be doing?"

"Max, we go through this every time you leave. I haven't planned every minute of every day, and even if I had, I don't see why I'd give you an itinerary. You don't give me one for your time in Marseilles."

"More bicycling?"

"I may ride to Roussillon with Robert."

"And what else?"

"And I'm going to hike. I haven't done that yet."

"Where?"

"I don't know."

"If madame will forgive me for intruding," Madame Besset said, bringing the cheese tray, "there is an excellent hike above Saint-Saturnin. That is the town, if you remember, we will move to after we sell the farm to our son. I know it well. If you park in the square and walk behind the church, you will find a stairway of Roman steps. I think you will be very pleased with what is at the top."

"What is at the top?" Max asked.

"A medieval town now in ruins. Collapsed castles, homes, an old roadway."

"It sounds wonderful," Stephanie said. "That's where I'll go."

"Take a camera," Max said. "I'd like to see pictures."

"Yes."

I am deceiving Max. I'm doing it very easily. I wonder if I ever deceived anyone before.

She began to tremble and could not stop. *Something is wrong; what is wrong with me?*

"Sabrina, what is it?"

"Madame!"

Max helped her to her feet, waving Madame Besset away. "We'll be in the library; you can bring our coffee there."

He led Stephanie to a couch and held her so she would not collapse while she sat down. "Can you tell me what it is?"

"No." She was breathless, as if she had been running.

He sat beside her. "Close your eyes. Lie back. Shall I call the doctor?"

"No."

"Do you feel ill?"

"No. I don't know how I feel." She lay against him, her eyes closed. Gradually her trembling eased. She opened her eyes. *Alice in Wonderland* lay open on the table in front of her.

"I could tell you my adventures—beginning from this morning," said Alice . . . "but it's no use going back to yesterday, because I was a different person then."

That has something to do with the way I feel. But I don't know what.

I was a different person then.

Yes, of course. I knew who I was; I had a name, memories, a past, a future.

But is that really what it means?

I don't know. I have to think, I have to try to understand—

"Feeling better?" Max asked.

"Yes. Thank you." She sat up. *Later. When I'm alone.* Madame Besset brought in a tray with coffee and slices of tarte tatin. "Tell me what you'll be doing in Marseilles."

She poured coffee, they talked quietly in the library, and it became an evening like any other. And then it faded from her mind, more quickly than she would have thought possible. She was busy with Jacqueline; she and Max drove to Saint-Rémy where she shopped for clothes; she drew plans for the redesign of the dining room. And she thought about Thursday. And then Max was gone. And Thursday had come.

"Your Madame Besset is wonderful," Léon said. "I've never been here."

They were walking on a wide, rocky path, the remains of a Roman road far above the town of Saint-Saturnin. On either side was a tumbled stone wall, here and there intact: black stones carefully set atop each other almost a thousand years earlier to mark the main road of the fortified town. The road began at a ruined castle overlooking the fertile valley far below, and stretched for more than two miles, past dozens of *bories* where families had lived, now little more than heaps of mute black stones.

"I wish I could bring the people back," Stephanie said, "and watch them farm and go shopping and play and . . . Where did they get water?"

"There may have been a river down there." They peered over the cliff into the valley below. "Dried up now, but we know that without water there could have been no town."

"So many people, so many stories." They walked slowly, beneath the blazing sun. They wore shorts, lightweight T-shirts and billed caps, and small backpacks. Léon had a sketch pad in his pocket and Stephanie's camera was hooked to her belt. "Did anyone write their stories? Is there a history of Saint-Saturnin?"

"I don't know of one. But I have histories of Provence in my library; I'll see what I can find."

"All gone," Stephanie murmured. "We should write everything down, everything, every day. We don't think about it, but otherwise it can vanish so completely . . ."

"Nothing vanishes." Léon's voice was casual, but he was being careful, searching for the words that would allow her to talk about herself. "Everything is here surrounding us, wherever we are. It's what I try to show in my paintings: the other lives and memories that are part of us even though they're voiceless and invisible. They haven't vanished; it's just that we haven't figured out how to find the key that will open all those locked doors."

They were alone in the ruined village. Bushes and flowers grew out of walls, clinging to bits of earth between the stones, lizards whipped across the road and into the shade of shrubs, birds flew protectively about their nests in the crevices of shattered homes, and the *genêt* bushes were in bloom, perfuming the air.

"My life has vanished," Stephanie said. She did not look at Léon. "You're right, of course, it's somewhere, in letters I wrote or work I accomplished or in people's memories. But not in mine. Not in my memory. I have none."

Thank you, Léon breathed silently, and knew then how desperately he had wanted her to be open to him, and knew, too, in that moment that he loved her. But, my God, he thought, my God, to live without memory: such terrible loneliness . . . "And Max?" he asked.

"He says he can't help me."

"Tell me all of it—can you?—from the beginning."

"The beginning," Stephanie said wryly. "A very recent one. Eight months ago. October."

They walked a little apart from each other, drinking from their water bottles as the sun moved higher, and she told him everything, even her faintness of three nights earlier, and the passage from *Alice in Wonderland*. By the time she finished, they had left the ruined village behind and were in open fields of tall wild grass, hot and dry, dotted with low scrub bushes. A small farm was in a hollow on their right, with a donkey in a small fenced enclosure and a child throwing a ball against white sheets swaying on a clothesline. Ahead was the edge of a forest.

Léon took Stephanie's hand. "We'll find a place to sit and have our picnic."

Stephanie felt his firm clasp and the rhythm of their matched steps. She was relaxed now, and happy, and there was a singing inside her. She had told him more than she had told Robert; more than she had told Jacqueline. She had talked to him as if she had been talking to herself.

The path led into the forest and they gave a small gasp at the sudden coolness. In a few minutes Léon stopped. "Grass, leaves, a small room. A place for lunch." He ducked into a grove of trees near the path and when Stephanie followed, she found herself in a small green space with walls of leafy branches and a ceiling of cloudless sky. Pale forest grasses covered the ground, drooping over the fallen leaves of many seasons, black and weathered to pliant softness.

Léon took from his backpack cheeses, saucisson, a container of wrinkled black olives in herbs, and a round loaf of roughly shaped bread. "Wine," he murmured, finding a flat place for the bottle, "glasses, knives, napkins. And grapes. Whenever we're ready. Now?"

"Not yet. It's so cool and quiet; I'd just like to sit for a while."

"Well, then." He pulled from his pocket his sketch pad and a crayon and with swift, easy strokes began drawing her. She sat a few feet away, her back against a tree, her legs stretched out, her head turned to watch him.

"As you will see when you visit my studio," he said, his eyes on his paper, "I have painted little else but you since our bicycle trip. If that displeases you, you must tell me."

"It pleases me."

He looked up quickly. "Why?"

"Because people in paintings have a life of their own. I know they're frozen in time, but they reflect what they were and hint at what they will be. If you paint me, I think it will be me and . . . not me. It might be the person I was. I'd like to see what she looks like."

He nodded, as if to himself. "An interesting idea. But is that the only reason you are pleased?"

"No. I like knowing that you think about me."

He laughed. "Most of the time, it seems. And do you think of me?"

"Yes. I shouldn't. I have a husband, a home . . . I shouldn't be . . . I have responsibilities and obligations—"

"But you see I have not asked you about them—nothing about your marriage or your home—nor have I told you about my own involvements. And you have not asked me. None of that has any place here."

"Why not?"

"Because there is too much we don't know yet."

"You mean I'm hurrying things along."

"I mean you are not joining me in holding them back. Come," he said, seeing the confusion on her face, "we'll have our lunch. And I want to talk to you about memory."

"What about it?"

He filled their wineglasses, then broke off a piece of bread and spread it with cheese and handed it to her. "Often, when I'm in the middle of a painting, I stand back from the canvas and look at what I've done and see something very good—an arrangement of shapes or colors, an altered landscape, a portrait—and I have no idea where that good thing came from. I didn't think about it before I painted it; I hadn't done it before. It just appeared."

Stephanie nodded. "From all your experiences for—how many years? How old are you?"

"Thirty-six."

"All your experiences for thirty-six years, stored in your memory, waiting for you. Because you remember everything, back to the time you were four years old."

"I don't remember everything; no one does. You're right that the experiences are waiting for me, but that's what I'm saying: they're waiting for all of us. Yours are waiting for you. And you'll find them. They'll come unbidden, as mine do when I paint, or you'll make connections with things you see and hear and read. In fact, some already have come to you, when you called the little girl Penny and mentioned Mrs. Thirkell. And you said you told Max that you'd moved around a lot, and you told me my painting reminded you of van Gogh. It's all there, Sabrina, everything you've ever done, your thoughts, your loves, your hates and fears and the wonders of your—how many years? How old are you?"

"I don't know."

"Ah. Of course. Well, we will declare your age. What do you think? I think thirty-one, perhaps thirty-two. Would one of those suit you?"

She was smiling. "And when is my birthday?"

"Oh, today. Why not? What better way to celebrate than this? Today, June thirtieth, you are thirty-one years old and this is a celebration." He refilled their wine-glasses. "So you have thirty-one years of loves and hates and fears and wonders and maybe a few things you'd like to forget permanently, all inside you, waiting for you, like an attic in an old house, dusty and whispering of secrets. Everything from the past is piled up, stacked away, pushed back to make room for more. But a wind comes, a hurricane, an earthquake, and things in the attic shift: some reach the top and come to us with no rhyme or reason, or we reach in and pluck something out—"

"*I can't do that!* Don't you understand? I can't reach in—"

"I know that. I'm sorry; I do understand that. But I believe that you will."

"Why?"

"Because you are young and strong. Because you try very hard and don't accept what has happened with tears or resignation. Because you have already remembered some things."

"And because you believe in gnomes and elves."

"And magic."

They shared a smile. The grove where they sat was hushed and still. The leaves drooped; the birds slept in the afternoon heat. No voice, no sounds from farm or city broke the silence. Stephanie bit into the earthy crust of the bread; the cool, smooth cheese melted on her tongue; the cold Chablis flowed to the back of her throat, and it all had the slow grace of a dream. She watched Léon begin drawing again, his crayon making a faint swish on the heavy paper. She liked the way he looked: his short blond hair almost white against his deep tan; his lean, muscular body a little tensed as he drew, as if every nerve was concentrating, as if all his energy nourished the fingers that moved so swiftly and surely over the paper. His blue shirt was streaked with perspiration, his mouth was faintly smiling, his green eyes were looking down—

He looked up and met her gaze and their eyes held. And that was like a dream, too, Stephanie thought, because it did not need logic to be natural and right that he was all she saw, or wanted to see.

He did not move, but it was as if he reached out to her. "I would like to help you find your past if you will let me."

"Yes." She stretched out her hand, and he took it. *This is where I belong; here and nowhere else.*

They sat that way for a long time, their hands clasped. Léon's sketchbook lay at his side. The hot, still air held them suspended, the grass and leaves felt moist beneath Stephanie's bare legs, a trickle of perspiration ran down the side of her face. Within her, the turmoil of the past months stilled. Her thoughts drifted, her breathing was light, a small pulse beat in her palm where Léon held it clasped to his.

After a time he stirred. "I was wrong. I do need to know about your marriage."

Stephanie's heart took a small lurch, as if she had been walking on level ground but had fallen suddenly down a step she had not seen. *My life is full of beginnings, and this is one of them.*

But she did not know how to begin, and the silence stretched out.

"You don't remember anything about marrying him," Léon said finally. "Or talking about a future with him. Or being in a motorboat after the explosion. But you do remember some of the things the doctors told you in the hospital. Did you talk to them about Max? Or your marriage?"

"I don't remember. Max bought all my clothes, I remember that; and they were always perfect, the right colors, the right size. And he stayed with me until he knew I would recover; then he went back to his company, and came and went. Then Robert found the house in Cavaillon and Max furnished it with pieces he'd had in storage somewhere, and his art collection. He'd owned your painting of the Alpilles for ten years, he said; he'd bought it at Galeries de Rohan in Paris.''

"That was when I painted it. It was in my first show at the gallery. I've shown there ever since.''

"In Paris? But we have your paintings at Jacqueline en Provence.''

"I do that for Jacqueline. A few only. Most go to Rohan. But you are only giving me information that anyone can see. I want to know about what is unseen.''

"I know.'' And then it came, more easily than she would have thought. "I don't love him. I've tried, but there is such a gulf between us of *not knowing* . . . I mean, I think he knows more about my past than he tells me, but I have no way of proving that, or even testing him. It's a feeling, no more, but so strong that I can't trust him. I believe him when he says he loves me and he's very good to me: he's let me do things he'd rather I didn't do, like work in the shop with Jacqueline and cook with Robert—''

"Why should you not do those things?''

"I don't know. He certainly doesn't want a helpless woman who lolls on a chaise all day eating bonbons and humming French love songs—''

Léon was laughing. "A charming picture. Did he tell you that was what he didn't want?''

"No, I asked him one day if that was what he was waiting for. He found it amusing, too, but he didn't tell me what was wrong with working with Jacqueline and cooking with Robert. He does like it, though, that I'm redecorating the house and adding on a studio for myself.''

"Because you are at home when you do it.''

"Yes. And because . . . it fixes me more permanently there.''

"Have you given him reason to doubt your permanence?''

"I haven't given him any reasons to be sure of me.''

Léon's hand tightened on hers, and she shook her head.

"I'm not proud of that. I owe him everything: my life, a home, a chance to make a real person of myself, Robert's friendship . . . I'd have nothing if it weren't for Max."

"But you think he is lying to you."

"Oh . . . such a harsh word. I don't know. I just can't be sure of anything with Max. I like him, you know; he's a good companion and he's a bulwark when I'm frightened or feeling lost, but there's something about him that makes me think of danger, or of dangerous people . . . maybe both. I know that sounds foolish; I know he'd be astonished if I told him that, but I feel it and it won't go away, even when I'm relying on him the most."

She paused. "I can't imagine myself changing the way I feel about him. Ever."

Léon's breath came out in a long sigh. "And what will you do?"

"I don't know. I've thought of leaving him, but there are so many reasons not to . . . I don't want to hurt him; he's done nothing to deserve that. And I'm afraid. I know so little about anything, I don't know where I'd even begin if I were on my own. Now that I have a job, soon perhaps I can think more seriously about leaving. But not yet. And there is one more thing . . ."

She looked at their clasped hands. Her voice was very low. "I will not move from being dependent on Max to being dependent on someone else. I will not exchange one protector for another."

"No, that would not be good. And there is no reason for you to do it. But what of us?"

She looked up at him and gave a slow, impish smile. "You're not offering to be my protector?"

"No. Though I would protect you if the need arose."

Oh, I like that, Stephanie thought. That he knows there is a difference. And then she took a long breath and plunged into the future. "I want to be with you."

"Then we'll be together. We'll discover all that we do not know and create our own memories." It was as solemn as a ceremony, Stephanie thought, with their clasped hands to mark it.

After a moment Léon said, "I've been with someone for a few months. I'll end it as soon as I can."

"I'm not asking you to do that. And I'm not—"

"You're not leaving Max. But it would not be fair to my friend to continue; we don't love each other, but we're good friends and I've always been honest with her."

"Jacqueline said the same thing about the man she sees. It sounds so simple."

He looked at her curiously. "Did she tell you the name of the man?"

"No, just that they have a good—" Stephanie stared at him and caught her breath. "No. It can't be. Léon, it can't be!"

"Why not?" His voice was gentle. "I told you my paintings were at her shop because of her; we've helped each other for a long time. And about a year ago we were both at a place in our lives when we needed companionship. We didn't want love; we wanted warmth and solace, and that was what we gave each other. She's a remarkable woman, you know; a very dear friend."

"She's been a friend to *me*. She gave me a job, she teaches me every day, we talk . . . about everything. I can't hurt her; I can't do anything that might hurt her."

"Sabrina, this is not between you and Jacqueline; it is between Jacqueline and me."

"No, no, don't you understand? I talk to her about Max and she told me about you; we were two women, talking, trusting each other. She's the only woman friend I have— well, there's Madame Besset, but that isn't at all the same—and I won't take and take from her and then steal someone away, someone she cares about . . ."

"You cannot steal me; what are you thinking? That I am like one of those silver spoons in your shop that you can tuck inside your coat and carry away on tiptoe?"

A small laugh broke from Stephanie. "I'm sorry; that wasn't a good word, but—"

"And as for Jacqueline caring about me, she does so as a friend, not as a serious lover. I told you that. Evidently, so did she."

"She told me you need each other."

His eyebrows rose. "She said that?"

"Yes."

"Just like that?"

"She said that you have a good time and need each other and if you parted tomorrow she would miss you very much."

Léon contemplated her. "Sabrina, I know Jacqueline well. I do not believe that was all she said."

Stephanie looked away from him. What did she owe Jacqueline? Loyalty, gratitude, love . . . but not a lie. "She said she would miss you very much for a while, but she would wish you well for the pleasure you had together. And you would do the same for her."

"She was right. Now please listen to me. Jacqueline and I have not looked for love from each other, and so we have not expected permanence. Each of us knew that what we had could change at any time, and then we would be friends of a different kind. That's what she told you: we would wish each other well. How many people are lucky enough to find that when they need it? A loving friend who brightens a dark corner of our life, who chases shadows away, who strives to make us feel better about who we are and what we are doing. Jacqueline and I did that for each other. But we never touched the mystery in each other, or even tried—" He saw Stephanie's eyes widen. "So she told you that, too. It seems she told you everything that was important about us. Now I will tell you what is important about you and me."

He turned Stephanie's hand within his and kissed the palm. It sent a shock through her and she gasped, and he kissed the same spot again, feeling her tremble. "I love you, Sabrina. I want to be with you and help you rediscover the world and yourself, and you will help me discover the world from this day on. We will be together as little or as much as you want, I'll do whatever you want, and someday . . . Well, that's enough. Predictions are folly; we have enough to learn about each other to fill the present. We'll build the future as we go.''

A powerful joy flared within Stephanie. She had no past, and no real belief that she ever would find it, but now she saw the outlines of a future, a place to belong, where she would not be lost again. She felt a delight in herself that she had not felt before: delight in her youth and strength, in her mind that could learn and remember what it learned, in her work, in the affection of friends, and in this man's love. Exhilaration buoyed her up: she was part of the earth and the sky, in this place, at this time. She was whole, and she was happy.

Almost without moving, they were in each other's arms. Stephanie put back her head. ''I love you,'' she said, and the words were a song that had been locked within her, waiting for a chance to soar. When they kissed, her mouth opened to Léon's and her arms drew him down to lie on her. She desired and she loved, and for Sabrina Lacoste, whose memory was eight months old, it was the first time.

CHAPTER 13

"*M*orning, Mrs. Andersen," the garage attendant said. "How long for you today?"

"About three hours, Juan." Sabrina slipped the ticket he gave her into her purse and took her briefcase and small suitcase of samples from the back seat. "How was your friend's wedding?"

"Oh, that was one great party. They better stay married after that send-off. Nice of you to remember. You want your car washed today? I've got time."

She started to say no, because that was Cliff's job, but Cliff was at soccer camp every day, coming home exhausted from some fierce determination that drove him from morning to night, and why not have someone else do it? "Yes, please. And would you try to get the stain off the back seat? I think it's ice cream, or maybe pizza."

He grinned. "Yes, ma'am. Kids, they are a trial. And put it on your bill?"

"Yes."

She walked from the cool garage to the heat of Dearborn Street, humid air heavy with fumes from cars and trucks, the smell of chickens turning on spits in a nearby restaurant, the faint spicy scent of carnations at the florist next door. The end of July, she thought. This has to be as hot as it gets. But then, why did Madeline say August is usually worse?

At the Koner Building the door swung open as she tried it. Vern was there, she thought, surprised; usually he sauntered in after she and Koner had been waiting for fifteen minutes.

Her footsteps echoed as she climbed the stairs to the room they had cleaned out to use as an office. "Good morning," Vernon Stern said. "Have I impressed you?"

"You have." She smiled at his grin, self-deprecating but eager, like that of a small boy who had lain in wait to spring a surprise. He was extraordinarily handsome, she thought as she did each time she saw him: his blond hair curlier than usual in the humidity, but still looking perfectly groomed. He was carefully craggy but polished, wearing jeans and cowboy boots and a blue silk shirt open at the neck.

"That's the goal: to impress." He took her suitcase and laid it on the folding steel table in the center of the room beside his rolls of drawings and the morning newspaper. "What is this? It feels like you packed rocks."

"A few wood samples and paint chips; mostly tiles and quartzite. So, yes, basically I packed rocks."

They laughed together as Sabrina opened her briefcase and took out three thick loose-leaf binders. "These are the specs; I finished them late last night, so I haven't gone over them. I'd appreciate it if you'd let me have your comments within a week."

He was scanning one of them. "Very good. Looks very complete. Quartzite in the foyers of the double apartments. I like that. And in the foyers of the smaller ones?" He leafed back. "Slate. Verde. Good choice. And six-inch floor moldings; wonderful. I hope Billy goes for the expense; they're the only ones that look right in a vintage building. You have a good sense of tradition—the best of it, anyway. I haven't met many designers who do; it's more European than American.'' He looked up at her. ''You've had fun doing this.''

''The best designs come when it's fun.''

''I agree. I wasn't criticizing. My dullest buildings are the ones designed to clients' idiosyncrasies; no fun at all. In fact, I detest them.''

''Why do you do them?''

''Because when you're on your own and dependent on the whims and whispers of the public, you keep your eye on what's truly important, which is keeping your name visible and memorable while doing your best to create excellence. Success and fame are wondrous things, though; they do make it possible to say no. And I think I'll be there in a few years.''

''I hope you will. It gives you such a feeling of strength, of being in control of who you are through what you're doing.''

He looked at her curiously. ''Now, how would you know what it is to depend for survival on the vagaries of fickle, wealthy, slightly bored socialites and know-it-all corporate types?''

''I've read about it.''

''Which means you don't want to tell me. Hints of a colorful past. I'd like to hear about it.'' Sabrina was silent. ''I'm serious; I really would. You're a fascinating woman, Stephanie; I can't find a category for you. Suburban housewife, antique dealer, terrific interior designer . . . but more than that, much more, and I'm damned if I can put my finger on it.''

''Why should you?'' she asked coolly.

''Because I don't like mysteries. I'm a very literal guy: I design buildings, I don't write poetry. You told me you'd grown up in Europe, so that explains your accent, and I suppose your feel for tradition, but there's something else, sort of a second person somewhere; you're so guarded, almost secretive. It's a challenge, getting close to you.'' He waited, but Sabrina met his eyes and said nothing.

"You know, that's hard to do: to say nothing. Most people try to fill a silence. You're not a babbler; I find that fascinating, too." He paused again. "Well, someday, perhaps; I don't give up easily, you know." He looked again at the notebook and skimmed more pages. "Double doors into the master bedroom suite?"

"I know you drew a single door, but it's at the end of the gallery, with a vestibule behind it, and I thought if we could find old stained glass it would be more dramatic from both sides."

"It would. Nice idea. Have you some ideas for locating the glass?"

"I'd try Salvage One first. And I have a list of other possibilities."

"So you know Salvage One. A designer's dream."

"Yes, but a nightmare, too, don't you think? All those bits and pieces of buildings that have been torn down—doors, windows, fireplace surrounds, sinks, grates, wall sconces—fragments of people's hopes and dreams and tragedies. I always feel as if a whisper follows me through all the floors, saying that everything is fragile, everything dies, and we should write down everything we do and think; otherwise it will vanish so completely . . ."

"Yes, I've felt that. But more than that: that we shouldn't believe in anything too devoutly, because it will soon be gone."

"Oh, no. It has nothing to do with trust and belief and love; just because something is fragile is no reason not to believe in it. Maybe it's a reason to believe in it even more; then we'll try to protect it."

"You have faith. I admire that."

Their eyes met and they smiled. Sabrina thought how much she liked him, and liked working with him. "Is there anything else in the specs you want to talk about now?"

"Well, let's see." He turned more pages. "What are the question marks? Decisions you haven't made?"

"Items where you and Billy and I disagree. He thinks

the quartzite is too expensive, for example. I hope we can settle most of them today."

"I'm sure we can." Stern closed the book and laid it down. He sat on the edge of the table, lightly swinging one foot. "Where do you do your work? Do you have an office?"

"I'm using our attic until we figure something out. Why?"

"Our firm has an extra room; it's yours if you want it."

Her eyebrows rose. "That's very generous."

"No, it's quite selfish. I want to see more of you." His eyes, improbably blue, gazed at her, and Sabrina was conscious of her Indian gauze skirt over bare legs, and her sheer cotton blouse with a deep V neck. He took her hand. "I enjoy talking to you, Stephanie, and working with you. I think about you when we're not together; you sneak up on me while I'm doing other things and then you stay there and I like it, I like the idea of your being with me. I like your quietness and your mysteries, I like the way you think, and you are wonderfully beautiful. Every time we finish up here I feel cheated because I want more of you, and it's seemed to me that you feel the same, that you wished you could stay." He paused briefly, as if waiting for her to agree. When she did not, he added, "And we make a good team; I can see us working on a lot of jobs together, even bigger than this one."

Sabrina nodded thoughtfully. "We do work well together." She was thinking how astonishing it was that a man so smoothly put together could be so crude. That shows how far I've come from London: it wouldn't have surprised me at all in those days to find a perfectly groomed member of a perfectly groomed society making a proposition and dangling at the end of it the temptation of more and bigger jobs through his influence.

She thought of Garth and smiled to herself. The idea of any other man in her life was incomprehensible. Once she had been able to visualize herself at dinner or the theater or in bed with a man she met; now she could not even imagine it. No one, ever, but Garth, she thought; how ridiculous for Vernon Stern to fantasize that I long to stay with him when it's time to go home.

I liked him, she thought; and now I don't. Now I just admire his work.

"Good," he said and smiled his boyish smile once again. "You can move into that room whenever you want; just let me know so I can tell the secretary you're coming."

"Oh, I won't be using it." She slipped her hand from his and moved away. "I do thank you, Vern, but I'm quite happy where I am."

She thought of stopping there, since that said everything about her life, but she went on, her voice friendly but a little distant, as if she were thinking aloud about an abstract problem that had nothing to do with him; as if, in fact, she had already forgotten what he had said. It gave them a chance, she thought, to continue to work together comfortably, on this job or any other.

"I do believe in things; I do have faith in what I can do. But I have faith in luck, too, and in magic. Because it seems to me that the world is so complicated, with twists and turns that can transform whole lives in an instant, if we find love and work and a family and a home, and if we can hold them together, a lot of it is because of luck and magic. And that's too special and rare to toss away for an adventure. It would be like daring the gods to repeat a miracle, and I'm not brave enough to do that."

There was a silence. Stern turned to the table and slowly unrolled his plans, as if taking comfort from the reality of them. He anchored the corners with a large stapler and a tape dispenser, and in another minute turned back to Sabrina.

"Lucky lady," he said lightly. "It seems those gods used my allotment of luck and magic to make me an architect. A good one, a great one, some people say, but when it comes to all those other good things—love and family and home—I haven't done so— Stephanie? What is it?''

She was looking past him, at the table. He had pushed the copy of the *Chicago Tribune* to one side when he unrolled his plans, and Sabrina was reading the headline of the article in the center of the front page, over a picture of the Administration Building of Midwestern University: "House Committee to Investigate University Use of Government Funds."

"Excuse me," she said, and picked up the paper.

Congressman Oliver Leglind, chairman of the House Committee on Science, Space and Technology, announced today that he is launching an investigation into college and university use of government grants in response to complaints that the system is rife with irregularities, waste and fraud.

One of the universities under investigation is Midwestern University in Evanston.

Roy Stroud, chief counsel to the committee, listed MU's Professor Garth Andersen as one of those who will be asked to testify. "Professor Andersen has admitted that some universities are guilty of excesses," Mr. Stroud said today, "but he also accused the committee—before a single witness has been heard—of 'fabricating plots to whip up the anger of voters with a slash-and-burn rampage across the campuses.' "

Other professors who will be asked to testify, according to Mr. Stroud, are . . .

"Excuse me," Sabrina said again and rushed into the corridor where they had hooked up a portable telephone. Billy Koner was walking up the stairs. "Vern's in the office," she said, and dialed Garth's number at the university.

"He's here? He's turned over a new leaf?"

"I doubt it." The ringing went on; she pictured Garth's

office, empty. "Billy, I won't be able to stay this morning. The specs are in the office. You and Vern can go over them and call me."

"No, no, that won't—" He stopped as she bent her head to talk privately on the telephone. "I'll wait for you in the office," he muttered and left her alone.

"He's in the lab, Mrs. Andersen," the secretary said. "Professor Collins had to go out of town and asked Professor Andersen to take his lab class and it's an especially long one; it's the last of the summer session. Is something happening? Three reporters have called this morning."

"Can you get a message to him in the lab?"

"I can go over there. Is that what you want me to do?"

"Yes. Please. Tell him to call me . . . no, I'll be on my way home." *I wanted a phone in the car, but Garth said it was an extravagance. I thought, after Mrs. Thirkell, a car phone would look like nothing, but I thought wrong.* "Tell him I'll call him in his office in fifteen minutes. And, Dalia, keep the reporters away. Can you do that?"

"Why don't I suggest he use Professor Collins's office? No one will find him there."

"Oh, very good." Wonderful, unquestioning Dalia; she should get a raise, Sabrina thought. "Do you have that phone number?"

She wrote it down, then, starting back to the office, had another idea and dialed her home number. "Mrs. Thirkell, have any reporters called this morning?"

"Three or four, my lady. All wanting Professor Andersen. I told them I had no idea when he would be home."

"Thank you." We are blessed with discreet women, she thought. "You can continue to say that all day. And if I'm not back when Penny and Cliff get home from camp, please tell them to stay home and wait for me."

Billy Koner and Stern were waiting for her, the *Tribune* spread out before them.

"This is your husband?"

"Yes. I'm sorry, Billy, but I have to leave."

"Because of this? What's the problem? He goes to D.C., tells them he spent the money on research or whatever, and he comes home. 'Course he shouldn't have said that about fabricating plots, that wasn't smart, if you'll forgive my saying so, but they don't hang people for that. So how come you have to hold his hand?"

"I want to be with him. When Roy Stroud was here he made it clear that he and Leglind are looking for a very big story with heroes and villains. Leglind is the hero; who do you think will be the villains?"

"Your husband? He's just a professor. These guys like bigger fish: CEOs, bank presidents, stockbrokers . . . they make good stories because the dollars are bigger and nobody loves them except maybe their dogs. You're too uptight, Stephanie; it comes from being connected to a university. You people lose touch with reality."

Impatiently she shook her head. "Leglind wants a ladder to climb on and he thinks he's going to get it from universities. He doesn't like professors and they're an easy target because they're so insulated they don't see what's coming until they've been run over by it."

"He doesn't need a ladder; he's head of one of the most powerful committees . . . Listen. I know Oliver Leglind; we grew up together. I put more money into his campaigns than people in his own state, than anybody, probably. He isn't going to run over anybody, and whatever you mean by a ladder, he isn't looking for it."

"I didn't realize you knew him. Then you'd know better than most people what he's thinking. He is a powerful man, but maybe the House isn't enough for him. Does he want to be in the Senate? Has he ever talked about the White House?"

Koner's face changed. After a minute he said, "They all talk about the White House."

"Really? All of them? Well, that may be, but right now I'm only interested in what Oliver Leglind talks about. He's built a reputation for being hard-nosed about the budget, except for projects in his own state, and now it looks as if he's going to get hard-nosed about professors with government grants. And they're sitting ducks because they can't show that every dollar they get leads to a product that you can buy at Wal-Mart. And if I can be of any help to my husband when Leglind goes after him, that's where I'll be, for as long as it takes.''

There was a pause. Koner picked up the newspaper. ''It says here, 'Professor Andersen has admitted that some universities are guilty of excesses.' ''

''That was Roy Stroud supposedly quoting Garth; I wouldn't take it on faith. But suppose he did say it. There are excesses everywhere. One definition of government is excess.''

Koner laughed. ''Right. They do know a lot about excess in Washington. So. Your husband isn't going to whip up some genes that I can buy at Wal-Mart?''

Sabrina smiled. ''I'm afraid not.''

''But he could change cattle or whatever, you know, getting more milk or leaner beef or whatever. Things we eat, right?''

''There are researchers working in those areas.''

''At your husband's university?''

''Yes. As long as they have the money. You can't have research unless someone pays for it.''

''Why don't the universities pay for it?''

''They do, as much as they can.''

''And they don't waste the government's money?''

''They probably do; I don't think anybody's found a way to make every penny productive. Have you, at home, or in remodeling this building?''

''I watch every penny.''

''That isn't what I asked. No waste, Billy, anywhere, in any of your projects?'' She waited. ''Well, that's not the main point anyway. I want to be with my husband, now that your friend has gone after him, and that's where I'm going. I'll call you—''

Koner grunted. ''Maybe I'll have a talk with Ollie. See

what he's up to. He's gonna be looking for money pretty soon; they always are, in the House. Damnedest thing; they get elected and they haven't even warmed their chairs before they're asking for money for the next campaign. I don't know how he has time to go after professors or anybody else. But what the hell, you're right: there's plenty of waste around. He could find it blindfolded; he doesn't have to go after it here. Listen. I'll talk to him. So today you can stay with Vern and get the specs finished. Right?"

"No, today I'm going to be with Garth. If you want—"

"It's Friday! You'll be with him all weekend!"

"If you want to talk to the congressman, Billy, you'll be doing it on your own, not as our representative. But I'll be interested in what he has to say. Call me at home. Anytime."

She shook hands with him and with Stern, picked up her briefcase and ran from the building, then walked quickly the half block to the garage.

"I never washed it, Mrs. Andersen; you said three hours."

"It's all right, Juan; next time."

On Sheridan Road she pulled into a gas station and called Garth. "Have you seen today's *Tribune?*"

"Just now. There was a copy in Chuck's office. Don't worry about it; it's a nuisance but we'll handle it."

"I'm on my way home."

"You don't have to do that."

"I want to. Garth, I think it's more than a nuisance."

She heard him tapping a pencil on the desk. "Well, so do I. But I haven't had time to think it through. There are exciting things happening here; I saw Lu this morning, and his paper . . . well, I'll tell you about it later."

"Is it finished? Are you submitting it?"

"It's finished; I'll send it in next week. I'm glad you're coming home. There's a lot to talk about."

"Garth, you won't talk to any reporters, will you? I should tell you about Billy Koner before you do."

"What about him?"

"He knows Leglind; in fact, it sounds like he's Leglind's pot of gold. He says he's going to talk to him. I'll tell you about it at home."

But when she parked the car in the driveway and walked up the front walk, Garth and Lu were sitting on the front porch swing, deep in conversation. Garth came down the steps and kissed her. "I couldn't send him away; he's too keyed up. It's a defining moment for him; he really isn't a student anymore: he's a scientist."

Sabrina turned to smile at Lu. "But he doesn't look happy."

"I know. I asked him if something was wrong. He said no. He could be worrying about the journal accepting his paper, but I've told him a dozen times I'm sure they'll accept it, which means it could be published before the end of the year. I don't know what's bothering him; I haven't pursued it."

"No, we have other things to think about."

Lu came down the steps. "I'll be going. If we could talk again, Professor—tomorrow, perhaps . . ."

"Lu, this weekend won't be a good time. But we've covered everything; there's nothing to do now but wait to hear from the editors."

"Once you submit the paper."

"I told you I'd do that next week."

Lu hesitated, then nodded. "Thank you." His voice was polite, flat, almost distant.

"How odd," Sabrina said, watching him walk away. "You're far more excited than he is. Did you say he was keyed up?"

"Almost manic when he arrived. Almost sleepwalking when he left. Maybe I will try to see him tomorrow."

"Garth, how about paying some attention to Professor Andersen and the crusading Oliver Leglind?"

He chuckled and put his arm around her as they walked up the porch steps. "I'm glad you're home. I'm glad you're with me. I love you."

They held each other and kissed. "Oh, your arms feel good," Sabrina sighed. "I miss them when they're not around me. I miss you, too." But after a minute she pulled away with a smile. "Too hot for extended kissing. Oh, iced tea. How wonderful."

"Courtesy of Mrs. Thirkell. She was making it when I got home."

"Is she here?"

"Shopping. Back soon." He dropped ice cubes into two glasses and filled them from the pitcher, beaded with moisture in the heat. They sat close together on the swing, holding hands. "What did your Billy Koner say?"

"I gather he's going to tell Leglind to take his fangs somewhere else."

"Why would Koner do that?"

"Either because I convinced him that universities aren't cesspools of waste and corruption, or because he thinks I won't spend time on his building if you're being hounded."

"And why would Leglind listen to him? You said something about a pot of gold."

"He made it sound as if he single-handedly funds Leglind's career. That could mean giving a lot or raising a lot; probably both."

"Did you ask him to talk to Leglind?"

"Garth, of course not! In the first place, I'm not even sure it's the best thing to do."

"It may not be. What did you tell him?"

"That if he did talk to Leglind he was doing it on his own, not as our representative, but of course I'd be interested in what he has to say."

"That sounds fine." Garth drained his glass and refilled it, and they sat in silence.

"You lost your temper with Stroud," Sabrina said.

"I was imprudent. I told myself to be polite, but that was after I hadn't been."

"And the quote about excesses in universities?"

"Not accurate. I said if there were excesses, that still wouldn't be an excuse to attack all research."

"A slash-and-burn rampage."

"Not the best choice of words."

"No." She smiled at him. "I love you, and you shouldn't have talked to him when you knew how angry you were."

"You're right. It's happened before. I should know better."

"When do you think they'll call you to testify?"

"September, October, maybe later. They don't seem to be in a hurry. They're concentrating on maximum publicity for a while."

"You've got the money for the institute, though."

"Most of it. It would be worse if we'd just begun our fund-raising. Still, I'd rather all those people of goodwill wouldn't be reading in their newspapers for the next couple of months about money going down the drain at Midwestern U."

"Is that what you're worried about?"

"That's part of it. I suppose my job as director would be on the line if they decided the institute is a boondoggle."

"Not for you; no one would accuse you of enriching yourself."

"Glory and fame. Keeping my name visible."

Sabrina thought of Vernon Stern. "That's important for some people; it's never been for you."

"Tell that to the congressman."

They were silent again. Beyond the shaded porch the humid air hung from the sky like a faintly rippling curtain, making the street look like an old painting, faded with time. Sabrina stirred, turning her hand within Garth's. "I said something today about writing down what we do and think: that we should write it all down because without warning it could vanish."

"An unhappy thought. What we have won't vanish."

"I was thinking of our street, our solid, secure, comfortable street. And it really is . . . but it's also a place where bad things can happen.''

"Which we will face together. And vanquish." They heard the telephone. "Damn, where is Mrs. Thirkell when we need her? I'll be right back."

Sabrina gazed at the ripples of heat. *Bad things happen. But not as bad as if we weren't together, all of us, our family.*

Garth came back and refilled their glasses. "That was Claudia. Your Billy Koner doesn't waste time. He called Leglind, evidently before you'd even left the building, and Leglind has called Claudia to say that their interviews have shown that the irregularities at Midwestern are innocuous compared to those at other institutions and because his time is limited he will be dealing only with the most egregious cases; therefore, none of us will be called to testify."

"What an easily bought congressman he is."

Garth put his arm around her and kissed her. "You're wonderful; have I told you that recently? Of course that's the real issue: not whether we have to testify or not, but whether a congressman is for sale. Claudia is furious; so am I. It's bad enough that he's for sale, but the other half of it is that he's letting that newspaper story dribble off into silence, leaving the innuendos floating around with a life of their own. We're not going to let him get away with it."

She pulled back to look at him. "You're going to demand a retraction. But you don't have any leverage. Unless you're going to use Billy again, and I can't believe either one of you would do that."

"Of course not; aiding and abetting the purchase of a congressman? Not the kind of thing we're known for. No, we're going to Washington. The congressman needs to have a conversation instead of issuing decrees. Claudia's secretary is setting it up, probably sometime next week."

"Do you think the congressman wants a conversation?"

"No, but he's going to have one. It wouldn't be smart

to refuse to see the president of a major university and the director of its Institute for Genetic Engineering whom you have vaguely accused of malfeasance, if not fraud. Now, that would be a juicy story for the newspapers.''

''I'm glad you're going. Both of you. If we could put this whole thing behind us—''

''It would be a brushfire, not a conflagration. That's the idea. You know, it seems our lives are made up of brush-fires: little crises that could scorch a life, even burn holes in parts of it, but not do long-term damage, even though when we're in the middle it seems that they might.''

''We spend our time putting out fires? It sounds awful. And frenetic.''

''Call it problem-solving. It sounds better.''

They laughed quietly, then sat, relaxed, gazing at the street, drinking the ice-cold tea, their clasped hands a little sweaty, their bodies languid in the heat. ''We could go inside where it's cool,'' Garth said.

Sabrina shook her head. ''Not yet. I like the idea of sitting with my husband on a front-porch swing in the middle of the afternoon; it feels very peaceful and old-fashioned.''

''Like courting.'' They smiled and kissed lightly, then sat again in silence, watching cars pass and neighbors come and go and the smudged shadows of trees lengthen across the pavement. Then the summer camp buses pulled up at the corner and children ran from them, backpacks bulging, hands full of trophies and projects. Penny was one of the first, and she was sitting on the steps near Sabrina and Garth when Cliff dragged his feet up the walk, scowling.

''I didn't think you'd be home,'' he said to them.

Garth's eyebrows rose. ''That's our greeting?''

''Sorry. Hi. Why are you sitting out here? It's too hot.''

''It seemed like a good idea, for a while,'' Sabrina said. ''Did the heat get to you?''

Cliff squinted as he looked at her from under the thatch of hair falling over his forehead. ''Why?''

"You look pretty grim for someone who's just come from camp. I thought you liked it."

"It's okay."

"It was fantastic two days ago," Garth said.

Cliff shrugged, then shot a glance at Sabrina. He leaned against the step railing, kicking at small stones on the front walk.

"Lu Zhen was there," said Penny. "He said he came to watch Cliff play."

"I didn't think he ever took time off," Garth said. "But he did say he'd talk about soccer in China; has he been doing that, Cliff?"

"A few times."

"He said he finished his paper," Penny said. "Does that mean he's going back to China?"

"Soon," Garth replied. "He's finished his postdoctoral work with me, and he's said he'll go back as soon as his paper is accepted for publication."

"Did you send it to *Newsweek* or *Time* or *People* or what?" Penny asked.

Garth smiled. "None of the above. Papers like Lu's go to professional journals, in this case *Science*. But I haven't sent it in yet. I'll do it next week, after I go over it."

"Again?" Sabrina asked. "I thought it was finished."

"It probably is, but I've only read it in pieces; I haven't had time to read the whole thing, start to finish. If it hangs together as Lu's described it, it will be a major breakthrough, something to make us all very proud of him."

Cliff kicked a stone and banged his shin against the porch railing. "Fuck it!" he cried and sat down, rubbing his leg.

Sabrina met Garth's eyes. "Why don't you and Cliff go inside where it's cool?" she said. "Maybe you'll make us a pitcher of lemonade; we seem to be out of iced tea."

"Good idea. Come on, Cliff, let's resupply the family with cooling beverages. I'm sorry," he said to Sabrina in a low voice. "I got carried away. It *is* an amazing project, you know; I'll tell you about it later."

He kissed her and stood up. "Cliff?"

"Yeh." He slouched through the door as Garth held it, then followed his father into the kitchen. The air in the house was cool and dry, and spontaneously they grinned at each other as they felt it buoy them up. "*Crazy* to sit out there," Cliff said.

Garth took lemons from the refrigerator. "I'll cut and you squeeze. Okay?"

"Sure."

They worked in silence, Cliff pulling down on the juicer's handle with such vigor that lemon juice splashed on the counter and on his shirt. Garth made no comment. He finished slicing the lemons, then scooped sugar into a tall glass pitcher. In a few minutes Cliff poured lemon juice and water into the pitcher. Garth stirred with a long spoon. They stood side by side, gazing intently at the sugar dissolving in the pale yellow liquid and at the small bits of lemon swirling wildly, chased by Garth's spoon.

Cliff went to the freezer, filled his cupped hands at the ice maker, and dumped the cubes into the pitcher, splashing lemonade on the counter. He looked at Garth, waiting for comments about the messy counter, about the splashes on his shirt, about his unwashed hands putting ice in the lemonade.

"Let's sit in here," Garth said. "I imagine your mother and Penny will be along soon."

Cliff did not move. "I've got some stuff to do in my room."

"In a while. I want to talk to you. It's important, Cliff."

Cliff shrugged and walked to the couch. Garth took glasses and the lemonade pitcher and followed him. "I thought we'd talk about Lu Zhen, since he seems to be a sore point in our house."

"It doesn't matter."

"Why not?"

"You said he was going back."

"Of course he is; that's been the idea from the beginning."

306

"I mean, like next week or something."

"I'm pretty sure it won't be that soon. I think he'll wait to hear if his paper is accepted for publication, and that usually takes a few weeks."

"You said it would be faster this time."

"It may be; I hope it is. But what difference does it make, Cliff? Lu is a student of mine and a guest in this house and no more than that; why can't we talk about him and even have him to dinner without your behaving as if war's been declared?"

Cliff shrugged.

"Am I supposed to know what that means?"

"I don't like him!"

"Well, that's something we've all noticed. The question is, why?" Garth poured lemonade, letting a few ice cubes slip into each glass. He looked at the tight muscles of his son's face and the disconsolate look in his eyes, and he ached for him, twelve years old, trying to find his place in the world, afraid of losing the place he had and that, until recently, he had never doubted. "I'll tell you something about Lu," Garth said reflectively. "Most of the time he's afraid. Some of my students are driven by ambition, some by a desire to do good, a few by greed. Lu is driven by fear. Everyone at home seems to have laid the most appalling expectations on him; it's a little like a Brothers Grimm fairy tale where the prince is sent out to slay the dragon, defeat the trolls, find the treasure, win the princess and get back to the palace in time for dinner."

Cliff gave a reluctant laugh. "He could just tell them to leave him alone; he's not their slave."

"I don't think he can tell them that. The government is paying his tuition and his rent, and his parents scrape up whatever they can spare for his food and clothes. The point is, he's a good scientist driven by fear, and I'm his advisor, and I want to help him. But that has nothing to do with how I feel about my own son."

"Yeh, it does," Cliff said after a moment. " 'Cause you get all excited when things happen in the lab; you talk about lymphocytes and all that stuff like they're people, I mean, you know, like you think they're terrific, and him, too, and you sit and talk and use words I never heard of, and I'm not smart enough to do any of that and I never will be—"

"Hold on." Garth set down his glass and turned to face Cliff on the couch. Why haven't we ever had this talk? he wondered. Is there something wrong with me, have I been too absorbed in my work and, lately, with my wife, or do other fathers and sons go along the same way for years without talking about their feelings, taking love for granted and assuming everything is fine? "You don't know how smart you are or how smart you will be. You're still trying things out and discovering things about yourself. I expect you to do that for a lot of years. If you pointed to something tomorrow and said, 'That's the kind of person I am and that's what I want to do for the rest of my life,' I'd be disappointed. I don't want—"

"You'd be *disappointed?*"

"Very disappointed. I don't want you to be like Lu, Cliff; I want you to be young for a while and not lock yourself into a room that may not be right for you. Even if it is right, I don't want you to settle into it too soon. You know"—he sat back, looking at Cliff with a smile—"you already have more confidence in yourself than I had at your age, and you're more balanced. All I ever wanted was to be a scientist; I was absolutely convinced that nothing else was interesting or worth my time. Then, later, I realized how many empty spaces there were in my life and I started spending time on history and literature and art, and having a good time with them. You're ahead of me in that."

Cliff shook his head. "I'm no good in school."

"You're okay. You're not giving it your full attention yet. We don't know what kind of a student you'll be when you decide that school deserves as much attention as soccer. But there's no hurry; you're giving yourself a chance to try everything. I admire that."

"Admire . . ." Cliff's voice trailed off. He was eyeing his father as if weighing his seriousness.

"Because it means you're curious, open to new ideas, ready to take on the whole world. I'm trying to tell you, Cliff: that makes me prouder of you than anything, even winning at soccer. I'd always love you, but on top of that I admire you for the kind of person you are. And I like you. I like to be with you. I'm grateful for that. I think it's the most special blessing of all: to like our children as companions."

Cliff was staring at him intently. The muscles in his face had relaxed; the disconsolate look was gone. He was absorbed in everything Garth said, reorganizing the way he thought about their relationship. "What about Lu?"

"What about him?"

"Well, you could say all that about him: you like him and you like to be with him and he's like a companion 'cause he's smart and he can talk about the things you want to talk about . . ."

"Cliff, I have a son. I love you and I like you and you're the only son I want. You're one of my three favorite people in the whole world and I want to talk to you about whatever you're interested in and I want you to listen to me when I talk about whatever I'm interested in. That sounds like a good deal to me; in fact, it makes me feel pretty lucky whenever I think about it."

There was a long silence. "You don't care what grades I get?"

Garth smiled to himself at his son's pushing to find the boundaries of his father's love. "I'd rather you didn't fail any courses."

"But if I did?"

"I'd be sorry."

"Why?"

"Because I'm unhappy when you're unhappy and I think you would be: you don't like to fail at anything. And then it would mess up your soccer; they don't let you play, do they, if you fail a course?"

"Uh . . . no." He picked at a scab on his knuckle. "Mom said that stuff once; she said I was curious about the world and I could learn a lot if I tried."

"Well, sometimes if we hear something twice it's easier to believe it. Maybe you'll believe it now."

"But when I asked her to go to the principal, you know, tell him something for me, she wouldn't do it. She said it was my problem, like she didn't care."

"She didn't tell me that. *Was* it your problem?"

"Well, yeh, but, you know, she used to go to school and explain things . . ."

"And now she doesn't. Do you really think that means she doesn't care about you and love you? Or just that she thinks you're so smart and grown up you can handle a lot of things without your mother running interference for you?"

"I suppose."

"You suppose what?"

"That she thinks I could do it without her."

"And did you?"

Cliff nodded.

"It sounds to me as if your mother thinks you're pretty special, the way I do. Look, Cliff . . ." Garth put his arm around his son. "Why don't we relax around here? We've got a wonderful family, one of the best, and we live in a good house in a good town, and we have a lot of fun together. I guess if we looked for problems hard enough we'd find some, but why should we? Let the scientists look for problems; they thrive on them. All the scientists in the world would vanish in a cloud of bewilderment if suddenly there weren't any problems. But right here, in our house, in our family, I love you and your mother loves you and what we all ought to be doing is enjoying each other, not growling about *maybe*s and *what-if*s. What do you think?"

Cliff sighed. He was resting against his father, still picking at the scab on his knuckle. "Sounds okay to me. Are you going to invite him to dinner again?"

Frustration rose in Garth. Cliff felt it in the tension of his body and he shrank into himself.

"Much too hot," Sabrina said, coming in with Penny close behind her. "I do like being outside, but there's a limit, and we've passed it." She made a swift survey of Garth's arm around Cliff, and of their faces. "Did I miss something?"

"Cliff wondered if we'd be inviting Lu to dinner again," Garth said, his voice carefully neutral.

"Oh." Stubborn Cliff, Sabrina thought. A long talk with your father, a good one, it looks like, but everything you heard will have to be absorbed over time, and meanwhile you have to push and prod, at least once more. "Well, I'm sure we will," she said matter-of-factly. "We'll probably have a farewell dinner for him when he's ready to go back to China. We always do that for visitors, don't we?"

She smiled at Cliff. "We'll have to be very nice to him, so he'll know we wish him all the success he's hoping for." She poured lemonade for herself and Penny and decided to do a little pushing and prodding of her own. "I think you might be especially nice to him, Cliff, since you haven't been in the past."

Cliff scowled.

"You're a host here, too, you know; this is your house as much as ours, and hosts have responsibilities to their guests."

"Yeh, but—"

"And it's always a good idea to be extra nice to someone when you're pretty sure you won't ever see him again."

"Oh." The scowl faded. "Well, yeah. Sure."

The back door opened and Mrs. Thirkell came in, struggling with shopping bags. "Cliff, could you—"

"Sure." He jumped up. His face was bright. He pried two bags from her grasp. "How come you don't drive? It'd be a lot easier."

"Because in this country you drive on the wrong side of

the street and it's unnatural and I want no part of it." The telephone rang and she swooped down on it. "Put everything on the counter, Cliff, if you please."

Garth stood and put his arm around Sabrina. "Thank you. Maybe, between the two of us, we've taken care of it."

"Mommy," Penny said, "did you forget? You were going to ask Daddy about the party tonight."

"Party?" Garth asked.

"Penny's been invited to Carla Shelton's house and she doesn't know who else is going."

"Shelton? Is that a new name? I haven't heard it."

"They're new in town."

"It's Carla's birthday," Penny said. "Can I go? She lives in that big house that we walked past, the huge one that was for sale for such a long time."

"But you don't know who's been invited, Penny, and we talked about that, remember?"

"My lady," Mrs. Thirkell said, "Princess Alexandra is on the telephone."

Sabrina looked at her uncomprehendingly. Alexandra?

I am standing in a kitchen in Evanston, Illinois, talking to my molecular-scientist husband and our eleven-year-old daughter about a party that perhaps she shouldn't go to, while our twelve-year-old son unloads groceries. What place does Princess Alexandra Martova have here, even on the telephone?

"My lady?"

"Yes. Thank you, Mrs. Thirkell." She took the telephone into the breakfast room. "Alexandra? Where are you?"

"Chicago, the Fairchild. Honey, I know this is unforgivable, but we're just here overnight, and would you and your husband come down and have dinner with me? Antonio's doing business from now to midnight and I'd love to see you. I didn't know we'd be here; we were flying from London to somewhere—Detroit? Pittsburgh?—where Antonio had people to see, and all of a sudden he told our pilot to go to Chicago instead. So I thought . . . You know, I miss Sabrina, and I thought how nice it would be to be with you for a while. Do you mind my saying that?''

''No.'' Sabrina closed her eyes and for a moment was Sabrina Longworth again, in London, talking to Alexandra about plans to go to a restaurant that night, talking about the next party, the next country weekend, the next cruise . . . the next cruise, Max's yacht, a cruise off Monaco, an explosion . . .

''Honey? If you're too busy—''

''No, I'd like to see you. But why don't you come here? We'll have dinner and talk as long as we want.''

''At your house? But you don't live in Chicago.''

''I don't live in the next county, either. It's about twenty minutes by taxi. Or . . . don't tell me Antonio hasn't hired a limousine; that was always the first thing—'' She stopped. *Why do I do that? I slip back so easily; you'd think by now . . .*

''It is amazing to me,'' Alexandra said into the silence, ''the little things Sabrina told you about us. Yes, we've got a limo, and I'd love to come to your house. Eight o'clock?''

Sabrina smiled, thinking how long it had been since eight o'clock was the earliest anyone would consider having dinner. ''Fine. I'll see you then.''

''*Mommy*,'' Penny said. She had come into the breakfast room. ''Can I go? Barbara's going.''

Sabrina switched her attention. ''You didn't tell me that before.''

''I forgot.''

Garth had joined them and he and Sabrina exchanged a glance. ''It sounds all right,'' he said. ''Vivian wouldn't let Barbara go if she was worried.''

Sabrina nodded slowly. ''Ten o'clock, Penny.''

''*Ten o'clock!* Mommy, it's Friday night!''

''You're right. Ten-thirty.''

''Mommy!''

313

"That's the deadline, Penny, and you know it. When you're twelve you can add half an hour."

"Barbara has till midnight."

"I don't believe it."

"Well . . . when she's home and they're having a party . . ."

"But when she goes out?"

"Ten-thirty," Penny said reluctantly, then impulsively threw her arms around Sabrina. "It's okay, I don't mind. Can I wear my new dress?"

"Yes, but it needs hemming. Ask Mrs. Thirkell."

Penny ran to Mrs. Thirkell and Garth and Sabrina turned to each other. "You're wonderful with her," Garth said. "She wants restraints—they all do, really, especially and mostly the indulged ones—and somehow you've always known that."

Always. Since September. At first it was easy to be strict because it's always easier with another woman's children, but then it was because they were mine and I worried about them and feared for them and, mostly, loved them.

"I love her. I love Cliff. I love you." She put her arms around him and kissed him.

"What did Alexandra want?"

"An evening of talk. She's coming to dinner—at eight o'clock, which shows that she has no children. I can't imagine her in this house, but it seems she wants to reminisce. You don't have to stay and listen."

"I thought I'd go to my office. It would be a quiet time to go over Lu's paper. Would you mind?"

"Of course not. Can you pick up Penny at ten-thirty, or be home so I can?"

"I'll pick her up."

They kissed again and stood in each other's arms as the sun streamed into the breakfast room and the bright voices of their children danced around Mrs. Thirkell's directions and words of advice. My home, my place, my love, Sabrina thought. The thought was sharper because she had slipped into her London self as soon as she heard Alexandra's voice, and for a moment it had seemed as if she held both lives in her hands and then, without hesitation or regret, had opened the London hand and let that life slip away.

"No, I won't live there ever," she said to Alexandra that night. They were alone in the library, a pot of coffee and the last of Mrs. Thirkell's apple pie on the table before them. "That was Sabrina Longworth's life, and my life is here."

Alexandra contemplated her. "You look gorgeous; night and day from the way you looked in London last time I saw you. Of course that was a ghastly time, that funeral, and then everybody gorging themselves at her house as if they were afraid they might never eat again . . ."

"Or be alive," Sabrina said quietly. "People eat after funerals to convince themselves they're still alive and healthy, everything functioning, death unthinkable."

"God, you sound just like her; that's something she'd say, in just that voice." Alexandra tilted her head and studied her. "You look like her and you don't. After the funeral, when the hordes were descending on the food, I kept watching you, and I thought I was crazy because I was sure you were Sabrina. I would have laid bets on it. But now I wouldn't be so sure. You're . . . oh, I don't know . . . softer than Sabrina was. No, that's not it. Quieter, not as much on edge."

"Happier, maybe."

"Oh, I don't know. Sabrina had some worries—didn't we all—but she was pretty happy, you know; we had a good time."

"I know." Sabrina smiled at her, glad to be with her. She was tall and willowy, with light blue eyes that turned up at the corners and pale blond hair falling sleekly down her back. She wore cream-colored silk pants and a matching short-sleeved blouse, and emeralds and diamonds at her neck and ears and wrists. Sabrina pictured herself in her French cotton sundress, with a Katherine Hayward amber necklace and earrings, and ballet slippers on her bare feet, and knew she was as perfectly dressed as Alexandra, but she also knew that she had lost the sleekness that radiated from Alexandra: a final polish that had been part of her London life when she was always on display. And I don't miss it, she thought, smiling at Alexandra. "You look perfect. Are you as happy as you look?"

"Honey, I find this hard to believe, but I am. I like building towns in Brazil; it's the first time in my life I've really felt useful. And I've fallen in love with Antonio, which is a good thing to do with your husband. I have Sabrina to thank for that; he learned a lot from her before she sent him packing."

"Antonio learned . . . ?" Sabrina was amazed; he had seemed impervious to any influences when she knew him. But it was Stephanie who broke with him, and she must have done it with a kind of innocent finality that Sabrina never had been able to muster. "What did he learn?"

"That other people, even women, have their own ideas and their own agendas that are as legitimate as his. I don't mean it's a heartfelt belief all the time, only sporadically, so I need to remind him, but he's doing better, and I've never had as much fun as I'm having now. I wish Sabrina could have known."

"She would have been glad for both of you."

"So what are you going to do about London? I thought you'd merged your shops, there and here."

"I did, but it isn't what I really want. It's incredible how much energy a house and a family take—"

"You're just finding that out? How old are your kids?"

"Eleven and twelve. No, of course I knew it, but everything doubled or tripled when I tried to juggle all of it with London. And when I thought about it, I realized I didn't want to be a juggler."

"No, I see that. Sabrina would have tried it; she probably could have made it work. But you're more focused here; you're really wrapped up in all this. I'm sorry Garth couldn't stay tonight; I like his looks. Smart and sexy, and, my God, the way he looks at you . . . every woman's dream. And I thought we'd have your kids, too; are your nights always this quiet?''

Sabrina laughed. "Hardly. Penny's at a party; Cliff is upstairs with a friend, playing computer games.''

"And Garth's at work.''

"He thought we'd like some time alone.''

"He was right, actually; I like this." There was a pause. "I have a question.''

"I thought so.''

"You *thought* so?''

"I thought there was a reason you came to Chicago. Straight from London.''

"You know, you're really unbelievable. Sabrina used to do that: just about read my mind. It's disconcerting, honey; it was then and it is now.''

"But you still have a question.''

"I do. Is Ambassadors for sale?''

"The only one who could have told you that is Sidney Jones, and I asked him not to tell anyone yet.''

"Well, some lawyers have generous hearts. I called him because I knew he was your solicitor and I told him it has been my lifelong dream to own Ambassadors and I would be crushed if you sold it—''

"Your lifelong dream?''

"A small exaggeration. I've been dreaming about it for the past couple of months. Honey, I could run it—I'm back and forth from Brazil all the time—and I want to do it. I want something of my own, apart from Antonio, and also . . . it would be like keeping Sabrina with me. I'll need some experts to help me until I learn a lot more than I know now, but London is crawling with experts. And wouldn't you rather sell to me than to a stranger?''

"Yes. I'd be very happy if you owned Ambassadors. The price is one million pounds.''

Alexandra burst into laughter. "You don't waste time,

do you? You even converted the money into pounds. That's without the inventory?''

"With the inventory."

"Then you're cheating yourself."

"I don't know the market in London these days. If you think I've cheated myself when you sell the pieces in the shop, send me half the purchase price. Then you're on your own."

"Honey, am I missing something? You've got it all thought out. Did you know I was going to do this? How could you?"

"I didn't know, but I think it's wonderful. You're right: I didn't want to sell to a stranger. I feel the same way about my house, but that probably—"

"Yes, Sidney told me about the house. I don't need it; I have my own and you made it so wonderful I wouldn't give it up. But I have some friends who are looking for a place; would you mind if I told them about it?"

Sabrina felt a moment of panic. It was all being taken from her. She had thought it would be a slow process, interviewing people, checking references, cataloguing inventory, all giving her time to let go slowly, to say farewell to what she had been. Now it was being snatched away from her and instinctively she put out a hand to hold it back.

But I don't want to. And as soon as she thought it, her panic was gone; her reluctance vanished. "That would be fine," she said. Her hand was still out and she put it on Alexandra's arm, and then they were holding each other, and both of them were thinking about Sabrina Longworth. "Thank you," she said at last. "I thought it would be so hard to do all that, cut the ties and turn my back on it . . . but this way it's almost like keeping it in the family. Do you think we could do all the paperwork by September? I'd like to have it done by my birthday."

"The nineteenth, right? Well, why not? Even lawyers ought to get through the paperwork in six weeks." She stood up and went to the small bar in the corner of the room and, as casually as if she were, in fact, a member of the family, she poured two glasses of port. "I'd like to drink to that."

"Yes. And to more visits. Would you come to Chicago again?"

"Honey, Antonio believes there are two places in the world: Brazil and Europe. Why don't you come to see me? I'm in Paris a lot; I'll be in London more than ever now; and we just bought a house in Provence, between Cavaillon and Gordes. You'd be welcome; you and your family. Oh, what a great idea! The kids would love it. Say you'll come. Not now; it's too hot. But in the fall . . ."

"I'll talk to Garth. He has to be at the Hague in October and we're going to be in Paris for a week after that, just the two of us. We might come to Provence for a couple of days; we'll talk about it."

The telephone rang and Sabrina looked at her watch in surprise. "Ten o'clock; maybe Penny wants to come home early. Excuse me."

When she answered it, Garth's voice was hurried, abstracted. "I have to stay later than I'd expected. Can you get Penny?"

"I don't like to leave Cliff alone."

"I thought Alexandra would still be there."

"Garth, what is it? What's wrong?"

"I'm not sure yet. I'll tell you about it when I get home."

"Is it Lu's paper?"

"It may be. *Is* Alexandra still there? Can she stay while you get Penny?"

"I'm sure she will. I'll take care of it, Garth. And I'll wait for you."

"I'll be home as soon as I can. I love you." Garth hung up and turned back to his desk, where the neatly printed pages of Lu's paper, with perfectly spaced paragraphs, formulas, and footnotes, were spread out before him.

Lu had been working for two years to find a way to produce mice with rheumatoid arthritis identical to that in humans so that scientists could rapidly test new treatments to alleviate and cure arthritis. To do this he had begun with a person who had rheumatoid arthritis, and isolated and removed genes that controlled the formation of joint tissue. Once the genes were isolated, he cloned them, collected fertilized mouse eggs and injected the cloned genes into the eggs, and then transferred the eggs to the oviduct of a foster mother mouse.

He went through the same procedure with the same person to isolate and remove genes that produced lymphocytes that attacked the joint tissue, causing arthritis. When he had two strains of mice with the two kinds of genes, he mated them. His theory was that their progeny would have rheumatoid arthritis identical to that of humans.

Garth had worked with Lu on his program of isolating and cloning the genes, and of producing two strains of mice that could be mated. They had celebrated together when Lu succeeded in producing a mouse with the gene that controlled the formation of human joint tissue. But after that Lu had withdrawn into the harder part of the project: producing a mouse with the gene with instructions for producing lymphocytes that would attack joint tissue.

And I was busy with the institute, Garth thought, hunched over the papers on his desk. And with my wife. And for a year I haven't paid enough attention.

He had thought from the beginning, two years earlier, that Lu would find it was not a single gene that controlled the development of lymphocytes, but two, perhaps more, which would complicate the project even further. But Lu had created his transgenic mice—mice with foreign genes—with a single gene controlling the development of joint tissue and a single gene controlling the development of lymphocytes. That was the reason Garth thought Lu had taken such a giant step forward.

But something nagged at him as he read the paper. He remembered other experiments with lymphocytes that had been ambiguous as to the number of genes involved; he recalled conversations with other researchers who said there had to be several genes, and papers that concluded there was much still to be learned.

But Lu's paper, elegantly constructed, said the issue was resolved.

Well, hallelujah, Garth had thought since Lu had told him. But beneath the celebrating, questions remained, and they became insistent in the silence of his office in the empty Molecular Biology Building at nine o'clock on a Friday night. And so, after reading the paper a third time, he reached for the telephone to call his friend Bill Farver. Seven o'clock in San Francisco, he thought; probably still at work. He called Farver's office at Farver Labs and found him there. "I thought you'd like to be the first to know that Lu Zhen says he's done it. I'm going over his paper now."

Farver's voice rumbled over the telephone, sounding as if he were in the next office. "Transgenic progeny with human rheumatoid arthritis? Garth, that's fantastic. Hats off; a hundred hats off. Of course I'm crushed; I don't like coming in second."

"How close are you?"

"Well, we're having trouble with the second gene for the lymphocytes; I don't know how long it'll be. I'd like to see Lu's paper; see how he did it."

Garth stared into the dark corners of his office. He and Farver had not talked about details; in a real sense they were competitors and only now, when he thought this part of the race was won, had Farver been so specific. "What have you tried?" he asked casually.

They compared notes on experimental techniques, Lu's and Farver's and others in Farver's lab, and then Farver said, "I just don't see how he did it, Garth. Two of my researchers swear there has to be a second gene, that there's no way you could end up with rheumatoid arthritis in a mouse with only one gene; you've got to have both. 'Course that's not the word of God from Jerusalem, but they've done a hell of a lot of work on this and I'm inclined to think they're right. Have you checked out Lu's work?''

Garth started to snap that of course he had; that that was his job as Lu's advisor and the director of his postdoctoral research project . . . but he got no further than opening his mouth. He hadn't checked out Lu's research as it progressed. He'd been busy, he'd trusted Lu, and he'd wanted him to succeed. ''I'll look at it again,'' he said.

''Your name is on Lu's paper, right? Have you sent it anywhere?''

''No. I wasn't ready.''

''Good thing. I always knew caution deserved more credit than we usually give it. Listen, let me know what you find, will you? If he's right, if we've missed something here, you could help get us back on track.''

''You'll hear from me. And, Bill, thanks. I appreciate your sharing all this.''

He gathered the pages of Lu's paper together and absently squared the corners. If Farver was right, the progeny of Lu's transgenic mice would be perfectly healthy: no sign of rheumatoid arthritis. Their parents would have had the gene for producing joint tissue, but they wouldn't have had two genes for lymphocytes. And therefore . . .

He left the light on in his office and walked through the building to Lu's laboratory. The mice slept or scampered or sat meditatively as he moved past them, reading the labels on their cages. When he found the ones he wanted, he drew blood from the tails of five of them and took the samples one floor down, to the testing lab. He glanced at his watch as he placed the test tubes in an agitator. Almost ten. He wouldn't be finished in time to get Penny. He called home from the telephone on the wall, gazing at the test tubes as he listened to Sabrina's voice and pictured the two women in the library, curled up on the couch, comparing lives, reminiscing.

''I'll take care of it, Garth. And I'll wait for you.''

''I'll be home as soon as I can,'' he said. ''I love you.'' His thoughts were on the test tubes, shining at him, light from the ceiling fixtures flashing off the glass and the bright red fluid as the agitator tilted the tubes up and down, like a playground seesaw.

He put the blood into the analyzer, then stood at the computer printer, waiting. A watched printer never prints, he thought, and strolled around the lab, stretching his neck, clenching and opening his fists. He did not come here often, though in his student days and the early days of his teaching at Columbia he had spent as much time analyzing blood as had all the other researchers. I'm getting away from the real work, he thought, and there isn't anything I can do about it. Not if I want to run an institute and advise students. And pay more attention to them than I've paid to Lu in the past year.

He heard the printer start up and he crossed the room to watch the paper roll from the machine. The columns of numbers printed out, one slow line at a time. And even before the printer stopped, even before he tore the page at its perforations to take it back to his office, Garth knew that the blood samples showed no sign of arthritis, or of any disease. The mice were healthy . . . and Lu's paper was a fraud.

CHAPTER *14*

_____

Stephanie heard a key turn, the front door open and close, the key locking it again, and she pictured Jacqueline walking into the coolness of the shop from the July heat on the cours Gambetta, adjusting a vase here, a lamp there as she approached the back room.

"Good morning, did you have a pleasant weekend?" Her voice seemed preoccupied. "Did you and Max do something exciting?" She opened a closet in the corner and exchanged her walking shoes for high heels. "You're very quiet, my dear. Is something bothering you?"

"Yes." *This is not between you and Jacqueline; it is between Jacqueline and me.* She heard Léon's voice, felt his arms around her in the cool forest clearing where they had made love. But it had been four days since then, with a weekend in between, and she could not stand it any longer; she had to talk to Jacqueline. Because it *is* between us, she thought, and she and Léon must have been together this weekend, and I can't go on pretending everything is the same, because nothing is.

"Well, then, we must talk about it." Jacqueline sat on

324

the edge of the table and reached out to put her arm around Stephanie.

"No, wait, please. I have to tell you . . . I thought, this weekend, you might have . . . you would have seen . . ."

"I was not here. I was in Paris from Friday afternoon to late last night. What would I have seen if I had been here?"

"Léon."

Jacqueline's body stilled, as if poised to listen, perhaps to flee. "So." Her voice was a murmur. "I did not guess it was you."

"What do you mean? You said you weren't here; you didn't talk to him."

"But he came to my house on Saturday and when he found I was gone he left flowers and a letter. I did not open the letter; it was late when I returned and I was tired and I left it for this evening. Because when a man leaves flowers and a letter, my dear, it means only one thing. Come now, don't hide your face; let me look at you."

Stephanie met her eyes. "I didn't know. And then he told me, but by then everything had changed."

"By then you were in love with him. And he with you, of course, since he has written me a letter." She smiled faintly. "Léon and I once promised each other we would not linger, half in and half out of the door, if we met someone else."

"I'm sorry, Jacqueline, please believe that. I wouldn't have—"

"Of course you would have. It is clear that this was meant to be; you could not have fought it without destroying yourself. You must not even think that you would have turned away from it; that would have been wrong. And what are you sorry for? Loving Léon? There is no better man anywhere; why would you be sorry you love him?"

"I'm not sorry I love him. I'm sorry that you must be hurt by it."

"Oh, well, hurt . . . we all are hurt now and then; otherwise we are dead. I am glad—" Her voice caught on the word, and she cleared her throat. "I am very glad for both of you, but for you especially, my dear Sabrina, because you are young and—"

"So are you!"

"Yes, but not as young as you. And not in so much need."

"We all need companionship and love, and someone to—" Stephanie broke into a nervous laugh. "Jacqueline, doesn't it seem to you that this is a very odd conversation?"

"Odd? I don't think so. I would say civilized."

"But neither of us has said anything about my husband."

"Well, no, but we are talking about you, what you need, which does not necessarily have anything to do with you and Max."

"But I'm *married*."

"But that is a problem only if you wish to marry someone else and have children. But I suppose . . . well, I suppose you do. Is that it?"

"We haven't talked about marrying or having children. It's just . . . loving him. Making love to him. Wanting to be with him even when I'm with Max, and I'm *married* to Max, I have responsibilities to him . . ."

"Oh, my dear, you sound like an American." Jacqueline paused. "Maybe you are; wouldn't that be a surprise? No, really, you can't be; no American speaks French as you do. But to have such ideas . . . Why can't you love someone besides your husband, especially when your marriage is not what you would like it to be? Are you being less kind to Max? Are you hurting him?"

"I will. Just as Léon hurt you."

Imperceptibly, Jacqueline's face became harder, almost masklike. And Stephanie understood that for the past few minutes she had been playing a part, conversing animatedly about Stephanie and Léon as if they were characters on a stage and she could analyze them, even help write their script while all the time staying apart, coolly interested but uninvolved.

But she was not uninvolved. *That is a problem only if you wish to marry someone else and have children.* She had not been able to say Léon's name. Stephanie saw how carefully she held herself, her back straight, her head high, as if she might shatter like a piece of rare porcelain if she let one muscle relax or one emotion burst to the surface. There was a desolate pride in that straight back and high head and Stephanie thought of how she would feel if Léon had written her a letter and sent flowers, and tears came to her eyes.

"Ah, you will not cry," Jacqueline said. "Neither of us will cry. Instead we—" There was a knock at the front door. Jacqueline and Stephanie exchanged a glance: they knew who it was, and for just a moment they were two women sharing a secret and, because of that, closer to each other than they could be to any man. But then it was gone. Jacqueline sighed. "I'll let him in." But Stephanie stood with her and they walked together into the showroom.

When the door swung open, Léon saw them both at the same time. "Good morning," Jacqueline said formally and stood aside.

He walked into the dimly lit shop and stopped beside a table where one of his smaller paintings stood on an easel. His voice was neutral as he greeted both of them. "It occurred to me," he said to Jacqueline, "that you might not have read my letter."

She smiled faintly. "How well you know me, Léon."

Stephanie winced. "I should leave. I'll be in back."

"I want you to stay," Jacqueline said. "We are all friends, isn't that so? And of course, Léon, you are right; I did not read the letter. I left it for tonight."

Léon looked at both of them. "It seems that by now it isn't necessary."

"Of course it is necessary. I will have it as a memento. In that sense it is far better than a conversation on a

327

Saturday morning, which would have left me only with echoes.''

"I called again on Sunday," he said quietly.

"My maid told me. That was very thoughtful, to make sure I had not come home early and faced Sunday afternoon alone, with only flowers and a letter. It was very like you; you have always been the most thoughtful—'' She took a few steps from them and stood with her back to them, one hand resting lightly on a gilded desk.

Stephanie started toward her, but Léon put his hand on her arm, and at that moment Jacqueline turned. The mask was gone from her face, but Stephanie thought she looked almost austere, her bones chiseled and sharply shadowed. There might have been tears in her eyes, but it was hard to tell in the dim light; they had forgotten to turn on the lights in the shop when they came to answer the front door. She contemplated Stephanie and Léon, who stood close together, his hand still on her arm. "How lovely you are together. You make each other more beautiful. That is a gift that love brings . . . and its mystery, of course. It is so special, that part: sharing and enjoying the mystery of each other."

She put her hands lightly on their arms, an embrace, a blessing. "I like knowing that you have found each other; I like being reminded that there are mysteries and discoveries always waiting for us." She kissed each of them on the cheek. "I love you both. I wish you much joy."

Stephanie breathed a sigh of gratitude and started to put her arms around Jacqueline, then hesitated.

"Oh, come," Jacqueline said. "We love each other, yes?"

"Yes. Oh, yes." They held each other. "I do love you. You've been so wonderful to talk to. I want you to be happy. I want you to have everything you want."

Jacqueline gave a small laugh. "So do I. And we still will talk, yes? As often as before. I would miss it if we did not."

"Yes." Stephanie concealed her doubt. She could talk

to Jacqueline about Max, but never about Léon. There are always compartments and hidden places, she thought, where we allow some people in and keep others out; our lives are tangled webs of secrets and deceptions.

A shudder ran through her. "What is it?" Jacqueline asked, feeling it in Stephanie's body, but before Stephanie could answer, another knock came at the front door, and they saw a face peering in.

"Oh, damn," Jacqueline said crossly. "Ten o'clock. Why can't people come late to do their shopping, the way they are always late for dinner parties?"

"I'll turn on the lights," Stephanie said, and went to the back room to flick on all the switches and bring the shop to life.

"And I will go to work," Léon said, joining her. "Are you all right? For a minute you looked faint."

"I'm fine. It was that feeling I've had before. But it goes away."

In a corner of the room they embraced and kissed, and Stephanie let herself flow into him, part of him as he was part of her. "I love you. I'm glad you came this morning."

He kissed her eyes and the corners of her mouth. "I adore you, I want you, I want to be inside you and next to you and across the table from you, and running through fields of lavender with you, and bicycling with you to every spring that is the source of every river, of life, of love . . . My God, I am running on like a drunken amateur poet. My love, we have many things to talk about."

"Yes." She was so happy she thought she could not contain it all inside her. "I'll call you, is that all right? I don't know when I can—"

"Yes, yes, call me. At my studio or at home. Anytime. Midnight, dawn, noon, I'll be awake, thinking about you, wanting you, most likely painting you. Call me. I love you."

Stephanie watched him walk through the shop. He stopped to speak briefly to Jacqueline and kiss her cheek, and then he was gone. She stayed where she was, giving herself another minute before going to work, holding on to his voice and his touch and the look in his eyes.

"Sabrina," Jacqueline called, her low voice carrying through the shop, "would you please bring the Terre d'Homme pitchers that came in this morning?"

And at that moment, Stephanie thought of Max, and her exhilaration vanished. I have to tell him, she thought. Tonight. Whatever Jacqueline says, what I'm doing is wrong, and I have to tell him . . . tell him I want to move out of his house, get a divorce, be free to . . . to do whatever I decide to do. *My love, we have many things to talk about*.

She carried the box of pitchers into the shop. Several customers were there, and then more came, and Stephanie thought of Max again only when she was driving out of Cavaillon and up the hill to their small enclave at the top. Her hands were tight on the wheel; she was rehearsing.

I'm sorry, Max; you gave me a life, but now I have to make my own.

I'm sorry, Max; I like you and I'm grateful to you, but I've fallen in love with—

I'm sorry, Max, but I think it's time I lived alone.

I'm sorry, Max; I don't want to hurt you, but I've met someone else and I have to be with—

I'm sorry, Max, but I can't live with you any longer because I don't love you and I think you're keeping things from me; you're not honest with me; I think you don't even want me to remember who I am, or anything about my past . . .

That was it, she thought as she drove into the garage. That was the reason she wanted to leave. She turned off the engine. It was all true, but it wasn't why she was leaving. She was leaving so she could be in Léon's bed, and spend her days and nights with him, and love him. She didn't love Max or trust him, and that had been true from the beginning, in the hospital, but she had stayed with him, because it had been secure. She felt a wave of despair. *I haven't grown up at all. I'm going from one safe haven to another, just the way I did when I went from my father to school to Garth.*

Garth.

The name echoed within her. Garth, Garth, Garth. Stephanie concentrated on it, trying to hold it still, trying to connect it to something else. But there was nothing; it meant nothing to her. Garth, Garth, Garth. Not a name she heard in Cavaillon; not an ordinary name. Was I married to him? Maybe I just lived with him. *Who was he? Who was I?*

"Damn it!" she cried, and hammered the steering wheel with her fists. One fist struck the horn and the sound blasted through the garage. In an instant the door opened and Madame Besset ran to her.

"Madame, madame, what is it?" She opened the car door. "Oh, how pale you are. You are ill, you have hurt yourself . . . Here, let me help you . . ."

"No, no, it's all right."

"It is not all right, madame, you are trembling. My God, what has happened? Come, take my arm . . ."

Stephanie held on to Madame Besset's ample arm and stepped out of the car. When she looked up, Max was there. "I'll take her, Madame Besset; please bring us something cold to drink." He put an arm around Stephanie's shoulders and led her into the house and into the living room, cool and shaded from the afternoon heat. "Sit down. Now tell me what happened."

"Max, who is Garth?"

"Garth? I have no idea."

"I never talked about him?"

"No. Does he have a last name?"

"I don't know."

"That's what happened in the car just now? You thought of a name?"

"Yes, and it was so clear . . . I never mentioned him? You're sure?"

"Sabrina, I've never heard that name. I would have

remembered if I had; it's not a common one. You think you knew someone named Garth? Have you any idea who it might have been?''

Stephanie searched his face. His arm was around her, and his eyes were close and steady. She knew he was telling the truth. Often she was not sure; there was a flicker in his eyes or a slight tightening of his mouth that she thought meant he was lying or hiding something, but now there was none of that. The name meant no more to him than it did to her.

''I think I was married to him. Or lived with him.''

''Impossible.''

''Why?''

''Because, my dear Sabrina, you would have told me. That much we did talk about.''

Madame Besset brought a tray with bottled water, a small ice bucket, and a bowl of fruit. ''Lunch is ready, monsieur, but I did not know if madame would be hungry.''

''Shall we have lunch?'' Max asked. ''I have something to talk to you about, but I won't until you feel ready.''

Stephanie felt a chill. ''Is something wrong?''

''Something might be, but it is manageable. Come; shall we have lunch?''

Subdued, Stephanie followed him onto the terrace, where the table had been moved to a corner shaded by a plane tree. They looked out on their small grove of cherry trees, stepping down the hill and, far below, the roofs of Cavaillon and the green valley beyond, shimmering in the heat. Climbing roses covered the wall behind them, white and pale pink, flickering with butterflies. ''Such a beautiful spot,'' Stephanie murmured.

Max served them from platters of cold sliced pheasant and marinated vegetables. ''There are thousands of beautiful spots in the world. So many places you haven't seen that I'd like to show you.''

''You mean you want to travel? Why? We haven't been here very long.'' Her eyes widened. ''Because of something that's gone wrong? You want to run away, is that it? Max, tell me what's happening."

He saw the fear in her eyes and backed off from what he had planned to say. She was already confused about this name that had popped up. And who the hell was Garth? Max Stuyvesant and Sabrina Longworth had moved in the same social circles in London and nowhere in those circles was there anyone named Garth. Well, probably someone from her childhood. He wondered if it was a good sign or a bad one that she would retrieve a memory from that far back. Did that mean less chance or more that she would remember everything? But it had been eight months; surely if amnesia lasted this long, it was unlikely—

"Max, tell me what is happening!"

"Nothing that you have to worry about." He filled their wineglasses and made his voice casual, almost indifferent. He'd have to prepare her: lay some groundwork. He could wait a couple of weeks before telling her they were leaving Cavaillon, and he would use that time to make sure everything was organized for him to operate from another place. "I told you, I can manage it. We don't have to talk about it today; it can wait."

"What can wait?"

"Talking about what we're going to do. It's not urgent; I want you to forget I said anything."

"I don't forget anymore. And if you're in trouble I should know about it."

"I'm not in trouble."

"You said something might be wrong."

"Well, it might be. But nothing has happened that you need to know about or worry about." He took her hand between his. "I'm touched by your concern. It means a great deal to me."

I've fallen in love with someone else. I'm leaving you.
She looked away, trying to find a way to begin.

You think, because I'm worried about you, I must love you. But I don't. I'm concerned because you've been good to me and I don't want you to be in danger, but I don't love you. I love someone else and I want to be with him, so I'm leaving you.

She could not say it. If Max was in trouble or in danger she would not walk out on him. And there had been something in his voice today that she had not heard before, something in his face she had not seen, just a flicker, but it was so startling to see even that tiny flare of anxiety in Max's eyes and to hear it in his voice that she could not say she was leaving, or even let him know that she was thinking about it.

But I can't share his bed and go on as his wife . . .

"I'll be away for a couple of weeks," he said as Stephanie remained silent. "I hate to leave you, but I have to see some of my people in a few places and I'll be on the move the whole time; otherwise I'd take you with me."

Relief swept through her and she looked down so he would not see it in her eyes. "Your export and import people?"

"Yes."

"And will they help you solve your problems?"

"I expect to have all the information I need after I talk to them. You'll be all right, won't you? You have Madame Besset and you seem to be close to Jacqueline; and you can finish the house while I'm gone. Surprise me. You can give me a tour when I get back."

Two weeks, Stephanie thought; two whole weeks. He'll work out whatever is wrong, and when he comes back, I'll tell him I'm leaving. And in the meantime I'll find a place to live. Because I have to do that. I'll be with Léon, but I have to be by myself, too.

Maybe, if I'm alone, I can concentrate and put things together and remember. Laura. Mrs. Thirkell. Penny. Garth.

She repeated the names to herself. They meant nothing. No faces came with them, no voices or conversations, no clasping of hands or sharing of smiles. Laura. Mrs. Thirkell. Penny. Garth.

Nothing.

But I will remember, she thought. Robert thinks I will; Léon thinks I will. One day it will all come back.

"—worried about my being gone?" Max was asking. "If you're really upset I can try to break it into shorter trips and be home in between."

"No, I'm not worried; I'll be fine. And I will finish the house; I think I can do it in two weeks. I need to find curtains for the bedroom; I think sailcloth . . ." And they talked about the house, and the orders Max wanted her to give the maintenance man and the gardener, and how she should forward his mail to the Marseilles office, and a dozen other topics, and buried in their conversation was the fact that both of them had decided that day not to tell the other what was most urgent to each of them. And in protecting each other by keeping silent, they were perhaps closer than at any time since Stephanie had awakened in the hospital and Max had told her he was her husband.

Stephanie held that closeness to her when he left the next day. He had bent over the bed to kiss her goodbye before the sky was fully light, telling her he loved her and would miss her and would call every evening. "Take care of yourself," she had said, and when he saw the worry in her eyes, he bent down and kissed her again, and then took his suitcase and was gone.

Stephanie and Madame Besset conferred on what they would need in the house for the next two weeks, she gave Max's instructions to the maintenance man and the gardener, and then she went to work early, and when the telephone rang she picked it up on the first ring.

"May I see you this afternoon?" Léon asked.

"Yes."

"I'll be outside at one. Or earlier, if you can."

"No, Jacqueline expects me to work until one."

And exactly at one he was outside the shop in his small car. "I want you to see my studio. And I've prepared a feast for you. Will you come with me or follow me in your car?"

"I'll follow you."

"How much time do we have?"

"As much as we want."

"As much . . . Max is away?"

"Yes."

He touched her hand, then waited while she went to her car, and in a few minutes they had left Cavaillon behind. They drove on narrow, curving roads past neat fields of melon and potato plants and stubby grapevines sprouting new leaves; past stretches of pale green wild grass slashed by brilliant swaths of orange-red poppies. Here and there painters wearing broad-brimmed straw hats sat in folding chairs before large canvases. Their arms were stretched straight out, extended by brushes that swirled, dabbed, swooped across the canvas to create visions of vivid poppies against a backdrop of green-black trees that marked the corners of farmers' fields and, on the horizon, the softly rounded hills and terra-cotta hill towns of the Vaucluse.

Oh, it is so beautiful, Stephanie thought, as if she had never seen the valley before. In the stillness of the fields that drowsed beneath a blue-white summer sky she felt herself moving soundlessly, without volition, dreamlike, suspended above the earth. The landscape floated past her, and the heat and molten light and piercing color of the poppies were inside her and enveloping her at the same time. She was part of everything, she took everything into her, and as she watched the back of Léon's head as he drove, she felt how wonderful and wondrous it was to be alive.

Léon turned onto a road that climbed above the valley floor, and she recognized the way to Goult, where she and Max had had dinner. But before they reached the center of the tiny medieval town, Léon turned onto an even narrower road and then, sharply, into a driveway barely wide enough for the car, walled on both sides by an impenetrable mass of trees and bushes and vines.

Once inside the wild tangle of that natural wall, Stephanie drew in her breath at the riot of color in flower gardens that seemed to have sprung up naturally but were in fact planned by an artist for harmony and scale. And tucked among them were small patches of herbs, vegetables, and salad greens: tall spires of frisée, feathery mizuna, white-flowered arugula, red oak leaf, pea vines, fronds of fennel. Sectioned by flagstone walks, the gardens filled every inch between the roadside hedge and the house.

Stephanie parked behind Léon and stood beside him, looking up at the house. It was built of rough-hewn weathered stone and was perfectly square, two stories high, with windows evenly spaced and three chimneys in the sloping tile roof. A child's drawing, Stephanie thought with amusement, and wondered briefly where she had seen a child's drawing of a house. But she let it go as Léon took her hand and led her to the heavy wooden door. "The studio is in back, but I want you to see the house first."

They walked into a central hall that cut through the house to the back door. Square, high-ceilinged rooms opened off either side of the hall, with polished stone floors, fringed Moroccan rugs, and couches and chairs of leather or intricately patterned wool. Huge paintings hung on the walls, abstracts by Tàpies and Rothko, a great blue horse by Rothenberg, drawings by de Kooning and Morisot. "My favorites," Léon said. "I don't hang my own work in my house."

They went through the back door to another building, a smaller version of the house, set amid more gardens and shaded by cypress trees. Léon unlocked the door and stood aside for Stephanie to go ahead of him. He stayed back, watching her as she stood in the center of the room beneath a twenty-foot ceiling. Under a hard bright light from a north-facing glass wall, there was color everywhere: canvases covered with an explosion of colors in slashing angles and flowing curves that spilled over into a confusion of paint-spattered chairs, tables, ladders, easels, high stools, and benches. Fluorescent fixtures hung from the ceiling, two potted tree geraniums covered with blooms stood near the window, a radio played Mozart, an armchair and daybed were covered with fabrics designed by Claire Goddard. Rolls of canvas stood in a corner near a coat tree missing an arm, a coffeepot stood on a small sink, and the tables were buried beneath books, thumbed and tattered magazines, pots of brushes and pencils, and stacks of sketch pads.

And on all the walls, tacked close together, were pictures of Stephanie.

Stunned, she turned in place, seeing herself repeated in charcoal sketches of a few swift lines, in washes of watercolor, in the bolder lines of crayon, in pencil, in pastel. She was sitting on the rocks at Fontaine-de-Vaucluse and in the forest at Saint-Saturnin; she was pensively drinking coffee at an outdoor café, lighting a lamp at Jacqueline en Provence, reading a book, daydreaming beside an open window. But most of the pictures were portraits, her face filling the canvas in full view, in profile, or turning away, the painter desperately trying to stop her before she escaped.

And always, in the curve of her mouth, the angle of her head, the shadow in her eyes, there was a sadness, a sense of loss underlying every other mood that Léon had caught. "Even when I smile," Stephanie said wonderingly, and looked back at him. "Is that true? It's always there?"

"So far. Sometimes more strongly than others."

Their eyes met across the studio and she wondered that he saw so deeply into her. He had not moved since she walked into the room and she realized how great was his capacity for stillness. She recalled it from their picnic at Saint-Saturnin: he settled into place, observing and reflecting, his imagination transforming what he saw, creating paintings in his mind so that, when he stood before a canvas, it was as if he played it all out, like a fisherman with his line.

"How do you see that in me? No one else sees it: Robert, Max, Jacqueline . . ."

"Perhaps I look more closely because I love you."

"But you see more than most people, in everything."

He smiled. "You're right; there's more to it than love." He closed the door and walked into the studio, absently picking up a tube of paint and replacing it in its rack. "The first law of painting—I'm sure writers would say the same thing about their work—is to take in everything unfiltered, without thinking about order or even meaning. The important thing is to concentrate and absorb. When we're young we hear only our own voice and we pay our most ardent attention to what touches us; many people never get beyond that, no matter how old they are. But anyone who wants to create must learn to see and hear more than the obvious and the personal. It's like sitting by a lake and suddenly seeing a trout break the water and leap up to catch an insect. When it leaps, you realize you've been seeing ripples all along—faint, but enough to let you know the trout was there. So you train your eye and you concentrate, and after a while, under calm surfaces you see other worlds, parallel to the visible one, and far more complex." He gave a rueful laugh. "I'm sorry; I'm sounding pompous."

"You sound like a man who thinks about what he does and understands it and loves it."

"In this case, with these drawings, I love you. I've been waking up at night and drawing you, and drawing you while I eat and walk in the woods, and when I'm supposed to be working on two paintings I've promised my gallery in Paris by the first of September. I found great joy in it, perhaps because I imagined you were thinking of me all those times I reached for chalk and pencil and paint."

"Yes."

Stephanie moved closer to the paintings and studied each one, walking slowly around the room. And suddenly she found herself before an oil painting, the only one in the collection, and it was of two of her.

"My two Sabrinas," Léon said, standing beside her.

In the painting, two women, identical except for their dress, faced each other, faintly smiling, so absorbed in each other that they had shut out the rest of the world. The light slanted across them at such an angle that one Sabrina was in sunlight while the other was in shadow.

Stephanie gazed at the painting for a long, silent time. She felt strangely happy, almost buoyant, held fast by the two women; she did not want to walk away from them. "It's very strange," she said at last. "I know I've seen this before. But that can't be, can it?"

"No. I painted it yesterday and last night. Perhaps you dreamed there were two of you? The Sabrina you can't remember and the Sabrina you are today?"

"I suppose . . . That must be it; what else could it be? Léon, I want to buy this. May I?"

"You will not buy it, what are you thinking? It's yours, all of these are yours. You need not ask; take what you wish."

"Thank you. Just this one. It makes me feel at home. That's where I'll hang it: in my own place."

"Your own place?"

Still looking at the painting, Stephanie said, "I'm going to find a place to live in Cavaillon. I can't live with Max anymore."

Léon drew in his breath. He turned her to him. "You're sure? You must not leave him because it is what I want."

"You didn't tell me you wanted it."

"No, of course not; how could I do that? I thought of it all weekend, but I knew it had to come from you. And you must be very sure, because you've lived with him and you feel loyal to him."

"But I don't want to spend my life with him. I want to spend it with you."

He studied her face, then sighed as if he had been holding his breath, and he kissed her, his mouth opening hers as his arms tightened. Stephanie felt their bodies fit together, shift and nestle in small adjustments until there was no space between them. She felt again the heat she had felt in the car, the dreamlike suspension, the brilliant colors exploding soundlessly around her. Heat and light and colors were all inside her and enclosing her; she was open to everything, part of the hugeness of life. Her arms were around Léon, her hand on the back of his head as they kissed, and suddenly a fleeting image came, of a white hospital room and a fog of nothingness. But it vanished as soon as it had come: there was no room for it in what surged through her now: the unfathomable vivid wonder of loving and of being alive.

"We could delay lunch," Léon murmured.

"Yes. Later."

They moved together to the daybed in the corner and lay on it and took off each other's clothes, Stephanie's gauze skirt over bare legs and her sheer cotton blouse with a deep V neck, and Léon's duck pants and short-sleeved shirt. "Thank God for summer," he said, "so little, and so easily removed."

Stephanie laughed with the joy of their bodies touching. This time, with hours before them, they explored each other, tasted each other, learned the outlines of each other's body. Léon's hands, a painter's hands, moved over her body as if he were discovering and revealing her at the same time. And Stephanie's hands, which had learned to identify the carvings of antique furniture and jewelry by touch as well as by sight, curved around the muscles and bones and hollows of Léon's body, memorizing him, making him hers.

In the wash of white light that poured through the glass wall, every angle of their bodies was accentuated, every pore, every fine hair, every pale vein that pulsed beneath their touch. "This is what I am doing when I draw you," Léon murmured, his mouth moving down Stephanie's body from her lips to her throat to her breasts. "I am kissing you and whispering to you and feeling the silk of your skin under my brush, and then"—he moved to lie on her—"I am inside you and you are pulling me deeper, making me one with you . . ."

A low laugh rippled in Stephanie's throat. "You can't do all that and go on drawing."

"No. Which is why I am not drawing now."

"I love you," Stephanie said, and touched his face. And then their bodies moved together and spoke for them, and they were silent.

Max and Robert sat in the small motorboat, sharing sandwiches and a thermos of coffee. They could not make out each other's face in the faint light from the distant shore, but they talked casually, like good friends. The intense heat of the early evening had eased, and they sat back, in shirtsleeves and chino pants, breathing deeply of the fresh sea air.

"Thank you for being here," Robert said. "I would have asked someone else, but my friend got sick so late, the time was getting short—"

"It's all right, Robert. You needed help and you knew I'd be here."

"But you were on your way home."

"I'll still go tonight; you know that. As soon as we've finished, we'll all drive back."

"It's not difficult, you know, but it always goes more smoothly with two. So I do thank you, and so will Jana when she gets here; it is a great favor to both of us. Sabrina will be glad to see you; this has been a long trip, has it not?"

"Two weeks."

"A long time away from her."

"Too long. It's the damnedest thing: I think I go a little crazy without her. After a few days it gets hard to eat and sleep. I don't understand it; I act like a smitten adolescent." He heard himself with surprise. It must be the darkness, he thought; otherwise I'd never have said that. But this is almost like talking to myself. And Robert is never judgmental. "Anyway, I won't leave her again. We may even go away."

"You mean take a trip? No, that was not in your voice. What did you mean, Max?"

Max considered telling him, then decided against it. He

had changed some of his plans and made new ones in the two weeks just ended, so it was impossible that Denton or anyone else would know them, but still, the fewer who had any information at all—even including Robert—the safer he would feel. "I meant a trip. We haven't traveled together. Is that the freighter?"

"Ah. Yes. On time."

They watched through binoculars as the freighter from Chile made its slow way toward them. "Five minutes," Robert said. "Ten at the most."

Max heard the tremor in his voice. "Why are you nervous? You just said it wasn't difficult. And you've done it often enough; it ought to be as simple as a game of croquet."

"My friend, croquet is filled with snares for the unwary."

"But you're not unwary."

"No. And I'm not usually this nervous. I suppose it's because she's so small, almost like a child, and so I think of her as a child, as vulnerable as a child."

"Robert, she's been teaching peasants how to fight for their rights in a country that tears people like her to pieces; she wanted to go there and you wouldn't have sent her if you'd thought she was as vulnerable as a child."

"I know. But still, so small, in such a harsh world . . ."

"Which she thinks she can make better."

"She is making it better. She knows that; they all do, all the young people who go off so bravely to wherever there is injustice. They all come from privileged families; have I told you that? They are wealthy, well educated, accustomed to luxury and the indulgences of a world that admires and rewards wealth more than poverty. But they find their way to me because they need something more, something they can point to and say, 'I did this and in my own small way I made the world a better place.' "

Max was silent, thinking of his life: smuggling and amassing wealth. The boat rocked gently; the freighter was almost up to them. Robert leaned down and lit a lantern, shading it with his cap.

"And that is why you help me, my friend. So that you can say in the cold hours before dawn when all of us are most anxious about ourselves, 'I did this and it helped Robert, who helps many others; in my own small way, I made the world a better place.' And now we must signal." He looked back for a moment. "We're lined up with the last dock?"

"We're exactly where you wanted to be."

"Then she will know where to look."

He balanced the lantern on the gunwale of the boat and slid his cap across it and away, four times, then waited a moment and did it twice again. He and Max stowed the thermos and unfolded a large blanket. Robert repeated the signal with the lantern three times, and then they waited.

This was the first time Max had come with Robert to pick up one of the fugitives, though he knew of many of them, since they often hid in a Lacoste et fils crate when a piece of equipment was being returned to Marseilles. Max's people fitted the crate with a small amount of food and water, and evacuation bags, and when the freighter was at sea a bribed crew member would open it. Freighters always carried thirty or forty passengers—travelers willing to forgo the comforts of a regular sailing ship for a bargain price and whatever romance they found in traveling on a working freighter and eating with the captain and crew—and Robert's young people, staying quietly in the background, blended unobtrusively with them until, approaching France, it was time to rendezvous with Robert in his small boat.

But this night, as Robert handed Max the binoculars and then took them back to focus on the freighter, no figure slipped over the side; no one swam to them to be hauled into their boat and wrapped in the large blanket. Max took the binoculars from Robert, and when the freighter slid silently past and he turned to watch it, he saw uniformed men on the dock. "Something's wrong. We're going in."

"A few more minutes." Robert's voice trembled. "Give her a few more minutes."

Max started the engine and kept it at a low idle while the freighter docked. He was furious. He was the one who bore all the risk: his company, his shipment, himself. "You're sure she left Chile?"

"I'm sure. I had a telephone call. You're right, Max, we must go in. My friend, don't be so angry yet. She may be hidden."

"She damned well better be." He revved the engine and swung the boat around. "What the hell made you think you could trust a girl to do something like this?"

"Max, she is a woman, not a girl, and of course I trust her. You yourself said she has been living a life of danger in a country where they tear people like her to pieces. Why should she not be successful as a stowaway?"

Max did not answer. They docked at the Lacoste et fils warehouse, and from there they went to a bar near the docked freighter. It was jammed with crews from freighters up and down the Marseilles dock, the air thick with cigarette smoke, the noise deafening. Robert, less noticeable and memorable than Max, slipped through the crowd, listening, asking questions. He returned to Max, who had bought two beers, and they found a place to lean against the wall. "Customs. They'll make a special search of the cargo. They choose at random; they chose this one. We have to—"

"They just happened to choose this one the night your girl is on board? How do we know they weren't tipped off?"

"We don't. But it would have had to come from Chile—"

"Or whomever they bribed on board."

"Yes, but then they would be looking for a stowaway, and the police would be here. All they're talking about is a routine customs check. Well, not routine, but a more thorough one, and they do those often. At random. We have to think about—"

"Fuck it," Max muttered.

"Max, this is not like you. You knew there was a risk; there's always been a risk, every time you've helped us bring someone out or in. Why is this night different from all other nights?"

"I don't know."

But he did. He felt things were closing in. For the first time he wondered if going to Los Angeles was realistic, or Rio, or Buenos Aires, or anywhere else. Since October he had behaved as if he was living a normal life, married, working, relaxing in short car trips around Provence. Not hiding, not on the run. But it was all pretense. Nothing about his life was normal. He was not married, he was in hiding, and soon he would be on the run. He had brushed all that aside because he wanted what he wanted, and he had ignored reality. *Like a smitten adolescent.*

Christ, he thought, I've got to get out of here.

And he meant all of it: Marseilles, Cavaillon, France, Europe.

While there was still time.

"We have to think about Jana," Robert said. "But we have to know what they're planning. I'll be back."

He made his way toward the bar again while Max stayed where he was, jostled by the crowd, watching through the swirling haze of smoke until two customs officers pushed into the room and fought their way to the bar. Robert stood near them, then motioned to Max to meet him outside.

"They're searching the cargo tomorrow; all they did tonight was stay with it until it was unloaded and locked in their warehouse. Max, she's in there, I know it. If we can get her out, no one will know. But of course the warehouse will be locked . . . and guarded." He turned to look down the dock. "Do you know which one it is?"

"At the end. No, the other end, the farthest from mine. One entrance and one guard. We'd have to take care of him."

Their eyes met. "I'll do that," Robert said. "But first I need the key to your car."

Max gave it to him. "I'll wait here."

He walked around the corner and leaned against the wall, away from the entrance to the bar. When Robert returned, dressed in his cassock, his hair and beard neatly combed, Max's eyebrows rose. "This requires prayer?"

"My friend, prayer and clothing have nothing to do with each other. I have been praying since Jana failed to appear. But what I am going to do requires trust, and this garb inspires trust, even though, sadly, in this case it will be misplaced. Now, you will leave the guard to me and I will tell you when we are ready for the next step."

Max put his hand on Robert's arm. "You'll be careful."

"I try always to be careful. Thank you, Max, for your concern."

They walked the length of the dock to a row of darkened warehouses, each with a lighted window beside the entrance. Robert went to the window, leaving Max behind. He pulled a bottle of cognac from beneath his cassock, took a drink, then struck the window with his knuckles and let himself fall just below it, flinging himself against the building.

The door swung wide and the guard stood in the opening. "Who's there?" He was short, with a broad chest and shoulders, hugely muscled arms and a paunch that hung over a wide belt. "What the hell . . . Father? Father, you shouldn't be here."

"Just celebrating," Robert said thickly. "Nothing wrong; just a little tired after all the celebrating." He grinned at the guard. "Getting transferred to Paris."

"Paris," the guard snorted. "That's no reason to celebrate. Full of fags and weaklings, and they take you for everything you got. You know what's good for you, you'll stay here."

"Well, but I have to go." Robert struggled to sit up, and held out the bottle. "Have a drink in my honor, even if you don't like Paris."

"Can't, Father, I'm working."

"Just one, to wish me well. Now you've got me worried about how I'll get along there."

"Well, one . . . what the hell." He took a swig from the bottle and wiped his mouth with the back of his hand. "But that was to you, Father; not to Paris or anywhere but Marseilles."

"Then we should drink to Marseilles. A great city."

"Well, why not?"

Another bottle appeared from beneath Robert's cassock. The two men sat together beneath the illuminated window, drinking to the guard's wife, to his four sons and three daughters, to his brothers and sisters, to his grandfather who worked in an olive oil cooperative, and then to the olive oil cooperative. Robert was faking it with small sips but still he thought perhaps he could not hold out against the guard, until at last he saw the guard's head nod, jerk up, nod again, and at last stay down, his chin on his chest, gentle snores lifting the edge of his undershirt.

Robert walked to the corner of the warehouse, and Max joined him. "That gentleman has a capacity of truly staggering proportions. He has a key ring but I don't think we can get it off his belt."

"Then we'll take the belt. But first bring him inside."

They dragged the guard into his room, then unfastened his belt and pulled it through his pants loops. He snorted as they took off the key ring and the keys clattered together.

Max bent over him. "Sound asleep. How much did he drink?"

"Just under one bottle."

"He'll have a good time explaining that tomorrow; more likely he'll fabricate a sudden attack of flu. Hold on while I check the logbook."

He ran down the columned entries in the book on the guard's desk until he found the shipment being returned to Lacoste et fils. "Fifth floor. We'll walk; I don't want to chance the elevator. And we'll move fast, Robert; I don't know how often someone comes to check on the guards."

He unlocked the warehouse door and they used the light from the guard's office to locate the stairway before locking the door behind them. Max jammed the key ring into his pants pocket and they made their way to the stairs. The staircase had windows at each landing, so they kept their flashlights off, guiding themselves in the blackness by keeping a hand on the wall. They climbed fast and steadily, counting five floors until they came to a steel door that Max eased open. "Ten minutes; less if possible." He was breathing hard and thought fleetingly that he was out of shape; he ought to ride a bicycle like Robert, whose breathing had barely changed.

The windowless floor was pitch black and they turned on their small flashlights. There was a sudden scratching, and then a scampering sound. Robert spun around. "Who is that? It may be—"

"It's not your girl. It's a rat. The warehouses are full of them. You start on the left; I'll go to the right. Hurry."

Narrow aisles stretched the length of the huge room between ghostly crates that loomed up in the narrow beams from their flashlights: crates as big as rooms and smaller ones stacked to the ceiling. Playing the flashlight beams on the shipper and destination stamped on each crate, they moved swiftly up and down the aisles, in dead silence. No sound penetrated from the dock below; the scampering had stopped. Max thought he might have suddenly gone deaf and he tapped his flashlight on a crate, for reassurance. Then, in the next aisle, he found his crate, and said, "Robert. Here. Quickly."

"Where are you?"

"Here." He shone the flashlight on the ceiling and Robert used the pinpoint of light as a guide to make his way up and down the aisles to him. "The crate is here; there's no sound from inside."

"She doesn't know your voice. She'd be very still. Keep talking. It helps me find you."

"Shall I recite poetry? Or tell tales from the Arabian Nights? Hurry, damn it; I want to get out of here."

"Max, I can't leap over these crates and fly to you."

"You haven't tried."

Robert chuckled. He felt very close to Max, their voices mingling in the darkness, danger hanging in the air. He turned a corner and saw Max holding his flashlight up to the ceiling, and he grinned, even knowing Max could not see him, because he had found him and they were together. "Thank you for the beacon. But what now? How do we open the crate?"

"With this." Max handed Robert his flashlight, took a chisel from his pocket, and began to pry open the side facing them.

Robert held the flashlight. "Do you remember the time I said I felt that we were two boys smoking behind the barn where the grown-ups couldn't find us?"

"How does it happen that a priest understands the rush one gets from danger? Most priests live unnaturally secluded lives; you're an anomaly, and even you—"

"There are more of us than you think, my friend, who believe that God looks kindly on action."

"But even you don't court danger; you simply do good."

"There is nothing simple about it. No, I don't court danger, Max, but I recognize its seductive nature. One could get hooked, as the young people say."

"Well, maybe you do court it; probably we all do. No game would seem worth the candle if it had no danger and we weren't sure that it had the potential to explode in our faces." He eased the heavy wood from the crate; it screeched faintly as it pulled away from its nails.

"Jana!" Robert exclaimed. He knelt as Max pulled the wood aside. "My dear, dear Jana!"

She was sitting between the wheels of the front-end loader, her knees to her chin, her arms around her legs. "Robert?" Her eyes, enormous in her small thin face, looked up at them blindly and Robert lowered his flashlight and reached in to help her out. She staggered a little, holding on to him. "I'm sorry; I've been here for a while."

"When did you hear about customs?"

"About six hours ago, and I got back in here right away; I thought I shouldn't wait."

"Very wise. Jana, this is my friend, Max Lacoste. We have him to thank for getting you here. Max, this is Jana Corley."

"We'll talk later," Max said impatiently. "Is anything left in here? Food? Water? Evacuation bags?"

"No. We cleaned it out on board. We thought they might have dogs."

"So if we hadn't found you . . ."

"I would have been very uncomfortable."

"Admirable." He made a swift survey of the interior of the crate, then took a hammer from his belt and hammered the crate shut. "Hurry." He led the way to the staircase and they ran down it in the darkness, their hands on the walls for guidance.

They had been in the warehouse for seven minutes.

Max locked the door and handed Robert the key ring. "You and Jana put it on him; I'll watch at the corner." He was breathing hard again; his legs felt rubbery. *Damn it, I'm in lousy shape.* He looked to left and right along the empty stretch of dock. *I'll go with Sabrina on her bike rides; maybe go back to tennis. When we leave France, I'll get back in shape.*

Robert and Jana joined him and he led them around the corner of the warehouse to the street behind it, and then through an alley to another street, this one brightly lit, lined with bars, cafés and strip joints. Prostitutes stood at street corners, couples strolled, a family with a baby in a backpack stood debating where to eat. Music blared from open doors to the sidewalks where men sat at tables drinking beer, playing cards, bantering with passersby and with the prostitutes who wandered over for companionship, then drifted back to their corners.

"The car is this way," Max said, but Robert put a hand on his arm.

"Perhaps we could get Jana something to eat before we leave. It's a long ride to Cavaillon."

"I'd rather get started; it's after midnight. Jana, can you wait a couple of hours?"

He looked down at her. It had been dark in the warehouse but now they were standing beside the brightly lit window of a café. Customers on the other side of the glass were only a few inches from them, talking and gesticulating, but Jana was not looking at them; she was looking at Max and as their eyes met, he knew she recognized him.

They all come from privileged families; have I told you that?

Jana Corley, Max thought. Small, blond, thin, extremely pretty, with a tilt to her head and an easy walk that showed she had been brought up with wealth.

They are wealthy, well educated, accustomed to luxury and the indulgences of a world that admires and rewards wealth more than poverty.

In other words, she came from the social circles in which Max Stuyvesant had been visible and prominent. Corley, he thought again. He had met a Corley—Richard, Ramsay, Ralph, something like that. He owned factories in Manchester, Max remembered, and had a home somewhere outside London. They had met, he thought, once or twice at Olivia Chasson's garden parties. And Jana could have been there.

What were the chances that one of Robert's idealistic young people would know Max Stuyvesant and would be smuggled into France in one of Max's crates on the one night that Max was there?

Not one chance in a million.

Except that it had happened. Because such things did happen all the time. People marveled at such coincidences, but they shrugged them off, saying "Small world" . . . one more proof that life was strange.

And so Max Stuyvesant, with a new name and newly

bearded, his hair dyed since he had last been in London almost a year before, stood on a raucous harbor street in Marseilles at twelve-thirty in the morning in the middle of July, and looked into the eyes of a blond radical activist and knew that she knew him.

Jana's eyes widened as their look held. "What did you say your name was?" she asked.

"Max Lacoste." His large body was very still. He expects me to expose him, Jana thought. She felt the unreality of everything that was happening: she was tired and stiff and keyed up from the last twenty-four hours, and now she was talking to a man she had last seen drinking champagne at a garden party in Kent, a man who was allowing everyone to believe him dead. And now he expected her to expose him. But why would I? she thought. He's helping Robert, and Robert is the best man in the world and he probably knows what's going on with him a lot better than I do, and Robert says he got me out of Chile. I'm not going to mess up his story, whatever it is. What good would it do?

She held out her thin hand. "How do you do. It's because of you that I'm here?"

"It was my company's shipment."

"And it was your people who gave me food and water in Chile?"

"Yes."

"And you were here to open my prison. I do thank you. You must think very highly of Robert and of what he's doing."

"We are good friends," Robert said. "Jana, shall we get you something to eat?"

"No, thank you, Robert, but I can wait. How long is it to . . . where are we going?"

"To Cavaillon. You'll come home with me just for tonight; tomorrow you return to London. It's two hours to Cavaillon, probably less, with Max driving. But you should have something—"

"Robert, I'm fine."

"Just a minute." Max went into the café. He returned shortly and handed her a paper bag. "Ham sandwiches and coffee. You can eat in the car."

"Thank you." But he was walking ahead and she and Robert walked quickly to catch up to him.

In the car, she devoured a sandwich, drank the coffee, then curled up on the back seat and fell asleep. She woke only long enough to realize they were in Cavaillon, to see Max's long look as she said goodbye, and to feel Robert's hand under her arm as he helped her up some stairs and onto a couch already made up with sheets and a light blanket.

The next morning there was barely time to discuss her work as they drove to Avignon, where she would catch a plane for Paris and then London. "A vacation," Robert said. "We will not talk about any more work for you for a while. You were in Chile for eight months; that is a long stint."

"I just want to know what you're thinking of, for me."

"I'm not, not yet. There is time, Jana; don't you want to play for a little while? Don't you have a young man to see?"

"Yes, but—"

"Then for now that is what you should be doing." He kissed her on both cheeks and held her close. "I am so proud of you. And grateful; you keep my hope alive. Now go; you'll miss your plane. I'll call you in a few weeks."

He is so good, Jana thought, and that was what she told Alan that night, when they were in his bed in London. "He doesn't want anything for himself; he just wants people to be happy. And to see justice done."

"I'll bet he gets a kick out of it, though," Alan said lazily. He lay beside her, his head propped on his arm, stroking her body. "God, you're thin. It looks as if you haven't eaten for eight months."

"I ate what the peasants ate. What does that mean: he gets a kick out of it?"

"Oh, cops and robbers, cowboys and Indians, bad guys

and good guys. It's a lot more exciting than sprinkling holy water."

"He does more than that; he runs a school."

"So it's more exciting than running a school."

"Well, of course it is. But he really thinks he can make the world better. For everybody, but especially for poor people."

"I know, you tell me that all the time. But everybody likes excitement, you know: danger or just a few thrills. You do, or you wouldn't go to those places. In fact, I want to talk to you about that."

No, Jana thought; not now. I like you, someday I might love you, but right now I don't want to get married; I don't want to stop what I'm doing. I'm only twenty-six; I'm not ready to settle down.

She cast about for something to change the subject. "Alan, do you remember Max Stuyvesant?"

"Sure; he was killed when his boat blew up. Last year, wasn't it?"

"Well, I'll tell you something if you promise to keep it to yourself."

"Whatever you want."

"No, I mean it, Alan; I think we should keep it a secret."

"Then you shouldn't tell me. I tend to talk."

"Do you? I never thought that. Well, then, I won't."

"I only do sometimes. For you I'd keep quiet. And now you've started; you have to finish it. Something to do with Max? A sly fellow, you know; he owned Westbridge. Remember that story?"

"Yes. Would you really keep it to yourself?"

"Word of honor on my titled ancestors' graves."

"You don't have titled ancestors."

"One of them was a duke, somewhere in there; I never paid much attention; it always seemed overrated to me. I mean, look at Denton Longworth, for God's sake; does he look like nobility to you?"

Jana laughed. "No, nothing like the fairy tales. Have you seen him lately?"

"Oh, here and there. We belong to the same club and you know how everybody goes to the same parties. They're all incredibly dull, I might add, when you're not around. Denton's all right, you know; he and Max were close friends."

"I didn't know that."

"Well, actually I didn't either, but he went ballistic when Max was killed. He kept after the police to find out if Max was really dead or not, kept saying Max wasn't the type to die, he had the luck of fifteen cats, that kind of thing, on and on. I never saw anybody as cut up as he was. Are you going to tell me the secret about old Max?"

"Well . . . I saw him in France."

"You mean his ghost? Come on, Jana, you don't believe in ghosts."

"I saw Max Stuyvesant. He isn't dead. He's alive and living in a little town called Cavaillon . . . well, actually, I'm not sure he lives there; he took Robert and me there and then drove off. But he must live around there, because when we left Marseilles he said he was going home, and he looks just the same except of course for his beard and I think he's dyed his hair. Wasn't it red?"

"With lots of gray," Alan said absently. "You're sure it was Max?"

"Of course I'm sure. I saw him at Olivia's a few times . . . in fact, the first time I saw him there was years ago, and Denton was there with Sabrina—you know, his wife? Before they were divorced. Anyway, I saw Max at Olivia's a few times, and then his picture was in the paper in all those stories about Westbridge. It's very strange—"

"Strange! It's crazy. Why would he let everybody think he's dead? Maybe he doesn't know who he is; maybe he lost his memory."

"No, he knew I recognized him. He was waiting for me to say something."

"Well, did you?"

"No. Alan, he was helping Robert; he got me out. I owed him something. And it was his company's crate that I was hiding in; if I'd been found, he could have been prosecuted."

"He could have wriggled out of it. Said he didn't know how you got in there."

"Still, it would have been hard for him. I mean, I'm sure his company is reputable and he isn't doing any smuggling like he did with Westbridge—"

"He smuggled you."

"That's different. That's doing good. For Robert."

"Well, that part's crazy, too, if you ask me. It doesn't sound like Max Stuyvesant, cozying up to a priest and helping him fight for the rights of poor people."

"Well, it was Max and he is doing good and that's why I didn't say anything. I mean, maybe he's trying to make up for what he did with Westbridge, so why not let him? I mean, I haven't any right to give him away, and I'm not going to. And neither are you."

"No, right, of course not. Except, you know, it isn't really fair to people who really care about him not to let them know—"

"Alan! You promised!"

"I know, but, you know, reporters . . . police . . . people like that shouldn't know. But what about his friends?"

"If he wanted them to know he would have told them himself."

"Well, it's hard to pick up the telephone and say, 'I say, old chap, this is Max Stuyvesant and I know you think I've been dead for lo these many months, but the fact is . . .' "

Jana was laughing, but she was uncomfortable. "You promised you'd keep it a secret."

He shrugged. "Whatever. Now, how about if we stop talking about Max? I haven't seen you in eight months and I think—"

"Yes," Jana said, and put her arms up to encircle his neck. "Yes, that would be lovely."

"And you'll stay with me through the weekend?"

"Till Monday. I told my parents I'd be home then."

"Oh, well, we can put it out of our minds, then. Monday is three whole days away."

And so it was not until the middle of the next week, when he went to his club, that Alan ran into Denton Longworth at the bar and told him, in absolute confidence, that he'd be pleased to hear that his good friend Max Stuyvesant was alive and well after all, and living in France, somewhere around Cavaillon.

CHAPTER *15*

*G*arth locked the blood samples from Lu Zhen's mice in the refrigerator in his office, locked the office and left the biology building, letting the door slam shut and lock behind him. Anger and pain propelled him across the campus; he was almost running, furious at Lu, furious at himself, and as hurt by the betrayal as if he had been dealt a body blow. The air was heavy and hot even now, at one in the morning, with no breeze from the lake to lighten it; the streetlights were softly smudged in the humidity and the trees seemed to droop and sleep. The campus was so quiet Garth's steps were loud on the paved walk. Lights burned in dormitory windows and he pictured students at Friday night parties or hunched over their desks or in armchairs, reading. Lu Zhen was behind one of those windows, perhaps writing to his family that his esteemed Professor Andersen would soon send his paper to a professional journal; that the years of study and sacrifice were about to culminate in widespread applause and a triumphant return to China.

Almost triumphant, Garth thought. Almost. The esteemed professor was careless, put his name on a fraud, and came close to sending it out for the world to see.

Lu should know. He pulled up in his headlong rush across the campus. *Why wait until tomorrow? I should tell him what I've found, that his paper won't be published, that he's through here.* He turned back toward the dormitories, but this time his steps dragged and soon he stopped again. He wanted to go home first; he wanted to talk to Sabrina.

He turned again and strode through the high Gothic gate at the corner of the campus and then past darkened houses through empty streets to his home. His house was not dark: the porch lights blazed and the curved windows of the upstairs bedroom shone for him. He let himself in the front door and took the stairs two at a time. Sabrina met him in the center of the room and put her arms around him and kissed him, and the tension in his body began to ease.

She smiled at him. "Coffee and cake in the library. Unless you want a drink."

"A drink and then coffee. Thank you, my love."

They walked downstairs, arms around each other. Garth felt her fine bones beneath her light silk robe, the smooth grace of her muscles as she moved, the strength of her body holding him, matching his steps. He was filled with the continuing wonder of it: that there was a door always open to him, lamps lit for him, and love to welcome him. "God, it's good to be here. I was so damned furious, and all I wanted was to talk to you about it."

In the library, he mixed Scotch and water and added ice. Sabrina had turned on a table lamp, and its soft light picked out the familiar shapes of furniture and books and stacks of magazines and journals on the tables and the floor, and Garth sighed, as if he had come to sanctuary. "Oh, what about Penny? Alexandra stayed while you picked her up?"

"Yes. I hope she had a good time; she didn't talk much. I'll ask her about it tomorrow." She poured coffee from a thermos and curled up in a corner of the couch. "Now tell me. What happened with Lu?"

"He faked his results. The experiment didn't work, but he wrote it up as if it had. Brilliantly conceived, beautifully constructed, and every word a lie."

"The experiment didn't work or he made mistakes in doing it?"

"It didn't work. It couldn't have." He gazed at her thoughtfully. "You don't seem surprised."

"I am surprised."

"But not shocked. You never did trust him, did you?"

"Not lately. But I wouldn't have guessed anything like this. I just thought he'd grab all the credit, use you to get ahead, that kind of thing."

"That kind of thing and a lot more is exactly what he did. And I should have caught it earlier. I'd been worried about his results off and on, but he had such confidence and I had confidence in *him* and I didn't watch closely enough. Then tonight I called Bill Farver and he told me they'd been having exactly the problems I'd been worried about. Lu knew about them—I'd mentioned them and he had to come up against them in his work—but he evidently brushed them aside. He could have called Bill or other biologists around the country to compare notes, but he was too damned arrogant—"

"Would they have told him? Isn't there a lot of competition in research?"

"Yes. You're right: they might not have told him. But if he'd asked, I could have called Bill a long time ago. I wasn't paying enough attention, I know that now, but all Lu had to do was ask me to find out what directions other researchers were going . . . he knows I would have done that. But he was so damn sure his way was the only way . . ."

"Or he was afraid."

There was a pause. "Could be, but I think more likely he was so convinced he'd found the answer that he was like a horse wearing blinders. Or maybe it was both: he was afraid and he isn't someone who lets himself question his own theories. But then, when the experiment failed . . .''

He stood and paced the length of the room. He felt Sabrina's eyes following him as he prowled. He loved that feeling of being in her sight, as if he were being held, caressed, encouraged to be himself without posturing, because she loved him as he was, and always would. An uncritical love, he thought, meeting her clear look, that made him far better than he would have been without it.

He moved restlessly back and forth, fingering objects on shelves and tables, skirting piles of books on the floor. "The damnedest thing is that he thought he could get away with it. He's working in one of the hottest fields in science today, along with hundreds of others, all of them ready to replicate experiments the minute they're published, to build on them and take the research even further. He knew that no one could replicate his experiment, because it didn't work, but he went ahead; he built an elegant structure over a rotten foundation, as if elegance were all that mattered. And I wasn't watching. I should have been meeting with him every week, forcing him to explain and defend every step of his experiment. But I trusted him. And I was careless.''

"I don't suppose," Sabrina said thoughtfully, "that this is the first time this has ever happened in scientific research.''

Garth gave a rueful laugh. "No, you're right; of course it's not the first time. Or the last: there are always people who will fake results if they're at a dead end. I've never understood how they can do it, any more than I can understand Lu, but I know they're out there. Some of them land on the front page of the *New York Times,* which is where I would have been if I'd sent in Lu's paper. And I wouldn't have been director of a genetics institute, here or anywhere else. I'd have been lucky to keep on teaching; Claudia would have been under a lot of pressure to get rid of me.''

He contemplated the dark fireplace, neatly swept for the summer. "I was so proud of him."

Sabrina heard the despair in his voice, and ached for him. "He gave you every reason to be proud. There was no way you could have known that he'd do this."

"But he lied about more than his work. He not only faked his research and put his career at risk, he put mine at risk as well, and that would have harmed all of us. All those nights he sat at our table, acting as if he liked being part of our family . . . that was another lie."

"He did like it." Sabrina went to him. "He missed his family, he liked being part of ours, and he likes all of us. He adores you, Garth; remember when I told you that? I've watched him looking at you and I know he loves you. It makes me wonder . . . are you sure he really knew all the implications of what he was doing?"

"He's been working with other scientists; he's very smart. He knew."

"But when you talk to him, you might try to find out what he was thinking, instead of straight out accusing him. He may not have thought it through. I just can't believe he'd purposely put you in danger."

Garth thought about it. "I don't know. Maybe. More likely he knew what he was doing and regretted it, but whatever he felt for me wasn't strong enough to overcome the pressures from his family and his government. Well, I'll know tomorrow morning." He took her in his arms. "Do you know, the only thing that cut through my anger tonight was knowing I could come home to you. No one else helps make my world as clear as you do. It's hard to keep believing that we can create order when things get messy, but somehow you do that for me; you help me believe it—"

As no one else has ever done. He thought that but could not say it, could never say it. He could never say that he and Stephanie had lost their way so long ago that for years they had been unable to make for each other, as he and

Sabrina had done, a place to belong and a sense of self that was fixed and solid in a shifting world.

"—and I keep wanting to thank you," he said, "to tell you what you give me each day, every day . . ."

"But you do the same for me. And it always seems new and wonderful and even surprising, and then I feel so grateful, because I'm where I want to be, and I'm with you, and I never want to be with anyone else, and it is so good to love you—"

His mouth met hers, and Sabrina closed her eyes as her arms curved around the familiar shape of his shoulders and his body fitted itself to hers. It was all familiar now, as welcoming as the rooms and lighted windows of their home, and they grew more confident in their coming together with each week and month of knowing that what they had was solidly theirs, not something balanced precariously on the edge of a deception. They kissed and held each other with the effortless merging of a swimmer slipping through water, weightless, almost without form, but at the same time sharply aware of an individual self, exultant and powerful, independent but still buoyed up and stronger for what was shared.

"Upstairs," Garth murmured, "or it's going to be the carpet right here. I've been wanting you all evening."

Sabrina laughed. "You were thinking about faked DNA all evening."

"Part of me was. The other part wanted you. There's always a part that wants you." He turned, his arm still around her, and started for the stairs.

"The lights . . ."

"Mrs. Thirkell will get them in the morning. You wanted me to get used to being coddled; look how well I've done."

Sabrina laughed again and Garth heard in her laugh love and contentment and delight, and felt a rush of well-being, that he had brought all that to life. *If a man can give that to the woman he loves, he ought to be able to do anything.*

Moonlight filled their bedroom, the shadowed corners

black against the pure white light, the patchwork quilt on the bed a soft pattern of pastels, the only color in the room. Sabrina threw back the quilt and they lay on the cool sheet in the cool room, their mouths and hands rediscovering each other, and then Garth was inside her, so easily, so naturally it was like a conversation, their bodies weaving together as had their voices in the library. But it is a conversation, Sabrina thought fleetingly. Whatever we do, wherever we are, we're talking to each other. But it's complete only when we're together.

Garth smiled at her and said, "Yes, my love," and brought his mouth to hers.

They were awake until almost dawn, and all those hours together were, to Garth, another affirmation of his need for her, not only when something terrible happened, but also when everything was good. He held her with a fierceness that came from knowing how devastating it would be to lose her, and he knew from her response that the same lurking possibility also haunted her—that something would separate them: illness, death, or the kind of unforeseen event or mad idea that had brought them together less than a year before. And, caught in the whimsical tangle of chance and probability, they made love with an intensity that seemed greater with each passing week, as the stakes grew higher and their defenses disappeared.

Garth could still feel that intensity and see Sabrina's smile the next morning as he crossed the campus, light-headed from lack of sleep, so deeply in love that it seemed impossible that he inhabited a world in which there was fraud and fear and confrontation. And the buying of congressmen, he mused, thinking beyond his meeting with Lu Zhen, in a few minutes, to two weeks ahead when he and Claudia would go to Washington, and then thinking beyond that to the politics of a university, the rituals of grant applications, the research projects that were fruitful and the others that ran aground, the time-consuming needs of students who deserved the best he could give them. All of it was part of the world he and Sabrina inhabited, but none of it, he told himself in what was almost a vow, no major problems or minutiae, would come between them. They would be vigilant, they would be protective, and whatever attention and energy it required, they would not let anything come between them.

He had called earlier, telling Lu to meet him at ten, and when he bounded up the stairs he saw him waiting beside his office door.

"Professor, good morning." Lu smiled broadly and held out his hand. "Are we going to discuss the note to *Science* announcing my discovery? I wrote it last night; I have it to show to you. They will publish it in their next issue, yes? And then, later, publish the paper. Of course that should not take long, as you said: major discoveries are published quickly. So"—he took a sheet of paper from his briefcase—"here it is; I think you will find it says everything it should."

"Perhaps not everything." Garth unlocked his office door, propped it open, and sat at his desk.

Lu brought a chair close to the corner of the desk, his favorite spot, and leaned forward, still holding his letter, still smiling. "And what is it I have left out?"

"An explanation of how you expect other scientists to replicate your experiment."

Lu's eyes widened in surprise. "Replicate? But of course . . ." And then, as Garth gazed at him steadily, the words sank in, and very slowly his smile faded.

Garth unlocked his top drawer and took out the bound copy of Lu's paper. He went to the refrigerator in the corner of the office and brought to the desk the vials of blood samples he had taken the night before. Finally, he took from a drawer in a file cabinet the computer printout from the blood analyzer. He lined everything up on the blotter on his desk. Lu watched his fingers as he squared them.

"I won't submit your paper to *Science*, or the note you've written. I'm sure you know why."

366

"No. I don't understand. You put your name on the paper; you said you would submit it on Monday."

"I also told you I'd go over it this weekend. I read it through last night and something in it bothered me, an assumption about a single gene. We did discuss this, you know, several times, though I didn't follow it up; I was distracted by other things."

"But it is a single gene! If you read my paper, you know that I proved it!"

He looked bewildered and painfully earnest, and for a brief second Garth wondered if he could be mistaken: if he had taken blood from the wrong mice, if the blood analyzer had malfunctioned, if Bill Farver had been wrong . . .

Impossible. Every one of those things would have had to occur simultaneously last night, and that was so unlikely as to be impossible. Lu Zhen was a consummate actor; he knew that, too. "I took these blood samples from your mice last night. This is the blood analyzer printout. You know what it says; you've probably got stacks of identical ones in your files. Or did you destroy them when they kept showing that your mice were healthy?" There was a silence. "Perhaps you'd like to read this one." He held out the long sheet of paper for Lu to take.

Lu's hands remained in his lap. He gave an almost imperceptible shrug. "Well, but you know, Professor, it doesn't matter. Somewhere in going through the experiment, I made a mistake. That was not good, I acknowledge that, but it was only procedural. Of course it affected my results, but not the research project itself; all I have to do is repeat the experiment correctly and the results will be exactly as my paper says. And other scientists will be able to replicate it and see its truth. Professor, I *know* I am right, and that is what is important: the theory and the experiment, not my procedural mistakes. So you see, there is nothing to worry about."

Garth was stunned into silence. He contemplated Lu Zhen as if trying to identify a new species. Lu gazed back at him confidently, one scientist to another. The silence lengthened. A ball thumped against the building just below the office window; students clattered past the open door on their way to the laboratories at the end of the corridor. There was no other sound. It was Saturday; most students were studying; most professors were mowing lawns or doing errands or lying in a hammock with a beer and a book: for them it was a normal weekend. But for Garth it was the end of a dream, and the pain and anger he had felt the night before stabbed at him again.

He showed none of that. He sat motionless, and the minutes passed, and soon Lu could not endure the silence. "So you will send in the paper. And the note."

"No, of course not; you don't know what you're talking about. You've written a fairy tale and called it a scientific paper and called yourself a scientist. You're not a scientist; you have no right to be part of the scientific community. We spend our lives dedicated to research, with absolute fidelity to that which can be proven; we search for connections—cause and effect, beginning and ending, living and dying—and follow them wherever they lead us, and if they take us down blind alleys we look for other paths, and when we find what we're looking for, or come upon something serendipitously, we stay with it until we've proven and proven again that it works, that it's correct and others can follow us, that we've made an advance, however small, in the long journey of science and a new beginning for—"

"Professor, this is the talk you give to freshmen; I've heard you. It is also in the introduction to your book. It's very impressive. But very little in the real world is so clear-cut. You know this; you deal with politicians and businesspeople and they always bend the rules. I bent some information, that is all, because I *know* my experiment will work; I know the results will be found by others. This is my truth and I *am* a scientist and I am as serious about it as you say all scientists should be."

"You would throw science out the window," Garth

said evenly, though his anger was growing, more so since he had been caught repeating himself, something every professor dreads. "You'd publish a lie because of a crazy arrogance that you know the truth in spite of experimental findings that show you're wrong."

"I'm not wrong! Professor, Professor, this works! You have been so excited . . . and now it will bring great glory to you and your institute . . . you will be famous! Even the Nobel Prize!"

Garth felt a flash of contempt. "I called Bill Farver last night, in Berkeley. He's been working on the same premise as you; remember we talked about that? He and his team have concluded that there must be at least two genes, perhaps more . . ." He laid it out, describing other theories and experiments, each deliberate word carefully chosen to leave no doubt. When he finished, Lu was looking past him, out the window, his face drawn, his cheeks hollow, as if he had grown old while listening.

"I had no evidence of that," he murmured. "All the steps I went through, and there was no sign . . ."

"There were signs, and we talked about them," Garth said flatly. "You chose another direction."

"All scientists do that." Lu looked at Garth, and now he was pleading. "We decide what we'll pay attention to and what we'll ignore. I did the same thing every scientist does. Professor, I can use so much of what I've done; it wouldn't take me long to go back and develop a new approach. I know I could find the answer and beat those people in Berkeley; I know more than they do—"

"You don't know a damn thing. You've got a good mind, Lu, but you're driven by arrogance and ambition and fear, and even the best mind isn't a match for all that. You're right: we do decide what we'll focus on, but we don't do it at the beginning; we do it when we know more about our options. You were in a hurry, so you decided at the beginning what you'd find and then you tailored your experiments to find it. And when it didn't work, you wrote down a bunch of fake blood-test results and let me put my name on it.''

"But I thought . . . when I did it again, without whatever mistakes I'd made—''

"The whole goddam project was a mistake! Don't you understand that? And what the hell does that have to do with letting me put my name on a paper that was full of faked numbers? Even if you were right and the experiment worked the next time, I'd be listed as advisor and coauthor of a fraud. That was the bonus you were going to leave me with when you went back to China.''

Lu's eyes narrowed. "You'd survive. You're famous. Everyone says you're one of the best, and you've got your institute and your family . . . you've got everything. But if you don't send in my paper, you rob me of everything. I couldn't go home; I couldn't go anywhere. I couldn't even get a job without a reference from you. I'd have nothing!''

Troubled by the desperation and resentment in Lu's voice, Garth said, "I think you should go back to China. You have your doctorate; you can get a job there. Perhaps some of your other professors will give you a reference. I won't pursue you or tell anyone what you've done, but if anyone—''

"You mean you'll write a reference for me?''

"Good God, after today? I said perhaps others would. If you go back to China I won't publicize what you've done. But if others ask me, I won't lie.''

"You don't have to tell them. No one would be forcing you.''

"Science would force me, my belief in science and in myself as a scientist. If you understood that, none of this would have happened.'' He stood up. "I have to leave now; I promised my family I'd spend the afternoon with them. Here's your paper; there are a number of things in it that you can use again, especially in the first half of the experiment. You did that part well. I admired you. I'm sorry''—he cleared his throat—"I'm sorrier than you will ever know that you couldn't be the kind of scientist I thought you were.''

Lu gave him a long look of pure hatred. He took the bound pages from Garth's hand and left.

Garth let out his breath and realized he was shaking. Damn him, he thought; damn him for the brutality of his stupidity and arrogance. But stupidity and arrogance were always brutal; Garth knew that. He just had not expected it in a young man of such brilliance.

He returned the blood samples to the refrigerator and locked it, then locked his office door. Outside, the heat rose up like a wall to meet him. He was wearing a short-sleeved shirt and khaki pants, and before he reached the campus gate they were wet. It was like swimming under-water, and he imagined himself doing a butterfly stroke, pushing the humid air aside so that he could reach his home.

And forget Lu, he thought, at least for a while. Forget the disappointment and my own failures, and how close I came to disaster. He walked down the somnolent streets. The houses and trees seemed to fade away in the heat, and Garth felt like a ghost in an abandoned town. He met no one else on his walk, though he heard shouts and laughter and splashes from backyard swimming pools, and a few blocks ahead he saw the mail truck making its slow way toward him. He turned up the walk to his house and opened the front door. Cool air curled about him, drawing him inside. What a good place to be, he thought as he closed the door. In so many ways.

He passed Mrs. Thirkell, humming in the kitchen, and went to the second floor. Young voices came from Penny's room. He glanced inside and saw Barbara Goodman and Penny facing each other cross-legged on the floor between the twin Jenny Lind beds, so absorbed they did not look up. A few feet away, Sabrina was sitting on the curved window seat in the round turret at the end of the hall, partially hidden behind a folding screen. She put her finger to her lips and he walked quietly to her and kissed her.

"Was it very hard?" she asked, her voice low.

"Sad and infuriating. Are you eavesdropping on Penny and Barbara?"

"Yes." She moved over so he could sit beside her. "I couldn't get her to talk about the party last night, and then I heard them—"

"—Tinkertoys," Penny was saying. "You know, gears and wheels and stuff, but nothing inside."

Barbara giggled, then her voice came, as earnest as Penny's. "But they're not really like that; they look fantastic, and they wear, you know, these great clothes that my mom won't buy for me, and they do everything! Nobody stops them the way everybody stops us!"

"I know. Except that . . . well, it's like nobody's paying any attention to them."

"Right! They're so lucky . . . I mean, don't you hate it when people are always telling you what to do and when to be home and whatever *they* want?"

"Well, yes, but . . . well, you know . . . maybe nobody cares about what they do. Or cares about them. Or loves them."

"Who doesn't?"

"Well, their parents."

"Oh, sure they do. Parents always love their kids. It's in the genes. Ask your dad."

"But my mom says they're like Tinkertoys because they're sort of empty inside. And she says they don't know anything."

"Oh, come on, Penny, they know everything! And they have all the fun, and you know it. I mean, didn't you want to go upstairs with them at the party last night?"

There was a pause. "Sort of."

"You did! I saw you watching them. And when they asked you, you said you'd be up later."

"Well, you know, if you say no, they make fun of you. And I didn't tell my mom and dad that they were going to be at the party. I mean, I just said you were going. So I thought . . . if something happened, I couldn't talk to my mom about it. I mean, if I did, she'd know I lied—''

"You didn't lie, you just didn't tell her everything. You shouldn't tell her everything anyway; it's babyish."

"It's not! I tell you things!"

"It's different with friends."

"Well, she's my friend, too. She always says the right thing."

"Yeh, like Tinkertoys."

"Well, it made sense when she said it. Why wouldn't you tell me last night what they were doing upstairs?"

" 'Cause you didn't come up and I wanted you to. I mean, *I* went up there when they asked me and you said you would and then you didn't. It was like you didn't care about me."

"I kept thinking about it . . . I wanted to but I didn't want to, I mean, I really wanted to, but they scare me, you know, I can't help it. They talk so loud and they tell jokes I don't get and they make me feel stupid. What were they *doing*?"

"Oh, lying around on those leather couches and sort of sliding off them and laughing and telling jokes and drinking beer and stuff, and the TV was on. They were in that little room, you know, with all that leather furniture."

"I didn't see it."

"And Arnie and Vera had sex."

"They did? Right there?"

"No, of course not. I mean, somebody said they should, but they said they weren't into that. They went into one of the bedrooms."

"I hate Arnie. He was one of the ones who threw me around that day at recess. I hate Vera, too. She laughs at me. What . . . what did *you* do upstairs?"

There was a silence.

"Barbara! You didn't!"

"No. I really wanted to, you know, see what it's like—I mean, it's all they talk about, practically—and they only

373

like the kids who do it, but Joey started pulling me out, you know, to this bedroom, and then he, uh, put his hand here and he stuck his tongue in my mouth and it was so awful, he tasted like beer and he was *sucking* and I thought he'd pull my tongue out . . . yech! I hated it!"

"He was sucking on your tongue? That's gross."

"Right. It was."

"So what did you do?"

"Knocked him down."

"Knocked him *down*?"

"Well, I pushed him and he fell backwards. There was this hassock behind him, you know, and he fell over it."

"Was he mad?"

"What do you think?"

"Well, what did he do?"

"He called me things. And everybody laughed."

"At Joey?"

"No! At me!" Her voice fell away. "They said I was stupid and a tease and a cunt. And they made this circle around me and you know, kind of danced? And I was in the middle, and they were saying cunt, cunt, cunt . . . I hate that word. It was so awful; they were so *mean*. They were never like that before."

"Not to you. Because you always sort of hang around them, like you like them. I hate it when you do that."

"I don't like them, not really. I mean, I mostly hate them. And I never went with them after school or anything, when they asked me, but, you know, I couldn't stand it if they laughed at me all the time the way they did last night. The way they laugh at you. And they really are cool, Penny, and I really do wish I was like them and they liked me."

"They turn lovemaking into fucking."

"What? That's really weird. What does it mean?"

"They make it not loving. You know, ordinary, like a handshake. Or scratching an itch."

"An itch!" Barbara giggled. "Who says it's like an itch?"

374

"My mother."

"Oh, you're always talking about your mother! I mean, she's really nice, but she doesn't know anything about sex; she's too old."

"She knows everything. About sex, too, I'll bet; she and my dad are always kissing. And one time he had his hand here, you know, sort of moving his fingers over it, and my mom said, 'Wonderful hands,' real low, and gave this little laugh like she was *so* happy, and I wished I could feel that way . . . someday. They thought they were alone, you know, in the kitchen, and lots of times, on Saturday and Sunday mornings, their bedroom door's shut and one time Cliff and I listened and we heard them talking and making all these . . . sounds, you know?"

Garth tightened his arm around Sabrina as she rested against him on the window seat. "Maybe a soundproof door?"

She smiled. "I think as long as it's part of our loving each other, there isn't anything she shouldn't hear."

"And I knew they were . . . doing it," Penny finished triumphantly.

Barbara sighed. "I never get to hear anything like that. My parents don't kiss much, at least not that I can see. And they close their door at night, and they get up early, before me. It'd be neat to hear them sometime. I guess they don't do it a lot." There was a pause. "She said it was an itch?"

"It shouldn't be like scratching one, she said. But when kids do it, that's what it's like. And she said it was like something else, too . . . I forget. Oh, like an after-school sport."

They giggled. "Soccer and softball and gymnastics and fucking," Barbara said, her voice rising. "They could put it on the bulletin board and we could check off which one we—"

"Ssssh!" Penny said.

Barbara's voice dropped only slightly. "But wouldn't you like to try it? I mean, find out what it's really *like*? I

375

mean, they talk like it's the greatest thing and I don't know what they're talking about and it makes me feel *little*, like they're grown up and I'm still a baby.''

"My mother says we should wait to find somebody we really love and share things with him; then it would be making love instead of, you know, fucking.''

Garth kissed Sabrina's cheek. "What a smart mother Penny has,'' he murmured.

"She didn't say that!'' Barbara exclaimed. "Did she? Does your mother really say 'fucking' to you?''

"Sure. Well, not a lot, she says it's not a good word, but you know, one time I said the kids at school were talking about fucking and masturbating and . . . you know. So we talked about it.''

"Well, it's easy for her; she can talk about itches and stuff because she doesn't have to go to school with those kids, so what good is that?''

"She says they're infants,'' Penny went on doggedly, "and the reason they laugh at us is probably because they're scared but they can't admit it.''

There was a pause. "She thinks they're scared?''

"That's what she said. That they got in too deep and don't know how to get out and don't know where they're going. Something like that.''

"Well . . . I don't know. They don't look scared to me. They didn't look scared last night.''

"I bet they were, though.''

"They didn't look like it. And when Arnie and Vera went into the bedroom, they didn't, either.''

"Did you watch them?''

"They closed the door.''

"So how do you know they did it?''

"They said so, when they came back.''

"So what did you do then? You didn't come downstairs right away. Did you try anything?''

"Sort of.''

"*You did?* You didn't tell me!''

"I meant to. I was going to today.''

"What did you try?"

"Uh, coke. They were snorting it."

"You did *coke*?"

"A little."

"How much?"

"I don't know. It didn't look like very much."

"Could you feel it? I mean, how did you *feel*?"

"It sort of tickled my nose."

"But how did you *feel*?"

"Nice. Like everything was fine. They stopped laughing at me and they liked me and I felt grown up and . . . good. It was really nice."

"Then what did you do?"

"Oh, sort of hung out, but they didn't seem so nice after a while. They got mean, like always, and they were telling jokes that I didn't get, so I came downstairs and that's when, you know, they opened the dining room and everybody started eating, so I did, too."

"And that was all?"

"Yeh, it wasn't, you know, fabulous or anything. It just felt nice for a little while. You could try it and see for yourself, they'd give you some, they've got lots. Or, you know, if we wanted to do the rest of it, we could ask Vera or somebody and they'd, you know, tell us where they'd be after school or on weekends."

"And do coke, you mean?"

"Well, sex, too. You know. I mean, I don't know about itches and all that stuff, but they keep saying it's so much fun and we could find out what it's like. They'd let us; they told me they like virgins."

"Oh." It came out as a terrified gasp and Sabrina started up, but Garth held her back. "She doesn't need us," he murmured, and slowly she settled back, but her hands were clenched. "I can't believe they're saying these things."

"So what do you think?" Barbara asked.

"I guess not," Penny said, her voice becoming stronger as she spoke. "I mean, I really don't want to. My mother says those kids are messing up a lot of things because they don't know who they are or how—"

"They know who they are! That's dumb!"

"No, like, they don't know what they can be, you know, how they'll feel about things when they grow up. Really grow up, you know, because there's all those things waiting for us—love and adventures and stuff—and we don't know what we'll really want later on, so we should wait. You know, be really grown up before we do grown-up things. So I guess I'll wait."

Sabrina sighed. *Maybe that's the best thing I've ever done.* She tilted back her head and met Garth's eyes, and they kissed, as lovers and parents, and Sabrina felt a rush of thankfulness for everything that was so good.

"Anyway," Penny finished, putting forward her last argument, "if my mother ever found out, she'd ground me for a year."

"A year! That's awful! That's not fair!"

"I know. She thinks it is, though. She says it's important for my growing up. And I guess I . . . sort of . . . believe her."

"You do?"

"Well, you know, when she's talking she makes everything sound like she's right."

"That's just because she's your mother."

There was a pause. "Maybe it's because she's really right."

Garth chuckled. "I like the way Penny thinks."

"Well," Barbara said, drawing it out. "Well, I guess . . ."

"What?"

"I guess I won't do it if you won't. Like, if we did it together we could, you know, talk about it. But I don't want to do it without you."

"Any of it?"

"I guess. But then they'll start laughing at me again."

"Oh, well. We could talk Chinese at them."

"Chinese? How? We don't know any."

"I know a little bit. Lu Zhen taught me; he's really nice. When he comes for dinner again, I'll ask him for more words and then I'll teach you."

"It's a lot harder than French, isn't it?"

Their voices changed; now they were relaxed, with no residue of their earlier tension that had seemed to Sabrina to be close to hysteria. They talked about their French teacher for the school year beginning in just a few weeks, and the sixth grade play, and some sweaters that Barbara wanted to buy because all the girls were buying them. A few minutes more and they were on their feet, talking about food. "Mrs. Thirkell always has something; she's wonderful," said Penny. "My dad says she's like the sun and the British Empire, that she never sets. I guess that means she never sits down, or she's always there, something like that."

"You're so lucky," Barbara said. "I mean, having her is like being rich, isn't it? Or a princess or something."

Their voices moved down the hall to the stairs and faded away. Sabrina was laughing softly. "You didn't tell me about Mrs. Thirkell never setting."

"I'd forgotten I said it. How nice that Penny understood it. I hope she understands how much she owes you."

"She understands that she got help when she needed it. And she isn't afraid to acknowledge it. I'm so proud of her."

"So am I. But mostly of her mother." They sat quietly, gazing through the turret's curved windows at the front yard below, shimmering in the heat. A neighbor, looking wilted, walked a wilted Dalmatian on a long leash; another neighbor gazed at a lawn mower in his front yard, gazed at the sky, then shrugged and put the lawn mower away. "It's better inside," Garth said. "It's amazing how many reasons I find to say that. Which reminds me: Claudia and I will be going to Washington week after next, just for the day."

"Yes, she called me. We had a long talk. It was very strange; she asked me how I'd handle them."

"Leglind?"

"And his sidekick. I can't believe that she really needs help with them."

"What did she say?"

"That she was looking for something that would lead to a public retraction, and she had some ideas but she wondered how I'd handle it."

"She didn't say why?"

Sabrina gestured slightly with her hand. "It seems that Lloyd Strauss told her I'd had something to do with solving a sex-for-grades scandal last year."

"A little more than something, my love. You did it all. Of course Claudia would have heard about that. And she likes you; she told me she values your friendship. Well, did you give her any suggestions?"

"We talked through a few of them, and there was only one that we thought might work, though we weren't happy about it. And of course everything could change when you're there."

"What was it?"

"Well, it was very simple, if you can ever call blackmail simple. I thought she might tell Leglind about the publicity you're working on for the institute: the donors and so on, and the opening ceremonies with guest speakers and politicians, and that you'd like him to be part of it, but if he's on record calling for an investigation of the institute as a waste of money, and then the university publicly applauds him for his support, it would sound like a bribe, even though everyone knows how interested he is in science . . . well, you get the idea."

"I do. As blackmail it's very good."

"You don't like it."

"Not any more than you do; it's a depressing way to get things done. It doesn't even matter that people use blackmail all their lives, mild forms of it—well, maybe not quite so mild—and find prettier names for it than blackmail or bribery or whatever it comes down to."

"But what you mostly don't like is that it probably will work."

"That's the most depressing part. In spite of all the good people who find their way to Congress, the ones who usually leave the biggest impression are the corrupt and craven ones. I know it's not only Congress, it's everywhere, and my friends in the social sciences say it's naive to expect anything else, but still it's depressing. And Claudia thought it was a good idea?"

"She thought it sounded more practical than appealing to Leglind's better instincts."

"Since he has none. She's right. Well, we have an appointment a week from Monday; we'll know then."

"Are you dividing up what you're going to say?"

"She wants to do most of the talking. I'm looking forward to it; I've never even heard her raise her voice, much less lecture a congressman."

As it happened, Claudia did not raise her voice in Oliver Leglind's office; she spoke so softly that the congressman had to strain to hear her. "We appreciate your seeing us on such short notice," she said, and watched with quiet amusement as Leglind and Stroud exchanged a quick glance of surprise at the gentle voice issuing from a woman six feet tall with slicked-back gray hair and oversize glasses. "It was, of course, gratifying to hear from Mr. Stroud that we had been exonerated, but it was quite dismaying as well."

The congressman frowned. He was a small man oddly out of proportion, his arms too long for his torso, his legs too short, his eyes peering narrowly from beneath heavy brows. He had thick hair so carefully waved it was clear it was his pride and joy. Garth knew he could be mesmerizing in front of a crowd, working it to a frenzied pitch with dark tales of government waste so dire it threatened the very core of the American way of life. But he was not swaying a crowd now; he was looking puzzled and a little impatient. "I thought you'd be pleased. I was told that you weren't happy with us, that you'd told Professor Andersen not to testify—''

"No one told me any such thing," Garth said. "I was prepared to testify; Mr. Stroud and I discussed that."

"Right. I heard about that discussion, Professor. You seem to think I'm not a curious person. You said *if* I gave a damn about science. You made some comments about my making up plots."

"I did, and I apologize. Those were ill-considered remarks that I regret making. I'm ashamed of them."

Leglind was silent. Garth was amused, as he always was at how disarming an apology is. Few people, poised for battle, can charge forward after those simple words: *I'm sorry. I'm ashamed.*

"Well, now, that's generous," Roy Stroud said. "Not too many people are manly enough to admit their mistakes. But I think the congressman hasn't been told why you're not happy with our decision. And why you're here."

"Because you've left us hanging," Claudia said. "We're in limbo out there where accusations float around but never quite come to earth."

"What? I'm sorry, I don't quite get that."

"She means we didn't say we were wrong about their university," said Leglind flatly. "But nobody can say that, because there hasn't been any testimony, and there isn't going to be any because that's the way you want it. At least that's what we were told. So if that's why you came, you've made the trip for nothing."

"Oh, I don't think so. We came because we want to discuss with you the opening ceremonies for the Institute for Genetic Engineering." Garth saw the twist of distaste in the corners of her mouth as she spoke the lines she and Sabrina had discussed, painting in glowing terms a picture of national and international attention, of wealthy donors including Billy Koner, of guest speakers who included Nobel Prize winners and political leaders from around the world. She held out a list of names. "They're confidential for now, but we brought them for you, because of course you belong among them.''

She paused, then reminded them of Leglind's call for an investigation of the institute as a waste of money. ''So how can we include you in this group of supporters whom we are publicly applauding? Others would say we were trying to bribe you. Everyone knows of your deep concern for science, and of course the institute is on the cutting edge of research and teaching, but still, we can't ignore your public statements. Of course,'' she added, ''a retraction now, almost ten months before the May dedication and opening ceremonies, would stand on its own. But that is not in our hands. We came all this way, Congressman, in the hope that you could help us resolve this dilemma.''

Delicately, almost reverently, Leglind took the list of names and held it at arm's length. Stroud handed him his reading glasses. He read it several times, top to bottom. ''Roy,'' he said at last, ''you didn't offer coffee to our guests.''

The *Chicago Tribune* for August 20 lay on Sabrina's attic worktable as she worked on the final set of specifications for the Koner Building. It had been ten days since the paper appeared with Oliver Leglind's statement printed on the front page, and Sabrina still glanced at it now and then as she worked.

It is the duty of all of us who are dedicated to democracy to study and investigate the information that comes to us. When, in our diligent and relentless search for truth, some information turns out to be false, to protect the reputation and integrity of all those involved, we must be swift to admit our error. Such was the case recently with Midwestern University and its Institute for Genetic Engineering. This institute, on the cutting edge of research and teaching, when opened next year will be a beacon to science and the world. The House Committee on Science, Space and Technology received information questioning the financial underpinnings of the institute and the university's handling of government grants. The committee would have been derelict in its duty had it not investigated those allegations. Having done so, committee staff found the institute, under Professor Garth Andersen, to be a model for other institutions; it found Midwestern University's use of government grants to be fully documented. There is much that is wrong in this great country of ours, and it is our duty to find it and root it out, but we must also applaud all that is magnificent, and make sure . . .

All those high-flown words, all that dancing around, to hide the fact that he cares only about his own power, his own publicity, his own agenda. And that he's for sale.
Sabrina turned back to the long table in front of her, covered with samples of carpeting and drapery fabrics, tiles, wood flooring, faucets, textured plaster for walls, and cut sheets of lighting fixtures. The specification books that she had first shown to Vernon Stern and Billy Koner had grown to twice their original thickness as the design of each room of each apartment was described, with samples of materials pasted in, and the names of the manufacturers and dealers who sold them. She had just inserted into the book the latest changes, and now she was packing the samples in boxes to be sent to the contractor for ordering. It was the biggest job she had ever done, and as she taped shut the last box, she felt content and a little sad that it was over. On the floors below, her empty house drowsed in the dense August heat, and Sabrina felt as if she were protecting it, like a bird nurturing the eggs in her nest. Everything was silent and still, Mrs. Thirkell on her day off, Penny and Cliff visiting friends, Garth in Chicago on a mysterious errand, which Penny had predicted at breakfast was probably to buy Mommy a birthday present. ''Be-

cause it's only two weeks," she said, "and Cliff and I already did ours."

Two weeks, and it will be one full year that I've lived here, one year that I've been Stephanie Andersen, one year since I began to love this family and feel that it was mine.

But a year ago she had had two lives, two homes, two businesses. Soon she would have only one, when she signed the papers transferring ownership of Ambassadors to Alexandra. The house in Cadogan Square was still Sabrina's, but Alexandra's friends had agreed to buy it and would take possession in December. And then I will have one place, Sabrina thought: one home, one family, one business, one center to my life.

Shafts of late afternoon sunlight dancing with dust motes lay like white ribbons across the worktable, empty now except for the boxes she had just packed. Finished, she thought; so many things are being finished. But so many are being started. That's the fun of a family: never knowing what will be around the next corner.

She carried the boxes to the head of the stairs for the UPS driver to take them to his truck, took a last look at the bare worktable, and left the attic, running lightly down the stairs. The telephone rang as she reached the kitchen.

"Stephanie, Vern Stern; I'm just checking on the samples."

"They're ready; I'll send them tomorrow."

"Good. I wasn't worried, but I like to check."

"You don't have to apologize. I'd do the same thing."

There was a pause. "I hope we connect again soon," he said. "I'll miss working with you."

"I've enjoyed it. And I've learned a lot from you; I was going to write to thank you for all you've taught me."

"Write? So formal. We could have had dinner; you could have told me then."

"No, we couldn't," Sabrina said easily, "unless you'll come here. I've invited you often enough."

"Someday I might take you up on it. You know, there's

a downside to being watched over by your friends; there's always the end of the evening when they wave goodbye from their cozy hearth and you go off alone. I'm not saying I'm not glad to have a place at my friends' tables; I am. But you're different, for me, and right now I'd rather not see you happily married and ensconced and ensnared.''

"Friends are glad to see that in their friends' lives. I'd be glad to see it in yours if you found it.''

"Well, who knows? I do envy you, Stephanie; you make the most of where you are. So many people don't, you know; they keep running after something else: money or fame or a bigger house or car or a new wife or husband . . . if it's there to want, they'll want it. But there's a serenity in you, like a fixed star; you know who you are and what you want to do with your life and whom you want to do it with. I was hoping some of that would rub off on me. Maybe if we do a few jobs together, it will.''

A fixed star, Sabrina thought as they hung up. After a lifetime of feeling unconnected. Garth doesn't have to buy me a birthday present; he's given me the best I could ever have. He's helped me find my place.

She heard the front door open. They're home early, she thought. She went to the living room and stopped abruptly in the doorway. Lu Zhen stood in the middle of the room. His face was haggard, his eyes were huge and darting, his tie dangled around his neck, and in his hand was a small black gun. He stared at her in shock and anger. "You weren't supposed to be here.''

"Lu, for heaven's sake, what are you doing?'' He waved the gun toward her tentatively, as if waiting for someone to tell him what to do next. "*Lu, what are you doing?*''

His head jerked back, his arm stiffened. "Mrs. Andersen, sit down. Please.''

"Not until you put down that gun. Lu Zhen, what is the matter with you?''

"You must sit down, Mrs. Andersen. I order you to sit down.''

"I will, Lu, we both will, but first give me the gun." Her heart was pounding. This couldn't be happening; such things didn't happen to anyone they knew. "Give it to me." Her voice came out hoarsely and she cleared her throat. "I'll put it away and I won't tell anyone about it. Professor Andersen won't know—"

"Professor Andersen!" He spat the name. "He's the one I came to see. You were supposed to be at your work; no one was supposed to be home." He raised the gun. "Sit down!"

Sabrina sat on the arm of a chair. "Why do you—"

"*In* the chair! *In* the chair!"

She let herself down, her eyes fixed on him. "Why do you need a gun when you come to this house?"

"Because there's nothing else to do. But I will not talk to you; I will talk to the professor and no one else."

"I don't know when he'll be home. Why don't you sit down while you wait?"

"I will not sit in your house anymore!"

"Oh, won't you!" she flared, forgetting the gun for a moment. "We've been good to you, we've made you welcome here as if you were a member of our family—"

"I have never been a member of your family! No one ever cared a damn for me!"

"That's not true and you know it; for two years we cared greatly for you. I know you miss your family and haven't made many friends; you're alone far too much. But why do you blame us, when we've tried to give you a family and a home to come to?"

"That isn't it," he muttered.

"What is it, then? Lu, I'll try to help you, but not if you threaten me with a gun. Good heavens, is that the way you treat your friends?"

"I have no friends in this house."

"Well, whose fault is that? We were all your friends once, and you liked it here: you couldn't wait for the next invitation. Now put that gun down; I can't talk to you while you're holding it."

"I need it."

"For what? To shoot me?"

He shook his head. He was very pale and his hand hung at his side, the gun pointing at the floor. "I don't want to shoot you."

"You don't want to shoot anyone. You know it would only make things worse. Lu, give me the gun. It's a terrible thing to stand there like that: it makes us enemies."

He stared at her and she thought she saw him waver, but then the front door opened and Garth came in, followed by Cliff and Penny.

"What the hell—!" Garth exclaimed.

"Stay back!" Lu cried. "Move over there, all of you!"

"Lu, what are you doing with a toy gun?" Penny demanded.

Cliff shoved her with his shoulder, moving her with him toward the stairs. "Maybe it's not a toy."

Garth stormed in, his hand outstretched. "Give it to me. God damn it, *give me that gun!*"

"Don't come any closer!" Lu's voice rose in hysteria. "Stay away from me!"

Garth stopped, his body straining forward. "You will not hurt anyone here, do you understand that? *I'm* the one you're angry at; you leave them alone or I swear I'll tear you to pieces. Come outside; we can talk—"

"I won't go anywhere with you! You want to ruin my life!" He swung around as Penny and Cliff reached the stairs. "Come back! You can't go anywhere! You'll call the police; do you think I'm stupid?"

"Leave them alone!" Garth started for him, but Lu swung back, pointing the gun at Garth's head.

"I hate you!" Penny screamed. "I thought you were nice, you were going to teach me Chinese, but you're mean and I hate you!" She ran to Sabrina and flung herself in her lap, crying. "Why do people have to be mean?"

"I'm not mean," Lu said, the child in him breaking through, but the gun was steady and his face was as steely as before. "*You're* the ones . . . ." His voice rose. "You think you can take somebody and smash him . . . *ruin* him!''

Cliff saw him bring the gun up. ''Don't!'' he shouted. ''Don't! Don't! Don't!''

Sabrina cradled Penny, bending over her to shield her small body. She was terrified. He could kill them. The television news was full of stories about angry, irrational people who thought the solution was to kill and who found it too easy to get hold of a gun. She tightened her arms around Penny. *They can't die. Penny and Cliff can't die; they're just beginning their lives*. Panic filled her and she stretched forward to cover Penny's tense, wiry body, which was pressing into her lap, straining to disappear into her mother. *Don't let her die, don't let Cliff die, please, please don't let my children die*.

''DROP THE GUN!'' Garth roared and lunged forward.

Lu scuttled sideways, to the far corner of the room, waving the gun at them. ''What will you do if I don't? You can't do anything!''

''I told you, we'll go outside and talk—''

''Talk! What good is talking? We talked in your office and I hear your voice all the time, telling me what you'll do and what you won't do, and I know you won't do a fucking thing to help me. You're jealous of me; you *want* me to fail. You think I'll get ahead of you, I'll get a Nobel Prize and be famous, and you'll be stuck here in your goddam institute. But I deserve to get ahead of you! Do you know how I worked for two years on my project? Harder than you ever worked in your life. You don't know what it is to work like that; you have everything, you Americans, you think the world comes to you and gives you everything and you take and take and take and what do you give? You do whatever you want, and if you don't like what somebody does, you throw him away, like a piece of trash! Well, I'm not trash! I'm as good a scientist as you are—better!—and I did my research and my experiment and *you said they were brilliant*, and now you fucking will do what I tell you because now I have the power! You will call the people at *Science* and tell them you are sending in my paper and it is very important and they should publish it right away.''

''All right, I'll do that, I'll call them, but only after you come outside. Come on, we'll go outside; I'll take the telephone with me and I'll call them from the porch.''

Lu narrowed his eyes. ''You don't really mean that. You're just saying it to get me out of here. You think you're so smart, you think you can fool me, but you wouldn't call them, I know you wouldn't, because you're too jealous, you know my paper is better than anything you've ever done in your whole life.''

''That paper is a fraud,'' Garth snapped before he could stop himself.

''It is not a fraud! It is not a fraud! *You said it was important!* You were wrong to listen to those other researchers; they lied to keep secret what they're doing. They're jealous, too, because I'm young and just beginning; you should have known that. Because my paper is not a fraud, and I have to get it published so I can go home!''

''No one will be able to replicate the experiment. Can't you get that through your head? The whole scientific community will know it won't work.''

''It will work. They just have to do it right. Anyway . . .''

''Anyway, by then you'll be in China, is that it? And you think Chinese scientists won't know what's going on in molecular biology in the rest of the world?''

''I'll take care of that when I'm there.''

''How?''

''I don't know!'' His voice rose in fury and frustration and without warning he pointed the gun at the ceiling and fired. Instinctively Garth leaped back. Penny screamed; Sabrina cried, ''Lu!'' The sound of the shot rocketed around the room; flakes of plaster fell on their heads.

''Lu, *listen*, please listen,'' Sabrina said urgently. ''It won't do any good if you hurt us; it will be worse for you. Put down the gun. Lu, *put down the gun.*"

But Lu barely heard her. For a moment he had looked stunned, but then desperation again held him in its grip. "See, it's not a toy, see, Professor, I mean it and you'll do what I tell you because you're afraid, aren't you? The big professor is afraid! You think everybody is afraid of you, all the little students, but some of us are as big as you, and now you're the one who's afraid! How does it feel? Does it hurt? I'll make you hurt if you don't do what I tell you and call the journal. Call them! Right now!"

"And after I call them, what will you do? Just walk out of here? Or will you think you should shoot us because we'll come after you?" Garth took a step forward. "You've boxed yourself in, Lu, and if you don't give it up now you'll do yourself incalculable harm." He took another step.

"Stop!" Lu cried.

"Think about China; you have a chance there. Your academic record is excellent; you'll get a teaching job there; you have a future. But not if you use that gun." He took another step. "Think about China, Lu; they'll know, they'll hear—"

Oh, Garth, my darling Garth, Sabrina thought through her fear. Always believing in reason. But there are so many times when reason isn't enough.

"Don't come any closer!" Lu yelled. "You don't know a damn thing about China. I'll be fine there; I'll take care of everything. But first I have to have my paper published! I have to have a name!"

"Based on a deception."

"NO! It's good science. And if you don't do what I say"—he took a long step forward and swung the gun toward Sabrina—"I will kill all of you. You don't think I will, but I will, because I don't care!"

His eyes followed the barrel of the gun and for an instant he was looking at Sabrina and Penny. And in that instant, Garth and Cliff flung themselves at him and slammed him to the floor. The gun went off and Penny screamed.

"Garth!" Sabrina leaped up, leaving Penny cringing in a corner of the chair. "Oh my God, my God . . . Garth! Cliff!"

"All right," Garth said. He sat up and knelt beside Lu, who was crumpled beneath Cliff. His body shook with silent sobs. Cliff straddled him, stunned by what he and his father had done.

"How did we do that?" he asked Garth. "How did we know, so we jumped him at the same time?"

"We make a good team." Garth took the gun from Lu's limp fingers and stood up. "All right," he said again, and took Sabrina in his arms. "I thought I might lose you. My God, the thought of anyone hurting you . . . or Penny or Cliff . . ."

"I know." She laid her head on his chest and felt the pounding of his heart. "We were all afraid for each other."

"Daddy?" Penny asked. "What will he do when Cliff lets him up?"

"He won't do anything. He's outnumbered." Garth realized he was still holding the gun. "Cliff, put this in the library. We'll get rid of it later."

Cliff's eyes were wide. "Sure," he said, awed by his father's trust. He eased himself away from Lu's body, waiting to see if he would move, but Lu stayed where he was, his head in his arms, his shoulders heaving. Cliff took the gun from Garth and held it gingerly by the handle, pointing it at the floor and walking almost on tiptoe to the library.

"He can't do anything," Garth said again to Penny. "It's over."

"But the gun went off."

"We'll look for the bullet later; it's probably in some furniture. The most important thing is that we're all right."

Sabrina knelt beside the chair where Penny still huddled. "It's over, sweetheart. Lu did a terrible thing, but he's sorry and no one was hurt. All of us who love each other are still here; we have each other and we're fine."

"I was so *scared* . . ."

"We all were. It was very scary. But now we don't have to be because everything is all right. Penny, listen, now we can say it's over, and feel safe again."

Penny's eyes were still wide with apprehension. "I thought our house was always safe."

"Well, it is, isn't it? Here we are; we're all fine, thanks to your dad and Cliff's amazing flying tackle. We'll talk about it at dinner, all right? But first we have to take care of Lu Zhen, and maybe you'd like to go upstairs while we do that. Okay?"

"Is Cliff coming up, too?"

"Why don't you ask him? I have a feeling he's in the library, thinking about everything that's happened."

"If he's not there, can I come back?"

"Of course."

She went off, and Sabrina sighed. There were tears in her eyes. "It isn't safe. We pretend it is, but the world is full of dangers and they can invade our most private places, the ones we trust to protect us. How can we tell Penny that?"

Garth held her close again. "We tell her we'll do our best to protect each other, wherever we are. That has to be good enough for all of us. I suppose the only true sanctuary is in love and responsibility, but even they go only so far. After that, we have to rely on caution and luck. My love, you were wonderful."

"I was terrified."

"So was I."

They held each other quietly, their heads bowed. Thank you, Sabrina said in a silent prayer. Thank you for this gift of time, more time for us to love each other and help our children grow up.

"I suppose I should call the police," Garth said at last, "but I don't really want to. What do you think?"

"I don't know. He's so unstable I don't think we can just let him go. What he ought to do is go home right away and let his parents take care of him until he can sort out everything that's happened and make a fresh start. But someone should be with him until he leaves; do you know of anyone?"

"I don't know of any friends . . . Oh, there's a chemistry professor from Hong Kong, unmarried, young; Lu's spent some time with him. I'll call him. He's completely reliable; I can tell him the whole story."

"No!" Lu jumped up. "Don't tell anyone. Please. Especially Professor Shao Meng; he . . . he thinks highly of me."

"You can't be alone," Garth said flatly. "Shao Meng is a good man and he could have been your friend if you'd gone to him. He may keep this to himself; it will be up to him how many other people know about it. You have no choice in this; you've forfeited the choices you once had."

"He won't like me anymore."

"You'll have to deal with that. Sit down while I call him. Sit down! And stay there."

Lu slumped onto the edge of a chair, his hands dangling between his knees. When Garth went to the telephone in the hall, Lu shot a glance at Sabrina. "You don't care that he's destroying me."

"Oh, what a fool you are. He's saving you. What future would you have had as a scientist after your fraud was discovered? This way, you'll go home with your Ph.D. and a clean slate."

Lu muttered something.

"What did you say?"

"There are lots of Ph.D.'s. I wanted to be famous."

"Maybe you still will be. But not if you keep on lying to yourself."

"I didn't lie. The others did. Professor Andersen was wrong to listen to them."

Sabrina gazed at him in amazement. *Still clinging to it, after all that's happened. There is no limit to people's capacity for deceiving themselves. And perhaps that is the most devastating deception of all.*

"And now you don't like me anymore," Lu said.

"Of course I don't. You almost ruined my husband and then you came here threatening to shoot me and my whole family. Why should I like you?"

"I didn't almost ruin him."

"Lu, stop lying to yourself! My God, can't you face the world as it is and stop retreating into fantasy?" She looked closely at his bleak face. "I'll bet you can. Late at night when no one is around and there's nothing in the silence but your thoughts, I'll bet you admit to yourself that your research was no good. You may push it away in the daytime, but I'll bet you tell yourself the truth late at night, when there's no one to face but yourself."

He glared at her. "What I tell myself late at night is my own business."

"Yes," Sabrina said quietly. "We both know it is."

In a few minutes Garth returned. "Shao Meng is on his way. Tomorrow he'll put you on a plane for China," he said to Lu. "As soon as you get to his house, you'll call your parents and tell them. If you give him any trouble, we'll call the police."

They all waited together, without speaking, until they heard a car turn into the driveway. Sabrina and Garth flanked Lu and walked him to the front door, then watched Shao Meng's car disappear down the street.

"God, what a waste, what an unbelievably self-destructive waste," Garth murmured. "So much promise, so much hope . . ."

"There's still promise, and hope, too," Sabrina said, and took his hand as they walked back to the living room. "It could be that he'll grow up after this."

"It takes a long stretch to believe that."

"I don't mind stretching. Right now I feel rather optimistic."

"An amazing feat."

"Oh, it's not so hard. Look what we've come through.

Leglind, Penny's and Cliff's crises, and now Lu. I think we've done pretty well. Especially in this Wild West scene; no one got hurt and there's only one small scar on the ceiling. We have a lot to be grateful for."

He smiled. "Yes, we do." He sat in an armchair and brought Sabrina to sit in his lap. "I think of that a lot. How much we have, and how we should always be aware of that, never let it fade into the background."

They kissed, and then Sabrina sat straight, her hands on his shoulders. "I have something to tell you. I probably should have earlier, but I was waiting to be sure everything would go through. I'm selling Ambassadors, Garth. Alexandra is buying it, and Blackford's, too, as a matter of fact; we'll sign the papers in a couple of weeks. And some friends of hers are buying the Cadogan Square house. We'll close on that in December."

Garth studied her face. "The shop and the house. A clean sweep. You're sure this is what you want?"

"Very sure. I've thought about it for a long time. I don't want two lives, my darling; I can barely keep up with all the drama in this one."

He chuckled and they were kissing again when Penny and Cliff ran down the stairs. "Oh, sorry," Cliff said, and took an awkward step back.

"For what? You're not bothering us; we're having a good time." Garth smiled at his children, their faces flushed, their eyes bright with that strange combination of pleasure and embarrassment that children feel when they see their parents embrace. His gaze took in the quiet living room and he saw in his mind the other rooms of his house and he knew that for most of the time they were indeed a haven against most of the winds of chance. Then he turned to his wife, who had just chosen their life as the only one she wanted. He held her close again until she lay against his chest. "A man's castle," he murmured.

Sabrina smiled. "A family's," she said.

CHAPTER *16*

---

*I*t was early September, two weeks after Max's trip to Marseilles, when Stephanie walked into the living room and saw that three paintings, among them Léon Dumas's painting of the Alpilles, had disappeared. Max was talking on the telephone in his office and she stood in the doorway, waiting until he hung up. "Max, what happened to the paintings?"

He looked surprised, as if whatever he did should be obvious to everyone. "I sent them away."

"What for?"

There was a pause. "To be cleaned."

"*Cleaned*?"

"Well, stored." He shoved back his chair. "Sit down, Sabrina; I want to talk to you."

"Oh, not here." Instinctively she had tightened inside, fending off something that sounded unpleasant. "Why don't we take a walk? We never do, and it's such a beautiful morning, I hate to stay inside."

He shrugged. "If you like." He put his arm around her and they walked outside, along the terrace to the flagstone walk that led to the front gate. The sun was burning off an early morning haze, and as they walked at the side of the road, the air was soft and warm and scented with lavender and thyme and late summer roses. "I've left you alone too much lately; I apologize for that."

"You've been so busy." Stephanie had been grateful for his late nights; they had freed her from refusing to make love to him. But now, glancing at him, she saw new lines in his face, accentuated by the sun's glare, and she felt a rush of concern. "You're worried about something. Is that what you wanted to talk about?"

"Yes, but not walking; I can't talk to you this way."

"Oh, Max, of course you can. You just prefer to do it the way you planned, in your office. You always have to be in control." She waited, but he made no response. "Where did you send the paintings?"

He took her hand, surprised once again by her quick perception. Somehow he had assumed that a woman with no memory would be slow to understand hidden meanings and the trail of clues that devious behavior left behind, but instead, he was always dodging her instinctive understanding.

"I'm sorry," he said. "I've been making plans that include you, but I didn't want to tell you about them all at once. I thought you'd be uncomfortable with change."

"Sometimes I am. What change?"

"My business. And our home."

They reached the end of the road and turned to walk along the edge of the plateau. Beside them the cliff fell steeply away, studded with low bushes, stunted trees, and pocked gray boulders deeply embedded in the earth. After a few minutes they came to an ancient church, straight-sided and windowless in gray stone with a small steeple and bell tower. A wooden gate was at one side; Max pushed it open and they walked into a tiny courtyard dominated by a wide spreading tree. A row of tombstones worn smooth by the centuries stretched along the stone wall. They sat on a small bench beneath the tree and Max put his arm around Stephanie. He kissed the top of her head, and they sat quietly for a moment, but he was too restless to stay still; he moved back so he could look at her. "You've been here before."

"Yes. Robert told me about it. It's a good place to think. Max, tell me what this is all about."

"I never knew it was here. Is the church locked?"

"Yes."

Beneath the tree the air was cool and still; not a sound broke the silence. "A hideaway," he murmured. "Except, of course, that it's a dead end."

"Do we need a hideaway?" In the silence, Stephanie sighed with impatience. "Where did you send the paintings?"

"To a warehouse in Marseilles."

"Why?"

He looked around as a man came into the courtyard wearing a leather vest, black work pants and a slouch-brimmed black hat. He nodded when he met Max's eye, and ambled over to the stone wall, looking over it at the roofs of Cavaillon.

"We'll go back." Holding her hand, Max led her to the wooden gate and back to the road, and looked over his shoulder as they walked toward their house. They walked between stone walls and high wrought-iron gates that allowed glimpses of stone houses set amid broad gardens, fountains, statues and towering trees. The sun-washed stones seemed luminous beneath the deepening blue sky; the roses were gold and pink, the leaves of the plane trees dark green, almost black. Max was touched by the purity and soft harmony of the scene. He looked back again and saw that the road behind them remained empty, but still he could not relax; he hurried on toward their gate. "I'm putting a number of things in storage to be sent to us wherever we are."

"You're planning to leave? Why? You'd leave Cavaillon?"

"Sabrina, we talked about this: all the places you haven't seen, places far more wonderful than this. We should start thinking about them, about other countries, other cities . . . Why would you want to stay cooped up in this little corner of the world?''

''I'm not cooped up. I like Cavaillon; it's my home. It's the only home I know.''

''You'll make others. We'll make them together.''

''I don't want others.''

''You may not have that choice.''

Stephanie pulled her hand from his. ''I do have a choice.'' They reached their gate and Max turned in. ''Can't we stay outside? Why are we going in?''

He took her arm. ''I'm more comfortable inside.''

''I'm not.'' Stephanie thought of Léon: of making love beneath the trees of Saint-Saturnin, eating lunch beside the sunlit waves of the Sorgue, bicycling past gnarled vines bowed down with grapes. Léon was fresh air, sunlight, the silver sheen of the moon, the warm, moist earth, and when they were together they were part of the earth, taking their strength from it and from each other. She could never say that about Max. Max was enclosures, interiors, secrets, manipulations, artificiality. Max was not part of the earth because he was determined to twist it to his purposes.

In the living room he sat on one of the couches, making room for Stephanie, but she perched on the arm of a nearby chair. ''I won't leave Cavaillon, Max.''

''You will.'' He held her gaze as if he could bend her to his will. ''You have nothing but me. Do you think that that woman in the shop will carry you indefinitely while you learn a trade? Do you think anyone in town gives a damn whether you live or die?''

''Robert cares.''

''Robert may not be here.''

She looked up at him sharply. ''*Robert* is leaving Cavaillon?''

''Not right away. But he may have to. ''

''Why?''

''For his own reasons.''

"And what are yours?"

Max went to the bar and poured a drink. Stephanie raised her eyebrows. "You don't drink in the morning."

"This morning I do."

"You're only doing it to keep from talking to me. Max, tell me whatever you have to say; you can't put it off forever. I want to hear all of it. Including," she added abruptly, suddenly seeing everything as part of a pattern, "how you make your money."

She had taken him by surprise; he shot her a look. "You didn't believe what I told you?"

"No. Well, partly. But I never believed that you told me everything. And now I want you to."

He paused, then shrugged. "Well, then." He returned to his chair and contemplated his drink. "There is a man who works for me in Marseilles, an artist, a brilliant engraver who—"

"What is his name?"

Max paused again. "Andrew Frick. I protect him; that name must not be repeated."

"Protect him from what? The police?"

"Among others. Andrew engraves money. Superbly. And I sell it, in large quantities, to people all over the world. Some of them use it for personal needs; some use it to bring down a government by undermining their country's currency; some use it to get prisoners out of jail, to arm private armies, sometimes to build schools."

"You make and sell counterfeit money." She remembered his locked desk, his secretiveness, the times she had wondered whether he was involved in something criminal. She felt sick. And then something else occurred to her. "How do you get it to them?" He did not answer, and after a moment she said, "You ship it to them. In construction equipment."

"Yes."

"You smuggle it."

"Yes."

"Why?"

"Because the amounts are too bulky to carry, and in luggage they could be found by customs——"

"No, I mean, why do you do it?" She forced herself to look at him, trying to see what he was thinking. She had lived with him for more than eight months, enjoying his companionship, depending on him, but she did not know what he was thinking. His gray eyes were as flat and unrevealing as they always were, even when they were making love. "Why, Max? You don't really need to, do you? Couldn't you make as much money—or, anyway, enough to live on—doing something that isn't criminal?"

He went to her and took her hands, kissing the palms. "I love you, Sabrina; you've made these months the best I've ever known. You've made a home for me. You gave me a place to belong. You're the most beautiful woman I've ever known, and the most intriguing, and I want you with me, wherever I am, whatever I'm doing."

"Why do you do it?" she asked again, her voice cool.

He hesitated, then smiled faintly, a little sadly. "Because, my dear, smuggling is all I've ever known. It's the way I live; it's what I do best."

"But that's ridiculous; you know so many things, you could do almost anything."

"Well, then, it's what I like best."

"But it's the reason you're in trouble, is that right? Because the police found out? Or someone else did, someone who could expose you. That's why you want to leave Cavaillon."

"Partly."

"Well, what else is it? What else have you done? You haven't"—she caught her breath—"you haven't killed anyone."

"No." The irony of it made Max furious. He could not tell the truth, even now, when he was ready to because he loved her. He could not tell her about Denton, or that they were both in danger because Denton had tried to kill them once, because to do so would be to tell her about Sabrina Longworth, about the past he had kept from her. "I haven't killed anyone; I'm not at all sure that I could. We'll leave Cavaillon because we have to, because my business requires it."

"That's not true. You're running away. But you'll always be running, won't you, and hiding inside houses instead of being free? Something will always come along that will make you run and hide. I won't be part of that. Even if I wanted to leave Cavaillon, I wouldn't run away with you."

"We won't be running. We'll buy another house; we'll discover a new place. We'll be together. My God, Sabrina, as long as we're together . . ." He looked at her and knew, with a heavy sinking inside him, that their being together was not an argument that would move her. But he went on, pushing the words at her, trying to make her feel what he felt, if only by the force of his voice. "I thought of California, perhaps Los Angeles. You'd have mountains there, and the desert and the ocean as well. Far more than you have here. Or Rio de Janeiro. I know some people there; they'd help you find another antique shop, or you could start your own. We'll make a new home. And we'll be together."

Stephanie shook her head. She tried to stand up, but Max still held her hands and pinned her in place. "Am I a prisoner?" she asked angrily.

"You can't walk out on me when I'm talking to you."

"I can walk out any time! Good God, Max, I've just begun to make a life and you're trying to force me to run away from it. I won't do it! I want to stay here. This is my home and I love it, and *it's familiar to me* and that's the most important thing in the world right now, to be surrounded by things that are familiar. Just because I went to China once and decided to try a new life for a while doesn't mean I want to do it forever! It was just— Max!"

She was staring wildly at him. There was a ringing in her ears . . . *To try a new life for a while*. What does that mean? *What does that mean?* "Max, did I go to China some time before the explosion?"

"I have no idea. If you did, you never told me about it."

"Why would I go? Max, help me! Didn't I tell you anything that might be a reason for me to go there?"

"No. And I don't believe you went there. Perhaps a friend . . . or perhaps you were thinking about it."

"I went there," she said flatly. "And I was running away." But that was all she knew; the fog had closed in and nothing was left. She had pulled her hands from Max's, and now, caught in the fog and the frustration of trying to cut through it, she went to the door.

Max stopped her. "You're not walking out on me. We're still talking about this."

She saw a flicker of emotion in his eyes: fear, she thought, or perhaps only worry. The lines in his face seemed to deepen as she gazed at him; behind the mask of his beard he looked almost drawn. He's sixty, she thought; it can't be easy to think about moving to a new country and changing life at sixty. Especially alone.

And so, once again, she knew she could not tell him about Léon. Not then, not ever. He would leave alone, knowing the partial truth that she could not bear the uncertainties of a new place or of a life on the run. He could live with that far more easily than with knowing she had fallen in love with another man.

She shook her head again. "I won't leave Cavaillon. Everything I want is here."

"You don't even know what you want. You don't know anything yet."

"I've learned enough to know what I want."

"Nothing lasts; don't you understand? What you think you have is only what you see today. It won't be the same tomorrow or next week or next year."

"Yes, that's how you live. I understand that. But I believe things do last. This town, my friends, this house, this—"

"You won't have this house."

"You'll take it away from me?"

"You can't afford it."

"Oh. Well, then, I'll find something small. Robert or . . . or Jacqueline will help me. And I'll get another job if she can't use me full time. And Madame Besset can always find a new position; she knows everyone."

"You belong with me." He heard the plea in his voice and silently cursed himself. Max Stuyvesant did not plead with anyone. Once again he turned away from her, and as he did he saw on the terrace the man in the leather vest and slouch-brimmed hat who had been in the churchyard. He was leaning against a tree, lighting a cigarette. As he flicked away the match, he looked up and met Max's eyes.

"Christ, she told someone. That damned girl, Robert's fucking do-gooder . . ." He strode to the terrace door. *Confront them; they can't think I'm afraid.* "What the hell are you doing here? Get out! Marcel!" he shouted, and the gardener appeared around the corner of the house. "Get him out of here; he's lost or drunk. And after this, God damn it, keep the gate locked."

He turned back, his hands jammed in his pockets. "I'm sorry."

"What did you mean? What girl?" Stephanie was frightened by the fury in his voice and by the fear, naked now, that lay beneath it.

"Sabrina, listen to me. We don't have much time. I've made my plans; I'm ready to leave, and you're coming with me. You're my wife; you belong with me. There's nothing keeping us here. You've built up a fantasy about Cavaillon because it's all you know, but that's the way an infant thinks of its crib. Any place in the world can be home; there's nothing, anywhere, that can't be duplicated. Come." Without moving from his place by the door, he held out his hand. "Come with me. I love you; I'll take care of you. You're my wife, Sabrina; you belong with me. I'll give you everything you want; I'll make you happy. Sabrina, I promise you I'll make you happy; we'll have a good life."

"No." She stood near the door at the far side of the

room. She pitied him for pleading when she knew he thought of himself as a man who never asked for anything, and she feared for him because of his sudden desperation. But another part of her felt detached, already cut off from him, wanting to have nothing to do with him. "You talk as if I belong to you. But I don't. And I don't belong with you. I don't like the kind of life you make for yourself, Max."

"You don't have to like it; you don't even have to know about it."

"If I stayed with you, I'd be as involved as you are because I'd be living on what you make. I can't be part of that, Max; I won't be part of it. And I can't be on the run all the time, hiding, looking over my shoulder—"

"God damn it, I'm leaving, do you understand that?" He was furious with her for fighting him, for refusing his pleas, his logic, his love. "This isn't a game, Sabrina, it's real, and I'm leaving. Do you know what that means? Do you know what it will mean to you to be alone? You have no idea what that's like."

"I won't be alone."

"You're depending on Robert—"

"I'm depending on myself."

"You can't."

"I can! Stop telling me I can't! You've tried to keep me dependent on you, Max; I know that. You haven't wanted me to recover my memory; you've wanted me to be a little girl, needing you for everything. But I'm not a little girl and I won't be your little girl ever again, and that's not a game, either; that is real."

He waited another minute, his eyes locked fiercely on hers; then he wheeled and left the room. Stephanie stayed where she was, trembling from his intensity and her own. But with him gone, the room was silent, as hushed as the land after a storm, and gradually her trembling stopped. It was over. *I'm depending on myself.* Soon she and Max would part, probably never to meet again. She was touched by sadness. He had been good to her; they had made a home. But everything she had heard and felt that morning wiped out the sadness, and let her think with equanimity of the moment of his departure, when she would touch his hand and kiss him goodbye for the last time.

But she did not touch him or kiss him goodbye. He stayed in his locked office for the rest of that day, and when she awoke the next morning he was gone. It was five o'clock; she had set her alarm because she had planned a bicycle trip up Mont Ventoux and had to start before the day became too hot.

Madame Besset was already in the kitchen, kneading bread dough. "Monsieur must have left very early, madame; he was gone when I arrived a little while ago. Will he be away long this time?"

"I don't know." Stephanie stood in the kitchen, holding her cup of espresso, feeling as if the earth had shifted beneath her feet. He was gone. Not just a short business trip this time; he would go thousands of miles, and he would stay there. She was alone. No, not alone, she thought, but she felt the emptiness of the house, its high-ceilinged rooms, the furnishings that she had bought and arranged over the past months, the gardens heavy with fall blooms, the well-stocked kitchen with Madame Besset its focal point.

You won't have this house. You can't afford it.

She walked to the back door and looked through the glass at Marcel, cutting that day's flowers for Madame Besset to arrange.

Who owns this house?

For the first time in months she was engulfed in the emptiness of not knowing who she was or where she belonged. The fog closed in and panic rose inside her. I don't belong here. I don't belong anywhere.

"A few days, madame?" pressed Madame Besset. "It would help in my marketing if you could tell me—"

"I told you I don't know!" She took a breath. "I'm sorry, Madame Besset; I really don't know. I'll tell you as soon as I can." She wanted to get away from Madame Besset's bright black eyes that saw so much and guessed much more. "I'm going to ride up Mont Ventoux on my bicycle; would you make a sandwich and fill two water bottles for me?"

"Yes, madame. That is a formidable ride."

"I know. I may drive the lower part of it." She went back to the bedroom and swiftly dressed in skintight bicycle shorts, a loose short-sleeved shirt, and bicycle shoes. In a small waist pack she stowed her wallet and car keys, sunscreen and a lightweight jacket, and the sandwich and grapes Madame Besset had given her. She slipped the two water bottles into the sleeves on either side of the pack. "I'll be back by midafternoon," she said to Madame Besset.

In the garage she strapped her bicycle to the rack on the back of the car, tossed her helmet and gloves into the front seat, and backed out of the driveway. A car was parked nearby with a man in the driver's seat wearing a black hat pulled low over his eyes. He seemed vaguely familiar and Stephanie nodded to him as she drove off. It was five-thirty in the morning.

The air was cool, the sky a faint blue-pink, and every leaf and blade of grass seemed clear and sparkling in this brief crisp interlude before the day's heat descended. Stephanie drove fast and easily, passing the trucks that barreled down the narrow roads. Once they had terrified her; now she thought of them only as obstacles to be calculated so that she had time to pull back in front of them before an oncoming car reached her. For such an early hour, the roads were busy, and she concentrated on driving, glancing now and then at farmers in the fields, women hanging out wash in the early coolness, and schoolchildren walking along the roads with yapping dogs chasing each other about their heels. Ahead of her loomed the chalky summit of Mont Ventoux with its radar station and huge television mast outlined against the pale sky.

She slowed when she reached the village of Bédoin, built on a small hill with Mont Ventoux rising majestically behind it. The narrow streets were deserted at this hour, except for the market area where men and women in long aprons were setting up tables and arranging on them fruits and vegetables or stacks of baskets and tablecloths while others hung newly killed chickens upside down, set out rows of cheeses in refrigerated cases, with long curving sausages dangling above, opened barrels and jars of a dozen kinds of marinated and herb-infused olives, and stacked loaves of bread of all sizes and shapes, some almost three feet across. Near the market area was the main square with the mayor's house at one end and the soaring stone church at the other; in the other houses that faced the square people slept or rose to make their breakfast. Everything was normal; for this village, the earth had not shifted. But Stephanie saw all of it as if for the first time because for the first time she was alone.

The summit of Mont Ventoux towered more than four thousand feet above the valley floor, and Stephanie drove partway up its heavily wooded flank before beginning her ride. At a curve in the road she pulled into a grove of cedars, out of the way of other cars, almost hidden from view. She put on her helmet and bicycle gloves and fastened her pack around her waist. It was six-fifteen when she began the ride up the paved road that cut back and forth between cherry and peach orchards and forests of beech and oak, cedar and pine that gradually gave way to scrub that thinned with the thinning air. Through the leaves Stephanie caught glimpses of the TV tower at the top, beckoning her on.

Her body had settled into a rhythm that made her feel she was flowing up the mountain, breathing hard, muscles straining, but exhilarated with her own energy and the cool air swirling about her. Thoughts and images drifted through her mind and she let them come and go without trying to hold on to them.

Max is gone.

I have the house.

But who owns it?

Robert will know; he found it for Max.

Robert will tell me what I can do. Stay for a while, then sell it.

Max should have the money, but how will I get it to him?

And where will I go?

I could live with Léon. He wants that. And I want it. No, not yet. I told him I was going to live alone. *I'm depending on myself.*

He understood; he always understands.

I love Léon. I love Léon. I love Léon.

The words sang within her to the rhythm of her body. Her muscles began to ache; she downshifted until she was in the lowest gear and rode more slowly. She pulled out her water bottle and squeezed a stream of cold water into her mouth as she rode, then twisted to replace it in her pack. As she turned back, a car passed her, surprising her; she barely saw the driver's black hat as she swerved to the right, skidding in the gravel at the side of the road. *Have to be careful; I might break my wrist.*

What an odd idea, she thought, but her mind was slowing to the same speed as her legs, and she let the thought go and pushed steadily upward, keeping her eyes on the summit. It was closer now and the trees were almost gone; soon they would disappear entirely and only the white stone of the highest elevation would remain, a white cap with the television mast like a feather in its center. The sun was higher, but as she climbed, the air grew cooler. She breathed deeply and thought of nothing but one more revolution of her legs, one more and then one more, and then she made the final turn in the road and she was at the top.

Gasping, she leaned her bicycle against the low stone wall and drank deeply from her water bottle, draining it, then opening the other. It was eight o'clock in the morning and at the base of the mountain the heat was building, but here, at six thousand feet, the air was cold and Stephanie began to shiver. She pulled out her jacket and put it on, zipping it up to the collar. She was alone; it was too early for tourists, and the restaurant was not yet open. The only sound was the steady rush of wind that gave the mountain its name. Stephanie left the bicycle and, nibbling a bunch of grapes, walked slowly around the summit, circling the white and red air force radar station and the long, low building housing scientific and television equipment, gazing at the scene below.

The Provençal plain spread on all sides like a verdant ring, and beyond it in a great circle of green and buff and blue were the Alps, capped with snow, the Lubéron, the Pyrenees, the Rhône Valley with its broad river winding in lazy curves to the horizon, shining silver in the sun, Marseilles and the lighthouses of the Berre lagoon, and the Alpilles chain that Stephanie had first seen in Léon's painting. *Léon should be here; we should be seeing this together. So much beauty, so much magnificence, such a glorious world.*

She felt a piercing happiness. *Everything is waiting for me: a new life, a whole life, with Léon. Because I will remember, however long it takes, and then I'll be the person I was and the person I am now. And I'll have everything I could ever want.*

She was smiling to herself, in love with Léon, with life, with all the possibilities that awaited her, when a shadow fell near her and she looked up into the face of a man who had come up behind her. He held a gun, so small it looked like a shiny silver toy palmed in his gloved hand, but it was aimed at her, and it was so close that her arm brushed it in turning. She gave a sharp cry and he gripped her arm with his other hand.

"Shut up. Don't say anything, just stand here, just the way you are, like you're looking at the view. People may come."

"What do you want?" Her voice sounded strange to her. "I don't have much money, you can have what I've got, it's in my pack. Take—"

"Shut up! Keep your voice down!" His black slouch hat almost touched Stephanie's forehead and their bodies were so close she could see small scratches in his leather vest. "I don't want your money. I want your husband. Where is he?"

"I saw you yesterday! In the churchyard. And this morning you were outside our house, in your car."

"*Where is he?*"

"I don't know."

"The fuck you don't." He pushed the gun upward into Stephanie's breast and she gasped. "I was outside your house all night; he didn't leave, but he's not there now. Where is he?"

"He did leave. He's gone." Now it was real, the man, the gun, the darkening sky. She was trembling and breathing rapidly; the gun cut into her breast and the man's face, so oddly cherubic with a tiny nose above full, red lips, was so close to hers she could feel his breath. Léon, Léon, Léon, she thought wildly; I can't die; we haven't even begun. "You're hurting me. What do you want?"

"Where did he go?"

"I told you, I don't know! I can't tell you! Please stop . . . you're hurting me."

"You stupid cunt, I'll stop when you tell me where the fuck he is. He didn't go to Marseilles; I checked. *Where is he?*"

"I don't know!" *He knows about Max's warehouse in Marseilles. What else does he know? Where does he come from?* "What do you want him for? What do you want of us?"

"I want him. I don't give a fuck for you if you tell me where he is."

"I can't tell you. He left while I was asleep; he didn't tell me where he—"

"You're lying." He tightened his grip on her arm, twisting it until she cried out.

"I'm not, I'm not. Please, that hurts, please leave me alone, there's nothing I—"

"Christ, this is like a fucking conversation. Okay, you're coming with me; if you won't talk, you'll take me to him."

"I can't!" Her fear exploded. "Damn you, I don't know where he is! We don't live together anymore!"

He was taken aback. The gun relaxed slightly against Stephanie's breast. "Since when?"

"Last night. He left and he's not coming back and that's all I know."

"Bullshit. I saw you at that church, all lovey-dovey; there's no way he was about to walk out on you."

Stephanie looked at him in despair, not knowing what else to say. "He's gone. He's not coming back."

"Fuck." He looked around as a tour bus pulled into the parking area a hundred feet away. "Come on, we're getting out of here."

"Why? I can't tell you anything! Can't you just leave, please, just go away? I told you, *I swear*, there's nothing—"

"Shut up!"

Men and women in straw hats and brightly printed cotton shirts and dresses, with cameras slung around their necks, were streaming out of the tour bus. The man pushed Stephanie before him along the low wall until they had rounded a corner and were behind the radar station. "My car's over there, around the corner," he said and gestured with the gun toward the end of the viewing area where Stephanie had left her bicycle. "You walk nice and quiet right next to me, and keep your mouth shut."

"Where are we going?"

"To your husband, like I said." He eyed Stephanie's long bare legs, then once again nudged her breast with his gun, this time a little playfully. "We might stop and have some fun on the way, though." Swiftly he reached down and shoved his hand between her legs. "Nice. Real nice. There's no hurry, is there? He'll be waiting for you, wherever he is."

"No!" Stephanie cried, and in desperation said, "If you touch me I'll never tell you where he is."

The man cocked an eyebrow. "See? I knew all along. And you'll tell me, you little cunt; you think you won't, but when I get through with you, you'll—" Raised voices came from the direction of the tour bus. "Get going, to the car." He jammed the gun against Stephanie's ribs and edged her with him to the corner of the radar station. He stopped there, gripping Stephanie's arm to keep her out of sight, and casually looked around. A few feet away stood the low building housing television and scientific equipment, its door closed. It was built in the shape of an L, and he pushed Stephanie before him across the small open space to the sheltered corner at the back of the low building.

They stood there, waiting. Stephanie's body was like ice, her breathing shallow, her muscles taut. She was terrified of the cheerful smile on the man's cherubic face and the way his eyes raked her. She could still feel the pressure of the gun barrel pushing into her breast and his hand between her legs. She looked around, but there was nowhere to run; the rock-strewn, treeless summit was bare except for the two vacant buildings and the tourists cheerfully exclaiming in German over the view, their cameras clicking.

But within a few minutes they were leaving. Cameras and binoculars were put away and they climbed inside the bus, the driver counting as they mounted the steps. The door swung shut with a hydraulic hiss and they were gone.

"Now." The man pulled Stephanie's hand through his arm, like a gentleman taking a stroll with his lady. But at that moment a car sped up the road, careened across the parking area, and scraped the man's car as it stopped beside it. "What the fuck—" he began and then he saw, around the corner of the building, as Stephanie did, that the driver was Max.

"Hey. How about that." As Max opened the door and stepped from his car, Stephanie felt the arm clamping hers relax, and she whipped her hand free and ran toward Max.

"Max, go back!" she screamed.

"Sabrina! Where are—" Stephanie heard a pop behind her, like a firecracker, and saw Max stagger and fall against the car.

"Max!" She stumbled and fell to one knee, then got up and ran on. Her knee stung and she saw blood running down her leg. "Max, go away, he's after you—"

"Get down!" Max's voice was a grunt, and as the gun fired again he and Stephanie dropped to the ground at the same time. Stephanie crawled rapidly along the pavement, grimacing with the sharp pain of her cut knee, until she turned the corner of the building. She heard the gun fire again, twice, as Max made a dash from his car to the other side of the building; then there was silence. She moved farther until she came to a recessed doorway and she huddled within it, holding her legs to her chest. She could not see either man; there was no sound but the steady rush of the wind. Then suddenly Max was there, silently putting his arm around her, pulling her against him. Blood from her knee stained the front of his shirt, but there was blood, too, soaking the upper part of his sleeve.

"Max, he hit you—"

"Hush." He kissed her, a brief, despairing kiss. "I love you. I couldn't leave you. Stay here. *Stay here.*" And then, his bloodied arm dangling, he left the doorway. He searched along the edge of the building until he found a large rounded stone, and took it with him as he moved away from Stephanie, back in the direction from which he had come. She watched him as he moved crablike, keeping his right side close to the building, until he reached the far corner. He turned and threw the rock the length of the building to the corner closer to Stephanie. It struck the wall, and as it took a bounce on the pavement, he disappeared around the corner.

Stephanie waited. Drawn back into the doorway, she saw only the shadow of the man as he peered around the corner where the rock had struck. Almost at the same time, another shadow joined it and then both shadows disappeared as Max threw himself on the man's back and they crashed to the ground. They fought on the pavement amid the sharp stones, grunting, cursing, rolling over each other.

Max felt the man trying to choke him, one hand driving knifelike against his larynx, and he slammed his knee into the man's crotch and heard him yowl as he relaxed his hand on Max's throat. Max was older but taller and heavier and so driven by terror—*he'll kill her; he won't be satisfied with me because she can identify him*—that nothing could hold him down. The man's black slouch-brimmed hat went flying, blood streaked the pavement, and then the shiny silver gun skidded along the ground.

Stephanie leaped from the doorway and swept it up. "Max!" She crawled closer to the writhing men. "Max, the gun!"

"*Merde!*" Max roared at the man and flung him off. He grabbed the gun from Stephanie's outstretched hand, aimed it shakily with his left hand—but he's right-handed, Stephanie thought, and then realized that it was his right arm that had been hit—and fired.

The man screamed and clutched his stomach. Max fired again, but his body was sagging and the bullet hit the building. "*Merde,*" he whispered, this time to himself.

Stephanie crawled to him and put her arms around him, cradling him. "We've got to get to the car; get you to a doctor. Can you—"

"No, wait. Have to rest." His breath was rasping in his chest and he slumped against her. "Too damn . . . old for . . . this sort of . . . thing."

"Max, who is he?"

"Sent by . . . someone. To kill me. Sabrina, get out . . . out of Cavaillon; they want you, too."

"No, he said it was only you . . ."

". . . a lackey . . . doesn't know anything. That's why I . . . came back. To get you. Couldn't leave you." He shifted his arm, grunting with the pain. "He was . . . at the house?"

"Yes, in his car, when I left this morning. He was in the churchyard yesterday, too; you saw him. Max, *who sent him?*"

". . . doesn't matter. As long as you get out . . . get away . . ."

"What good will it do? He found you this time."

"Chance. A stupid accident. A favor for a friend . . . a good deed . . . should have known better . . . not the type to do good deeds . . . and it backfired. It won't happen to you. Listen to me—"

"How did you know I was up here?"

"Madame Besset. And he'd been on our terrace, so I knew he was around. Went out the back at midnight; didn't see him, but I knew he was . . . somewhere . . . so I had to come back . . . couldn't leave you. Then I saw his car. Christ, so close . . . he could have killed you . . . shouldn't have left you alone. Sabrina, get out, get out, you're not safe!"

"You didn't say that yesterday."

He gave a weak bark of laughter. "I thought . . . love . . . and being together . . . Christ, what a fool, to think that love was enough."

Stephanie was crying. She held him to her breast, her head bent over his. She had never cared for him so much. "Max, I've got to get you to a doctor. You can crawl, can't you? Where are the keys to your car?"

"Left them in it." He raised his good hand and caressed Stephanie's face. "So beautiful . . . made my life bright. Sabrina, listen . . . listen . . . if I don't make it—"

"Don't say that! Max, we're going to your car. Come on, now, I'll help—"

"—call Robert. He'll take care of you. He knows what to do. *Call Robert.* Say you will."

"Of course I will; I'll call him anyway; he'll help us. Now come on, Max, please, I can't carry you . . ."

"Try . . ." Grunting, he tried to push himself up, using his good arm, and at that moment the other man gathered himself together and leaped upon them, knocking them backwards. Stephanie's head hit the pavement and for a moment the world was black. Max was on top of her, crushing her, and she could not breathe; blood throbbed in her head, bursting against her eyeballs. She dragged breath into her lungs and tried to scream, but no sound came. I'm going to die, she thought, and heard the gun fire, and fire again, and with a fierce effort she thrust herself up and pushed Max off her.

She opened her eyes and saw the building nearby, blurred and wavering, and clouds trailing like torn ribbons across the deep blue sky. She felt cool air on her face and a terrible pain at the back of her head, and then her vision cleared and she saw Max's head near her own, unmoving.

She took long gasping breaths and slowly came to her hands and knees. She stayed there, swaying a little, her head down, then moved stiffly to Max. Blood covered the front of his shirt; he was staring at nothing. "No, no, no," Stephanie whispered, and laid her face against his and held her fingers to the side of his neck to find a pulse. "Max, please be alive, please be alive." But there was no response; there was no pulse. She stayed there for a long time, until she told herself that he was dead.

She sat up and gazed at his face, the deep lines that had only recently appeared, his halo of grizzled hair, his tight gray beard. She put her hand over his eyes and closed them. "You didn't have to stay," she whispered. She was crying again. "Oh, Max, you didn't have to stay. You were gone; he didn't know where. You were safe. And even when you came back, when you saw his car, you could have turned around. You could have run."

A few feet away, the other man sprawled across piles of rocks, blood soaking his pants. His eyes stared at the sky. And from the other side of the building came the sound of a tourist bus lumbering up the hill.

They were hidden from the main parking lot and viewing platform by the long side of the building. Without thinking it through, Stephanie knew she had to hide them. She did not know what Max had done or who had sent his murderer and still might want to kill her, and since she could explain nothing she knew she had to keep this a secret, at least until she could talk to Robert. Robert would know what to do. Robert knew more than she did.

So, crying, gasping with pain as she struggled with their deadweight, she dragged Max and then the gunman around the corner to the inside angle of the L-shaped building, and piled rocks in front of them. If tourists came around to see the view from this side of the summit, it would be almost impossible to make anything out in the deeply shadowed rock-filled niche where they lay.

She bent over Max and touched his face. She kissed his closed eyes and his mouth. "I'm sorry, Max. I'm sorry I couldn't love you; I'm sorry I couldn't stay with you. I'm sorry I can't stay with you now or take you down with me. If I could . . ."

The brakes of the tour bus squealed; the pneumatic door hissed as it opened. In Spanish the driver told his passengers how long they had to admire the view, and not to wander down the mountain or stand too close to the edge. Over his voice came the sound of another bus, close behind, with another load of tourists.

Stephanie took off her torn jacket and brushed herself off, wiping her bloody knee with tissue from her pocket. She ran her fingers through her hair and took deep breaths, trying to still her trembling. She wanted someone to hold her, she wanted to cry in someone's lap, but there was no one. *I'm depending on myself.*

But Robert will help me, she thought again. Max said he'd know what to do. I have Robert to help me with everything. And Léon . . . oh, Léon, my love, when I feel a little stronger, when I don't come to you as a child, then we'll be together.

It had been only a few minutes since the buses had arrived. She was still trembling, but she was able to stand straight, her head high, and she walked away from the protection of the building, moving quickly, purposefully, to Max's car, ignoring the buses and anyone who might be looking. The key was in the ignition; she turned it, backed out of the lot and drove down the mountain.

* * *

It was after nine o'clock that night before it was dark enough for Robert and Stephanie and Andrew Frick to drive up Mont Ventoux unobserved. When Stephanie had arrived that morning after driving recklessly, almost blindly, through the streets of Cavaillon, she and Robert had held each other and wept together, wrenching tears that were perhaps the only ones that had ever been shed for Max. Then, exhausted, she had fallen asleep on the couch in Robert's apartment, and Robert struggled with the tears that would not stop and with a sense of unreality as he called Andrew and made the arrangements Max had laid out for him.

Confident Max, invulnerable Max, the consummate schemer and manipulator and survivor . . . how could he be gone? For all that he had done that forced Robert to turn a blind eye, for all that he had been that Robert bemoaned—what a great man he might have been had he turned his talents and energy to true leadership!—for all that, he had helped Robert when Robert needed him; they had been friends; they had loved each other.

Robert did not know what job Andrew Frick had with Max, but his name and telephone number were among Max's instructions, and so it was Andrew, crying, cursing Max's killer, who drove Robert and Stephanie in his van up Mont Ventoux as the sky darkened and a sliver of a moon rose over the Alps. "The main thing is, the police can't know," he said.

"No," Robert agreed. He had wrestled with that problem all day, and concluded that there was too much at stake for the police to investigate the shooting death of Max and his assassin. Robert's obligation now was to Sabrina, and Max had told him that she could be in danger. A police investigation would expose her, her picture would be in the newspapers, other unknown men might come for her. And whatever Max's business had been, it was obviously not one that would withstand police scrutiny, and that could harm Sabrina, too. There was Max's

Swiss bank account, which Robert would turn over to Sabrina, there was the title to the house and the cars, there were valuable antiques, all of them hers now. But perhaps not so easily hers if the police were brought in. She could be left with nothing but the taint of having been Max's wife.

So, my dear friend, we will give you a private funeral, and make our private farewells. And since you were a private man, it seems right that that is what we do.

"Neither of them can be found," he said to Andrew.

"Right. We'll have to take care of both of them."

On the summit of Mont Ventoux, so dark when they turned off their headlights that they could not see each other, they found the bodies where Stephanie had left them, behind crude piles of rocks. Andrew drove close to them and the three of them lifted them into the back, dimly lit by the van's ceiling light. Then Andrew retrieved Stephanie's bicycle and helmet and locked them in the rack on the back of the van.

"That man's car," Stephanie said. "There may be something in it."

"He never gave you a name?" Robert asked.

She shook her head. "Or where he came from. But Max knew. He wouldn't tell me, but he knew who sent him. He knew who wanted him . . . dead."

Andrew put his arm around her and squeezed, thinking that this was the most gorgeous woman he'd ever seen, and trust Max to keep her a secret. Old Max, sixty, he'd said once, sixty years old and good enough to get this incredible woman. Christ, he thought, what the hell am I going to do without Max? Not that I can't find work—I can always do that—but he made it so much fun.

They found the car still parked unobtrusively in a corner of the parking lot, a rental agency sticker on its license plate. Inside, they found another gun, three passports with different names and countries of origin, a map of Provence, a thermos of coffee, a half-eaten sandwich, and a photo of Max torn out of a glossy magazine.

"But he has no beard," Robert exclaimed.

"And his hair is red; I never knew it was red," Stephanie said. "He looks so much younger." She felt a deep sadness; she had known almost nothing about him.

"I liked the beard," Andrew said. "He always seemed a little wild, you know, outside everybody's predictable lives."

"Yes, that was Max," Robert said softly. "He wouldn't let himself fit into a category. Or a way of life."

"Come on," Andrew said impatiently. He gathered up everything but the thermos and sandwich and put it all in the glove compartment of his van. "Let's get out of here."

They drove down the mountain and pulled into the grove of cedar and pine trees where Stephanie's car was still parked. Only this morning, she thought. A lifetime ago. Fifty feet into the woods, while Stephanie held a small flashlight, the men took shovels from the van and dug two graves. "Not close to each other," Robert said. "I don't want that man lying beside Max."

"Wherever," grunted Andrew. "Just so the son of a bitch who sent him doesn't know where he is. Hey, that'll keep him awake, right? His guy disappears, no sign of Max, no nothing. He won't know what the hell happened. I hope it drives him crazy."

It was midnight when they laid the two bodies in the graves. A light breeze whispered through the small clearing, lightly touching the perspiring men and Stephanie's tearful face.

"Our Father," Robert said quietly. He took the flashlight from Stephanie and turned it off, and the three of them stood in the pitch-black silence, holding hands. "We bring you Max Lacoste, in an unconventional way, but nonetheless in a spirit of love and grace. He was a man who wandered far from your path, a man who lived a life we would not emulate but for which we cannot entirely condemn him. He was a complicated man, a devious man, but a caring man. He was a man who, even when outside the law, cared for others, did good, and shared what he had in money and energy and talents. He could have been much more . . . or much less. He was never able to be completely happy, though he knew happiness as well as sadness, wealth and loss, love and fear. He was my friend and the friend of others. Had he lived, he might have turned his great talents to the service of others. I will always believe that that might have happened, if he had lived. Now we commend his soul to you. In the name of the Father, the Son, and the Holy Ghost . . . amen.''

Stephanie, crying, heard Andrew crying. Then she saw the flashlight's thin beam move to the other grave, and heard Robert say a brief prayer for the soul of the murderer. "Now," Robert said, and with Stephanie again holding the flashlight the men shoveled earth into the graves, tamped it down, then dragged branches and fallen leaves over them.

Stephanie knelt where Max was buried and pressed her palm to the earth. My husband, she thought. Somehow it never seemed right to me that we were married, just as it doesn't seem right, even now, that Sabrina is my name, but he cared for me as a husband would, and that was what mattered.

"My dear." Robert's hand was on her shoulder, and she rose and went with him to her car, and he drove it while Andrew followed in the van, all of them locked in their thoughts as they drove through a sleeping Bédoin, past the darkened villages and farmhouses that dotted the rolling plain, and so back to Cavaillon. "And you will stay with me tonight," Robert said to Stephanie. "I don't want you to be alone in your house."

She looked at him through drooping eyes. "You think there are others, and when they don't hear from that man they'll come looking for me."

"We don't know that."

"But you think it. That's why you want me to stay with you."

"It's possible. I don't want to take the chance."

She was too tired to argue. "But I want to talk to Andrew first."

Robert left them alone in his small living room, and she asked Andrew about what Max did in Marseilles, and he told her. "There's a huge market all over the world for counterfeit money, hundreds of millions of dollars a year. Max was providing a service, and I was honored to be part of it. He was a hell of a guy to work for, Sabrina, and a hell of a good friend. I mean, he cared about people and he loved being alive and making things happen. I thought he was like a puppet master, you know, sort of keeping the rest of us dancing."

"Yes," Stephanie murmured. "What was the good deed he did?"

"Good deed? No idea."

"He said the reason they found him was some kind of coincidence. He was doing a favor for a friend and it backfired."

Andrew shrugged. "Got me. He didn't talk to me about his private life."

"Does Robert know?"

"About the good deed?"

"About any of it. The counterfeiting, the smuggling . . ."

"Christ, no. Max told me never to tell him. He really cared about Robert, you know; he wouldn't have laid that on him. Anyway, he didn't really trust anybody, even the people he cared about. Oh, sorry, I didn't mean—"

"It's all right. I know he was like that."

"Look, Sabrina, if you need help, if you need anything . . . I'll get you out of here, I'll take care of you; I mean, if you'd let me—"

"Thank you, Andrew, but I'm fine. I have Robert and . . . I have friends."

Robert. Friends. She thought about them all night, sleeping fitfully on the small couch, waking with a start, thinking she heard Max's voice, or Léon's or Jacqueline's, or Madame Besset beating egg whites for a soufflé, or the bell at Jacqueline en Provence announcing a customer. Sometimes she was sure she heard the dull thud of soil being flung into graves. At dawn she stayed awake, and that was how Robert found her, curled up, one hand under her cheek, her eyes wide and thoughtful.

"What is it you look at so intently?" he asked.

"I'm trying to see the future." She wore a pair of Robert's pajamas that were only slightly too big, and as she sat up, her hair tousled, her cheek red with the imprint of her fingers, Robert thought she looked like an innocent child.

"Part of your future is secure," he said, and told her about Max's money. "You're a wealthy woman, Sabrina; you'll need someone to help you handle your money and Max's investments. I know two people, one in Marseilles, one in Paris. Let me give you their names."

Stephanie took the cards he held out. *A wealthy woman. But all I want is what I have: a home, a job, friends . . . and Léon.* "Robert, I have a friend. Someone very important to me. I'd like you to meet him."

He gazed at her without expression. "Did Max know?"

"I never found a way to tell him. I wanted to, but . . . You see, he was leaving Cavaillon. And I was staying."

"He told me you were leaving together. But not for a while."

"He left last night. I wouldn't go with him."

"Because of your friend?"

"Partly. But mostly because this is my home and I didn't want to start all over again somewhere else."

"Max was your husband."

"I couldn't go with him, Robert. He told me things about his life, things I couldn't be part of . . ." A shiver went through her. "I can't believe we're talking about him like this; I keep thinking he'll walk in the door and be angry because we're talking about him. He didn't like people to talk about him, or to know anything about him."

"But I knew him, at least I knew some sides of him, and I don't believe he would have left you behind."

"He didn't want to. He tried to persuade me to go. But he knew I didn't love him—I think you knew it, too, Robert—and when I refused, he had to leave. He knew they'd found him, whoever they were, and he didn't have much time. But then he came back. He said I was in danger, too."

"And so you must leave after all. As soon as possible."

"Where will I go? Robert, I have nowhere to go; I don't know anyone anywhere but here."

"I have friends; I can send you to them. Or is the real reason that your friend does not want to leave?"

"I haven't asked him. I love him, Robert, and I want to marry him, but I have to know what kind of life I can lead before I ask him to be with me."

"But you must leave. How can you hesitate, after yesterday? If you want your friend with you, you must ask him to leave Cavaillon, but in any event, Sabrina, *you cannot stay here.*"

"Yes, I know, I know, I just can't decide right now . . . Robert, right now I just want you to meet him and get to know him."

"To give you my blessing."

"Yes."

"And to marry you?"

"When we're ready . . . if you would . . . there's no one else I want."

"But then what is it you want now?"

"I want you to tell me you're happy for me. I want you to be glad that I've found someone to love." Tears came to her eyes. "I want you to be my family."

Robert kissed her forehead. "This afternoon, then. Can you reach him that quickly? We'll have lunch at Café Hélène. A family lunch."

Café Hélène was a converted house, white stucco, square and solid on its street corner, its tables shielded from the traffic by a high stucco wall. Stephanie and Robert were led through a narrow arch to a tiny walled courtyard fragrant with roses, with a single table set for three.

When Léon arrived, he took Stephanie's hands and kissed them. "I was worried. I called all day yesterday. I even called Jacqueline, who said she does not keep track of you on Sundays."

"So much has happened . . . I have so much to tell you. Léon, this is Father Robert Chalon."

They shook hands, taking stock of each other, liking each other. "I've seen your work," Robert said. "You have a great talent."

"But what has happened?" Léon took Stephanie's hand again, and sat beside her while Robert told him what had happened on Mont Ventoux. As he talked, Léon moved his chair closer to Stephanie's, his grip tightening on her hand. "Terrible, terrible. How terrifying to be there . . . alone. With the winds and the dead. Dead," he repeated, his voice barely a murmur. "Dead. So suddenly, so crazily. We never thought . . ." He put his arm around Stephanie and turned her face to his. "All I want is to be with you always, to help you when you need it, to shield you from danger so that never again could you be alone on a mountaintop in such terror . . . my God, I would do anything to keep you from that."

"I thought of you," Stephanie said. "I talked to you. I said I couldn't die because we had barely begun."

He laughed quietly. "We'll take care of each other from now on. And Father Chalon will watch over us both."

"Wherever you are," Robert said, and then they talked about all that had happened and all that might happen. They sat at the small round table for the whole afternoon, remembering Max, learning about Robert's work and how Max had helped it, trying to imagine the danger facing Stephanie.

"We'll leave," Léon said at last. "Why would we stay where there is any danger at all? Nothing keeps us here; we'll choose a town where we can begin everything new, where we can be as private as we wish. Oh. I know the place. I have friends in Vézelay; I use their guest house and studio whenever I visit Burgundy. We'll go there. No one looks for anyone in Vézelay; there are too many tourists. Everyone becomes anonymous.''

"A beautiful town," said Robert. "But close to Paris. Less than two hundred kilometers, I believe.''

"Far enough," Léon said. "We can slip in and out for theater and music and galleries, and live as we wish in Vézelay. Sabrina, does that sound good to you?''

"Yes," she said. And she did not say that there might be people in Vézelay who knew her, or in Paris, or anywhere else they might go. Until she remembered who she was, there was nowhere she could be sure she would be anonymous. But why talk about that now? She was with Léon. The terror of yesterday and the black sorrow of the burial in the forest were behind her. She remembered her piercing happiness on the summit of Mont Ventoux just before the murderer arrived. *Everything is waiting for me . . . a new life, a whole life, with Léon. Because I will remember, and then I'll be the person I was and the person I am now. And I'll have everything I could ever want.*

It would never seem that simple again, she thought. She knew now how the calm of a sunlit day could be shattered and happiness swept away. She knew there would be other shadows in the years to come, new discoveries, sudden meetings that she could not even imagine. But if they held on to each other, to what they would build together, nothing would be as terrible as that lonely moment on the summit of Mont Ventoux. *Because we'll be together. And we won't let anything tear us apart.*

"Well, then, Vézelay," Léon said. "A very special place. A good place for us. How soon can you be ready?''

"The house . . ." Stephanie said. "Madame Besset. I can't just walk out.''

"Madame Besset and I will pack up everything in the house and send it to you when you're ready," Robert said. "You should leave very soon. You should not go back to that house at all.''

"No, you'll stay with me," Léon said. They talked about storing the antiques and the art from the house, and

428

paying Madame Besset and moving Léon's furnishings and his studio. "Formidable but not impossible," Léon said to Stephanie with a smile. "And we start with a visit to Avignon. I have some supplies to pick up; can you come with me? We can make lists of everything we need to do."

Stephanie shook her head. "I can't just walk out of Jacqueline's shop. I'll ask her how long she needs me."

"It is more important that you leave," Robert said. "I could tell her for you."

"No. Thank you, Robert, but Jacqueline is my friend. I'll tell her I'm leaving in . . . one week."

Léon met Robert's eyes. "Less," he said. "We'll go the day after tomorrow. What we cannot pack, Father Chalon and Madame Besset will finish for us. But first Avignon, yes? Will you come with me tomorrow afternoon after you finish in the shop?"

"Yes," Stephanie said. She was remembering a shop Max had shown her, filled with antique maps. She would buy one for Léon. She had not yet given him a gift and suddenly, urgently, she wanted to.

"I'll pick you up at one," Léon said, but when he arrived at the shop the next afternoon Stephanie was still inside, helping a customer. He watched through the window as she appeared and disappeared, moving from the front of the shop to the back. Seen through the glass and the cluttered window display, she se med dreamlike, a beautiful woman wearing a white summer dress, drifting among fragile antiques. Nothing lasts, Léon thought. He gripped the steering wheel. The hell it doesn't. This will last. What we create will last.

Stephanie opened the car door and leaned across to kiss him. "I'm sorry; we were so busy. Jacqueline was wonderful. I hope we can ask her to visit us in Vézelay. Do you think she'll come?"

"Someday. I went to your house today. Madame Besset and I packed your clothes and I paid her for September. I told her you'd left town."

"What did she say?"

"That she'd always thought you and monsieur had many secrets and she would not be surprised at anything you did. She hopes you remember her fondly."

"She knows I will. She taught me to drive."

"And Robert taught you to cook."

"And you taught me to love. How long will we be in Avignon?"

"Not long. And tomorrow we go home to Vézelay."

Stephanie sighed. "Once I thought I should live alone for a while before coming to you. I thought I needed to learn how to do that."

"And now?"

"I want to be with you. I like to hear you say *home*. And I don't know what all the tomorrows will be like."

"Whatever they're like, we'll face them together." They drove in the hazy heat through villages with a row of shops, a church, and a square where men in black played *boules*, rolling the silver balls across the smoothly swept dirt while families watched and applauded, and then they were driving through one of the gates in the old stone wall that encircled Avignon. In the distance they saw the great towers and domes of the Palace of the Popes. Léon found a parking place near the river and got out, stretching his legs. Stephanie reached into the back seat and put on a wide-brimmed straw hat with a long red and orange scarf tied around the crown. Léon drew in his breath. "So lovely . . . I'll paint you like that, in Vézelay, beside a wall of bougainvillaea. Is the hat new?"

"I just bought it; I loved the colors. Where are we going?"

"To Monet Fournitures Artistiques. This way." They walked to the Place de l'Horloge, and stopped for a moment beside the carousel of brightly painted horses and elephants and great thronelike seats, turning to the accompaniment of hurdy-gurdy music. Stephanie gazed at it, unable to tear herself away. "Isn't it wonderful? Such a happy place for children."

Léon took her arm and they moved on. The heat built up in the square; people took off their jackets and draped them over their arms. Stephanie took off her hat, combed her hair with her fingers, and put it on again. They left the square and came to a cobbled street along the Sorgue River, the air cooler here, mossy waterwheels turning lazily at the river's edge and, on the other side of the Rue des Teinturiers, a row of antique shops.

Stephanie recognized one of them. "Léon, we have to go in here. I want to buy you something."

Inside, she moved around a large table, lifting heavy folios, each one holding a map encased in protective sheets of plastic. "Oh, this one. Do you like it?"

Léon's eyebrows rose. "It's quite wonderful. Very rare. A Tavernier. But do you have any idea what it costs?"

"It doesn't matter. I want to buy you a present. I want to buy you this."

A small man, stooped over a cane, came through the doorway. His white hair was in disarray; his white beard was trimmed to a neat point. "Yes, madame?" He quoted a price.

"Fine," Stephanie said.

Léon was poring over the map. "Superb. I've always looked for one." He and the shop owner compared the map to others; Léon said that he was a painter and looked at ancient maps as works of art. They talked for a long time, answering Stephanie's questions, enjoying each other. Then Léon said to Stephanie, "I'd like to wait. Do you mind very much if we don't buy it today? I'd like to be sure where we'll be living before I start dragging it around. It could be sent to us later."

"Oh. If that's the reason . . . yes, of course. But I do want to buy it for you. And I won't forget. We'll wait," Stephanie said to the owner of the shop.

"I can hold it for you. If you have a card, monsieur . . . ?"

"No, plenty of canvases, but no cards."

"We'll call you," Stephanie said, and as they left,

Léon took a final glance at the map, lovingly put back in its case by the little man with white hair.

"You're wonderful," he said as they walked to Monet Fournitures Artistiques, the art supply shop. "I've wanted one of those all my life." Inside, Léon greeted a tall woman with broad shoulders, round cheeks and oversize glasses that made her look like an amiable owl. They talked about oils and watercolors while Stephanie wandered around the shop, enjoying the riot of colors, the display of brushes lined up by size like a military formation, stacks of canvases in graduated sizes, and palettes hanging from long rods. When the woman went in back to find some gesso, Léon put his arm around Stephanie. "My darling Sabrina, you are very patient."

"I'm having a good time. Max never liked to browse in shops. He just looked in windows."

"Husbands aren't supposed to love shopping."

"Some husbands might."

He smiled. "Perhaps we'll come across one."

The woman came back and wrapped Léon's order. "Thank you, monsieur. I hope to see you again soon."

"I hope so. But the next shop will be in Paris," he said to Stephanie when they were outside again. "I'll have to find a whole new set of shopkeepers."

Stephanie stopped in the street. "You're turning your life upside down because of me."

"There is no better reason in all the world."

They kissed beneath the trees of Avignon, and then they walked on, arm in arm, in love, free of the tentacles that seemed to reach for them in Cavaillon. "Soon," Léon murmured. "A new life. I feel like an explorer beginning a new adventure."

Two adventures, Stephanie thought. The one we make together and the one I still travel alone: finding the other half of myself. And I will. Soon. Léon will help me. And who knows what I'll find in Vézelay or Paris that will be the key I've been looking for all this time?

Part III

Part III

CHAPTER *17*

In Avignon, on a hot October afternoon, Sabrina stood at the counter of Monet Fournitures Artistiques. She wore a wide-brimmed straw hat with a long red and orange scarf tied around the crown, and she spoke with the owner of the shop about two people who had been there a few weeks before.

"The woman did not tell me her name," the owner said. "But when I was in the other room, she and her friend were talking together and he called her by her name. And she spoke her husband's name."

Sabrina looked at her, waiting.

"Her name was Sabrina," the woman said. "And the husband's name was Max."

The colorful shelves seemed to tilt around her and Sabrina put a hand on the counter to steady herself. *Sabrina and Max.* She had come to Avignon looking for a ghost. And she had found two of them.

It could not be coincidence. Someone was deliberately impersonating Sabrina Longworth, even going so far as to create a man named Max. But why? Everyone thought

Sabrina Longworth was dead; why would anyone impersonate a dead woman? It made no sense. Unless . . .

Unless . . .

Unless she was Stephanie. Stephanie Andersen, still playing the role of her sister Sabrina. Stephanie . . . alive.

She couldn't be. There was no way . . .

But who else would look exactly like her and be named Sabrina and be with a man named Max?

What if she hadn't been killed? What if she was alive? *Oh, my God, Stephanie, if you really could be* . . .

"Madame," said the woman, and Sabrina saw that she was offering a glass of water.

"Thank you." The glass was heavy and deeply ridged, a bistro glass, comforting in the hand. "I need to know more about them. Please believe me, I was not that woman."

"Then, madame, she could only have been your twin sister; such an astonishing resemblance—"

"I must know more about them. Please, is there nothing else you can tell me?"

"Nothing, madame. I had not seen them before. The man, the painter, most likely does not live in Avignon; otherwise, I am sure he would have been in my shop many times. I would guess he is from a nearby town, perhaps Les Baux; many artists live there."

"And . . . the woman? Where might she live?"

"I cannot say. But even though they spoke of a husband, they seemed to me like two people who live together. Or perhaps . . ."

"Yes?"

"I did think that perhaps they were running away together. There was a kind of urgency—" A customer came into the shop and the woman put her hand briefly on Sabrina's. "That is all I can tell you, madame; I wish I could be more helpful."

"Yes. Thank you." And then she was in the street again, in the early afternoon heat. Crowds walked past, heading purposefully to cafés; shopkeepers hung Closed signs in doors and windows. Lunchtime, Sabrina thought vaguely. One o'clock. My flight from Marseilles to London. And tomorrow, to Chicago.

But she could not move. She stood in the shade of a plane tree, her thoughts chasing each other.

Her name was Sabrina. And the husband's name was Max.

Sabrina and Max. Not so many miles from Monte Carlo, where there had been an explosion . . .

The street emptied. She leaned against the tree, breathing rapidly.

To live another life. Stephanie in Hong Kong, one year ago. *An adventure, Sabrina! A week. Just one incredible week.*

And Sabrina hesitating: *You might get greedy.*

Was that what had happened? Had she wanted more? Had she wanted a lifetime, and so she and Max had arranged to disappear?

Stephanie would never do that.

Her name was Sabrina. And the husband's name was Max. Not so many miles from Monte Carlo.

And the man in the map store, angry because she insisted she had never been there, had said, *I understand that you are not especially interested in maps—that you deal with antique furniture instead . . .*

"Dear God," Sabrina said aloud. "I don't understand."

But . . . if Stephanie was alive . . .

Stephanie. Alive.

Her other half, the part of her that she had lost a year earlier and still mourned, still ached for, even in the midst of the greatest happiness she had ever known.

Stephanie. Stephanie. Stephanie.

She had to find her. Whatever she found, whatever it meant, whoever that woman was, she had to find her.

You deal with antique furniture.

Almost running, she retraced her steps through the sun-baked streets to the shaded stone courtyard of L'Europe.

Lunch was being served to well-dressed guests who looked up in surprise at Sabrina's flushed face and hurried footsteps, and she walked more slowly into the lobby and upstairs to her room.

I'll call, she thought. I haven't time to run all over the countryside from one antique shop to another—

Time. The flight from Marseilles to London. And tomorrow morning, from London to Chicago.

She looked at her watch. One-thirty in Avignon. Seventhirty in Evanston. They'll be at breakfast. My family will be at breakfast. My husband and children will be at breakfast.

The words sank like stones. *My family. My husband and children.*

Garth, Garth, Garth.

She clamped down on the thought. Not now. Later. Now is for Stephanie.

Stephanie. Alive.

Oh, Stephanie, I love you, I've missed you, sometimes I've felt so empty . . .

But if she is, what does that mean? She's been gone for a year. She let us think she was dead.

Why would she do that? Because she still wants to be Sabrina Longworth? Married to Max?

Max would want to disappear. That would not surprise anyone who knew him and could imagine what he would do when he heard that reporters were working on a series of stories exposing Westbridge Imports, art forgeries, and smuggled antiquities. Max Stuyvesant would have made careful plans and then, one day, vanished, and no one would have been surprised.

But would Stephanie have wanted to share that exile with him? Could she be so much in love . . . ?

But her husband. Her children. Her sister. *How could she let us think she was dead?*

Wait . . . wait. She's not alive. How could she be? It's all a coincidence . . . an impostor . . .

But there were too many coincidences, and the longer

she thought of Stephanie alive, the more real it became.

She hunched over in her chair, her hand trembling as she waited for the hotel operator to connect her to Evanston. Mrs. Thirkell answered, solid and comforting, and then Garth was there.

"Oh, my love, my love," Sabrina said, the words breaking loose before she could stop them.

"What is it? What's wrong?" His voice, quick with concern, resonated inside her; she shut her eyes and felt his warmth, his lips on hers, the weight of him . . .

"Nothing." But she was trembling so violently the word was barely a whisper. I'm sorry, she told him silently. I haven't lied to you since you found out the truth about me; I believed I never would lie to you again. But I can't tell you about this. I have to follow it myself; I have to find out what happened, because, in the deepest way, this is between Stephanie and me. I'm sorry, my love, I'm sorry, but I have to talk to Stephanie by myself—

Talk to Stephanie?

I can't talk to her; she's dead. She's been dead for a year and I've had to get used to being without her. But if . . . if somehow she's alive, then I have to talk to her by myself and find out why she's done this. She'll talk to me; we always could talk, about everything.

She took a breath. "Nothing's wrong; it's just that I miss you, I love you . . . I miss all of you. I hate being away; nothing is any fun without you."

"Well, that's easily solved."

"I know. I'm working on it. Now tell me what's happening at home."

"You're not coming back tomorrow."

Oh, Garth, you know me so well, you understand things before I say them.

"No, I'm staying on for a few days. There are some things I want to look at, for Collectibles."

"Are you still in London?"

"No, in Avignon. I'm going to call some antique dealers in Provence; I don't know how long it will take."

439

He was silent. He knows I'm lying, Sabrina thought. I came to Provence without telling him; I'm not being forthcoming now. He'll wonder if I'm being pulled back to Europe, to my old life; if a year of domesticity was enough.

"Garth, this came up all of a sudden; I hadn't planned it." She heard the pleading in her voice, but there was nothing she could do about it; she was pleading with fate, that everything would be fine. "Nothing's really changed. I'll meet you in Paris in two weeks, after your conference, just the way we planned it. Cliff and Penny will go to Vivian's and you and I will have our week alone."

"Of course we will," he said easily. "Now tell me what else you've been doing."

Sabrina sat back in her chair, breathing more easily. What was wrong with her that the first thing she thought of was that Garth would be angry or fearful? He knew that she had sold Ambassadors and her house on Cadogan Square; he knew she no longer wanted even a partial life in Europe. I'm seeing plots everywhere, she thought. "I saw Sidney Jones and signed the papers for Ambassadors; it's all Alexandra's now. But I spent a lot of time there, going over the books, talking to Brian, checking the inventory . . ."

"Handling withdrawal pangs."

She smiled. "Something like that. It wasn't hard; it just had a sort of melancholy about it. Like graduation."

He chuckled. "I like that. By the way, do you know what hotels you'll be staying in before you get to Paris?"

"Not yet. I'll let you know as soon as I do."

"Good. Our children are clamoring to talk to you; this is fair warning before the sound you hear goes up a few decibels."

"Thank you. I love you, Garth."

"I love you, my dear one."

Then Penny and Cliff were on extension phones, chattering about school and sports and friends, their voices riding over each other, evoking their life in Evanston: the three-story frame house with high-ceilinged rooms, polished wood floors, tiled fireplaces, shelves of books, a basement and an attic where unexpected treasures could be found, the kitchen with its sagging couch where everyone sat at some time during the day. *My* house, Sabrina thought, remembering the warm embrace with which it held their family together.

Still, she felt a tug of impatience as the children talked and as soon as she hung up she opened the telephone book to antique shops and galleries, and thought of nothing else but this task. This search. For Stephanie.

She began with shops in Avignon. She had admired Arjuna earlier that day, and so she called it first and asked if a woman named Sabrina Longworth worked there.

"No, no one by that name," said the owner, and was about to hang up when Sabrina said quickly, "Or anyone named Sabrina? Whatever the last name?"

Again the answer was no. But now Sabrina knew what to ask: there was no reason to think that Stephanie would have continued to call herself Sabrina Longworth if she was in hiding with Max. They would have taken a new name.

If it really is Stephanie. If she really is alive.

But that thought was growing fainter. By now Sabrina was searching not for a ghost but for her sister.

She telephoned antique shops in Avignon, Arles, Les Baux, and Saint- Rémy all that afternoon and evening— "Is there someone working in your shop named Sabrina?"—with no success. The next day, on a chance, she skipped to the east and called shops in Aix-en-Provence and Saint-Saturnin, but again had no success. After a quick lunch, with the map before her, she called shops in the small towns between Aix and Avignon: Apt, Fontaine-de-Vaucluse, Carpentras, Orange, Gordes, Roussillon. And late in the afternoon she came to Cavaillon, and called Jacqueline en Provence.

When a woman answered, Sabrina asked the question automatically; she had repeated it so often she barely heard herself say the words. "Is there someone working in your shop named Sabrina?"

"Sabrina? Is that you?" asked the woman

Sabrina's heart pounded. "You know her?"

"Is this a joke? Sabrina, where are you?"

"Please, does Sabrina work there?"

"Well, I don't understand . . . I could have sworn it was your voice . . . No, Sabrina no longer works here; she's left town. Who is—"

"Can you tell me where she went?"

"No. Who is this?"

"A . . . friend. I must talk to you about her. I'll come to see you. What time do you open tomorrow?"

"Ten. But I would not tell a stranger—"

"I'll see you then."

That night she did not sleep. She sat in a café in the Place de l'Horloge, watching the carousel revolve, watching the people, watching the hours pass on the clock tower. *I'll know tomorrow. They worked together; they would have talked. This woman will know her.* At dawn she packed and checked out of the hotel and took a taxi to the train station, where she rented a car and drove the forty miles to Cavaillon. She pretended she was Stephanie, looking at farmers preparing their small fields for winter, driving along high walls of meticulously pruned cypress trees that stopped abruptly to reveal snug stone farmhouses set back from the road, each with its own swimming pool and neat gardens. She heard a rooster crow, and then another, as the sky grew bright. If Stephanie had been in Avignon, and worked in Cavaillon, she would have driven on this road. She would have seen these fields, these houses, heard these roosters. So different from Evanston, so different from London . . .

The traffic became heavier as she approached Cavaillon, and it took her a while to find the center of town. She reached it just before ten, driving around the central square with its fountain topped with a sculpture of metal spikes like the rays of the sun. Exuberant drops of water flew out from the fountain, sparkling in the morning sun, landing on Sabrina's car. She barely noticed; her gaze was fixed ahead or glancing down briefly at the map on the seat beside her. Following it, she drove past small shops and cafés to the cours Gambetta and, turning onto it, saw Jacqueline en Provence, in the center of the block, its gold lettering beckoning her on.

There was no place to park; she left the car jutting into an alley and rushed to the shop, pushing open the front door and stopping only when she found herself in a narrow space with furniture, floor lamps, and baskets of linens blocking her way. The air was faintly musty, the light soft and diffuse, the furnishings mellow with the polish of generations. *My favorite kind of shop. And Stephanie's, too.*

"Sabrina! My dear, I thought you had gone. You've changed your plans?"

A tall woman, austerely beautiful, her ash blond hair pinned loosely back from her face, came from the rear of the shop, her hands outstretched. "I was worried about you; such a quick farewell, without an address or an explanation . . . you and Léon both. I couldn't imagine that he would leave his studio, just like that . . . and what of Max? I was quite concerned. You both just vanished. So much mystery."

Sabrina's hands were held tightly and she was silent for a moment, caught in the absurdity of what was happening. *Sabrina, who is playing Stephanie, being mistaken for Sabrina.* She shook her head in despair. *Will there ever be an end to this deception?*

"Not a mystery?" the woman asked, seeing Sabrina shake her head. "Then what is it?"

She wished she could tell her the truth; she liked her. But there was nothing she could learn here. *Without an address or an explanation . . . you and Léon both.* Léon would be the artist buying supplies in Avignon. Both gone, vanished, and this woman knew nothing about it.

Sabrina felt a sinking within her. Stephanie—if it is Stephanie—didn't want this woman to know anything. They worked together, but she left without an address or an explanation. *I can't even ask her what Sabrina's last name is.*

"My dear, what happened?"

"Oh, it's so complicated," she said in frustration. "I came to find out . . . a few things."

The woman frowned. "This is very strange. A woman telephoned yesterday, asking about you. I would have sworn it was your voice."

Sabrina shook her head, and then remembered that both the woman at Monet Fournitures Artistiques and this woman had spoken of an urgency: *Perhaps they were running away together.* "Has anyone else been asking about me?"

"No one. Well, your friend the priest, Robert, came to retrieve a jacket you had left here. He was quite evasive when I asked him if he knew where you'd gone. But that's not what you meant. Sabrina, are you afraid of someone?"

Someone else to ask. A priest who knows more than he wants to tell. I can find a priest named Robert; that shouldn't be hard. She moved toward the door, impatient to be gone. "I don't know. There are so many things I don't understand. I'm sorry; I'd tell you everything if I could. Perhaps later I'll come back and tell you everything. I'm sorry . . ." She opened the door and rushed to her car.

She looked for steeples and drove toward the one that seemed nearest and in a few minutes she came to a large church with an attached rectory and school. I'll ask inside, she thought; they'll know every priest in town.

She saw no one in the church, so she went to the school. Its double doors opened onto a large corridor stretching to left and right; directly opposite was a door with a translucent glass window, and the word "Director." Sabrina knocked once and went in, and found herself in a small anteroom with an empty desk. An open door led to an office where a small man with a neatly trimmed beard shot with gray sat at a desk. He looked up, then leaped to his feet. "Sabrina! My dear, what can you be thinking of?

Why have you come back? Where is Léon? Have you both gone mad?"

He knows. He knows everything. Sabrina walked into his office and closed the door behind her. "I must talk to you. Is it all right to talk here, or will we be interrupted?"

"What is it? Has something happened to Léon?"

"That's not why I'm here. Please, I must talk to you and it will take quite a while."

Frowning deeply, he studied her. "My dear, you are very strange. Well, then, come. My apartment is the quietest place, and for a change no one is sleeping on the sofa."

He glanced at her with a smile, but Sabrina did not even pretend to understand. She would tell him the truth. And he would take her to Stephanie.

He led her outside and along the building to a door that led upstairs to a tiny apartment: a living room with a couch, a chair, a lamp, and a small sink and hot plate in a corner. A narrow bed could be seen through a partially opened door. "Would you like tea? Or coffee?"

"Tea. Thank you."

He brewed it on the hot plate, his back to her. They were silent; both tense, both expecting a surprise.

"So, my dear." He put two thick white mugs on a small bench in front of the sofa and sat beside Sabrina. "What is it that you wish to tell me?"

"A complicated story. And I will ask you to help me when I've finished."

"I will always help you when you need me, Sabrina; you know that."

"Yes." She gazed at him. A good friend. A good man. She sipped her tea, then put down the mug and folded her hands in her lap. "First I must ask you to tell me your name."

"You are serious?"

"Yes."

"Well, then. Robert Chalon. As you have known for almost a year."

445

"Thank you. Now I would be grateful if you will let me speak without interruption."

His eyebrows rose. "So authoritative suddenly. But of course, my dear, if you wish, I will not interrupt."

"Well, then. My name is Sabrina Longworth. I was born in—"

"Sabrina! Your memory has returned! Oh, what a wonderful gift; why did you not tell me immediately?"

Sabrina stared at him. *Your memory has returned.* Why had she never thought of that? It explained everything. And it seemed so obvious: the yacht, the explosion, injuries . . . and a year of silence because Stephanie did not know who she was.

But why did she think her name was Sabrina?

Max.

Both of them had survived and he'd told her that her name was Sabrina. Sabrina what?

"My dear Sabrina, please go on. I'm sorry; I did promise not to interrupt."

Not Longworth; the name was new to Robert. So something else.

"Sabrina?"

"It's not what you think. Please, let me tell the whole story. I was born in America and grew up in Europe. I lived in London, I was married and divorced, I owned an antique shop. My sister married a professor in America and had two children. Her name was—is—Stephanie Andersen; she is my identical twin, and she is the woman who was on the yacht with Max."

Robert's face was frozen, stunned; he leaned forward, his eyes locked on hers.

"One day, in September of last year, we took a trip to China together and decided to change places, just for a week. We both needed to get away and we thought it would be a lark, an adventure, and no one would know and no one would be hurt. But deceptions"—the word caught in her throat—"deceptions don't work that way."

She told it all then, from her broken wrist to the explo-

446

sion on the yacht, her mourning for her sister, the passionate love that had grown between her and Garth and the children, the life they had made together.

"Last month a friend called and said she had seen me in Europe. She said it had to be"—the words caught again—"my sister or a ghost."

"And it was both," said Robert when she did not go on.

She nodded. After a moment Robert poured their cold tea into the sink and brewed another pot. "A most incredible story."

"I know. So fantastic it seems to have nothing to do with everyday life. But it's all true."

He unwrapped two tea bags. "All of us lead fantastic lives, you know. I would not deny the drama of any life." He tilted the teapot and refilled their cups. "Of course your story goes beyond that: it is fantastic and outrageous. I believe it and I am sorry for it—from a whim you have reaped a maelstrom—but it is not productive to talk about that now." He sat beside her. "The explosion on the yacht. You don't know what happened before it?"

"No. Stephanie called from London the day before she left. That was the last time I talked to her. The next day . . . a telephone call . . ." A tremor ran through her.

"You miss her greatly."

"We were so much a part of each other; it was as if a piece of me had died, as if something inside me had been torn away. That didn't change, no matter how happy I was . . ."

"My poor child," Robert said, understanding what torments crouched, waiting, for both sisters. But he had said enough; it was not the time to say more. This woman still had to come to terms with the reality of a sister who lived, and how she would welcome her back.

Sabrina had fallen silent again. She was exhausted, but pleasantly comfortable. "You're very easy to talk to."

"I hope so. Sabrina always thought so. But it is Stephanie, isn't it? I can't think of her that way."

"Please tell me where to find her."

"She and Léon have gone to Vézelay."

"Vézelay? In Burgundy?"

"Yes, fairly near Paris. A lovely town filled with tourists. They thought they could be anonymous there."

"Why should they be? What are they afraid of? Are they hiding?"

"Yes . . . perhaps. We're not sure, but it is possible that Sabrina—Stephanie—is in danger and it seemed wise for them to leave. They wanted to start a new life since Max—"

"Max. Is he here?"

"No, he—"

"He was the one who told her she was Sabrina, wasn't he? When she lost her memory. Of course he had only known her as Sabrina. What did he say her last name was?"

"Lacoste. The same as his."

"The same? Why?"

"Because she was his wife."

"But she wasn't. She wouldn't have married him; she couldn't have."

Startled, Robert said, "No, of course not. Of course not; she couldn't have married Max. But he told her he was her husband, and she had no information that would contradict that. Although she told me often that she did not *feel* married to him, even though he was deeply in love with her and she was grateful to him for the home he gave her. But I should tell you that Max—"

"I have to find her. How do I get to Vézelay? I have a car; I can drive. If I leave now—"

"My dear, wait until tomorrow. You look worn out. One more night won't make a difference and I could help you by telling you something of her life, of the things that have happened to her."

"No, I know you want to help, but I want to see her, I want to hear it from her. And I can't wait another night; my God, to know that she's alive—I have to find her!"

"But there is something else. I told you that your sister may be in danger. Things have happened here—"

"Danger from whom?"

"We don't know. But—"

"You don't know? Then why are we wasting time talking about it? Good heavens, are you saying I should be frightened? Whatever it is, Stephanie will tell me about it. And we'll share it."

"Léon is with her."

"That doesn't matter! It never has. Whoever else came into our lives, there was still the two of us. Nothing ever changed that."

But now something could. Garth . . . Penny . . . Cliff . . .

She shook her head roughly. Not now. Later.

"Please, I can't stay and talk; please tell me how to get there. And where she lives."

"Well, then." Robert rummaged in his desk and found a map of France. In the margin he wrote an address and telephone number. "It's a little more than five hundred kilometers, and you are not familiar with the roads. If you would like, I can come with you."

"No. Thank you, but I can't . . . no one but the two of us."

He nodded. "I understand. Now let me show you . . ." They bent over the map and Robert marked the route. "It is not a difficult drive, but some of it may be tedious. And if you get tired, you must rest; don't push yourself." He met her eyes. "But of course you will. My dear, I wish you well."

Tears came to Sabrina's eyes. He feared for her, and for Stephanie, too. She bowed her head and he took her in his arms like a child and held her with a slight rocking motion.

"You are a strong woman, my dear, but sometimes strength is not enough. If you need me, I am here. For both of you. I hope you will always remember that."

"I will. Thank you." Sabrina took the map, with the

most direct route to Vézelay brightly outlined with a yellow marker. "You must have been a very good friend to Stephanie."

"And to you," Robert said and they exchanged a smile as Sabrina gently closed the door, then ran down the stairs and down the street to her car.

Stephanie and Léon lingered over coffee in the long, slow evening, drifting in reverie, reaching out now and then to touch each other and exchange a smile of wonder. They were together, and no one but Robert knew where they were.

Cavaillon, and the violence and fear that had come to it, had been left behind. They sat in the courtyard of a small, square two-story stone house with a steeply pitched orange tile roof, hidden from the street by a high, rough stone wall covered on both sides with bougainvillaea. The pale purple blossoms hung in lacy clusters from long looping branches that tumbled over the stones and the white wooden gate set deep into the wall. The scent of the flowers mingled with that of the roses and wisteria in the courtyard, the coffee in small porcelain cups, the spicy pears in a glass bowl on the table.

"Like honeysuckle and red wine," Stephanie murmured.

Léon looked at her quickly. "Yes. Where? A garden?"

She tried to hold on to the brief flash of memory. "It must have been. Honeysuckle bushes and red wine. And people, lots of people. A party. Léon, there was a party! And it was in a yard, not a garden, a yard, and the bushes, the honeysuckle bushes, were all around it."

"Yes, good, and who was at the party? Who were the people, Sabrina?"

After a moment she shook her head. "I don't know. I can't even see myself there. Oh, I hate this, I feel so unconnected when I see a flash of something and then nothing else; it's like finding a sliver of china and never knowing what the bowl or vase it came from looked like."

"But you're not unconnected."

"No." She smiled at him, grateful for his quiet presence, and his love. "Not anymore."

They held hands on the table and the calm of the evening enfolded them and they returned to their reverie and sense of wonder. The sun had gone down, but still the light held, shadows more sharply creased, the sky above their small enclosed courtyard arching gray-blue, streaked with peach and lilac clouds. Muted voices came from beyond the wall; somewhere a violin sang a plaintive folk song of Burgundy. Stephanie, fully in the present, breathed deeply, sensually, and stretched her arms above her head. "I love you," she said, and Léon stood behind her and bent to kiss her neck, his hands on her breasts.

"We've come home," he murmured. "My darling Sabrina, we have come home."

Later, they cleared the table together, stacking the dishes in the sink, and went out, to walk through the town. Vézelay was built on a hill, the streets leading steeply to the great basilica of La Madeleine at the top. In the growing darkness, Stephanie and Léon strolled past low stucco buildings, holding hands, looking into shops and art galleries so tiny they were barely wider than their open doorways. Above were apartments, shutters open wide in the soft air. Geraniums bloomed on windowsills and in wooden planters and clay flowerpots spaced along the stone sidewalk and beside every entrance. Interspersed with the shops were houses turning a blank face to the street, showing to the throngs of tourists only their locked front doors and garage doors so old they were deeply fissured, held together in wildly random patterns by the square handmade nails of another age.

The tourists were leaving, walking down the hill to their buses, and the higher Stephanie and Léon walked, the quieter the town became. Soon, at the top, they were alone. "Now, briefly, Vézelay is ours," Léon said in amusement. "Until tomorrow when the buses return."

"I like it both ways," Stephanie said. "Even when it's

so crowded we can't walk up the street, everyone is so happy. They like being here and they're always smiling."

He kissed her lightly. "And so am I, it seems." They walked around the great church with its tiled conical roof topped with a cross and the narrow arched windows that reminded Stephanie of eyes open in surprise. At the far end of the flat summit was a stone wall overgrown with grasses and wildflowers, and Stephanie and Léon perched on it and looked over it, down the long, long slope to the flat green fields of Burgundy outlined by rows of trees and the lazy bend of the Cure River, a sinuous ghost in the fading light. In the two weeks they had been in Vézelay, it had become their favorite spot. "A destination for pilgrims over a thousand years ago," Léon had said when they first visited it. "And still today, for aren't we on a pilgrimage to find safe haven and a home?"

They sat there until it was almost too dark to see; then they turned and walked back the way they had come. "Come to the studio," Léon said suddenly when they were near their house. "I want to show you something. I was going to wait, but I want you to see them now."

He had rented a studio above a wineshop and charcuterie; it was flooded with light from the north and east and large enough for the wide canvases he had begun painting in his studio in Goult. At the top of the stairs he unlocked the door and threw the light switch. From the doorway, Stephanie saw the two portraits of her that he had almost finished when they left Provence and, on another wall, a series of paintings that were new. Léon stepped back and she went up to them, moving slowly from one to the next.

They were blocks and fragments of color, but within the abstract breakdown of form could be seen the essence of each painting: four children playing, sitting, hiding, sharing secrets, urgently racing to a destination unseen.

"Of course they'll get more abstract, more essential," Léon said as Stephanie gazed at them for a long time. "But this is the beginning." He put his arm around her. "What is bothering you?"

"A dozen paintings of children."

"Yes?"

"We've never talked about children."

"Of course not. We were getting acquainted. And you were married. I never felt it was urgent, did you?"

"But you've never even said you like children. Or that you want them. I still don't know if you want them."

"I've always liked them. I find them baffling and secretive, and it's a little daunting the way they often make one feel extraneous, but they're really quite fascinating and likable, even lovable. Why are you laughing at me?"

"Because you're so solemn, as if you're analyzing aliens. Children are just like us; they're just more open about everything. Even when they're secretive, they're more honest about it than we are."

"I don't know what that means."

"Oh, that they want to be found out." She had moved closer to the row of paintings pinned to the wall, so engrossed in them she was almost talking to herself. "They leave clues so others will stop them from doing something they know is wrong. Cliff made sure I'd find that radio and those other things in his room; he didn't even try to hide—"

She turned slowly. She was pale, her eyes as startled as those of a sleeper awakened by sudden light.

"Who is Cliff?" Léon asked.

"I don't know. It sounds as if he's . . . my son."

"Or a brother?"

"Oh. Yes, I suppose . . . But he would have to be much younger."

"That would not be so unusual." He drew her to him. Her face was against his neck; he could feel her quick short breaths, the trembling of her slender body. He held her until the trembling subsided and she drew back.

"What if he's my son?"

"Then we have a greatly complicated situation. And I think we will know, one way or another, before much more time passes; it seems to me you are remembering more these days, are you not?"

She made a gesture of frustration. "As I said: flashes. Bits and pieces."

"But from them you will build a past; one day they will all fall into place, like the chips of marble an artist embeds into a mosaic. Each is valuable but meaningless; then suddenly it is part of a whole and tells a story. Do you believe this?"

"Yes." And, hearing him say it, she did. One day she would know.

"But we will not let ghosts and fancies interfere," he said, and kissed her again. "We are going to make our own life, and take what comes each day and conquer it. We will talk about having children, because of course I want them. I never did before, but now I do, and I think that must be why I made these paintings. Often I find my dreams on paper before I know I have dreamed them. What do you think?"

"Yes." She felt herself curl up inside, as if she had told a lie, and she knew she should not do this; she had no right to take Léon into the emptiness that was always with her, no matter how happy and content she was. But she loved him and he was her whole world, and so she kissed him and said, "Yes, I want to have our children."

"And Robert will marry us here, in Vézelay. My love?" His face was close to Stephanie's; he kissed her almost chastely. "Will you marry me? Do you know, I have never asked you that."

"Yes," Stephanie said once again. "Yes, yes, I want to marry you. But . . . not yet. We don't know what I'll remember. We could wait a few months, a year, even more; what difference does it make as long as we're living together?"

"I want to marry you," he said quietly. "I don't want to wait. I don't want to live with you in a way that makes it impossible for us to build a family. I want everything with you, Sabrina, not just a living arrangement. I will not force you, but I feel strongly about this."

And that was enough. Whatever lay ahead, they would

share it. "Then we should invite Robert to Vézelay," she said.

"We'll call him tonight."

He turned off the light switches and locked the door. They walked down the narrow stairway to the dark sidewalk, faintly lit, and made their way down the middle of the deserted street to their gate. Léon pushed it open and they walked into the courtyard, where one candle still burned on the olivewood table where they had eaten their dinner. Golden light spilled from the windows of their house, turning to gold the wisteria vines climbing around them, the bougainvillaea on the stone wall, the single rose on their dinner table, their faces as they turned to each other. "I love this house," Stephanie said. "I love you. Thank you for giving me all this."

He gave a small laugh. "I'm the one who is grateful. Once my only center was painting; everything else revolved on the periphery, casual, not essential. You've given me everything that is essential. You've made me complete."

He unlocked the heavy wooden front door and they went inside and up the stairs. "The dishes," Stephanie murmured.

"Terribly important," Léon said dryly, his long thin fingers unbuttoning her white shirt. "I greatly fear they will wait for us."

They lay on the bed and came together with a passion that had been growing since they left Cavaillon. Nothing they had known before was as powerful as the love they shared and the response of their bodies in their own home, together in a small town where no one knew them. When, much later, they lay side by side, smiling at each other in the lamplight, Stephanie kissed him and said, "I think I could be content with this and nothing else. If I never know any more about myself than I know now, it might be enough."

"Not forever, I think. But it doesn't matter. Whatever you discover, I can't imagine it changing what we have.

Something this powerful can't be shattered easily. Or at all. Good heavens, is that the doorbell? No one in Vézelay is up this late."

Stephanie felt a stab of fear. "Could someone have followed us?"

"No, no, there is no chance. You know that. Robert's friend has been watching your house; no stranger has been near it. And we left from my house in Goult, not from Cavaillon. Perhaps it is a peddler; shall we ignore it?"

"Yes." But when the bell rang again and then again, Stephanie unaccountably began to tremble. "It's something else. Something . . . something . . . oh, what's wrong with me?"

Léon sat up. "You're afraid. I'll go."

"No, I'm not afraid, that's not it. It's just . . ." She leaped out of bed. "I have to go. It's for me."

His eyebrows rose. "How do you know that?"

"I don't know." She pulled on a silk robe of peacock blue and green that Léon had bought for her in Avignon, and ran her fingers through her long hair. "I'll be right back."

"I'm coming too. Wait for me. Where did I put my robe?"

"I think it's in the other closet. It's all right, Léon; don't bother. I'll only be a minute."

She ran down the stairs. She heard Léon go into the other room and open the closet and pictured him fumbling through clothes they had not yet completely organized. At the bottom of the stairs she crossed the small foyer and opened the door. "Yes, what can I—"

She was looking at herself.

"Stephanie!" said the vision. "Oh, Stephanie, thank God—"

A long scream broke from her, shattering the quiet night. And then the world went black.

CHAPTER 18

"*Sabrina!*"

Léon, at the bend in the stairs, heard Stephanie's scream and hurtled the rest of the way down and into the foyer. In the dim light he saw Stephanie on the floor and a woman bending over her, her long chestnut hair falling over her face. *Just like Sabrina's hair . . .* The thought came and was gone as Léon shoved her aside. "Get away from her!" He took Stephanie into his arms and lifted her. He heard the woman say, "Léon, please, let me help," and thought, as fleetingly as before, *How the hell does she know my name?* before he carried Stephanie into the living room and laid her on the couch.

"Sabrina, my love, my love." He sat with her, cradling her against his chest. And then he looked up at the woman, who had followed him, and felt his body go rigid with shock. "My God. My God. Who the devil—" The woman reached out to touch Stephanie's hair. "Get away from her! Leave her alone!"

Leave *us* alone, he thought, because he was filled with fear. Sabrina in his arms; Sabrina standing beside him

457

The room seemed to tilt; he could not think. And so he denied the other woman and bent over Stephanie, seeing only her, murmuring to her. "Wake up, Sabrina, wake up, my love; it will be all right. Whatever it is . . ." He breathed in the scent of her hair and brushed his lips across her cheek, watching her eyelids flutter. He felt he was holding his whole world in his arms, this woman who was the core of his life, and he was filled with terror because he knew her past had come into their home and could take her from him.

How lightly he had talked of it! How easily he had told her she would remember everything and then they would deal with it together. Fool, fool, fool, to be so naive. Now, at this moment, he knew that the past could never be so casually dismissed: it could always twist and shatter the present, and only a fool would think otherwise.

"My love, my love, it will be all right." Like a child trying to ward off invisible dangers in the scary corners of his room, he repeated it. "You'll be all right. *We'll* be all right." And, like a child, he added to himself, *We will, we will, we will.*

"Léon, please, please let me . . ."

The woman was standing close by, reaching toward Stephanie, *yearning* toward her, Léon thought, and he could deny her no longer. He looked up. "You're her sister."

"Yes."

"She didn't know she had one. And a twin . . ." He stared at her, his artist's eye comparing them. "It's uncanny. I could have mistaken you for her."

She nodded gravely. "Many people have." Once again she reached out, and this time Léon did not stop her as she took Stephanie's hand in hers and bent to kiss her. And then, suddenly, as her lips touched the warmth of Stephanie's cheek, her legs buckled and she sank to her knees beside the couch and laid her cheek on Stephanie's.

Stephanie, Stephanie . . . She wept and it seemed she could not stop. She looked at Stephanie through her tears and gently brushed her hair back from her face. *I did that before, in the funeral home, a year ago. I laid my head on the side of Stephanie's coffin and wept in that awful dark room until I thought I would tear apart. How can she be here now?*

"I don't know, I don't know," she murmured. She kissed Stephanie's forehead, her cheek, her closed eyes. "So wonderful . . . magical . . ." She looked at Léon. "I thought she was dead."

Instinctively he had tightened his arms as if to keep Stephanie to himself, safe from even the touch of the past. But the past was here: the past was this woman, kneeling beside the couch, her hand on her sister's hair, her body leaning toward her as if desperate to take her from Léon into her own embrace.

"Is she married?" he burst out. "Does she have children?"

Sabrina froze. Her hand fell to her side; she swayed a little, away from him. Her mouth opened, then closed. The words would not come.

Stephanie stirred and Léon bent to her. "My love, my love . . ."

Her eyes opened. She saw only his face. "Léon? I thought Sabrina was here. I saw her and everything came back . . . it was like a flood . . . I couldn't stand it; it hurt. Isn't she here?"

"Sabrina? But, my love, you're Sabrina."

"Stephanie," Sabrina said.

Stephanie turned. A low cry broke from her. She wrenched free of Léon's embrace, and then she and Sabrina were in each other's arms.

Two identical faces, wet with tears, pressed together as they embraced so tightly it seemed they had merged into one. They held each other for a long time, not moving, silent tears falling softly in the silence of the house, the silence of the night.

Quietly Léon moved away, through an archway that led to a small library. He could see them sitting on the couch, but he stayed in the shadows and watched them. He could not believe it even now: two stunning women, identical in every way, even to the curve of their arms and fingers as they embraced, the lashes on their closed eyes, their voices murmuring each other's names, saying they loved each other.

Stephanie, he thought. Her name is Stephanie. But Max called her Sabrina, and so we all did. And they were speaking English. American English, not British. Effortlessly, without an accent, Sabrina—*no, her name is Stephanie*—was speaking to her sister in English. American, he thought. She's American. I never guessed.

"I love you," Sabrina said. "I couldn't bear it that you were gone; I've missed you so much."

Stephanie shuddered within her sister's arms. "I didn't remember anything about you. I remembered other things, other people—flashes, really, not connected to anything—but I never remembered you. I love you, I love you, but I didn't remember you. Why didn't I? Oh, Sabrina, so much has happened! How will we ever put it all together?"

Sabrina gave a shaky laugh. "We'll start at the beginning. But not yet. Let's not talk yet; let's just be together—"

"No, we have to talk. We have to. I lost everything—did you know that? It was so awful: like walking through a fog, through *nothing,* just—"

"—emptiness," Sabrina said. "I thought of that when I thought about you, everything gone: an awful—"

"Nothingness. That was it. I knew the names of things, and languages—isn't that odd?—or maybe not. One of the doctors told me I was repressing things about myself because I'd had some kind of conflict that caused pain or guilt . . ." She and Sabrina exchanged a quick look; then Stephanie veered away from it. "So there was nothing about myself. Nothing. Except, somehow there must have been something, because it never seemed right that my name was Sabrina. And Léon painted a portrait of me, a double portrait, and when I looked at it, it made me feel so

460

happy . . ." She shook her head. "I can't believe it. It's all back, as if nothing had happened. But I don't know anything about you, what you did, what's happened— Oh! Penny and Cliff! Have you seen them? Do you know how they are?"

There was a pause barely the length of a heartbeat. "Yes. They're fine. You're right; we have to talk. Do you think we could make some tea?"

"Oh, yes, let's. We can't just stay here; I want to know everything. Let's go to the kitchen. Oh, but Léon—" Stephanie looked for him. "Léon?"

"Yes." He was beside her, thinking: Penny and Cliff, Penny and Cliff. She said those names once and wondered if they were her children. "What would you like? Shall I make you some tea and then"—he forced himself to say it—"then I'll leave the two of you alone."

A look of confusion swept over Stephanie's face. "No." She stood up, and Sabrina stood with her; they clung to each other, arms around each other's waists. "Would you mind?" she asked Sabrina. "I want Léon to know everything."

"If that's what you want."

"I know you'd rather it's just the two of us, after so much time . . ."

"Yes. But we'll do what you want." Sabrina extended her hand. "Hello, Léon. I'm glad to meet you."

Through his bewilderment and cold fear, he saw the swift understanding between them, the unspoken assumptions, the powerful love, and knew he could not break that bond, nor would he even try. It was theirs alone, and it changed everything: it turned his world and Stephanie's upside down. But he liked this woman: the love she had for her sister; her warmth and directness. She would not lie or participate in others' lies, he thought. He took the hand Sabrina held out to him and saw the shadowed look in her eyes and wondered what part of this incredible meeting was causing her pain. "Léon Dumas," he said. "But I don't know your name."

461

"Sabrina . . . Longworth." Her tongue tripped on it. "But also . . . Stephanie Andersen."

Stephanie frowned. "That was a long time ago . . . and it wasn't for real."

"But they told us you were dead and I couldn't—"

"*Dead*?" Stephanie stared at her and suddenly all the events of the past year seemed to surround her, pieces fitting into place. "Lacoste . . . Max Lacoste. Sabrina Lacoste. But he was Max Stuyvesant, and I was Stephanie Andersen. He didn't know that, of course; he thought I was you, so when he told me my name was Sabrina, when he said I never had children and he'd never heard of Garth, that was the truth, as far as he knew it. But he said we were married, and I never married him; how could I? He made that up, I suppose, when the yacht exploded, and he changed his name and let everyone think we'd been killed. He made us disappear. Of course you thought we were dead; what else could you think? And then"—she looked wildly at Sabrina—"*then you couldn't change back*."

"You and Max weren't married?" Léon asked. He could make sense of nothing but that.

"No. Oh, Sabrina, that's what you meant about my being gone." She kissed Sabrina's cheek. They were still standing together, their arms around each other, their hands moving, stroking, caressing in constant reminders that this was real. "You meant you thought I was dead. But there wasn't a . . . body. How could you think—?"

"I don't know. We have to figure that out. But first I want to know about you. Everything. Robert wanted to tell me but I—"

"You know Robert?"

"That was how I found you. I'll tell you the whole story when you tell me yours . . . or we can take turns, but—"

"But not standing in the living room." Léon felt he had to do something, say something, to restore a sense of reality. He felt he was losing Sabrina . . . no, he thought, Stephanie. I must remember, her name is Stephanie. It seemed to him she was disappearing into her sister, the two of them merging as their voices, identical voices, overlapped and they held each other as if they could not ever again be torn apart. And what they said made no sense. "Come; we'll make tea and then you can talk. I'll stay if you wish."

This time Stephanie hesitated. She glanced at Sabrina. "It might be better if we're alone."

Léon's fear rose again, but he only nodded. "I thought so." He led the way to the kitchen, a long narrow room with tall wood cabinets, a worn wood floor, and a high window at one end above a planked table and four wooden chairs with rush seats. Léon switched on the ship's lantern above the table and went to the stove.

"Léon, I'll do it." Stephanie finally left her sister's side and went to him, her arm around his waist, her head on his shoulder. "I'm sorry. I love you; I don't want to hurt you. But there's so much . . . everything is so mixed up and I can't tell you about it, not yet . . . or maybe I should . . . Oh, I don't know what I should do!"

Léon hesitated, afraid of confusing her even more. But then he thought, the hell with it. He had his fear to deal with, and he had to try to balance the sisters' almost mystical closeness. He took Stephanie in his arms. "I love you. And you love me. We haven't dreamed this; we haven't chased a fantasy or clung to each other out of desperation. We came together freely and offered to each other all that we had and all that we were, and it didn't matter what we had been before. From the moment we loved, our past had nothing to do with the life we were building together. We knew that we would change each other, and our lives would change, and *that was what we wanted*. That was what made us happy. I want you to remember that."

"I will," Stephanie said gravely. "I couldn't forget it." She reached up and touched his face. "I love you. But everything is so complicated . . . I'll tell you about it later, I promise. I'll tell you all of it. But Sabrina and I have to fill in our lives, and we have to do it in our own way, and I don't see how you can be part of that.''

She was changing as he watched her, growing stronger, more positive, more sure of herself. Because now she has a self, he thought. The recovery of her memory and her sister beside her have filled in all the empty spaces that I alone, and all the love in the world, could not fill.

''I'll be upstairs,'' he said, and kissed her, and felt her respond with the passion she had shown earlier that night, and that was what he took with him when he left the room, a passion that could not—if there was any meaning in the world—be taken from them.

Stephanie stood at the stove, her back to Sabrina, waiting for the water to boil. As soon as Léon left, she had begun trembling and now she could barely lift the kettle. ''Let me help,'' Sabrina said at her shoulder.

Stephanie did not turn around. ''I'm afraid.''

''We both are.''

The words they had not said, the questions they had not asked in the rush of emotions in rediscovering each other, hung in the room.

Will you try to take your children? What will you do about Garth? Do you want to come home? It's my home now, my . . .

Will you walk away from my family? Will you make room for me with them or will you fight? It's my family, my home, my . . .

But they could not say them aloud.

Sabrina poured steaming water into a red-patterned teapot. ''Tea bags,'' she murmured, and Stephanie opened a drawer and took out a handful, then reached up and brought down two mugs in a red and white pattern that matched the teapot. ''Oh, it's not fair!'' Sabrina cried. She stared through sudden tears at the cheerful mugs. ''You're back, we're together . . . we shouldn't have anything to be afraid of; we should be rejoicing, celebrating, singing, dancing . . .''

But there was too much between them besides joy and

discovery: they were mired in the quicksand of what they had begun one year ago.

At the table they held hands, their heads close together. "Tell me what happened to you," Sabrina said. "Where were you when you couldn't remember anything?"

"In a hospital in Marseilles. I woke up and Max was there and I didn't know who I was. But I don't want to talk about—"

"And that's when everything seemed empty. Like a fog. That was how I thought of you. As if you'd disappeared into a fog, a cloud, an emptiness, all of space."

"Yes, yes, that's what it was! And everything was muffled and I felt so *alone*. Even later, when I'd feel happy . . ."

"Yes, even then," Sabrina murmured.

"You know; of course you know. You always know. What were you doing? Sabrina, I don't want to talk about me; I want to know about my family and what you've been doing, where you've been—"

"I'll tell you later. I want to know about you, and about Robert and Léon and that shop you worked in, and everything else. All of it."

"No!" She jerked her hand from Sabrina's. "I have to know about my children! How did you tell them? Do they hate me? They thought I was dead! They thought I'd run off from them and then I was killed—"

"So did Garth."

"Yes, but . . ."

"What?"

"He wouldn't have cared. Things were so bad between us . . . you must have found that out right away. I was afraid to tell you in Hong Kong; I was afraid if you knew, you wouldn't change places. But it must have been obvious. He barely knew I existed, and all I wanted was to get away from him. And when you broke your wrist and I stayed in London, I was so relieved; I just didn't want to go back to him."

Sabrina tightened her muscles, trying to still the tremors that ran through her.

"What's wrong?" Stephanie leaned forward and took Sabrina's hands in hers. "What's wrong? Why are you shaking?"

Sabrina shook her head. "I'll be all right. Just give me a minute—"

But Stephanie's fingers were moving over Sabrina's, feeling the rings on her left hand. She spread her sister's fingers across her palm. "You're married! You didn't tell me. We've been talking all this time and you never said a word. Who is it?"

Sabrina looked at the dark window giving back their reflections: the only people in a darkened world. She took a breath, as if plunging off a cliff into the unknown, because there was no way to hide it or to soften it.

"Garth," she said.

Stephanie dropped her sister's hands and shoved her chair back, the legs scraping on the wood floor. "What are you talking about? *Married to Garth?* That's crazy; you couldn't be. You didn't even like him. It's been a year; there's no way you could live with him that long, much less marry him. And anyway, why would he—" Her breath came in short bursts; her face was flushed. "Why would you make up something like that? You're not married!"

"We were married last Christmas. Stephanie, listen—"

"I don't believe it. Why? *Why would you?*"

"Because we love each other." Sabrina's tremors had stopped; her body was cold, her voice flat. She would tell the whole story and then somehow they would go on; they would decide about the rest of their lives. She wished she could have put it off and enjoyed the miracle of being with Stephanie, but that was like a child's prayer that everything would be easy. "I told you I couldn't change back. The world thought Sabrina Longworth was dead, so I couldn't be her, ever again. I was living Stephanie Andersen's life and I knew it was wrong, that it couldn't go on, and I tried to leave Garth, over and over again, but something always came up, something with the university or the children or the trip to Stamford, and then he figured out who I was and . . . kicked me out.''

"He figured it out? When?"

"Just before Christmas."

"*Christmas?* From September? All that time he didn't know? Didn't even have a suspicion?"

"He had reasons for overlooking things, for finding explanations. He wanted to believe I was his wife."

Stephanie flinched. After a moment she said, "Was there a funeral?"

"Yes. In London."

"And you didn't tell him then?"

"I tried to. Stephanie, let me tell it all, from the beginning."

"So he finally got it and kicked you out." Abruptly her thoughts switched to Sabrina, and, as it had been through all their lives, it was as if she were inside her. "What a terrible time for you; what an awful thing, to lose everything, to have someone tell you you can't have it anymore or even come close . . . But you didn't lose it, did you? You're still there?"

"I went back. Garth came—"

But Stephanie had plunged into herself again. "So when he kicked you out, he told Penny and Cliff, and they hated me. Didn't they? I know they hated me. He told them I'd left them to play a silly game because they weren't as important as—"

"Stephanie, he didn't—"

"But it was only going to be for a week! They could understand that, couldn't they? And then later they thought I was dead, so maybe . . . maybe they didn't hate me so much."

"He didn't tell them. We've never told them. They don't know."

Stephanie stared at her. "They don't know I've been gone all this time? They think you're their mother?"

"Well, damn it, that was the idea, wasn't it? You wanted me to convince them of that when you asked me to take your place." Sabrina drew in her breath. "I'm sorry. Yes, they think I'm their mother. They *know* I'm their mother; I have been, you know, for over a year. And I've been Garth's wife since December. Stephanie, I'll tell you the whole story, but please let me tell it all; don't say anything until I'm finished. Please."

"You took over my family. *You stole my family!*"

"What are you talking about? I didn't steal anyone! They weren't sitting on a shelf waiting to be stolen; they're human beings who love and who need love, and I went to them because you asked me to, and I stayed because—"

"Because you wanted them for yourself!"

"Because I love them! Because you were dead. Because they became my family!"

The kitchen was silent. The two women sat so still they might have been sculpted in their chairs, leaning slightly forward as if wanting to touch but unable to; as if a barrier, more formidable than anyone could measure, kept them apart. Stephanie could not make sense of it. For over a year, with so many chances for mistakes and blunders and nostalgia for another way of life, Sabrina had played a part so brilliantly she had swept a whole family into her embrace and they had loved it enough to make her a part of them without ever wondering if she belonged there. Well, she doesn't, Stephanie thought. She's an impostor. She's only been filling in.

From upstairs came the sound of something being moved across the floor, a lamp, perhaps, or a chair. Oh, Léon, Stephanie thought, what are we going to do? She pictured him upstairs, unable to sleep. "He's sketching," she murmured. "He does that when he's worried about something or he can't sleep. He fills pages: people, landscapes, fantasies, dreams . . ."

"You love him very much."

"More than . . . almost more than anyone. We were going to ask Robert to marry us."

Sabrina burst through the barrier between them; she jumped up and put her arms around Stephanie, holding her close. Stephanie's head was against her breast; she felt her tears and her warm breath through her blouse. "I'll tell you everything that's happened. And then you'll tell me. We can't think about what comes next until we do. Oh, I wish it was just the—"

"—two of us. I know. We could have such a good time, just being together. Finding out again—"

"—how wonderful it is. How perfect. Whatever else happens—"

"It is perfect." Stephanie looked up at Sabrina and instinctively they laughed together. "It's not the same with anyone else; how could it be?"

"I know." But Sabrina's smile faded and she stood with her head bent. Because it had been perfect when they were growing up and, later, when they had separate homes and separate lives and had turned to each other for support and encouragement, but now, when they were caught in a tangle of conflicting needs, she did not see how it could ever be perfect again.

Stephanie went to the stove. "We'd better have more tea. It's going to be a long night."

Sabrina watched her fill the teakettle, and then she began to talk, even before Stephanie returned to the table. She began with Brooks's call from London, telling them the yacht had exploded off the coast of Monte Carlo and everyone aboard had been killed. She described the funeral and her frantic attempts to tell everyone that it wasn't Sabrina who had died; it was Stephanie. "But they all said I was in shock; poor Stephanie Andersen, in shock, distraught, incoherent. And I suppose I was. I broke down and said sometimes I couldn't tell who I was, Sabrina or Stephanie, and that was when Garth took me away."

In her mind Stephanie saw Sabrina fall beside the open grave, crying, *It wasn't Sabrina! It wasn't Sabrina who died!*; she heard people gasping and saw Garth leading Sabrina away. But Sabrina had left something out. "Before that, before the funeral, why did you think it was me, in the coffin?''

"I don't know. The room was dark and I was crying, everything was blurred . . . but it did look like you. I remember how dark it was—there were a few candles, that was all—and everything seemed hazy because I couldn't stop crying . . . but still . . . I don't know. Maybe we'll be able to find out sometime . . .'' She fell silent. "Shall I go on?''

"Yes."

She told Stephanie everything in that long year: how she had helped Garth in the sex-for-grades scandal at the university that had almost cost him his job; the job offer from a company in Connecticut and their visit there; her growing love for Garth and the children, their love for her. And then she came to Gabrielle's telephone call—*I know what the two of you look like and I'm telling you, I saw you, or her. Or a ghost*—and her trip to Avignon, and then Cavaillon.

It was dawn when she finished: the sky over Vézelay lightening to pearl gray and then a soft wash of color that turned the bougainvillaea to pink and gold. From upstairs came the sound of a door closing, footsteps, another door.

Stephanie sighed. "Why did you come looking for me? You didn't have to. You could have gone back, to Garth and Penny and Cliff. I might never have remembered who I was."

"You don't mean that. You know why I came here. I had to find you; you're part of me."

"Yes." Stephanie smiled faintly. "Thank you. What an odd thing to say. Thank you for finding me, for giving me back my past. Thank you for loving me."

But now what? Will you walk away from my family? Will you make room for me with them or will you fight? It's my family, my home, my . . .

They sat quietly, staring blankly ahead, and turned together as Léon came in. He stopped short, arrested by the sight of those identical faces, identical poses, even an identical exhausted droop to their shoulders.

"I'm going to the studio," he said casually, as if this were an ordinary morning, with an unremarkable visitor. "I'll be there all day, if you'd like to walk over later on."

Stephanie tried to focus on him. Nothing in Sabrina's story seemed to have any connection with Sabrina Lacoste and the life she lived in France, or with Léon Dumas, whom she loved and wanted to live with for the rest of her life. She felt a sinking inside as she thought of her two lives, each like a seamless sphere. *How will I ever put them together?*

"Come at one; we'll go to lunch." He said nothing about the bewilderment on Stephanie's face; he ached to hold her and comfort her but at the same time his anger was growing because she seemed to be shutting him out, his beloved Sabrina who . . . *No, damn it, why can't I remember? Stephanie, Stephanie, Stephanie.* He wanted to demand information, but he knew she had to tell him freely who she was and what she had been, and whether she wanted his help in patching her two lives together. He could not force any of that on her. "One o'clock," he said again. "We'll go to Melanie's."

Sabrina glanced at Stephanie's frozen face and said, "We'd like that. And I'd like very much to see your studio."

Léon walked the length of the room and kissed Stephanie. "I love you." He nodded to Sabrina. "I'll see you at one."

Then they were alone again. "Are you too tired to go on?" Sabrina asked. "Should we wait?"

"No, I don't want to wait. I want you to know what I've done, what it's been like . . ."

They made coffee, and Stephanie warmed croissants in the small oven and filled a dish with red pears. "Let's sit outside; I like it there."

They sat at the table where she and Léon had eaten dinner . . . a lifetime ago, she thought. The sun was higher now, lifting over the houses across the street, warming the old stone wall, the painted wooden gate set deep within it, the rough flagstones of the courtyard. A nuthatch sang in the chestnut tree spreading above them; blue jays swept across the open sky. From the street beyond the wall came the clang of iron shutters being raised by merchants opening their shops, the laughter of children skipping down the hill to school, the rumble of German and Spanish, English, French, Italian, Swedish that accompanied groups of tourists, cameras clicking, making an early pilgrimage to the basilica at the top of the hill. "What a lovely place," Sabrina said. "No wonder you chose it."

"We chose it because Léon has a friend here who found us the house and the studio. We didn't have time to look around."

"Why not?"

"Wait. I'll tell you the whole thing. I don't understand all of it; there's so much we don't know. But . . ."

She told Sabrina everything, from the moment she'd awakened in the hospital and looked up into Max's face to the day she and Léon left Cavaillon. Sabrina listened with a sense of wonder that they had been so far apart for a year, living in different cultures, speaking different languages, and yet they both had worked in antique shops, had made new friends and fallen deeply in love, and had been in danger, had faced a man with a gun and felt the helplessness that comes when reason is not enough.

When Stephanie finished, Sabrina stirred. "Terrible, terrible. What you went through . . ."

"It was worse for Max," said Stephanie, almost coolly, and Sabrina drew back a little.

"Are you mourning him?"

"He was good to me and he—"

"He lied to you about being his wife; he hid your past from you—at least what he thought was your past—"

"I don't forgive him for that. But he cared about me, he was good to me, and he died in a terrible way."

"And almost took you with him."

"He saved my life!"

"But what got you there in the first place? He was running, Stephanie, hiding . . . from what? Most of us aren't living with men who are being stalked; what was he up to? Probably some scheme like Westbridge; there's no reason to suppose he'd do anything legal for a change."

"Westbridge? Max's company? What about it?"

"Oh, you don't know. No, how could you? The stories came out last December. They smuggled antiquities out of Third World countries; they had customers who paid millions of dollars for a vase or a funerary sculpture or a piece of a mosaic floor . . . anything and everything. They faked rare porcelains, too, but that was almost a sideline. If Max was doing the same kind of thing in Marseilles . . . what did he do there?"

Stephanie hesitated, strangely reluctant to expose Max, even in death, even to Sabrina. But they had to talk about it; too much hinged on Max, in London and perhaps in Marseilles. "He made counterfeit money and sold it around the world."

"Good Lord, he never changed, did he? I suppose he smuggled it in; how else would he do it?"

"Yes."

"What was his company?"

"Lacoste et fils."

"He never had sons."

"He liked the sound of it. I suppose he thought that any company with a father and sons had to sound respectable."

"And who worked with him?"

"Oh, he had people in a lot of countries. I don't know who was here, except for Andrew. Andrew Frick. The engraver. An artist, Max said. A genius."

"Where is he? We ought to talk to him."

"I don't know. He's disappeared."

"You mean you called or went there?"

"Robert tried to find him after Max was killed, but he'd vanished. The telephone at Lacoste et fils was disconnected, and there was nothing in the office or the warehouse: Robert called the police and they broke in and found nothing. Not even a piece of paper.''

"Frick cleaned it out?"

"Or someone else; I don't know how many people worked there."

"You never went there?"

"No. Max said I'd find it dull. And then, after I met Léon . . ."

"You wanted to stay home when Max went to Marseilles."

Stephanie nodded. Their eyes met. "It was never right between us. I tried, because I knew he cared for me and I was grateful for all that he'd done, but I never felt really married to him."

"Because you weren't. Even Max Stuyvesant couldn't fool you completely."

They smiled together, sharing the small joke about Max—always so certain of his irresistible powers of persuasion—and it struck Sabrina that for this brief time she and her sister were living entirely in the moment: being together and puzzling something out, as they had done through all their growing up when they had relied on each other for companionship and love and understanding.

But her thoughts were moving ahead. "So Max could have been killed because of what he did in Marseilles. But he said you were in danger, too. Meaning Sabrina Longworth was in danger. And that could only have been because of something that had happened in London. And London was Westbridge."

"I didn't have anything to do with Westbridge."

"You're sure? You were there for five weeks. Long enough to hear something or repeat something."

"I didn't. You were there for years, it was your life; I was only borrowing it."

"Wait, maybe it was this. Do you remember, just before you left for the cruise, you wrote a letter to me. You thought I'd read it after we switched back. I found it at

Ambassadors after you'd—after I thought you'd died. You said in the letter that you'd told Rory Carr he could tell you nothing you didn't already know."

"I remember that. He was taken aback when I said it. But . . . *Rory Carr?* You think he was working with Max?"

"He confessed to that. It was part of the whole West-bridge story. You said in your letter that he'd been fishing for information about Olivia Chasson's Meissen stork, the one that turned out to be a forgery."

"The one I broke."

"That was brilliant, Stephanie. I wouldn't have thought of it; I'd been going crazy trying to figure out how to tell Olivia I'd sold her a fake."

"Oh, it was such fun. I made it look like an accident and I felt so good about doing it for you . . ."

"And Rory asked you about it."

"Yes."

"So he probably thought maybe it wasn't an accident, that you'd broken it deliberately, and then he would have panicked, thinking you knew all about Westbridge."

"I didn't."

"But you implied that you did when you said you knew everything there was to know. When I read your letter about that, I was sure that was why they blew up the yacht; they were after—"

"*Blew it up?* Max said it was the boiler."

Sabrina put her hand on Stephanie's. "That's the one part I didn't tell you. It was a bomb. Under your stateroom."

"A bomb . . . But all those other people . . ."

"Whoever did it wasn't concerned about other people."

Instinctively Stephanie curled her shoulders against a world that had such people in it. After a moment she said, "But it couldn't have been Rory. If he worked with Max he wouldn't have killed him; he would have picked a time when I was alone."

"Rory and Ivan Lazlo—"

"Ivan Lazlo?"

"Max's secretary, years and years ago; he was in with Rory in Westbridge. These people seem to hang around forever. They confessed that they'd planned to blow up the yacht and one or both of them set the bomb. And they were after both Max and Sabrina Longworth. They said they'd had some quarrel with Max, but I don't believe that anymore. I think they were working for someone."

"Someone else was after us? Why?"

"I don't know. But Rory and Ivan are in jail, and some-one found out that Max was alive and learned where he was living and sent someone to kill him, and I don't think Rory and Ivan are smart enough for that, or have the right connections. But someone did it, and we have to find out who it was. Because . . ."

Sabrina turned her hand and Stephanie clasped it, and suddenly they were girls again, with Sabrina explaining something and Stephanie putting her trust in her sister. Their handclasp tightened and Sabrina closed her eyes, treasuring the warmth that flowed between them.

She opened her eyes to the cloudless sky and the bright sun filtering through chestnut leaves and the song of the nuthatch descending in sweet trills. "Because now there are two of us. And you can't stay in hiding forever. And however all this works out between us, one of the first things that's going to happen is that the news will get back to London that Sabrina Longworth is alive. And Max could be, too, as far as that goes."

"Max is dead!"

"Who knows that? You and I and Robert and Andrew Frick, who's disappeared. The murderer couldn't exactly report back: he's dead and buried. So whoever gave the order will be wondering about Max, and then he'll hear that Sabrina Longworth is alive. And he'll probably try again."

Stephanie froze, her coffee cup halfway to her mouth. "But then, which one of us . . . ?"

"I suppose whichever one he sees first, you or me. So we have to find him and stop him before he hears that you're alive."

"How?"

"I don't know. We'll have to figure that out. I think we'd better go to London, though; that's where it starts."

Their eyes met.

"I'll call Garth. He wants to know where I'll be staying. He's leaving tomorrow for a conference in The Hague; we're meeting—we're supposed to meet—in Paris next week."

"You won't tell him!" Stephanie exclaimed.

"I can't lie to him. I've already—"

"Sabrina, please! You don't have to lie; you just don't have to tell him! Please, please; you've got to give me some time. It's too soon; it's all happened so fast, I don't know what to . . . What am I going to tell Penny and Cliff? I've got to think about it; I've got to think about what I'm . . . what I can . . . I mean, I can't just walk in and pretend I've been there all this—" She stopped. That was what they could not talk about; not yet. That was what Sabrina had done: walked into a house that was not her own and built a life of love and cherishing . . . built a family.

He wants to know where I'll be staying. Léon will want to know where I am, Stephanie thought. And I want to be with him. But my children are with Garth.

Sabrina had pulled back, her body shrinking away. Stephanie saw the bleak emptiness on her face and knew she was thinking of Stephanie Andersen reclaiming her life: slipping smoothly into the house in Evanston, into her family, leaving Sabrina to return to London. Alone. As if the past year had never been.

But I couldn't do that, Stephanie thought. Garth would know. I couldn't fool Garth.

She looked again at Sabrina's desolate face, and tears came to her eyes. "I'm sorry, I'm sorry, I don't know what to think or what to say . . ." She leaped up and walked around the small courtyard, arms crossed, hugging herself as if to hold inside all the emotions that were clamoring for attention. She looked at Sabrina across the space between them. "Please don't tell him, Sabrina. *Please*. Not until I know what to do, what to say . . . how to talk to Penny and Cliff. Oh, God, it seemed so simple when we started . . . remember? But what do I tell them now? That I left them because I wanted a little adventure all to myself but now I'm back and ready to be their mother again? I can't say that; I have to think of something else, another way to . . . I can't do it! I can't face them! Please, Sabrina, please, I beg you, please give me some time!"

"All right." Sabrina's voice was so low that Stephanie did not hear the despair in it. "But just for a week. Just until we meet in Paris." Until who meets in Paris? an inner voice asked, but she pushed it away. She felt drained. She would keep the secret for Stephanie, but it could destroy everything she and Garth had built when he learned that she had kept it from him for a week that her sister was alive.

But isn't it destroyed anyway if Stephanie wants her family back?

"Then we can go to London right away." Stephanie's voice was calm now; she had averted a crisis and put off a decision. "That's the most important thing right now, isn't it? If you're right, if someone really will come after me . . . or you . . . or us . . ."

Her voice took on another kind of anxiety, the kind Sabrina recognized from when they were young: fearful, edgy, but also oddly confident, because Sabrina was there and Sabrina had always been the one to lead the way into adventures and find the way out of them. "We'll find them, won't we? We've got to! You're right, I can't stay in hiding forever, but I can't go through anything like that again . . . If you knew what it was like on that mountain, watching that man and Max and feeling so helpless . . . It comes back at night, you know; I wake up and I'm up there again and that man is so close to me, and then Max is telling me I'm in danger . . . Oh, you're right, you're right, we have to find out who it is and . . . stop it. Somehow. What shall we do in London? Talk to Rory Carr? We could make a list of people Max knew—''

Sabrina stood up. "I'm going to call home. They'll just be getting up.''

"Home,'' Stephanie murmured. Her rush of words stopped; she stood, drooping, beside the wooden gate, holding a trailing vine of bougainvillaea. My home is with Léon, she thought.

And Sabrina paused at the door to the house and looked back at her sister, gazing intently at the tangled vines of pale purple flowers, fragile-looking but tough. My enemy, my love, Sabrina thought. We've spun a web that has no way out.

CHAPTER *19*

---

*L*éon drove them to the airport and Sabrina went alone onto the plane, leaving them to say goodbye.

They stood in a corner, away from the crowds. The sun streamed through the glass wall, and Stephanie closed her eyes against it. Léon held her to him with a kind of fatalism. "Through this whole mad story, this remains: I love you. And I'll be here. I'll wait as long as you need."

"But not forever," she murmured.

He smiled faintly. "Forever has a great deal of flexibility. I don't know how long mine would be. But you're right: I won't wait if you show no sign of being able to make up your mind to come to me."

She opened her eyes. "I love you, Léon. I want to marry you. I can't imagine living with Garth ever again. But . . ."

"But Penny and Cliff. I understand that. They're wonderful in those pictures; she showed us so many I felt I almost knew them."

"So many," Stephanie echoed, remembering the shock of seeing the small leather-bound album that Sabrina carried in her purse. Twenty photographs of Penny and Cliff playing, studying, reading, digging in the garden, grinning into the camera or making gargoyle faces and striking poses, Cliff in a muddy soccer uniform, Penny painting at an easel on the screened-in back porch, the two of them on bicycles with Garth. Stephanie barely looked at Garth, but she could not take her eyes off her children. How could they have grown so much in only a year? They had a poise, a confident stance, a lift to the head that she did not remember. She had not even recognized their clothes. She had ached to hold them and she had studied each picture for some sign of unhappiness or insecurity. But she had found none. They were all prospering, she had thought: secure, comfortable, loved. And the house had looked neater than she remembered it: newly painted, the warped boards on the front porch replaced and stained, the bushes trimmed. So many pictures, she had mused, leafing through them again and again. Most parents are satisfied with one or two. And then she remembered that Sabrina was not even a parent. Or maybe . . .

She shook off the memory and kissed Léon, clinging to him, afraid to let him go. "I'll call you. I can't decide anything until we know what we can do in London, but I'll call you, I promise, every day."

"I can still come with you; there are seats on this plane. It might be better—"

Stephanie was shaking her head. "I told you before, Léon, we have to be together and figure out who we are and what we're going to do, and no one can help us with that. We got ourselves into this and somehow we'll get ourselves out."

"You may. You may find it impossible. And meanwhile you could be in danger. If you would go to the police—"

"We can't. I told you: if we went to them the whole story would come out and Penny and Cliff would . . . oh, God, read about me in the newspapers, hear about me on television, that I left them . . . You said you understood that, Léon; I have to tell them myself.''

''And when will you do that?''

''When I know what to say. And how to say it.''

''But first you'll go off on this crazy adventure in London, the two of you, after you told me you'd had enough of crazy adventures.''

''But we're in danger. You just said that. We have to do this.''

''Yes, all right, I understand that. But at least let me come with you. I don't know how much good I'd be at protecting you, but you might need help; how do you know what you're getting into?''

They heard the final boarding call for the plane. ''We'll be careful; we'll be all right.'' She kissed him. ''I'll call you, I love you, please don't forget. I love you.''

He held her for one last moment. ''I want to do so much for you. But you'll have to let me.''

''I know.'' She tried to promise him that she would, that they would do so much for each other, but she could not promise. ''Thank you for saying that; thank you for wanting it for me. Please trust me; I'll try . . . I love you.''

In the plane, Sabrina was sitting in the aisle seat, her hands folded loosely in her lap. She looked up. ''I thought you might want the window.'' A glass of orange juice was on the small tray between the wide leather seats, and she held it while Stephanie slid past.

''Thank you. I would like to see Paris again, even if only from above; it's been so long. Do I look all right?''

Sabrina smiled. ''Like a woman in disguise.''

''But it's all right?''

''Yes, of course; you look wonderful.'' They had chosen their clothes the night before, dressing for London in October: Stephanie in a gray wool pants suit Max had bought for her, perfectly tailored, with a high-necked sweater and a wide-brimmed felt hat pulled low over her forehead, almost touching her dark glasses. Her hair was in a braid tucked beneath the hat. She wore no makeup. Sabrina wore a wine-red wool dress with a long triple strand of pearls and carried a matching cape; her hair fell in long waves below her shoulders, her makeup was distinctive. "We look perfect," she said and looked up as the steward came with his tray of drinks.

"*Madame Lacoste, voulez-vous un jus de fruit ou du champagne?*"

"*Jus,*" Stephanie said, looking directly at him, and when he had served her and left, she grinned at Sabrina and lowered her voice as she switched to English. "He didn't even look twice."

"Because we don't look the same, not much, anyway. But we shouldn't push it in London. I don't think we should be seen together at all."

"Until we feel safe. And then—" An amplified voice gave instructions in French and English as the plane moved away from the gate, and Sabrina leaned closer to hear her sister's faint voice. "And then I won't be Sabrina Lacoste anymore."

Sabrina looked past her, out the window. They had made an unspoken agreement not to talk about the future. First they would do whatever they could in London and then they would confront themselves. They both knew it was cowardly, but they wanted these few days together, to rediscover what they had been to each other in the past. *Because whatever we do, it's going to change again. And we don't have any idea how much we can salvage.*

She saw the vast sprawl of Paris tilt as the plane banked and turned north. The gold dome of the Invalides gleamed in the morning sunlight, the Eiffel Tower's web of girders was silhouetted against a pale blue sky. She thought of Garth at The Hague, giving his talk, joining in seminars, part of a community of scientists. "Yes, it's a good conference, one of the best," he had said on the telephone the night before. "But I'm having trouble concentrating. All I want to do is meet my wife at L'Hôtel on Sunday."

Five days from now. I have five more days to be Stepha-

*nie Andersen, Garth's wife, Penny and Cliff's mother, a
homemaker and interior designer from Evanston, Illinois.*

The silver ribbon of the Seine meandered out of Paris
into the green countryside and suddenly Sabrina felt a rush
of relief. They were free. The land and its entanglements
lay thousands of feet below, they floated through sparkling
sunlit space in a cocoon of leather and tapestry and shining
metal, and they were together.

Stephanie turned from the window and met her eyes.
"We're free. Isn't it amazing? And wonderful? I wish we
could just keep flying for . . . oh, a long time."

Their hands met, their fingers twined. "We'll have to
figure out how to feel this way on the ground," Sabrina
said.

"Oh, if we could."

The steward returned. "*Madame Lacoste, Madame
Andersen, voulez-vous du vin? Du café? Nous avons une
variété de pâtisseries . . .*"

"*Café et pâtisseries,*" Sabrina said, and Stephanie nodded. They held hands until he brought trays set with linen,
crystal and china and offered them a choice of pastries in
a woven basket. He filled their coffee cups.

"*Merci,*" Stephanie said and turned to Sabrina. "I do
like being waited on. Part of the magic of London was
Mrs. Thirkell. And even though I loved being alone with
Léon in Vézelay, sometimes I missed Madame Besset."

"They sound like two of a kind. Another thing we
shared all year. I like your friend Robert."

"Oh, yes. Wasn't it wonderful that he came to Vézelay
before we left?"

"Yes, but that was no accident. He came to help. He
was afraid he'd find chaos and disarray—"

"Léon furious or perhaps even gone—"

"And the two of us at swords' points, or something like
that; anyway, having a lot of trouble loving each other."

They laughed softly, remembering Robert as he had
stood in the doorway, dressed in a bright red shirt and blue
jeans, gazing solemnly from one of them to the other, then

smiling and holding out his hands. "Two amazing women. Beautiful, intelligent, energetic, and very, very foolish."

"Yes," Sabrina had said. "If you came to tell us that, we've already discussed it more than once."

"I came to help. But you seem to be fine. I'm comforted by the way you look at each other; you haven't lost love or trust." He looked around. "And Léon?"

"At his studio," Stephanie said. "He'll be here soon for dinner. You'll stay with us, Robert, won't you? We have an extra room."

"Gladly." He looked closely at her. "No more nightmares about Mont Ventoux?"

"Yes, but Léon is wonderful, and getting away from Cavaillon helped. But I've missed you."

"And I've missed you. Our little town is quite dull without our talks and our cooking lessons. And without Max. I loved him, you know. We talked often; he called almost every day, sometimes on business, but usually just to chat."

"What kind of business?" Sabrina asked.

Robert hesitated only a moment. "He helped me smuggle young people into countries of great poverty and political repression, and, when necessary, out of them."

Stephanie stared at him. "But he was smuggling counterfeit money; that was why I wouldn't go away with him."

"Wait." Robert closed his eyes briefly. "Money. In those large pieces of equipment. He always had huge crates coming and going: returns, he said. I thought the returns were high. And Frick . . . Frick made the money. Max once called him his Dürer. I thought he was joking, but I should have caught on: Dürer was a brilliant engraver. Oh, Max, Max, I made use of you, I loved you, and you were everything I didn't want to think you were. All the clues were there and I ignored them because I chose not to know."

Sabrina thought of Garth in the beginning, ignoring clues so that he could believe Sabrina was his wife. *We*

*shape the world to our own needs and desires, and when
we can't, sometimes we call it a disappointment and other
times we call it tragedy.*

"Smuggling young people?" Stephanie asked. "For
what?"

"To help poor people resist despots. To help them organize and protest, sometimes to take the land that right-
fully should be theirs, sometimes simply to manage their
own villages without interference. All those activities are,
of course, illegal in those countries, and so, when the
governments begin to close in, we bring the young people
home. Max helped me bring a young woman out shortly
before he was killed. That was an adventure: we were like
two boys."

"A good deed," Stephanie said suddenly.

"Yes, he did many."

"No. I mean, I know he did, but I meant something
else. He told me that he did a good deed and, because of
it, that man found him and killed him. He said it was some
kind of coincidence."

Robert stood with clasped hands, his head bowed.
"Jana," he said at last.

"What?"

"The young woman we brought out. Jana Corley. I
thought she and Max looked at each other in a way that
seemed . . . well, it was just a passing thought, but it
seemed to me that they knew each other."

"Corley," Sabrina said. "I know a Tabitha and Ramsay Corley. He owns factories in Manchester; they have a
home in Kent."

"Her mother's name is Tabitha," Robert said slowly.
"She told me that once. But Jana is discreet; she doesn't
talk about our work. I can't believe she would talk to
anyone about someone helping me, as Max was that
night."

"Well, we'll find out," Sabrina said decisively. "We
wondered where we'd start in London. Now we know."

Robert held their hands. "Take care, my children. You

are so lovely and full of life, but you know that there is evil in the world. You did a foolhardy and dangerous thing when you traded places; now you must be exceedingly wise and cautious and thoughtful.'' He kissed their foreheads and Sabrina felt it was a blessing. ''I wish you well. You must write to me, or call. We must not lose each other.''

The plane flew over the flat fields of Normandy and then the English Channel, speckled with tiny whitecaps like flecks of snow. The coast of England was visible at the top of Sabrina's window. London, she thought. Home for so many years. Home, work, friends.

''Will we stay at Cadogan Square?'' Stephanie asked.

''Yes, for the last time. I sold it to Alexandra's friends, but they won't take possession until—''

''You sold it? You sold your house?''

''I have another one.'' The words whipped out before Sabrina could stop them. She set down her coffee cup with a shaking hand. *How are we going to keep from talking about who we are and what we're going to do?*

The steward removed their trays; there was a bustle in the cabin as passengers slid their tables into the slots in the arms of the seats, put away computers and briefcases and prepared to land.

''Do you want to be the one to talk to Jana?'' she asked. ''You were living with Max; it makes sense for you to do it.''

''Oh. Yes, if you'd like.'' And they both knew that by veering away from it they had decided, once again, that they could keep from talking about it as long as they both wanted to.

Stephanie's face was averted; she was watching the land come up to meet them, and thinking about touching down at Heathrow. It was so nice up there, she thought; now I have to face things. Except . . . not alone. Sabrina will help me. She'll get us through this. Somehow.

The house on Cadogan Square was dark and chilly, huddling against the rain that drummed from a leaden sky.

Sabrina made a fire in the sitting room while Stephanie ran to the market and brought back food for lunch and dinner. They both were at home in the neighborhood and in the house, moving easily through its rooms, and both felt the strangeness of that but did not comment on it.

"Shall I call her?" Stephanie asked. "I don't want to go all the way to Kent if she's out of town."

"She might have a flat in town." Sabrina paged through the telephone directory. "There's a J. Corley in London, near Berkeley Square. It's worth a try."

"That's so close. I think I won't call; I'll just take a chance."

"I'll have lunch ready when you get back."

Stephanie called for a taxi and Sabrina watched her, marveling that she was so comfortable in London and Cadogan Square after such a brief time. But why not? she thought. How long did it take me, in Evanston?

Stephanie found a raincoat and hat and umbrella in the foyer closet and dashed from the front door to the taxi. As they crawled through the traffic, she looked at the streets and buildings and undulating lines of black umbrellas with bewilderment. London, ageless and familiar, felt like home. But she had felt the tug of belonging as she looked at the scenes of Evanston in Sabrina's photograph album. And Cavaillon had been home. And Vézelay was home now—or anywhere, with Léon.

What's wrong with me? Can't I even say where I belong?

Jana Corley's apartment was in a curved row of flats, gray and dripping in the rain. Stephanie rang the bell and when a young voice came over the intercom, she said, "I'm a friend of Robert Chalon."

A buzzer sounded; she opened the door and climbed two flights of stairs. Jana was waiting, thin and blond, wearing a sweatsuit and heavy socks, her eyebrows still raised in surprise at Stephanie's announcement.

Stephanie held out her hand. "Sabrina Lacoste. And you're Jana Corley?" She kept her hand in Jana's and walked her back into the flat. All the lamps were on, and a small gas fire burned in the grate. The bewilderment Stephanie had felt in the taxi was gone: she felt strong and purposeful because she was doing something she and Sabrina had planned together. "I'm a friend of Robert's; I lived in Cavaillon until a short while ago. I lived with a man named Max Lacoste. But I think you knew him as Max Stuyvesant."

Jana's face became wary and she pulled away. "Max Stuyvesant is dead."

"He was thought to be dead. He's been living in Cavaillon. You know that. You met him there, when you were with Robert."

"But I didn't say anything. I mean, I didn't tell him I recognized him; it was obvious that he didn't want me to. I guess Robert didn't know. And I could understand it, you know; if I'd been mixed up in that Westbridge business I'd have wanted to duck out, too. And I figured maybe he was sort of doing penance for it."

"Penance?" Stephanie asked.

"Well, you know, he was working with Robert; you do know they brought me out of Chile? They even did this routine, it was like a movie, when I was locked up in a warehouse in Marseilles: Robert got the guard drunk so Max could take his keys, and they broke open the crate I was hiding in . . . I was never so glad to see anybody in my life. So if Max was working with Robert, he was doing good, and I thought it might be to sort of balance Westbridge and whatever else he'd done. You know, after Westbridge everybody laid the most incredible exploits on him; it was mostly envy, I think. Like he'd lived out their fantasies. I'm sorry, I didn't offer you anything. Would you like tea? Or soup? I'm heating some for lunch; anything to keep warm. I hate October; all of a sudden it's winter. What do you take in your tea?"

"Nothing, I don't want anything, thanks. I have an engagement for lunch. I need to ask you something."

"About Max? Did he send you here?"

"I'm trying to find out if you told anyone you'd seen him in Marseilles."

"No, of course I— Oh. Well, I did, as a matter of fact. I shouldn't have, but Alan absolutely promised he wouldn't tell anyone. We hadn't seen each other in a long time and I was . . . well, you know, I was very relaxed and I sort of let it out. That didn't get back to Max, did it? I can't imagine how it would."

"Who is Alan?"

"My fiancé. Alan Lethridge. Well, he's not exactly my fiancé, but I call him that sometimes, when I'm feeling fond of him. But, you know, he promised he wouldn't tell anyone and I'm sure he didn't. I'll ask him, if you like."

"I'd like to ask him myself. If you'll tell me where to find him . . ."

Jana frowned. "Did something happen?"

"I'm just looking for information. And it would be helpful if I could talk to Alan."

"Well." She went to the desk and stood beside it indecisively, then shrugged. "I guess Alan can take care of himself." She wrote on a pad of paper and handed the sheet to Stephanie. "He's usually home by four."

"Thank you."

Jana followed her to the door. "Say hello to Max for me when you see him. I don't care whether he wants to stay in hiding or not. He did a good thing for me and I'll always be grateful."

"Thank you," Stephanie said again. "I'm glad to hear it."

In the taxi she gazed unseeing at the streaming window, thinking of Max, whom Robert had loved and Jana admired, who tried to control everything and everyone around him, who lived by his own rules whether he was doing good or breaking the law. *They even did this routine, it was like a movie.* I couldn't love him, she thought, but I could have tried to get to know him better, to understand him. I wish I had.

Sabrina had set the small table in the sitting room, and

Stephanie warmed herself at the fire before sitting down. The lashing wind and rain made the room hushed in dry snugness, and Stephanie sighed as Sabrina poured a white wine. "So lovely. Maybe we could make time stop for a while."

"Yes, we keep thinking that."

Sabrina filled their bowls from the soup tureen, and it occurred to Stephanie that her sister was acting as hostess, pouring wine, serving soup in her own home. *Has she already decided to come back here? What is it she wants?*

"Tell me about Jana," Sabrina said, and as she listened to Stephanie's brief report she thought how well Stephanie looked, how confident in relating her conversation. *Does she think she can do whatever she wants, with Penny and Cliff, with Garth, with Léon? With me? She can't believe I'll just walk away from them; she knows now what they are to me.* "So Alan is next," she said when Stephanie finished. "Do you want to talk to him?"

"Oh, no, it's your turn. Unless you'd rather not. Have you ever met him?"

"I've met his mother, but I never liked her. Xanthia Lethridge. As I recall, no one ever talked to her because she couldn't keep anything to herself; it would be all over London the next—" Her eyes met Stephanie's. "Maybe it runs in the family. I'll call him; if he's in town I'll see him tomorrow."

Alan Lethridge lived in a town house filled with his parents' discarded furniture. "Awful stuff, isn't it?" he said to Sabrina, leading her into the drawing room. He was tall and thin, with a handsome, eager face and long hair; he wore blue jeans and an oversize sweater. "No wonder they got rid of it. But I'm too lazy to shop and I wouldn't know what to buy anyway. I'm waiting for a princess to rescue me and turn the place into a palace. Won't you sit down, Mrs. Andersen? What can I do for you? I remember I met your sister somewhere a long time ago, but I don't know where."

Sabrina sat on the edge of a hassock and waited until he

sat nearby. "I'm trying to find Max Stuyvesant and I thought you might be able to help me."

"Max? *Max Stuyvesant?* What are you talking about?" There was a clamorous silence; Sabrina could almost hear options running through his mind. "Is this some kind of a joke? Max is dead."

"He was presumed dead. But didn't you find out that he was alive?"

"Me? I didn't find out anything. How could I? I didn't know him; I never saw him. I mean, I did once in a while, I mean, people do, you know, at parties or the races, but we never talked; the fact is, I'd barely know him if I saw him."

"But I think you heard he was alive and told someone."

"I didn't." He looked at the ceiling, seeking help. "I mean, I didn't hear he was alive, so naturally I couldn't tell anyone anything."

"I think you did tell someone. And it's important that you tell me who it was."

"Nobody! Look, I'm sorry, Mrs. Andersen, but obviously I can't help you, so if you don't have anything else . . . I mean, I'm sorry to be rude, but . . ." He stood and looked down at her.

Sabrina stood beside him. He was indeed being rude, and the only reason for that was fear. "This isn't a game, Alan. It's very important; in fact, someone could be in danger—" Panic flared in his eyes, his mouth tightened stubbornly and he strode to the door. A mistake, Sabrina thought, at least a mistake until she and Stephanie decided how much to tell him. She followed him to the door, her voice casual now. "If you remember something, please call me. I'm staying at Lady Longworth's house and I'll be there for a few more days."

"There's nothing to remember." Sabrina thought he sounded like Cliff, mumbling, grouchy, guilty.

"He's lying and he's not very good at it," she said to Stephanie, at home.

"Is he afraid?" Stephanie asked. "What would he be afraid of?"

"Maybe Jana. If she's the princess he's waiting for, he wouldn't want her to know he broke his promise, especially if there are serious consequences. We have to decide how much to tell him, in case we want to talk to him again."

"Why can't we just tell him what happened to Max?"

"Because . . ." Sabrina got up to add a log to the fire. They were in the upstairs sitting room, where they spent most of their time, the drapes pulled shut, the fire casting a flickering copper glow on their faces, cashmere afghans lying lightly over their laps as Sabrina lay on the chaise and Stephanie curled up in a deep armchair. A tea service was on the table between them, and now and then they exchanged a smile because it was so good to be together in this warm, private place. "Because I don't think we should tell anyone."

"But why not? How can we find out who sent that man if we don't tell people what happened?"

"I don't know. I just think it's best not to tell anyone, at least for now. It's just a feeling I have. We can talk about it some more if you want; I'm sorry I can't give you a reason."

"No, it's all right. I trust you." Stephanie leaned forward and lifted the quilted cozy off the teapot to refill their cups. "But if Alan won't tell you anything, what do we do now?"

"Talk to Lazlo and Carr. I don't know how close they were to Max, but we do know they worked for him and they quarreled over their forgery business. Maybe somebody talked to them about Max, or asked questions that seemed unusual, or . . . Oh."

"What?"

"I just remembered. The oddest thing. One day last spring, when I was over here, Denton came into Ambassadors and asked me if I'd heard from Max."

"*Heard from Max?*"

"Yes, I thought he'd gone crazy. But when I said Max was dead, he said he was *presumed* dead, that they'd never found a body. And he thought he might have called me."

"That's sort of scary, isn't it? What did you tell him?"

"That Max was his friend, so if he were alive he would have called him, not Stephanie Andersen in America. And then he said . . . wait a minute, I'll try to remember . . . He said, 'Well, if he does surface—' and then he apologized for putting it that way—'if he does and if he happens to call you, would you let me know? I somehow can't believe he's really dead, you know. He always seemed indestructible to me.' And there was something else, Stephanie. I think he was afraid."

"Of what?"

"I don't know. But I'm going to call him."

She spoke briefly on the telephone, then hung up. "Hunting in Germany. Back on Friday."

"Well, but he couldn't really know anything, could he? It was just some kind of weird thing. Does Denton do weird things?"

"He wasn't crazy when I was married to him, if that's what you mean. And he wouldn't be frightened without a reason. Well, I'll talk to him on Friday. Or maybe you'll do it; you might be better with him. But first we'll find Rory Carr or Ivan Lazlo. Maybe both of them."

At her desk, Sabrina called Michel Bernard and Jolie Fantôme, who had written the newspaper articles exposing Westbridge Imports and Max Stuyvesant. "They're on assignment in Canada, Mrs. Andersen," said their assistant. "Can I help?" And when Sabrina told him what she wanted, he said, "Carr and Lazlo are London, both of them, at Wormwood Scrubs Prison in Shepherds Bush. They're in the lifers unit, you know, so they get only one VO—sorry, visiting order—a month, and it's only for ninety minutes. So you'll have to find out if they've had a visitor for October. They may not have, since it's early in the month. If you need me for anything else, please call. Good luck.''

"They're in London," Sabrina said. "Wormwood Scrubs Prison. Not far: Shepherds Bush, on the west side. Shall we each take one?"

"Oh. Yes, why not?" They looked at each other and burst out laughing. "Remember Dmitri?" Stephanie asked.

"And Theo, poor Theo, our—"

"—chauffeur. And those swimming parties when one of us would dive in and nobody knew—"

"—which one of us came up at which end of the pool."

"And one of the embassy secretaries giving us a lecture and getting us mixed up and you'd say—"

" *'I'm* Sabrina, Miss Derringer, that's Stephanie,' and she'd get so furious she'd just about choke on those eighteen strands of pearls she wore every day . . .''

They were laughing and they moved into each other's arms, holding each other tightly in the sheer joy of being together. "It's the same," Stephanie whispered. "We haven't lost any of it."

Yes, we have, Sabrina thought bleakly, but she did not say it because she did not want to shatter this time together. Right now they were caught up in the hunt, following it with the closeness and delight that had once been the most important things in their lives, and so this brief time itself became the most important thing in their lives, for as long as it lasted.

But too much has changed. And this is the last time. We'll never have it again.

The visiting room at Wormwood Scrubs Prison was narrow and low-ceilinged, with a long table for prisoners and their visitors. Impassive guards watched for the slightest movement that was out of the ordinary. The noise increased as visitors arrived; voices bounced off gray walls and the gray floor and ceiling. As she walked into the room Sabrina felt that the world had turned to gray, leaching the color from her blue and green plaid suit, her blue hat and blue leather gloves. And when she took off her gloves her hands looked pasty beneath the unforgiving lights.

Through a far door, Rory Carr walked in, dressed in gray. His silver hair was slicked back, but that was all that was left of the impeccable art dealer Sabrina remembered. The skin of his neck hung in folds, his eyes were sunken and restless, the pouches beneath them puffed half-moons sliding down his cheeks. But his voice was almost the same: as unctuous as if he oiled it regularly. "Mrs. Andersen, I am very glad to see you. I've wanted for a long time to express to you my profound regret at the death of Lady Longworth. I sincerely hope you will believe me when I say that I had nothing but admiration and affection for her. I never knew she would be on the yacht when Ivan proposed his mad scheme. Of course I had no influence on his infantile and destructive behavior, but had I known, I could have tried to stop him. It haunts me that I might at least have tried."

"No influence," Sabrina murmured. The newspapers had reported that Rory Carr had been indicted as a principal—an accomplice, aider and abettor in the heinous crime—and found guilty of murder.

"None whatsoever." Carr's voice deepened. "Lazlo is an animal; no one can deal with him. But foolishly I believed him and trusted him, and I am paying for my foolishness by being forced to greet you in these depressing surroundings."

Sabrina sat in the hard straight chair and folded her hands on the table. The room was filling up and the clamor of dozens of voices crying, swearing, demanding, begging, forced everyone to speak even louder to be heard across the width of the table. She looked at Rory Carr's ruined face and told herself that he had been a partner with Lazlo in murdering fourteen people and in trying to murder her sister. She waited to feel hatred for him, but she felt nothing. Stephanie was alive and Carr's life was over.

So she could talk to him and make him feel she was not an enemy. "No one can deal with Ivan? I thought Max Stuyvesant dealt with him. And with you."

"Well, Max . . . Ivan worked for Max for many, many years. At least fifteen. He did Max's bidding."

"Except when he put a bomb under his stateroom."

"Please." Carr held up his hand. "I can't bear to think of it. Max was one of my favorite people, a good friend, a superb art aficionado, an absolute genius in smuggling. I admired him enormously."

"Then it will please you to know that there is a rumor that he is alive."

"*Alive?*" Carr's body seemed to surge across the table. A guard moved forward and he sat straight again, staring at a far wall. In a moment he smiled a gentle smile. "Dear Mrs. Andersen, that is not possible. Your credulity is charming—very American—but whatever you have heard cannot be true. I would be delighted if it were, but really, there is no way that Max could be alive. He was killed on his yacht last October. Everyone knows that."

"There is speculation that in fact he wasn't killed; that he's been living in France."

"Speculation? A vague word. What does it mean?" His condescending voice roughened at the edges. "Believe me, Mrs. Andersen, he is not alive!"

"You mean no one else has suggested to you that he might be living in Provence, running an export company in Marseilles, perhaps smuggling counterfeit money into Third World countries?"

At the addition of each new detail, Carr's face sagged farther, like taffy oozing off the edge of a spoon. "Of course not. Of course not." In the surrounding din, a small pool of silence spread between them. "My God . . . could that be possible?" His glance raced around the room. "You're serious? There is evidence that Max is alive? Mrs. Andersen, you must tell me! Is he alive or not?"

He had skidded from patronizing to terrified, and it

seemed clear to Sabrina that he was telling the truth: no one had told him. So he was not the one who had sent an assassin to Provence. Someone else had, most likely the same person who had ordered Lazlo and Carr to kill Max on his yacht, someone so powerful that Carr was terrified. Of what? Of being punished, perhaps killed, even inside Wormwood Scrubs Prison, for failing to kill Max on his yacht?

"Well?" he demanded. "Is he alive or not?"

"I can't tell you. But if he is, he would be very grateful if you cooperated with the police and told them who ordered you and Lazlo to set the bomb—"

"What? What's that? No one ordered us—my God, what are you saying? Ivan set the bomb because he was afraid of Max, afraid Max might kill us. We'd had our little business, you know, small forgeries, nothing major, but it was a nice living. But Max thought it would lead the police to Westbridge, and we quarreled . . . But you know all that; you read it in the papers. What did you mean about someone ordering us?"

"Perhaps I'm wrong. But suppose there is someone. He's not in prison; we'd know about it. So he's outside. How did he manage to put you and Ivan here for years while he went on with his life as if nothing had happened? I know Ivan isn't too bright, but I thought you'd be too smart for that."

"I am. I know what I'm doing."

Sabrina tilted her head thoughtfully. "So someone has promised to take care of you when you get out. Money or a job, maybe a house in some warm climate? Come on, Rory, what did he promise you? Even lifers can apply for parole after enough years; you'd still have time to enjoy being set up somewhere. Who was it?"

"I don't know what you're talking about."

"Well," Sabrina said after a silence, and stood up.

"You're not going!" Carr exclaimed. "Our ninety minutes aren't up."

"I might as well, if you can't tell me anything."

"Tell you what?"

"Whom you're working for."

"I just told you! Is that why you came? Because you imagined . . . Mrs. Andersen, Ivan did it! By himself! I did nothing, though I confess I knew about it. But no one else is involved! I assure you, I swear to you, no one else!"

His face was shiny with terror and Sabrina felt a rush of triumph because she knew she was right. But there was no pleasure in reducing Rory Carr to terror; she was sick of the whole thing. "Well, as I said, I may be wrong. But I certainly thought there were signs that pointed to someone else."

Carr's head jutted forward. "Why?"

"Oh, rumors; you know how people talk."

"More rumors? My God . . . But no one has anything to talk about."

"Would Max, if he were alive?"

"No. Nothing."

"How about the man who told you to kill Max?"

"*I told you* there wasn't anyone."

"But just as a hypothesis. If someone ordered you and Ivan to kill Max, he'd have something to talk about, wouldn't he? Maybe in bed with someone or in a bar or at a party where everyone was bragging about something or other . . ."

"No! It's a crazy hypothesis."

"Well, crazy or not, perhaps he sends you money and writes to you and does what he can to make you more comfortable. *Does* anyone write to you or send you money?"

"No."

"I'm sorry to hear it. You have indeed been abandoned. How about visits?"

"No."

"No visits?"

"Not since—" Carr pressed his lips together, struggled with the idea of saying more, then shrugged. "Not for a couple of months. Nicholas used to visit both of us, but he stopped. Of course he's having financial troubles and I gather he and Amelia have gone their separate ways, but still, he's a free man and I'm in here and it's quite selfish of him to worry about himself so much that he has no time for me. I miss our talks about art. I should think he misses them, too; he doesn't have so many friends, you know; he's not generally a lovable person.''

''Perhaps he'll come back.'' Sabrina stood up again, anxious to leave. Her heart was pounding. Nicholas. Nicholas, who had tried twice to wrest Ambassadors from her and had been worried about her looking too closely at the finances of Ambassadors and Blackford's . . . Nicholas might have known about the forgeries, might have joined forces with Rory and Ivan to add to his income and then decided to kill Max if Max had threatened to expose him.

No. He isn't smart enough, she thought. Also, he's a coward.

But he knows something. He must, or why would he have come here? Why would fastidious, self-centered Nicholas have come to Wormwood Scrubs Prison month after month to talk about art with Rory Carr?

She started to ask Carr if Nicholas had worked with him, but changed her mind. It would be best to go to Nicholas.

''No one comes back,'' said Carr mournfully. ''No one cares. And Max isn't alive. No one could have survived that bomb. The police said the same thing, you know; no one could have survived.''

''Goodbye, Rory.'' Following a guard, Sabrina hurried through the prison to the cold sunshine outside, the clear air, the distant horizon. She drove to a hotel where Stephanie waited, and while she told Stephanie about the conversation she changed into black slacks and a black sweater while Stephanie put on the blue and green plaid suit, the blue hat, the leather gloves. ''He's terrified,'' Sabrina said. ''I'd guess Ivan will be, too. And if he doesn't mention Nicholas, be sure you do.'' And then she waited for Stephanie to return.

It was almost an hour before she did. "He's mean and stupid,'' Stephanie said contemptuously. "And he looks like a ferret or a weasel or whatever they are: as thin as a rope and he *slinks*; he almost bends around corners. Why would Max have anything to do with him?''

"I gather he was efficient. Did he say anything about Nicholas?''

"He talked about everybody but himself. Can't we talk in the car? I really want to get out of here.''

"Give me a minute.'' Sabrina twisted her hair on top of her head and pulled on a black hat with a floppy brim that left only her long, graceful neck exposed. She fastened a black fur-lined cape at her throat and put on oversize dark glasses. She and Stephanie stood before the mirror while Stephanie applied more lipstick, combed her hair so that it fell loosely over her shoulders and down her back, and adjusted the small blue hat at a sharp angle, leaving her face free. "Pretty good,'' Sabrina said, looking at their distinct images with approval. "I'll pick you up in front in about twenty minutes.''

Dressing up and playacting, she thought as she went to a taxi stand and directed the driver to take her to the hotel. For all the seriousness of what they were doing, and the deadly crime at the core of it, they were having fun, like children playing a game. Having an adventure. Doing something for a lark. A shiver went through her. *Just this time. We won't do it again. Whatever happens, after this we'll never playact anymore.*

Stephanie was waiting in front of the hotel, and stepped quickly into the taxi as it pulled up. "I never want to go to a prison again,'' she said as the driver turned around for the drive back to Cadogan Square. "Nobody seemed to like anybody; most of them were blaming each other for everything.''

"You mean Ivan?''

"Everybody. The prisoners blamed their families and

the families blamed the prisoners, and they all blamed somebody else for whatever they'd done, like the landlord or the police or the foreman at the factory . . . Oh, Lord, what an unhappy place. It makes me feel so lucky . . .''

"Yes." They fell silent and only began talking again when they reached the green expanse of Kensington Gardens, alive with the cheerful voices of children playing, and turned onto Gloucester Road to go home. "Did Ivan say anything about Nicholas?" Sabrina asked.

"Mostly he blamed everything on Rory Carr. He said no one could deal with him. I said that Max had, and he said Rory did Max's bidding, and I said, 'Except when he planted the bomb under his stateroom,' and he said—''

"Did you really? That's exactly what I said. What did he say about Nicholas?"

"That he didn't come to visit anymore. Amelia left him, he said, and he's got financial problems, but it's a dirty trick to think only of himself and let Ivan rot. I was going to ask him if Nicholas had worked with them— could that be possible? It seems incredible to me—but I thought if they *did* work together they could still get in touch, and why let Ivan know I was even thinking that?''

"Yes, that's what I thought. And I just wanted to get out of there."

"Let's go see Nicholas, shall we? Right now." Stephanie saw Sabrina smile and she laughed a little self-consciously. "I know how it sounds—like somebody on a hunt—but that's how I feel, and now we have a new clue and I can't wait to do something about it."

Sabrina looked at her watch. "He usually leaves at three. We'd better wait till morning. Do you want to be the one to talk to him?"

"I don't know. We should think about what we'll say."

"Maybe . . ." Sabrina smiled to herself. "Maybe we should take turns. Shake him up a little."

"Would it? Maybe we should."

"Oh, I don't know. It was just a thought. Another game."

They turned to look at each other. "We're getting so good at them," Stephanie said.

"Yes." In a minute Sabrina leaned forward. "There used to be a little grocery store here, but I don't see it; I guess we'll go to Harrods."

"What for?"

"Dinner. We didn't buy enough yesterday."

"Oh, Sabrina, can't we go out? There must be lots of places in London where nobody knew you and it won't mean anything to them if they see us together. Please, can't we?"

"I thought the whole idea was that we wouldn't be seen together."

"I know, but now that we're here it doesn't seem that anything could hurt us. Doesn't it seem that way to you? I know that Max was killed, probably by somebody from here, but that doesn't really mean we're in danger."

"I think we could be."

"Well, maybe. It's hard to believe, though, when everything is so normal, people going about their business . . . What do you think could happen? Do you think someone is going to shoot us if he sees us together?"

"I don't know. But that part of it isn't a game. You saw Max get killed, Stephanie; whoever caused that to happen isn't a normal person just going about his business; he's somebody who thinks he has to kill to protect himself. Do you really want him to know Sabrina Longworth is alive?"

Stephanie was silent. "Well." She sighed. "I just thought it would be nice to go out together. It's fun to playact, but it's been so long since we did things together, and I was thinking that we might not be together like this again . . . at least, not for quite a while."

"Oh. Well, we'll think about it. I suppose we could go out of town. Maybe tomorrow night. First we have to decide what we're going to say to Nicholas."

At dinner in the sitting room, before the fire, they wrote out questions and practiced asking them, as if they were rehearsing a play. But the next morning, when Stephanie walked into Blackford's, Nicholas gave her no chance to ask any of them.

He came to greet her, bouncing on his small feet, hands outstretched, a merry smile on his face that did not reach his eyes. "My dear Stephanie, what a surprise, a splendid surprise, to be sure, but still . . . why didn't you let me know you were coming? I would have arranged a festive board at the Savoy to make up for last time."

Stephanie gazed at him, frowning slightly; she had no idea what he was talking about.

"Well, of course you would prefer to forget it; I assure you, so would I. Believe me, Stephanie, never have I done anything like that. To walk away and leave a woman alone in a restaurant . . . good Lord, it twists like a knife inside me whenever I think about it. You have my apology, my heartfelt, *agonized* apology; I can't imagine how I could have done it; it's not in my character—but of course you know that; we've been good friends since your dear sister left us, and you know it is not my way to do such things. Well, now we can put that behind us and go on as before. Let me show you what I've done with the shop . . . a few new pieces, not as many as I'd like, but the economy, you know, and a slow summer—"

"Is that the real reason, Nicholas? Are you sure it has nothing to do with your finances?"

He swung around. "Good heavens, what a question. Has someone been talking about me? Might you have gone to Amelia before coming here? I hadn't thought you were close to her. But if you did, you heard many false-hoods and I should tell you . . ."

Stephanie was silent until his litany of complaints about Amelia, which slid smoothly into mistrust of Brian's work at Ambassadors, ran down. When at last it did, she said, "I haven't talked to Amelia. I'd rather hear from you what your finances are."

"But they're fine, why wouldn't they be? Business is always slow in the summer; by now you should know that. I'm quite dismayed, Stephanie; I thought we understood that it was to our mutual benefit to be friends in a trusting association, and not allow suspicion to cloud our relationship.''

''Suspicion? All I did was ask about your finances. I thought if you've been in trouble for a few years—''

''I have not been in trouble! Good Lord, Stephanie, you Americans see dark plots everywhere . . . it must be all those gangster movies. Have you really nothing else to think about?''

Frustrated, Stephanie contemplated him. ''You're doing well; everything is fine—''

''Exactly. Exactly.'' A jovial smile creased his face.

''—and there's been no reason in the past few years for you to look for other sources of income.''

His smile faded. ''What an odd thing to say. Are you fabricating another plot?''

''Plots depend on secrets, Nicholas, and if anyone has them, you do. You'll have to excuse me; I have another appointment.''

Stymied, angry, she took a taxi to Cadogan Square. ''I was no good at all. I didn't get anything out of him.''

Sabrina stepped into the skirt Stephanie had taken off. ''You can't be subtle with Nicholas; he sees it as weakness.'' She buttoned Stephanie's blouse and pulled on her tweed blazer. ''You wore a hat, didn't you?''

''Your brown cloche. It's amazing how many clothes you still have here.''

''I only took the ones that are right for Evanston.'' She veered away from that subject. ''Have you told me everything he said?''

''Yes. It wasn't exactly a long conversation.''

''Well, we're about to begin the second act.''

She studied Blackford's windows before going in. They were dusty and the displays were the same she had seen when she was there in the spring. Sloppy or uninterested or broke, she thought. Maybe all three. She pushed open the door and a small bell announced her arrival.

Nicholas appeared from the back room. Annoyance

spread over his face. "My dear Stephanie, more questions? This does begin to resemble an interrogation."

Sabrina took note of the dust on the furniture, the visible price tags that should have been tucked away, the ragged displays of books and cushions, a lampshade askew. "What an interesting choice of words, Nicholas. One thinks of prisoners being interrogated. Is that what you see in your future?"

His bouncing feet stilled. He sighed. "We're back to gangster films again. Really, my dear Stephanie, you have a narrow, uninformed view of the world, quite American, of course, but I thought some of your sister's knowledge and sophistication would have rubbed off on you."

"I would have thought 'narrow and uninformed' describes anyone whose main vocabulary is insults. Is that the only way you can talk to me, Nicholas? I came back because we never discussed your finances, or how you augmented them when Blackford's started to go down—"

"*Augmented?* I told you—"

"You told me nothing that was true or useful. Your shop looks as if you've abandoned it already; I assume, in your mind, you have."

"Ridiculous. Blackford's is my life. I would have nothing if I lost it. This is a temporary slowdown, nothing else. I'll recover from it; I always do."

"You've lost the ability to recover. At one time you were a good dealer, Nicholas; you knew antiques and you had a real love for them. But now you're just hanging on: a frightened, failed businessman stupid enough to ride on the coattails of the wrong people."

"Good heavens, what's happened to you? You were quite reasonable this morning. It's quite confusing, Stephanie, and I haven't the faintest idea what you're talking about."

"Your partnership with Rory Carr and Ivan Lazlo."

Nicholas took a step back. Dust motes hung in the air and he seemed to waver in their midst. "I don't know anything about Rory Carr and Ivan Lazlo."

"You know everything about them. I've just been to Wormwood Scrubs. They told me you'd stopped—"

"You went to Wormwood Scrubs?"

"—visiting them. They're angry that you're free and they're locked up. They say you're being selfish and only worrying about yourself. Rory says he misses your talks about art."

Nicholas's face was ashen. "They shouldn't have said anything."

"Why not? What did you promise them?"

He shook his head. His hands twisted around each other; one toe tapped spastically on the wooden floor. He looked at it as if willing it to stop, but it had a life of its own. Still looking at it, he said, "You see, it was a brief madness, Stephanie. Madness. I knew it, but I couldn't stop it."

Sabrina's steady gaze betrayed none of the relief that swept through her. Not a bad bluff, she thought. "Yes," she said, encouraging him.

"That's all." He looked up and backed farther away. "There's nothing else to say. It's over."

"Hardly. I have contacts in London, you know, through my sister. I think the authorities would listen to me if I went to them."

"But you wouldn't! What would you gain? I told you: it's over. Westbridge is gone, and in any event I would have stopped; I worried about it, you know, all of it."

"All but the money. And that was much more important than your integrity and your honesty with your customers."

He flinched. "I didn't *want* to do it, you know. That's what I meant about a madness . . . You won't tell anyone, will you?"

"Not today. Today I'm looking for information."

"About what?" It was a whisper.

"How it worked. All of it."

"And you'll keep it to yourself?"

"At least for today."

"That's not very reassuring, Stephanie." He waited.

Judith Michael

"Well, of course there's no proof . . . it would be your word against mine. And who would believe you? You're an American."

Sabrina burst out laughing. It unnerved Nicholas, and his hands fluttered, but in another minute he brightened, as if he had convinced himself that now they were friends. "Come on, Nicholas," Sabrina said. "Tell me how it worked."

"Well." His foot tapped; he put both hands on his thigh to still it. "It really wasn't so much, you know. I did need money, and they needed a reputable gallery for the forged pieces Rory couldn't sell anywhere else. I did fret over it, but it was so absurdly easy and no one questioned the authenticity of the pieces and after a while it was just another business. Of course it was wrong—I knew that— but we all do wrong things in our lives and I wasn't really harming anyone; I'm really a very productive member of society. I certainly don't deserve to be punished; I provided a service and ran my little business very quietly. It really was quite little, you know; quite tiny compared to Max's. He and his partner were the important part of Westbridge: Rory and Ivan and I were little cogs in a very big wheel."

"Partner? There was nothing in the newspapers about a partner."

"Well, I don't know absolutely that there was one." Nicholas was talking faster, the words spurting out as if they had been bottled up and now, at last, shot forth to point in the direction of this anonymous person left over from Westbridge, still free, still without worries. "But, you know, I was puzzled by how easily Max found clients—princes, kings, presidents, the wealthiest of the international set—and he always knew what art they wanted for their collections. I asked him about it once, but he brushed me off as if I were a fractious child; he was quite abrupt. So after a time it occurred to me that he must have someone high up, perhaps even a member of royalty, who had access to these people all around the world and could

508

set things up. Of course I had no proof, but it seemed to make sense."

"Yes." Each person leads to another, she thought. All of them tangled in webs of secrets and schemes . . . and murder. "And I'm sure you found out who it was."

"To my deep regret I did not. It wasn't as if one could ask his secretary if Max had a silent partner; as far as I could tell, he kept his records in his head and did most of his business at his club. One never knew whether he was mingling socially or doing business there."

"What was his club?"

"The Monarch. On Regency Street."

"Thank you." She turned to the door, then turned back. "By the way, Princess Alexandra Martova is buying Ambassadors from me. I think it would be best if you sold her Blackford's."

"Sell Blackford's? Never. You're being quite high-handed, Stephanie. Sabrina never would have spoken to me in such a way; she would have understood that this shop is all I have left in the world. I'm not surprised you're selling Ambassadors; after all, it's not as if you're really part of London. But I will not even discuss selling Blackford's."

"You may change your mind. As you say, what you did was wrong, in fact it was criminal, and Rory and Ivan may not keep that to themselves forever."

"They have no reason to talk about me. None."

"Because you promised to take care of them? Money, a house, a warm climate?"

"Good God, no! I said I'd do what I could if they needed help, but I don't have the resources to support them for the rest of their lives."

True, Sabrina thought. So it was someone else who had made that promise.

"But what if you can't give them any help at all? They already feel betrayed by you, Nicholas; would they tell the police about you if you gave them nothing?" She opened the door. "Of course, if you sold Blackford's you'd have enough money to protect yourself, maybe even to start another shop, something on a smaller scale.''

Nicholas stood with his head bowed, his hands clasped beneath his chin, as if in prayer. He stood there for a long time. "What would she pay?"

"Fifty thousand pounds for the inventory and your client list. I'm sure that list is quite small by now."

His head came up. "Fifty thousand! That's nothing. The reputation of Blackford's—"

"Has gone steadily downhill. And it will be worth nothing if your involvement in the forgeries comes out. Fifty thousand is what I will suggest that Princess Martova pay.''

Nicholas looked around his shop. The tapping of his foot was loud in the silence. "I'll have nothing left."

An appropriate punishment for the forgeries, which, after all, no one can prove.

At last a long sigh came from his slack lips. "Have her solicitor call me. I'll talk to him. I don't promise that I'll accept such an absurd offer, but I'll talk to him."

"Goodbye, Nicholas." She closed the door softly behind her.

In the gathering darkness, she hesitated; then, on impulse, she took a taxi to the Monarch Club on Regency Street. "Wait for me," she said, and started up the steps of the gray stone town house, one of three, side by side, that made up the exclusive men's club. Women were not allowed inside, but she planned to talk to the concierge at the doorway.

She stopped halfway up the steps. Above her, Alan Lethridge was coming through the door, laughing heartily at a friend's remark. He met Sabrina's eyes. "Hello again," he said, still smiling, and then he remembered their conversation and his smile faded. He stood a few steps above her while his companion went on, not realizing Alan had remained behind.

"Alan," Sabrina said pleasantly. "I think we should have a talk."

His companion turned. "What's up, Alan? They're waiting for us."

"I'm late," Alan said to Sabrina. "I'm meeting Jana."

Once again she thought how much like Cliff he was: sullen, angry, but unable to push past her, held by the authority in her voice and stance.

"This shouldn't take long," she said. "We'll just take a short walk."

He looked helplessly at his companion. "I guess I'll meet you. Tell Jana I'll be there in a minute. As soon as I can."

Sabrina took his arm and they strolled along the street, past the shops closing for the evening, past restaurants poised for the evening to begin. "You didn't tell me you were a member of Max's club."

"Why should I? I don't see why you give a damn whether I am or not."

"I give a damn because you told me you'd barely recognize Max if you saw him, that you never saw him except at parties and maybe the races, and you never talked to him. And I'm wondering why you lied about that."

Alan walked beside her, slouching, his hands in his pockets.

"You knew Max," Sabrina said, so softly that Alan had to lean sideways to hear her. "And Jana told you that Max was alive when everyone thought he was dead. And you passed that on. But you weren't thinking about what you were doing. Why do you think he was hiding in France? What if his life was in danger? Max has always had enemies; everyone knows that. What if you put him in danger by talking? Do you know what you've done?"

"I haven't done anything!"

"You broke a promise. You exposed someone who was hiding from danger. You put him at risk."

"You don't know that for sure!"

"How do you know? You don't know very much, Alan. You talk too much without thinking about possible consequences. Now I'm asking you one more time. Who was it? Whom did you tell?''

"Christ, why do you care so much? What difference does it make?''

"It makes a difference. You don't need to know why.''

"*Why?* Is he dead or something?''

"Do you want that on your conscience?''

"I just want you to leave me alone!" He stopped walking and stared at his shoes. "I promised Jana . . .'' He scuffed one shoe on the sidewalk. "Denton," he blurted. "He'd been out of his mind, you know, wondering if Max was really dead—they didn't find the body, he kept saying that—so I thought he ought to know that Max was alive. Put his mind at rest. I told him in confidence. Absolute confidence. I'm sure he kept it to himself.''

Sabrina was staring past him at the trees spaced along the street.

It occurred to me that he must have someone high up, perhaps even a member of royalty . . .

Max and his partner were the important part of West-bridge.

He'd been out of his mind, you know, wondering if Max was really dead—they didn't find the body, he kept saying that.

Kept saying that. Denton Longworth, frantic about whether Max was really dead or not.

Maybe Rory Carr and Ivan Lazlo hadn't been the only ones who were worried about Max getting rid of them because they were endangering his business.

Maybe Denton had had a falling-out with him; maybe Denton was trying to take over Westbridge; maybe Denton had threatened to shut the business down if it didn't go his way.

Crooks could find so many things to quarrel about.

Denton would have heard from Rory Carr that Sabrina Longworth had told him, one day in her shop, that there was nothing he could tell her that she did not already know. He would think she'd figured out the forgeries for herself, or that Max had told her.

Plenty of reasons for Denton to want both of them gone.

But then, after the explosion, why did Denton identify someone's body as that of Sabrina Longworth? He'd been married to her; he knew what she looked like.

Something we'll have to ask him. Among a lot of other questions.

She dismissed Alan, who was gone in an instant, and stopped at a telephone to call Stephanie. "I'm on my way home. I have a lot to tell you. And tomorrow Denton will be back from his hunting, and we're going to pay him a visit."

CHAPTER 20

"*I* expect him by noon tomorrow, Mrs. Andersen," Denton's butler told Sabrina when she called. "If you wish to call then . . ."

"No, that won't be possible. Just tell him I'll be there at two. It's very important that I see him; make sure he understands that."

"If you could tell me the nature of your call . . . he likes to know in advance . . ."

"I know he does. This is confidential and urgent. He'll know what it's about."

She turned to Stephanie. "That should get him. He'll think I've heard from Max. That was the last thing he asked me: to call him if I did." She ran a finger around the rim of her teacup. They were sitting in their usual places in the upstairs sitting room; in three days it had become a habit, one they already looked forward to. How quickly we make nests for ourselves, Sabrina thought. And settle into them, and mold ourselves to them and make them our definition of happiness. We didn't think about that a year ago when we started this caper.

"He'll be upset," Stephanie said.

"I'd guess that panicked would be more like it. You know, I can't really believe it. In spite of everything we've heard, how could it be Denton? He wasn't brought up on the streets; he had everything anyone could want. And besides, he's such a lightweight."

"Is he really? I always thought he had power: a viscount and all that."

"Titles don't mean power. Anyway, I don't think Denton would know what to do with power if he had it. As far as I know, he only cares about himself and making his world pleasant."

Their eyes met. "That's why it could be Denton," said Stephanie. "Protecting his pleasant world." They gazed at the leaping flames in the fireplace. "Do you know, almost the first thing you ever told me about him, when I came to your wedding at Treveston, was that he strolled through the world as if it were one of his Treveston gardens."

Sabrina smiled faintly. "I remember. I thought it was wonderful, that kind of confidence. But in fact it's far different from confidence; it's a supreme arrogance that I suppose makes just about anything possible. Including murder."

Stephanie put down her cup. "Let's go somewhere. We can't sit around and think about Denton all night; how incredibly depressing. And you did say you'd think about going out to dinner. Did you find a restaurant?"

"Yes, but—"

"Sabrina, please!"

"Well, I read about a new Italian place in Cambridge. I haven't been there for years and I don't know anyone there. It's about an hour and a half away; if you don't mind the drive, I think we'd be all right."

"Then let's go."

They dressed in evening suits with short skirts and long jackets with beaded lapels, Sabrina in black, Stephanie in deep blue. They took capes from Sabrina's closet, and then Sabrina called a limousine. "The first rule for strange places is, always make sure you have a way to get home."

Their eyes met in the mirror. They had not done that when they traded lives. Such a simple rule, and they had forgotten it.

They looked away. "Time to go," Sabrina said.

The limousine drove slowly through the early evening traffic, weaving among high black taxis and small MGs and Volkswagens that skittered along the road like children thumbing their noses at authority. At intersections, streams of workers flowed past and vanished as they plunged into the earth, descending on escalators to tube stations far below. Locked in their thoughts, Sabrina and Stephanie watched through tinted windows as the neighborhoods changed, the crowds thinned and then disappeared, and only a few cars moved through the streets.

They were in the suburbs: neat cottages and half-timbered houses, blocks of apartments sprouting forests of television antennas, children playing in front yards, shops, schools, a hospital. And then open fields and dense forests, deep green in the fading light. Sabrina remembered a line from Blake—"England's green and pleasant land"—and she thought of how long it had been her green and pleasant home but now was a country for others. She could not imagine living there again.

She glanced at Stephanie, gazing out her window, absorbed in . . . what? Her children? Her husband? Léon? How far away she is, Sabrina thought, and touched Stephanie's hand lying on the seat between them. Stephanie turned and smiled briefly, and then they turned away again, into their own thoughts.

The limousine slowed as it reached Cambridge, driving past the mellowed red brick buildings of the university and through narrow streets lit by gas lamps and the illuminated windows of shops. "Wait, could we stop?" Stephanie asked suddenly. "Look, Sabrina, what a lovely shop. Ballard's. Have you ever heard of it?"

"No, it must be new."

"Let's go in, shall we?" When Sabrina hesitated, she said, "Please, Sabrina, we're so far from London, what harm could it do?"

"Oh, I suppose it's all right. It's been a long time since we went to an antique shop together. We'll be about half an hour," she said to the driver, and they walked to the shop.

The entrance door, of old leaded and stained glass, opened into a wide, shallow room, dimly lit and filled with European and American furniture, clocks and chandeliers from three centuries. "What an incredible collection," Stephanie said. "Jacqueline would love it." There was no shopkeeper in sight and she and Sabrina moved slowly through the room, looking at telltale details that could distinguish a genuine piece from a reproduction. "Georgian," Sabrina murmured. "Just right for Billy Koner's lobby. Vern would love it, but Billy would say it's too old-fashioned."

"Who are they? Billy Koner and Vern."

"Billy owns the building I told you I designed. The one in Printer's Row. Vern is the architect."

"And Vern likes Georgian furniture? Isn't that strange, for an American architect?"

"He's more interesting than most of them." She looked up as an enormous man came into the store, his bald head shining as he flipped a light switch near the entrance.

"So sorry, my dear," he said to Sabrina, peering at her through his glasses. "I stepped out for a pint and ran into some friends." He did not see Stephanie, who was shielded by a large armoire. "Closing in half an hour; I'll be in the office back there if you need me."

"Tell me about Vern and Billy Koner," Stephanie said when he was gone. Sabrina described them, and her designs for the apartments, the lobby, the elevators and stairwells. "I loved that job; it was the biggest I've ever done, and the most fun because of Vern. And Billy, too; I like him. Vern and I played a game, guessing how long it would take to convince him of something we both knew was perfect.''

"Did you convince him?"

"Most of the time. Sometimes he dug in his heels, but then, why not? It's his building."

"It sounds wonderful. Much bigger than Max's town house, and that's the only job I've ever done."

"But you had a good time. Did you buy all the furniture?"

"Good heavens, no; he had tons of it in storage. He took me to see it one day and I couldn't believe it; he had so many pallets in the warehouse it was like opening one treasure chest after another."

They were sitting on one of the sofas now, close together, their voices low. Stephanie described her remodeling of Max's house around his massive furniture, covering the walls with suede, adding Oriental rugs and bringing in low lamps because he liked the rooms dim at night. "It wasn't as good as your design of Alexandra's house—I couldn't get the same light touch you had—but Max was pleased. He said it was the best house he'd ever had."

After a moment Sabrina said, "You really became me, didn't you? I didn't realize, from our telephone calls, how perfectly you made my life your own. I knew you were having a good time, but it was more than that, wasn't it?"

"It was magical; it was a fairy tale that I'd dreamed about and envied as long as I could remember. And the most incredible thing was that I couldn't seem to do anything wrong. It was the only time in my life when everything went perfectly: I went to auctions and parties and dinners and I did what you would have done, and I did it well. I don't understand how that happened, but it did and it was so wonderful I didn't want to give it up. The problem is, I became you, but you did better: you became both of us. I don't know how that happened, either, but somehow the whole time you were Stephanie Andersen, you never stopped being Sabrina Longworth. I was so sure you'd be bored and furious that you had to stay there, but you were happy. So what happened? You changed them; is that it? Somehow you changed Garth and Penny and Cliff so they fit in with the way you wanted to live. How did you do that?''

"I didn't change them. They changed me."

"No, don't you understand? You were still Sabrina. You are now. You're both of us. So who am I?" Her eyes were pleading for an answer. "Who am I, Sabrina? You know who you are, but I've lost myself."

Sabrina took Stephanie in her arms. "You're my sister and I love you." Stephanie laid her head on Sabrina's chest like a child, her breathing slowing as if she would settle there for good.

"Closing, my dears, sorry, but it's time."

The voice came from the office and Stephanie shot upright with a small laugh. "The voice of doom. *Closing.* Coming to an end. Oh, Lord, I'm getting morbid. Let's go to dinner."

The Italian restaurant had a small front room with a bar and a larger room with tables and high-backed booths. Sabrina had requested a booth and they were led to one in the corner, drawing stares as they walked to it. "Not one familiar face," Sabrina said as they sat opposite each other.

"You didn't expect any." Stephanie leaned out of the booth to look behind her. "I like the room."

Sabrina, facing the room, nodded. The walls were of rough plaster hung with watercolors of Italian hill towns and harbors; the floor was tiled in white stone, crisp paper covered the cloth on their table. "It could be Italy; they've done a nice job."

The waiter, wearing an open-necked shirt, black pants, and a towel wrapped around his waist as an apron, brought glasses and a bottle of Chianti and took their order. "Tell me again about Penny's puppets," said Stephanie, and Sabrina thought how like a child she sounded, asking for a bedtime story. Over the past three nights, in their long evenings together before the fire, she had told Stephanie everything about Penny and Cliff she could think of, but still Stephanie asked for more.

As if she's memorizing things for her return, Sabrina thought, but she talked to Stephanie calmly and steadily, as if the thought had never been.

"—so somehow her teacher arranged with Kroch's to display Penny's puppets in the window with her name on a card in front of them—" She stopped, looking across the restaurant, her face frozen.

"What is it?" Stephanie's voice rose in alarm. "What's wrong?" She turned, but the booth was too high for her to see over it, and before she could slide to the front to look out, Alexandra was there, bending down, hugging Sabrina.

"My God, Stephanie, what a place to find you! Is this for antiques or academics? Garth giving lectures—" She turned to the other side of the booth and sucked in a loud breath. She staggered and grabbed the table, staring at Stephanie. Her mouth moved but no words came.

"Sit down, Alexandra." Sabrina held her arm and pulled her down beside her.

She sat, her eyes on Stephanie. She looked from one sister to the other. "I don't . . . How could . . . *Who are you?*"

As she asked that of each of them, the waiter arrived with bowls of risotto. "Ah, there are three signorinas for dinner?"

"Later," Sabrina said and waited until he left. She pushed away her dinner and held Alexandra's hand between hers. "My sister wasn't killed on Max's yacht; she escaped, but she lost her memory and only regained it two weeks ago. But that's only—"

"Sabrina!" She rose to lean over the table, stretching her hand to Stephanie. "Oh, my God, my God, I can't believe it . . . Sabrina!"

"No, wait," Stephanie said. "That's only the beginning."

"We'll tell you all of it," Sabrina said, "but first we owe you an apology."

Alexandra turned to her. "For what? You don't owe me anything. Sabrina was the best friend I ever had, and when she was gone, it was as if you took her place. I mean, when I visited you in Evanston I almost felt—"

"You were in Evanston?" Stephanie exclaimed in surprise.

"I forgot to tell you about that," Sabrina said to Stephanie.

"So what's the apology for?" asked Alexandra.

Sabrina and Stephanie exchanged a look. "You tell it," Stephanie said.

The waiter returned. "Is there anything- -?"

"More wine," Sabrina said.

"Just a minute." Alexandra took a pad of paper from her purse and wrote a brief note. "Give this to Mr. Tarleton when he comes in, with my apologies. My would-be dinner companion," she said to Sabrina and Stephanie. "Now, go ahead. You're apologizing—for what?"

"We played a trick on you. You were a loving friend and we tricked you, and both of us hated doing it, but we were in so deep by then—"

"Am I supposed to know what you're talking about?"

"No. I'm about to tell you." Sabrina paused impatiently while the waiter filled three wineglasses. He looked at them curiously. "That's all," Sabrina said, and, reluctantly, he left. "First of all, I'm Sabrina; that's my sister, Stephanie. Thirteen months ago we took a trip to China . . ."

Gradually the restaurant emptied. The waiter drifted by as he crisscrossed the room. He removed the cold risotto. Unasked, he brought espresso for three. Soon all the waiters were clustered near the kitchen door, relaxing. Talk and laughter still came from the bar and a few diners dallied at tables near them, but Stephanie felt the change in the atmosphere: the evening coming slowly to an end, busboys clearing the last dishes and spreading fresh tablecloths and white paper on the tables, waiters changing into their street clothes, the owner preparing to make a final swift appraisal of his domain before closing and locking the door.

Closing. Coming to an end.

She shook her head and turned back to Alexandra, who, all through Sabrina's story, had looked back and forth from one of them to the other, listening, looking, wondering. By now she was no longer disbelieving, as she had been when Sabrina began, but she was still stunned, clinging to every word.

"—and we came to London a couple of days ago, to try to figure out what happened. We never went anywhere together, but we thought we were safe in Cambridge, that no one would know us. What in heaven's name you're doing here—"

"A new restaurant, and the owner is a friend and he asked me to show up so he'd get a mention in the gossip columns. You and I used to do this a lot; we did it a year ago, as I have good reason to remember, since that was the night you introduced me to Antonio. Oh. But it wasn't you, was it? It was Stephanie, and you were in America, being her." Alexandra's eyes flashed to the ring on Sabrina's left hand. "You haven't said anything about that."

"That's a separate story."

"But I visited you, and you had the most wonderful family . . ." She saw Stephanie wince. "I'm sorry, I didn't mean . . . well, yes, I did; that's what I saw. And all that time you'd found Léon. I have one of his paintings, by the way; I bought it at Galeries de Rohan. I liked the way Sabrina described him. Is he really that wonderful?"

"Yes."

"And you've told him all of this?"

"Yes."

"I can't believe it. It is the most fantastic, unbelievable, incredible story . . ." A slow smile lit her face. "You two are amazing. You know, I don't even mind it that you fooled me; good Lord, how many times have I wished I could do the same thing? I've looked at other women and wanted to be them, just for a little while . . . What the hell, there was a time, some years back, when I wanted to be Sabrina.''

"A tangled web," Sabrina murmured.

"Yes, a good way to put it. But who could have guessed the things that would happen?''

"We never even tried to predict what could happen," said Stephanie. "We just talked about how to make it work for a week.''

"Well, it did. And for a lot longer. You were perfect. And you must have been having a good time; everybody in London said how happy you looked all that fall.'' She looked at Sabrina. "Both of you, right? Building new lives. Well, I have to hand it to you; you'd win best actress at Cannes hands down.'' She saw Sabrina's face harden and glanced again to her left hand. "Sorry, that was dumb. You weren't acting, were you? Not after a while. But why didn't you tell *me*?'' she suddenly demanded. "We were as close as friends could be. When we all thought you'd been killed, and you came back as Stephanie to bury her— *oh*. For God's sake, *whom did we bury that day?*''

"We don't know. We can't understand it. I was in the funeral home for a long time; I sat by the coffin . . .''

"But you said it was dark,'' Stephanie said. "Just a few candles. And you were crying.''

"Yes, but my own sister . . . Well, maybe that was it; I really didn't see anything clearly. I saw what I expected to see.'' Slowly she repeated it. "What I expected. Everyone does that, you know; that's why Stephanie and I were so successful; people arrange reality to fit their expectations, and they'll go through all sorts of contortions to make the world seem logical rather than take something seriously that doesn't make sense at all.''

"I did that,'' Alexandra said to Stephanie. "Remember, at my dinner party, you told a story about Greece, when you were young, and you said, 'Sabrina saved me.'

We all thought it was very odd, but you covered it up somehow and that was that. It never occurred to any of us . . ."

"Why would it?" Stephanie said with a faint smile. "Who would try such a crazy trick?"

"Yes, but wait a minute. Didn't Denton identify the body?"

"He did, and that really doesn't make sense," Sabrina said. "I'm sure he wasn't crying his eyes out when he did it. That's one of the things we're going to ask him."

"Both of you? Didn't you tell me you'd been taking turns?"

"Yes, up to now." She and Stephanie smiled at each other. "But I think this time we'll go together."

Alexandra's eyes gleamed. "Won't that be something to see. You know, I was never fond of Denton; he didn't seem to connect with anybody, me included: we were all background to whatever he was doing to make himself happy. But I never would have pegged him for a murderer. It makes me wonder about some other people I know in the upper ranks, so to speak, of society, here, South America, everywhere. Do you think it's dangerous, going to see him?"

Sabrina thought about it. She met Stephanie's worried frown. "He'll be confused when he sees us; we'll definitely have the advantage. And I'll bet he never does his own dirty work. I think we'll be all right."

"You're just going to walk up there, both of you, and ring the bell?"

"That's the idea."

"It has great possibilities. I'd love to see it. Can I go along? I promise I'll stay in the background; you won't even know I'm there."

"No, but we'll tell you what happens. Where are you staying?"

"Claridge's. I've been meeting with Brian at Ambassadors. I love that shop, Sabrina. I love owning it."

"You're probably going to own Blackford's, too. I'll tell you all about it later."

"Blackford's? It's gone downhill."

"That's one of the reasons you're getting it for fifty thousand pounds. You'll do wonders with it; even from Brazil, you'll do better than Nicholas has."

"Probably, but I didn't even know I wanted it. Well, good Lord, another mystery. You're sure you won't take me with you to see Denton?"

"No, and you didn't really expect us to. We'll call you tomorrow, after we see him. It may be late afternoon."

"Then I won't be here. I'm going to Paris."

"Oh." *So am I, to have a week with my husband. But when he finds out I've lied to him, when he finds out that Stephanie is alive—*

And what happens before that, when Stephanie and I finally talk about everything we've avoided for three days?

"We're going, too," Stephanie said, and avoided Sabrina's swift, surprised glance. "We'll be in Paris tomorrow night. We can call you there."

"Oh, good. Why don't we have dinner together? And really eat it this time. I'll be at Relais Christine; where will you be?"

Stephanie looked at Sabrina.

"L'Hôtel," Sabrina said. Her hands were clenched in her lap.

"Perfect; we'll be just a few blocks from each other. I'll call you tomorrow night. No, Antonio meets me tomorrow night, and it's beyond his understanding that I'd be able to think of anything but him on the night of our reunion. How about Saturday morning?"

"Fine," Stephanie said. "We have all day Saturday."

Sabrina was silent. *All day Saturday. Before Garth arrives on Sunday. All day to talk, to decide what will happen on Sunday, at least the part of Sunday we have any control over.*

Sabrina signaled for the check. "Listen," Alexandra said abruptly, "I want you to know I love you both. I guess if I knew Stephanie better I'd see differences between you, but to me, right now, you're both Sabrina and I love you. I'm sorry, I know how crazy that sounds, but—''

"It's all right," Stephanie said. She put her hand on Alexandra's arm, almost as if to steady herself. "I don't know who I am, either."

That night, as she did every night at midnight, Sabrina called home. They were ready for her: Cliff on the couch in the kitchen, Penny in Garth's study, and Mrs. Thirkell waiting nearby to say a few words when Cliff let her have the telephone.

"You sound excited," Sabrina said to Cliff. "What's going on?"

"Nothing." There was a warning note in his voice that was clearly meant for Penny on the other telephone, and Sabrina knew that something was indeed going on. Her heart sank, because she was sure it was some kind of homecoming surprise, and there might not be a homecoming if Garth would not allow it. Maybe he'll banish me as he did before, she thought, as he has a right to do, and I'll lose them, lose them all, and Penny and Cliff will think I deserted them, just as I did last December.

But if she did not come home, would Penny and Cliff know it?

If Stephanie went home with Garth, would Penny and Cliff know it?

Would they see differences even greater than the ones they had found excuses for a year ago?

Would they demand an explanation because they'd know something was wrong, that the mother they loved had changed?

Tears stung her eyes. "Cliff, if you're planning something for when I come home—"

"We're not," he said, sounding relieved, and Sabrina was taken aback. What were they up to?

She listened to their talk about school and friends and a

painting contest Penny had entered, and she laughed at their small jokes and puns, and when she hung up, she told herself that she wouldn't think about whatever they were planning. It was probably a present they were making at school, and there was nothing she could do about that. *They'll give it to me or they won't. I'll know on Sunday.*

At six the next morning, as she did every morning, she called Garth in his hotel at The Hague. Seven in the morning there; his only time to talk before his conference sessions began. Curled up in her sitting room, with Stephanie in the guest room down the hall, Sabrina knew that her voice was subdued, almost strained with the effort of measuring every word, but she could not make herself sound carefree and lively, even when she concentrated on trying.

"A lot of talking to people," she said, avoiding outright lies. "Nicholas is selling Blackford's . . . Oh, Alexandra is here, getting organized at Ambassadors with Brian, and she's buying Blackford's, too." She talked about London and the weather and packing up the furnishings and art at Cadogan Square and shipping them to Evanston, and then she said, "I don't really want to talk about me; tell me what you've been doing."

As he talked, she could tell, because she was so familiar with every nuance of his voice, that he knew something was bothering her. But after the first night, when she had been evasive, he had not pressed her. He described the scientists at the conference and their papers, the attention his own talk had received and the little sight-seeing he had been able to do; he told her he had heard from Claudia that the *Chicago Tribune* was doing an investigative series on Congressman Leglind and the effect congressional hearings had on university research, and Sabrina asked enough questions to keep him talking about all of that and more for almost an hour.

"And that's enough," he said at last. "Everything else will wait. You haven't told me your hotel in Paris."

"L'Hôtel. It's on the Left Bank, near the Boulevard Saint-Germain. Do you know what time you'll be there?"

"Early. Probably about nine-thirty. I have a surprise for you; I'm telling you now so you can wonder about it for a couple of days."

"You too? Penny and Cliff are planning something . . . Garth, what's going on?"

"Were they mysterious? I'll have to ask them about that. My love, you'll have to wait until Sunday. I've started counting the hours."

"It will be here before we know it," Sabrina murmured. "Oh, Garth, I love you; you're so much a part of me, my life, my dreams . . . I'm sorry," she said and willed her voice to lightness. "I'm being dramatic. I miss you. I love you. I'll call you tomorrow from Paris."

When she came downstairs, Stephanie was waiting in the kitchen with café au lait and croissants. "Not exactly an American breakfast," she mused. "Isn't it odd how French I've become? Do you know, for ten months I didn't speak English or hear English spoken. Now and then a word would break through and I'd find that scary because I had no idea what it meant, but otherwise everything I said and thought was in French and I never thought twice about it. Isn't that unbelievable? Even my language was lost." She was concentrating on carefully folding napkins. "Were you talking to Garth this morning? I came down early and I heard your voice when I went past your room."

"Yes. And I talked to Penny and Cliff last night. They're fine: busy and happy and brewing some kind of mischief."

"Mischief?"

"They denied it, but I could hear it in Cliff's voice. I suppose they're making something in school; they've done that before."

"Yes, I remember."

Withdrawn again, they ate their breakfast and then the telephone rang. Stephanie went to answer it, because every morning at ten—how ritualized we have become, Sabrina thought—Léon called.

She looked up when Stephanie returned. "What is it?"

"He wants to buy a house." She sat down and held her cup in both hands. "He found an old house high up, near the basilica, and he wants to renovate it. There's a building about fifty feet away that would be perfect for his studio; he'd make a covered passage to connect it to the house. It's very big, the house is; he says it has . . . plenty of room for children."

With a small gasp, Sabrina shrank into herself. Stephanie was staring out the window, her thoughts far away. And then the telephone rang again and after a minute Sabrina rose to answer it.

"Stephanie? Denton Longworth here. I understand you called, you wanted to come over at two? Of course you can, but you could just tell me now what it is you want; you don't have to come all the way here . . ."

Alert now, hearing the thread of alarm in his voice, Sabrina glanced at Stephanie, and mouthed, *Denton*, before saying calmly, "It's not that far, and I don't like to have important conversations on the telephone."

"Well, then, why not come right away? You don't have to wait; I mean, I'm here, and I don't have any plans . . . I got back early, you know, and there's nothing on my calendar until later . . . You can come now!"

"What a good idea. I'll be there in twenty minutes."

In the entrance hall, she and Stephanie stood before the tall mirror. They were wearing tweed slacks and gray cashmere sweaters they had found in Sabrina's bureaus: not identical, but close enough. They both wore a strand of pearls and pearl earrings; they both pulled on long charcoal gray coats, one belted, the other not—"but he'll never notice," Sabrina said. Their makeup was identical; their long chestnut hair, falling below their shoulders, was identical. "We'll do fine," Stephanie said. And they left the house to walk to the taxi stand.

Denton's tall gray town house was so narrow it reminded Stephanie of a passenger on a crowded bus, his arms clamped to his sides. It stood on a street of equally narrow houses near Saint James's Square and within walking distance of the Monarch, the club where Sabrina had seen Alan Lethridge. Closed drapes and a deeply carved front door made it look as if it were fending off visitors, but before Sabrina and Stephanie had a chance to lift the brass knocker, the door was opened wide and the butler stood before them.

"Mrs. Ander— Good God!"

Decidedly un-butlerlike, Stephanie thought in amusement. She had been tense and fearful, in spite of Sabrina's confidence, but the thought came to her that this, too, was a game, another game among all those they had played as children and in the past year, and alongside her fear a spark of anticipation flared up.

"Good afternoon, Bunter," said Sabrina. "I believe we're expected."

"Mrs. Andersen?" His eyes, wide and staring, slid back and forth so he did not have to declare himself speaking to one or the other.

"Yes," Sabrina said simply and walked past him into the house.

She remembered it so well it was as if she had been there the day before. Nothing had changed; it was furnished exactly as it had been when Denton's parents bought it for them as a wedding gift. Even the floral arrangements seemed the same. With Stephanie close behind, she walked through the echoing marble foyer, ignoring an archway that led to the main salon, heading instead for a closed door that, she knew, led to a small study. *Less room for Denton to maneuver*.

"Please, if you would . . ." the butler said helplessly, standing in the archway, indicating they should follow him into the salon.

"We'll wait in here." Sabrina opened the door. Across the room, standing beside a leather-topped desk, Denton was on the telephone, his back to them. He heard the door open and turned and saw Sabrina and Stephanie side by side. There was a suspended moment that seemed to stretch endlessly; then a small sound escaped him, the telephone fell from his hand, and he crumpled to the floor.

"My lord!" The butler sprang to Denton's side, lifting him to a sitting position on the floor. "My lord, my lord!"

Still wearing their coats, Sabrina and Stephanie sat on one of the leather couches and waited. The room felt like a cave, Stephanie thought, with brown velvet drapes pulled tight across the high windows and a brown and black Bokhara rug stretching from the heavy mahogany door to the brown marble hearth of the cold fireplace. She watched Denton's head roll against the butler's arm, and saw his eyes open and look toward the doorway where he had seen them. When he found it empty, he looked slowly to the left and saw them sitting together on the couch, two identical women, their heads tilted at exactly the same angle, watching him with interest.

He closed his eyes, then slowly opened them, willing the vision to disappear. "Denton, we want to talk to you," Sabrina said briskly. "Get up now. Perhaps Bunter will bring you some tea."

"Scotch," Denton said automatically. He stayed where he was, his eyes moving from Sabrina to Stephanie, his small mustache quivering in the round face that usually was rosy and smiling but now was stiff and pale, the lips barely moving. "You were dead. I saw you."

"My lord, let me help you up." The butler stood, bringing Denton with him. He lowered him onto the other leather couch, then hung up the telephone, which had been dangling over the edge of the desk. "I'll bring tea, my lord."

"*Scotch.*" His eyes were on Sabrina and Stephanie. "You found someone—a double—God, it's a perfect match. What was it, plastic surgery? What for? Christ, you could have killed me . . . the shock . . . I could have died. What the hell do you think you're doing?"

"But we didn't die," Sabrina said.

"We're both here," Stephanie said.

"Stephanie Andersen and Sabrina Longworth."

"You see, two people got off the yacht before it went down."

"And they've been living in France."

"Quite well, and very anxious to talk to you."

They looked at Denton expectantly.

"Got off the yacht . . ." Denton echoed hoarsely. He cleared his throat. "It's a lie. I saw your body. I identified you."

"Yes, we've been wondering why you did that," Sabrina said. "How closely did you look at the body?"

He stared at them helplessly. "I don't know."

"Oh, come now, Denton, of course you do. What did you see? Hair that looked like mine? A face that looked a little like mine?"

"But it would have been bruised and swollen," Stephanie said. "And there would have been cuts all over it. That's what we've been forgetting; that's how I looked when they took me to the hospital. It took weeks for the bruises to disappear and the swelling to go down."

"So someone could have resembled you—"

"There was someone!" Stephanie turned to Sabrina. "There was a woman on the yacht who did look like me. She was taller and thinner, but there was definitely a resemblance, and her hair was almost the same as mine—in fact, Max teased her: he said she'd obviously found my hairdresser and had it colored and styled like mine, and someone else asked her if she'd hired my dressmaker so she could look like me. If she was badly bruised—"

"*Two people*?" Denton demanded, and they turned to him.

"What did you tell the undertaker?" Sabrina asked.

"*Two* people got off the boat?" he asked. "Who was the other one?"

"One thing at a time," Stephanie said. "What did you tell the undertaker?"

"*Who was the other one?*"

The butler came in, carrying a tray with glasses, an ice

bucket and a bottle of Scotch. "If the ladies wish a drink, or tea . . . ?"

"Nothing," Sabrina said. "And I think we won't need to be disturbed again."

"Christ, you sound just like her. Christ, I can't be-lieve—it can't be . . . you really are Sabrina?"

"Really," Stephanie said solemnly. "I got off the yacht before it sank. What did you tell the undertaker?"

"Christ. Sabrina. Christ. I was so sure . . . It looked like you. Not a lot, I suppose; you're right, the face was all bruised, the eyes were swollen shut, and they'd cut your—her—hair; it was so matted they couldn't comb it, they said, and there was a lot of confusion, people all around, the press, you know, and relatives of all those other people, so I just glanced—you know I can't stand the sight of dead people, it makes me sick—and said it was you, and then I gave them a picture of you and told them to do the best they could with makeup and whatever tricks they have, for the funeral, you know. I thought it was the least I could do."

He took a breath, adjusting, adapting. "But this is fan-tastic! Incredible! Wonderful! It was a terrible shock, ter-rible, terrible, to all of us, Sabrina"—he looked from one sister to the other, reluctant to ask outright which of them had once been his wife—"everyone felt it; we all were devastated. What happy news we have to tell everyone now! A miracle! I'm glad you came to tell me, though I must say it was not kind of you to play that shocking trick, showing up without warning . . . I really might have had a heart attack, you know, and there was no reason for it. We're not enemies, you know. By the way"—it came out carelessly now—"who *was* the other person who escaped from the yacht?"

"But you already know the answer," Stephanie said. "You know that Max escaped and you know he's been living in France ever since it happened."

"*Max?* Good God, how would I know that? Escaped? Alive? My God, my God, another miracle. It's almost too much to believe. But of course I knew nothing about it; how could I? Why would you think that?''

"Because we know a great deal about you," Sabrina said. "We've talked to Nicholas about Westbridge Imports and he told us about Max's partner—''

"Partner? Wait, this is . . . Nicholas said Max had a partner? He's lying. I knew Max and I never heard him talk about a partner. Never. Westbridge was all his: his money, his ideas . . .''

"Nicholas didn't say anyone else had money in Westbridge. He said someone was lining up customers for smuggled antiquities and giving Max information about them, and places to find specific works of art to be stolen and smuggled out . . . that sort of thing. Someone who moved in wealthy circles. Someone like you.''

"I would never do such a thing. It would be a betrayal of my class.''

Sabrina and Stephanie gazed at him in contempt. Denton poured more Scotch, the neck of the bottle rattling against the edge of the glass. "Max and I were friends. That was all.''

"You worked together," Stephanie said, and coldly lied. "Max told me that.''

"When? What are you talking about?''

"When we were living together," Sabrina said and watched with amusement as Denton's eyes swiveled to her. "I lived with Max for almost a year; surely you knew that, Denton. When you tracked him down, didn't anyone tell you he had a wife?''

"Wait. Wait. One thing at a . . . Lived with him? You lived with him? And what does that mean . . . *tracked him down*? What are you talking about?''

"I lost my memory in the explosion," Stephanie said, and Denton's eyes swung back to her. "Max told me I was his wife, and I believed him and lived with him. He told me everything. He told me about you. He told me we were in danger.''

Denton's glass stopped halfway to his mouth. "Why?''

"Because," said Sabrina, and Denton's eyes jerked from Stephanie's face to hers, "you'd tried to kill him once, with the bomb on the yacht. He knew it—"

"*I* tried to kill him? You're mad. I had no reason, no reason, no reason to kill anyone. What do you think you—"

"That's why he was living in France under another name. And he knew that if you found him, you'd try again. So he told me we were in danger, and in fact—"

"Stop it! This is insane. You're making this up, the two of you . . . What is it, some kind of game? Going back and forth . . . what the hell for? Making these outrageous statements . . ." He seemed to gain strength as he talked. "Absolutely outrageous. Based on nothing but some kind of fantasy. You're still trying to get back at me, Sabrina, is that it?" He looked at Stephanie, then at Sabrina, then back again, and finally settled on some neutral point between them so he would not have to decide which sister was which. "Haven't we been divorced long enough to become friends? What do you want? Money? Is that what you're here for? I don't pay blackmail. Even if I did, I haven't anything to give you, so you're wasting your time. Wasting your time! Coming in here . . . how dare you come into my home and brazenly accuse me of . . . of . . ."

"Murder," Sabrina said. "We're not interested in money, Denton; we're interested in what you've done. You see, we also talked to Ivan Lazlo and Rory Carr."

His face darkened. He put down his glass. "You bitch. You didn't talk to them. Even if you did, they wouldn't tell you anything."

"You seem so sure of that. I suppose that's because you promised to take care of them when they get paroled. Even if it took another ten or fifteen years, they'd still be young enough to enjoy whatever you've promised them."

"This isn't a game," Stephanie said. "You and Max quarreled about Westbridge, and Rory told you I'd made a foolish remark that I knew everything there was to know about the forged ceramics. So you had reason to want us both gone, and you told Ivan and Rory to get rid of us. Was the bomb their idea or yours? It really doesn't matter; you gave them an order and they carried it out, which makes you guilty of murder.''

''But Max wasn't killed!''

''Fourteen other people were on that yacht. They were all killed.''

''And then,'' Sabrina went on, ''you found out that Max was alive, in Cavaillon, and you sent another one of your henchmen to kill him. You're not very creative, Denton; you always think of killing when you feel threatened. Of course, as you've discovered, what seems to be an obvious solution doesn't always work.''

''I have no henchmen; I sent no one! How the hell many times do I have to tell you that? As far as I knew, Max was dead.''

''You were never sure of that. You weren't sure last May, when you came to Ambassadors and asked me if I'd heard from him. I thought he was dead, Denton; you weren't sure. And then, a few weeks ago, you heard that he was alive. You heard it from someone in your club. You see, we've talked to him, too. We've talked to all of them. Rory Carr, Ivan Lazlo, Alan Lethridge, and of course Nicholas. No one is lying for you, Denton; they're all quite willing to talk.''

Denton sagged. His chin was embedded in his chest and he looked at them from beneath heavy eyelids and saw them close together on the couch, arms touching, bodies touching, wearing the same clothes, their voices overlapping. They seemed to be one person, vengeful, relentless, implacable. He lowered his eyes and looked at his hands, twisted in his lap, and tried to think of a way to ask if Max was still alive.

''I saw the man you sent,'' Stephanie said casually. ''He followed us home once, from a church we'd visited. He hung around our house. He was still there after Max left.''

"Left," Denton echoed. He looked up. "*Left?*"

"Yes. I woke up one morning and he was gone. He'd told me he was leaving, so I wasn't surprised; it was just more sudden than I'd expected. I left Cavaillon after that; Max had told me your man might be after me, too. The way Rory and Ivan had been when we were on the yacht." She gazed at Denton. "Max told me," she added dreamily, "that he would always come back."

With a grunt, as if the breath had been knocked out of him, Denton slid all the way down on the leather couch. His heels dug into the rug, his head sank lower onto his chest. Burt, the man he had sent to Cavaillon, had called to say he had located Max, and that was the last Denton had heard. He had not called again; he had not checked out of his hotel. But he was never there when Denton called, again and again. There was no way to know what had happened: if he had tried to kill Max and failed, or if he had given up without trying because Max seemed invulnerable.

He *was* invulnerable. The son of a bitch wouldn't die.

Denton had always been in awe of Max Stuyvesant. He believed there was something mystical about him, as if he were a djin, larger than life, moving among them but not one of them, ruthless, unstoppable, untouchable, a force that Denton never could emulate or even understand. After the yacht had exploded and he had identified the body of Lady Longworth, Denton had haunted the waterfront for days, pestering the police for information about any bodies found far from the sunken ship, insisting that the search continue, that he would pay for it, that he had to know whether the one man still unaccounted for had survived or not.

In the end, he had left Monte Carlo without knowing anything, and slowly, in the following months, as nothing was heard of Max, he began to believe he had indeed been killed, blown to pieces in the explosion, or trapped somewhere at the bottom of the Mediterranean, beyond everyone's reach. Until Alan Lethridge had told him that Max was alive.

He knew then that he had been right all along. Max was a djin: a creature of magic who either had come through that powerful explosion unscarred or else had died and then come back to life.

Max told me that he would always come back.

And either he had escaped Burt's gun in Cavaillon or Burt had killed him and once again he had come back to life, scaring the hell out of Burt, who took off, never to be seen again.

At the moment, Denton could believe either one.

He'll be after me.

His head came up as if the words had been spoken aloud.

He knows I've tried twice; he'll kill me before I can try again. And there is no place I can hide.

Sabrina and Stephanie were watching him intently, following the expressions that raced across his face. "Of course you can tell the police what happened," Sabrina said conversationally. "You'll go to prison, of course, but I suppose you have as much chance for parole as Rory and Ivan. And you're a young man—forty-one, isn't it? When you get out, you'll still have many happy years with your friends."

I'll never have any happy years. I'll always wonder where he is, when he'll show up. I'll always be looking over my shoulder . . .

"I think you should call the police," Stephanie said seriously, her voice warm and encouraging. "You'll feel much better about everything."

But not safer. Even prison isn't safe from his reach.

"Call them," Sabrina said firmly: it was an order. "Of course we could do it, but it would be better if you did. Or would you rather call your solicitor? Yes, I'm sure you would; you always find other people to do the difficult work for you. Call him, Denton; let him take care of informing the police."

*But even prison is safer than this house or anywhere
I might go: cruises, the races, country houses, ski re-
sorts . . . Prison would be much harder for him, and it
would give me time to think of some way to get to him
before he can get to me. That's what I need—time—and I
know I'll figure out a way to beat him.*

As if in a dream, he rose from the couch and went to the
desk. It was out of his hands. He saw Sabrina and Stephanie exchange a look and knew they had triumphed completely, but it was too late to care about that. He turned his
back and picked up the telephone, and with a leaden finger
slowly dialed his solicitor's office.

CHAPTER *21*

---

*A*t last, in Paris, they talked.

They arrived on Friday evening and left their luggage in the sitting room of their suite at L'Hôtel. "Let's walk before dinner, shall we?" Sabrina asked, and they went out as they were, in the walking shoes and pants suits that they had put on for travel after coming back to Cadogan Square from Denton's house, Sabrina's a sleek gray with a thin stripe and Stephanie's a brown and black tweed. They walked a little apart from each other in the mild evening air beneath the bright lights of Paris. The closeness, the oneness they had felt in Denton's study, was gone. Sabrina tried to find a way to recapture it, remembering their pleasure in sharing London, wishing they could share the magic of Paris in the same way, but she could not do it. There were too many words waiting to be said. Say them! she cried silently to Stephanie. We only have tonight and tomorrow before Garth arrives. Tell me what you want. I don't know what I can do, what rights I have . . . Tell me what you want so we can talk about it.

But Stephanie was silent and so they walked in silence,

crossing the Seine on the Pont Neuf and turning to follow the river past the ancient Palais de Justice and the extravagantly sculptured Hôtel de Ville. The apartment buildings of Paris crowded in upon each other and upon the river. Their steep roofs, punctuated by dormers, hung like heavy eyebrows over gray or buff stone facades; scrolled ironwork curved around balconies or guarded high arched windows, and at the windows lace curtains or fringed draperies framed a small sculpture, a lamp, an arrangement of flowers.

"And behind every window a private story," Sabrina mused aloud, providing an opening to conversation. But Stephanie did not answer, and so they walked on, amid the crowds strolling on the riverbank past lighted boats tied up below, some decked out as restaurants. Then they left the river and turned down a quiet side street until they came to the Rue de Rivoli and turned once again.

"Where are we going?" It was the first Stephanie had spoken since they left the hotel.

"This was always one of my favorite walks," Sabrina said. "From the Left Bank to the Place des Vosges. It's so old it's almost a history of Paris. I used to walk here all the time, when I was at school. There was a little café called Trumilou on the Right Bank; I wonder if it's still here."

Stephanie put a little more space between them. *You were at the Sorbonne and I was at Bryn Mawr. Later, that was one of the things I envied, part of your whole life that I envied. And never stopped envying, so that when I thought of changing places, it seemed I'd wanted to do that all my life.*

And now what? What do I want from you now?

The Place des Vosges lay before them, a vast square of four-story town houses, once the homes of royalty, surrounding a fenced park. "It was in ruins," Sabrina said, "but most of the houses have been renovated and it's become very chic. Vern Stern told me that an American, Ross Hayward, did one of them: brilliantly, he said. It was unusual to have an American architect working here."

Stephanie gazed at the elegant buildings with steep mansard roofs and shuttered windows. "Did you ever design any houses in Paris?"

"No, just in London and the countryside."

"But you could. You know French interiors as well as English, and you have contacts here."

"I do, but I'm not working in Europe anymore."

They stopped in the middle of the sidewalk and the crowds parted around them, giving them quick sideways glances as if feeling the tension building between them. "Let's go back," Stephanie said.

They walked back and crossed the Pont d'Arcole to Notre-Dame. They stopped on the broad plaza facing the great gray mass of the church, tilting their heads back to gaze at the towers and flying buttresses illuminated against low clouds that shone a pale gray from the lights of the city. No other city, Sabrina thought, had such beauty at every turn, such a wealth of evidence of the brilliance of the human imagination. So the two of us ought to be able to solve our little problem, she thought wryly. Compared to the conception and building of Paris, it should be a breeze.

"It's nine o'clock," she said as they turned to walk again along the Seine. "I made a reservation for dinner, if you feel like it."

Stephanie's eyebrows rose. "When did you do that?"

"Before we left London."

"Where?"

"Laperouse."

"I've never been there."

"The food is good and it's very quiet."

"You're always arranging things." A faint note of resentment trailed through the words, and Sabrina said quickly, "We can go anywhere; what would you like?"

"I don't know. I don't know Paris."

"Well, a bistro?"

"Yes. Something small."

"Let's see if we can get into Benoît. Do you want to walk? We'd have to go back the way we came."

"Yes, I love to walk."

It's such a good way to put off talking, Sabrina thought, and in fact they did not speak again until they were seated across from each other in Benoît's tiny dining room with figured wallpaper, lace curtains stretched across the bottom half of the windows, and a few small tables, most of them along a banquette that stretched the length of the room. The maître d' led them to the only unoccupied table and Stephanie slid onto the banquette. Briefly, Sabrina debated sitting beside her, but instead took the chair the maître d' was holding for her on the other side of the table.

"We'll order right away," she said, "and we'll have a bottle of the Pichon-Lalande." She looked quickly at Stephanie. "Unless you'd rather have something else."

"No, that's fine." The maître d' brought the wine, displayed the label to Sabrina, poured it, waited for her to taste it and nod her approval, and all the while Stephanie seemed to be gathering herself to begin, like a diver in the moment when every muscle is tensed to push off from the board and into the air. "Everything should be fine, shouldn't it?" she said at last. "We don't have to be afraid anymore that someone is after us; we're together, we're in Paris, we have people who love us . . ."

"What do you want to do?" It came out so abruptly that Sabrina repeated it more softly. "What do you want, Stephanie?"

"Everything. I want all of it." She gave a rueful laugh. "That's what got us into this mess, isn't it? I wanted everything. To be Sabrina Longworth just for a little while and to have my own life waiting for me so that I could go back whenever I wished. As if the world would stand still for me while I lived all the fantasies I'd ever dreamed of. Like a child. Children see the world that way."

"I wanted it, too," Sabrina murmured.

"But your world changed and you changed with it and

made it all yours. I didn't change, not enough anyway, and now I don't know where I belong.''

"Where do you want to belong?''

"I don't know. But wherever it is, I want Léon to be part of it. I can't imagine living with Garth again. We had nothing together when I left for China, only misunderstandings and anger and frustration, and we both wanted out. I know he was relieved when I left; he probably hoped I wouldn't come back.''

"He hoped you'd come back and make your marriage work.''

Stephanie shrugged. "I didn't see any sign of that. I'm not even sure he felt that way until you came and somehow made him want it. But it doesn't matter, don't you understand? I don't care what he wanted.'' She leaned forward, the words, after so long a silence, pouring out. "I did care once, but after a while it seemed that his work was more important to him than I was, much more interesting and . . . *valuable*, and that just wore me down. I suppose I wore him down, too; maybe that's what happens in marriages that fail: people grind each other down until they just don't fit together anymore. I don't know what you found in him; maybe he changed after I left, or you're better for him, so *he* was better. Maybe because you weren't Stephanie, he wasn't Garth. Wouldn't that be odd? But it doesn't matter. We can't ever live together again. I'd feel that way about him even without Léon. But I want my children.''

A long sigh escaped Sabrina; that was what had been lurking at the edges of all their conversations in all the days they had been together.

"I think about them all the time, you know. When I saw those pictures in your album I almost couldn't stand it, I wanted to hold them and hear their voices, the way they talk so fast, both at once, sort of tumbling over each other, so excited, so in love with being alive . . . Oh, God, Sabrina, I miss them, I feel empty without them . . . Do you know, once, in London, Gabrielle was having trouble with Brooks and she came and sat in my lap and I said without thinking, 'Hush, dear Penny' . . . Oh, why didn't I go back then, why did I have to go on that cruise . . .''

"One last fling," Sabrina reminded her, knowing she was being cruel.

"I know, I know, I still thought I could have it all; I thought I could push it a little further, and then still further, and nothing would change: there wouldn't be any price to pay. That was a fantasy too, but I wouldn't let myself think about it because I didn't want to go back to being myself. Because it was myself that I didn't like; I never stopped loving my children and I never forgot them when I lost my memory; they were always inside me. One day, when I was in Aix, there were some schoolchildren on an outing and a little girl got separated from them and I was taking her back to her group and I called her Penny. She asked me why and I didn't know why, but I thought—I even told Max—I thought that must be my daughter. He'd told me I wasn't married when we met—and of course that was the truth as far as he knew it, since he thought I was you—but after I met that little girl I thought he'd lied or something, and I must have been married. Another time I told Léon that Cliff had made sure I'd find a stolen radio in his room. It was so strange, I had no idea what it meant, except that it sounded as if I had a son named Cliff. I even remembered Garth's name once. It came out of nowhere.''

The waiter brought their dinners, sliding them deftly onto the table, though they were leaning so close to each other there was barely room. He glanced at their identical faces, so beautiful it was difficult to believe that there could be two of them, but he did not linger; he refilled their wineglasses and left. He respected discreet conversations.

"I'm not even sure I want to live in America again. I could live in France, you know, with Léon and Penny and Cliff. That's what Léon wants. He wants us to have children—so do I—but that doesn't change anything: I want Penny and Cliff.''

The words were hammer blows, shattering the crystal of Sabrina's life. She felt numb, as if the only way to keep her life intact was to cut off all feeling. She sat back and took a sip of wine and looked at Stephanie without expression. "And what will you tell them?"

Stephanie flushed. "I thought . . . I thought you would . . ."

"Tell them for you? No. I won't do that. Or were you thinking I'd walk away and let you walk in, in my place? Why should I? They're not a set of dolls to be passed back and forth, depending on the day of the week and what suits us. We fooled them once and it took Garth a long time to be able to live with that, and I won't be a party to trying to fool him again. I love him, Stephanie, I love all of them, they shape my life, but even if that weren't true . . . good God, you can't play with people that way!"

"You said Penny and Cliff still don't know."

"It doesn't matter. They're human beings and you can't toy with them as if they're not. Besides, they've grown up in the past year and I'm not at all sure they could be fooled again. Maybe at first, but not over time. They're still as self-absorbed as most children, but they're smarter than most, they're curious and observant and loving, they see a lot and they listen and they try to fit what they see and hear into a view of the world that makes sense. And after a while, if things don't make sense, they ask a lot of very tricky questions. Stephanie, I know them! And I won't have them hurt!"

"*You* won't have them hurt? They're my children, not yours! You were the one who said they aren't dolls to be passed back and forth . . . Who do you think you are to tell *me* you know them, as if you can just walk in and take over and be their mother—"

"I am their mother," Sabrina said icily. "I did walk in and take over. I did it because you begged me to."

A shudder swept over Stephanie. She pushed her untasted food away. Her mouth drooped. "That's what I'd have to tell them, isn't it? That their mother wanted to be somebody else and so she . . . walked out on them.''

The pain in her sister's voice cut across Sabrina's anger and she started to reach out to comfort her. But her hand fell back to her lap. My enemy, my love, she thought, as she had before. They faced each other as if they were strangers.

''Yes,'' she said bluntly. ''That's what you'd have to tell them.''

''But there must be some way to say it so that it doesn't sound so awful . . .'' Stephanie clasped her hands as her thoughts swung wildly from one side to the other. ''There has to be a way to make them understand. Everybody has crazy ideas; they'd understand that. Kids always think about doing things that seem crazy and impossible . . . If I could make them feel what I was feeling at the time, I know they'd forgive me. It might be hard for them, but they would, I'm sure they would.''

She looked at her hands. ''No, they probably wouldn't. They probably couldn't. It would destroy everything they believe in, the goodness of their mother''—she looked at Sabrina—''*both their mothers.* They'd hate us both, wouldn't they? Children believe the world is reliable and predictable, and if I told them what I'd done, what *we'd* done, the world would seem crazy. Not reliable. Not something they could count on.''

Around them was the murmur of quiet conversations, an occasional boisterous laugh, the chime of wineglasses meeting in a toast, the clatter of dishes from behind the swinging doors that led to the kitchen. But a hush enclosed Stephanie and Sabrina's table, and even as they faced each other it seemed to Sabrina that they were speeding away from each other, faster and faster, like a film gone haywire, and soon they would only be small specks, no longer, or ever again, recognizable to each other. And she did not know how to stop it; she thought perhaps there was nothing they could do but watch each other disappear.

Stephanie shifted in her chair. ''But I have to tell them,

don't I? Denton's solicitor will go to the police, and the whole story will come out; everyone will know I'm alive—I mean, Sabrina Longworth is alive—and Penny and Cliff will hear it from television or newspapers or other people if they don't hear it from me. Or from you.'' She looked at Sabrina's face. ''No, you said you wouldn't do that. And I couldn't ask you to. I couldn't ask you to tell them you're not their real mother.''

I am their real mother; I've become their real mother.

''But they'll hear it anyway; an hour, a few hours after Denton's solicitor goes to the police the news will be everywhere and that would be the worst way of all; then they really wouldn't forgive me. If I told them, at least they'd know I'd been honest . . . finally. But honesty isn't really something we can claim, is it?''

I've been honest in my year with them. Everything I've done has been done through my love for them; they know that.

''No, I'll have to tell them, that's all there is to it. They're my children, and I want them, and if they're hurt, they'll get over it. Children are resilient; they bounce right back. Anyway, I don't believe they're really completely happy; they must know, deep down, that something isn't the way it ought to be. When they—''

''They are happy,'' Sabrina said sharply, unable once again to hold back the words. ''They've had a wonderful year. They've been happy and loving and loved. They haven't felt anything was missing—'' Not fair, she thought. She had no right to claim her sister's children just because they had had a good year.

''I don't believe that,'' Stephanie said firmly. ''They must have a feeling, even if they don't understand it, that something is wrong. And when they know I'm their real mother they'll be happy because things will seem right again and they'll want to be with me and no one else.''

The waiter came with raised eyebrows, and when Sabrina nodded, he removed their full plates. ''It was not good, madame?'' he asked each of them.

"C'était excellent. Malheureusement nous étions distraites."

"Nous reviendrons," Stephanie said. She looked at Sabrina, her eyes bewildered. "It feels so natural to speak French, but it feels right to speak English, too. It's as if I'm always caught somewhere between two people, whatever I do. Whatever I decide."

Outside, in the mild evening, they retraced their steps back to L'Hôtel. Stephanie walked past the fine antiques furnishing the sitting room of their suite, past a table with fruit and a bottle of champagne sent by the manager, to the terrace, filled with late autumn flowers. She leaned against the low wall, gazing at the steeple of the church of Saint-Germain-des-Prés. "It's terrible, what we're doing," she murmured. "I hate it, I hate it, but I don't know what else to do."

Sabrina was in the doorway behind her. "What do you hate?"

"Hurting you." She did not turn around. "You knew that's what I meant; you always know what I mean. I hate hurting you. But wouldn't it be enough if you kept Garth and I took Penny and Cliff?" She heard Sabrina's sharp intake of breath and she swung around. "I'm sorry, oh, God, Sabrina, I'm sorry, I don't know what's wrong with me, I sound like a vendor haggling in the market. It's just that I feel so trapped . . . that there's no good way to untangle what we've done . . . and I love you and I know you love me and I need you—we've always needed each other; we've always been closer to each other than anybody, anywhere—but still . . ."

"Still we're further apart than we've ever been."

"Yes."

The width of the terrace stretched between them. Sabrina's arms came up and Stephanie leaned forward, as if to move into her embrace. But at the same moment, Sabrina's arms fell to her sides and Stephanie leaned back against the wall. The terrace seemed to widen between them. They looked at each other in the faint light, identical faces, beloved faces, separated by all that they themselves had set in motion. Around them, the scent of chrysanthemums and stock seemed painfully sharp; the distant sounds of traffic suddenly rose to a clamor.

"I'm going to bed," Stephanie said and, in a flurry of movement, crossed the terrace, passed Sabrina in the doorway, and disappeared into the bedroom. Sabrina stood where she was, watching the church steeple fade as the lights of the city went out one by one. It was very late; the hotel slumbered. On the street below, a dog barked, a man said good night to friends, a pair of motorcyclists revved their engines and roared off into the distance. In the silence that followed, as clearly as if they were beside her, she heard her children's laughter and the clatter of their feet as they dashed about the house. She closed her eyes. I won't give them up. I won't give them up. I won't give them up.

What does that mean? I have no way to keep them without destroying their love for me and for Stephanie.

She was crying. She turned from the terrace and walked blindly to the closed door of the bedroom. The lamp beside her double bed was on; in the other bed, Stephanie lay curled up on her side, her back to the room. Silently, Sabrina closed the door of the marble bathroom and washed her face and undressed, then slipped between the cool sheets of her bed. She could hear Stephanie's irregular breathing and knew she was awake, but she said nothing; in her separate space, she lay awake through the night, thinking of home and imagining Garth holding her hand, as he did every night as they fell asleep and every morning as they awoke and turned to each other to begin a new day.

When the sun reached their room, Stephanie threw back the covers and stood up. She glanced at Sabrina's closed eyes and thought, She isn't asleep, I know she isn't, she didn't sleep any more than I did, but she doesn't want to talk. And even if she did, what can we say to each other?

She walked past her sister without speaking and closed the bathroom door quietly behind her.

She showered and washed her hair and dried it, combing it with her fingers. She dressed in the clothes she had brought into the bathroom with her, then eased open the door and went back into the bedroom. Sabrina was not there.

She's gone! Stephanie thought wildly. Garth will be here tomorrow, and she's left me to face him. I can't, I can't, I'm not ready! I don't know what to say to him; I don't know what to say to Penny and Cliff. I'm not ready; she can't leave me here alone!

She ran into the sitting room. Sabrina was sitting on the terrace, wearing her silk robe. Coffee and a covered basket were on the table beside her next to a folded copy of *Le Figaro*; she had not opened it.

"Oh, thank God," Stephanie said. "I thought you'd gone."

"Not yet." Sabrina's face was pale and Stephanie saw a reflection of her own sleeplessness and uncertainty in her sister's eyes.

"Are you going to wait for Garth?"

"I haven't decided anything about tomorrow. Have you called Léon?"

"Not yet."

"What will you tell him?"

"I don't know. I don't know!" She stood in the doorway. "What should we do today? We have to do something, don't we?"

"Alexandra called while you were in the shower; she wanted to have lunch. I told her I was thinking of Giverny or the Marmottan for today, and she said she'd like to go along and she'd be here about ten."

"Giverny or the Marmottan?"

"Well, anything to do with Monet. When I was in school here, whenever I had a problem I took refuge in his garden or his paintings. There's something about their perfection, even while it's not quite real, that always made me feel there was a core of serenity I could reach, even if it took a long time."

"A core of serenity. Oh, if only . . ." Stephanie shook her head and, after a moment, said, "Is there more coffee?"

"Of course. And croissants. I'll take a shower and then we'll ask the concierge for the train schedule to Giverny."

Stephanie sat down as Sabrina went to the French doors. But as she reached for the pot of coffee, Sabrina came back and bent down and kissed her on both cheeks.

"Good morning, Stephanie. I love you."

Stephanie turned and put her arms up. "Oh, I do love you, Sabrina. I love you and I'm sorry, I'm so sorry, but there's nothing I can do about it! I wish . . . I wish . . . oh, God, I don't even know what I wish!"

Sabrina knelt beside the chair and they embraced, their cheeks together, their eyes closed. The sun warmed them. "I'll get ready," she said, and left quickly, while Stephanie's eyes were still closed.

Stephanie poured coffee and bit into a croissant, barely tasting it. She gazed for a long time at the church of Saint-Germain-des-Prés, thinking of people stopping in on their way to work, looking for something. *A core of serenity.* And maybe they find it, she thought, unless they've gotten themselves into the kind of mess we have.

But if we hadn't started this whole crazy thing a year ago, I never would have met Léon. I wouldn't have met Robert or Jacqueline; I wouldn't have found out all the things I could do in London; I wouldn't have been Alexandra's friend.

But I would have had my children.

And taken them for granted, the way I used to do.

She was dizzy. She closed her eyes and opened them to the brilliant sun and still nothing was clear. I want it all, she thought again, with despair—*all, all, all*—haven't I learned anything? She felt herself tense with the impossibility of it, and then she thought, Well, no one can have it all, I know that, but it would be a lot easier to accept whatever I can have if Sabrina would decide what we're going to do, so I wouldn't have to—

She was ashamed, and she gripped her hands in her lap. *I'm sorry, Sabrina: I'm still trying to get you to take the responsibility for my life.*

The knocker on the door of their suite startled her. The maids, she thought, walking through the sitting room. They can come back when we're gone. She opened the door.

"Mom!" Cliff yelled, and flung himself against her, pushing her backwards into the room.

"Mommy, *bonjour, bonjour!*" Penny was dancing up and down in her excitement as she burrowed against Stephanie under Cliff's widespread arms. "Daddy taught me that, did we surprise you? We did, didn't we? That was our surprise! You didn't know we were coming!"

Stephanie staggered beneath the onslaught of her children. Joy flooded through her and she bent her head and clasped them in her arms.

"You didn't know, did you?" Cliff demanded. "We kept it a secret, didn't we?"

"Yes, you did," Stephanie whispered. "Oh, I love you, I love you, I love you, I love you . . ." She could not stop saying it. Her lips were against the upraised faces of her children, her body opened to their warmth and electric energy, and she felt faint and stumbled backwards again.

She heard the door close and looked up, over the heads of the children, into Garth's eyes.

Shock struck her like a wave, and she looked quickly away. She had cut him so completely out of her life that it was incredible to see him this close, with the children there, almost as if they were the family group she had long since denied. And he had been reaching toward her with a love in his eyes she had not seen since their first years together, sending a stab of jealousy through her that her sister had brought that out in him where she herself had been incapable of it.

She shook her head as if to fling off her thoughts. She had registered, in one swift second, that there was more gray in his hair than she remembered, that his lean face had a gentleness she did not remember and that he was far handsomer than she remembered, but then she withdrew from him and returned to the clamor of her children. That outstretched hand, the love in his eyes, were not for her, and she could not tell him she wasn't Sabrina. She wasn't ready. She could not even greet him as if she were his wife. If he didn't like it, that was too bad; what right did he have to spring this surprise on her? She would deal with it later. Maybe he would just go away and leave her with her children.

With the children and Léon.

"You smell different," Penny said accusingly. "Are you wearing perfume? You told me you don't like perfume."

"Oh. Well, most perfumes . . . Maybe it's my shampoo; it's a new kind. Tell me about your plane trip. And how come you're here. I thought . . ."

Huddled together, they moved past the closed bedroom door and onto the terrace, Penny and Cliff's high, excited voices propelling them along. Garth stayed where he was, cold with shock and fury. This woman was not his wife. He had known it the moment their eyes met. He had lived with Sabrina for thirteen months and he knew her as he had never known another human being, and this woman was not Sabrina.

This woman was Stephanie.

Not killed in an explosion. Not buried in London. Not mourned for a year. Instead, living in . . . well, wherever the hell she'd been living; what difference did it make? Wherever it was, she would have had to be in hiding, since she was supposed to be dead. But here she was, traveling with Sabrina, sharing a hotel suite, having a couple of weeks together—was that why Sabrina had come to London so often in the past year, to visit her sister?— then going back to whatever life she was living now.

Sending Sabrina back to Evanston.

They hadn't been satisfied with playing at a new life for a few months; they'd wanted it for good. And so the deception had never ended.

He watched Stephanie's radiant face as his children chattered about O'Hare Airport in Chicago and De Gaulle in Paris, and about their trip. They were so full of new adventures that they asked her nothing about herself; they looked directly at her but always through the haze of their self-absorption, adjusting reality—if indeed they needed to—automatically as they went along.

As I did once, Garth thought. But never again.

"Look, Mom, they gave us these neat little kits; see, the toothbrush folds up—"

"And there's a mask, Mommy, look, and some of the people wore them when they went to sleep and they looked so weird!"

Garth watched them, his face frozen. *Why didn't she tell me? If they wanted to make it permanent, that was what I wanted, too. Why in God's name didn't she tell me so we could deal with it together, make our marriage valid, live an open life . . .*

Because she would have had to tell the children.

But we could have done that together.

Could we?

What would we have told them?

That the woman they thought was their mother had fooled them. That their real mother had waltzed off one fine September day and stayed away for a month before she was killed—well, supposedly killed—without making any effort to see her children or talk to them in all that time. Could we have told that to Penny and Cliff?

"And a comb and these funny slippers. Why would you wear slippers on a *plane*?"

"And they gave us a book of crossword puzzles and we did *six* of them!"

Of course we could have told them. They're strong children, and with enough love we could have found a way to help them deal with it. It would have been better than living a lie. If she'd told me from the beginning, she and I could have worked everything out, made a life together. And now we can't. Now we have nothing together.

I will never be deceived by her again.

His muscles were taut beneath his cold skin, like wires wound on a spool almost to the breaking point. His face was rigid, his eyes blank, hiding the turmoil of his thoughts as he watched Stephanie and his children. She never looked at him.

God damn it, look at me! Look at what you've done to us, to all of us . . . He took a long step toward her and saw her flinch—so she was aware of him; she knew exactly how much distance was between them— and he stopped. There would be no confrontation in front of Penny and Cliff. Not now, not until he'd had time to think of some way to bring them up to date on how their mother and their aunt had made fools of all of them again and again and then, most devastatingly, again. He felt he would explode with the rage within him; he wanted to tear his children from that woman's arms and take them away, cradled protectively, shielded even from the sight of her. But he did not move. He would wait until he could get her alone.

Or get Sabrina alone.

Where was she? It was no longer a question of his dealing with one impostor or the other; now, for the first time since this damned game had begun, he would face them together.

But he could not ask Stephanie where her sister was until he could get her away from Penny and Cliff. And how the hell was he going to manage that?

There was a knock on the door behind him and he jerked around. If that was her— No, of course it wasn't; she wouldn't knock. The maids, he thought. Good; they might distract Penny and Cliff. He opened the door.

"Garth!" Alexandra exclaimed. "Good heavens, a day early? Husbands should never do that to wives, you know, it's—'' She saw his stony face and his rigid stance. "Oh, my God." She looked beyond him, at Stephanie and the children close together on the terrace, and turned back to him. "I gather that's Stephanie, and she told you."

"Does the whole world know?"

"Almost no one. Did she tell the whole story? Where she's been?"

"She told me nothing. We haven't spoken."

"Then how did you know?"

He gazed at her in silence.

The color rose in her face. "Well, I guess, if you really do find that kind of love with someone . . ." She looked again at the terrace. "Where's Sabrina?"

"I don't know."

"And from the sound of your voice you don't care. But I don't believe that, and I'll bet you don't either." She gazed at Penny and Cliff. "I think we've got to get the youngsters out of here so you can explode. I do believe you're going to any minute now." She strode past him, to the terrace. "Penny and Cliff! What a fabulous surprise!"

"Is *everybody* in Paris?" Cliff demanded.

"The whole world, at least. Don't I get a hug?"

They ran to hug her, and Stephanie looked up, as if just awakening. "I forgot. Giverny . . . the Marmottan . . ."

"Slight change in plans. The grown-ups have a lot to talk about so the younger generation is going to be whisked away." Casually she put her arms around Penny's and Cliff's shoulders. "Come on, you two, we're going to give your parents some time together. I'm taking you to my favorite café, a few blocks from here, as it happens; there's a magician there every day at eleven-thirty, and I'll treat you to lunch and café au lait."

"A magician?" Cliff echoed. "A French magician?"

"Probably. I think nationality doesn't have much to do with it."

"We're too young for coffee," Penny said.

"Maybe in Evanston, but not in Paris." She was shepherding them through the sitting room.

"What kinds of tricks does he do?" Cliff asked.

"You should never ask that, Cliff; most of the magic of a magic show is surprise. It's like love," she added, fixing her gaze on Garth until he met her eyes. "There are always surprises; love is supposed to be able to roll with them, instead of getting knocked out. That's the magic part: something to hold on to even when you're not sure what's going on around you."

"Can we really have coffee?" Penny asked. "I mean, we're not any older, just because we're in Paris."

"You're older than you were yesterday. Anyway, it's half hot milk. That's what café au lait is: coffee with milk. If you don't like it, we'll switch to hot chocolate."

"How about wine?" Cliff demanded. "I mean, as long as we're in Paris . . ."

Alexandra laughed. "That's a bolder step. We'll discuss it on the way. Garth, you and Stephanie take your time; you can join us later."

"No!" Stephanie had moved swiftly from the terrace, terrified of being alone with Garth and having to tell him who she really was. "We'll go with you." She was so nervous her movements were jerky as she sidled past Garth and opened the door. "Come on, let's go, let's go."

Alexandra looked at Garth. "I'd be glad to take them; it would be a treat for me."

"No!" Stephanie cried. "*Come on!*"

"Come on, Daddy." Penny took Garth's hand. "Isn't it amazing to see Alexandra in Paris? And we'll all have café au lait!"

"Half milk," said Cliff. "It sounds awesomely boring. Can't we do something else, Dad, until time for the magician? Like climb the Eiffel Tower?"

"And walk off all our angst," Garth murmured, and only Alexandra heard the bitterness in his voice.

Cliff frowned. "What's an angst?"

"Anxiety, depression, worries, problems."

"I haven't got any. So can we *go*?"

"Daddy, let's go!" Penny cried.

They were tugging at his hands, and Garth saw beneath their excitement the first faint signs of worry that something was wrong: their mother wanted to go with them to the café and their father was holding back, and why was that? And they hadn't even kissed, and they always kissed, all the time, even when they hadn't been apart for two weeks. Garth met their eyes, tinged with apprehension, and gave in. He let them lead him out the door behind Alexandra, who, with a brief shrug of resignation, had followed Stephanie into the corridor.

L'Hôtel was lavish with antiques, marble and velvet; Garth had noted them peripherally when he arrived, thinking mostly of Sabrina and the surprise he and the children had planned: two days in Paris for the four of them and then a week for the two of them alone while Penny and Cliff flew to London, where Mrs. Thirkell waited at Cadogan Square to take them under her wing for a few days before taking them home to Evanston. It had seemed like such a good idea at the time. Now, taking the velvet-lined elevator to the lobby and walking blindly past pink marble and a soaring curved staircase, he knew that it was clearly the worst idea in the world.

No, it was a good idea. Based on what I thought . . .

Not thought. Knew. I knew the way things were between us. I didn't dream it or willingly deceive myself. I brought Penny and Cliff to Paris because we were a family in the best sense of the word.

The sun's glare stopped him just outside the entrance and he shaded his eyes, watching the others a few paces ahead. Alexandra and the children looked back when they realized he was not with them, but Stephanie looked fixedly ahead, her back stiff. And in that stiff back, Garth saw the Stephanie of their last quarrel, thirteen months ago, just before she went to China: the Stephanie who had not returned.

Sabrina had returned. Sabrina, who had shown again and again how deeply she loved them.

She wouldn't do this to us. She wouldn't live a lie,

pretending to mourn her dead sister—pretending to marry me!—pretending in every way that made us lovers and friends and husband and wife, and brought magic into our home.

I don't believe that. I do not believe that.

But . . . magic and surprise, Alexandra says.

Well, I am surprised.

"Daddy, come on! It's just a few blocks, Alexandra said!"

"Garth." Alexandra waited until he caught up to her. "Tell me what you want. We've got to do something to help Penny and Cliff; they keep asking me if everything is all right. They ask Stephanie, too."

"And what does she say?"

"That everything is fine and she loves them."

Garth shaded his eyes again and looked at his children. "Can't you think up a story about my wanting to be alone with . . . their mother? You've already said it once; add some window dressing. Make it sound romantic, if you don't mind stretching the truth to the breaking point."

"Garth, don't pass judgment yet. And don't be so bitter. You don't know the whole story. You don't know what she's been through."

"I don't give a damn what she's been through. Nothing would justify the lies, the pretense—"

"Wait a minute." Alexandra's eyes were wide with surprise. "I didn't mean Sabrina. I meant Stephanie. You don't know anything about her."

"I don't want to. Why the hell should I? You think that after she's been romping around the world for more than a year without a sign that she gave a damn for her family, I should start worrying about what she's been through? Oh, Christ, Alexandra, I'm sorry; I shouldn't dump it on you. If you still want to take Penny and Cliff for a while and give them some story to explain it, I'd be very grateful."

"I'll take care of it; I love being with them. We'll be at Le Petit Prince, on the Seine; keep going to the river, then turn left. You can't miss it. Take as long as you need; we'll be very happy watching the magician.''

Garth watched her stride ahead and scoop Penny and Cliff into her orbit. But already his thoughts had moved on.

She identified the body. She went through the funeral. If she wasn't pretending, how did that happen?

Whom did we bury that day?

They had always been so close, Sabrina and Stephanie; in some ways mystically close. Had he ever really known either of them? Had he really been a part of Sabrina, or had he deluded himself about the magic of this past year, fabricating what he wanted to believe just as he had willed his belief that she was Stephanie those first three months before he figured out the deception?

No, damn it; she loves me as I love her. I know that. I know that. Some things can't be faked.

Once before, he had felt this unraveling of certainty in a world gone haywire: last Christmas, after he had kicked Sabrina out and she had fled to London. Alone, in the late night stillness, he had thought, *Things fall apart; the center cannot hold.* Now, on the Rue de Seine on a brilliantly sunny day in October, he longed for a center that could hold, a stable center, a place where trust could live.

He could hear Alexandra pronouncing French phrases and his children repeating them, frowning in concentration. But they kept looking back, too, and their frowns then were for Stephanie and Garth, a little distance back, not near each other. Garth lengthened his stride and caught up to her. ''We're going to talk. Alexandra is taking care of Penny and Cliff.''

''Not now, later, please, not now.'' Stephanie looked to left and right, into tiny ateliers and shops, as if some place might offer escape. She could not talk to Garth. He thought she was Sabrina and she did not know how to act like Sabrina with him; she had no idea what they were like together.

I just want my children. I just want to be with them and think that everything will be all right from now on.

"Not now," she repeated to Garth, her voice rising. "Later, later, not now." Sabrina wouldn't have said that, of course; Sabrina would have greeted him with the same love that he'd had in his eyes when he came in the door. He'll think I'm angry, tired of him, maybe he'll think I've met someone else. Well, that's too bad. I'm doing the best I can. I can't face anger and accusations and . . . hatred. She shook her head again—"Not now!"—and walked swiftly on.

Sabrina sat in the bedroom of the hotel suite, behind the closed door, her hands limp in her lap. Why hadn't he told her he was coming a day early? Why hadn't he said he was bringing the children? She could have planned for it; she and Stephanie could have been prepared. Why had he thought it should be a surprise?

But those weren't the important questions.

How could he have believed I was the woman who answered the door? How could he have been fooled again, after the year we've had together?

But it seemed he did believe it. And had gone off to a café with his children and with Stephanie. The Andersen family, on an outing in Paris.

She sat beside the window overlooking the street and the church steeple, but what she saw was the house in Evanston, the bedroom she shared with Garth, the kitchen where Mrs. Thirkell reigned and Penny and Cliff helped make dinner and brought their schoolwork to their parents for help or admiration, the dining room where they had welcomed Lu Zhen because he had no love in his life and they had so much.

I helped Garth with Lu Zhen. I helped Cliff with some of his problems and I made it easier for Garth to talk to him. I helped Penny believe in herself enough to withstand the sexual pressures at school. I was a friend to Claudia and helped her put the squeeze on a disreputable congress-man. I finished the design of the Koner Building.

I could say that I've done a good job in Evanston; I wrapped things up nicely, no loose ends dangling. I could say that my story there is finished; that it's time for me to leave.

In her mind she saw Garth's smile of greeting as it would have looked when Stephanie opened the door to their suite. She sat in the bedroom, seeing his smile, feel-ing his touch. *Oh, my dear love, forgive me. Everything got so complicated . . . The only thing that stayed simple and clear was my love for you and the children, but I couldn't separate it out from all the rest. I'm sorry, I'm sorry. I love you.*

Alexandra swept the children into the café and in a flurry of energy held their attention by commandeering a table and imperiously demanding menus, sparkling water and café au lait. While they waited for the magician, she wove elaborate stories about the posters that covered the walls; she told them how one of the waiters got his large red nose, why madame peeked out from the kitchen but never took a step into the café, why the dog was curled up in a corner looking so mournful. She was exhausted by the need for such continuous creativity, but she was exhila-rated by their enthralled faces, and so she went on and on, silently wondering why the magician had chosen this day of all days to be late.

Outside, Stephanie stood at the window and watched the backs of her children's heads, bent forward to be close to Alexandra. Once in a while Penny jumped a little in her chair; she always did that, Stephanie thought, when some-thing brought her a special delight. The minutes passed, the crowds flowed around her, leaving her a little space of her own. Behind her, couples strolled along the Seine or sat on benches, eating lunches from paper bags. Through the glass, Stephanie watched Alexandra talk and caught glimpses of her children's laughing faces. They looked up eagerly as a red-mustached man in a tuxedo and top hat came to their table. He carried a large basket, and after saying something to Penny and Cliff, he gestured over the basket with a white-gloved hand, and instantly a hat made of brilliantly colored feathers appeared on Penny's head. Her eyes wide with wonder, Penny reached up to touch it. She took it off, and she and Cliff turned it this way and that, looking inside it, trying to find the secret to the trick. Like their father, Stephanie thought. Believing everything has an explanation. But then she saw them look at Alexandra and the magician, laughing with delight, and she knew they believed in magic, too.

She put her hands on the warm glass window. Something was happening to her: she felt like a stranger. Outside, looking in, not able to hear what her children were saying, not able to share their laughter and wonder and delight. But I'm not a stranger, she thought; I'm their mother. She repeated it aloud. "I'm their mother. They love me. I'm their mother. *I'm* their mother."

But still, she was standing outside the window, cut off from them, from their thoughts, from their excitement, from their animated conversation with the magician and with Alexandra. How did they know Alexandra? Oh, yes, Sabrina had said she'd been in Evanston. Why? Sabrina hadn't said. Something else that had happened while Stephanie was gone, one of dozens, hundreds—too many, perhaps, for her ever to know them all.

I'm not part of their life anymore. And it's my own fault, nobody else's; I walked away and never thought that I might lose them.

But I can find my way back; I can be the center of their lives again, really and truly their mother again, I know I can. It will just take time, and I'll have to be so careful . . .

But what if I can't? What if I've changed so much—or they have—that they'll know that I don't belong with them? How will I explain that?

Maybe I wouldn't have to. I could just tell them how

much I love them and how sorry I am that I left them; wouldn't that be enough?

She saw her children waver through her tears. *It ought to be enough to tell your children that you love them. Love ought to be enough to smooth over anything.*

But if it isn't . . .

Abruptly she turned and walked back the way she had come, her head bowed, tears running down her face. Garth, watching from a few feet away, took her arm, gripping it so that she had no choice but to walk with him toward the hotel. "Where is she?"

Still crying, Stephanie barely heard him. "What?"

"Sabrina. Where is she?"

She looked at him wildly. "What are you talking about?"

"You know damn well what I'm talking about. For God's sake, Stephanie, you can't believe you two could fool me again." He stopped and stared into her frantic eyes. Stephanie. The real Stephanie. But Sabrina had been his Stephanie for so long, the only woman he . . .

I can't think about that now.

He walked on, almost dragging Stephanie with him. "Whatever you've been up to, however the two of you managed to make everyone think you've been dead all this time, I won't be part of your games anymore."

"Wait, you're wrong." Relief flooded her. He knew. She didn't have to tell him. "Sabrina didn't—"

"Wrong? You didn't let all of us think you were dead? You haven't been living another life for the past year? And Sabrina wasn't having a good time fooling me again— another deception, a very successful one? She's been calling me every night for the past two weeks, lying about what she was doing and whom she was with." His voice shook with fury. "Lying . . . my God, you're both experts at that. And now you want something else, so you've come back. A year ago you wanted out and you got out, you did whatever the hell you wanted to do, and now you want something else. Well, what is it? If you think for one minute you're going to take those children away from me—"

"You're hurting my arm!"

"Hurt isn't something you have much right to talk about." He stopped beside the iron fence that ran along the Seine, and held her in front of him, once again staring into her face. The image of Sabrina. Uncanny, he thought; even now she could be Sabrina. But there was something that made her Stephanie, a woman he did not love, a woman he could despise for what she had done.

She tried to pry his fingers loose. "I never meant to hurt you. I did want to get away, to have another life . . . I wasn't happy—you knew that!—but all I wanted was a few days; I thought I'd be back in a week and we could try to start again. I never wanted to hurt you!"

"You chose a peculiar way to demonstrate it." He eased his grip on her arm. "But nobody forced it on you; you chose it and went through with it and now it's done. And if you've come back to take Penny and Cliff, you can forget it. They're staying with me. I don't know what you've done for the past thirteen months or whom you've done it with, but you've managed to go all that time without a single phone call or letter to your children, and as far as I'm concerned—as far as any judge would be concerned—that disqualifies you from having anything to do with them. Are you listening to me? Damn it, look at me! They're the most important thing in the world to me right now, and I'm going to make sure they don't know what's been going on: you're not going to tell them and neither is Sabrina. My God, you two bitches, toying with a couple of children who never did anything to you but love you and depend on you—"

"Garth, stop, stop . . . Listen to me! Sabrina didn't know I was alive. She didn't toy with Penny and Cliff, or with you. She loves you. It was terrible for her to lie to you every night, but she did it for me, because I begged her to. I couldn't face you and the children; I didn't know what to do, so I asked her for a little time . . . and then we had to find out who was after us . . . Oh, God, it's so complicated; I can't explain it all.''

"She didn't know you were alive?"

"No. My God, Garth, she thought she'd buried me!''

Before he could stop it, joy flooded him. *She didn't know.* He had barely heard the rest—someone was after them?—all he knew was that Sabrina had not lied, had not pretended to be his wife, his love . . .

But then, looking past Stephanie at the sun-speckled crowds beneath tall horse chestnut trees, he thought, Why should I believe that? It's too easy. They lie too well, both of them. "She sat beside a coffin for a whole afternoon and said goodbye to her sister."

"I know; we've talked about that and we think we know how it must have happened. It's part of everything else, the whole year that I was in London and then France . . . Garth?" She looked into his eyes, trying to read them. She thought there was less anger; he seemed to be listening, weighing what she said, and she remembered how he always took time to repeat to himself what he heard so that he could incorporate it into what he knew, and evaluate it. The scientist, Stephanie thought, and knew she had never tried to understand that part of him. "I could tell you the whole story, but it would take so long . . . and Sabrina ought to help me tell it.''

"Where is she?"

"I don't know. She was in our bedroom at the hotel.''

"While the rest of us were there?"

"Yes.''

"There was a closed door; was that it? Could she hear us through it?"

"I'm pretty sure . . . yes, she could. I forgot she was there. The children, the shock of seeing you . . . I didn't think. But she can tell you . . . we can tell you everything, if you'll just listen. Garth, believe me. She didn't know. She thought I was dead and she was in love with you. She is in love with you.''

He studied her face. "Can you think of any reason why I should believe you?"

"You're a scientist; you ought to be able to recognize the truth."

He gave a short laugh. "Scientists are often fools."

"But you aren't. Sabrina said once that you weren't a fool, but we fooled you; she was trying to get me to come back because she was worried about what we'd done. I think she loved you then, though of course she wouldn't tell me. But I wanted more time; I wanted one last cruise"—a shiver swept over her—"and she gave it to me." Her voice dropped, and Garth leaned closer to hear her. "She's always done that. All our lives she's done what she could to make me happy. And I've relied on her to do it. I've never been as strong as she is; I've never had the same kind of belief in myself; I've never been as free in my imagination or my friendships or my work, or any other way. That was why I envied her. So I . . . used her. And she let me, because she loves me."

They stood on a cobblestone walk beneath a wide-spreading chestnut tree. On the far side of the Seine the massive gray stones of the Louvre seemed almost black, silhouetted against the cloudless sky. "Let's go," Garth said abruptly, and turned her with him and they walked quickly the remaining short blocks to the hotel. They took the elevator in silence to the top floor and in silence they stood at the door of the suite.

Stephanie raised a tentative hand to knock, but Garth reached around her and turned the knob and they walked in.

Sabrina was in an armchair on the terrace, her hands folded in her lap. She had moved from the bedroom, and that was all she had done. She looked up at the sound of the door; her eyes met Garth's and what should have been a joyous reunion after two weeks apart was instead a long look of doubt and anger, smoldering resentment, apology, and an attraction between them so powerful that even Stephanie felt it.

Sabrina stood up. "Where are Penny and Cliff?"

"At the café with Alexandra," Stephanie said, "and a magician to entertain them." She rushed to Sabrina, as if she had to move quickly to keep from changing her mind, and put her arms around her. "Too much is happening. It must have been awful for you, listening to us and then hearing us leave. I'm sorry we did that, but I couldn't stay here alone with— I mean, I was afraid. Everything happened too fast for me to think straight."

Sabrina's eyes again went to Garth.

"He knew right away," Stephanie said. "I thought he didn't, but he knew the minute he saw me. And then we all dragged him off to the café."

"You knew," Sabrina said to Garth. "You knew." And for the first time a small smile lit her face. "And did Stephanie tell you what happened to her?"

"No." Garth was looking from one to the other with the sense of unreality he had had since arriving that morning. Seen together, except for the clothes they wore, the sisters could have been one woman standing before a mirror, and as he looked at them his anger revived. It may have been true that Sabrina believed her sister to be dead, but, for all the love she professed for him, she kept from him the shattering revelation of Stephanie's survival. And now, seeing them together, he wondered if anyone ever could become as important to them as they were to each other. He did not know what to say to them, how to talk to them together. He told himself he did not want to talk to them; he would take his children home and get the hell out of both of their lives.

But Sabrina had taken a step forward, her hands out. "I'm sorry. I promised once never to lie to you again. I broke my promise and I can't tell you how sorry—"

"You broke more than that." Fighting against the ache to hold her, to kiss her, to awaken the smile that illuminated her face, he ignored her hands. He watched them drop to her sides and then he let his anger overflow. "I thought we had an understanding in our family that we wouldn't hurt each other, that our home was a place of safety, a refuge in a world that sometimes seemed cold and complicated and threatening. We got past your first lies—I thought we'd gotten past them—but now we're back where we started. There were dozens of chances for you to tell me what you were doing these past two weeks, but you'd decided—the two of you had decided—again!— how much truth the rest of us were entitled to.''

Stephanie had crept into a corner of the sitting room, shrinking from the anger in Garth's voice as if it were aimed at her. She stood there tentatively, wanting to escape into the bedroom but afraid to leave. Garth saw her behind him in the shadows, and he saw Sabrina in front of him on the sunlit terrace, and his rage built as he thought of them flanking him as they had flanked a year of his life without his knowing it. Impostors shaping his life. ''Well, it's over and I'm leaving and I'm taking Penny and Cliff with me. Neither of you will have them. It's monstrous to think that a family could be incidental to the whims of two bored women, that children could be passed back and forth like playthings, enjoyed for a while then tossed aside until at some point they're remembered and maybe longed for. I won't—''

''I didn't toss them aside!'' Stephanie cried. ''I knew Sabrina would take care of them; I knew she'd keep them healthy and happy until I came back, and she did, and now—''

''*Now*? You think you're coming back now?''

''Not to you. I couldn't do that. You don't want me and I don't want to live with you, Garth, not anymore. But I want my children. They're mine, Garth, I'm their mother! Doesn't that mean anything to you?''

''No. Should it? It hasn't meant anything to you.''

''That's not true; it has! I've wanted them every minute since I got my memory back—'' Garth's head swung sharply to her. ''That's what happened! You never asked, you never cared, but that's what happened to me, and we haven't had a chance to tell you about it, but if you'd let us, you'd understand; you'd change your mind. Sabrina"—she went to the terrace where Sabrina stood—"you've got to help me. I don't want to tell it alone; I want us both to do it."

" 'The whims of two bored women,' " Sabrina said icily, looking at Garth. "You know better than that. You're working yourself up to a rage—you tend to do that—and if you don't stop, we won't be able to talk at all."

"God damn it, don't tell me what I 'tend' to do. You knew for two weeks that Stephanie was alive, that you were making our whole life a sham—"

"*Our whole life?*"

"—and that nothing would ever be the same. You knew it and kept it to yourself. Because you loved your sister. That's a hell of an excuse. You say you love us, too. Is that the dividing line of your loyalties? If it's us and a stranger, you'll choose us; if it's us and your sister, you choose her."

"That's not fair."

"Why not? You did choose her."

"Briefly. And only once. I knew we'd see you soon—"

"More than once. There was the big one. You chose her when you faked being her so we wouldn't know she'd left."

"I didn't love you then. I haven't chosen anyone but you and the children since then. I did lie on the telephone, but I didn't see how I could do anything else, and it was only for a few days. I thought, on Sunday, tomorrow, I'd meet your plane and we'd be able to talk and . . . work things out . . ."

"You thought you'd have time to manipulate me again."

"Garth, please stop. I know you're hurt and angry, and you have good reason to be, but I never wanted to manipulate you and you know it. All I wanted was to live with you and make a life with our children that was good and loving and rewarding. I never wanted to fool you beyond that first week; I fell in love with you. And our house really was a refuge for me, a haven, and I did my damnedest to make it one for you and Penny and Cliff, too. As far as I know, I never hurt you, or them; I tried to make the three of you feel loved and cared for and protected. You know all this, you've known it for months, and I'd appreciate it if you'd try to remember what we've had together instead of sliding back to what you were feeling last December and reliving that whole awful time as if nothing had changed.''

"How much has changed if you could lie to me for the past two weeks?'' He heard himself fling the words at her and wondered why he could not let it go, why he kept harping on it. *I love you. I know you love me, I know you get trapped by Stephanie's demands. I need you; I don't want to live a life without you.* But still his anger fueled him and the harsh words poured out. He turned from the pain in Sabrina's eyes and looked at Stephanie. "You both think you can pick up wherever you want, whatever you've done, and go right on, like kids who break a window and then pretend it wasn't their fault. But this time you're not picking up where you left off; you can't blame someone else for what happened. I don't give a damn what you do with your life, but Penny and Cliff won't be part of it.''

"You can't say that! I'll fight you for them!''

"With what? Your passionate desire for a fling in London? A year away from them? They're staying with me. You won't see them again. Neither one of you will see them again.''

"Oh, don't keep going on like that,'' Sabrina said angrily. "Be angry, hold on to your anger if that's all you can do, but you don't know the whole story and you can't even think rationally about what to do until you've heard it. Why did you ignore Stephanie when she told you she'd lost her memory? Didn't you believe her? Or don't you want to hear anything that might change your mind about us? All we're asking is that you listen to us. Will you do that? If nothing else, it will satisfy your scientific curiosity.''

He smiled, then caught himself. He looked at his watch. A little after noon; his children were still being entertained by the magician. And by Alexandra. *Our guardian angel*, he thought.

''It won't take too much of your time,'' Sabrina said coldly.

He nodded. ''All right.''

''Let's sit out here.'' Her voice had changed again. Now that she knew that the whole story would come out, she let herself feel Garth's sense of betrayal and vulnerability in the unstable world he had discovered when he came to their hotel room, and her voice shook with her love for him and her desire to protect him. ''It's so beautiful; the terrace is so wonderful . . . and I'll get us something to eat; I think we need it.'' She picked up the telephone and asked for wine and coffee. ''And lunch,'' she added, and ordered seafood salad for three. ''I don't know if we'll eat it; probably not. Stephanie and I mostly send our food back these days: we haven't finished a meal in so long I can't remember it; I suppose if we were on a diet it would be . . . But we're not; we're just . . . Well, anyway, we can try.'' She was talking too fast and too much, but she was so nervous she thought she would fly apart. Garth had slowly followed them to the terrace, and as he did, she felt she could barely grasp the fact that the three of them were together, their roles so oddly skewed, all the secrets exposed, the future still unknown. *Except that Garth may, at any time, tell me to leave so he and Stephanie can work out how they'll share their children.*

Stephanie sat on the edge of a chair near Sabrina. Garth pushed a chair farther away from them before sitting down. ''Well?''

''Max got me off the ship,'' Stephanie said without preamble, and she told the whole story in a level voice, now and then looking at Sabrina, never at Garth, mostly gazing past both of them at the nearby steeple and at tall

573

thunderheads building on the horizon. Rain tonight, she thought absently even as she talked on, occasionally turning to Sabrina to ask her to take part, but for the most part speaking by herself for almost an hour.

When the waiter brought their order, Garth directed him to the terrace and, when he had left, closed and locked the door. That was their only distraction; the rest of the time Stephanie talked, and as she told her story, all the parts of her life came together: her years growing up with Sabrina, college, marriage to Garth, the birth of her children, her brief time in London pretending to be Sabrina, the months in France with Max, Robert, Jacqueline, and then Léon. And she saw herself standing outside the café, watching her children with Alexandra; she felt again the warm window beneath her palms, saw Penny and Cliff waver through her tears. It was the first time she had seen everything at once, and she began to realize that there were some parts of her that she could never recapture.

When she finished her story, they sat in silence. One of the bottles of wine was empty; the coffeepot on its warmer was half full. The seafood salad was untouched.

"But there's something else," Stephanie said at last, looking at her hands, clasped in her lap. "I'm having trouble making sense of who I am. I used to know, when I lived in Evanston, but I didn't like myself very much; that was why I wanted Sabrina's life. I wanted to be her a lot more than she wanted to be me; I really believed that I could put on a new life like a new coat, and then I'd be everything I wanted to be."

"And were you?" Garth asked. It was the first time he had spoken, and when Sabrina heard in his voice the curiosity of the scientist, she breathed a sigh of relief.

Stephanie's glance flickered toward him, then away. "It seemed that way. I knew I was only playing a part, but I was almost perfect because I'd been longing for it for so many years, and because Sabrina was inside me somehow, helping me without my realizing it." For a brief moment she looked directly at Garth. "I know we did a terrible thing, and I'm sorry, but for a little while I was so happy. I forgot how overwhelming the world had seemed every morning when I woke up; I felt I could do anything. But of course I knew, underneath, that I couldn't; I knew I was only playing a part, that I couldn't really be Sabrina because I'd left too much behind that I really cared about." Her glance slid past Garth's eyes again. "I kept wanting more and more adventures because I thought that was the way to stay happy, to forget the person I'd been, the one I didn't like. So I held on to being Sabrina; I couldn't let go. But, underneath, I knew I couldn't ever really step into Sabrina's life because of everything I'd left behind. I'd had so much, much more than I'd realized, and then I'd abandoned it, but it was always there, whatever else I did."

"You got what you wanted," Garth said, still with the absorbed air of the scientist. "You wanted to forget who you were, and you did."

Stephanie stared at him. "Yes, but I didn't plan to forget. The doctors told me I was repressing my life because I felt guilty about something I'd done. And they were right, but that didn't help me remember. But now, when I do remember, I don't seem to be anyone. I mean, I don't seem to fit in anywhere."

Sabrina took her hand. "You will. You haven't had enough time to get used to remembering."

"No, it's more than that." She took her hand from Sabrina's and turned her empty glass between her fingers. "I told you the other day that you kept on being yourself all the time you were being me. This whole year, you've been both of us. You knew what you wanted, you knew where you belonged and you trusted yourself to shape your future. I guess most people know those things and don't wonder about them at all, as if they've built a house and furnished it and they can go from room to room with their eyes closed, they know it so well, and they know it belongs to them and no one else, so it becomes a reflection of them and they see themselves every time they walk in the door.''

She looked again at Garth and saw an intense interest in his eyes. For the first time since their early years together, she felt the stirrings of pleasure that she had caught Garth Andersen's attention. ''But when I was in London all I wanted was to be Sabrina: I kept pushing Stephanie Andersen away. And then, in France, I was Sabrina Lacoste, and I made a life there, as whole as I could make it. So many lives, so many feelings, all mixed up inside me and I've lost whoever I was and I don't know who I am now. Or where I belong.''

A wren flew down to the terrace wall, pecked at a stone, hopped a few exploratory feet, and then, with a rush of small wings, flew off.

''All I have are my children. Don't you see? You've got to understand this: they're all I'm really sure of! I think about them and everything seems clear. I know they could give me what I don't have: I'd be their mother, so I'd know who I am, and we'd make a life together, and I'd know where I belong.''

Sabrina leaned forward to pour from the second bottle of wine. She waited a moment to steady her hand before she refilled their glasses. ''I thought it was the parents' job to help children find out who they are and where they belong.''

Stephanie flushed. ''That's a cruel thing to say. I'm trying to be honest.''

''So am I. Penny and Cliff already have what you're looking for. They've learned a lot in the past year. Or haven't you noticed?''

''Yes, I've noticed! Damn you, damn you, you know I have!'' She stared angrily at Sabrina through sudden tears. ''They're so different; how could I miss it? They're . . . stronger than they were.'' Her voice faltered. ''Bolder. More adventurous.'' And then she spoke aloud the words that had been gnawing at her since she had been with her children that morning. ''Like you.''

"Like both of us," Sabrina said quickly. "You brought them up for all those years before I got there."

"No. You know what I mean. All those years I envied you, it wasn't just for the life you led, it was because you were the one who reached out for adventures. You helped me come along when we were young, you even led me, and I was grateful . . . but it isn't easy being grateful. And then when I was living in Evanston, I'd get angry with myself for holding back when I knew you would have gone out of your way to meet somebody new or handle a problem or face a crisis instead of running from it. That's what you've given to Penny and Cliff. They won't grow up feeling angry at themselves for being afraid of adventures. They'll forge ahead. Like you."

For the first time, Garth felt a stab of pity for Stephanie. He knew she was right: in one year with Sabrina his children had grown more eager to rush forward and embrace whatever might lie ahead, more confident of their future. They were no smarter or nicer than they had been when they lived with Stephanie, but they were more able to take on the world. And Stephanie knew it.

Sabrina was conscious of Garth observing them. It was the first time, she thought, that an outsider had watched them work out the tensions and love and unfathomable closeness between them. But then she caught herself. An outsider? Her beloved Garth; Penny and Cliff's father. Sitting back in his chair, looking relaxed and casually interested, as Sabrina had seen him look many times when he was in fact intently listening, weighing new information, analyzing it and incorporating it into his world. There was nothing sloppy or careless about her beloved Garth: he was passionately curious about everything and, except when angry, willing to listen to anything, but it was facts he trusted; he relied on emotions only when they did not create havoc with an orderly world. He was not an outsider; he was part of whatever order she and Stephanie would create from the confusion they had wrought. He belonged with them; they were all part of each other now.

As if she were looking down from above, she saw the three of them held together as if by the strands of a spiderweb, invisible until the sun struck it at the right angle. Then, briefly, the connections and strength of the bonds became clear. Three of us, she thought, sitting together in Paris beneath a brilliant sun and a clear blue sky and a little wren who keeps swooping by to check us out: three people caught in a drama infinitesimally small on the world's stage but so enormous within the boundaries of our lives that it overwhelms us with its possibilities for happiness or despair. We are being very civilized about it all. But we are very frightened.

As the silence stretched out, Stephanie jumped up and stood a little distance away, leaning against the terrace wall, her arms folded protectively across her chest. "You've all changed, you know; it's obvious. You're not as hard as you used to be," she said to Garth, "even with all the terrible things you've said today. The way I remember you, your face always looked so stern, as if you were about to give a lecture or scold somebody. And, it's funny, but you seem more sure of yourself, too, like Penny and Cliff. I don't know what that means: maybe it means you've discovered there's more to life than genetics."

She saw him look at Sabrina; she saw their eyes meet and hold. "I guess," she sighed. "I guess that's it. And you're in love," she said to Sabrina. "I've never seen you when you really loved someone. I thought you loved Denton when you married him, but that was just excitement, wasn't it? You're different now. As if everything is in the right place and you can reach out beyond yourself and . . . soar."

Sabrina smiled. "I like that. It's what I thought about you, in Vézelay."

"Oh. I seemed that way to you? It seems like such a long time ago."

She paced with short, nervous steps, trailing her hand along the stone wall. "Maybe I was that way. I think I felt that way before I remembered everything. Then I got so confused . . .''

In the corner of the terrace she turned and faced them. ''You've made a new family,'' she said, almost accusingly. ''You've all changed so much, especially Penny and Cliff; they're so . . . oh, God, *they're so happy*. And I don't know if . . . if it would be best for them . . . I'm not sure . . .'' She closed her eyes. ''I don't know if I can do this,'' she whispered.

''Stephanie.'' Sabrina began to stand up to go to her, but Garth leaned forward and put a hand on her arm. She turned and met his eyes again, and in that moment, with the warmth of his hand holding them together, she chose to stay with him and let Stephanie find her own way, alone.

Stephanie opened her eyes. ''I don't think . . . when children are happy, anybody should take that from them. They're so beautiful, aren't they—Penny and Cliff? So full of life and joy and fun . . . They were dancing down the street with Alexandra as if they were going off to conquer Paris. They weren't afraid of anything! Well, yes, they were: they were afraid their parents weren't being loving to each other. And I guess they're used to seeing loving parents, aren't they? They're used to that. A house filled with love. *Aren't they?*''

''Yes,'' Sabrina said quietly.

Stephanie bent her head. She picked at a stone on the wall, just as the wren had pecked at it earlier, concentrating on it. ''All last night, when neither of us was sleeping, I was thinking about the four of you in Evanston, in that awful old house that always creaked and needed fixing somewhere, and in the kitchen, making dinner and eating together . . . I could see all the rooms so clearly, and all of you in them, being together . . . All those things you told me when we were in London, about their school and Cliff's soccer and Penny's painting and their friends, and that Chinese boy . . . all night I thought about you, the four of you, but mostly about Penny and Cliff, and I knew they were happy, and then when I saw them, it was more than I'd ever imagined . . . how happy and secure and loving they are in a . . . in a loving family.''

There was a long silence. The sounds of traffic were like ocean waves in the background, isolating the terrace with its three motionless people. "What I mean is, I couldn't . . . I couldn't imagine . . . forcing myself into that. Into what you've created. Because they don't think anything is wrong, anything is missing. I wanted to believe they thought that, but they don't. They're happy. Their world is solid and familiar and . . . stable. They're full of trust, not fear. As long as . . . as long as I . . . as long as I keep quiet.''

She looked at Garth. "I asked for them today because I thought if you said yes, we could work something out. I thought it would be so wonderful to have them that I'd do anything to make them happy and then they would be.'' A rueful smile touched her lips. "Instant happiness. I didn't have any new ideas about how we'd do it or what I'd tell them when they knew I wasn't Sabrina—because of course they would know; there's no way I could fool them for more than a few hours—I just wanted it to happen because it would be so wonderful. The same way I wanted to be Sabrina because that would be wonderful. As if I could wish into being a world that was wonderful. But what would I do when they started wondering why I wasn't like the mother they knew? I couldn't tell them the truth. I thought I could think of a way to do it, but there isn't one. They'd never trust me again. Children think their parents will always be there for them. I guess they find ways to handle divorce, but this wasn't a divorce: this was a game—Robert called it foolhardy and dangerous—and we played it so carelessly, as if we were playing with a deck of cards. How do you make children believe their world is stable and reliable after that? I can't do it. I can't take them away and pretend to be their—'' Her lips moved, but no sound came. And then, her voice almost inaudible, she said, "—pretend to be their mother, when they've already got one."

Sabrina felt a rush of wonder and joy that left her breathless, and then a terrible sadness. *Stephanie, you can't walk away from them forever; you love them so.*

But isn't that exactly what I want her to do?

Garth went to Stephanie and took her in his arms. She looked at him through her tears and then laid her head on his shoulder like a child. "I'm sorry, Garth, I'm so sorry, I'm so sorry; I didn't think about what I was doing, I just went ahead, and you deserved better, and so did Penny and Cliff; I'm sorry, I'm sorry—"

"Hush, it's over, it's over." Garth stroked her hair. "It's done; we can't go back." Over Stephanie's head, he met Sabrina's eyes and, jubilantly, felt once again the unalloyed wonder he had felt for a year whenever he looked at her and knew she was part of his life, part of him, and nothing could shatter that. "We wouldn't go back, even if we could," he said to her. "We've traveled too far; we've made too many discoveries."

"But we have to find a way," Sabrina said to him. "The three of us."

"Yes. We will." His love for her seemed to him so transcendent, their understanding so instinctive and complete, that he knew there could be no room, ever again, for a deception between them: no room, no need, no place in what they would build on that which they had already begun. In the damnedest way possible, he thought wryly, but we have made a beginning, and a good one, and from now on we'll . . . what had Stephanie said? Soar. From now on, we'll soar.

The wren had returned and was swooping in narrowing circles, looking for a place to land. Garth smiled. Stubborn bird. He'll find his place. We all do, if we're lucky.

He held Stephanie away from him. "Listen to me. You're not going to walk completely out of Penny and Cliff's life. We won't be a party to that. We'll tell them the same truth we'll tell everyone else: that their Aunt

Sabrina wasn't killed in the explosion, that she lost her memory and has been living in France since January, that she's recovered her memory and loves them and wants to see them as often as possible, even more often than she used to. And that we'll visit her in Vézelay or wherever she's living, as often as we can.''

Stephanie was staring at him, standing stiffly within his loose embrace. With a sharp movement, she pulled away and walked to the other end of the terrace and stood there, her head bent, her hands over her ears. *There is no end to a deception once it begins.*

She saw Sabrina walking toward her and turned her back, leaning her forehead against the stone wall, still holding her ears. *On and on and on: endless ramifications, circles and more circles, layers and layers piling up, until it becomes a new truth.*

And this was the new truth: that she would play a part in her children's life. Not the part a mother expected to play, but a part that would allow her to see her children grow, and give her opportunities over the years to tell them how much she loved them and wanted what was best for them, wanted them to be the strongest, happiest people they could be.

On the fringes, Stephanie thought. I'll always be on the fringes of the Andersen family, the one to wave goodbye when they go off together to their home, their shared experiences, their private stories and jokes, their plans for tomorrow and the next day and the next.

It isn't enough.

It's better than nothing.

And in that moment she gave up Stephanie Andersen and took to herself Sabrina Longworth. Not the Sabrina she had replaced in London, but a new one, entirely hers. Somehow she would make a life from that name.

Garth saw the slight straightening of her shoulders and knew she had made up her mind. It occurred to him briefly that they would have to find a way to get a divorce. We don't really have to, he thought: if she's going to be Sabrina, she's been divorced from Denton for years and she's never been married to me. But I think we'll all want to do it as soon as possible, and put an end to as much as we can of this crazy adventure.

"Stephanie," Sabrina said.

Stephanie turned. "Wrong name," she said shakily, trying to smile, and then they were in each other's arms. And if their world had turned upside down and they could not yet fathom how they would deal with the twists and turns of the coming years, they were still together, they had not lost each other, there would still be a voice at the other end of the telephone line, saying, "You understand, you always understand."

Stephanie held her sister as if she could never let her go, but then, steeling herself, she kissed Sabrina on both cheeks and stepped back. "I can't see Penny and Cliff now; I can't talk to them yet. I have to get ready to be their Aunt Sabrina, and that's going to take a while."

Sabrina studied her face. "You're not going back to Vézelay?"

"Not yet. I'll call Léon; he'll understand that nothing has changed between us, that I want to spend my life with him, but right now I have to be alone for a while. I think I'll stay in Paris for a few days and then probably go to Cavaillon to spend some time with Robert. I'll let you know where I am." She stepped back farther, putting more distance between them, until she was beside Garth. "Thank you for forgiving me. And for letting me be part of Penny and Cliff's life. I promise I'll be very good to them. A good aunt. I've never been an aunt. An adventure, Sabrina!"

She turned to the French doors that led to the living room and looked from Garth to Sabrina with a wavering smile. "I think you'd better go, don't you? Your children are waiting."

"Yes," Sabrina said, "in a minute." She walked past Stephanie into the sitting room and took from her purse the small photo album she carried at all times. "This is for you. I'll send more as we take them."

Stephanie held the album in both hands. She opened it and turned the pages. "My sweet Penny," she whispered. "And my very handsome, grown-up Cliff." She rested her fingers on a picture of the two of them grinning at her from the backyard of their house. "Thank you," she said to Sabrina. "I love you."

Sabrina kissed her. "I love you . . . Sabrina. You'll come to visit us in a little while. Please. Please."

Garth put his arm around her. "Time to go." He kissed Stephanie's cheek. "We'll talk to you soon. And see you soon."

His arm around Sabrina, they walked to the door and into the corridor without looking back. But Sabrina could not help it. She glanced quickly into the room as the door closed and saw Stephanie standing alone, one hand clutching the photo album, the other raised in farewell.

Then she and Garth were in each other's arms for a long silent moment until, together, they turned to walk down the corridor. Hand in hand, Garth and Stephanie Andersen walked to the elevator, to the lobby, to the street, where, a few blocks away, their children waited.